A legion of men knew her
as the Wild Rose.
But only one
Knew her secret.

The Wild Rose was the title she had taken and
the legend she had created—the beautiful blond
aristocrat who roved the highroads at the side of
England's most notorious highwayman—and
matched him, valor for valor, reckless deed by
reckless deed.

But the Wild Rose was more than a legend. She
was a woman, with a woman's needs, a woman's
hungers, a woman's weaknesses . . .

. . . and now the one man who possessed the
truth about her had turned the flood tide of her
power into a current of all-consuming passion
pulling her ever closer to the abyss . . .

RAPTURE . . .
You'll thrill to it!

Rapture

by

Rosamond Royal

POPULAR LIRBRARY • NEW YORK

RAPTURE

Published by Popular Library, a unit of CBS Publications,
the Consumer Publishing Division of CBS Inc.

Copyright © 1979 by Rosamond Royal
All Rights Reserved

ISBN: 0-445-04359-8

Printed in the United States of America

First Popular Library printing: September 1979

10   9   8   7   6   5   4   3   2   1

To Destiny, which guides us all,
this book is dedicated.

There are many kinds of love—old and new—and not the least of these is the love of a mother for the child of her lost lover. . . .

The Island of Majorca

1638

A blaze of sunlight spilled down through the fig tree's silvery branches, reached scorching fingers through the palms that cast wavering shadows across the courtyard, and turned to breathtaking scarlet the deep-red roses that rioted over the balustrade and stone pillars of the big house at San Telmo. Excited servants bustled about in the heat.

There was going to be a wedding!

Only the sixteen-year-old bride was not laughing. *She* sat white-faced, with her fingers twined tightly together, in an upstairs room behind a locked door before which a guard was mounted. Her moonbeam-fair hair cascaded like glistening gold over her tense shoulders, and her horrified gray eyes stared at the high-necked white wedding dress, the overflowing heavy white lace veil that lay spread across the bed, with the despairing fascination one might give to a striking snake. They had lied to her! The man she was to wed was not young, not handsome, not good. He was called The Whip and he lashed men to death for his pleasure. Dear God, they were going to wed her to a monster!

Hurt to her heart by her daughter's dazed expression of horror, Rosamunde, the girl's beautiful mother, gazed at young Elaine with compassion, and her own hands clenched fiercely. Rodrigue's brother had done this—he had tricked them both to satisfy his wife's ambition! Margarita aspired to become a lady-in-waiting at the Spanish court, and The Whip's power and influence— bought by this infamous marriage—would secure that place for her. Young Elaine was to be the sacrifice to that ambition.

Rosamunde's heart ached for her daughter, and on her lips trembled the words she dared not speak: *I am going to save you, Elaine, though it cost me my life. You will never wed The Whip.*

Suddenly she could not bear to look at Elaine, suffering there. Instead she turned, a shimmering woman with sinuous grace, and walked to the window, stood looking out through the bars so recently placed there—how well they knew her temper! How wise they had been to remove Rodrigue's pistol from the room, for she would surely have shot her way out, whatever the cost!

Below in the hot courtyard servants ran busily about, preparing for today's nuptials. In a few moments old Juana would come to dress the bride for the ceremony. In a day or two at the most she, Rosamunde, would be dead.

For it was her intention, with the aid of trusted Juana, to save Elaine by dressing *herself* in that long concealing white bridal gown, let that heavy white lace veil drape over her own face. She and her daughter were the same height, the same coloring—only their eyes were a different hue, for hers were vivid emerald green. But she could keep those eyes cast down. Their figures, save that the young girl's delicately molded breasts were a shade less developed, were identical. Their voices were near enough—and she would mumble shyly.

She would take Elaine's place before the altar—but she dared not confide that to Elaine, for proud young Elaine would never accept such a sacrifice from her. Juana would bring drugged wine and Elaine would drink it, all unknowing, "to give her fortitude" for the coming ordeal.

Rosamunde's mind raced ahead. The marriage would be by proxy, for The Whip never traveled. In the ceremony which would shortly take place in the vaulted family chapel of the great house at San Telmo, young Elaine—no, *Rosamunde!*—would be wed to The Whip's jewel-encrusted sword, held point down by that smirking Frenchman with the broken nose! By jolting coach the bride would be transported to The Whip's stronghold of La Calobra on the far side of the island. The journey would take at least two days.

That would give Juana time to effect Elaine's escape.

For once at La Calobra there would be no turning back. Women had been known to leave that forbidding pile—but they left it greatly changed, their faces forever blank with horror. And when the groom—that horrid groom!—lifted the bridal veil from the bride's slender shoulders, he would find himself cheated. Young Elaine —although she did not know it now—would be far away.

Rosamunde had no illusions about how The Whip would greet this unwelcome impersonation. Once arrived at La Calobra she could count her future in hours, perhaps in minutes.

No! Her valiant heart rebelled at that. *She would escape, she would rejoin Elaine, she would find a ship to carry them away from this accursed island!*

Standing there by the barred sunlit window, she had the feeling of having done it all before, and for a treacherous moment her own wild venturesome past rose up before her. And she was back home in England, sixteen again, and rebelliously facing a barbarous marriage.

The year was 1620.

1

The Highwayman's Lady

One   *Rosamunde*

England 1620

I   *Her riotous pale-gold hair tightly coiffed and*
haloed by the candlelight that suffused the cavernous
drawing room of Kenwarren House, Rosamunde Langley
missed the last note of her song under the insistent aggressive scrutiny of the handsome peer who leaned forward, his glowing brown eyes beaming suggestively into
hers. He was Lord Matthew Waverclay, wealthy, twice a
widower and of an unsavory reputation. Resentfully, sixteen-year-old Rosamunde remembered hearing Louisa
murmur languidly behind her fan, "Pay some attention
to Rosamunde, Matt. You are focusing too much on
me. James will surely notice." A cynical smile curving
his narrow cruel mouth, Lord Matthew had promptly
eased himself to Rosamunde's side and insisted she sing
to Louisa's accompaniment on the harpsichord.

Rosamunde had protested fatigue, but James, the elderly earl of Kenwarren (and Louisa's husband), had be-
stirred himself in his velvet chair. "Sing, child," he
echoed.

So Rosamunde had sung a ballad in her clear light
voice—and missed the last note under the pressure of
that bold aggressive stare. Now she lifted her chin and
her green eyes flung back a challenge to Lord Matthew
as he lazily moved to block her path. Biting her soft
lower lip, she swept her heavy skirts around to pass him,
and his lace-cuffed arm, moving apparently in an acci-
dental path, knocked the ivory fan from her hand. As
both bent simultaneously to pick it up, his dark head
brushed her fair hair, scented with lemons. His strong
lazy fingers were first to retrieve the fallen fan, and when

he reached forward to return it to her, his hand idly brushed the soft thrusting crests of her young breasts, so well concealed under the thick heavy brocade of her gown. Rosamunde stiffened, but Lord Matthew, with a lofty smile, turned back to Louisa, the lady who sat at the harpsichord, her creamy fingers tracing a desultory tinkle that sounded almost like laughter.

Red with mortification at this double insult, and forced to make her way stiffly in the big flounced wheel-farthingale that cloaked her young loveliness, Rosamunde proceeded to a handsome carved straight chair and sat down primly. She was abruptly conscious that the eyes of her guardian, the earl of Kenwarren, rested on her thoughtfully. *Better he watch his young second wife Louisa!* thought Rosamunde irritably. Everyone at Kenwarren House knew Louisa had many lovers and played the old earl for a fool. Why, she'd even heard that new maid, the bawdy Lutie, say to Mull, the housekeeper, "Her ladyship's after Lord Matthew now, ain't she? Sure, she's fair bustin' out o' her dress tonight!" And Mull had tittered coarsely, "Well, the mistress is bound to show the two best points she has left!" At this reference to Louisa's fading if overdone charms, Lutie had slapped her thigh and howled. Both had stopped abruptly as Rosamunde hurried down the corridor past them. Rosamunde had pretended not to hear. She always pretended not to hear when matters concerned Louisa, of whom she was very apprehensive.

For had not Louisa, immediately after her marriage to the old earl, promptly seized and tossed away all of Rosamunde's gowns? True, she had replaced them. Under the guise of bestowing warm generous gifts, Louisa had managed totally to conceal Rosamunde's young glowing beauty under the stiffest fabrics one could find. Great billowing wheel-farthingales to hide her graceful limbs, huge awkward padded sleeves which hid her slender arms and from which only her small hands stuck out below lace cuffs, shapeless bodices with long-pointed stomachers, gigantic wired ruffs to cover her white slender neck, furbelows, flounces—Rosamunde could hardly walk in the

13

clothes Louisa had so sweetly bestowed upon her. And as for her hair! It was pulled back so tightly that the skin of Rosamunde's forehead was taut and her eyebrows felt permanently elevated—and over all was stuck an elaborate headdress made of stiffened lace and fabric that completely altered the shape of her head. Only her heartrendingly lovely face showed, clothed in the sheerest of pink-and-white complexions, lit by large iridescent green eyes shaded by thick dark lashes. Those eyes were heart-stopping. Louisa had been able to do nothing about them. She had eagerly suggested that Rosamunde was shortsighted and should wear spectacles, but Rosamunde had retorted that her vision was excellent and proved it by shooting an arrow through an arrowslit of the round tower such a long distance away.

The thought of that arrow shot made her blush. For Lord Matthew had been there, standing beneath the shade of the May-flowering beeches of Kenwarren Park. He had insisted on setting Rosamunde's hand to the yew bow, placing his arms bindingly about her as he did so. Lord Matthew had a cruel mouth and no kindness in his gleaming brown eyes, which were hard as agates, but Rosamunde had felt her heart beating uncomfortably fast against his taffeta doublet and had hated her own feminine betrayal of emotion beneath these assaults of his undoubted masculinity.

Now from her straight chair she could see Lord Matthew, one arm resting on the harpsichord, his broad back bent over Louisa as if to hear her better, and guessed he was peering down the front of Louisa's startlingly low-cut rose satin gown—even the lovely colors Louisa had sequestered to herself; Rosamunde was left with ugly shades of brown and taupe and dark indeterminate hues unsuited to her fair young loveliness.

As if that was not enough, tonight Louisa was mockingly urging her lover to pay some attention to Rosamunde to divert attention from her own infidelities! Rosamunde's slender fingers clenched together achingly. Even though at sixteen she was all too conscious of the debt she owed to her elderly guardian for keeping her at vast Kenwarren

House under his protection, all too conscious that she was an impoverished charge almost completely dependent on his kindness, she knew there would come a time when her patience with Louisa would snap. A time when her green eyes would flash and her soft lips curl and her light voice fling words at the dark voluptuous overdone beauty that once spoken could never be unsaid.

Rosamunde was not a fool. The face that looked back at her daily from her mirror was a reckless face. She knew that someday Louisa would torment her once too often, drive her too far.

And on that day she must be prepared to strike out for herself, for she had no hope that James, earl of Kenwarren, so besotted with his second wife, would aid her against Louisa. In that battle, Rosamunde must lose. So she was being very cautious and so far she had held her tongue.

At the harpsichord Lord Matthew said something to Louisa, and her laughter tinkled and her fan swept up. Rosamunde heard her reply in a low tone, but she could not make out the words. That it was about her she had no doubt, for Lord Matthew promptly turned his cold amused countenance toward Rosamunde, his dark eyes alight, his expression that of a fox on the prowl for chickens. Doubtless Louisa was again urging him to pay attention to her! Well, Rosamunde had no desire for Lord Matthew's attentions. Rich he might be, fashionable he might be. But he was twice a widower and old enough to be her father! That he was hard and strong and made an elegant leg in his satin knee breeches and took his snuff with an air did not recommend him to her. Her dislike of him had been instantaneous and absolute. Now, seeing him approach across the Turkey carpet, she abruptly rose and turned to her guardian.

"I am tired," she stated. "Have I your permission to retire?"

The bag of bones who was the old earl stirred and nodded.

Rosamunde fled, finding her way through the maze of corridors that led to her room. Kenwarren House was a handsome home, but the miserly earl kept it in a run-down state—just as he kept his horses and his outbuildings in a run-down state. Only with dark Louisa did he unloose his pursestrings, even allowing her to squander his money on low-cut dresses to attract the many admirers of her overdone charms and on frightful frumperies for Rosamunde, who greeted each new item with shock.

Having traversed the dark corridors with a lighted taper, Rosamunde opened the door to her bedroom with a sigh and sought refuge within. This room with its oriole window and its familiar squarish furniture represented a safe haven to her, for it had been her room through most of her young life.

Now she placed her taper carefully on the table and struggled out of the big enveloping gown. She could have waited for old Betts, who would have been glad enough to help her—and who undoubtedly would be along later with some warm milk—but she could not wait to rid herself of the hateful thing. She tossed the offensive dress over a chair, removed her petticoats and huge farthingale and chemise, and slipped with relief into a thin white night rail, suitable for the warmth of the summer night.

Pensively she leaned on her arms, staring out of the open casements at the moon-bathed countryside. Out there beyond her sight were dairymaids tossing in the hay with their lovers, bright-stockinged legs thrashing as they giggled. And fresh-faced young farm girls looking shy-eyed at the bashful young rustics who came to call and sat on hard wooden benches dreaming of the day they'd wed and bed. Down country lanes all over England on a fine night like this maids were walking hand in hand with light-footed lads who sighed and stopped to kiss them in the shade of gnarled old trees. And downstairs Louisa was no doubt arranging her own bedroom tryst with Lord Matthew—a daring tryst with Lord Matthew slipping quietly into her bedroom, as did her other lovers, while the old earl snored in his adjoining room next door.

Rosamunde sighed. In all the world, only she did not have a lover. How her heart dreamed of him! Tall he would be and brave. A man of steel who bent others to his

16

will but did not bend. Wealthy? She doubted it. So many things she put before gold. But when he held her in his arms, this man whose face she could not see, she would become a woman, warm, yielding. Her senses would flare up to his touch and she would follow him anywhere, anywhere.

In the garden below a loud caterwaul sounded and a dark furry shape leaped from a low stone wall, to be swiftly followed in one pouncing spring by another dark furry shape. There was an instant yowling scuffle, which rose and fell. Even the cats had lovers. . . .

Ruefully, Rosamunde sniffed the air. It had the scent of rain in it. She smiled wryly. If those clouds that were building in the western sky portended rain, the cats might find their ardor dampened by a sudden downpour.

With a sigh she turned from her vigil at the window and slipped between the covers of the big square bed, tossing off all but the lightest sheet. She moved restlessly, and her hair spread out around her on the pillow in a golden torrent. Tomorrow might bring her the lover she dreamed of, tomorrow. . . .

Unaware of her beauty or the trouble it would bring her, she drifted off to sleep.

Flickering moonlight wavered through Rosamunde's oriole window, glanced across her sleeping form and high-lighted for a moment the hall door that opened swiftly to admit a man in satin knee breeches. So quickly did Lord Matthew Waverclay close the door behind him that it seemed barely to have opened at all, and his eyes were all for the hall outside—as became a man who was slipping into the bedroom of his host's wife. By the harpsichord after dinner, while the earl of Kenwarren drowsed in his chair, Lord Matthew had made his tryst with Louisa, and it was the voluptuous and insatiable Louisa he confidently expected to find waiting in the big four-poster. How could Lord Matthew know that, slightly befuddled by wine and hearing a servant's step on the stair, he had hurriedly taken a wrong turn in the endless corridors of Kenwarren House and had now admitted himself to the bedroom of

17

the earl's sleeping ward instead of the earl's pretty and faithless wife?

In the fitful moonlight the moon went behind a cloud as Lord Matthew turned at last to view the room, and he could barely make out the bed, let alone the occupant. Had the moon been out he would have been greeted not only by the sight of Rosamunde, one sleeping arm outflung across the pillow, but also, flung across the chair, the ill-fitting gown which had met with his derisive stare in the drawing room below.

Now Lord Matthew crept silently across the room. No word did he speak, for he knew the earl's bedroom to be but a whisper away, although Louisa had assured him that the door between would be bolted. He had bedded the lush Louisa on two former occasions—once in his great house near Salisbury, and once at a houseparty given by Lady Soames—but this was the first time he would take Louisa dangerously in her own house, within actual hearing distance of the earl. It loosed in him a sense of excitement, and his fingers trembled as he hastily discarded his rosette-trimmed shoes and divested himself of his satin breeches.

Hot to be about his wooing, Lord Matthew tossed aside the sheet that covered that dim feminine form on this summer night and plunged joyfully upon her. He was greeted with a gasp and a strangled cry which he took to be passion and hastily smothered with a kiss. His hand took possession of a warm throbbing young breast whose silkiness delighted him. His loins pressed in upon a smooth stomach, and his legs felt a pair of dainty limbs in wild motion—which he took to mean a desperate eagerness to be free of the light restriction of their enveloping nightdress. That he had aroused such unbridled lust in the woman he held in his arms filled Lord Matthew with pride. About to lose his hold on her wriggling form, he took a more determined grip, his lips closing down like a clamp upon the soft mouth that moved and twisted beneath his own as Rosamunde desperately tried to turn her head this way and that in her frantic efforts to elude him. It took Lord Matthew some moments to realize that the feminine body in his arms was struggling—actually bat-

18

tling to be free. But even this he mistook for passion. Dimly it was borne in on him that Louisa's familiar body seemed to have altered in some delightful way, that the silky hair that cascaded over the pillow and now mingled with his own dark locks smelled slightly of lemons—not the musky perfumes Louisa affected—and that the body pinned beneath him was of a singularly yielding sweetness, and thrashing about in panic.

To Rosamunde, Lord Matthew's onslaught had been as unexpected as it was terrifying. She had been wakened out of a sound sleep by the weight of a body falling on her, and when her green eyes had flown open in terror and her soft mouth opened to scream, a pair of hard punishing lips had smashed down upon her own, effectively silencing her. Half-smothered, she struggled against this heavy burden with the pawing hands, who held her cruelly tight and seemed bent on tearing the light night rail she wore from her softly rounded breasts. In shock, she realized that one of her attacker's knees was endeavoring to pry her legs apart. Instinctively, she kicked at him. Her breath sobbed in her throat.

With Rosamunde's violent exertions and finally her kick, which caught him at the ankle, numbing her toe but alerting him to the idea that all might not be well beneath him, Lord Matthew sobered a bit. Gradually it seeped through his wine-fuddled brain that he had made some terrible mistake, that the slight body that cringed in his arms was . . . not Louisa. And besides, the moon, which had coyly hidden, now beamed brightly through the oriole window and showed him that the hair spread out on the pillow was not dark—it was pale and shining.

With an abruptness that eclipsed his pouncing descent upon the slender body in the bed, Lord Matthew's head went up, and for a moment the bright moonlight revealed his astonished face as he stared down at the figure beneath him. Rosamunde's lovely young face, lit by wide angry iridescent green eyes, glared up at him. They were only a kiss apart, but in that flashing instant he could see the pulsing white column of her slender neck, her creamy shoulders and pearly breasts, pink-tipped and rising and

19

falling in a gasping rhythm as Rosamunde tried to get enough breath to speak.

"Lord Matthew!" she gasped. "Get out of my bed!"

But this pink-and-white vision with riotous pale-gold hair and skin a silken delight to the touch had fired Lord Matthew's passion past conscience or regret. His dark eyes red-rimmed, he muttered, "Faith, you've spent the evening inviting me here with your simpers! You'll not turn me out now!"

It was such an unjustified accusation that Rosamunde, enraged, brought her now free right hand around and struck him full in the face. His head jerked, and for a moment his eyes darkened and his teeth, shining white in the moonlight, closed together with a snap.

"Damned silken wench—driving me to frenzy!" he muttered, grasping the hand that had struck him in a grip that near paralyzed her arm and slamming it back onto the pillow. As abruptly as he had left her, he returned, his hard mouth smashing down upon hers with a violence that bruised her lips and nearly cracked her teeth.

Doubly shocked by the violence of his attack—especially now since he knew he had made a mistake and she was not Louisa—Rosamunde struggled with renewed desperation. But his hard-muscled arms and lean punishing fingers held her fast. They dug bruisingly into her tender flesh, and she heard fabric rip as her light night rail departed her body. His hands were now mauling her breasts hurtfully, and she would have cried out had she had the breath or opportunity, but that clamping mouth was robbing her of her senses. Giddily she fought, writhing to this side and that. But his lordship was obdurate. The weight of his body was flung across her slight form, and try though she might she could not elude him, although her hips moved swiftly this way and that across the soft mattress.

Panting, perspiring in his efforts to subdue this green-eyed wildcat he had captured but not yet tamed, Lord Matthew made a violent effort to thrust between those thrashing legs—and was rewarded, as Rosamunde's mouth jerked free from his lips, by a scream that echoed through

20

his head as she twisted violently away from his male hardness. The scream seemed to echo and reecho, and in a maddened way he realized that *her* scream was not the only scream in the room. A candle's glow cast long shadows against the wall, and from the open doorway behind him burst a woman's screams, peal after peal, to mingle with those of the girl on the bed.

Once again interrupted, Lord Matthew sat up. His head swung around to view the author of this intrusion. The sight of an elderly aproned maidservant agawk in the doorway and screeching loudly met his furious gaze. Cursing, sputtering, Lord Matthew leaped up, and Rosamunde, relieved of his weight, was able to scramble off the bed, her lovely naked figure sylphlike in the moonlight. Inwardly she thanked God for old Betts, who stood solidly in the doorway, clutching in one hand a candle that shook and in the other a tankard of warm milk for her young charge. Betts had been of the opinion that Rosamunde was catching cold. So long had she administered to the ills of those who lived in Kenwarren House that she had waited to come up until she'd finished her other chores, intending to wake Rosamunde and make her drink the milk. Instead she had been greeted by the sight of the pair thrashing about on the bed, and it had rattled her wits.

In moments the entire household was in an uproar. Betts was still screaming—in spite of Lord Matthew's roars to be silent—when Louisa, the earl's dark-haired, dark-eyed wife, rushed in still clad in the elegant rose satin gown she'd worn earlier. Louisa's practiced eye took in the situation at a glance: Rosamunde blushing and clutching the shreds of her torn night rail around her, Lord Matthew red-faced and furious, scuttling back into his handsome breeches as best he might. Ah, it was clear enough! Rosamunde—and *her* lover!

"You are a harlot—a very harlot!" shouted the enraged Louisa, tossing back a head of dark curls. "Seducing a guest under our very noses!"

It was too much. Rosamunde's self-control snapped. Disheveled and as enraged as Louisa, she shouted, "Seducing! *Your lover* tried to rape me!"

Just at that moment the earl arrived, tall, gaunt, his bony head covered by a stocking cap. At Rosamunde's shouted accusation he turned pale, but he grasped his wife's arm to hold her back from physically attacking the angry half-naked girl. His frozen face silenced his ward, but she kept her eyes fixed on him expectantly nonetheless, anticipating from him at least rough justice.

Even that was not forthcoming.

The nightcapped earl cast barely a glance at his furious wife, whose arm he held in a viselike grip. But he cast more than a malevolent glance at his guest, Lord Matthew Waverclay, hastily adjusting his satin breeches to cover himself.

Red-faced at this cold inspection, Lord Matthew reared up to his not inconsiderable height and gave his host back a look of some desperation. How well known in the household was his affair with the earl's wife he did not know. But he could hardly admit that he had been headed for Louisa's room and had blundered instead into young Rosamunde's. Lord, how silken had been her bare shoulders beneath his impatient hands, how matchless her ripe young breasts beneath the thin night rail he had succeeded in ripping off when that dunce of a maidservant had burst in and set up a howl! With a last jerk he finished adjusting his trousers and slipped into his rosette-trimmed shoes. Once again fully dressed, he straightened up before the earl and his lady and tried to assume a truculent air.

That air was lost on the earl, who flashed a look from his discomfited guest to Rosamunde, a slender eloquent figure in the remnants of her white night rail, her green eyes furious. The earl considered that wayward figure, that soft unrepentent mouth. He turned to consider the Lady Louisa by his side. It occurred to him that the very youth and dash of sixteen-year-old Rosamunde might have served as a spur to Louisa's wild flirtations—for he was not unaware of them, though he did not suspect how far those flirtations had led her.

"Matt, I did not think it of you," he told his guest coldly. "But since you've debauched the girl, you'll rectify the situation by marrying her. At once."

22

Before that pronouncement, the elegant Lord Matthew paled. And beside the gaunt earl, Louisa drew in her breath sharply.

"But I swear to you I did not—" Lord Matthew whirled almost in appeal to Rosamunde, and his voice faded. For this was a Rosamunde far different from the shapeless dowdy girl Louisa made her appear by day. This new glowing Rosamunde was a different sight altogether—a sight to make his blood course feverishly through his veins. Her golden hair cascaded like shimmering light over gleaming white shoulders. Round trembling young breasts were deliciously revealed as they thrust forward against the torn material of her thin white night rail. Bedazzled, his gaze roamed over her sheer flawless skin, her slight but elegant figure, small-boned and tiny-waisted, and his hard brown eyes gleamed with a new light. He was seeing clearly that he had made a mistake in choosing for seduction the wife over the ward. Rosamunde was tall and slender; she stood proudly. She would carry clothes well— if they did but fit her. She had a natural grace and dignity of bearing and fearless eyes that even now tried to stare him down. Such a regal beauty would preside well over any great household—indeed, she would preside well over his own great household at Waverclay Court.

And in bed . . . ah, in bed. He ran his tongue over his cruel sensual mouth, remembering the touch of her, the faint delightful perfumed scent of her, the elegance of her slender body. In bed . . . what he could *not* do with that sweet body in bed!

"I was carried away," he said shortly. "It was the wine." And then he rushed on in a hoarse voice to proclaim that the match was what he himself would wish. His face was bland as he met Louisa's frank glare. "Indeed," he added haughtily to the earl, "on the morrow I had planned to seek her hand from you, James."

The earl gave him back a grim smile and released his wife's trembling arm. "It seems you pressed your suit a bit early, but I'll overlook that."

"I will not marry him!" cried Rosamunde, trembling. "Nothing could induce me!"

23

Lord Matthew's brows elevated and his cruel mouth twisted derisively at the corners. Quite casually he took out his snuffbox and expertly extracted a bit of snuff, inhaled. Rosamunde watched him grimly, it was a habit she hated.

"Your opinion is not being solicited," snapped the earl. "You are my ward, and as such, I will see you do what's best for you."

Rosamunde would have given him a hot reply, but Lord Matthew announced with a sigh that he regretted that he could not stay to immediately consummate the marriage but pressing matters required his presence at his seat of Waverclay Court on the morrow. He would, regrettably, be forced to leave them.

At this reprieve, Rosamunde breathed a deep sigh of relief, but the earl gave Lord Matthew a suspicious look. Testily he insisted that both his ward and himself would accompany Lord Matthew back to Waverclay Court on the morrow, lest Lord Matthew's memory prove faulty. The banns would be published and the marriage of his sullied charge would take place as soon as possible.

Lord Matthew smiled thinly and snapped his snuffbox shut.

Outraged, Rosamunde again found her voice. "I will not marry Lord Matthew!" she cried wildly. "You cannot force me."

"You are my ward," pointed out the earl heavily. "You will obey me in this matter."

"I will *not* obey you!" flashed Rosamunde. "My mother never meant me to be forced into marriage with a rapist!"

Lord Matthew's lowering expression boded ill for his bride-to-be.

"Mind your tongue, girl," commanded the earl crisply. " 'Tis your future husband you're insulting."

"I'll run away!" threatened Rosamunde, driven too far.

Immediately she regretted that remark. The earl considered her with narrowed eyes. "Yes, I believe you might," he murmured. With determination he took several sashes and, grasping her wrists and ankles, tied her firmly to the bedpost.

24

"An excellent idea," approved Lord Matthew coldly. "She will have time to reflect upon the honor I have done her in offering her an old and respected name." He swept out of the room with never a backward look at fuming Rosamunde or pale shaken Louisa. As if to see him at last to his proper bedroom, the earl followed him down the hall.

Old Betts had long since set down the milk and fled. Now Rosamunde, bound to the bedpost and humiliated, found herself alone with Louisa. Louisa's dark eyes were flashing as brightly as the diamond rosettes in her artfully wired-up hair. The creamy tops of her full breasts—scandalously revealed by her low décolletage—rose and fell wrathfully. Her richly embroidered overgown whirled as she strode angrily about, turning at last to face the rebellious young girl tied to the bedpost.

"Rosamunde, you are a fool!" cried Louisa, clenching her hands together and wincing as her big rings cut into her flesh. "Lord Matthew is—he is not right for you."

"But he is right for *you*, is he not?" flashed Rosamunde. "Why did you not speak up for me? He is *your* lover! You knew he was but seeking your room and stumbled into mine!"

"How dare you say that?" Louisa drew herself up so that her diamond rosettes quivered. Suddenly it occurred to her that this marriage at least would rid her of a lustrous young rival for attention in her own household—a too beautiful young girl who was increasingly difficult to keep looking plain even though she had tried her best.

"I say it again!" cried Rosamunde in a fury. "All the household—indeed, all the countryside—knows of your lovers!"

Her passion, which had been white-hot, now draining away, Louisa considered her husband's ward. Yes, it would be well to be rid of Rosamunde, and as for Matthew—well, he would still come visiting, leaving his young wife at home, no doubt . . . . She gave Rosamunde a sour look. "Matt will know how to deal with you," she promised ominously. "He has had two wives, and I hear he took a whip to the first, who displeased him."

Rosamunde's iridescent green eyes widened. With her quick mind, she saw at once the direction of Louisa's thoughts. Ah, it had been no secret to her that the older woman was jealous of her youth, of her beauty. Without a murmur she had endured the hideous hairdo, without protest she had worn those shapeless padded farthingales that Louisa had thrust upon her. But this—!

"I will *not* marry your lover!" she panted, white-faced, straining against her bonds. "I will kill myself first!"

Louisa's eyebrows lifted. She gave Rosamunde a contemptuous look and swirled out, slamming the door. A key turned in the lock, and Louisa's derisive laughter echoed down the hall.

Left alone, Rosamunde stared down in horror at the bonds that held her. She was—she *must* be dreaming! From this nightmare she would surely wake! But her body told her that it was no dream, for strange wild stirrings had been aroused within her. She, who had never known a man's arms, had been grasped and held and roughly fondled. And now painfully it had come to her that she was young and in her heart no longer a carefree girl but a woman—and ready for a man to love her.

But that man was *not* Lord Matthew Waverclay! Thinking about him, her teeth ground. Ah, what a fool she'd been not to have had it out with Louisa long ago! Telling herself Louisa's jealousy would fade, that Louisa would eventually relent and let her have pretty clothes and the attentions of suitors—for surely every girl dreamed of having amorous suitors vying for her hand. She had practiced forbearance as Louisa kept all the young men away and glided swiftly between her and such houseguests as Lord Matthew. Playing a waiting game, Rosamunde had let Louisa work her cruel way upon her, striving to make her plain, keeping her dressed like a frump. And her reward was to be denounced as a seductress and banished to the bed of a lecherous and cruel man! So violently did she rend at her bonds that her slender wrists were rubbed raw. At last, panting from exertion and pain, she desisted.

Brute force would not break her free, she realized bitterly. She would have to use her wiles if she hoped to escape Lord Matthew.

2   *Morning found Rosamunde drooping in her bonds,* numb with fatigue. Breakfast was brought to her by old Betts, who tch-tched as she untied her. It was only some hot gruel and milk, but it gave Rosamunde strength. Betts left when one of the maids came to help her dress, and as the door opened to admit the girl Rosamunde saw with a sinking heart that the earl himself stood guard outside her door to prevent her escape. Had her room not been located high above a stone terrace that fronted on a garden, Rosamunde might have struck the girl aside and tried to go out by way of the window. As it was, she massaged her numbed hands and raw wrists and allowed herself to be garbed in a dark-gray damask traveling dress with shapeless padded sleeves and a sloping neckruff, yellow-starched, with considerable stiff lace at collar and cuffs. Rigid busks held the stiff pointed stomacher in place and made it almost painful to wear, and the whole dress seemed heavy and stiff enough to stand alone, for none of it conformed to her fair young body.

Trembling with anger—for she could hardly have been more uncomfortable; the great billowing damask skirt spread out over a farthingale barely small enough to go through a coach door—Rosamunde brushed the maid aside and dressed her own hair. Dressed it not as Louisa had willed it, but more fashionably, high over a roll in the front and caught up in a shining bun at the back, in a manner that set off her sweet face to perfection. She glowered at her shapeless reflection in the mirror. Indeed she'd half a mind to rip the hated farthingale off, to rip all her clothes to shreds! But the maid would undoubtedly be punished, and anyway that would only bring another condescending gift from Louisa—some gown twice her size that buxom Louisa had been about to discard as too old-fashioned—so there was naught to be accomplished by that.

In a cold voice she announced herself to be ready. Ironically, the earl held open the door, seized her arm as she would have eluded him. Holding her with a grip so firm she winced, he escorted his ward down the main stairway, followed by her small trunk in the arms of a burly footman.

Rosamunde looked about her wistfully as they made their descent into the cavernous hall below. Kenwarren House had been her home since her mother, second cousin of the earl's first wife, had brought her here as a child. The earl's first wife had been fond of her young cousin; their warm friendship had endured and even blossomed during the long lingering illness that had made the earl a widower. Surprisingly the two kinswomen, the younger and the older, had died close together—the earl's lady of tuberculosis and Rosamunde's mother when the new hunter she was riding had shied at a snake and tossed her headfirst into a stone wall.

For a time both Rosamunde and the earl had endured loneliness in the great stone pile of Kenwarren. And then Louisa had come into their lives and changed everything. Years younger than the earl and quite poor, she had seized upon his offer of marriage and come with glittering eyes to the great house at Kenwarren. She had gazed upon Rosamunde with distaste and mentioned at once that the girl's clothes needed alteration—she would see to it. She had remarked to the earl that Rosamunde was too . . . *forthcoming.* Young men had been kept at a distance. In *her* hive, Louisa intended to be the only queen bee.

Now as Rosmunde trailed down the familiar stairway beside her guardian, she recalled wistfully running down these same wide stairs to be enfolded in her mother's loving arms, recalled playing here as a child with a gray kitten, romping outside with the gamboling hunting dogs, and then as a young girl dreaming of a lover carrying in armloads of fragrant flowers from the garden to deck this gloomy hall. For a moment her green eyes filled with tears. She felt forlornly that she was seeing these stairs and this hall for the last time.

Her tears dried rapidly at the sight of Louisa and Lord Matthew, standing together at the foot of the stairs. They had obviously been having a warm conversation, for there were two bright spots of color on Louisa's cheeks and his lordship looked discomfited. Without comment, the earl swept forward, dragging Rosamunde, and reluctantly Lord Matthew followed them.

Moments later they were seated in the green coach, the three of them, with Rosamunde's small trunk on top, along with the liveried coachman and a footman. Blazoned on the side of the coach were the crest and arms which identified it as belonging to the earl of Kenwarren. Rosamunde's last sight of the house was of Louisa's yellow taffeta skirts flouncing in through the big oaken doors to be lost in the gloom of the great hall.

She lifted her chin and stared stonily ahead of her as the coach rolled down the tree-lined drive and out past the big stone gateposts. But as she reached the main road a hopeless feeling overcame her.

If only . . . if only her father, Jonathan Langley, had lived. Her wild father. . . . Her set face softened as she thought of him. She had seen him but half a dozen times in her life, for he was always off to foreign wars, seeking his fortune. A younger son who had married a penniless bride against his father's wishes, his family had never forgiven him. And his reckless gallantry had led him eventually to disaster and death . . . on the block. Rosamunde winced; she did not like to think about it.

Her mother's sweet face had gone gray as ashes when she heard her Jon was dead. The light had gone out of those dreaming eyes forever, leaving a blank emptiness. Perhaps that was why she had ridden the new hunter so fast. Perhaps she had not cared when she was hurled through space to crush out her life against a gray stone wall. . . .

In any event, there was none to save Rosamunde now. Head held high, her face a calm mask, she sat with a thumping heart as the coach rolled on.

Their pace was leisurely, and at an inn known as the Ox and Bow they stopped for lunch. Rosamunde scarcely picked at her pigeon pie, and she watched with distaste as Lord Matthew and the earl, while complaining about the food, ate generously, washing it down with great tankards of ale.

Shortly after leaving the Ox and Bow it was discovered that their coach had a defective wheel—the earl never being one to waste money on unnecessary repairs, his equipage was always breaking down. Lord Matthew vented a deep sigh and pursed his thin lips. The earl drummed his fingers. Slowly they limped back to the Ox and Bow, and at a nearby smithy repairs were made to the faulty wheel.

Rosamunde bethought herself of escape, but she was closely watched. In the private room of the establishment, the earl, who pretended to doze, opened one eye whenever she so much as moved. As the minutes stretched into several hours, Rosamunde grew increasingly desperate.

At last, filled with a fine sense of panic, she found herself on the way again, the green coach moving south across the storied Salisbury Plain.

Beside her, sunk in thought, sat the bony earl, a grim skeleton of a man whose bones, one felt, should rattle as the coach bounced. His long sleeveless overgown of velvet was clutched around him as if the day were chill. His thoughts were upon his young wife, Louisa, and he continued to ignore his companions just as he ignored the wonders of the Salisbury Plain which they traversed. Tonight, God willing, would find them at Waverclay Court, which lay to the north of the cathedral city of Salisbury, split by the beautiful River Avon. Past hills on which the Romans had camped centuries before, hills fortified and held by Saxons and by Normans, they jolted, but always his mind was on Louisa . . . sumptuously lovely dark Louisa, whose roving eye had not escaped him.

He was inclined to blame all of Louisa's excesses on Rosamunde. If the girl were not so strikingly beautiful, Louisa would not, he felt, be driven to flirt with her fan or with her bold brown eyes that held out promises of delights. Something about young Rosamunde, who seemed not to know the stunning effect of her beauty, brought out the devil in Louisa. He frowned and turned to regard his ward with disfavor. She had a reckless face—as had her father before her. It had brought to him and those who loved him only grief. Yes, best to be rid of her, and quickly, before she soured his relationship with Louisa. And though he'd had a qualm or two that Matt might be too old for the girl—and never for a moment had he believed Louisa's hysterical accusation that Rosamunde had attempted to "seduce" Matt—he was now firmly convinced of the wisdom of his choice of suitors.

Lord Matthew would have a firm hand on the reins, and Rosamunde needed a firm hand. There was a wildness about her sometimes that disconcerted the earl. Now he turned to consider her from beneath lowering brows. To her unattractive garments he gave no thought. Instead he brooded on the fair pink-and-white complexion, the soft rebellious mouth, the long lashes that swept her cheeks and shadowed her brilliant green eyes—and her glorious fair hair swept fashionably up from her forehead and now in perilous danger of falling down to sweep over her slender shoulders as the coach tossed her about. A beauty now, and in another year or two the whole countryside would be in an uproar about her, he thought cynically. Best to turn her over quickly to Lord Matthew. Matt was twice a widower—he'd know how to keep the chit in line!

Rosamunde, as if she felt the pressure of these thoughts, turned briefly to regard the earl. His cold expression gave her no comfort. It had given her no comfort when they passed Stonehenge, where a circle of ancient monoliths pointed to the sky, and she had no doubt it would give her no comfort when they reached Lord

Matthew's seat of Waverclay Court, which lay to the north of Salisbury. Irritably, she moved away from the earl.

Across from her, her foppish betrothed recrossed his knees. Those knees were a miracle of ribbons and bows. Rosamunde despised those knees, and her expression showed it. Her head lifted, and coldly she met Lord Matthew's eyes. While always half asleep by day, he was waking now and considering her with a hard lecherous stare. She fidgeted and moved uneasily under that look as a low grumble of thunder was heard in the west and fleecy gray clouds moved across the dying sun.

It was late when they stopped to dine at a tiny inn that ordinarily would have been beneath their notice. The earl was for spending the night under its thatched roof, but Lord Matthew angrily insisted that his business at Waverclay Court was pressing and they must with all speed push on.

So it was under a pale moon and low scudding clouds that threatened rain that the green coach careened behind galloping horses over the dangerous stretch of road that led south toward Salisbury. The coachman knew he must now make up for lost time. For the moon was up, and all knew that highwaymen prowled these roads by night. Inside the coach the three passengers bounced and jolted, Lord Matthew muttering they'd best pray that the coach not lose a wheel and land them all half dead in the ditch.

Within, Rosamunde's pale-gold hair was coming loose from its pins as the coach rocked. Her rebellious green eyes were fixed with loathing on her betrothed, whose cynical expression said that once wed he'd bring her to heel. In the main his gaze never strayed beyond her bouncing breasts trapped in their stiff tight bodice, and Rosamunde reddened and crossed her arms over them in fury —immediately to uncross them in a wild attempt to keep from being flung across the coach into his arms as the right front wheel struck a rock. Righting herself, she promptly recrossed her arms over her breasts, and her scathing gaze raked over Lord Matthew.

Although the earl beside her was dressed in rather

sober garb, Lord Matthew wore a wealth of romantic ringlets beneath his large plumed hat and a large falling ruff above generous slashed sleeves of red velvet. His Venetian breeches narrowed over his thighs and were shaped to button below the knee, where they became a mass of ribbons. Rosamunde's lip curled.

Lord Matthew was not entirely proof against Rosamunde's derisive inspection of his person. He turned with a sneer to the earl.

"Your ward seems displeased," he said carelessly, his offhand tone conveying how little Rosamunde's opinions counted.

Roused, the grim earl gave him an impatient look. "What can you expect, Matt? We're forcing the girl against her will." He turned irritably to his ward, bent on making her the scapegoat. "Had you not flaunted yourself so, you wouldn't have inflamed Lord Matthew to enter your bedroom."

Rosamunde turned to him a fearless glance. " 'Twas Louisa who flaunted herself. Lord Matthew but mistook my door for the door to Louisa's room." Her head snapped back as the earl's hand cracked against her cheek.

"Say no more about Louisa," he gritted through his teeth. "She is my affair, not yours!"

Rosamunde sat calmly. A red mark on her white face from his blow was the only indication that he had struck her. But anyone who had looked into her green eyes at that moment would have been alerted at once to danger. She was young, but she had courage. Now she clung as best she could to her precarious perch in the bounding coach and considered her chances if she were to throw open the door and fling herself out. Broken bones possibly . . . and *that* would seal her fate. No, she must find some other way to escape Lord Matthew. At Waverlay Court she would be hard put to keep his hands from her body unless . . . perhaps the earl would guard her from him until the banns could be read; it might give her time to escape.

"When you are wed—" began the earl in a more civil tone. But he never finished his remark, for he was interrupted by a shout from the coachman out front as the horses rounded a curve, saw something dead ahead of them in the road and shied. The coachman sawed on the reins; the stallion with the white forelegs skidded and lost his footing. All four horses went down in a tangled heap of reins and thrashing hooves. Behind them the green coach careened wildly and pitched over onto the soft earth at the side of the road.

Inside, the earl's words were cut off by a violent lurch as the coach seemed to leave the road altogether and then to descend upon it with a sickening thud as it overturned. Rosamunde, flung from her seat upon Lord Matthew, felt the crack of her shoulder against his jaw. She was knocked nearly senseless. After a stunned moment, she lifted herself up, extricated her arms and legs from Lord Matthew's scrambling figure and crawled at last out of the coach door, which the two cursing gentlemen within had managed to claw open. Eyes upon the rutted moonlit roadbed below, she jumped down in her awkward farthingale, realizing with relief that she must be unhurt, for her legs held her firmly.

As she raised her head, it was a tingling sight that met her astonished gaze.

The trembling horses had righted themselves and stood hopelessly entangled in the reins. Sprawled on the ground, the coachman had both hands in the air; the footman who usually rode beside him was nowhere to be seen. Behind Rosamunde, who stood rooted, Lord Matthew pulled the cursing earl, who had sprained his ankle, from the coach door.

Rosamunde stood at gaze, her feet as rooted to the Salisbury Plain as if they had grown there. Before her, etched against the wild night sky, was a tall rider, occupying the center of the road. Lean and formidable in stance, he sat astride a big black horse with a prominent white star on its forehead. Easily he bestrode the saddle, and his serviceable leather boots reached halfway up his lea thighs. Above his broad shoulders a wide-brimmed black hat with a gray plume shadowed a pair of gleaming eyes under straight black brows, and the rest of his face was
34

covered with a dark silk scarf. In the breeze that had come up at twilight his short black cloak whipped about him and ruffled the gray plumes of his hat—but nothing ruffled the pistol in his steady hand that drew her astonished gaze. It was pointed—at them!

"Stand and deliver!" he said in a ringing voice, and Lord Matthew and the earl swung around to face this horseman whose pistol was pointed unwaveringly at Lord Matthew's head.

"By God," muttered the earl. "It's—"

"Hard Harry!" gasped Lord Matthew, and Rosamunde's nerves tingled anew as the name of this famous highwayman passed his lips.

"So some call me," supplied the rider, on a faintly humorous note. "Now that we've established that, hand over your valuables, good sirs, and be quick about it."

Rosamunde stared at the highwayman, fascinated.

The tall man who sat so competently astride the big black horse was known the length and breadth of England. His exploits on the highroads had earned for him the name of Hard Harry. It was rumored that he was a gentleman, down on his luck, who had taken to the road for a living. As wily as he was formidable, Hard Harry worked alone, and never for long in one place—which was perhaps why he'd never been caught. Of late he'd been reputed to be in the north of England. Certainly none of them had thought to meet him this night on the road to Salisbury.

"Do as he says!" cried Lord Matthew nervously as the recumbent coachman made a twitching movement. "Can't you see the fellow's got a pistol pointed at me?"

Rosamunde, looking up into that dark face, so nearly hidden by the enveloping broad-brimmed hat and the scarf, was held by a pair of the steadiest gray eyes she had ever seen. For a moment as they regarded her startled face she thought they held a twinkle.

A moment later the earl's footman, concealed where he had fallen on the other side of the coach, rose up and hurled Rosamunde's small foot trunk at the highwayman's head. It glanced off his broad shoulder, but it knocked the gun from his hand and it fell to the dusty road.

As an instant reflex, Rosamunde, who was closest, leaped for the gun and snatched it up.

"Good girl," crowed Lord Matthew, reaching inside his satin coat for the small pistol she knew he carried.

A sudden madness came over Rosamunde. Why should she, being forcibly carted away by these two men, come to their aid? Better the highwayman than they! He had looked upon her kindly—he might even help her escape. And escape she must before the gates of Waverclay Court clanged shut behind her!

Without hesitation she turned and pointed the gun at Lord Matthew. Her face was wild—and resolute.

"If you touch your pistol, Lord Matthew," she said in a tone almost as cold as the highwayman's, "I will kill you." To emphasize her words, she cocked the pistol.

Lord Matthew, already pale, turned white as parchment in the moonlight.

"Your ward's taken leave of her senses, James—speak to her!" he sputtered to the earl.

"Rosamunde!" cried the earl, wincing as his weight fell on his injured ankle. "Rosamunde, consider!"

"I have considered," said Rosamunde calmly. "And I prefer to take my chances with this gentleman than to proceed with you two."

Beside her the highwayman, who had drawn his sword, sheathed it, vaulted lightly down from his horse and in a swift fluid motion took the pistol from her. "I'm obliged to you, my lady." He bowed urbanely. "And now if you will do the honors and relieve these gentlemen of their valuables—I trust you will know where they are and what they might be?"

Rosamunde frowned up at him. "There's a price to my help."

The highwayman sighed. "There always is."

Rosamunde flung back her fair head and took a deep breath. Her lovely face looked very reckless in the moonlight. "It is that you take me with you."

If the lean highwayman was startled, he did not show

it, but the earl's bony old face turned white with rage. "Rosamunde!" he thundered. "*Think*, child! This man is a common thief who'll end up being hanged at Tyburn!"

The highwayman laughed. "Like as not," he drawled. "But there's something in what the old gentleman says. You wouldn't like the road, my lady. It's very rough, it is."

"It's better than marrying Lord Matthew," said Rosamunde grimly, nodding her head at his fuming beribboned lordship.

The highwayman's cold gray eyes looked interested. "Why, so it would be," he said lightly. "And sure you've done me a favor this night. So I'll take you wherever you wish to go, my lady. And where we'll go, you can be sure Lord Matthew won't follow." He watched alertly as she extricated rings and purses and even—with a grim look at her late betrothed—a gold snuffbox.

"This watch," she faltered, looking down at the earl's large gold timepiece. "His money he can replace, for he has much of it. But the watch was a gift of his first wife, who was very good to me. I like not to rob him of this remembrance."

Hard Harry gave her a strange lingering look. "Then we'll let the old gentleman keep his watch," he said promptly. "For I confess I owe ye a debt, mistress—perhaps my life."

The earl gave Rosamunde a stony look as she gave him back his watch.

"And his signet ring," she added, troubled. "It was his father's."

The highwayman sighed. "He may keep that too. And now, mistress, if that trunk's yours, I'm afraid we can't take it." He was storing the loot in his saddlebags as he bade the footman truss up the three men with thongs cut from the reins.

" 'Tis good riddance," said Rosamunde bitterly, "for 'tis filled with clothes bought by Louisa to make me look ugly." She watched as the highwayman deftly inspected the bound wrists and ankles of the men and, having declared them tight enough, tied up the footman himself.

He hesitated, then with a muttered "Horses should not be left in this condition," he untangled the reins so that the horses stood comfortably. He gave them an encouraging pat and turned to Rosamunde. "I'd take one of them for you to ride, my lady, but they're huge beasts and would be remarked."

Rosamunde shrugged. She knew the miserly earl made them double as plowhorses. "I care not how I go—as long as I am rid of Lord Matthew."

"Filthy wench," growled Lord Matthew from his seat on the ground beside the coach. "And to think I'd considered giving you honest marriage! Faugh! A roll in the hay is too good for you!"

The gray eyes smiled down on him. Lord Matthew flinched as a lean hand shot forward and grasped the lace at his throat, gave it a cruel twist. "I'm sure you wrong the lady," the highwayman said pleasantly. "She's obviously in no mood to roll in the hay with *you!*"

Lord Matthew's eyes popped as there was a ripping sound and the lace came away—to be abruptly stuffed into Lord Matthew's mouth.

"That," said the highwayman easily, "will encourage you to keep your thoughts to yourself until we're out of earshot. You gentlemen are in no danger. There will be someone along this road at least by sunup—though you may perchance find it a little damp." He looked toward the west, where another thunderclap sounded, sniffed the air, which was damp with rain, and turned to Rosamunde, who stood silently watching him. "What's your name, my lady?"

"Rosamunde Langley."

"Oh? Well, could we rid you of that vast cage, Rosamunde? For I doubt me you can ride in it."

He was speaking of her farthingale! Rosamunde blushed furiously. "A moment," she said in a smothered voice, and retreated behind the overturned coach. Somehow she struggled out of the farthingale and left it there by the road—it stood alone on the ground like a giant deserted birdcage. As she hurried back, she stumbled and nearly fell. For her dress, relieved of the great hoops over which it had been spread, was now far too long. She scooped up her skirts with a flash of pretty ankles.

"That's better," approved the highwayman dryly. "And now it's up behind me, Rosamunde, and hang on, for I'm known to travel fast and we'll have our ale in Devizes on the morrow!"

Lightly he swung her up behind him, and they rode off toward the north, leaving the four men sitting in the dirt beside the overturned coach, regarding their departure bitterly.

They rode north until they had crested a low hill and were out of sight of the coach, and Rosamunde ventured with a frown, "Was it very wise to tell them where we were going?"

She could feel laughter ripple the broad back around which her arms were twined to keep her seat.

"But my lady, this is all the distance north we travel. The gullible will now seek us to the north toward Devizes. The crafty will be well aware that I'll double back and go in the opposite direction, and so will seek us in the south. So we'll fool the both of them—we'll travel east toward Winchester. There's even an inn on the road that's safe for me." As he spoke, a shaft of lightning lit the sky and another loud thunderclap sounded. "And there's rain to cover our tracks," he added comfortably. "A lovely thing, rain—and there's so much of it in England."

He wheeled his well-schooled horse about and struck off from the road, stopped by a little brook in a grove of trees and vaulted down, lifting Rosamunde down to the greensward beside him. Contentedly, the horse began to drink from the cool tinkling water, and the highwayman removed the scarf from his face and smiled down at Rosamunde.

"You've a pretty face," he observed. "But there's enough dress there for two of you, lass."

"I know," muttered Rosamunde, nettled. She was looking up at that bold countenance nervously. Hard Harry's face was lean and weathered, darkened by sun and wind. So dark, indeed, that his smile was a white gash in that dark face. And his eyes beneath those straight black brows were of so pale and misty a gray as to be almost white in the sudden shaft of moonlight that gleamed on his thick dark hair. They were eyes of an exceeding steadiness, and indeed his whole countenance was the most resolute that Rosamunde had ever looked upon. A face to make men quail. His body was large and competent, with a wide span of shoulder, yet slim-waisted and graceful. She saw that the look of breadth which had first struck her came from his broad shoulders and strong neck upon which his alert hawklike head was placed. And his hands . . . a gentleman's hands, she thought idly, slender, strong and well-shaped. Hands admirably suited to the reins of a gallant steed or—to offer to a lady in a dance.

She blushed a little as she realized she was staring and looked quickly away. When she looked back she saw that he had taken his scarf and wet it in the stream and was now applying it to his horse's forehead. Rosamunde gasped. He was washing the white star from the black horse's head!

"It is very clever of you to disguise your horse so," she blurted.

"A good trick," he acknowledged indifferently, and having finished, reversed his cloak. Instead of black, he was now cloaked in green. He plucked the feather from his hat and stuffed it into his saddlebag, replaced it with a green one. "They'll be looking for a man in black astride a black horse with a white star," he told her. "Not for a green-cloaked man with a green-plumed hat astride a coal-black stallion. But you"—he studied her with a frown—"you'll be harder to mask. Could we rid you of that ruff, my lady?"

Awkwardly aware of her frumpery appearance, Rosamunde hastily removed the yellow-starched neckruff, and he stuffed it into the saddlebag. A light rain began falling as he prepared to remount. He took off his cloak and swung it over her shoulders. "To keep your finery dry," he explained, and Rosamunde climbed up behind him. He guided his horse carefully down the streambed and out upon the grassy bank lower down. It was raining harder now. "That will wash out our tracks," he observed contentedly.

Through the night, cross-country, they rode. Rosamunde, with her arms clasped tightly around his waist, and having endured so much during the day and night just past, began to feel sleepy. The hard feel of his swelling back muscles against her breasts was comforting, and she leaned her head against his broad back and dozed. She came awake with a start when the horse leaped over a small obstruction and Harry's hand swiftly grasped her thigh to hold her fast.

"Don't sleep yet, my lady," he said softly. "There's time and enough for that."

Tingling as she felt the gentle pressure of his hand on her thigh, Rosamunde straightened up. Somehow his touch had roused in her thoughts that she now knew should have been with her all along. For in her anxiety to escape a noxious marriage to Lord Matthew Waverclay, she had quite overlooked something else.

She was seated behind England's most notorious highwayman, riding over wild country to she knew not what destination. And now she had overthrown what little protection she had had from her guardianship.

She was alone with a wild stranger riding over a dark and unknown plain.

3 *Rain began to patter down. All night they rode* through a steady drizzle. By dawn the rain had increased in intensity and the wind whipped her wet cloak about. Hard Harry seemed to know where he was going. Rosamunde was grateful for that. In a daze of fatigue she lay against his back, her arms locked about his waist so that she would not fall out of the saddle as again and again sleep overcame her.

"Hang on, my lady," the highwayman encouraged her. "There's a deserted barn just over the next rise. We'll shelter there."

Too tired to be afraid, Rosamunde sighed and opened heavy-lidded eyes to see ahead a rickety wooden structure, its roof mostly gone. It looked inhospitable in the dim pinkish light, but as Hard Harry swung her down and stood her up on her unsteady legs, she saw that it had been used fairly recently for the storage of hay—indeed there was still some hay left in one corner, which the big black horse fell upon greedily.

Harry took the now soaking cloak from Rosamunde's slender shoulders and hung it over a low rafter to dry. Rosamunde looked about her uncertainly in the dimness as Harry busied himself currying down the wet horse. "If you need help getting your dress off, I'll be finished in a minute," he flung over his shoulder.

Help in getting her dress off! Rosamunde jerked to attention and threw a worried look at that broad back. Did this highwayman really think she was going to peel down to her petticoats in the presence of a strange man? Irritably she wrung water out of the hem of the sodden gray damask. Her efforts accomplished little, for the huge dress was now so heavy and soggy with water that she could hardly stagger around in it. She sank down on a wooden beam that had at some time fallen from the roof and tried to wring out her wet hair.

In the pounding rain she did not hear Harry's light step behind her. His voice sounded so close in her ear that she started. "Come now, can't have you catching your death in wet clothes. Off with it, child!"

Child! To be asked to take off her clothes and called a child in the same breath!

"I am not a child!" she flashed, turning to look at the tall highwayman who bent over her.

42

Harry chuckled. "Now you sound like one," he said. "Hold still—there!"

To her horror, she realized he was deftly unfastening the hooks that held her dress together in the back. She tried to squirm away, but her efforts were futile. Beating down her protests, he peeled it off—she was thankful for the dimness, for her face was crimson—and tossed it over the low rafter beside her cloak.

"Petticoat," he said coolly, and she jumped as she felt his competent hand at her hip.

"I'll do it," she said incoherently—for it was clear he would brook nothing less, and she'd no mind to be fighting him in this deserted barn! Quickly she undid the petticoat and stepped out of it, held it at arm's length and retreated from him swiftly as he took it.

Feeling quite naked in her long white chemise—for no man had ever before viewed her in her underwear, save Lord Matthew in her night rail—she watched as he disposed of the petticoat in the same fashion. She was relieved—and perhaps just a little piqued, though she would never have admitted it—that he did not even glance at her. Instead he rummaged through a saddlebag and from it produced a white ruffled garment, which she saw was a man's shirt.

"Dry yourself with that," he instructed, tossing it to her. "And then snuggle down in the hay. 'Tis clean enough. You'll be dry and warm in no time."

Apprehensively, keeping a nervous eye on him, Rosamunde did as she was bid, snuggling down in the hay and rubbing herself dry. Although the highwayman had taken no liberties with her—save in his insistence that she remove her clothes, and she observed with some relief that he had not removed his own—she now viewed her situation with rising alarm. She vowed inwardly that she would not sleep, lest this lean highwayman pounce on her in the night as Lord Matthew had. But as time passed and the sodden sky grew lighter and still nothing happened, she decided to rest her eyes a bit. Her last sight of him, before her eyes closed, was of a dim seated figure leaning against a post, looking out into the glancing sheets of rain. But though she had vowed to remain awake, the monotonous beating of the rain on what was left of the roof and her own tiredness defeated her. Dreamlessly, she drifted off to sleep.

On the Salisbury Plain the bound riders seated glumly beside the overturned coach had had good luck. No longer than an hour had they sat miserably in a light rain before another coach had lumbered up, and the occupants rendered them assistance. Indeed, the occupants had turned out to be neighbors of Lord Matthew Waverclay and had taken him and the earl (their coach having broken its wheel) to Waverclay Court, before they departed on the short run to their neighboring house.

In the handsome pile of Waverclay Court, the earl, wan from his recent experiences and looking more than ever like a cadaver, had been deposited upon a large canopied bed in an upstairs chamber. His aching leg had been propped up, and he had been plied by dutiful servants with hot buttered rum.

Alone downstairs in his echoing ancestral hall, Lord Matthew Waverclay, now clad in a handsome brocade dressing gown laced with silver threads, paced the stone floor as he sipped Canary from a large crystal goblet. Even more than his recent humiliating experience with the highwayman on the road, his mind was tormented by the memory of a shimmer of pale silken hair that had been gossamer to his touch, by the gleam of rapidly rising and falling breasts, pink-tipped and delicately molded, by the rousing touch of dainty white limbs and satin thighs. In his nostrils, flaring now with wrath, lingered the faint flowerlike scent of a fair young body that he had almost—but not quite—possessed. He strode about vengefully and kicked at his dog, who departed his usual place on the hearth with a mournful yelp.

Another face, another scene tormented his lordship's mind. It was imaginary but to him as real as truth—and as maddening. He could picture the lean highwayman, who had so airily ridden off with Rosamunde, stopping at some bawdy house that passed for an inn and hustling the
44

frightened young girl upstairs. Could see him strip her on some tumbled bed still warm from the last occupants. Could see him feast those hard eyes that had been so steady above the pistol—indeed, that had struck terror into his lordship's heart—on the whole lovely length of her. Could imagine him clasping that fair scented body to him and having his way with her.

Light seemed to explode in Lord Matthew's brain at the thought, and he smote the goblet in his hand with his fist, to be rewarded by cut fingers. With an explosive curse, he hurled the broken goblet at the hearth with all his strength, and bright shards of glass flew about to scatter on the stone floor.

Shaking, his face pale as he stared down at his bloodied hand, Lord Matthew swore a great oath that he would be revenged on Hard Harry, by heaven he would! Yes, and he would have Rosamunde too! He brought his fist down on the massive table before him with such force as shook the wood.

Calming himself, his lordship sat down at that table, drummed his bruised fingers upon the polished wood and pondered. Where would Rosamunde go? Indeed, what doors would be open to her?—eventually, when the high-wayman had done with her, or when she had escaped him as Lord Matthew half thought she would, for her sudden seizing of the dropped pistol and turning the situation to her advantage had convinced him of her resourcefulness. Where would she go? Not home to Kenwarren House, for she would fear the old earl's vengeance. Where then? Had not the earl, as they had talked together on the way here, given him a clue when he had discussed Rosamunde's parentage?

Suddenly Lord Matthew sat up, his dark eyes gleaming, and again smote the table with his fist. A short barking laugh escaped him. God's teeth, why had he not thought of it before? There was but one place the girl *could* go!

Pleased with himself, he lounged back in his chair, poured himself another goblet of Canary and drank the night away.

With a complete disregard for his guest's age or injured

45

leg, Lord Matthew roused the earl at dawn, striding unceremoniously into the chamber where the earl lay sleeping. Lord Matthew was dressed for travel, and his sword hung from his baldric, into which were thrust two large pistols. The earl, noting this display of armament as well as his friend's evil expression, sat up, wiping the sleep from his eyes. As he moved his nightcapped head, he groaned.

"Gad, ye're about early, Matt," he muttered, testing his injured ankle and wincing.

"We must talk," said Lord Matthew in a terse voice, pulling up a chair by the earl's bedside and crossing his handsomely booted legs. From the tops of those polished boots, lace spilled in profusion. Seated, he offered the earl snuff from an enameled box.

The earl shook his head. " 'Tis too bad the highwayman got your gold snuffbox, Matt. I know you were fond of it. Do I take it from that brace of pistols that ye're off to bring him to justice? If that's your intention, ye'd have done better to set off after him last night!"

Lord Matthew ignored that jibe. Delicately he took a pinch of snuff between thumb and forefinger, snapped the box shut and sat back and regarded his elderly guest through heavy-lidded thoughtful eyes.

"Of course, James," he said with slow deliberation, "you understand that I cannot marry your ward now. Not after what has happened."

The earl sighed. "Is that what you woke me to discuss?" he asked peevishly.

Lord Matthew considered him. After a pregnant pause he added, "But I would still be willing to offer her my—ah—protection."

The earl looked up at him sharply. "I take your meaning, Matt," he said brusquely. "Ordinarily I'd object, but after last night, I wash my hands of her. What you do with Rosamunde is your own affair. If you can find her."

"I have a feeling I shall," said Lord Matthew. He rubbed his gloved hands together, a sinister look on his face.

"Shall what?" asked the earl bluntly.

"Find her," said Lord Matthew on a steely note. "And the reason I have waked you so early, James, is this." He proceeded to explain, and the earl, a bit hesitantly, agreed. Afterward Lord Matthew snapped his fingers, and his secretary, who had been hovering in the hall outside, appeared with ink and a quilled pen and a parchment already drawn up. The earl's eyebrows lifted when he saw the document had already been drawn up for his signature, but he made no comment. He dipped the quilled pen in the proffered inkwell, and when it was sealed with melted sealing wax, affixed the imprint of his signet ring.

Eyes gleaming coldly, Lord Matthew rose. "Take your ease, James," he said loftily. "I'm off, but all my household will be at your disposal while I'm gone."

From the bed the earl grunted a goodbye and watched him go.

Within the quarter hour Lord Matthew, ignoring entirely the "pressing business" that had brought him home, departed Waverclay Court. Astride a fine bay horse and accompanied by a brace of grooms, he rode toward the north.

His face as he rode was very grim, and the grooms looked uneasily at each other. They had not seen him in such a state since he had whipped poor Lady Mary, his first wife, insensible—an act that had very probably led to her death by pneumonia, as he had tossed aside the whip and stalked out leaving her lying locked in a cold room in midwinter with the windows wide open. Now, riding behind his lordship, they muttered to each other, for the winded coach driver had told them a wild tale about Lord Matthew's new betrothed turning a gun on him and taking off with a highwayman. They rightly guessed that his lordship's abrupt leavetaking had to do with this rebellious lady, and they pondered uneasily upon the awful vengeance his lordship would wreak on the unfortunate maid when he found her.

It was a grim entourage that rode north through the morning light across the Salisbury Plain.

Nestled deep in the hay and happily unaware that Lord

47

Matthew had taken to the road in pursuit of her, Rosamunde slept soundly and late. When she awoke the sun was high in the sky and the air smelled damp and fresh. Outside she could see sparkling meadow grass, not yet quite dried by the sun—and the black horse, knee deep in that grass, grazing contentedly. Although she saw that his cloak was still flung over the rafter, Hard Harry was nowhere in sight.

Rosamunde stretched deliciously. The sleep had made her feel quite refreshed—and hungry. She sat up and looked about for her dress.

It was gone.

She sat bolt upright. Her petticoat was gone too! What was she to wear?

At that moment she glimpsed Harry striding through the meadow. He was dressed differently this morning, in plain country clothes with leather jerkin, which she guessed must have been in his saddlebags. But even in the distance she knew him by his dark swinging hair that gleamed in the sun and by his confident broad-shouldered stride. He was carrying something over his arm. Rosamunde scrounged down in the hay and watched him approach with some trepidation.

"Ah, you're awake," he said, bending low beneath a broken rafter to enter the barn and smiling down at her. "There's a village nearby and I got us some food there —and another dress for you."

He tossed the pile of brown cloth he'd been carrying over his arm to Rosamunde with a careless gesture. "Try it on. I think it will fit."

Rosamunde caught the dress. "My own dress—" she began, confused.

"—was too conspicuous," he finished for her. "At least in this you'll look a demure country lass instead of the lady in gray damask they're combing the countryside for at this moment!"

"Turn your back," said Rosamunde severely.

"There's a stream just past the corner of the barn," he said, still imperturbable. "Hidden in those trees. You'll be wanting to wash. Here's my shirt to dry you."

Again he tossed her the ruffled shirt of the night before, which lay on the hay beside her. "And a comb for your tresses."

He'd thought of everything! Astonished, Rosamunde accepted the shirt and comb, and with the new dress draped around her shoulders, made for the stream clad in her white chemise.

Bathing was a shivering delight. The cold sparkling water made her young body feel fresh and alive, and the woods about were thick and green and concealing. She felt like a wood nymph as she shed her shoes and stockings, slipped out of her chemise and stepped into the knee-high water, bending over to splash it over herself until her pearly skin was pink and rosy.

She stood in the cold stream and toweled the upper part of her body dry with the ruffled shirt, then shook out her tangled hair and combed it. The dress, she saw, was not new as she had first thought it. It was well worn, and like its petticoat, of a soft brown linen of a type worn by country girls. She stepped from the stream and held it up, before getting into her chemise—it would make a good disguise, she realized. Harry had chosen well.

So rapt was her attention on the brown dress that she had no warning when a long arm clamped around her waist and a hand was abruptly clapped over her mouth. She dropped the dress and for a moment struggled against this new restraint in horror, then bit the hand. She felt the taut figure behind her wince—and then it came to her addled mind that it was Harry's arm that held her, Harry's voice in her ear.

"Quiet, lass," came his urgent whisper. "There's a wagonload of gypsies heading for the old barn. Best they not see us. I've managed to get Nightwind"—she knew Nightwind was his big horse—"into the woods; 'tis but a step from here. But you'd best dress quickly, for they may come this way looking for water."

He removed his hand from her mouth.

She was trembling. "I—I'm sorry I bit you," she mumbled.

His other hand—a bit lingeringly—left the satin skin of her naked waist. But his expression was impersonal.

" 'Tis all right," he said indifferently. "Wild creatures often bite when you come upon them unawares."

Wild creatures! She was standing here stark naked with only her long pale golden hair to screen her from his view—what could he expect?

"Turn your back," she ordered stiffly.

Harry obliged her. There was a soft sound as his feet moved on the grassy bank. She stole a look at him. He was standing at his ease with his back to her, watching keenly in the direction of the barn. Her whole body flushed crimson with embarrassment that he had seen her thus in the rude—indeed, must have had a good look, since he had slipped up on her out of the woods. With fumbling fingers, she hurried into her chemise, her shoes and stockings. She was about to step into her petticoat when he muttered, "Someone's coming," turned and swept her up in his arms, grasped her dress and petticoats and struck out through the woods, whence she could hear a soft whinny.

Rosamunde, seething with indignation at being carried about summarily in her underwear by this autocratic stranger, was stiff with fury and mortification when he reached the black stallion and put her down. With a glare, she bent to the task of getting into her brown petticoat.

Over her protests, he helped her into the soft brown dress. As she smoothed it down over her hips, she realized it was an excellent fit.

"How did you get it?" she said, puzzled.

"I found a girl your size carrying a basket of eggs and traded her your dress for it," He grinned. "I told her I'd stolen it and she'd best hide it for a year. When last I saw her she was slipping home through the woods. She realized your gown's value—faith, I think she may keep it hidden longer than a year, for she assumed it was stolen and she won't want it taken from her!"

Rosamunde grimaced at the memory of the ugly gray damask. She wondered if this simple farm girl knew it was supposed to be worn over a great wheel farthingale which
50

would hardly go through doors. She much preferred the tired worn rag she was wearing now—which at least fit her young curves daintily—to the rich gown she'd just lost.

" 'Tis good to look at you, country lass!" he said merrily, stepping back a pace to view her. "Come, we'll ride a bit and break our fast beside some stream."

This time he took her up before him, holding her lightly with one arm around her waist, and she was very aware of the feel of his hard thighs against her legs in her worn skirt, and of his arm that brushed her soft breasts as they rode. With each jog of Nightwind's hooves the cordlike muscles of that lean arm brushed her, and through the thin worn material she was uncomfortably aware of his strong sinews against her bouncing breasts. Little tingles of feeling swept through her—pleasurably. She was very annoyed with herself that she should be so upset when she could see by stealing a look at Harry's dark countenance that he was completely unmoved.

In that, Rosamunde showed her innocence of men. Harry was almost painfully aware of his light soft burden, and the gossamer brushing of her sweet young breasts was burning the very sinews of his arm. He had not intended to spy upon the maid, nor indeed to frighten her, but when the gypsy cart had showed up, it had seemed wiser to be quickly away. The sight of that pale slender lustrous body standing knee-deep in the sparkling water had brought him to a jolting halt, and for a moment he had drunk in like strong wine the sight of cascading golden hair that broke over white shoulders and flowed down again to fall shimmering between her round pearly pink-tipped breasts.

Last night she had been an overdressed child with a lovely rebellious face. This morning she had abruptly changed into a woman, with her fair young body a vision of loveliness in the dappled morning light, and the brook water still sparkling along her slender naked thighs and dainty hips. His mind was still filled with that sight, and it took an effort of will to keep the arm that her breasts brushed so delightfully from trembling.

Rosamunde, in her innocence, thought he looked grim.

51

At last they stopped by a bend in the stream that wound through the woods and alighted. Rosamunde watched him undo the linen napkin he had brought from the village and from it produce dark bread and cheese and cold mutton and wine. He gave her a merry look. "Food is plain on the road, but 'tis usually plentiful."

Primly she sat down and partook of this repast.

Having polished off his share, Harry leaned his long body back against a tree trunk, arms clasped behind his head, long legs asprawl, and considered her as she daintily finished her meal. She kept her eyes cast down, aware of his scrutiny—for she was still painfully remembering that he had come upon her while she was nude, and it was hard to face him.

"Where is it you wish to go, my lady?" he asked. "I'll keep my part of the bargain to take you there— wherever it may be."

Rosamunde set down the last bit of her cheese. "I've nowhere to go," she admitted sadly.

"And how is that?"

She sighed. "You will perhaps have heard of my grandfather, the earl of Arne. But you will surely have heard of my father, Jonathan Langley, who lost his head on the block."

The hard gray eyes held a flicker of renewed interest. "His crime?"

"His crime was friendship," she said frankly. "And loyalty—but not to his king."

"Ah, well," he said indifferently. " 'Tis difficult to be loyal to James."

"So my father found," she said wryly. "He and Sir Walter Raleigh were old friends. They fought together under Drake when Drake destroyed the Spanish fleet at Cádiz. It was unthinkable to my father that such a man as Raleigh should be tried for treason. And at the last"—a wistful little smile curved the corners of her soft mouth— "when they were going to behead Sir Walter in the Old Palace Yard, my father hastily assembled a group of Sir Walter's friends to snatch him from the block."

She had his interest now—there was a glint in his eyes as if he saw somewhere a kindred spirit.

"Unfortunately they were betrayed and got not even within sight of the Old Palace Yard. They were arrested, tried, convicted—and my father went to the block as had Sir Walter, in spite of all my mother's entreaties. I—I did not see the execution, but it broke my mother's heart. She was never the same afterward." She looked down and studied her hands. "I think the earl would have turned us out then, but his wife would not hear of it. She was my mother's kinswoman, and had taken us in years before when my father first went to fight overseas. The only real home I ever knew was Kenwarren House." Her voice was melancholy. "Then she died—of consumption. And shortly after her my mother died too, in a hunting accident. I was the earl of Kenwarren's ward—and ours was a house of mourning. Until Louisa came." Her voice hardened. "The earl had lost no time in marrying again, and Louisa was his new wife. She was years younger than he and—and I suppose you would call her pretty." She wrinkled her nose in distaste "At least, many have. Louisa did not want a young girl living in the house. 'Twas she who insisted I leave off mourning—at first I thought it was because she wanted more cheerful surroundings, but now I know 'twas because black silk made my skin too white!" Her tone was bitter. " 'Twas Louisa who plunged me into stiff old-fashioned farthingales, for she wished no competition in her own home!"

He looked surprised at that, and lest he think she had been competing with Louisa for the attentions of the elderly earl, she said quickly, "Louisa had many lovers. Last night one of them—Lord Matthew Waverclay—came into my bedroom and—and assaulted me while I was sleeping." Her cheeks grew pink.

His eyes narrowed. "Waverclay? The fellow in green satin breeches in the coach?"

She nodded, adding in a hurried voice, "I am convinced he blundered into my room by mistake, thinking he had found Louisa's room. But I could not fight him off, and even when the moon came out and he could see

53

I was not Louisa, he did not stop but grasped me the tighter!"

Harry's jaw hardened.

"But a maidservant came in to bring me some warm milk and set up such a howl as woke the household. The earl said Lord Matthew must marry me—"

"To save his own face, no doubt," murmured Harry.

"And when I said I would not, he tied me to the bed-post, where I passed the night. The next morning he and Lord Matthew took me by force into the coach, and we were on our way to Lord Matthew's seat near Salisbury when—"

"When I happened along."

"Yes. The earl is a vengeful man. And Louisa hates me. Now that I have thwarted their plans, I can never return to Kenwarren House." She shrugged hopelessly.

He frowned. "Have you no one to go to? No people anywhere who would help you?"

Rosamunde thought about that. "My mother was orphaned like myself—she had no close kin. But my father had a brother . . . you see, my grandfather and my father were at odds over my father's marriage to my mother; he'd chosen an heiress for his wild son to wed— and instead he married my mother, penniless but beautiful. After my father was arrested, my mother and I went to see my grandfather, hoping he would appeal to the king. But he would not see us." She sighed. "I remember the house—Langley Grange. The grounds were lovely. I thought of my father growing up there . . . but we were not received. My father's brother was away. My mother was frantic; she said even if his father would do nothing, his brother might still save him—but he was on the Continent, and our message must not have reached him, for we never heard from him. But last year I heard that my grandfather had died and my uncle—my father's brother—had succeeded to the title and estates. So," she added reluctantly, "it is possible that I would find a welcome at Langley Grange with my uncle."

Harry thought about that. " 'Tis worth a try," he said

at last. "I will take you there and we will see how you fare."

"No." To his surprise Rosamunde lifted her head and spoke up firmly. "I will not go to my kinsman as a beggar seeking alms. Consider how it would look! To arrive with naught but the dress on my back! I must"—she cast about for some alternative—"I must find some sort of employment so that I may at least arrive outfitted and in a decent manner. Think you—think you that is impossible?" She faltered.

A glimmer of admiration flickered in Harry's eyes. He liked spirit, and this wench had an uncommon amount of it. "Have you given thought to what you would like to do? What kind of work?"

For a moment she was confused, for it had never before occurred to her, highborn daughter of the aristocracy, to consider toiling for a living. She had been brought up to marry—and to marry well. "I read and write," she said naively. "And speak a little French and play the harpsichord—badly."

"I doubt we can place you as a scribe," he said dryly. "Nor yet as an interpreter or musician—good or ill. Tell me, can you cook?"

She shook her head sadly; Kenwarren House had been well staffed.

"Well, you can certainly serve ale at an inn. That takes no experience, and your pretty face should serve you well."

"I suppose so," she said reluctantly. Suddenly her level gaze met his, her green eyes fearless. "What of you?" she asked. "You saw last night that I could handle a pistol. Indeed, I am a fair shot, for it was my father's pleasure that I should learn. Could you not use a staunch companion at your side? Could you not take me with you? At least for a season?"

Harry gave her an astonished look. "On the road, you mean? Faith, I'd not thought of it. My lady, sometimes there are ambushes set up for such as I. You saw what it was like last night. A chance throw by the footman, but it caught me unawares. Had you not seized the pistol, I'd have been shot down where I sat or trussed up and taken to jail and hanged—could I not have cut my way out of it with my sword. 'Tis a dangerous game I play, and not one of my choosing."

Rosamunde digested that. His dark face looked a bit sad, she thought, and she wondered what had first set his booted foot upon this road he took.

"Were you always a highwayman, then?" she asked curiously.

His grim laugh rang out. "No, I was not born one, although sometimes, faith, it seems so! I was born a gentleman, on a country estate, my father's only son and heir. When I was eleven years old my father was implicated—unfairly—in the Gunpowder Plot. He was arrested along with Guy Fawkes, tried and executed. Our lands were seized, my mother and I fled to London. Her people turned us out. We found cold meager lodgings that winter, and I—but twelve then, though big for my age—took to the road to support her. I lied about my intentions, for it would have broken her heart. But when I came back with the first purse I took, I was already too late—she'd caught cold in our drafty rooms, soon her fever was high, and she was swept away by it. I think what shocked me most was the ease with which she died—she just slipped away from me; one moment she was there and the next she was gone." He was silent for a while, his face moody. "I felt my life was shattered when she died, and I cared not for God or man. The highways became my home, and I've lived on them ever since—and that's fourteen years now."

Rosamunde looked into that dark reckless face, imagining the boy he had been—confused, hurt, proud . . . and bold.

"You haven't told me your name," she said softly.

He turned to consider her, and his gray eyes were cold. "My family name has not passed my lips since the day my mother was buried," he said. "On that day I swore a great oath that I'd never speak it unless I could own up to it proudly—not as a landless hunted wanderer. But my mother called me Harry, and so you should."

They looked into each other's eyes, these two outcasts, and a silent bond was forged between them.

It was Harry who broke first under the steadfastness of those wide green eyes. He rose restlessly. "We'd best away. The inn near Winchester that I spoke of might have need of a barmaid, Rosamunde. 'Tis called the Hare and Hound."

4   *Meekly she accompanied him, mounting up at* once and modestly trying to keep her round breasts from bouncing against his arm as they rode. In that attempt she was completely unsuccessful, and Harry grew restive as they rode, occasionally shifting his position as if he found the saddle uncomfortable. He looked quite fiery by the time they had arrived at their destination, a small half-timbered inn build in the old queen's time and nestled off the beaten track among a grove of trees. He alighted and lifted her down in silence, and she followed him across the trodden grass. It was dark by now and the candlelit windows looked inviting. Laughter reached them from inside. And the burly innkeeper threw up his head and bellowed a coarse welcome as Harry strode into the room with Rosamunde following.

Friends he had and plenty, Rosamunde saw, for in this crowded room all were smiles to greet him. Looks of admiration they gave him too—the women, at least; there was envy in the eyes of the men. Soon Rosamunde came to understand that this was no ordinary inn, but a favored haunt of "gentlemen of the road" and those of like kidney. She saw about her town rakes gone to seed and carefree cutthroats home from foreign wars. The women were wanton indeed. They wore fine clothing (probably stolen, she learned later), but the hems of their gowns were filthy, and Rosamunde saw to her surprise that at least two of the dresses were torn with no attempt made to mend them or even to pin the torn parts together—skin and undergarments showed through. The bleary eyes of these women narrowed at sight of wide-eyed Rosamunde, so young, so lovely. Then they went back to whatever they were doing—drinking ale, playing at dice, telling lewd jokes—but their shrill voices had a higher key, their raucous laughter a kind of desperation. Had she not been so innocent, Rosamunde might have guessed these downhill bawds saw in her something they had lost—or never had at all: a sweetness, a dewy freshness, a flung challenge to life. As it was, she cast down her eyes at the way these wenches teased the men, brushing by them with a sidling gait that let a rounded hip caress a lean thigh, and leaning far over the tables as they tossed out the dice or dealt the cards, the better to display their large breasts.

Harry saw Rosamunde's discomfiture and frowned. He was leading her across the room when a rich seductive voice cried, "Why, 'tis Harry!" And Rosamunde turned to see a handsome red-haired girl clad in stained green satin flounce into the room and hurry across to Harry—and stop, hands on hips, at sight of Rosamunde.

"Hello, Nell," said Harry grimly. "We'll have some supper, the lady and I."

Nell gave him an affronted look and tossed her red head. "There's little of the great joint left, and what there is, is hard to chew," she declared.

"We'll take potluck, Nell." Imperturbable, Harry seated Rosamunde at the end of the long common board and himself on the wooden bench beside her. "Perhaps you can find us a bird and a pasty? Best you have—we're hungry tonight. Some wine for the lady, Nell. Ale for me."

Muttering, with another glowering look at Rosamunde, Nell flung away to fetch their dinner.

"Who was that?" asked Rosamunde.

"Nell? A friend," said Harry in a noncommittal tone,

and Rosamunde looked at him sharply, for she'd been well aware how Nell had looked at him, how the voices around them had stilled as Nell had looked her over and only risen again when Nell turned away.

"That woman is your mistress," she stated doggedly. "Deny it if you can!"

"Nell is her own mistress," said Harry irritably. "And favors whom she pleases."

Rosamunde was silent at that, waiting for her wine.

Harry, apparently leaning back at his ease, was looking around him with discontent. He was seeing this place with new eyes. Well enough it had been for him when he rode in dusty and tired and eager for a safe hole to hide in, ale for his gullet and hot embraces, but now . . . He cast a troubled look at Rosamunde, sitting with her slender back straight and her chin high, ignoring the bold glances that came her way. A highborn lady, and he had brought her here! It irked him as he drank his ale.

Vexed, he addressed himself to the plump bird and pasty Nell brought. She favored them both with a sullen look as she banged down the trenchers. "And would the *lady* like more wine?" she drawled, running a hand along the back of Harry's neck as she spoke.

"No, thank you," said Rosamunde quickly.

Harry reached up and disengaged Nell's hand from his neck. "I'll have another tankard," he said.

Nell gave his dark hair a sudden pull with her free hand and danced away from him with a laugh, while Rosamunde sat startled at this outrageous behavior.

Harry, as if to relieve himself once and for all of the problem of Rosamunde, called over the innkeeper. She listened as Harry dickered over the terms of her employment. She was to have a private room and a latch on her door; he was most particular about that. The innkeeper's eyes twinkled as he agreed, and he beckoned to his wife. A stout puffing woman, she lumbered over and rested her greasy hands upon the table.

At his "The little lady's seeking work," her small eyes raked over Rosamunde's ripe form as if she might have been a young shoat ripe for butchering. Her expression grew sly.

"Aye, the girl can serve ale," she agreed, dismissing with a sniff any other abilities Rosamunde might possess. She turned abruptly at a new distraction. A scuffle had arisen by the door, where a big robust fellow with a florid face had pounced smiling on a tall slattern and borne her screeching to the floor.

"See to your sister!" shrilled the innkeeper's wife. "She's at it again!"

"Melly, do be getting yourself out from under Bob Benton—you're blocking the door!" the innkeeper chided raucously.

Pinned into the corner by Bob's large frame, Melly flung him a murderous look, and her claws dug ungently into Bob's amorous face. This attack was rewarded by a loud curse and a relaxing of the big arms that held her as Bob, putting a hand to his face and crying in mock horror, "Blood! She's wounded me!" struggled to his feet.

Eyes snapping as she pulled down her dirty taffeta skirts, the innkeeper's sister came up off the floor like a squalling cat, spitting curses at Bob—who laughed at her—and flung away.

In horror, Rosamunde turned to Harry. "You might at least have *helped* her," she accused.

"To unseat Bob? Aye, she battles with him daily, but on which side she's fighting one can never be sure," Harry told her cynically.

The innkeeper's wife sniffed, but the innkeeper smiled merrily at Rosamunde. " 'Tis true, young mistress. We think it likely they will marry, for Bob cannot keep his hands from Melly, and she turns up wherever he is!"

"Ha, marriage is it?" railed the innkeeper's wife. "And I suppose we'll support that drunken lout Bob as well as your sister?" She turned to Rosamunde, her voice tart. "You can start at once, girl. We've a full house tonight, as you can plainly see—Nell's overworked and Melly's no help, spends all her time teasing Bob!"

Harry protested that Rosamunde was tired, but Rosamunde shook her head. "Best I start now," she muttered, and Harry saw how firm was the set of her jaw. He guessed she was shrinking inwardly, and drummed his knuckles as she leaped up, seized his empty tankard and followed the innkeeper's broad-beamed wife to the kegs of beer and wine. She came back with a brimming leathern blackjack of ale, which she set before him.

" 'Tis a handsomer tankard than the pewter one Nell gave you." She indicated the black leather tankard with a winsome smile. Harry leaned back, basking in that smile, and watched her fair head move briskly through the throng as she next brought a round of ale to a table in the corner.

In that corner were some of the worst rakes in the territory. Lounging on long benches with booted feet upon the table, hats askew, their hard eyes wandered over the new barmaid. Beguiled by Rosamunde's startling loveliness and gentle manner, they tormented her skillfully, saying things to make her blush. When, furtively, one pinched her as she served his ale and she jumped away with a small shriek, sloshing ale on the table, Harry half-rose to his feet, then grimly sat back down.

"Help her out, Nell," he growled, as Nell swung by, her arms full of empty pewter tankards. "She's new to this."

"Help your own doxy," said Nell dispassionately. She paused, watching him from her vixen's face. "Will you be taking her to your bed tonight, Harry? Or are you leaving her to someone else?"

Harry's hand tightened on the handle of his tankard. "She's to have a room with a latch on the door; 'twas agreed."

Nell shrugged. "Latches break easy." She considered Harry with sly interest. "Then if she's not your doxy, is it my bed ye'll be seeking tonight?"

"I'm off down the road most likely, Nell," Harry said with a restless gesture. "But what of Dick Brue? I don't see him, but will he not be here to bed you?"

"Dick's no substitute for you, Harry—I like your gentlemanly ways!" Nell gave a luxurious sigh and moved her hips suggestively.

But Harry failed to notice the invitation. "Dick's jealous of you, Nell," he said bluntly. "You'll drive him too far with your wayward ways and he'll kill someone."

"That's my affair."

"You can see the girl's new," he muttered, returning to what was on his mind. "And having a hard time with that wild bunch over yonder. You were new to this yourself once. Can ye not help her out a bit?"

"I told you I'll not help your new doxy," said Nell in a clear biting tone and flounced away.

After that Harry watched Rosamunde's progress through narrowed eyes, drinking lightly, refusing to be drawn into a game of cards or joining a tippling group by the big fireplace. Hat over his eyes, he appeared to sleep.

On through the evening Rosamunde worked, her head held high, miserably aware that these rough men were making sport of her, determined not to let them get the best of her. At last, as she bent over to set down a flagon, one reached up slyly underneath her skirt and pinched her bare bottom. Green eyes flashing, Rosamunde turned and gave him a slap that knocked his head back. With a snarl he came to his feet and seized her slender wrist with a ferocity that made her wince.

From the end of the common board, Harry came awake. His voice rang out. "Let the lady go, Jack," he said coldly.

The one called Jack, who had Rosamunde's wrist in his savage grip, growled something unintelligible.

Harry was on his feet—a threatening rise to his full commanding height. Abruptly his naked sword appeared in his hand. "Release her!" he thundered.

Jack paused and studied Harry. "Ah, what matters it?" He flung Rosamunde's arm away so that she staggered against the table. He sneered. "You cannot stay to protect this pretty partridge, Harry. Mayhap I'll not be here, but there'll be others to have her on!"

Harry was striding across the room. "Apologize to her!"

"Aye, I'll apologize," cried Jack, falling back and half-laughing but watching his dangerous adversary narrowly. "We're friends, Harry—why quarrel over a wench?"

The cold gray eyes considered him, but the sword was sheathed. Jack breathed easier, and the watchful crowd went back to whatever they'd been doing before—the fight was not to take place. Grimly Harry retreated to his seat, again seemed to doze. Now, however, covert glances were cast at Rosamunde's protector. No one in the room was fooled into believing Hard Harry was asleep.

Abruptly Rosamunde received better treatment. But when Nell passed by her, Rosamunde saw tears in the girl's eyes.

The door swung gustily open and a pair of swaggering and dusty gentlemen in plumed hats came in laughing. One of them was tossing a velvet purse into the air and catching it. He paused at sight of Rosamunde and his brown eyes glinted.

"Well, a new one!" he murmured, arms akimbo. He smiled. "Come here, wench!"

Uneasily, Rosamunde took a step toward him. She cast an anxious look at Harry. Harry continued to doze.

The new gentleman held forth the velvet purse in a teasing gesture. "Ah, don't be shy, wench," he encouraged. "Half of what's in here is yours if you'll but go up those stairs with me!"

Rosamunde blushed fierily. She could very well guess what "going up those stairs" meant. "I am barmaid here," she stated in a level voice. "And that is all. I am not for sale like the ale or the wine."

"But I mean not to buy you," retorted the stranger with a broad smile. "I mean only to pleasure you for an hour or two. Come now, what's the harm, wench? Ye'll be easing a weary traveler! Here, give me a smack and you'll have a sample of what's to come!" He reached out for Rosamunde, who eluded him.

From the end of the common board, Harry sighed and rose to his feet. "Hold, Jarney," he said equably. "The wench is mine."

Jarney turned slowly to face him. He frowned. "But you lay claim to no lass, Harry."

"To this one I do."

"Ah, so that's the way of it? Well, I've a fancy for her. Will you wager her for this?" He shook the velvet purse; it jingled faintly. "'Tis a good price if you win!"

Harry glanced at Rosamunde, whose steady green eyes met his with boundless confidence. A bleak smile lit his dark face. "Nay, I'll not wager her favors," he said softly.

Jarney gave a sulky shrug. "I'll see how I fare with her after you've left," he remarked airily.

"That you will not," corrected Harry. "She rides with me. Come, my lady."

Rosamunde's green eyes lit up. He was taking her with him! He would not leave her here with this riffraff! She sprang to his side, and moved beside him to the door, seeing him toss a few coins on the wooden table to pay their bill.

"At least," drawled Jarney, "tell us your name, wench."

"Her name is Trouble," said Harry heavily. "With me. For any man who thinks to touch her. Remember it, Jarney."

Together they went out into the cool night, Rosamunde happy and Harry frowning.

"I liked it not there," she confided.

"Nor did I like it for you," he said. "It was a mistake bringing you here. It must have been this life I've been living that made me err so. Any fool could see that you could not stay there—even I."

"But I can ride with you," she pointed out proudly. "Or could, had I a horse."

"The horse is no problem," muttered Harry. "But ride with me—that's out of the question. You could not keep my pace."

Riding was one thing Rosamunde did superbly well. She flushed and was silent at this rebuke. Harry seemed to come to a decision. He strode back to the door of the inn, beckoned to the innkeeper, who came out and gazed at him questioningly.

"I've need of a horse for the lady," said Harry. "I've a snuffbox here of gold, and a ring. Give me the best

64

beast you have, one with strength and wind and gentle manners for a lady."

"I've just the thing, Harry," said the landlord, studying the snuffbox and ring covetously. "Name of Graylady." He brought out a sleek gray mare, and Harry walked around the horse, slapping her flanks, pulled back her mouth to view her teeth and smiled.

"She'll do. We'll be needing a saddle too." And when the horse was saddled, "Up you go, Rosamunde." He offered his cupped hands to her small foot and she sailed up into the saddle.

"Rosamunde," murmured the landlord, scratching his chin as they rode away. "Sure and she's fair as a rose. . . ." And went in to tell Jarney the wench's name was Rosamunde.

Walking the gray mare beside Harry's mount down a rutted track that was barely a trail at all, Rosamunde patted Graylady's head and stroked her silky mane. She gave Harry a slanted look through her lashes. *Mine*, he had said. *The wench is mine. . . . She rides with me.* She had thrilled to his words, thrilled to the hard fit look of him, his strong commanding walk, the way he moved his broad shoulders always as if he were wearing a cloak.

Now beside her he was frowning in puzzlement. "I know not what to do with you, Rosamunde," he admitted frankly. "I cannot take you marauding with me—and yet I cannot leave you."

Rosamunde sighed. "It was a sinful inn. There must be others."

"All inns are sinful with such a face and such a figure as yours," said Harry tersely. "You overtempt a man." Rosamunde colored and straightened proudly in the saddle. Left-handed compliment it might be, but it ranked high among the few she had received.

The night air was damp, and shortly it began to rain. Rosamunde wondered if Harry would go back to shelter in the inn; he rode on. The shower ended, but left them soaked. They had ridden for almost an hour in sodden clothes when Harry turned from the narrow track they had been following and guided them up a hill, winding

65

carefully in the shadow of broken stone walls she could only half-see in the darkness. Abruptly the moon came out and she saw before her the ruins of an old round tower that must have stemmed from Norman times. Its thick stone walls were ivy-covered and steeped in decay. It had such a haunted look that Rosamunde hesitated for a moment when Harry dismounted, lifted her down and bade her enter a dripping black hole of a doorway.

"Lonely it looks, but in my profession there's safety in loneliness," he told her ironically. " 'Tis one of my stopping places when I'm in the neighborhood. Few ever come here, yet there's grass on this hill for the horses and there's a spring nearby."

With some trepidation, Rosamunde stepped inside, stood still while her eyes became accustomed to the darkness. She blinked when Harry, soft-footed beside her, lit a candle which showed her she was in a round bare room with a pile of hay in one corner and a stone stairway winding up into darkness. She would have gone up, for she was accustomed to sleeping on an upper floor, had in fact already set her foot on the first stone step, when Harry's arm stayed her.

" 'Tis best to sleep near the doorway," he explained. "In case of trouble." And in response to her nervous look, "I'll guard you well, my lady. No wild beasts will attack you."

Rosamunde bit her lip and looked quickly away at the irony of his tone. Wild beasts—she was not thinking of wild beasts! At the inn he had said, *She is mine.* And there was more than one kind of attack for a girl to guard against.

She shivered as he took her hand and looked up at him with dark questioning eyes. "Come, we'll find the spring," he said gently, and led her out through the wet grasses.

Harry's big black horse was already there, and the gray mare had followed him. Their coats sleek in the moonlight, they were drinking greedily of the clear cold water that bubbled up between some ancient stones. Rosamunde knelt on the wet stones and drank the cold water as Harry did, from her cupped hands. It was bracing as wine. She rose from her kneeling position on the stones and tossed back her wet fair hair, gleaming pale in the moonlight. And found Harry looking at her, an unreadable expression in his shadowed eyes.

Once again she was struck by his countenance, for a more resolute face she had never seen in her life. He had left his wide-brimmed hat inside, and his long gleaming dark hair swung to his shoulders in the silvery moonlight. From beneath straight black brows a pair of level gray eyes regarded her very steadily, and she looked quickly away, made uneasy by that look, and pretended great interest in smoothing out her wet skirts. Hard Harry they might call him and highwayman he might be, but it came to her in a rush that here was the kind of man she *ought* to have had for a betrothed—not that evil Lord Matthew Waverclay!

He turned to look at the round tower, an eerie shaft in the moonlight. "Men lived here once," he mused, "and this was their watch tower. Now"—his voice was ironic —"it belongs to the birds—and me."

In silence, sensing his somber mood, she accompanied him back over the wet grass. Swiftly, by the weak light of the guttering candle, he spread the pile of hay in the corner into an inviting bed. " 'Tis not been disturbed since I put it here," he murmured complacently, as he bent over the hay, patting it down. "And 'twill make a soft bed for you, my lady. Not so soft as the great house you've left, not yet so soft as the bed in the great house you were bound for when I met you. But safe for a while at least."

"I prefer this bed to either of those," said Rosamunde, kicking off her sodden shoes.

Harry rose, stood looking down at her. "We'll be cozy here for the night—though there'll be a great lack of the polite society you're used to."

Rosamunde looked up at him with a wry smile. "I've set myself beyond society. When I pointed your pistol at Lord Matthew, I was lost to that—I can never go back."

For a bleak moment, in complete understanding, they looked back at each other—they, the dispossessed. Then his smile flashed in his dark face. "Faith, I've forgotten something. If it's still here, I've a gift for you, my lady."

She watched him take the stone stairs three at a time, disappearing upward into the darkness. His boots rang hollowly. A few moments later he returned with a woman's dress flung over his arm and handed it to her with a jaunty gesture. "Something dry to wear," he said.

Rosamunde gave him a look of astonishment and took the dress from him. It was very shabby, and in the guttering candlelight she could see that it was of a sleazy material and an old-fashioned cut used by country women. But it looked to be near her size.

"How did you come by it?" she asked, amazed.

Harry laughed. "The lass who was wearing it preferred the dress I gave her and left her old one here."

So he had brought women to this tower before! Rosamunde hid her embarrassment by bending over the dress. Harry had trysted here with some woman. And why should that give her pain? "Where—where is she now?" she muttered. "She might come back for it."

Harry shrugged. "She was on her way to London when last I saw her, with a few gold coins I gave her to speed her on her way. She'll not be back. She'd no mind to spend her life as a drudge or a dairymaid—no, she'll not be back."

In wonderment Rosamunde fingered the worn material. Harry was very successful with women, she realized, remembering the lingering looks Nell the barmaid had given him. All the women in the inn had tried to catch his eye, and one had brushed him with a large ripe breast as she passed, but he'd seemed not to notice. Plainly he did notice *some!*

"Where—where are you going to sleep?" she asked hurriedly.

It came to him suddenly that, though shivering in her wet clothes, she was afraid to undress. A new experience for him, for the women he knew were only too eager to undress in his presence, stripping voluptuously to excite his senses. This child-woman was not like that. "I will sleep across the doorway," he said, "to guard the entrance.

After you've called to me to say you've gone to bed." His gaze softened as he studied her. "Spread your wet clothes on the stone stairway, my lady. 'Twill help them to dry." He was off jauntily, whistling a small tune.

Rosamunde remained where she was until his whistle died away—which meant he'd be well out of sight of the doorway. Then with a sigh of relief she began unfastening the hooks of her bodice. Her clothes were a sodden mass around her, and her very bones ached, so tired was she. In a haze of weariness she stripped off her wet clothes right down to her bare skin, and spread them carefully over the stone steps to dry. The night was warm and damp with only a light breeze blowing. Too tired to fiddle with fasteners, she wrapped the big-skirted dress around her and sank down into the straw, burrowing in. She meant to watch for Harry's return, she meant to keep a vigil herself, but the night sounds lulled her.

"I've gone to bed," she called drowsily, and saw through her lashes Harry's tall form as he came through the door, blew out the candle and sprawled like a big dog in the moonlit doorway, guarding the entrance. Oddly his presence gave her an enormous sense of security—which was foolish, she knew, for surely in this lonely place it was he she had to fear. She wondered idly what the girl had been like who had worn this dress that was wrapped loosely around her. It smelled woodsy, as if she might have lain in it on a pile of fresh boughs. Rosamunde's cheeks grew hot at the thought, for Harry might have lain on the boughs with her!

There was no sound from that sprawled shape in the doorway. Plainly her highwayman was asleep. The night sounds receded; she too had fallen asleep.

She awoke to bright moonlight and the feeling that she was not alone. In her fright and confusion she could not immediately recollect where she was and looked around her bewildered at the single door, the tiny high-up window that cast a shaft of silvery light across her body. Her eyes widened as a big form materialized out of the darkness. She would have screamed, but the figure swooped down and a big hand was instantly clapped over her mouth.

"You're quite safe, my lady," a reassuring voice she recognized as Harry's told her. "I know I startled you when I rose thinking I heard something outside. 'Twas only the horses. But you must not cry out, for sound carries a long way here, and 'tis best not to alert any wayfarers to our presence here."

"I'm sorry," she murmured in confusion, as he released his grip on her mouth. He was kneeling beside her, and she thought he looked very fit, his eyes held a smiling gleam. For the first time Rosamunde realized that the dress she had wrapped around her when she went to sleep had come loose from her body as she tossed and turned in sleep. Now in the summer night she was horrified to realize that her round breasts—indeed her whole body—were bare and silvered in the moonlight to Harry's admiring gaze.

With a gasp, she reached out, groping for the dress to rectify the situation. But Harry's long arm intervened. Leaning down, his warm mouth closed over hers, and his sinewy arm, reaching beneath her bare back in the straw, pulled her toward him. Firmly, but with a gentle pressure that took no account at all of her thrashing efforts to be rid of him.

A feeling of forbidden pleasure stole over her, a rhapsody of the senses. These steely arms that held her fast were pleasant arms, this lean body pressed hard against her own warm naked one was a body to which her own responded vibrantly. Against her will, she surrendered herself to him, to the stolen magic of these moonlit moments.

Abruptly Harry stiffened and drew away. She was not to know the effort it cost him, for that tempting display had been almost more than his resolve could bear. But the lass had risked her life to save him on the road, and he'd not repay that by taking her virginity! A pulse beat in his forehead and his very blood sang in his veins, but with a mighty effort he dragged his arm away from her and heaved himself up, staring down for a last moment at her

70

lovely face, her parted lips and wide eyes, dark pools in the moonlight.

"I'm still not sure of the sound I heard," he said in a colorless tone—no sign there of the tight grip he was keeping on himself in the face of that lovely body so temptingly bared before him, as she clawed through the hay to pull her dress over her. "So I think I'll just have a look around. I won't be back for a while." He paused. "Don't look so frightened, my lady. There's no cause."

Heart thudding, but at least with her dress now covering her, Rosamunde sat up.

"If I looked frightened," she said defensively, "it was because just two nights ago Lord Matthew plunged on me in my bed to rape me. And when I woke and saw you there I thought—I thought I was back there at Kenwarren House and he had me again!"

"Ah . . . " murmured Harry. "In your bed, you say?"

Rosamunde shivered, remembering. "My guardian said he had debauched me. That was why he insisted Lord Matthew must marry me."

Then the lass was not a virgin? For a moment Harry stood studying her. Rosamunde, hurrying through these confidences in a muffled voice, did not realize she had given him this impression. She was looking down at her hands as she spoke. When she looked up, he swung on his heel and was gone.

She sank back, watching the door through which he'd departed. So easily he could have taken her . . . and yet he had not. Her chance-met highwayman, she thought with a lump in her throat, was more of a gentleman ever than that peer of the realm, Lord Matthew, who'd have taken her against her will without mercy.

Hard Harry they might call him. Her heart scoffed. Faith, he was none so hard. He'd had a dozen opportunities to catch her unaware, to force himself on her with his superior strength—but he had not. A wisp of a thought occurred to her, hung like smoke in the damp air. Perhaps . . . perhaps he did not want her, but was only grateful that she had helped him on the road. And why should that thought prick her so? Why should her

71

reckless inner self, that self that shone so frank and free through the wide green eyes, be wishing, turning and twisting and wishing wistfully that he had not left her, but that he had stayed, that their bodies had melted together eagerly as one. . . .

Angrily she got up and dressed herself before he could return. These were naked thoughts. As if to shield herself from them she clothed her naked body, pulled the hay over her up to her neck. After a time he returned and again flung himself down in the doorway without looking at her. Sharply conscious of his presence there, she lay awake for a long time. Then, drowsily trusting, she sank deeper into her bed of straw and drifted off to sleep.

The next morning, with birds singing under a fresh clean-washed sky of azure blue, they mounted up and rode down into the woodlands. Rosamunde, now clothed in the country dress, with her own dress left behind, wondered for a moment if Harry would give that graceless gown to the next girl he brought this way. She cast him an irritable look, but he rode beside her with equanimity, the bright sun gleaming on his dark hair, lost in thought.

Through the day she noticed that he kept casting speculative glances at her and there was something hard and thoughtful in his eyes. She did not know why he watched her so, but she could feel the pressure of his keen gaze, which seemed to glide through the thin material of her dress and caress the very flesh below. Her heart beat a little faster, and his rapt attention gave her a sense of power that was heady and delightful.

In the late afternoon, Harry risked a country inn, leaving his horse behind some bushes with Rosamunde and walking in boldly as if he were some footsore traveler. He came back with a big sack slung over one shoulder—and in it cold meats and bread and cheese and a pudding and a pastry—and under his other arm a bottle of wine. "We'll feast tonight, my lady!" he declared blithely, bade her mount and led her deep into the green forest to a woodland glade of soft grasses ringed around by hoar old trees, where the sound of a stream rippled by out of sight through the dark branches.

72

There, while the horses nibbled contentedly at the green grass, he spread out the napkin and they shared their repast. A bee buzzed lazily by in the soft evening; there was a scent of wildflowers in the air, fresh and sweet. Rosamunde leaned back against the rough bark of a tree bole, kicked off her shoes and wriggled her toes in her stockings. She took dainty bites of the good country food and felt content.

Across from her, Harry watched her with glowing eyes. Before the banked fires in those gray eyes she was suddenly aware of the pressure of her soft breasts against the thin material of her dress, of the perhaps seductive way she leaned back against the tree trunk.

She sat up hastily and assumed a more proper posture, pulling down her skirts, but the fire in Harry's eyes did not dim. He handed her the last of the pastry, and as his fingers touched hers, something flickered between them like summer lightning.

"Don't you want it?" asked Rosamunde breathlessly. "You're hungry too and—it's your share."

"I'd rather watch you eat it," he said lazily, stretching his long form on the grass beside her and plucking a grass blade, testing it between his teeth.

She ate slowly, considering that long relaxed form. Every lean ounce of him bone and muscle, his steely sinews instantly doing his bidding. Like a lounging tiger, full of latent force and fire. Her gaze traced the hard lines of his face, softened now by a new gentleness of expression. And roved down the white linen shirt, for he had taken off his coat, and it now lay on the grass beside him supporting the brace of pistols he had taken from his belt.

Very serviceable they looked, and she wondered how often he had used them. She finished her last bite, and as she did so he turned over lazily toward her, throwing an arm across her thighs in the light dress.

"Rosamunde," he said softly, as she tensed. "Hast ever given a man a kiss for love?"

She shook her head, her throat dry as autumn leaves.

"Wouldst try it now?" he asked, his deep gaze compelling her.

It seemed not so wrong. . . . Under the sweet hypnosis of that deep voice, she leaned forward a shade, and Harry's dark face rose to meet her. His lips sought hers hungrily, and his arm went around her back and drew her down to his own lean body. Rosamunde felt a shock as those warm lips twisted down over her own, and moved convulsively as his probing tongue pressed through and found her own. A sweet unreason of the senses pervaded her, a warmth that was not of the night or even of Harry's warm body pressing close to her—but a warmth of her own, kindled through his lips. She who had so coolly held her guardian and her betrothed at bay with a stranger's pistol on the moonlit road felt suddenly small and frightened and yet at the same time curious and beguiled. Her resistance crumbling, she melted against him—and suddenly stiffened.

While his lips still held hers pinioned beneath his own, his hands were moving about her body, touching her, caressing her. He—he was undoing her bodice!

In virginal fright, she tried to pull away from him, but his fingers were strong as steel bands and urged her back toward him. Those fingers were inside her bodice now; his hand cupped her naked breast, nuzzled and tumbled its soft trembling peak. Small fiery flames shot through her, tingling and delightful. His hands seemed to be everywhere, teasing, caressing, rousing her skin to pinkness and her nerves to frenzy. Her head spun dizzily. This—this was love!

Slowly, deliberately, Harry played on her vibrant young emotions. Experienced with women, he fingered her artfully as a clever harpist might gently finger the strings to make beautiful music. His hand moved downward from her breast to span her soft waist, feel it shudder beneath the gentle pressure he applied. And on, trailing down around her hips, which she felt as a burning journey. He settled her more comfortably in his arms and withdrew his lips from hers to sink his face in the hollow of her throat.

He could hear the sobbing breath she drew and felt the latent passion in her awaken.

"No, Harry," she murmured. "No, you must not. We—"

"Hush," he murmured. "Don't spoil it." And his warm searching lips journeyed down her throat and bosom to seek her pulsating breasts, cause delicious tremulous bursts of sensation to swirl and envelop her.

"No." She pushed her hand against his chest. "Harry—"

One of his hands had left her, and she thought, with mingled relief and regret, that he was leaving. She felt his body, so close-pressed, sweep away from her for a moment, felt his arm brush her stomach, which recoiled delightfully from his touch.

A moment later she stiffened in real fright and tried to jerk away. His errant hand was parting her thighs, and his male hardness, warm and eager, was pressing against her yielding flesh. Even as she would have cried out to him to stop, his lips again closed with sweet strong pressure over her own and his maleness made its thrust.

Her head jerked so violently that she evaded his lips, and a wild cry broke from her lips. For a moment Harry's own head lifted and he stared down at her in stunned surprise.

"A virgin!" he muttered.

But so hot burned his blood within him at that moment that had she been thrice a virgin, he would not have stopped. She writhed beneath him protestingly, and he felt her draw in her breath with a strangled sob and desisted, stroking her hair as he might have stroked the mane of a nervous colt, murmuring her name. As she quieted trustingly he thrust again and this time ignored her caught breath and trembling and moved within her rhythmically, flawlessly, toward their perfect union.

In that first searing moment Rosamunde had gritted her teeth against the pain of that fierce relentless pressure within her, and then to her surprise she was conscious of a silken pleasure, a moving delight of the senses that made her cling the tighter to his straining body and move in harmony with him as if they were dancers on some far wild shore of love.

75

Their bodies moved and blended as she joined him in ecstasy, and she moaned and writhed beneath him, forgetting shame, forgetting fear, forgetting all but this lean sinewy man who held her, bending her to his will—which was now her will too. This man who fanned the flames of her passion until they swirled around her head in a roaring fire, threatening to sweep her away altogether.

At last, from the top of that tall tower of emotions that reached to the sky they descended silkily, like feathers falling lightly to earth, to lie like blown leaves, their limbs entwined, their bodies softly touching in the summer dusk.

She lay cradled in Harry's arm, and he bent and placed a kiss on her parted lips, running a warm hand down over her naked back with his other hand. Eyes closed blissfully, she shivered under that touch, and her lashes were a dark fringe against her rosy cheeks. And she had thought Lord Matthew's attack was all there was to love! Inner laughter rippled through her, joyous heady laughter sweet as honey. All her life she had been told it was wrong to lie in a man's arms and be fondled, yet—this was not wrong! Nothing so sweet and natural could be wrong! She lay back in the crook of Harry's strong arm and stretched, fetching a little blissful sigh.

When she looked up, Harry was bending over, regarding her tenderly. His face was dark above her own, but his eyes gleamed in the dusk. "A virgin," he murmured, nuzzling her ear with his lips.

"But no longer," she murmured, sighing, turning to press her face against her lover's chest.

"You are my first virgin," he said whimsically. "I've fought to avoid them."

Her head snapped back, and she looked at him in surprise. Something in his voice as he'd said that . . . But as she moved, her breast rippled, and his eye was caught by that soft movement. His lips found and held that pink tip, trembled it, tasted it. And the touch of her roused him so that his muscles hardened and he pulled her to him and took her again. With joy and tenderness, unafraid, she went into his arms, responding recklessly. He was hers. Her lover. This highwayman the world called Hard Harry.

76

Her Harry. She lost the train of her happy thoughts as their bodies blended and soft explosions of the senses lifted her up and swept her down a great wild river, only to lift her up again, higher and higher.

"Harry," she whispered. "Harry." The word was a silken murmur against his cheek. Lost in a bright wild world of his own, he seemed not to hear her, but his arms tightened about her as if to claim her forever.

That was the way she interpreted that tightening of the arms, that slight increase of pressure—a man staking a claim to his mate. Now and forever. For always and always.

Her world was tinsel-bright, laced with threads of gold. On a risky throw of the dice she had found her lover—found him beside an overturned coach in the moonlight—and she was ecstatic that he shared her own wild feelings.

The moon had long since risen when they ceased their lovemaking and, wrapped lightly in Harry's cloak against the damp night air, she drifted off to sleep.

5   *She was waked by the sun, knifing down fitfully* through the heavy overhanging branches to gild her dark lashes and warm her fair half-smiling face. But she woke slowly, her lips curved in a smile, and memories of moon-drenched kisses and tender caresses teamed through her mind in bright array. Her whole body quivered with memories of the night just past; every inch of her vividly recalled Harry's fiery touch, the power and sweep of his passion.

She stretched luxuriantly, the tips of her naked breasts peeping out from his enveloping cloak as she did so. Now fully awake, she turned to him, her face in the glow of morning alight with happiness. She saw that he sat beside her frowning, his chin and one hand resting on a drawn-up knee. At the haggard look of him, she sat up anxiously, leaning on one elbow, and reached out a tentative hand and gently touched his arm.

"Is aught the matter, Harry?" she inquired softly. For now he was her lover and surely his problems had become her problems.

Harry cast a troubled look at her. His brow was furrowed, and he looked somehow less reckless—less hard. "I like myself the less this morning," he muttered.

She did not apprehend his meaning.

"I took advantage of your innocence," he said bitterly, drawing his cloak up around her so that it hid her breasts from his view. Unaware that his gesture was a form of self-punishment, she blushed from embarrassment. "I thought from what you told me that Lord Waverclay had completed his rape."

Her blush deepened. "I had no knowledge of these things to judge by," she murmured. "My life has been too sheltered. When my guardian said Lord Matthew had debauched me and must marry me, I thought he *had* raped me—I took for granted that that was all there was to it. Now I realize that he had but begun to enter me before my scream and the maid's from the doorway roused the household and sent him tumbling off me."

Harry ran a hand through his hair. "I believed you'd been raped violently two nights ago and that I'd be doing you no great harm by showing you how a man *should* make love to you—gently and with regard for your feelings."

"But you did me no great harm," Rosamunde assured him wonderingly.

"When I realized I was mistaken and that you were still a virgin, I did not stop—therein I harmed you. And for that," he growled, "even though *you* may forgive me, I cannot forgive myself."

She sat up to protest, forgetful that the cloak fell away as she did so, burning his gaze. "But you are my lover, Harry!"

78

apron who shook her broom at her and snarled, "Begone, trollop! Begone! We want no likes of you here!"

Amazed that anyone would consider her a trollop, Rosamunde stumbled toward the town's only tavern. She had not planned to try for work there, but she felt a sense of panic at her lack of success. She took a deep breath and went briskly through a doorway into a room that smelled of stale ale and other foul scents. From behind the bar a woman raised up: big, buxom and overblown, her hair frizzed and of an unnatural hue of red.

"I seek employment," said Rosamunde hesitantly. "Might you have a place for me, perhaps?"

The woman came out from behind the bar with measured tread, big breasts bounding like melons, and looked Rosamunde over. She walked around her, considering her from every angle.

"Ye've found the right place," she breathed. "And there'll be customers aplenty for the likes of ye! We'll tell them ye're a virgin and they'll wear a path up the stairs to yer bed! Come share a glass o' ale with me and we'll talk terms. I've two girls upstairs, and as you can see, 'tis a small place. But I'll get rid of one of them and you can have her room. Though 'tis a small village, we do a good business from the countryside, especially on market days. Farmers and horse traders and apprentices—all eager to spend their money on a likely lass. Ah, word will spread fast that we've the bonniest lass of all on the premises!"

All of this came out in a burst before Rosamunde could interrupt, and the woman's jovial slap on the back near jolted her teeth.

"I—I did not have in mind to entertain men," said Rosamunde in a trembling voice. "But honest employment serving ale."

The big woman winked. "Aye, we'll call it that. And serve ale ye will until duty calls upstairs! Which won't be long with your looks, will it?" She looked archly at Rosamunde's bosom. "The lads won't need ale to warm them when they see those ripe little apples, will they?" She broke into a husky peal of laughter and dug Rosamunde in the ribs with a knowing elbow.

Rosamunde fled.

Dejected, she made her way back to the smithy, where the brawny perspiring smith had just finished shoeing the gray mare. Harry, long legs stretched out at his ease as he sat astride a stump, watched her brightly.

"It would seem there is little opportunity in this town for a woman of my talents." Rosamunde faced the smith, picking her words carefully. "Are there perchance some gentlefolk hereabouts who could use a—a governess for their children? Or"—her voice shook—"perchance a lady's maid?"

The heavyset smith laid down his bellows and gawked at her. "Such gentry as there be in these parts," he said, scratching his head, "have more maids than they can well use, and they pay them such a trifle as hardly keeps body and soul together. As for governesses—" He spat. "The only governesses be sisters and cousins of the gentry who'd rather support them in their houses than turn them out to almshouses and so become a scandal. Nay, ye'll not find such a job hereabouts, mistress." He chewed his lip. "There do be positions for dairymaids sometimes, but they must have experience. Are ye experienced with cows, mistress?"

Aside from occasionally having strolled through the dairy at Kenwarren House, Rosamunde had no acquaintance at all with cows. But—a dairymaid she'd be!

"Cows like me," she said defiantly. "I'm very good with them."

Harry gave her an astonished look, but the smith turned and pointed out a lane that led from the smithy. "Try at the dairy just past the stile—ye cannot miss the place. Tell Bates that I sent ye."

Rosamunde thanked him and hurried away down the lane. It was but a short distance before she came upon a stone dairy barn with a thatched roof. The place was devoid of cows, which were all out grazing at this time of day, but the farmer, a ruddy-faced fellow in a leather
84

jerkin that smelled of manure, put down his pitchfork and greeted her jovially.

Rosamunde explained her mission.

"Aye, I'm Bates. A dairymaid, are ye now? Mine has just left me. Ye can start at once. The new young milch cow jumped the fence this morning before milking and I've had no time to go looking for her. Ye can find her and bring her in and milk her."

"Where is she?" asked Rosamunde in a worried voice.

"Somewhere in the woods yonder—she's a brindle cow with no sense at all and is probably caught by now in some thorns."

Rosamunde gave him a doubtful look. "How will I know her?"

"She wears a bell," he said mildly. "She's new to the herd and won't mix yet—so she took off into the woods. The rest of them had the good sense to head for the pasture!"

Rosamunde gave him a bright unhappy smile. Filled with foreboding, she headed for the woods. The way was stony and uphill, over tree roots covered with wildflowers. She paused every few steps and listened intently for a cowbell.

She had almost given up, and was having a hard time pushing her way through brush and low-hanging branches and vines, when she heard a distant tinkle. Fighting her way through the vines that made the way almost impenetrable, she won at last to a thicket. Bates was right. His new brindle cow was woefully trapped in a clump of thorn.

The cow was skittish, and Rosamunde approached her warily. She did not want the beast to panic and plunge deeper into that thicket, which had already torn her skirt and scratched her arms. But the young cow seemed to understand that she needed help, and stood still while Rosamunde—pricking her fingers as she did so—pulled aside some thorny branches. Immediately they were removed, the cow gave a snort and trotted free. She zigzagged through some trees, gathering speed.

Rosamunde, hastily letting go of the thorny branches

and sucking the blood from her finger, plunged after her, tripping over roots, tearing herself away from entangling vines. Just when she thought she had the cow cornered, the cow would break free in another direction. Rosamunde followed doggedly, eventually pursuing the animal to a stream. There the brindle cow hesitated, floundering on the rocks at the edge, unwilling to plunge in. Her hesitation gave Rosamunde time to catch up, and by now she had plucked a willow switch and managed to guide the cow out of the woods and down the hill, following her in a mad dash back to the barn.

"I see she knew the way back," approved Bates, looking up from tossing out hay. "There's hope for her yet."

Rosamunde's hair was wild and tangled from its encounter with branches and vines. She swept it back from her perspiring face with a scratched arm and leaned panting against the whitewashed stone wall of the barn to catch her breath. "She's explored the woods, and now, like a disobedient child, she's for home and supper!"

"I see ye understand animals." He grinned. "There's the pail and stool. Let's see how well ye milk."

This was the moment Rosamunde had been afraid of. With all the aplomb she could muster, she seized the wooden pail and the three-cornered milking stool and placed it beside the brindle cow. Seating herself carefully, lest the tipsy stool tip over, she looked up—and saw that the cow had moved.

"Nice cow," she said mechanically, and edged toward her, dragging the stool. At last she had the cow almost pinned against the whitewashed wall and seated herself firmly again, aware of Bates' bright inspection behind her.

She pushed the bucket into place with her foot, seized a large pink udder and pressed gently.

Nothing happened.

She tried again, afraid she would hurt the cow. The young cow turned impatiently and gave her a resentful look.

Rosamunde tried another udder. And another—with no success. Wondering what could be wrong with her

86

technique, she grasped two at once and gave both a smart tug.

It was too much.

The young cow had had a bad day. Thrust into new surroundings, shunned by the herd, she had struck out on her own and become lost and entangled in thorns, and been bullied by a perfect stranger in flapping skirts into returning to the barn. Now with her udders uncomfortably swollen with milk, she was undergoing Rosamunde's inept attempts to milk her. In a sudden burst of irritation, she gave a loud moo and kicked over the bucket, the stool—and Rosamunde, who was tumbled backward into a pile of straw.

Rosamunde lay there for a winded second, regarding the young cow in helpless fury. As she struggled up she found herself looking straight into Harry's amused eyes. From nowhere his tall figure had appeared and was lounging in the barn doorway.

Stung by his amused surveillance, Rosamunde gained her feet with a bound and would have started for the cow again, but Harry stepped forward and blocked her way.

"Ye're no dairymaid, my lady."

"Aye, that's plain," sighed Bates ruefully from behind her. "The poor brindle's eager to be milked, but 'tis plain ye've not the hands for it."

"I guess that's true," admitted Rosamunde in a shaking voice.

"Since we're all agreed on that, there's no point lingering to discuss it," Harry said briskly. "Come, mistress, mount up. We've far to go by nightfall."

Rosamunde shot him a look. Far to go by nightfall? They were going nowhere together!

But she was tired enough to drop, and the sight of the newly shod gray mare waiting outside the barn door was too tempting to resist. Silently she flung herself up onto the saddle, ignoring Harry's proffered help.

A little way out of town in the afternoon heat, Harry halted his horse under the shade of a giant oak, seized her bridle and brought the mare to a halt.

"Will ye not let me do penance for my sins against you?" he asked pensively.

Rosamunde studied him with a frown.

"Ye have seen now what the world is like. Is it not better to seek your uncle's protection now, rather than waiting, say, for a year for your pride's sake and going to him with your face scarred perchance by a kick from a cow? Or with arms burned from some mishap at a bakery or a broken ankle from falling down some rickety backstairs laden with chamberpots?"

Rosamunde bit her lip. Indeed it seemed the only course offered. And she knew she'd never make it by herself, walking along the roadside. She'd be attacked by roving animals or roving men—and at the moment she was not sure which was worse.

"Now that my grandfather is dead, I should receive a welcome from the new earl, his son," she said slowly. "After all, he was my father's brother and bore him no ill will so far as I know. I told you that he was abroad when my father was taken and that we could not reach him in time to help us in our appeal."

"Did he write to you later?" asked Harry.

"Not so far as I know, but my mother was very sad for a long time and she might have received a letter and not told me. She could not bear to speak of my father, for the mere mention of his name brought tears to her eyes. I am sure that was why she could not see the high stone wall and rode toward it, giving no thought to whether her new mount could scale it—she must have been blinded by tears."

There was more than one way of committing suicide, thought Harry. And who was he to judge that lovely heartbroken lady who had hurled herself blindly at a high stone wall and snuffed out her life? But her going had left Rosamunde adrift and alone. His heart hardened toward the dead woman who had found it easier to die than to live and fight for her child's welfare.

"I'll take you to your uncle," he said decisively. "At least you can let me do that to atone for my hot blood."

" 'Tis far away," she said doubtfully. "The manor lies northwest of Nottingham on the River Trent."

Harry looked at the lovely lines of her—a face, a figure he was reluctant to let leave his sight. " 'Twill not be so bad a journey," he said carelessly. "Faith, on my way back I can find a few coaches with rich gentry inside whose purses I'll lighten. I know the road to Nottingham well, and we'll have no difficulty following the Trent northward. 'Tis a navigable stream. On which bank does Langley Grange lie?"

"On the west bank," said Rosamunde promptly. "The Trent washes the east front of the house. 'Tis lovely country." She sighed.

"And you shall no doubt live in it and enjoy it," said Harry gaily, giving her horse's flank a slap and urging his own black horse forward with his knee. Nightwind responded, and they rode on through the late summer afternoon and camped for the night in a grove of old trees where crickets chirped and birds made soft sleepy cries.

Rosamunde was almost reeling in the saddle when they stopped. Long exhausting walks and hot emotions, as well as their ride, had tired her, and she swallowed only a few morsels of the food Harry had managed to buy along the way, before she sank back, sound asleep.

Harry rose and stood looking down at her in the moonlight for a long time. His gaze was very tender. In that moment he would have given twenty years of his life to be somebody else—a man who could woo and win her and live with her openly in some village or shire. But he could not ask her to share his dangerous hunted life. Not when she had an aristocratic uncle who could give her all the things he could never give her—a safe home, protection from the law . . . an eligible marriage.

An eligible marriage . . . His mouth grew wry, for he had no doubt as he looked down upon this desirable heap of womanhood, this sleeping beauty curled up like an exhausted child at the root of a great tree, that she would marry—and soon. The lads of Nottinghamshire were not so dull that they would let this great treat escape them. They'd be battering down the doors of Langley

Grange within a fortnight of her arrival for a mere glimpse of her!

Feeling suddenly old and tired, Harry stretched his long length out on the ground—well out of reach of Rosamunde, whose soft lovely body tempted him more than he desired to admit. There was an ache in his throat as he studied the moon through the dark branches, and in the bleakness of his heart he understood for a stabbing moment that lady who had ridden her new hunter head on at a high stone wall.

It was long before he found sleep that night.

6   *But with the morning Harry was all urbanity again,* a jaunty young highwayman of his chivalry escorting a young lady in distress to her next of kin. Courteously he offered Rosamunde a bath at a cold swift-running brook, and himself bathed downstream cut off from sight of her by the brush. Afterward they breakfasted at a farmer's house, and Harry told the farmer's children outrageous lies about his narrow escapes sailing the seven seas. At another time Rosamunde would have been amused and her green eyes would have sparkled at his tales of savage natives and sea monsters, but his impending desertion of her still rankled. She was very quiet, long lashes shadowing her cheeks as the farmer's buxom young wife served them dark bread spread thick with yellow butter and bowls of fresh-picked berries and clotted cream, which they washed down with wooden tankards of fresh milk cooled in crocks in the springhouse.

Harry paid the farmer in silver pieces of eight—for

gold might have made them suspect—and they rode away with the farmer's excited children waving goodbye.

"They've little enough of this world's goods, but they live in the fresh air and sunshine and set a good table," mused Harry, looking back at the tiny croft with roses spilling over the whitewashed wall. "They lead a good life."

"Yes." Rosamunde returned his gaze with a level look. "And you added to their enjoyment of that life today. You tell very believable lies, Harry."

He winced, both forks of her comment pricking him. "And you," he said ruefully, "have a wicked tongue, my lady."

She shrugged. "I had not thought so, but then I am discovering new things about myself daily."

He gave her a sharp look, but she was serenely studying the gamboling of two squirrels in the great beech tree just ahead.

For the most part that day, Rosamunde rode beside him silently. Though she was grudgingly grateful to the debonair highwayman for his safe escort, she was not yet willing to relent and smile at him. He had, she felt bitterly, taken her virginity under false pretenses—what matter if he had misinterpreted her words? *She* would certainly not have been willing to sleep with him in any case if she had thought he meant to fling her aside the next day!

That she had not been flung aside but was being escorted with all haste and courtesy to her next of kin by a penitent Harry did not move her at all. Her heart was involved, and when the heart is rankled, barbs appear. These barbs shone as angry sparkles in her iridescent green eyes on those few occasions when she glanced at Harry, who rode along unconcernedly beside her. Barbed too was her speech, for she was angry with him for his too ardent courtship (in her own mind she called it rape and worse!) and even angrier over something she had so far refused to admit: she had liked it.

They camped that night by a clear spring-fed stream, and bathed in it as the sky turned from pink to blue. As she dressed in the shelter of the mulberry bushes that lined the bank, Rosamunde watched two black swans glide majestically by. The air was soft, and with her skin fresh and pink from her cold bath and all the beauties of nature around her, Rosamunde could not help feeling happy.

They mounted up, riding on through woodlands and meadows, skirting towns and villages where a hue and cry might be raised. Harry bought wheaten cakes and honey and cider at an inn they chanced on, and they ate them in a dappled woodland glade while a pair of angry jays scolded them from the branches.

Rosamunde, munching her wheaten cake, stole a resentful look at Harry. He was good to look upon, certainly, hard as the hickory against whose trunk he leaned, biting into his wheaten cake with his strong white teeth. A man to send tingles through any female heart . . . He had not been visibly impressed by her sulkiness of the day before, nor had he shown any change in his unswerving purpose to deliver her to her uncle. Was he made of stone that he could treat her so? He caught her puzzled resentful look and gave her a sunny smile.

"They told me at the inn that there's a fair being held at the market town up ahead. Shall we chance it, my lady?"

A fair! So he was not for delivering her so speedily, but would take time to dawdle at a fair! Her heart fluttered suddenly as she wondered if he was changing his mind about keeping her with him. Of course, she had not changed *hers*. She would not go with him now, even if he begged her!

"Would it be dangerous to be seen there?" she asked.

"Probably."

Somehow that answer disconcerted her. She frowned at him over her wheaten cake. "Then—?"

Harry took his last bite, rubbed his fingers on the linen napkin they shared, tossed it to her. "You seem sad, my lady. I thought it might divert you."

Rosamunde caught the tossed napkin. Not for worlds would she have let him think that prolonging this journey would please her! "It might be amusing," she said carelessly.

Harry hid a smile. There was much of the little girl in her yet, he could see, for all she tried to seem such a formidable woman.

They remounted, and a little way along Harry turned from the barely perceptible track they had been following and they crossed a wide ford. The silvery water glistened under the horses' hooves as they sloshed through and splashed silvery drops upon Harry's boots and Rosamunde's shoes. On the other side they found a wider lane, and soon they were mingling with carts and people riding horses or mules or simply walking into town, jogging gaily along this country road in their finery, many of them carrying produce—eggs and firewood and fat geese and chickens and berries and vegetables to sell at the fair.

It was easy to slip into the town with the throng, to give an honest-looking lad a coin to watch their horses, and to mingle with the fairgoers who milled about. They paused to watch an archery contest and then some acrobats and jugglers as they made their way among the stalls. Rosamunde had her fortune told by a dark-eyed gypsy, who shook her golden earrings and guessed her to be a lady's maid and promised her "advancement." Laughing, they went on, and Harry bought her glass baubles for her ears. She put them on, smiling—and suddenly realized that she'd been laughing and talking to him gaily ever since they'd arrived, all her anger forgotten.

She paused in the act of pointing out some hot cross buns, and Harry put out an arm to keep the moving crowd from jostling her. She lifted her head, and her green eyes looked wonderingly up into his dark smiling face. For the first time she faced her feelings honestly. Would she always love him? she asked herself. Even if he deserted her?

Harry seemed uncomfortable under the wistful scrutiny of those dark-lashed green eyes. "We'd best go, my lady," he said softly.

Without a word, Rosamunde accompanied him back to the horses, and they rode out of town amid the homeward-bound fairgoers under the dying rays of the sun. Overhead a burnt-orange sky darkened to a narrow golden glow in the west as the dusk settled down and they left the well-traveled lane once more for the unfrequented byways.

Rosamunde rode with a strange lightness of heart, as if time were suspended, and they would ride on forever, never reaching their destination. On these quiet lanes—scarcely tracks, for Harry knew all the back roads and shortcuts—she was alone with her lover.

And why should she not linger in his arms this night? Why should she ever let him go? Why should she not fight for him and keep him with her? She turned to him with witchery in her glowing eyes. Harry received the full burning impact of that look, and his breath caught. It was an invitation. . . .

Abruptly—though he hated himself for his alacrity in doing so—Harry found a campsight in the first glade he came to. He'd sworn an inner oath he'd not take her against her will, but if she'd a mind to . . .

He watched as she slid down from her mount and tossed back her long fair hair. She made a pretty picture standing there by the pale horse, the two of them gilded by a big yellow moon. Harry, passing by, brushed her soft hip in its brown skirt, and the touch burned him. He turned about sharply and gave her a tense measuring look.

"We've not supped. Are you hungry, my lady?" he asked hoarsely.

"No—not hungry," she said carelessly, stretching her arms above her head so that her lovely young form was the better displayed to his view. He stood rooted, hypnotized by her loveliness as, with a sigh, she smoothed the brown fabric of her skirt down over her lissome hips. Suddenly she turned and took hold of a button of his coat with two fingers, looked up at him with a wicked smile. "You are a fool, Harry," she said softly.

His heart was thumping in his chest, but with a wrenching effort he made his voice casual. "And why a fool, Rosamunde?"

"Not to take me with you." She turned away from him with a shrug.

Harry stiffened. So that was her game . . . using her

94

wiles to get him to change his mind, to take her with him. Not simple dalliance because the night was warm, the moon was yellow. Lest she see the disappointment mirrored in his face, he walked to the nearby brook, where Nightwind was drinking, passed the gray mare contentedly grazing nearby. Harry knelt and drank from his cupped hands at that brook, dashed cold water over his face, dried it with his kerchief. When he returned he saw that Rosamunde was lying stretched out beneath a tree with her head resting on her hands. She was watching him mockingly, but he withstood the tempting sight of her and brought over the food he had bought at the fair, spread it out on a large linen napkin between them and gestured toward it.

"You'd best eat, my lady," he said, stretching out on the grass. "We've a long ride ahead of us tomorrow."

"Have we, Harry?" She turned over, stretching like a small cat, tantalizingly displaying a white shoulder in the moonlight.

Harry bit into a roll and fought back his desire to take her. He knew she was playing with him, and he knew why: she did not wish to go to her uncle's, where life would be restrictive; she wished to keep the freedom of the open road of which she had had a taste. And he no less than she wished he could keep her with him.

"I have changed my mind about you, Harry," she said softly. "I think you love me after all."

"What leads you to that opinion?" he asked with a show of calm he did not feel.

"Oh . . . 'tis in your voice when you speak to me, in your eyes when you think I do not see you looking at me."

Harry winced and almost choked on the roll. Did he give himself away so obviously? He began to tie the ends of the linen napkin together. "I have had many women, Rosamunde," he said with a frown.

That irritated her. "And were their legs as good as mine?" she asked, deliberately lifting one shapely leg to be silvered by the moonlight. Her skirt slid down its silky length to her hip as she did so, and for a moment she inspected the leg with some interest. "Don't turn away from me, Harry. Consider—were those other women better to look upon than I am?"

Harry was shaken by the sight, but when he met her level gaze his mouth was grim. "I think none of them were as good to look upon as you are," he said shortly. "But that does not mean I will take you with me on the high-roads, Rosamunde."

"Ah, does it not, Harry?" She reached out and touched his thigh with her fingers, was rewarded by a startled lurch as his taut nerves reacted and the blood suddenly twanged through his veins. She laughed softly. "Tell me that you do not want me, Harry. Let me hear you lie."

"I will not lie to you, Rosamunde," he said, putting her hand away from him with an effort. "I want you."

"Then since you want me so much, why do you not take me?" She half-rose, leaned toward him and tossed back her bright hair. "All I ask is that you take me with you on your ventures instead of to my uncle's. Is that so much to ask?"

"Go to sleep," he said in a strangled voice, rolled over and kept his back to her.

She flounced away and lay back angrily upon the ground, studying his prone body scornfully. But it had been an exhausting day, and she was soon asleep.

In the morning, Harry woke first and rose, stood looking down at the sleeping girl. She was disheveled and lovely in her coarse country clothes, and an unwonted gentleness spread over Harry's hard face as he stood there. He'd have to be careful not to touch her, he warned himself, for she'd near broken his resistance last night, and if he took her again, it would be hard to put her away from him. . . .

And put her away from him he must do.

She woke and looked solemnly up into his eyes.

" 'Tis time to rise, my lady," he said, and left her to untie the linen napkin containing their breakfast while he went down to the brook.

When he returned they ate hungrily, for Rosamunde had eaten nothing the night before and the lone roll Harry had eaten had near choked him.

"We're too near a farm for a bath, my lady," he said as he finished. "I can hear cocks crowing over yonder."

Rosamunde nodded and went over and mounted the gray mare.

Thus companionably, but not as lovers, they rode the summer byroads north into Nottinghamshire.

Just south of Nottingham they passed a rocky hill crowned by a castle which had been built by William the Conqueror. They crossed the Trent and rode on into the town—rode in impudently and bought food at the sprawling market in the heart of the town.

"Nottingham was taken thrice by the Danes," Rosamunde told Harry, mindful of her long-ago Danish heritage.

"And no doubt they pillaged the place and raped all the women," said Harry ironically.

She shot him a look and laughed—Harry was no respecter of history.

From Nottingham they followed the River Trent north through showers. They sheltered for the night in the loft of a deserted barn and started out in the morning through a clean rain-washed countryside, where even the birds sang for very joy.

But Rosamunde was not joyful. Their northward march along the Trent meant they were nearing their goal. Even though she found excuses to dawdle for this or that reason, they must inevitably reach Langley Grange on the morrow.

Had she been able to see past Harry's calm resolute face into the seething caldron of his mind, she would have taken heart. For Harry too knew that Langley Grange was fast upcoming, and the wrench of parting with her was almost more than he could bear.

But he was determined to put a good face on it. *Let the lass go with apparent gladness, let her find her way without me*, he instructed himself. *Do not try to hold her, Harry. You can only hurt her.*

So he told himself.

But he studied her often as they rode, painting her portrait in his mind for future viewing on lonely nights as he galloped down strange roads, dangerous nights as he hid from pursuers in hedgerows and copses. In her coarse country clothes, riding with her straight back erect and her long fair hair streaming down about her slender shoulders, her slight body tempting and womanly . . . he would always remember her thus.

When the morrow came, she told him, "Today we will reach Langley Grange."

"I know." He sighed. "And now I wish you had the dress you started out in. 'Twas a rich gown for all its ugliness."

Rosamunde grimaced. "I hated that dress. 'Twas a reminder of Louisa's unkindness to me." She looked down at the coarse brown cloth she wore, fingered it. "If those who live at Langley Grange do not care for me as I am, perhaps they will not care for me at all." She gave her head a defiant toss.

"They cannot help caring for you," Harry said huskily, and rode on ahead before she could see the tortured look in his eyes. Rosamunde followed on the gray mare.

They had come to a bend in the river. Rosamunde, with a sinking heart, knew the great house of Langley Grange lay just ahead along that river. For the last hour she had been very pensive, knowing she was losing him. Now she stole a look at Harry. He rode silently, looking straight ahead. Her heart grieved. He did not love her. If he loved her, he would not let her go—he would take her with him. When the great house hove in sight above the treetops, Harry reined in his horse.

"I go no further, my lady," he said reluctantly. " 'Tis perhaps known that you left your guardian for a highwayman. It might go hard with you if they thought you had stayed with me."

"But—I would not tell them your right name," she blurted.

He smiled at that. "Nay, I know you would not. But 'tis best you invent some story that I left you but a few miles down the road from where I found you, and that kind strangers picked you up in a coach and took you north—or say that the earl sent you and the serving maid who accompanied you fell ill and was left at an inn and would return to Kenwarren. 'Tis doubtful they'd check your story. Tell them anything, my lady—except the truth."

Rosamunde stiffened. If Harry could be this nonchalant about their parting, so could she.

"I'll tell my own lies, thank you, Harry," she said crisply. "Thank you for bringing me here, and I'll now return your horse to you."

"Nay, the gray mare is yours. I gave her to you."

"She is yours again," said Rosamunde steadily and climbed off. She gave the gray mare a pat. "Goodbye, Harry," she said in a voice as expressionless as she could make it. But something about his level gaze broke her down. She turned swiftly and almost ran away from him, hurrying along the tall hedgerows that bordered the road.

"I'll wait for two hours at the bend in the river," Harry called after her. "If you aren't well received, walk back to the bend and I'll find you a place with a good country woman as I promised."

Rosamunde stopped in her tracks and turned, her face tortured. "Thank you," she whispered forlornly, and then stumbled on, her green eyes blurred by tears she angrily dashed away.

Soon she was walking down the long rather overgrown avenue of oaks that led to the great house, old when Henry the Eighth was king. It was an awesome pile, this home of her father's fathers, built in the time of the Plantagenet kings to serve as a fortress. Past old yews that had once been clipped into a formal garden she walked, awed as she approached by the large stones of which the house was built. Dark it looked, the windows seeming too small for its great size.

No one accosted her. The drive was deserted. Boldly she banged the heavy iron knocker of the peaked double front doors.

Those doors opened rather swiftly, creaking a bit as became old iron hinges, and a servant stared out at her, blinking. His livery was green and stained and worn, but at least it was livery.

"I am Rosamunde Langley," she said, her back very straight. "And would see my uncle, the new earl of Arne."

She thought the servant should show more surprise at the arrival of a niece of the house, but instead he scuttled back hastily and ushered her inside. Perhaps the earl of Kenwarren had written her uncle, she thought uneasily. Perhaps she was already a great scandal and would have to return to Harry at the bend in the river after all. The thought did not upset her.

In the dark and cavernous great hall the servant left her to peer curiously at the enormous stone fireplace and the ancient tapestries that hung threadbare from the great beamed ceiling, lost in darkness overhead. In the distance a wide stairway with an ornate railing wound upward. Her father had walked those stairs in his youth. . . .

But she was not left long alone. The servant returned swiftly and guided her through a small anteroom into a larger chamber hung with heavy dusty-looking green drapes and meagerly furnished with large cumbersome furnishings. On the walls were a number of moldering portraits in wide carved frames. These were her ancestors, her father's people. She approached one of the big pictures and studied it. The painted features of the man standing stiffly in armor did resemble her father a bit, she thought—though it was hard to tell, she had seen her father so seldom; he'd always been away fighting in foreign wars. The next portrait did not resemble him. Nor the next.

So absorbed was she in her perusal of the pictures that she did not notice a soft sound behind her.

"I had not expected you so soon," said a careless voice.

Rosamunde whirled to face the man who had just stepped out of the small antechamber and was now watching her with cold delight written across his handsome dissolute face. His glowing brown eyes held a sneer, and he stood easily watching her, encased in a suit of amber satin.

100

"Lord Matthew!" She gasped.

"My runaway betrothed," he said nastily and swept her a mocking bow.

Rosamunde did not hesitate. While Lord Matthew's head was bent over in his bow, his curls cascading, she dashed past him and rushed for the door through which she had come—only to collide with an older man, clad in dark shabby gray, who was just coming through it. He was bearded and looked very stern. As she crashed into him, his arms closed around her involuntarily, and he let her go slowly, keeping a tight hold on one arm.

"Let me go!" cried Rosamunde. "I will not remain in the room with this man!"

"Hardly a joyous greeting from one's betrothed," observed Lord Matthew. "Nor for your newfound uncle."

"I am *not* your betrothed," gasped Rosamunde, trying to shake free of her newfound uncle's grasp. "Sir, if you are indeed my uncle, I will ask that you let me leave here at once! I—I do not like your choice of guests."

For answer, her newfound uncle dragged her to the center of the room, almost threw her at Lord Matthew. His face was pale and a pulse drummed in his temple. There was nothing of her father about him that she could see. Nor any kindness in that stark spare countenance.

"You have disgraced our family name," he told her coldly. "It seems you have inherited this trait. My brother disgraced us as well—nay, he near ruined us with his treason. And it would seem you are just like him. This gentleman"—he indicated Lord Matthew, who now had hold of her, with a nod of his head—"offered you honorable marriage, and what did you do? At gunpoint you ran away with a total stranger and a highwayman to boot. It is no wonder he now refuses to marry you!"

"He—refuses?" Hope kindled in her green eyes.

"But he will at least keep you off the highways and from the gibbet. He will take you into his household and give you his protection at Waverclay Court. It is the most you could hope for under the circumstances."

His "protection" . . . not a wife but a mistress. Rosamunde paled but rallied. "I will not go with Lord Matthew

101

to Waverclay Court," she stated. "Nor can you make me do so legally. The earl of Kenwarren is my guardian, and I do not see him here. If I go to Waverclay Court, it will be because I am dragged there by force—would you conspire in the abduction of your own niece, your brother's daughter?"

Her uncle smiled thinly. There was only dislike in his eyes. "I see you would prefer your reputation to be bandied about in alehouses and taverns, that all might know of your scandalous escapades. But *I* would *not* prefer it. Lord Matthew, your much-abused betrothed, did not come to me empty-handed. He brought with him a legal paper signed by the earl of Kenwarren, turning over your guardianship to me. And since you can no longer hope for marriage, I now turn you over to Lord Matthew Waverclay for his disposal."

Rosamunde recoiled from this blow. She hardly felt the pain of Lord Matthew's steely fingers biting into her arm. "I do not believe you!" she cried. "The earl would not do this!"

For answer, her uncle strode to a small writing desk and took out a parchment signed and sealed with red sealing wax. On the sealing wax was imprinted the arms of Kenwarren—it had been made by pressing the earl's signet ring into it when the wax was hot.

Shocked by the sight of it, Rosamunde snatched at the parchment, and Lord Matthew promptly jerked her back.

"She would destroy the document," he explained to the older man. "You'd best keep it from her reach. This cat has long claws."

"I see that what you say of her is true," observed her uncle, returning the paper to the writing desk. "She is indeed treacherous. Why you would want her, I would not know."

That remark startled Lord Matthew. He glanced in amazement from the earl to the dainty beauty, fiercely struggling in his arms. "She is of a certain distinction in face and figure," he began.

"I see," interrupted the older man ironically. "You are a worshiper of beauty. Which is no deeper than the skin."

He pursed his lips and cast a look over the mantel at the portrait of his recently deceased and almost frighteningly homely wife. "There are better reasons for choosing a woman," he observed severely.

Lord Matthew, who could not think of any, forebore comment on the earl's lofty views, but kept a viselike grip on the struggling Rosamunde. "It may be," he said in a suave voice, "that if I can bring the wench to heel and teach her patience and obedience, I might once again consider marrying her."

"That," observed her uncle with a distasteful look at his lovely struggling niece, "would be almost too generous. My one request is that you remove her from my sight as soon as possible."

"Ah, but it is late in the day," said Lord Matthew smoothly. "I would beg your indulgence for rooms for us both for one more night. It is too late to start out upon the highways even with an escort—and who knows, her late companion may be prowling the roads with his brace of pistols."

Helpless in his strong grasp, Rosamunde thought of Harry at the bend in the river, expecting her to have been well received, and eager to turn back south again. Best they leave now! For if they chanced to pass Harry, she had no doubt he'd somehow effect a rescue.

"I don't wish to stay in your house!" she flashed. "A man who would speak ill of the dead—'tis no wonder my father never mentioned you. I don't doubt he was ashamed of the relationship!"

Her uncle's eyes narrowed and his jaw jutted out. She guessed he yearned to slap her impudent mouth. "You are more than welcome to stay the night, Lord Matthew," he grated. "Yes, and I'll give shelter to this hellcat too—but only because it is so late. I want her removed from my house with tomorrow's dawn!"

"I prefer an early start," agreed Lord Matthew, amused.

"A room will be prepared for the girl next to your lordship's. I trust you can keep her under control? I'll not have her rushing about the house with her venomous tongue, giving the servants grist for their gossip!"

"Perhaps we could have rooms tonight in a quieter part of the house?" suggested Lord Matthew. "I would not wish to disturb . . . " He left the sentence unfinished.

"I take your meaning," said his host quickly. "You may have rooms overlooking the river. That side of the house is quiet. Indeed, if you wish to give the girl a good thrashing and teach her manners, I'll not raise a hand to stop you. 'Tis no more than she deserves." He glared at his white-faced niece. "And I'll leave orders for my servants that no matter what transpires in the night they are not to come near your rooms."

A wolfish smile lit Lord Matthew's dissolute face. "I will hope to tame the wench," he said almost meekly. "And further hope that you will one day be my guest at Waverclay Court and can observe the fruits of my tuition, for I have no doubt she can be broken to my hand."

"A generous offer, but I've no wish to see my niece again. I regard it as a kindness that you take her off my hands. Since I do not care to receive her at my table, her supper will be sent to her room. You, of course, are welcome to join me."

Lord Matthew cast a thoughtful look at Rosamunde's high color and defiant mien. "It might be best if I too dine in my room this night and keep an eye on my charge here. She may well attempt to escape."

"A stout rope will do wonders for that," said his host bluntly.

"I'll not be needing it," said Lord Matthew serenely. "I believe you'll find her much gentler by morning when we depart."

His host snorted. "Faith, I should hope so, although I very much doubt it!" Arms akimbo, he stood and watched his guests leave the room in the wake of a frightened-looking servant. Lord Matthew was half-dragging a reluctant Rosamunde along beside him, his grip numbing her arm.

When they had cleared the door she turned to him. "I won't go with you to Waverclay Court," she panted. "I wouldn't be your wife and I certainly won't be your mistress!"

104

"I doubt you'll have much to say about it," Lord Matthew sneered. "But we can discuss it over supper. In the meantime, hold your tongue—your uncle prefers we have our discussions privately." He indicated the servant just ahead.

Rosamunde, biting her lips from the pain of his numbing grasp but too proud to protest, fought back a desire to scream. It would do no good, she realized, and—suppose he gagged her?

Down several long corridors and up and down flights of stairs they followed the servant to a secluded part of the house, and he opened the door to a chamber on the second floor, stood back as Lord Matthew thrust her inside, accepted the key, followed her in and locked the door behind him.

Freed from his imprisoning grasp, Rosamunde immediately rushed for the casement windows, threw them wide and stepped out upon a narrow balcony.

There she stopped.

A story below her, lapping at the very walls of the building, ran the River Trent, deep and green. It was very wide at this point, and Rosamunde did not swim. Death waited below. For a moment she swayed at the railing, wondering what it would be like to drown. But she was young and life was sweet and somewhere down the road was Harry. With a dangerous look in her green eyes she turned at bay. Lord Matthew had the key to the corridor door on his person—somehow she would get it. Somehow she would make her escape.

7   *"I see you are considering how you will get the key,"* Lord Matthew drawled unpleasantly, reading her

thoughts. "But I shall endeavor to make you desire it less."
He advanced on her, an evil figure in his amber satins,
and Rosamunde retreated, looking about her in a hunted
way for something to throw at him. About her was a big
square room, devoid of furniture save for a massive bed,
a high-backed chair and a sturdy chest on which reposed
a single heavy candlestick. She leaped forward and seized
upon that candlestick, but Lord Matthew was too quick
for her. With a giant bound he pounced on her and tore
the weapon from her hand. It fell with a heavy sound
upon the floor and rolled away.

Rosamunde, now caught by a grip on her right forearm, tried to jerk away, but Lord Matthew's strong left
hand maintained its grip. With an almost careless blow of
his right hand he slapped her so hard her head snapped
sideways, and she staggered backward with her senses
reeling. Again his right hand lashed out—this time to
grasp the right sleeve of her worn dress and give it a great
tug. Beneath this assault the thin material ripped free and
the whole sleeve came off in his hand.

With a gasp, Rosamunde managed to straighten up and
clutched with her free hand at her bodice. But another
violent slap knocked her head to the right, and her left
sleeve was torn away.

He let go of her arm and both his cruel hands found
her white throat and squeezed. Fighting for air, she pummeled him with her fists and kicked out at him, but he
shoved her writhing body against a wooden footpost of
the great four-poster and pinioned her legs with his own.
The beating of her fists against him he seemed not to feel,
and indeed there was an almost insane concentration in
his anger as those fingers about her windpipe blurred her
consciousness and made her sag to her knees.

As she fell the hands left her throat and snatched her
roughly upward by her bodice, which tore away along
with her chemise, so that she fell back against the bed
with her softly curved young breasts exposed to his furious gaze.

Gulping in air, still half-fainting, Rosamunde came up
from a dark pit to feel herself spun about. Dimly she felt
106

the material leave her rounded hips as skirt and petticoat and chemise were ripped away. As air came back to her straining lungs, she struck out again gamely at her brutal antagonist. But Lord Matthew was in no mood to brook argument from this wench who had for so long eluded him. He responded with an ugly snarl, and this time his bruising hands slapped her face this way and that, herding her across the room by the fury of his onslaught until at last her slight body sagged and he picked her up and hurled her violently upon the bed.

Half-stunned, Rosamunde lay there and watched in horror as he bent and picked up her torn dress, her petticoat and chemise, even her shoes and stockings, which had been strewn here and there during the fight. He strode to the balcony and flung them all over the balcony railing into the river below.

"That," he said, returning to stand over her, breathing heavily, "is what I mean when I say you will have less desire for the key. Even *you* would hardly care to run through the corridors of Langley Grange stark naked, to be seized and enjoyed by any passing lackey!"

As the force of that bore in on her, Rosamunde cast an involuntary glance of horror down at her own slender body. In the turmoil of the struggle she had hardly realized that all her clothes were gone, but it was true what he said. She was lying there stark naked. She made a grasp for the coverlet, and he jerked it away from her with a laugh, stood there devouring her with his hot insulting brown eyes. She scuttled away from him, made to cover her pulsating breasts with her arms and drew her legs together tightly, trying to shield herself from his insolent view.

Lagging footsteps sounded outside in the corridor, and Lord Matthew stepped back, picked up the coverlet and tossed it to her.

"Cover yourself," he ordered, and Rosamunde hurried to do precisely that. "I will remove it when I'm ready," he added negligently. "But there's no need for you to display yourself to the servant who brings our supper."

He straightened his wig, which had been knocked

107

askew, and flexed his shoulders in his satin coat, from which, Rosamunde saw, several buttons were missing. She was briefly, bitterly glad that she had been able to do at least some damage to his clothing.

Outside, halting footsteps passed their door, and Lord Matthew's gaze flicked over Rosemunde's wild rebellious green eyes and tumbled pale-gold hair, spread out in wild confusion around her on the pillow as she crouched beneath the coverlet.

"On second thought," he said, "I may decide to go downstairs to sup after all. But first I will tame you, my pretty wildcat."

He strode toward the bed. There was a rip in his satin sleeve from his recent encounter, but there was no diminution of his resolve, and the face that loomed toward her was just as merciless. Rosamunde shrank back, sliding her naked back up the pillow, pressing back along the headboard. As he reached the edge of the bed she skittered out of it, clutching the coverlet about her, and ran to the far side of the room.

Lord Matthew gave a nasty laugh. "I'll teach you to run from me!" he said coldly and darted forward with a speed she had not guessed he possessed. She sprang to the right to avoid him, but he plunged toward her and caught her by the legs, bringing her crashing to the floor, bruising her knees and arms. As she tried to struggle free of him, she lost the coverlet and was pinioned by a large hand around her ankle.

His other arm locked about her waist, and he managed to gain his feet with his struggling burden and once more hurled her upon the bed. He was about to follow when a knock sounded somewhere and a loud but muffled voice called, "Yer lordship? Supper, yer lordship. I've brought yer supper."

"I'm in here!" shouted Lord Matthew, halting his advance. "You may serve me here." He picked up the coverlet and balled it up in his hands, threw it at Rosamunde, who made haste to cover herself with it. With a high color and snapping eyes, he strode to the door, pulled the key from his pocket and flung it wide, keeping a wary eye on the girl on the bed. Realizing full well she'd have no chance to make it past him out the door, Rosamunde stayed where she was with the coverlet pulled up to her neck. She was well aware of the way her face reddened as the servant entered.

He was in almost as dowdy livery as the one who had met her at the front door, but younger, and he walked with a limp. After one curious look at the wild-looking young woman in the bed he kept his gaze carefully averted and carried in a small table on which reposed a silver trencher containing a leg of lamb, the gravy half-congealed, and a thin partridge. He limped out and received from a helper—a barefoot young girl who peered in curiously—a basket of bread and cheese and a large pastry. As he set these on the small table, the girl ran in to hand him a bottle of wine and a silver goblet, and Lord Matthew gave her such a scowl as sent her scurrying out again. But the liveried servant was not to be frightened by scowls. With maddening slowness, he limped about, arranging napkins, pouring out the wine.

When he had finished he made an awkward bow. "I be right back with the lady's supper," he promised.

"That won't be necessary," said Lord Matthew with a steely look at Rosamunde. "The lady isn't hungry."

Rosamunde, who hadn't eaten since breakfast, gave him an outraged look.

Lord Matthew saw the servant out, locked the door carefully behind him and called through the heavy wooden panels, "You can clear the dishes in the morning. Don't disturb us further this evening."

Rosamunde, from the bed, was considering whether she could leap up and reach that wine bottle and bring it crashing down on Lord Matthew's head before he could move to stop her. Reluctantly she had decided she could not, but at that "Don't disturb us," she shuddered.

Oh, Harry, Harry, she thought forlornly. *Why did I leave you?* And then in panic, *He said he'd wait two hours for my return . . . but Lord Matthew will keep me here till morning.* She had no guarantee Harry would take the road south. Perhaps he would turn west through Sherwood

Forest or strike north for Lincoln. Somehow, somehow, she vowed, she'd get back to him, no matter what Lord Matthew did to her. She'd find her way back to that terrible inn where she'd served ale to the highwaymen and wait for him there!

Lord Matthew seemed to enjoy her flushed discomfiture. He ate slowly. After a while his cold voice bit into her feverish reverie. "What is your highwayman's name? There must be more to it than 'Hard Harry.'"

"He did not tell me," muttered Rosamunde.

From taking a bite of partridge, Lord Matthew lifted his head to regard her keenly. "How so?"

Rosamunde decided to play for time. The wine bottle was not so very far away. Imperceptibly she moved toward it.

"He did not stay with me," she lied. "He set me down at the next crossroad and said he'd not be held back by riding double and let the king's men catch him."

"Ah, did he now?" murmured Lord Matthew. He looked pleased, and Rosamunde inched a little nearer the bottle. "And why came you not back to the coach to ask my forgiveness?"

"We had a scuffle at the crossroads, for I felt he had broken his promise to take me where I wished to go—which was back to Kenwarren House."

"Kenwarren House?" Lord Matthew leaned forward, fascinated.

"Yes. I knew that the earl would not punish me, but I hoped when he returned that I might get him to listen to reason and not betrothe me so quickly."

"So you started for Kenwarren House?" He was watching her as he took another bite of pheasant.

Rosamunde sighed. She had his attention focused on her more intently than she wished. It was hard edging toward the wine bottle under such intense scrutiny. "No —that is, I meant to go there, but in the darkness after he threw me off his horse, I knew not which way we had come. It began to rain and I took the wrong road and when morning came I found a small farmhouse. When I told them my story, the goodwife suggested I seek my
110

only kin—my uncle—and have him write to my guardian as to the way of things."

"Then you walked all the way here?"

"No." Rosamunde shrugged, a shrug that brought her body a little closer to her goal. In a moment she would snatch that bottle and bring it down across his temple. "Some strolling players happened by and did give me a ride in their painted wagon partway, and after that a farmer carrying vegetables to market let me ride behind him on his mule, and later on a lady in a coach."

"A lady in a coach?" Lord Matthew picked up the wine bottle and refilled his goblet. He kept his hand around the neck of the bottle as he considered her.

"Yes, a lady," she mumbled.

"Did she give you her name?"

"She told me she was the Lady Dorothy Wynbridge," improvised Rosamunde. "I did not give her my right name, and she tried to hire me as a lady's maid. I told her I was on my way to my mother, who worked as housekeeper at Langley Grange."

His fingers still curled around the neck of the bottle, Lord Matthew studied her thoughtfully. "So . . . he did not touch you?"

"The highwayman? No, he was anxious to get on. He but said what he did about us having ale together to anger you."

Lord Matthew decided he had not poured out enough wine. He lifted the bottle again and filled his goblet to brimming. This time he set the bottle down on his other side, away from Rosamunde.

She gave the bottle a haggard look. She could not reach it now, not unless she leaped across him. Sick with disappointment, she sank back and watched him slowly continue his meal. He seemed lost in thought. With a groaning stomach she watched him work his way even through the large pastry—and without having offered her any. Not for worlds would Rosamunde have asked Lord Matthew for a bite—she would have starved first. She divined this was a deliberate part of her punishment: not only would he work his will upon her, he would starve her as well.

At last he was finished. The silver trencher was piled with well-picked bones and broken bits of bread. The cheese and pastry were all consumed, the last of the wine swallowed. Lord Matthew—warmed by so much unwonted exercise before supper—had enjoyed his food. Partially to annoy Rosamunde, whose hunger he had guessed, he had been leisurely throughout. Now he daintily rubbed his fingers with his napkin and leaned back in his tall-backed chair, considering the rebellious beauty before him.

"In London," he said, "women outnumber men thirteen to one. Offers of marriage do not come often to penniless young women, even when they are good to look upon."

Rosamunde shot him a scathing look and went back to searching the room with her eyes. She was looking vainly for the heavy candlestick he had earlier knocked from her hand. It had been an ideal weapon and had fit her hand well.

"Your guardian, the earl of Kenwarren, knew this well when he proposed our troth. You would have done well to have listened to him, Rosamunde."

She could not see the candlestick anywhere; it must have rolled under the bed.

"You should go to London," she said in a brittle voice. "The choice is greater."

Lord Matthew stood up, flicked a napkin across his amber satin trousers to brush away the crumbs and tossed the napkin aside. "I perceive a certain bitterness in your tone," he said wearily. "Still, I am inclined to be generous with you, Rosamunde. Not that you deserve it." He saw that he was speaking to her shoulder and his voice hardened. "It may be that if you please me—mind, I say *please me*—I will reconsider and wed you after all."

Please him! Rosamunde felt sick. No doubt he expected her to toss aside the coverlet and open her arms to him, take him to her quivering breast—now that he had been so magnanimous as to mention marriage!

112

She would die first!

Somehow this night must be got through. Tomorrow, God willing, she would make her escape. She hoped the morrow would not find her too battered to travel, to go seeking Harry, for she'd no mind to submit to Lord Matthew without a battle. Her hands clenched and she kept her face averted as Lord Matthew shed his coat, removed his boots and began to remove his breeches.

"You will not bed me without marriage vows," she said evenly, managing to keep the tremor out of her voice.

He laughed shortly and kicked his way out of his trousers, swaggered toward the bed. "I will bed you and you will *plead* for marriage vows," he corrected in a cold voice. "And you had best still be mainly a virgin, for I had barely entered you in Kenwarren House before that damned scullery maid set up a howl."

Rosamunde lifted her head and looked fearlessly into his eyes. "I will fight," she said in a voice that for coldness matched his own.

"Good," he said sarcastically. "I should hate to see you lose spirit at such a moment."

She flashed him a look of bright hatred, and tensed as he bent over her. He snatched away the coverlet and reached out to fondle her breast, and she struck his hand away and reached up and clawed his face. At his enraged howl, she tried to slide off the bed and elude him, but his hand thumped down on her shoulder in a grip that made her wince; his fingers dug in, leaving blue marks.

"I'll tame this devil in you!" he cried hoarsely, and fell upon her like a savage, pinioning her hips beneath him, tearing apart her locked legs with his knees, forcing his way between her thighs as with his hands he held her wrists and arms outspread against the bed.

Desperately Rosamunde fought. She strained and gasped and writhed this way and that, but he was too strong for her and his weight held her pinned helplessly beneath him. Inexorably he was winning the battle, and with a sudden hard thrust that made her gasp he won his entrance. She was looking wide-eyed into his face at that

113

moment, and she saw his head rise up and a terrible snarl light his dark visage.

"Lying strumpet!" he cried. "You have cheated me! You are not a virgin—you have lain with that damned highwayman!"

She flinched as he raised his right hand and crashed his fist down into her face, blacking her eye and sending bright needles of light through her brain.

Rosamunde screamed and tried ineffectually to shield her face.

In fury he brought his left fist down upon her other eye, and her scream had a high keening sound of deep pain as her head was rocked right and left.

"Tonight a *man* will bed you!" he roared, and drove within her with such force that she felt sick and faint, and the pain in her loins matched the blinding pain in her head.

"That may be," said a steely voice behind him, "but that man will not be *you*, Waverclay!"

Neither had seen a man's catlike form drop from a window overhead to land lightly on the balcony outside. Absorbed in their struggle, neither had heard him spring through the open casements. But suddenly Lord Matthew was seized by the scruff of his shirt from behind and jerked bodily from the bed.

Through a red haze, Rosamunde's bruised eyes saw the violent form of Harry in action. *Harry!* she thought, dazed. *How did you get here? How did you know?*

Lord Matthew, his face convulsed with rage at being thus torn from his objective, staggered backward and then, righting himself, lunged viciously at the lean highwayman. At that point Harry delivered himself of such a blow as Rosamunde had never thought to see dealt by mortal man. He brought up his fist from the floor and drove it with all the force of his springing body into Lord Matthew's face. There was the violent crunch of bone on bone, and Lord Matthew's face exploded in blood as his nose was crushed. The force of Harry's blow lifted him off his feet and sent him smashing into the wall. Still

114

dazed, Rosamunde heard his head crack like an egg against that wall.

"You've killed him, Harry," she muttered thickly.

"I hope so," said Harry fervently, scooping her up. "Unfortunately there's no time to make sure. I was seen and the alarm is out. They'll be breaking down the door soon. Can you swim, Rose? Are you badly hurt?"

She shook her head, content to lie and ache in his arms.

"No matter," he muttered, crossing the room with her. "Don't be frightened and don't cry out. I'm going to drop you in the river, and I'll be right behind you—I'll hold up your head and get you to shore. Here we go, Rose." He dangled her over the balcony as far as he could, and dropped her down into the deep green water.

He need not have cautioned her against being frightened. As the cool water closed over her head, Rosamunde lost consciousness altogether.

A moment later Harry had split the water beside her in a clean dive, found her, and lifted her head above the waterline. With the swift strong strokes of the experienced swimmer—indeed, much of his boyhood had been spent swimming—he struck out into the center of the stream, letting the current sweep him along, swiftly passing the bleak walls of ◦Langley Grange and moving around a bend in the river, beneath overhanging trees that dipped into the water, out of sight of the windows.

Swimming rapidly, Harry breathed a deep sigh of relief. No shouts had sounded, no alarm been given. It might not yet have occurred to the occupants of Langley Grange that their unwanted visitor had left by the water route—his swift action had bought him time.

Striking out now for shore, he swam beneath low-hanging branches and lifted his limp dripping burden tenderly from the river. A very mermaid she seemed, so slight and naked, her pink-tipped breasts and hips gleaming with water, her fair hair streaming with it, and her wet dark lashes glued to her pale cheeks, where ugly blue bruises were beginning to show. Carefully he carried her through the trees, paused a moment and whistled. A low whinny answered him, and he changed direction slightly and soon was rewarded by the sight of the big black stallion and the gray mare.

He grasped the cloak he had thrown over his saddle and tenderly wrapped Rosamunde in it. She came to and smiled at him, a wan smile, as he laid her across his saddle and vaulted up behind her.

"I can ride, Harry," she whispered.

"I don't think so," he said shortly. "Rest as best you can, Rose. It may be a long night."

She did not protest. She cuddled against him, grateful to her bones that he had found her, that he had saved her. Harry nudged Nightwind with his knee and, leading the gray mare, struck out in a westerly direction. When a small rivulet crossed the path he led the horses down it, for he'd no doubt there'd be dogs shortly in pursuit.

The luck that had always been with him held, for they met no one and as night closed down clouds slid over the moon and obscured the stars. There was a low rumble of thunder in the west and the feel of rain in the air. Letting Nightwind pick his way carefully, Harry steered a course that would lead them into Sherwood Forest. The rain began, and Harry thanked God for it, for he had heard a distant baying and had little doubt what quarry the dogs sought. On through the sodden night they plowed, the horses, himself and his limp burden.

Rosamunde was little better than half-conscious through that long night. She slept fitfully and moaned in her sleep, waking sometimes with a choking gasp in the belief that she was still Lord Matthew's prisoner.

"He was waiting for me," she muttered once. "He had guessed where I'd go. My uncle had transferred his guardianship to Lord Matthew so he'd have no need to marry me. . . ."

"Hush, Rose, hush," said Harry huskily. " 'Tis over now." His arm around her tightened, and she slipped back into the halfworld of semiconsciousness, foggy and filled with bloody dreams.

Once, half-asleep, she murmured, "It hurts," like a reproachful child, and Harry swallowed. Those who knew him well would have been astonished to see tears in his
116

hard gray eyes—though it would have surprised none of them to know that inwardly his hard fist was smashing into Lord Matthew's face all over again.

By morning they were well away from Langley Grange, the tired horses walking sedately under the old oaks of Sherwood Forest. In the early light Harry found a wood-cutter's hut and a sturdy woman bending over a washtub, who looked up curiously as he approached.

"Canst give us shelter and a crust?" he asked. "I've gold to pay."

The woman gave him a doubtful look, peering suspiciously at the slight figure that lay across his saddle.

"The lass and I were eloping," Harry explained ruefully. "Her father caught up to us and near killed her. He locked her up, but I managed to help her escape through a window. We've ridden all night." His flat voice gave testimony to his weariness.

"Ah, the poor babe," murmured the woman sympathetically, clucking her tongue as she saw Rosamunde's bruised shoulder and blackened eyes. "That a father would do such a thing to his own! Bring her inside."

"I'll tend her myself," said Harry, dismounting and carrying his drooping burden into the hut, despositing her on a pile of fresh grasses in the corner. "If you could bring me some of that hot water from your fire?"

The woman nodded and went out to the big iron kettle that boiled on a tripod above the flames. She brought Harry a wooden basin of hot water and some clean worn linen. With great care he sponged Rosamunde's hurt face and bruised body, his strong hands moving as delicately as a woman's over her silken skin, a muscle clenching angrily in his jaw as each new hurt appeared. Rosamunde's eyes fluttered open, and when she saw who it was, fluttered shut trustingly. As gently as if she were a babe, he washed her and dried her with more clean linen the woman brought him.

"Such a fair little thing, poor child," murmured the woman sympathetically, and beamed her pleasure as Harry thrust a gold piece into her clawlike hand.

"Some food, if you can spare any. And this"—he thrust

117

another coin into her hand—"is to say you've not seen us. Her father would kill the lass next time if he caught her. He's vengeful and he's wily—he'll come seeking her and he'll tell you some convincing tale, like as not about guardianship or the law—but he's her father all the same."

The woman nodded. "May God strike me dead, I'll not tell," she said devoutly, fingering the gold pieces.

"Good." Harry settled Rosamunde down on a clean cover he had spread over the woman's bed and threw his cloak over her. "Have ye a dress she could wear?"

"Nay. My clothes would ne'er fit her—but wait. There's something here of my son's. He's away for a bit." She opened a rude box and pulled out a boy's breeches and shirt. They were crude country clothes and ill-fitting, but Harry looked at them, pleased. The cry would be out for a man and a woman—not a man and a lad!

"I'll need hay for my horses," he said.

"I've some grain." And as he rose, "I'll curry them down myself," she volunteered. "And feed and water them too, soon as I've set a dish before you."

Her "dish" was a thick hot soup flavored with herbs, followed by slabs of cold venison. With a wooden spoon, Harry carefully spooned some of the hot liquid down Rosamunde's bruised throat. She made a weak gesture to show that it hurt, and he realized as her eyes opened that she could hardly speak. The brute had choked her! With a hand that trembled with rage that he had not torn Lord Matthew limb from limb while he had the chance, Harry resolutely forced a little of the liquid through her pale lips.

"You need it, sweetheart," he said huskily. And at his bidding and the endearment, she took a little more, and winced.

"You . . . came back," she managed to whisper. "I could not believe it was really you."

"Aye," he said gently. "I was waiting at the bend in the river when I saw a piece of cloth coming down the river, caught on a floating branch. I jabbed at it idly with a stick and suddenly recognized it as part of your dress. You can
118

be sure I lost no time in getting to the manor house. When the door opened, I knocked the fellow who opened it senseless and was searching the upstairs rooms for you when your scream guided me to you. You were just below me—and I dropped out the window onto the balcony below and saw that he had you." His teeth ground. "Ah, that I had had the time to finish him off properly," he said in a voice of yearning.

She reached up a weak hand and stroked his neck beneath the thick shining dark hair that rested on his shoulders and spilled over his fine white linen shirt. Her gaze was loving. "I thought I'd lost you," she murmured wistfully.

"Never again, Rose," he said huskily. "I thought you'd fare badly with me, but it seems you fare even worse alone. I'll keep you safe."

Her eyes, bruised all around, looked up at him trustingly. She swallowed a little more soup and fell asleep like a child.

Fatigue weighing heavily on him, Harry took out his pistols and laid them by his hand and crawled onto the bed beside her. She lay in the curve of his warm body, and as she slept she nestled her hips against him gently. It made a tender fire in his loins, a lovely ache that yearned to be satisfied. With a gentle finger he moved his hands beneath the cloak, cupped her breast with his hand and brushed its soft peak with questing fingers. He was rewarded with a soft sigh and an involuntary movement of luxury. Rosamunde slept.

With a sigh of his own, Harry—careful of Rosamunde's bruises and within easy reach of his pistols—fell asleep too.

He woke to the sound of the woman coming into the hut.

"I hear dogs in the woods," she said, and he got up alertly. "No," she added, cocking her head and listening. "No, they're moving away now. Must be some hunters."

Harry looked at the sun, glistening down through chinks in the roof, gilding the single window and striking slanted light through the door. Faith, he must have slept the clock

119

around! He felt quite fit. Beside him Rosamunde had stirred and was smiling at him from her bruised face.

"Do you think you can ride, Rose?" he asked gently.

She moved and groaned. "I think so," she said in a slightly hoarse voice.

Harry frowned and touched her bruised throat. "Is it better this morning?"

She nodded. "It aches a bit. As does the rest of me."

"Aye. He used you ill."

"Not so ill as he would have had you not appeared. I think he would have killed me, Harry."

There was hell in Harry's eyes. "Let us hope I've rid the world of him," he muttered. "I should have stayed and made sure!"

The hut woman fed them a good breakfast of porridge and some berries she'd picked that morning. As they left she pressed on them a large bundle containing cold meat and bread and "bit of grain for the horses," and as a last gift, a battered man's hat for Rosamunde.

"I wish I had something to give her," sighed Rosamunde as Harry boosted her gently to the saddle.

Harry gave the woman another gold piece and bade her hide her gold well lest those who followed find it and know they'd come this way and slit her throat for it. She was waving as they set out, Rosamunde with her bright hair pushed up inside the shapeless countryman's hat, with a jerkin hanging loosely over her rough shirt. The trousers fit better, but not so well as to display her lovely figure, for which Harry was grateful. Shoes had been a problem and she was riding barefoot, her delicate feet and calves a temptation to keep Harry's eyes from the road.

"Where are we bound?" she asked. "Some 'safe' inn?"

"There may be no safe inns at the moment," he said grimly. "Not if the reward's large enough."

She digested that. "Your friends would turn on you?"

"Not my friends, but those who know me by sight and would make a shilling from any man's carcass."

"Where will we go?" she asked hopelessly. "Is any place safe for us?"

"I could leave you in keeping of some good farmwife,
120

for gold, while you mended," he said musingly. "But there are always those who'd come seeking, and a face and figure like yours are sure to be remarked. Best you stay in men's clothing—which becomes you well," he added with a grin, his eyes raking the soft hips and buttocks astride the gray mare. "Well . . . I've no great need of gold this season. Come, Rose, I'll take you to a place as safe as any."

Rosamunde wondered where that was, but dared not ask for fear Harry would change his mind and leave her instead with "some good farmwife" to mend.

8   *For several days they rode, avoiding towns and* dwellings, sleeping out on the lush summer grass. Their pace was leisurely, and the horses grew sleek on much grazing of summer meadows. Respecting Rosamunde's bruised, misused body, Harry made no move to touch her, save for helping her onto and off of her horse—and running his hand gently down her shoulderblades or waist as he did so. He had abandoned his plumed hat and now wore a wide countryman's hat and a sober leather jerkin he had bought from a farmer whose haycart they passed on a country lane. He left Rosamunde and the horses secreted for short periods in wooded spots and thick copses while he shopped in market towns, and brought back food in leathern bags and linen napkins. Rosamunde grew used to this strange gypsy existence and began to feel dreamily that they might ride on forever.

She kept no track of distances now, or directions. She cared not where she went, as long as Harry was beside her.

So it came as a shock when one day Harry speeded his

pace. "We must hurry if we are to reach our destination before dawn," he said.

Rosamunde, who had almost come to the conclusion that they had no destination at all but were wandering aimlessly, drinking in the beauty of the countryside, reveling in their love for each other, came alert.

A place of safety, he had said. She wondered if it would be again some small inn that catered to "gentlemen of the road."

Through copses and down little streambeds and twice across ruined stone bridges he led her, through a gentle rain that pattered ceaselessly. She was entirely lost and had no idea where they were when at last, the rain having stopped, they came to a clearing in the woods where some cattle stood in a little companionable group in the moonlight. Past them, through a grove of old oaks, she glimpsed the roofs of a manor house, and was startled when Harry rode boldly across the clearing toward it.

As they drew near he approached more carefully, keeping well out of sight of the windows. But she felt he need not have bothered, for as they came closer she saw that the wing toward which they rode was ruined, that the glazing was gone from the tall gothic windows, and that one end had tumbled down. The stones were a jumbled mass through which they picked their way.

Harry alighted and briskly set her on her feet. She waited as he opened a tall door that led into a stone-floored room and led their horses through. She followed him in and looked around her curiously. The moonlight through the door, and through a high window as well, showed her hay piled on the floor—taken from the haymow she had glimpsed by a distant outbuilding, no doubt—and a wooden tub which Harry picked up and carried away. He came back presently with the tub filled with water.

"Got it from a drain barrel." He grinned at her. Obviously her highwayman had prepared for his homecoming.

The horses, which he quickly rubbed down, fell to eating and drinking contentedly. Harry took her hand and led her down a long gallery, where their footsteps echoed
122

on the stones. At the end of the gallery he opened a door into a creditable chamber, bathed in moonlight.

"The best room of the lot," he said dryly.

Rosamunde stared about her at the stone fireplace and handsome windows. "I can't believe no one lives here," she said slowly.

"Ah, a caretaker lives in the far wing—the new wing." Harry nodded toward the great bulk of the house, which lay through a blocked doorway. "But he's old and feeble and almost entirely deaf and never comes near this ruined old wing. He believes it's haunted. All in the neighborhood do." He laughed grimly. "They've seen my light at night sometimes, I suppose—I am the one who haunts it."

She sighed. "It must have been a beautiful place once," she said wistfully.

"Ah, it was, Rose, it was." His voice softened.

"Who lived here then?"

"In better days I did," he surprised her by saying. "This was my father's house and the house of his father before him. I spent my boyhood here, and roamed these fields as a lad. Before my father was implicated in the Gunpowder Plot, and the king confiscated our lands and sent my father to the block. And when I'm working this part of the country," he added, "I stay here. John, the caretaker, sees my horse in the pasture among the cows and knows I'm back. If he guesses that I stay in the old wing, he tells no one. Indeed, he may think that I sleep in the woods, but he does not ask me. I give him a golden coin now and then to ease his lot, and bring him a bottle of wine now and again. Not that there's need to buy his silence—he was long in the service of my family before the estate was confiscated and sold, and now he serves the new owner, who never comes here, but only draws off such revenues as the estate produces."

"It's too bad the new owner has let the house fall down."

"Yes. It was in bad repair in my father's time, but nothing so bad as this. I remember it as it was, with lights and people and good times." He fetched a sigh. "Still, 'tis a safe place for me, Rose. I left here as a small lad, and I've greatly changed. None know my real name, so the authorities have no thought to look for me here. Should anyone stumble upon me here, I'd just be the son of the unfortunate former owner, come to view his lost patrimony."

She waited for Harry to tell her his real name, but he did not. Instead he lit a rushlight and rummaged in a cupboard and produced linen napkins and wooden spoons and a pair of the black leathern tankards they called "black jacks" and set them on a table. By that flickering light she surveyed him, still waiting for him to tell her his name. But his jaws were hard closed, and regretfully she decided that he would keep his oath and never tell her.

From the leathern pouch he had carried in, he now produced the food he'd procured at the last market town: coarse brown bread and cheese and a pudding.

"John will get us more when he goes to market," he told her. "You'll meet him in the morning. We have to be careful about the rushlight, for who knows, there may be lovers trysting in the hayfield who'd be curious and come and peek in through the windows."

"This place could use a woman's touch," she murmured ruefully, choking on dust as he brushed off a bench for her to sit.

"And you'll provide it, Rose," he said whimsically, pulling up another bench across from her and leaning his elbows on the table. "I note you're still limping," he added abruptly. "How badly did he hurt you?"

"It's mostly the riding," she said, "as well as—as the other." She gave an involuntary shudder as she remembered the terrible beating Lord Matthew had given her. "I'm all right," she said hastily.

Harry's face was grim as he cut her a thick slab of cheese with his knife, and she knew he was wishing he'd reached her sooner. Or that he'd never let her go to Langley Grange . . . perhaps he blamed himself for that.

"Harry," she said softly, reaching across the table to lay gentle fingers on his forearm, " 'twas not your fault. I never thought Lord Matthew would guess where I'd go."

Harry moved ever so slightly as if her light touch had
124

burned him. "No, But *I* should have thought of it," he said in hearty self-accusation.

Rosamunde gave him a melting smile and took a delicate bite of brown bread. "Neither of us knew him that well," she said in a rueful voice. "Think you if he is dead they will be after us for his murder?"

He shrugged. "Like as not," he said indifferently. "A man can be hanged but once." He paused. "Should they take us, I'll say you had no part in it, Rose, as indeed you did not. I'll say I abducted you."

She smiled wistfully. "Ah, they'd give the lie to that, Harry, the first time they saw us look at each other. And there's the earl to say I turned a pistol on him and Lord Matthew and went with you willingly. No, if you hang, I'll hang with you."

Harry reached over and touched her face. "Let's have no talk of hanging. Your eyes are better—the bruises are almost gone."

She nodded. "Aye, they've turned from purple to gold. I was an awful sight, wasn't I?"

"Never that." He shook his head and his voice grew husky. "You looked like some poor abused kitten that had been worried by a dog and then half-drowned. It hurt my heart to look at you."

She swallowed and looked down lest he see the tears bright in her eyes. Not since her mother's death had anybody worried about her, cared for her. And this man who heated her very blood and made it sing raspingly in her ears, whose touch could be gentle as gossamer or hard as iron, *cared for her*. It was in the way his hard face softened when he looked at her, in the miracle of his touch. Harry . . . her lover.

"I feel not a maid in these clothes," she said, swiftly changing the subject. "It seems wrong for a woman always to dress as a man."

"We'll mend this tomorrow," he said, and filled her black leathern tankard again with wine until she put up her hand to bid him stop. He watched her bemused as she drank it, and his love for her shone in his eyes.

Rosamunde had rolled up the sleeves of her coarse

shirt, and her delicate forearms seemed doubly feminine against the heavy material. The top of the shirt was undone against the warm weather and displayed a glimpse of fair white skin and occasionally, as she moved to reach for her glass, the top of her round breasts. She was completely unconcerned about this display with Harry, and did not notice the uneasy shifting of his shoulders as the impact of her beauty was borne in upon him. Desire for her poured over him like a hot golden shower of sparks, and it was a wrench not to move swiftly around the table and take her in his arms and make her his then and there.

But . . . he did not know how badly Lord Matthew had hurt her. Ill used she had certainly been. He would hold back his passions. Time enough for that tomorrow, he told himself sternly.

But when she rose to clear the table and brushed his shoulder with her soft breast as she reached across him, he jumped as if a white-hot iron had stung him. His very muscles quivered from her touch.

"Rose," he said hoarsely, and she turned and smiled into his eyes. He melted in those deep deep pools of iridescent green, deeper than the sea, wilder than dreams. "Rose," he groaned, rising quickly to get him away from her before his resolve crumpled. "I'll do that. Get you to bed, Rose." He indicated a pallet of straw in the corner.

Rosamunde was feeling better now. It still hurt a bit to move and there was a pain now and then from her recent mishandling, but she was young and strong, and even such a beating as she had taken was wearing off. She gave Harry a provocative smile and eased away from him. In spite of her slight limp, she moved lightly with a gentle sway of her hips that did him mischief.

In the faint glow of the rushlight, she turned her back to him and eased out of her shirt, thankful she was already rid of her hot jerkin. She pulled the shirt off her arms so that her slender shapely back was bare except for the silken cascade of her fair hair that streamed down it, and there was just a glimpse of one rounded breast as she turned slightly, wriggling out of the shirt.

Behind her, scalded by the sight, Harry dropped a

tankard, bent down to retrieve it and said thickly, "I'll sleep in the corridor, Rose, outside your door, so you'll feel safe." And fled before his hot blood beat down his good common sense that told him she was willing but not yet truly ready.

Rosamunde turned with a frown and watched him go. At first she had been grateful to him for his forbearance, for after the beating Lord Matthew had given her, every bone in her body had ached and it had been hard to ride, swaying in the saddle, without moaning. Now she was nearly mended and she yearned for him to hold her. She sighed.

After she had undressed, she took the rushlight and leaned through the doorway. "Would you like the light, Harry? The corridor is so dark, but in here the moon shines through bright enough for me."

She saw that he was lying on his back, relaxed, on a pallet of straw, but his body seemed to tense as he looked up at her. It was a stirring scene presented to his gaze: a slender white arm reaching through a silken curtain of hair, deepened to dusky gold in the flickering light, and above him a dangling glimpse of a pale satiny breast, rosy-tipped.

With the last of his willpower, Harry took the rushlight from her and blew out the flame. "Go to bed, Rose," he said in a muffled voice. And heard her light step, albeit slightly uneven still, going back to her own pallet.

Sleep was hard to come by that night for the lean young highwayman. Just three strides from him was the silken woman of all his desires, stretched out innocently in sleep. He could picture her there, silvered by moonlight, curled up with a sweet smile on her fresh young mouth, her body soft and warm and aglow. He had only to reach out and take her.

On her pallet in the room where they had dined, Rosamunde lay serene. She had some inkling of the effect she was having on Harry and was well content. And what if he did hurt her bruises a bit? Faith, she'd stand a bit of pain to have him hold her in her arms again. Why, he was treating her as if she were so fragile she might snap like

127

some flower stem at a touch! Tomorrow she'd take matters in hand!

But the next day she was still limping a little and sometimes wincing, and Harry's keen eye noted it. Rosamunde sighed inwardly. It was nice to be cared for—but there were limits!

The day brought other delights, however. Harry took her to meet old John. Boldly to the front door of the great house they marched, to bang its great iron knocker. After what seemed a very long time the heavy oaken doors creaked open and a bent old man appeared, clad in tattered velvet livery. His faded blue eyes widened in delight. "Master Harry! And you bring a lad with you!"

"Not a lad, John—a lady."

Old John leaned forward to peer at Rosamunde's country-boy clothes. She stood rakishly, smiling at him. "A *lady!*" he whispered in an awed voice.

"Aye, John. This is my Rosamunde. Should she ask aught of you, 'tis the same as if I asked it, for she is my life."

Rosamunde flushed happily at this admission of Harry's.

Old John nodded, gave Rosamunde a deep respectful bow and warmly ushered them into the high-ceilinged great hall. Warm summer air rushed in with them.

"Mistress Rosamunde," said the old servant formally. "'Tis my pleasure to welcome you to Master Harry's home."

"My home no more, John," corrected Harry. He stood in the dimness, looking around him. "Ye should air it more. 'Tis so damp the walls run rivulets."

John sighed. "With none to help me and down with the aches most of the time, Master Harry, 'tis more than a body can do."

"How are those aches, John?"

As John answered, vividly describing the pains in his back, Rosamunde looked around her. The house dated from perhaps the fourteenth century and was not as grand as those more recent ones built in Tudor times. But it had a serene charm. The floor beneath her feet was of big stone slabs, worn smooth with the passage of many

128

feet. This great hall occupied a vast space but was sparsely furnished. At one end heavy stone stairs, with a thick oaken balustrade, deeply carved, wound up into the dimness of the upper galleries. The door frames were of stone and peaked at the top, giving the place vaguely the air of some ancient abbey. Reaching up one wall was a huge stone fireplace in which a man could easily stand erect. And down the center of the room stretched a great trestle table, the wood somewhat battered as if it had been in use for centuries. How grand a chamber this had been when that great trestle was loaded with mighty trenchers and lords and knights and their ladies took their ease around it, warmed by the fire from that giant hearth! And with brilliant pennants emblazoned with heraldic emblems floating from the beams of that high-flung ceiling.

Her imagination took off, fired by the thought of minstrels playing their lutes from the high galleries as below tankards clashed together and spurs jingled and the company laughed and drank to each other's health and then the lords and ladies, having supped, began a merry dance over the great slabs of stone flooring.

Her face grew pensive. This might have been *her* house had she and Harry met in better days, had kings and their follies not intruded on their lives, had their parents lived and prospered, had . . . she smiled at herself for a fool. They were what they were—Harry a highwayman bound for the gibbet and herself his mistress, a woman the world counted lost to shame.

All the same she studied carefully the hunting scenes in the long moldering tapestries that hung down the dripping walls and determined that the house would indeed be aired. *She* would see to it.

That it now belonged to others who cared nothing for it made no difference to Rosamunde; this was Harry's ancestral home, and as such she would honor it.

Harry looked doubtful when she announced that she would see to the airing. He accompanied her, his long legs striding beside her shorter ones, as she moved eagerly through the great moldering rooms. Obligingly he opened

129

the windows for her—most of which were stuck and yawned open as if eager to drink in the warm summer air.

"Which was your room, Harry?" she asked softly.

"Yon chamber " He nodded toward a door, and she ran to it eagerly, searching for some signs of the little boy he had been. But it was a barren room, devoid of all save a huge bed with the shreds of a ruined canopy and a large heavy cupboard in one corner.

"All that could easily be moved was stolen after we were turned out," he told her, and she could feel the bitterness beneath the hard indifference of his tone. "Over here was my father's room—and this my mother's." He showed her two great chambers that adjoined, still boasting a few sticks of enormous furniture and a bit of moldering drapery. "My father had a fine collection of swords—all gone now. And my mother's room was a wonder of delicate needlework and—" He stopped. "This house makes me sad, Rose. I feel not that way in the old wing, for it was always deserted and near ruin. But this—it was home to me, Rose, and I remember it warm and bright and full of laughter."

Her green eyes blinked tears and she flung herself against him, glad old John had not come upstairs with them. "Oh, Harry, we can bring it back. I'll scrub and clean and polish, and John—"

"No," he said gently, pushing her away. "We cannot bring back the past, Rose. I am Hard Harry now, and not the earl's son and heir. Another holds that title now; another holds these estates in fee. 'Tis a highwayman you're with, Rose, a man with a slender grip on life and little future. I brought you here so that John would know you and protect you. Should you be found here on a day when I'm gone, you're but a wanderer in search of employment whom John has kindly let shelter in the ruined old wing—not Rosamunde Langley, for she is gone too. The maid is as gone as the lad I once was, nor can we whistle them back. But while this stout arm can defend thee, Rose, I promise thee its service."

Firmly he took her away from the rooms he had prowled in his youth, rooms that held so many memories
130

for him. But her heart had thrilled to his ringing tone. *I promise thee . . .* She swept down the stairs on his arm, her limp forgotten, feeling like a bride.

Below they found a smiling John, who had set out handsome silver tankards of wine for them.

"Ye'll remember these, Master Harry." Eagerly old John pointed toward the tankards. "They're the ones with the crest. I was able to save them for ye."

Harry smiled. "I remember them, John."

Rosamunde lifted her tankard and peered at the crest. A wolf rampant and the motto *I avenge.* She glanced at the hard wolfish face across from her. That Harry would avenge if he got the chance she had no doubt.

Then Harry bade old John join them, and the three of them toasted a bright future that Rosamunde, with a brimming heart, felt could still come to pass.

"Ye must be on yer guard for the haymakers when they come to the meadow," cautioned old John, wiping his mouth with his sleeve. "The cows wander down to the meadow by themselves and return when 'tis time for milking, but the haymakers would see the horses were they in the meadow—for ye've brought horses, I've no doubt?"

"Aye, two—Nightwind and a gray mare."

"And the haymakers might come into the old wing for rest and shade—or perhaps to hide for a while and pretend they're working—and perhaps they'd discover where you keep the horses."

Harry's eyes twinkled. "You know where I stable my horse then?"

"Aye, I've always known. But ye're alert, Master Harry, and I thought not the haymakers would ever catch ye napping. But now . . . " He cast a doubtful eye at Rosamunde, who was staring dreamily at the huge beams and great rafters overhead: beams from which pennants and tapestries once had hung, while war trumpets had sounded. . . . She came back to earth and listened. "I'll warn ye of the haymakers," John was saying. "For they always come tell me the day before they start to make hay. 'Tis because they want me to have water for them—and perhaps a bite of food."

"Hold them off, if you can, John," said Harry with a laugh. "Our horses are enjoying the rich grasses."

"If I can, I will do that. I'm known as a weather prophet, and I'll prophesy rain. I'll tell them the hay isn't ripe yet, or is overripe—ye'll see."

Rosamunde smiled at the old man's eagerness to help.

"I'll look around a bit myself before Harry takes me back to our hideaway," she said, divining that Harry wanted to speak to John privately. Through the enormous downstairs rooms she sauntered, loving them. All those great stone fireplaces—those silent hearths that once had crackled with roaring fires. And outside—gardens. Overgrown, but still gardens. She could see them through the open windows, trace overgrown pathways spilled over with musk roses. And there past that low broken wall was an herb garden! She spied rosemary there, and thyme. And yes, marjoram too. She must visit that herb garden, for her mother had taught her much about herbs.

On through a thick archway into another great chamber she walked. This was the buttery. She sighed. How she would have enjoyed living in this house . . . in better days. Sunk suddenly in gloom, realizing it was but a dream and could never be, she retraced her steps, heard Harry finishing a sentence ". . . if you can find such, John. If not, I'll off to the next town and see what I can find."

John nodded, looking important. His back was much straighter now that he had seen Harry, she realized. John too was beginning to hope. And his hopes were as frail as hers.

She trailed along when Harry went looking for John's old mule Tobias in the west pasture, wandering about among contented-looking dairy cattle chewing their cuds. He brought back the mule, who seemed to know Harry's hand and respect it, and hitched him up to a wagon and helped old John's creaking bones up into it.

"I'd go myself, but . . . " Harry left the words unfinished.

"I know, sir." John nodded vehemently. "Best you didn't."

And Rosamunde was left wondering if John really knew

all about Harry. Perhaps the two of them chose mutually to ignore the fact that this was not the young lord of the manor but Hard Harry the highwayman who sheltered here. She sighed and pondered. Strange were the ways of men. . . .

Harry left her for a stroll over the estate. She would have gone with him, but he refused sternly. "Only this morning ye were limping, and ye've walked enough for one day, Rose."

So she spent an afternoon of delight in the overrun herb garden, finding tansy and basil and, hidden under some riotous weeds next to a clump of wild garlic such as grew in the pasture and gave a terrible taste to the cows' milk, some mint. Much pleased, she straightened up as Harry rounded the corner of the house, beckoning to her with a long loaf of fresh-browned bread. She ran forward and drank in the delicious aroma of the new-baked loaf, saw that he carried under the same arm a bulging linen napkin which she guessed contained cheese, of which he was very fond, and other good things, and in the other several bottles of wine.

"I see you've found my mother's herb garden," he said. His gaze shifted to the low stone wall, overrun with ivy. "My dog Prince is buried over there." He nodded to a tangled area overrun with myrtle. "I see they've moved the stone I placed there as a lad."

His dog . . . her heart ached for him, his father's head gone to the block and his mother resting in some potter's field. She leaned down and pressed a quick kiss onto the back of the hand that clutched the wine bottles.

That lightened his somber mood. Harry leaned down and brushed her tumbled blond hair with his lips. "John asks that we sup with him of evenings, but he's old and the trip into town tired him, so I said we'd begin tomorrow night."

"Will that be safe?" she asked alertly. "Doesn't John have visitors?"

"From outside none can see into the great hall. Should anyone come—which isn't likely—we can seize our trenchers and be off with them down the long corridors before

John can unbar the doors. Actually there's more danger from our rushlight in the old wing. And there's less need for light if we take our evening meals with John."

She nodded her head, convinced. Then, noting that swinging from the arm that carried the wine bottles was a leathern sack tied with a thong, she asked, "What's in that?"

"This? Ah, this is for you, my lady!" He shook the leathern sack tantalizingly. "But you'll try it on back at your quarters—no need to gaze on it here!"

Try it on? Something to wear, then! She felt a glowing eagerness, for the country lad's clothes were rough-textured and abraded her skin.

Back in the old wing, Harry deposited the wine and the leathern bag and the loaf upon the table and stowed much of the contents of the linen napkin in the cupboard. "Against hunger in the night," he said lightly. And watched smiling as she spilled out of the leathern bag a soft full-skirted dress of a thin green material a shade lighter than her eyes, and a delicate chemise—not so nice as those she'd had at Kenwarren House but doubtless the best the village afforded. And a pair of slippers and stockings! She exclaimed at the slippers and hurried to try them on—it was hard to go barefoot in the overgrown yard. She lifted her foot rapturously—they fit! So either old John had looked with more keenness than she had thought at her bare feet or Harry had given him her measurements. Harry lounged nearby, telling her that John had given out the story that he was buying gifts for a cousin who was soon to be wed, in the hope that she'd invite him to live with her and her new spouse.

Rosamunde hardly heard him, so busy was she slipping the new cotton stockings over her legs.

"Turn around," she ordered haughtily when she saw Harry's eyes feasting on this rare sight of white knees and shapely thighs.

With a sigh, he did as he was bid. And shortly she spun around before him, fully dressed in her new finery, green eyes asparkle.

"You're a very witch in those clothes," he told her ruefully. "A witch to rend the heart of a man."

"But do I rend *your* heart, Harry?" she asked with a smile of pure deviltry.

"Aye, that you do, Rose." He pulled her toward him as gently as foam moves from the top of the waves to the shore, and held her as lightly as one might a bird, not to crush its wings. "Your bones are so delicate," he marveled.

"But I'm tall for a woman," she pointed out. "Which helped me masquerade as a boy!"

With loving fingers he smoothed back her fair hair from her upturned face, delighting in the silky feel of it, and slipped his hand down the back of her neck, felt her small shiver as he traced a path down her spine to the small of her back.

Reluctantly he let her go. "I'm riding out, Rose. It could be I'm working tonight. From words John let slip unthinking, 'tis best I scout out the country a bit."

She knew he was still afraid of hurting her, and her face fell.

"I'm completely recovered, Harry. Could—could I not come with you?" she asked in a small voice.

"Nay, I'll not risk you," he said grimly. "You'll wait for me here."

"But must I sup alone?" she asked plaintively.

"You'll not sup alone. There's John."

"John is all very well, but—suppose somebody comes, Harry?"

"Then you'll use the sense God gave you and hide in some likely place—either somewhere inside this house or perhaps in the woods by the river. There are trees with slanted boles you could climb and hide in if need be— you'll think of something."

She knew from his carefree words he was sure no one would disturb her, but she pouted, hating to be separated from him even for a night.

"I'd rather go with you," she said, tracing a light design across his shirtfront with coaxing fingers.

His chest thundered at her touch, and he drew away

135

quickly. "There's food and drink and fresh water, Rose. I'll be back before the dawn."

Swiftly he turned and was gone. She realized he had already saddled Nightwind when she saw him glide like a shadow through the dusk of the empty meadow and into the trees. She went down to comfort the gray mare, robbed of her companionship, patting her gentle head, looking into the soft eyes, feeding her tidbits.

She sighed and shrugged luxuriously. She was feeling *so* much better. Harry should have taken her with him.

"We'll go next time," she whispered to the mare, and the mare nuzzled her arm and gave her back a gentle whinny as if to say, *Yes, we will.*

Rosamunde joined old John for supper, but she refused to let him set the table in the great hall—all that distance to carry the dishes! Instead they ate companionably in a small antechamber with only one high-up window so that no one could look in and see that John had a guest for supper.

They did not talk much. Both were worried. Rosamunde looked into those faded blue eyes, across the crispy meat pie. She was sure John knew where Harry had gone, but she was equally certain he would not tell her.

She did not ask him any questions, and he did not volunteer any information. She supposed she was still too new a member of the family for him to really trust. After supper John insisted on hobbling back to her quarters with her and seeing her safe inside. She was uneasy about his making his way back through heavy weeds that might trip him, but he told her proudly that he knew his way about the grounds like a cat—and she had no reason to doubt it, since he had grown old in service here.

She had eaten lightly, and now she took off her dress and lay down in her chemise and tried to rest. The sweet-smelling summer grasses of her pallet were soft beneath her, but rest would not come. Feeling nervous, she got up after a while and dressed and then sank back on the pallet. Although she closed her eyes and tossed and turned about, sleep eluded her. The night wore on, and still she could not sleep. She found herself listening for small sounds. Was
136

that a hoofbeat soft upon the grass? Was that a whinny in the distance? Had Harry in his wanderings met with disaster—a coach with a strong escort perhaps which he had not seen? Was he lying now in his blood on the highway with that strong bronzed hand in its ruffled cuff slowly releasing its steady grip on the pistol, while the whole length of his long lean body released its grip on life?

Unable to lie still with these musings, she got up and paced about, stared out the windows into the darkness. Then she went out and stood in the shadows of the building's ruined stone walls, her feet and the hem of her dress getting soaked by dew.

Tension mounted in her, and she began to shake. She leaned against the stone wall and began to pray. Silently, feverishly. *Let him come back to me. Please, please God, let nothing happen to him.* Time passed. It must be nearly dawn. Why—had—he—not—come?

At last he came. Quiet as a shadow stealing out of the trees, leading his horse slowly. She saw at once that something was wrong. Nightwind had gone lame.

She stepped out of the shadows as Harry led the big black horse inside.

Harry looked surprised. "I took no purse this night, Rose. Nightwind slipped on a rock and went lame. I think it's no great matter, but—we'll see tomorrow." He seemed worried as he watered Nightwind, soothed him and curried him, bathed his swollen ankle and made him a soft bed of hay. Rosamunde watched, gone weak with relief that he was home, and eager to help—though Harry waved her away. "I'll do it myself, Rose." Her heart went out to him, for she knew how deeply he loved the big black horse.

When he had finished, Harry straightened up and she could see his eyes gleaming pale in the moonlight.

"You waited up for me," he murmured.

"I—I could not sleep," she confessed. "I kept thinking, what if you were taken? It tore at my mind."

He took a step toward her and his voice was husky. "Rose."

She stood very still as he took her lightly by the shoulders and drew her into his arms. His hands came up

137

through her tumbling hair that framed her upturned face, and his words seemed wrenched from his depths. "I would always return to you, for—you are mine, you know."

Under the pressure of that gaze, the burning touch of his hands and the nearness of his lean body, she felt her knees melting.

"Yes," she said, her reckless inner self answering for her. "I know that."

Up into his arms he swept her, like a gust of wind, carried her lightly back to the "best room," where he had piled the sweet-smelling meadow grasses for her to sleep on. Onto those grasses he laid her tenderly, brushed back the tangled golden hair from her pale forehead. "I have naught to offer you, Rose, not even a name—you know that."

"Yes," she said steadily, her green eyes, luminous in the moonlight, never leaving his face. "I know that, Harry. But—I do not care."

Harry needed no further invitation. With a sweet wild fire, his lips crushed down on hers, and she felt a tremor go through his lean frame at the eager warmth of her response. For her parted lips met and twisted upon his, and her tongue met his questing one in a fever of desire.

She felt him urge her dress down around her shoulders, pulling at the hooks in his impatience, until her white shoulders gleamed bare and at last the hooks gave way and her round breasts burst free, pale and silvered in the waning moonlight. He drew in his breath at that sight, and his lips, gentle and nuzzling, moved down to those pink-tipped mounds, caressed and nibbled them. With an arm beneath her, he turned her slightly to the side and completed the unhooking, slid first her dress and then her chemise down around her slender incurving waist and softly—undoing the top of her petticoat—inserted his two hands on the bare skin at the top of her hips and eased all down at once until she lay only in her stockings, having kicked off her sodden shoes.

He smiled down at her and removed her slippers and then her stockings, sending prickles up her spine and gentle pulsations through her whole being as his hands slid caressingly down her smooth thighs and eased the stockings down her calves and off her dainty feet.

Naked before him, even though the moon was nearly fled and even his face appeared blurred and pale in the dimness, she still looked up, wide-eyed and trustingly, into his gleaming eyes. But she shivered as his hands roved back along her ankles, up them to smooth the flesh around her calves, slid over her knees and moved caressingly along her upper thighs. She stiffened convulsively as his fingers reached that silky triangle of blond hair at the base of her hips, for of a sudden her last encounter with a man—an encounter of smashing vicious brutality—rose up before her and made her turn rigid.

"I'm sorry," she whispered, near tears. "It was just that—that—"

"You've naught to fear, Rose," he said in a voice so deep and intense it thrilled her. "I will make you forget Lord Matthew's brutal handling. Trust me, Rose. If I hurt you, if it's too soon and you're not mended yet, you've only to speak and I'll desist. For to hurt you would give me no pleasure, Rose." He bent and planted a light kiss on her smooth stomach, which quivered beneath his lips.

With that last caress, he disengaged himself and moved away from her. Rosamunde lay back with a madly beating heart, her own eyes large and dark, and watched as he disrobed, pulling off his boots, stripping off his white ruffled shirt and then his trousers.

She had yearned for him, but—yes, it was true; her recent bad experience with Lord Matthew had made her strangely timid now that the moment was at hand.

Rosamunde had never seen a man without his clothes before. Even Lord Matthew had been fully clothed except for—and she hadn't looked *there!* Of course, she had seen men stripped to the waist at work in the fields, big bulging muscles gleaming with sweat as they pitched hay and made shocks of the corn. But this man was different. His white body was like a statue in the garden at Kenwarren House, which everybody said was Greek. Long and lean he was, with an exceeding length of arm and breadth of shoulder. His shoulder muscles did not bunch but rippled—a swim-

139

mer's muscles, had she but known it, for as a boy he had been a great swimmer, and had proved it by bringing her unconscious body down the river from Langley Grange. His deep chest tapered to a narrow waist and lean hips, and his cordlike thighs marked him as a horseman. Only a light dusting of dark hair darkened his chest. Her eyes moved downward—she blushed and looked away.

He was moving toward her now, purposefully in the gloom. She tensed, half expecting him to pounce upon her as Lord Matthew had.

Instead he knelt beside her, and lovingly his lips and hands explored her young body, leaving a pulsing trail of fire that rippled through her innermost being and sent new aches and new desires racing keenly through her blood. His touch was magic. She moved and moaned under his touch—and forgot Lord Matthew, forgot his mishandling, forgot him forever. This was Harry, this was love. She reached out a gentle hand and smoothed it across his broad back muscles, felt a tremor ripple beneath her fingers.

Abruptly he slipped down into the soft grasses beside her and slid an arm beneath her, bringing her body up against him so that her soft breasts were crushed against his deep chest. He buried his head in her hair and ran his fingers down her back so that she moved and quivered beneath his touch.

"Rose, Rose," she heard him murmur. She did not know that he was holding himself back with an iron grip, holding his own passions in check until he ached from it, not to frighten this girl who had been so cruelly, so recently hurt by Lord Matthew. His jaw clenched with the effort not to move too soon, to hold back until she was fully ready to receive him. This girl to him was very precious. In the fading moonlight she seemed to him a silvery moth in his arms, beating her wings gently. He smelled the lemony scent of her hair and the haunting perfumed scent that was Woman, soft and yielding—and his. His.

Slowly his arms tightened about her. His very head was

reeling with the softness, the wonder of her. The wonder that she should be here in his arms.

Rosamunde, caught up in a bright flame of desire, stronger than she had ever known before, felt herself a stranger on a new wild shore. Her whole body pulsed beneath his fiery touch, and she clung to him passionately. With a little strangled sob she thrust herself forward against him.

Her passions mounted—and he could feel them mount. And intertwined with his own fiery passions he felt a strange pride and exhilaration that he could bring her this, that he could make her feel so, erase the hurt where hurt should never have been, and bring her joy. With a terrible tenderness he embraced her, as if it were the last night of their lives, and no woman before her had ever roused in him the exultation wrought by this green-eyed lass of sixteen summers.

Flawlessly, rhythmically, their passions built and crested. Rosamunde forgot her tensions; Lord Matthew was cast from her mind. She forgot all but the strong man who held her and the sweet small explosions of desire as she melted against him. Breast to chest, they could feel each other's heartbeats. Legs fierily entwined, they moved and fondled. Gracefully, as in some wild dance of the gods, they moved together in silken grace, and joined and parted and joined again. Up and up into a bright and wonderful world of their own passions' making they soared and winged and swooped and rose and fell on the waves of their pulsing sensations. Rhythmically, flawlessly, they moved toward their perfect union—and found it, gliding on bands of moonlight through the scented summer night in a whirling ecstasy that burned through them like a bright white flame, devouring, enchanting, all-consuming.

At last, at last it was over—tumultuous, intoxicating, feverish, but over, and they lay companionably together in the bed of summer grasses he had made for her.

" 'Tis a warm night, Rose." His voice softly interrupted her dreaminess. "Wouldst like to bathe in the stream?"

She nodded, still lost in this new world he had made for her. Harry rose. He stooped and swept her up in one

141

arm, threw his cloak over his shoulders. Then he carried her, running lightly through the meadow in his bare feet until, through the trees, she saw the stream, a silver ribbon in the last of the moonlight.

On the grassy bank he set her down, and they plunged in and stood ankle-deep in the cold running water and bathed themselves, splashed water on each other and laughed in the low intimate way of lovers. And afterward they lay naked on the soft grass by the stream—and there he took her again, with such warmth and tenderness that she melted into his arms as if she had always belonged there. His lips were eager, his body besieged her, and passion's bright flames swept them up above the trees toward the farther stars as their bodies twisted and twined and they rolled over and over on the damp grass, tasting, touching, holding, loving.

At last they lay panting and surfeited beside each other in the first pinkening light of dawn. Rosamunde turned her head to look at Harry fondly. Her lover. Her strong yet gentle lover. She lifted a hand and lazily ran a finger along his stomach, felt his strong muscles contract and saw his eyes darken as they opened to study her. He smiled and returned the compliment by nuzzling a pink nipple that quivered delightfully under this sweet assault.

So, lightly playing upon each other's passions, they lay there together. So silent were they, so rapt and interwoven in their thoughts, that two soft-footed deer came out of the forest and drank from the stream near them, never suspecting their presence. Birds came and drank, and little furry wild things rustled down to the water's edge. The sky grew pink with the promise of a warm fair day. Rosamunde's heart dreamed.

She loved the young highwayman whose long lean body lay stretched out clean and naked beside her.

Harry lay relaxed with his arms behind his head and studied the dark branches of the trees overhead. Since the moment he had left her sweet arms and lain here beside her on the soft dewy grass of the streambank, he had felt incredulous. He who had always taken women so lightly, caring a little for all but not overmuch for any one, was

142

overcome with worry about this one. Was she comfortable, was she well fed, was she warm, was she happy? Her every wish seemed of paramount importance, her desires a command . . . and he who had taken trollops and light women as lightly as they had accepted his hot caresses was moved almost to tears at the bruises still visible about the lovely green eyes that looked so trustingly into his.

But it was growing light; people might be about. He picked her up again, now languorous in his arms, and moved to the edge of the woods. He looked alertly about but saw no one. In the pink light of dawn he carried her back to her bed of summer grasses, deposited her tenderly and slept deeply beside her while the sun struck gold through the gothic window of the ruined old wing.

To Rosamunde, half-awake and drowsing, it seemed that the moon had given them silver and the sun had given them gold. An enchanted couple blessed with riches untold. . . . In the crook of Harry's arm she lay dreaming, with her fair hair tangled under his shoulder. They would marry, of course—someday. And Harry would by dint of some great luck find a new profession, a less dangerous one. And they would find a house too—not so grand as this one nor yet so dilapidated, but a cottage somewhere that they could call their own. And there would be little Harrys and small Rosamundes clinging to her skirts. . . . She lay there envisioning all this until she drifted off and slept like a babe on Harry's arm.

It was late when she woke, and she found him gone and saw that he had left breakfast prepared upon the rude table.

Surely he had not ridden out again! She leaped up and stumbled into her chemise. Fastening her petticoat as she went, she moved down the stone corridor to find Harry tending Nightwind, bathing the big black horse's strained leg, while those great intelligent eyes looked down at him in silent gratitude and understanding.

"Can I help?" she asked, and Harry looked up from his work and a smile lit his face.

"I'm just finishing. Nightwind will be all right in a day or two. Rest will do it." He sounded happy, and he gave

143

the big horse an affectionate pat. Then he rose, towering above her to that great height from which he smiled down on her fondly. " 'Twas a waste to dress, my lady," he murmured hoarsely, and with his fingers urged down the top of her chemise until her naked breast was cupped in his hand. He lowered his big dark head and nuzzled her throat gently, let his lips wander on down her bosom.

"I came to ask if you'd breakfast with me, my lord," she said lightly, trying to pretend her heart was not beating fast beneath his caressing hands.

"Ah, so it's breakfast you want?" Sleepy half-shut eyes considered her. "Well, we'll sup first of food and then of love. What think you of that, Rose?"

It was indeed what she wanted, but she bridled a little and shook out her fair hair, tantalizing him. He ran his fingers through that hair and she threw her head back to rest against his hand, beamed her green eyes up at him through dark slanted lashes.

"Faith, you're a very temptress, Rose," he murmured. And the words echoed and resounded in his heart. Who'd have thought that a maid of sixteen could hold him so in thrall that his heart burned at the sight of her and his very loins ached with a desire to take her and crush her to him and make her his? Who'd have thought it of Hard Harry, who'd taken his fun where he found it all across England?

Back down the corridor she minced beside him, making him slow his steps to match her shorter strides. She felt the impatience that was in him to have her again and glowed with the knowledge, reveled in it. Brushing his arm, she knew a pride and exhilaration and tenderness that were wholly new to her. A man wanted her—and he was the man *she* wanted. It was a golden gift.

They feasted on dark bread and cheese and hardly tasted their food. They feasted on each other with their eyes, and then, regardless that the sun was high, they spent the long golden day in gentle play on their bed of sweet grasses, exploring each other's bodies, making tender new discoveries, finding new delights. Harry caressed her as tenderly as one might caress a small kitten, careful not to hurt. And Rosamunde was as playful and gamboling as any small kitten, roguish and impish, happy as a child at this thing called love.

9   *That night they supped with old John in the newly* aired great hall. Supped on that great long trestle table Rosamunde had so admired. Old John would have served them and himself eaten in the buttery but that they insisted he join them at table and would have it no other way. The old man's eyes shone at this signal honor that he should dine with Harry and his lady, and he entertained them with tales of Harry's early youth. Ah, young Harry had ridden the wildest horses, he always swam the deepest rivers, and was a better marksman even than his father.

Harry grinned and shrugged off these evidences of an old man's fondness. But he chuckled and Rosamunde dissolved into laughter when John told how the grown-up Harry, home returned to find John having trouble with vandals ("They did break the windows of the hall and also steal, mistress"), Harry had, with John's assistance, covered his face with a hood made from a large linen napkin with only slits for the eyes, and tied about his body a huge white coverlet ("In the night it did not look to be a worn coverlet, mistress, but more like a Roman toga such as the statues in the garden used to wear before they were sold"). That night, when the vandals had come prowling, Harry had charged suddenly out of the trees waving a sword and a great tree branch. ("He did look unearthly, mistress, him roaring and howling like a wild beast and

145

all that white cloth waving in the wind, and they did break and run, near to fainting, and did never come back to bother us at all.")

Rosamunde shook with laughter, and old John, pleased that she had so enjoyed his story, urged on her more meat pie (it was his only culinary achievement, and he was inordinately proud of it; Rosamunde, who could not cook at all, the servants having done all that at Kenwarren House, was careful to encourage him and admire his efforts).

"'Tis very good, John," she said, taking another small portion.

Harry, who guessed she was not hungry, but only took this portion to please old John, gave her a soft look. "John will have you believing I was a wild lad," he said. "But not all of my ways were wild. I was interested in geography."

"So you could explore the world, no doubt?" guessed Rosamunde. "Like Drake and Raleigh and Smith?"

"I had thought to do such things—as a lad."

"Aye, Master Harry, and you would have done it too," said John sturdily, "save for the troubles that came upon you."

"Perhaps, John, perhaps." Harry's eyes were distant now, his gaze fixed upon some far horizon of his youth where dreams were fled.

"I had saved some of Master Harry's books against the time that he would return, but the vandals tore them up." Old John sighed. He was silent for a while; then he confided to Rosamunde, "'Tis lonely here without Master Harry. I do grow old, and 'tis good to have him back—and with so sweet a lady."

Rosamunde smiled at him and swallowed her last bite of meat pie. "Delicious," she said, and John beamed at her. He was a lovable old man for all his sometimes crochety ways, and frail. When he rose to clear the table she too rose to help him.

"Nay," said John, shocked. "'Tis not meet that my Master Harry's—" He paused, uncertain how to speak of her. "'Tis not meet," he began again, "that a lady of
146

quality should do menial things. And for me 'tis a pleasure," he added frankly, "for I do eat and drink well when Master Harry is home!"

Rosamunde would have insisted on helping him, but Harry put a detaining hand on her arm. He knew old John's ways, knew that it was truly a pleasure for the old man to serve the last of "the family," who would always be to him the rightful heir to the estate.

After their supper they walked hand in hand through the deep weedy grass that surrounded the old building. Rosamunde looked up, smiling at the rising moon that struck the tall casements and bathed the mellow old stones in an enchanted light. This was Harry's home, and on such a night it was easy to imagine that Harry was truly the heir, that they were merely out for an evening's stroll and would return to walk through mellow candlelight in the great hall up that carved stairway to beautifully appointed rooms where soft scented beds had been turned down by giggling servant girls. Easy to imagine . . .

Enchanted too was the night around them, with the soft sound of crickets, and little sleepy chirps of night birds, and the throaty croaking of frogs from the nearby stream. As they reached the doorway there was the wild cry of a loon and later the silvery wail of a little screech owl.

In the warm darkness they moved into the ruined old wing, down the stone corridor to the place that was theirs alone—inviolate. They lit no rushlight, for now Rosamunde was as aware of the objects in the room as was Harry. Rosamunde took off all her clothes and saw in the dimness that Harry was doing the same, swiftly, as if by mutual consent. She sank down on her soft pallet of sweet grasses covered by Harry's spread-out cloak, and reached her white arms up to him. Harry leaned down and she pulled his now naked form down to her, urgently.

"You won't leave me again, will you?" she murmured.

It was a foolish question, and she knew it. And Harry, as rapt as she, made some soft incoherent answer meant to soothe but yet not to promise. He lay with his weight resting on his arms and between and beneath them her

147

tempting body. Now he lowered his loins so that his manhood brushed her—he felt her quiver and was glad. His heavy dark hair fell down into that riotous fan of pale golden hair spread out around her sweet face, and as she moved and her nipples lightly brushed against his naked chest, he felt their fire and responded warmly, tracing with his lips a light pattern across her gleaming shoulders and down the cleft between her breasts, over her smooth stomach to her navel, feeling her slight gasp as he did so. And the loving nearness of him, the bright splinters of desire she felt at that nearness, made her forget for a time that his was a dangerous calling and he might be gone on the morrow.

"Ah, Harry, Harry, I love you so," murmured Rosamunde, feeling a wild free soaring of the senses as Harry's lips teased and caressed her. She moved her hips a bit to accommodate him the better, and Harry obligingly lifted the weight of his loins a bit so that she might move as she pleased. He slid down beside her with an arm lightly holding her around her slim waist, one hand gently cupping a round buttock as his lips made their way now along her stomach, now along her hip.

Responding to these small delightful assaults on the senses, Rosamunde turned her body on its side to meet him frontally. "Don't leave me, Harry," she whispered. "For I could not stand it."

This time he made no reply, but lifted his head and stretched out his long body, lifting her lightly until she lay on his chest with her long fair hair spread out over him like a bridal veil.

"If I leave, I will always come back, Rose," he said in a deep rich voice. "Depend upon it, for you are mine." For him it was like a marriage vow.

Ah, but that was not what she meant! She meant he must not risk himself, must stay here where if he needs must flee, they would fly together! But this was no moment for saying it, when her senses were leaving her, when her voice was incoherent, when her world careened dizzily under the magic of his lovemaking. With a soft sound in her throat she surrendered herself to the night and the

148

moonlight—and to Harry, whom she would always love. She pressed her hips and stomach and breasts tightly against him, crushing herself against him as a rose is crushed against the palm, her very body by its soft sweet pressure imploring him to take her, to make her his again —and yet again.

Himself half dizzy from the sweetness he held within his grasp, Harry's arms tightened about her, and his maleness rose to meet the challenge of her femininity. In heavenly bliss they melted together, their legs entwined, and she nestled there on his long body as might a small bird resting from its flight, then twisted about as her passions rose beneath the assault of Harry's ardor. His hands traveled up and down her silken body at will, and she trembled. He moved within her, and she gasped in pleasure. And with an ancient rhythm, older by far than the stones that rose on the Salisbury Plain, they moved together, joined by love and passion, and climbed to magical heights, impossibly high, their very beings blending into one as their love for each other was expressed in the most elemental way known to man and woman.

Harry held her, he loved her, his love was a devouring encompassing thing—to her a blessing and a treasure. Her heart was filled with happiness and her body knew many splendors there in his enfolding arms.

No words needed to be spoken over them to make her his. She was that already. And in silent beauty beneath the old and silvered moon they wordlessly plighted their troth again, each to the other, and knew without saying that nothing that ever happened to them would change the way they felt about each other. She was Harry's and Harry was hers. And together their passions led them on a fiery dance up some endless stairway to the stars.

From these glamorous heights of feeling and of passion unleashed, they floated down on a suddenly dissolved stairway, landed pillow-soft upon Harry's great cloak spread over the sweet meadow grasses. From being gods for a space they had become again human, stricken with needs other than of the body, beset by troubles from without.

149

"You *will* go away from me again—I know it," she murmured bitterly, fighting back unhappy tears.

Harry's sleepy arm held her to him. "We'll live one day at a time, Rosamunde," he chided her. " 'Tis the only life we have—can ever have."

And she pressed her lovely face against his chest and wet it with her tears. For what he said was true, and wishing would not make it otherwise.

As tenderly as if she had been a babe, Harry stroked her long silken hair and ran his hands down her back and hips. And the soft yielding feminine feel of her, and the sweet scent of woman in his nostrils, and the lemony scent of her hair, were an intoxication that woke desire in him again, so that his hands moved more masterfully now and smoothed the silken skin of her inner thighs and caressed her secret places until she shivered in his arms, her tears forgotten, and clung to him again. And once again they were speeding on their strange wild primeval journey that took them to such dizzy heights of pleasure and left them ever with no regrets.

When at last she drifted into sleep beside him, she promised herself fiercely that she would keep him beside her always, that she would never let him go.

Happy and heavy-eyed, they woke and took a before-breakfast splash in the stream nearby. And afterward nearly forgot to eat, for the sight of her lovely naked form silvered by the water was too much for Harry and he took her then and there, spreading her legs gently on the soft grass of the streambank and tasting the sweetness of her body, nuzzling her soft breasts with his lips until she was moaning beneath him, and then in wild ardor, clasping her to him feverishly, to strain beneath the great old trees while the summer breeze whispered a rustling melody through the trees.

Once again they dipped in the stream, and this time Rosamunde, seeing Harry's eyes light up as she stood knee-deep in the shallows and shook out her long fair hair, put a chiding hand flat against his chest and laughed.

"You'll die of hunger," she warned teasingly.

"My hunger this morning is not to be satisfied by bread
150

and wine," he told her, running a hand lightly over her wet stomach so that she took a swift gasping breath. "I crave a stronger draft, my Rose."

"Well, then you must wait for it," she laughed, pulling away and eluding him. "For I am famished for that breakfast you scoff at!"

"You're not a woman," he protested, coming out of the water with a bound and grinning at her from the bank. "You're a soulless water sprite come from the stream to tempt me!"

She stood before him combing her long hair with a wooden comb John had found her, and turned an impish shoulder to him which displayed her softly peaked breasts in profile to his tender gaze. She shrugged and they rippled gently. Harry's eyes lit, studying them.

"Rose, Rose," he said with a groan. "You do tempt a man past endurance."

She laughed, but kept warily beyond his reach. "If I am a water sprite, then I am a water sprite who'd see you fed!"

"Aye—you feed my body. But what about my poor bewitched spirit?"

"Your poor bewitched spirit will wait till after breakfast." She laughed, stepping lightly from the water, proudly conscious that he watched her luxuriant naked form with heated gaze. She walked about to dry herself, whirling her arms and pirouetting to let the summer air dry the shining drops that clung to her slender arms and dainty naked limbs. Harry lay on his back on the grass, his arms clasped behind his dark head, watching her.

A shining drop clinging to the pink peak of one soft breast caught the light and glimmered diamondlike—and Harry envied it. Another droplet rolled lazily down the valley between her breasts, and he watched its progress as it journeyed in silvery luxury down her smooth white stomach to disappear into the silky blond triangle of shining hair that nested between her thighs. She turned, shaking out her fair hair again, lazily conscious of the thoughts she inspired in him, and he was presented with a ripe

151

view of her straight lovely back, culminating in the delicious curve of her buttocks atop her dainty legs.

He sighed. So much loveliness, he felt internally, could kill a man. But it would be a lovely death. One eagerly sought.

"Rosamunde, Rosamunde—not the World's Rose. *My* Rose. My own Rose," he muttered, reaching out and claiming a dainty ankle.

Gently she shook him free. "Harry—" She reproved him with a soft look.

Reluctantly he desisted. And watched as she stepped with dainty naked limbs into her chemise, and then her petticoat.

" 'Tis a pity to mask so much beauty," he sighed.

Her eyebrows lifted as she slipped into her dress, turned to him to work the fasteners down the back. "And would you have me go naked?" she teased.

"Always," he said fondly, "in an Eden of our own." And pressed her slender waist with strong gentle fingers.

"Harry," she said in a dreamy voice, leaning back against him so that her back was a flame against his chest, *"this* is our Eden. Heaven has given it to us."

And an Eden in truth it seemed to them—a time of loving. For after breakfast, for all her weak protests made through slanted lashes, for all her turned shoulder that but invited him the more, he took her again, fondly, and so they passed the day in gentle pleasures.

It was for them a wonderful golden afternoon, and it stretched into a wonderful golden week of sultry summer days, of dips in the pool far down the stream that Harry showed her, of shared passion in the moon's white slanted light, a honeymoon of discovery and shared delights.

For his part, Harry never wished to leave her. He knew the time would come when he must return to the road, else they would starve, but he put that thought away from him.

But when Nightwind was well and galloping happily about the meadow with Graylady, when the weather was fine, with sultry days and pleasant nights, there was no longer any excuse for him to dally so, for the great fairs

152

of the market towns awaited, and rich purses were to be had as careless travelers roamed the highways.

Rosamunde had felt Harry's restlessness grow as the days passed, and one morning he told her that he was riding out, nor would he listen to her pleas for him to stay. Firmly he took her to old John and commended her to his care until he should return. Should anyone ask John about her, he instructed John to say Rosamunde was a destitute wench who had wandered by looking for work, and was helping him for her keep.

With shadowed eyes Rosamunde watched him ride away from her, the big black horse and lean rider disappearing into the trees. He would be back, she told herself staunchly. She'd urged him to take care, and his eyes had softened as he promised her he would. But—who could be sure of that? So many dangers beset the road, and Harry was by nature a reckless man. She felt desolate. If only he had taken her with him. . . .

That night she dined with John in the echoing cavernous hall and watched the guttering candle send wavering shadows up into the high old beams of the ceiling. Over her meat pie she asked John about Harry and his family in the old days.

She found John glad enough to tell her. "Master Harry's father, the earl of Locke . . . " he began, and she thought, *Ah, so they were the earls of Locke! Then this house must be Locke Hall.* Somewhere in the dim past, she thought she had heard her mother speak of it.

"What was the family name, John?" she interrupted carelessly.

"Waring," John said promptly, and she repeated to herself silently: *Waring. Rosamunde Waring, wife to the earl of Locke.* It was a lovely dream . . . but she knew it was not to be. She sighed. "What was Harry's mother like, John?"

"Oh, she were a fine lady. Sweet like yourself, and brave. But it fair killed her when her lord husband was taken. She waited not even to sup, she was up on her horse and away to London to petition the king for his life, and young Harry with her." He sniffled. "She did say to

153

me, 'Take care of all at the hall, John, for I will be back and my lord husband with me!' And so I did take care, but her journey was all for naught, for the king refused even to see her. And my poor lady did catch her death of cold in her drafty rooms in London and died there, for she were a delicate thing and could ne'er stand a draft."

It was her broken heart that killed her, thought Rosamunde, staring down the long empty board and seeing in her mind that wild ride to London, and all the struggles to see the king that had come to naught. Her heart ached for Harry's mother, who, like her own, had watched helplessly while her husband went to the block. "Is there a portrait of her, John?" she asked wistfully.

"There was, but the vandals slashed it when they overran the hall, and Lord Penwether—the new owner, him that has taken young Harry's rightful place—did order it and the other things the vandals had harmed to be taken out and burned. I did try to save it, but he wouldn't let me." John's face darkened.

Along with John, Rosamunde felt a stab of hatred for this moneyed lord who'd bought Locke Hall and now occupied "Harry's rightful place." Hated him with a blaze of impotent fury, for any day Lord Penwether could ride up and reclaim the hall from them—turn John out, and then Harry and she must needs fade away into the countryside.

"What of Harry's father?" she pursued. "Not frail like his mother, surely?"

"Nay—his father, who were named Harry too, was a merry lad and not overmuch for caution. Harry be the stronger, more like his grandfather, who was the stoutest warrior this part of the country ever knew. Looks like him. Is like him."

She felt a burning pride that Harry should be so like that stout warrior, his grandfather. "Is there a portrait of him, John?"

"Nay, they burned that too. But ye've a living portrait of him in Harry, mistress—for except that his grandfather were fair and Harry's dark, they're much alike."

She hesitated to ask her next question and poked at her
154

meat pie for a while before raising her eyes ro look steadily at John. "Do you know what Harry does, John, when he rides away?"

Old John caught his breath.

"Aye, I know, although we never speak of it, Harry and I. Nor would I ever tell it, mistress," he added earnestly. "Not even if they put me on the rack and broke my bones. But a gentlemen like Harry must make his way as best he can these days. 'Tis glad I am he found you, for it must have been lonely on the road for a man like Harry."

"Yes," she murmured reflectively, her green eyes deep pools in the candlelight, "I rather imagine it was."

But John's words set her to thinking.

She slept that night on the stone floor of the hall on a pile of clean-washed bedclothes, for old John would not hear of her going back to the old wing. Master Harry had bade him take care of her, and he could watch over her better here, he declared proudly. So although she would have preferred to watch for Harry to come riding back to her over the meadow from that room where he'd made love to her and which held such sweet memories of him, she deferred to the old man's wishes.

But sleep she could not. Wild visions of Harry shot and wavering in the saddle, or being hunted down with fresh horses while Nightwind staggered along winded, or lying in his blood on the highway while a booted foot stirred him, haunted her. She twisted and turned. Finally she got up and stood staring out the window, then came back to sit on the pile of bedclothes, hunched over and brooding, staring into the darkness with wide fear-deepened eyes.

By morning Harry still had not come, and she was sure he was dead. She was all for riding out to look for him, but John assured her fearfully that Harry would not like that, and would blame him if he returned to find her gone. Sometimes, John insisted, Harry was gone for days, yet always he came riding in with never a scratch. Ah, he boasted, he had a charmed life, had Harry!

155

Rosamunde gave the old man an anguished look. She could not swallow her breakfast.

That day she spent pacing the corridors, restlessly exploring the big empty rooms. At every sound outside she ran to the windows to look out, hoping to see a big black horse and a reckless rider come bounding out of the trees, but no one came.

Another day passed and another.

10   *It was with the waning moon of the third day* that he came to her. Like a shadow out of the trees emerged Nightwind, running in his impatience to be home in his meadow. Rosamunde, who had been standing pensively in the shadows of the stone building watching Graylady graze in the moonlight, had seen the mare's head lift and heard her sudden whinny. Heart pounding, she peered forward to see that big running shadow break from the darker shapes of the trees.

"Harry!" she cried. Careless that her thin slippers were getting sodden with the dew, she picked up her skirts and ran toward him through the wet grasses.

He vaulted off his powerful mount and swept her up into his arms.

"Ah, Harry, Harry," she whispered brokenly. "I thought for sure you were dead—or taken!"

"There, there!" His laughing face was reckless, exuberant. "Not dead—not even nicked. I've made a rich haul, Rose! A coachload of drunken dandies headed for a wedding celebration at some great manor. They had rings and gold chains and wedding gifts of plate. The weight loaded me down and I had to hide some of it—

the plate—deep under some brush. I'll go back for it as soon as the chase has died down."

"They could trap you with it, Harry," she warned. "If they find it, they'd know you'd return there and they could lie in wait in ambush to take you."

"Aye," he said more soberly. "So for your sake, Rose, I'll use caution and wait. They'll either find it as you say, and wait in ambush—but they'll tire of that and go away. Or they won't find it at all and I will. 'Tis some plate and silver candlesticks that were heavy and will fetch a good price."

"Was that what took you so long? Hiding it?"

He shook his head. "No, they were following close. I could not risk leading them here, Rose, so instead Nightwind and I led them a merry chase." He chuckled. "They'll be searching for me all the way to London!"

She smiled wanly at his sally, but her heart was clutched with fear and her hands felt cold. *They had followed close.* That meant he had been in terrible danger all that time. . . . She clenched her hands together to keep them from shaking. She who could be so brave for herself was drenched with fear for Harry.

"Come, Rose," he said. "Let's see you smile. I've brought you a necklace—of silver and seed pearls. 'Twas intended as a wedding present for the bride, no doubt."

"Poor girl," murmured Rosamunde wryly.

"Ah, do not worry about her! From the look of that coachload of dandies I cornered, she'll have at least a dozen such necklaces—and maybe some garnished with gold and rubies. 'Twas not the only coach making its way to the wedding—'twas just the one I selected."

Somehow that made her feel better, for she could not bear to think that the bride had been robbed of her only gifts. The necklace was delicate and lovely, and Harry clasped it round her neck and kissed her ear lightly as he did so. She stirred slightly under his touch and turned about in the moonlight that Harry might admire it. She was glad this necklace had not been wrenched from some woman's throat, but when she looked into Harry's smiling gray eyes, she knew that he was not the man to wrench

157

such things from women's throats. She was instantly certain that he had chosen his coach with care, perhaps observing the occupants as they alighted at some inn, and lying in wait to pounce on them later. A coachload of wealthy dandies . . . so much more dangerous than a coachload of well-dressed women with perhaps only an old man to guard them. But such had been Harry's choice, and such, she knew, would always be his choice. She felt a surge of pride in Harry, hard-driven, who yet chose his prey with such care. Such a man, she told herself angrily, should not have to resort to the highways to seek his living!

"Are you hungry?" she asked.

"Nay, I've eaten."

"Then," she murmured, giving him a silken look, "as soon as you've unsaddled Nightwind and watered him, perhaps you'll be for bed?"

"Aye, Rose—to prove how much I've missed you!"

She sighed, and drifted over the wet grass to the old wing, which to them was Eden. She was lying gracefully on her pallet of straw, with the moon playing witchingly over her body in its light chemise, when Harry strode in. He flung off his gauntlets, tossed aside his sword and struggled out of his boots while she watched.

" 'Twas all I could do not to ride straight back to you," he confessed. "Though I knew full well I had to lead my pursuers away, every crossroads was a wrench. I had to force myself forward past every turning in the road that led back to you."

They were the words she wanted to hear, and she gave him a smile of pure enchantment. "Then hurry out of your clothes," she said in a soft rich voice, "so I can give you the welcome you deserve."

Nothing loath, Harry almost ripped off his clothes and pressed her to him. Rosamunde went into his arms with a little sigh of contentment. And that night her love burned the brighter for having lived these past three days in terror that she had lost him.

But her loss of sleep had told on her. Morning found her eyes shadowed and dark, and Harry looked at her in
158

worry. "Faith, what's happened?" he asked. "Didn't you sleep at all while I was gone, Rose?"

She shook her head ruefully. "I kept thinking of you lying on the highway with your throat cut. It wasn't conducive to a good night's sleep, Harry."

He sighed and stroked her slender wrist. "You must not think about such things, Rose."

"Ah, how can I avoid it?" she cried, and thrust his hand away from her. "Oh, Harry, can we not eke out a crust some other way? Must you always be risking your neck for a living?"

He sighed. "I could go away and enlist in some foreign war."

"Oh, no, no—then I'd never see you."

"There's a price on my head, Rose. 'Tis not safe for me to linger too long in one spot lest there be someone who recognizes me and decides to fatten a lean purse with the reward."

"You mean," she said in a hopeless voice, "it must always be this way for us?"

"Oh, no." He kissed her. "Something may turn up. And if it does, we'll be quick to seize our chance, Rose. Life is full of odd twists and turnings. There may be a way out for us yet."

"If I had to wait all my life for it, Harry," she said, turning to him intensely, "I'd count us lucky if we could but show our faces to the world for what we are . . . at the end of it."

"Perhaps we will," he said in a husky voice. "Perhaps one day I'll be able to make you proud of me, Rose."

"Ah, but I am proud. It's not that!" She flung her white arms around him and pressed his long lean body close to her soft yielding one. "Ah, Harry, we'll sell the necklace to buy food so you'll have no need to ride out so much. 'Tis not necklaces I need around my neck—'tis your arms!"

Harry gave her a tormented look. He would have given his life for her and counted it worth the cost. Now he promised huskily in response to her wild muffled entreaties that he would indeed stay away from the road for a
159

while, that he would keep safe, that he would stay here with her at the hall.

Softly he caressed this lovely girl who sighed against him with broken words of entreaty for his safety. He was deeply touched at this clear expression of her love and caring. He was not given much to introspection, but now in his heart he looked back over his wasted life and asked himself in wonder what he had done to deserve her. If only he could give her his ancient name and title and his rightful patrimony . . . then there'd be no need to seek the road, then he could spend his days beside her, catering to her every whim.

He heaved a deep sigh. Those were daydreams. He was a highwayman and must risk his neck for gold on summer nights. He had no trade—and even if he had, the guilds were strict and held tightly to their own, they'd never let him in, nor had he years to spend in apprenticeship, for he must care for Rosamunde. He toyed with wild ideas of trading ventures in that great world he had dreamed of entering as a boy when he studied geography. And then he forgot them as Rosamunde's softness worked its will upon him and he was consumed with a great burning fire that swept them both up, so that their bodies yearned and strained together, and amid silken caresses and broken murmured words of love, they forgot their separation and her fears. Forgot the world and clung together as lovers, in a tangle of arms and legs and pressing bodies, savoring the delights of the flesh, atingle with desire and surging toward fulfillment.

Several days later the haymakers came, and Harry and Rosamunde led the horses out into the woods before they arrived, having been warned by John of their coming. From deep in the woods they could hear the shouts of the men as they scythed the long waving grasses and piled them with pitchforks into a great sweet-smelling mound. And each night that mound was lightened as Nightwind and Graylady were brought back to graze the moonlit meadow, and as Harry and Rosamunde, laughing, carried great armloads of hay to store in the old wing lest
160

the lumbering ox-drawn haycarts should carry it all away.

It was tiring work in the starlight, but work she loved. And when, wet with perspiration from their exertions, they finished at last and went back to the woods with the horses at dawn, they found a tinkling stream. There they took off their damp clothes and bathed in the dawn's light. Then they flung themselves down on the greensward beneath the heavy gnarled trees and exchanged kiss for kiss and sigh for sigh, and no one was the loser. Their passion flashed brighter than the gold Harry had brought home from the highways—burned brighter and more enduring than the hard metal for which men sold their souls.

On the haymakers' last afternoon—and old John was glad to see them go, for it was his duty to feed them their noonday meal—Rosamunde and Harry lounged on a small grassy bank far downstream where no whinny from their horses could be heard in the hayfield. They had made love in the dappled light of morning, and the memory of it held a lingering sweetness that cast a pale honey glow over the golden light of afternoon. Afterward they had bathed in the cold silvery water, and in the deepest green pool by the farther bank Harry had begun to teach her to swim, holding her graceful body lightly as he taught her the strokes that would carry her knifelike through the water.

When Rosamunde was tired from her exertions, they had lain by the bank letting the sun dry their naked bodies. Leaning on an elbow, Harry had admired the satiny length of her, and she had stretched coquettishly and rolled over like a kitten, teasing him with an impudent outstretched toe that tickled his knees, a questing finger that found his loins, causing his muscles to lurch suddenly. Finding his lady in such a playful mood, he reached out and pulled her to him and caressed her until her teasing spirit melted into passion. Joyously aroused, they clung together, rolling on the grass in a wild joining of body and spirit.

Their passions assuaged, they slipped apart and lay silent, considering the leafy curtain of branches overhead. Then Rosamunde had risen and, with a long lustrous look at Harry, walked into the stream again, bathed while he feasted on the beauty of her white thighs and whiter breasts. Then she had splashed out of the water and had sat down on the bank near him, letting the soft breeze dry her body while she wielded her wooden comb in her long wet hair, bringing it from its tangled disorder into pale wet strands of satin that clung to her gleaming shoulders and rounded breasts in a way Harry found disquieting.

He reached over to rest a lazy hand on her naked lap, and moved his fingers gently along her silken thigh. He loved to touch her. She was so soft, so feminine, so utterly woman.

Rosamunde gave him a questioning look, a wary look as if to say, *No, this time I am dressing.* And for a moment the wooden comb was held stationary in the golden cascade of her long hair.

"Someday I'll get you a golden comb, Rose," he said, thinking it a small enough tribute to her dazzling beauty.

"This wooden one is well enough, Harry," Rosamunde told him softly. Her eyes were deep-green pools of limitless promise as she smiled at him beneath the branches. " 'Tis your love for me that's the finest gold—I need no other."

Harry's throat suddenly closed up. He pressed her to him, hid her face against his deep chest so that she could not see how she had moved him with her simple declaration. It came to him in sudden fright that if he lost her, his life would be empty, nothing, that she was his all.

"That gold you'll always have, Rose," he promised her huskily. Her smile was blissful to hear him say it, and her lips moved softly against his chest, caressing it with small kisses.

But she had caught at his heart more sharply than ever before, and in that moment Harry swore to himself a great oath—that he would ever hew to her. He had found his woman, and like the lean gray wolf, he would take no other mate. It was a thing he would not have spoken aloud, but it was a vow that throbbed in the depths of him—throbbed even as her lips moving softly against his chest, made his loins catch fire and burn with a raging

162

desire to possess her, to bend her sweet body to his and taste of all her secrets.

Hard Harry, who had taken his fun where he found it all across England, was hopelessly in love with a slip of a girl who put all her trust in him. It was heady wine, and he drank deep of it, savoring each draught as if it were his last.

All summer they lingered there at Locke Hall, with Harry lazing about, rarely going out upon the highway. The horses grew fat and sleek, and Rosamunde and Harry spent pleasant hours brushing them, currying them, feeding them sweetmeats. Rosamunde plucked herbs from the overgrown herb garden and flavored tasty stews which Harry and John proclaimed little short of miraculous. Sometimes she bustled about the buttery with flour on her apron and a wide smile on her face as—taught by old John—she made great pies out of the peaches and ripe pears and cherries and apples that they brought her.

Knowing it could never be more than pretense, Rosamunde played house in the great moldering manor, pretending to herself, dreaming wild dreams that could never come true. Harry knew this, but he could not bring himself to dim those dreaming eyes with harsh truths. He let her have her summer in the sun.

Their rude awakening came when they were sunning themselves in the meadow, lying sprawled against the haymow listening to the humming of the bees and the lazy chirping of the birds. They started at the sound of hooves. Looking up, they saw through the distant trees a coach and six enter the drive, followed by numerous horsemen.

Harry leaped up and ran, bent over, for the old wing. Swiftly he saddled their horses while Rosamunde, who had followed as fast as she could, ran down the long stone corridor and bundled up their food and possessions unceremoniously into leathern pouches and linen squares. When the party had disappeared into the house, they rode their now well-laden mounts swiftly across the meadow and into the trees beyond.

"Think you they saw us from the windows?" she asked uneasily.

"Nay, I think they had no time to reach the windows," he said, frowning. "And the footmen were busy carrying in the luggage."

"Who do you think it is?"

" 'Tis obviously Lord Penwether come to affix his claim more securely to his moldering possessions. I feel sorry for John," he added harshly, "with all this great troupe bursting in upon him and not so much as a maidservant to help him!"

Rosamunde looked at Harry with compassion. Once again he had been booted out of the home of his fathers. He sat Nightwind with easy grace, silent and thoughtful. "We'll wait," he decided, "and speak to John later. He'll be disappointed if I do not tell him goodbye."

They walked their horses to the place where they had so often frolicked in the water and rolled in rapture on the grassy bank. But it was no longer a day for frolic. There beside the clear green pool where Harry had taught her to swim, she spread out a meal on a big square of clean linen and they ate, soberly, without talking much. Afterward they took the horses farther into the woods.

When dark came, Harry stole back to the house and spoke to John. He returned with a huge armload of hay, a thick slab of cheese and one of ham, and some fresh bread and fruit. He threw the hay down before the horses. "Lord Penwether has come to stay," he announced bitterly. "By tomorrow John will be up to his ears in scullery maids and chimney sweeps. I've cleared our traces out of the old wing so that no blame can be attached to him for letting it be occupied."

"Then . . . " Rosamunde bent to spread the hay so the horses could better share it. "What's to be done?"

"We cannot stay here," said Harry. "I'll have to find you some new place. Though offhand I know not where."

She touched his arm. "No new place, Harry. I'll ride beside you."

He shook his head irritably. "You know that's not possible, Rose. The road's too hard a life for a woman. We can meet and tryst like this for a time, but as for riding with me . . . " He shook his head.

"You think a man riding with a woman would be remarked?" she challenged him.

"I think *your* face and *your* figure would be remarked anywhere," he retorted in a quelling voice.

"Just so," said Rosamunde. Preoccupied with where to take her, Harry did not notice the strange inflection in her voice. She might almost have been laughing at him. "Then what will you do now?" she asked almost blithely. "Ride for that cache of plate you left hidden?"

He nodded. " 'Tis just what we need. With that, I can persuade some goodwife to care for you until I can return."

Rosamunde's mouth tightened at that and she tossed her golden head. She turned quickly away lest Harry see her expression.

"When will you go to get it?" she asked in a muffled voice.

" 'Tis some distance from here." Absently he told her the location. "I'll nap a while first"—his voice grew lazy and he took her by the shoulders, his meaning clear—"and then ride out for it."

"No." Surprisingly, Rosamunde eluded him. She sounded remote. "You'll need your strength," she said dryly.

Harry gave her a keen look, but he dropped his arms. She was fretting, he guessed, because he had refused to let her ride with him. He sighed. "If that is how you will have it, Rose," he said shortly, "I will ride for it now."

"Yes, that would be well," she agreed, brushing off her skirt. "Shall I wait for you here?"

He was startled. "*Of course* you will wait for me here—unless you hear people approaching. Then ride downstream and hide in any likely spot. I will find you. You'll hear me ride by, whistling."

He would whistle for her! She gave him a bitter look, but he did not see it. He was busy mounting up. Then he was riding away from her—at an easy pace, for he had some distance to go.

Rosamunde waited until he was well out of sight and then went into such a flurry of activity as would have

astonished Harry, had he seen it. Swiftly she tore some
of the linen into strips and bound them about her. Then
she changed into the country-boy clothes she had worn
when she had first arrived at Locke Hall, snatched up
what was left of the food and leaped astride Graylady to
follow hot on Harry's heels. She tried to stay well back,
but in the darkness sometimes she would see him silhouetted in the moonlight on the crest of a hill ahead of her
and realize that she was moving faster than she should—
for she only wanted to pace Harry, not to catch up with
him.

Dark and rustling, the night seemed to crowd in around
her, for these were unfamiliar roads, and twice she almost
lost her way. But Harry's directions had been clear,
and—even when she thought she heard a wolf howl
nearby—she reminded herself that if she screamed, she
was not so far behind but that he would hear her.

Another wolf call sounded, and she speeded her pace.
Graylady was toiling uphill now and the moon had scurried behind a cloud. It was clouding up for rain, she
thought uneasily, hoping the rain would hold off, for if
the road became mired the gray mare—not so powerful
an animal as Nightwind—might fall behind. And who
knew by what route Harry would return? She felt very
crestfallen at the thought that she might miss him at his
ultimate destination, the cache of plate.

She had just reached the crest of the hill and was peering through what seemed total windswept darkness when
the mare shied and she was suddenly swep from her saddle. She landed on her hands and knees in the road and
struggled to her feet just as the moon came out—to realize that the flash she saw just in front of her was the moonlight striking on a naked blade, and that the prodding she
felt in the front of her jerkin came from the point of a
sword.

Just as that knowledge was borne in on her, Harry's
strong face came onto view, and from this vantage point
it had a demonic look.

"Harry!" she gasped. " 'Tis me—Rosamunde!"

"Rose!" he cried, dropping the point of his blade and
166

hastening to brush her off. "My God, I nearly skewered you! What possessed you to try to slip up on me like that?"

By now Rosamunde had regained her composure. "It *was* rash of me," she agreed complacently. "And you *did* draw your sword, didn't you?"

"Indeed I did," he growled, sheathing it. "And would have run you through save that the moon came out from behind the clouds and gave me a look at you! For I like not being followed on dark byways, and I've been aware for some time that a horseman was following me stealthily, holding back whenever I came into view."

"I'd have come forward sooner had I known you'd seen me." She laughed.

He snorted. "What madness is this? Why did you not wait for me as I told you?"

Rosamunde stood with her feet planted, hands on hips. "The point is, Harry, you thought I was a *man!*"

"It was dark, Rose. I was not expecting you and—"

She stamped her foot. "You thought I was a *man,* else you would not have drawn your sword!"

He stared at her, bemused. "All right," he said in an altered voice. "In the darkness I did think you to be a lad about to leap on me. I was about to show you your error!"

She ignored that faint irony. She leaned forward earnestly, for she *must* convince him. "Harry—observe." Dramatically she pulled off her jerkin, paraded before him in her shirt.

"You've bound up your breasts," he noted, staring at her shirt in the moonlight. The wind rippled the material against her skin. "And your shoulders seem to have increased in breadth."

"Aye, I've bound my breasts down tight and made a padding that tapers to my waist, and built up my shoulders to give me a *boy's* figure. With my hair coiled up under my hat and pulled into a queue behind and tied, who'd think me a woman?"

"*I* would," said Harry flatly. "For I know you to be one."

"Harry," she said, drawing herself up with dignity, and

167

something sorrowful in her voice arrested him. "If you do not take me with you on the road, I swear to you I will strike out on my own."

"You tried that once before," he reminded her. "Remember the cow?"

But Rosamunde was not to be diverted by that barb.

"I remember," she said with dignity. "And indeed I may be buffeted. But still I will do it. Ah, Harry." Her voice was beseeching. "Grant me this—let me do it. You cannot know the agony I go through waiting, thinking you dead by the highway, run through by a pike, shot."

His hard eyes softened as he looked down at her anxious face. He brushed back a tendril of her fair hair with his fingers. "Rest easy, Rose. I've the devil's own luck— many have said it."

She stamped her foot. She was near tears. "But no one has luck forever. There could come a time when you'd need a staunch fellow at your back."

"And you think to be that staunch fellow?"

She nodded recklessly. Witch lights played in her green eyes, making him draw in his breath. " 'Tis true I have a short reach compared to you, and no great strength for a sword arm. But a pistol I can aim and shoot straight— and you saw for yourself that my hand did not shake when I aimed a pistol at Lord Matthew!" she added eagerly.

"Aye." He frowned. "I saw that."

"Then take me with you, Harry! Do!"

Harry sighed. Against his better judgment he had let the wench beguile him. He took her shoulders in his strong hands, wryly noting the padding. "There's a condition if I grant you this, Rose," he said harshly, and she looked up at him in surprise. "It is this: if I fall, if I be taken, you will ride away—you will make no wild attempts to save me, you will save *yourself*."

She flinched and shook her head. Harry's grip tightened. His voice roughened and he spoke between his clenched teeth. "I'll take you with me no other way, Rose. *Swear!*"

Reluctantly, knowing Harry meant what he said and that this was the only way she would ever ride beside him, she repeated in a faint voice, "If you fall, if you be taken, I will ride away and save myself. I swear it." A shiver went through her. "Oh, Harry, you cannot mean it!"

"I do mean it," he said grimly. "Think you I could know a moment's peace if I thought I was bringing you to your end?"

She looked down, unable to meet his blazing eyes.

He released her and straightened up. "I know well 'tis a foolish thing I do to take you with me at all," he growled. "But you will follow my orders and you will obey me in this, do you understand?"

"I have sworn," she said bitterly. "I will honor my oath."

Two   *The Wild Rose*

II   *In surging triumph Rosamunde remounted Gray-*
lady and rode blithely with Harry to find the cache of
plate. Beside her Harry was glum.

"Wait for me here," he said tersely, when they reached
a clump of trees.

"But—" she began to protest, when his dark frown
stopped her.

"If you ride with me, you will obey my orders." His
voice was testy. "Is that understood?"

She nodded her head and watched as he rode away. It
was understandable, she told herself, that he would wish
to go in cautiously, but she was restless and uneasy until
he returned, appearing so suddenly that she jumped.

He flashed her a smile in the moonlight and patted his
bulging saddle bags. " 'Twas all where I left it, hidden
under a new fall of leaves. We'll ride for Winchester and
turn it into ready cash now that you have decided to try
your luck with me on the road."

She thrilled to that—no more talk of leaving her with
a goodwife!

They rode on, circling the nearby village, and rested
for a couple of hours before dawn by a little stream. It
was damp there and Rosamunde felt the cold, but was too
proud to admit it. She was grateful when Harry tossed his
cloak about her shoulders.

"Why Winchester?" she asked him.

"In Winchester there's a fence who can convert anything to cash." Harry chuckled. "His name is Isaac."

"You have dealt with him before, then?"

"Many times."

Rosamunde huddled in the cloak, shivering. She was entering Harry's life now—his real life, not some passionate idyll that could not last, but his everyday existence. And it would include shivering in many gray dawns while they rested the horses, and many men like Isaac. She was glad when Harry reached for her and pulled her to him, warming her with his body.

"I will learn the ways of the road," she promised him in a small voice, and he held her the tighter. She thought he was going to make love to her, but he pulled away suddenly. "It is a hard ride to Winchester," he said. "Sleep awhile."

Thus commanded, she tried to sleep, comforting herself with the nearness of his lean body. Although she would not admit it, she was a little afraid of this entry into the life on the road—not for herself, but for Harry. She must learn these new ways quickly, lest she endanger him.

Before they rode on toward Winchester, she finished her transformation from lass to lad. While Harry watched, his dark face expressionless, she bound up her hair tightly, making a small neat queue in the back, and pulled her hat down to shade her iridescent green eyes.

"Do I not make a neat country lad?" she inquired proudly, and Harry nodded.

"Aye, you do, Rose," he agreed, but his tone was noncommittal and she sensed the reserve in his voice. That made her anxious as they took the road to Winchester.

Harry must have sensed her unease, for he kept up an easy conversation as they approached. Winchester was the ancient capital of England, he told her. Lying on the right bank of the Itchen, in Roman days it had been called Venta Belgarum. He turned his horse sharply to avoid three hooded lepers, shuffling along miserably at the side of the road. One of them cried out and held out a claw-

171

like hand for alms. Harry tossèd them what he could afford and the hooded creatures fell upon it, fighting over the coins by the roadside.

Rosamunde shuddered. There were sights like these all over England—indeed all over Europe, for leprosy was the scourge of the day. Unlike the Black Death, which came and went in great cataclysmic outbreaks, leprosy was the silent killer. It crept stealthily upon its victims. Like crime and taxes, it was always there.

"In Winchester is the shrine of St. Swithin," murmured Rosamunde hastily, trying to forget the pitiful lepers. "I remember one of the maidservants at Kenwarren House telling me about it as a little girl. A marvelous place, she said, full of gold and jewels."

Harry gave her a jaded look. "When Henry the Eighth looted it, Rose, he found the gold and jewels to be fake."

So even kings took to the road for pelf! Rosamunde sighed, but it made her feel a little better about the contents of Harry's saddlebags.

They rode past the ancient cathedral and into a rabbit warren of twisting streets full of little shops. Before one of these, a goldsmith's shop, Harry dismounted. This time Rosamunde accompanied him, tagging along silently into the dark musty-smelling interior, where a sallow-faced woman gave Harry a sharp look.

"I would speak to Isaac," said Harry, and the heavy velvet hangings behind her parted and an old man appeared. He gave them both a shrewd glance, and Rosamunde got her first glimpse of Isaac the Fence.

Her first feeling was of disappointment, for she had somehow expected someone flamboyant, and this parched-looking little man was hardly that. He had silver hair and yellow teeth and a long-suffering expression. His thin body was richly garbed in a long dark damask gown of the sort the earl of Kenwarren affected. It fell to his ankles, and the full sleeves of this robe were slit to reveal skinny arms clad in undersleeves of green velvet laced with gold.

"It has been a long time, Harry," said Isaac. "I thought you must have left this part of the country."
172

"I am returned." Harry smiled. "This lad with me is named Robbie. Look well upon him, for he is trustworthy and it may be that one day I will send him to you instead of coming myself."

Isaac nodded and turned to study Rosamunde. She gazed back at him steadily, and his gaze fell away. "We are going into the back room, Rachel," he said to the sallow-faced woman. "See that we are not disturbed."

She nodded, and they accompanied him through the hangings into a small back room with several doors. Rosamunde guessed there would be several escape routes from this room should the need arise. The main furnishings were a handsome table and several chairs, plus a scale for weighing gold.

Harry tossed the heavy saddlebags he carried onto that table and spread out the plate and candlesticks.

Isaac's eyes glinted. He studied the plate thoughtfully, hefted the pieces, and offered Harry a quarter of what they were worth.

Harry shrugged and his face hardened. He reached out to gather them up, saying he would take them elsewhere, but Isaac's querulous voice deterred him. Isaac protested that times were hard and warned Harry he'd have trouble selling them.

" 'Tis worth taking them to Benjamin at York for the price you offer—he'd pay much more."

"Nay, nay, be not so hasty." Isaac's tone had grown soothing. "There is no need to travel to York—and Benjamin of York would pay ye less than I."

Harry snorted and Isaac upped his offer. They haggled until Rosamunde grew quite tired, but in the end Harry received what he considered a fair price and Isaac counted out a trove of golden coins into a small velvet purse. Harry swept the empty saddlebags over his arm and picked up the velvet purse.

"Can ye recommend a safe house for the night, Isaac? Robbie is tired."

Rosamunde threw him a grateful look. Indeed, she was sagging with weariness. And Isaac directed them to a trim cottage on the edge of town with ivy spilling over a low stone wall in the front.

Harry knocked and a smiling white-aproned woman with floury hands came to the door. He mentioned Isaac's name and her smile broadened.

"Do come in," she said, moving her ample body aside so that they might pass into the cozy room. "If ye be friends of Isaac's, ye be welcome indeed. I've a nice room upstairs for as long as ye care to stay—and anything else ye'll be needing."

That last proved true. The next morning, after a languorous night of lovemaking, half-smothered in the softness of their landlady's fat goosedown mattress, they rose to a good breakfast of fresh country eggs and clotted cream and red apples and hot pancakes. No sooner had they laid down their napkins and risen from the table than their landlady, Mistress Revers, told them a bootmaker was waiting to see them if they desired his services.

Harry nodded his approval, but Rosamunde met Mistress Revers' twinkling hazel eyes in surprise. Later she was to learn that all manner of services were available at these "safe" abodes frequented by "gentlemen of the road," and that this particular bootmaker, who was tall and bony and glum, called at Mistress Revers' cottage whenever her stableboy brought word that there were extra horses in her stable. Rosamunde wondered briefly what Mistress Revers' neighbors must think of a woman who required the constant services of a bootmaker, and later in the day Mistress Revers graciously enlightened her, unasked. The thought had occurred to her as well, so she had spread word about the neighborhood that her husband had an affliction of the foot that caused intermittent swelling, and he fretted about it so that she must needs be calling the bootmaker constantly to try to give him relief. Shortly after that disclosure, Rosamunde had her first sight of Mistress Revers' husband, a portly gentleman with a ruff of fair hair, bleary blue eyes and a nose red from drink. He nodded cheerfully to Rosamunde as he went by. "Greetings, cousin," he said, and Rosamunde blinked.

"All our guests are 'cousins,' " said Mistress Revers in

174

answer to Rosamunde's blank look. "Remember to limp a bit, John," she called after her husband, and he promptly began to favor his left foot as he closed the front door and shuffled down the path that led from the cottage to the street.

"He's to the nearest tavern." Mistress Revers sighed. "If 'twere not for John's drinking, we'd to London and make ourselves a fortune, for there's many gentlemen there—and ladies too—in need of safe houses, and we've the knack of respectability. Ah, well, John has friends here to bring him home of nights if he's past walking, so perhaps 'tis best we stay in Winchester." She shook her head. "I had dreams of London when I was a young girl —but all men are alike, I suppose."

All but Harry, thought Rosamunde, with a warm rush of blood to her face. She was remembering how lovingly he had held her the night before, the soft words he'd murmured into her ear, there in the depths of that great feather bed.

"Ye're young yet," commented Mistress Revers wryly, as if in answer to the look on Rosamunde's face. "Ye've much to learn of men."

Rosamunde thought she knew all there was to know of Harry, but the way the older woman had mentioned "men" made her look up sharply—after all, she was posing as a man herself!

She saw Mistress Revers regarding her with some amusement. "Would ye like the loan of a chemise, young sir?" she asked Rosamunde roguishly. "For I'm thinking you must be tired of trousers and would prefer petticoats."

"You've—you've guessed!" stammered Rosamunde.

"From the beginning," nodded Mistress Revers. "Ye're much too pretty for a lad, and besides, the gentleman with you has such a protective air about him when he turns his gaze on you—I knew ye were his doxy from the start."

Rosamunde bit her lip. Mistress Revers had guessed her to be Harry's doxy; it had never occurred to her to speculate that she might be Harry's wife. And maybe she never would be, Rosamunde told herself gloomily. For Harry took a dim view of family life upon the road.

"Ye've not known the gentleman long, have ye?" asked Mistress Revers with a sly nudge of the elbow.

"Long enough," said Rosamunde in a choked voice.

"Ah, well, at least ye'll have boots if he leaves ye," said Mistress Revers cheerfully. "I gather ye've bound up your breasts, for ye do look too flat-chested to attract a proper man."

Rosamunde's gaze flew unbidden to Mistress Revers' overample bosom.

"My greatest attraction," the other lady said, noting Rosamunde's glance and bridling a little. " 'Twas how I got my husband," she added in a tone of confidential pride. "I managed to give him a wee peek of my bosom when he thought I did not know he was about. We had gone out berrying, a whole pack of us. I'd had my eye on John all along, but he'd never noticed me before—he were chasing after my cousin Agnes same as all the rest. Agnes had long yellow braids and a honeyed way of talkin' to men. Well, that day I determined I would have John— she could have the rest, but not him. So I located a bee's nest between two bushes and I called to Agnes, 'Oooh, look, here's the best berries!' and she hurried over and stepped right in the bee's nest and three of them stung her—would have been more but she ran so fast. I left her soaking her foot in the brook and moanin' and complainin' and went off to find John. He was a little distance from the rest, and I spied him through the bushes and made my way near him, never letting on that I knew he was there. Then I gave a little cry to attract his attention—I pretended I'd been scratched by the thorns of the berry bushes and did undo my bodice and let down my chemise to have a look. My John came crashing through the berry bushes and did embrace me then and there— and I let him, protesting all the while, but letting him have his way, for well I knew Agnes were just a tease and he'd got nowhere with her, nor ever would! Agnes were pretty in the face, but droopy-like when she unlaced her bodice, so I thought 'twere time to show my best feature, as it were. And I was right. Before the fall bonfires were

176

lit my John and I had jumped over the stile and were man and wife!"

Rosamunde was very embarrassed by this recital. She mumbled something and fled before her landlady could ask by what method she had "enticed" Harry into taking her with him on the road. She was indignant at that "at least ye'll have boots if he leaves ye." Harry would never leave her! Those lovely boots . . . her face softened. Even though she herself had been stunned at the price the bootmaker asked, Harry had promptly commissioned him to make a handsome pair of boots for her. She smiled, remembering how restive Harry had become as the bootmaker handled her foot and touched her dainty ankle. It was plain he did not wish any other man to touch her!

"We're in need of a tailor as well," he'd told the bootmaker.

"I know one, master." The bootmaker's glum face had split into a ghastly grin. "He be quick, expensive and"— he emphasized the word—"safe."

"Send him along," said Harry. "And a glover too if ye know a good one. Robbie's in sore need of a pair of gauntlets."

Later in the day the tailor, a pink-cheeked little fellow with a high chirping voice, came by and—while Harry watched, drumming his fingers—measured Rosamunde for a cloak, reversible like Harry's, and other garments of a young gentleman of fashion.

Rosamunde stood in the center of their sunny bedroom, being measured. The little tailor seemed the very picture of contentment. Uncaring that Rosamunde and Harry were a lawless pair—and undoubtedly he knew it—he was humming at his work. He had just finished taking the measurements for her new cloak, and she had been thankful the material she had wrapped about her arms to make her shoulders appear wider had not slipped.

But now he was about to measure her for a suit of green velvet. Rosamunde had fairly glowed as she selected the lush fabric. Indeed she had been so excited at the prospect of new clothes to replace her rude country attire that the method of acquiring those clothes had not occurred to her. Now she cast an apprehensive glance at Harry. It was one thing to be measured for boots or a cloak, but—trousers! That meant he would measure not only her hips and stomach and waist but from crotch to heel as well. He would be handling her!

He was concentrating on his work; he was just passing the tape measure around her bound-down breasts to take her "chest" measurements. Rosamunde was so tense that as his hand brushed her underarm and the fabric of her shirt suddenly tickled her skin, she gave a convulsive jerk in her nervousness and the binding that held her breasts slipped down, allowing one breast to bounce free. The little tailor, peering at his tape measure in concentration, suddenly found through the coarse material of the country shirt a round young female breast cradled in his hand.

Instinctively Rosamunde flinched away from him. The tailor's jaw dropped in consternation. His hand jerked away as if she had burned his fingers and he gave a little jump backward, peering with startled eyes into Rosamunde's reddened countenance.

"I—I be sorry," he muttered in confusion.

Behind him Harry sighed. "Your surprise is understandable," he said, rising to his full height and towering over the little tailor as he took the tape measure from his trembling fingers. "Perhaps I should have alerted you, but I wanted to see if she would be able to fool even you. Since she has not, I will take these measurements myself if you will direct me. As you can see, we will also be in need of certain padding. This present method of taping down her breasts is not a good one—any sudden lurch, as you have seen, can set them free. I would prefer you to construct pads to add breadth to my lady's shoulders, and a padded corselet of some type that will be comfortable to wear that will give her a figure that tapers boyishly from shoulder to hip. Can you do it?"

"Aye." The tailor's round-eyed gaze was still fixed on Rosamunde in fascination. "But I must know the lady's true measurements first, and 'twould be better if I did make the padding first and be sure of a comfortable fit

178

and then measure for doublet and cloak when she is wearing them. Although," he added thoughtfully, "I could take the measurements for the trousers now, allowing only for a little play for padding at the waist, since we will need no padding about the hips."

"No, we will need no padding there," agreed Harry wryly. "We will leave you for a moment, Rose, while you unburden yourself of that makeshift contraption you have wrapped around yourself."

They went out into the hallway and closed the door. Rosamunde quickly freed her lissome figure from the restraining wrappings—indeed, she was very tired of them. When she had slipped again into her rough country shirt, she called that she was ready and greeted them with a dazzling smile.

The tailor blinked. Confronted by the full splendor of Rosamunde's delightful figure, his practiced measuring eye noting how suddenly tiny "Robbie's" waist had become, how dainty her shoulders, how outthrusting her firm young breasts, he seemed content to stand and stare at her.

Harry gave him a sardonic look and proceeded to take the measurements. Rosamunde was covered with blushes and very conscious of Harry's hands, deftly measuring her in intimate places while the young tailor watched.

She was very relieved when the ordeal was over, but shocked when Harry abruptly pulled out two gold pieces, for it seemed to her the tailor was already asking a fortune for outfitting her.

"Ye might say these gold pieces are payment for your having discovered my lady's secret," Harry said slowly, "and for keeping it—for even the bootmaker did not guess."

At the sight of yellow gold, the tailor's eyes lit up greedily. "The bootmaker did remark her dainty foot and ankle," he declared in an eager voice, reaching out for the coins.

Harry dropped the coins into the tailor's hand and then seized the little man's wrist in a numbing grasp. "Ye'll not discuss her with him," he said softly. "Ye'll
179

keep my lady's secret and ye'll say nothing *ever* about this to anyone. Else I'll cut your throat for you," he added pleasantly.

The little tailor swallowed, and his pink face lost some of its color. "Never will I speak of it," he declared in a choked voice. "*Never!*" And fled, clutching the coins in trembling fingers.

"Do you think you can trust him? Do you think you can trust any of them?" wondered Rosamunde after he had gone.

Harry shrugged, but his face was bleak. "Who knows? It should be enough, if the price on my head is not raised."

Rosamunde shivered and turned away, staring out the window at the low ivy-covered stone wall below. For a moment she had forgotten that Harry's head had a price on it.

But when the tailor returned for fittings of the padding she was to wear beneath her clothes, he assured her earnestly in his high chirping voice that never would he have revealed her secret in any event. His cheeks pinked brightly as he added gallantly that to know such a beautiful lady was its own reward.

"He is enamored of you, Rose," Harry said dryly after the tailor had left. "So I think you need have no fear of him."

She need have no fear, but perhaps Harry might. . . . It was suddenly borne in on Rosamunde that her beauty might be a two-edged sword, for a man who wanted her might well see Harry as standing in his way, and betray him not only for gold but in the hope of replacing him in her affections.

"Why so sad, Rose?" Harry tilted up her chin and looked down into her eyes. "Did I not just tell you there was nothing to fear?"

"I am not sad." She faltered. "I was thinking how much I love you." Her arms went around him and tightened, holding him with all the force she possessed. "Oh, Harry, hold me!"

Harry laughed and caressed her fair hair. "Faith, I'll find occasion to reassure you again—if this is your response," he said, his eyes glinting, and picked her up and lightly carried her over to the big bed.

"We'll be late for supper," Rosamunde gasped, knowing well his intentions.

Harry laid her down and gently pulled back her shirt to plant a kiss on one pink nipple that trembled beneath this pleasant assault. "Mistress Revers will guess why we're a bit late and be all smiles, you'll see. I'm thinking her John isn't enough for her these days. Did you see how she dimpled at the young tailor? Had he not been so besotted over you he'd have been hard put to escape her!"

"Harry, you're a very devil." Rosamunde laughed, sinking back into the deep feather mattress and letting it envelop her, even as Harry's big body now descending upon her seemed to envelop her. She forgot her fears and gave herself up to the sweetness of the moment, to delights of the senses, and a love that would be with her to the end of time.

"You'll see I'm right," he muttered as they hurried downstairs, still a bit disheveled from their romp.

Rosamunde restrained a giggle and kept a straight face as she met Mistress Revers' smile of approval and conspiratorial wink.

"I said they'd be right down, John, didn't I now?" asked Mistress Revers of her husband. "No need to call them, didn't I say that?"

Bleary-eyed John grunted and bent his head to mumble grace, then fell upon his food as if famished while Mistress Revers kept up a running conversation with Harry. She eyed him roguishly and laughed so exuberantly that her heavy bosom bounced, and altogether was so lively that Rosamunde would have been amused had not her somber thoughts returned.

But even though her body felt lazily content, even though she still basked in the warm afterglow of Harry's love, Rosamunde's green eyes were shadowed as she picked at the plump pheasant and pease that had been set before her. She had just discovered one of the prices she must pay for accompanying her highwayman on the road: of those who learned her secret, she must let no man

181

become too enamored of her. Else the price of her haunting beauty might be a noose tightening around Harry's neck.

12   *Harry and Rosamunde lingered for a few days in* the cottage, enjoying Mistress Revers' good cooking, and long lazy afternoons of playful lovemaking in the big feather bed in the guest room. Sometimes in the mornings Rosamunde left Harry asleep upstairs and wandered downstairs to share a cup of morning chocolate with Mistress Revers. Looking around her, she never failed to be amazed, for scattered throughout the cottage—which looked so cozily ordinary from the outside—were objects of value. The table was always covered with fine linen for supper, and with a Turkey carpet when not in use, and the plate was all heavy silver of the finest craftsmanship.

"Do your neighbors not wonder how you come by all this?" wondered Rosamunde one morning, turning impulsively to her plump hostess.

Mistress Revers shrugged complacently. "I tell them 'tis all from my son, who is a planter in Barbados. 'Tis well-known he sends me money."

"Then he does prosper in Barbados?"

Mistress Revers looked surprised. "I know not if he prospers or not, nor yet if he is in Barbados. I have not heard from him for seven years, so he may well be dead. But I made arrangements with a friend in Southampton to post me letters from time to time, and all believe they come from Barbados and contain money." She laughed and took another sip of her chocolate.

Mistress Revers did indeed have a talent for the aura

of respectability, thought Rosamunde wryly, but she smiled at her hostess and looked out through the cottage window into the fall sunshine.

The Colonies, she thought dreamily. Now *there* was a place where a man and a woman could go—whatever they'd been in England—and make a new life for themselves.

But when from the depths of the feather bed she mentioned this to Harry, he told her that the American continent was a raw land full of savages, while Barbados survived precariously "in a Spanish sea."

Rosamunde was rebuffed but thoughtful. There had to be *some* way out for them.

Meantime they lingered on in the cottage, loathe to go, and Rosamunde did indeed borrow a chemise from Mistress Revers, and a pretty homespun dress too. It was good to be in skirts again, and she wore them blithely about the cottage. There were no visitors, for Mistress Revers had spread it about the neighborhood that her visiting cousins were fresh off the ship from Brussels and were "down of a mild distemper." Since it was rumored that there was plague in Brussels, the neighbors gave the cottage a wide berth. Harry and Rosamunde joked about this ruse, but they were glad, for it made their stay in Winchester doubly safe. And it was a relaxed time for them, lounging about in their room sipping good smuggled wine, playing hide and seek with smothered laughter in the big enveloping feather bed in which they sank down and down and down while it closed suffocatingly over their heads.

Rosamunde was almost sorry when her new clothes were delivered, for it meant that they would soon be leaving. But when Harry told her they could have rented a villa in France for a season for less, she realized unhappily that they could not afford to stay longer. Would it always be thus, she asked herself, paying exorbitant prices for things others bought cheaply? There was more than one price to be paid for a "carefree" life on the road. But her new clothes! The luscious suit of green velvet, the flowing cloak, the lustrous handmade boots, fashion-

183

ably wide at the top to display lace-point boothose, the leathern gauntlets stitched in green, and the white shirt of fine linen trimmed in a froth of Alençon lace. Happy and excited, she rushed upstairs to try them on, and Harry turned a chair about and sat down, leaning his arms on the wooden back, to watch.

She was still fascinated by the new padded undergarment the tailor had designed for her. It was indeed ingenious, the shoulder pads fitting tightly like sleeves over her arms and the garment ducking under her lightly bound breasts and coming up flush against them to taper down—with only slight padding about the waist to give her freedom of movement—to the hips. It was far better than the padding she had contrived!

Harry watched with an expression she could not fathom as she donned her new clothes. The shirt was so lovely, of fine white linen, daintily stitched, that she pressed it against her face before putting it on. She exclaimed with delight at the long-sleeved forest-green velvet doublet, tight-fitting and small-waisted—though not so small as *hers* had been before the padding!—with its points and the deeply pointed overlapping flaps that formed a short "skirt" over her full-cut green velvet breeches that reached fashionably to just above the knee, where they were decorated with rosettes of lighter-green satin ribbon. Wide shoulder pieces of the same forest-green velvet curved around the armholes and rested lightly upon the padding the tailor had contrived for her shoulders. Both front and back of the doublet were slashed to reveal a green satin lining that matched the rosettes at waist and knee.

"The rosettes will all come off," said Harry in an expressionless voice. "And can swiftly be replaced with yellow ones—a set of which the tailor has supplied us. The trousers too are reversible—notice the thin black canvas lining beneath. If necessary, you could change the color of your rosettes, reverse your trousers and cloak, and you would be wearing black—not green."

"But the doublet—it is not reversible."

"If the chase grows hot enough," said Harry grimly, "you could throw your doublet away."

She protested at that, fingering the lustrous material. "But it is so beautiful!"

"*Life* is even more beautiful," said Harry. "And to enjoy it, one must keep one's head from the noose."

She caught her breath at that, for he had reminded her of what she had all but forgotten, that these new clothes were, after all, a *disguise*.

Still, she could not help exclaiming over the green silk stockings, the handsome new wide-top boots and white linen boothose edged with lace points.

Harry forebore telling her that in a pinch those lace points would have to be discarded too.

At last in her new green velvet suit, booted, lace over-flowing her cuffs and spilling out in a misty froth to conceal her white throat, she stood before him and struck an insolent boyish pose. Green eyes sparkling, her lovely face flushed with pleasure, she preened before a frowning Harry, who circled about her, inspecting her as if she were a horse he was considering buying.

"You see?" she said proudly, turning about so that the overlapping velvet flaps about her hips swung a little. "None would guess that I am not a man. I can ride beside you as—as your younger brother."

Harry hid a smile. Garbed so, she looked indeed like a slight and reckless youth, and her costume lent her a boyish charm. But to Harry, who knew so intimately each curve of her lovely body, she gave herself away a thousandfold with every graceful movement.

"Come," she wheedled. "You'll not say I'm not a fair lad?"

"Nay, Rose, I don't say that." He studied her, a slight frown upon his dark face. "It could be I know ye too well—and for that reason feel that others can see through your disguise as easily as I do. Come, we'll test it. Our host tells me of a coach that arrived from Basingstoke yesterday. The driver was filled with tales of a highwayman who fell upon them. The job had all the earmarks of a friend of mine. If 'twas Will—he's called Wily Will in the trade—he has a favorite haunt, and he'll be holed up at the Hound and Kettle snug as a rug by now."

"The Hound and Kettle?"

"Yes. 'Tis a safe inn halfway to Basingstoke. Come, pack your things and I'll settle up with our hosts. Will has keen eyes. We'll try your disguise on him."

For all her brave words, Rosamunde's heart pounded a bit faster as she rode north beside Harry down a maze of country lanes through the lovely Hampshire countryside. They passed sparkling trout streams and fat cattle and rode boldly through sleepy little hamlets that lazed in the sun. It was night when they skirted some tall hedgerows and found a small isolated inn that bore the painted likeness of a hound and kettle on a board outside.

"Now," said Harry, dismounting and tossing Nightwind's reins over a hitching post. "We'll see if other eyes can winnow you out as easily as mine."

Too proud to show she was daunted, Rosamunde followed him to the low wooden doorway, went through it with a slight swagger she hoped was masculine. The candles in the room flickered wildly at the sudden draft, and all inside promptly swung around to see who was coming through that door. She saw there were kegs for tables and rude benches for seats in the common room, and the candlelight gleamed on polished pewter tankards—all of which were held immovable as the dozen men in the room surveyed the newcomers with hard eyes. Coolly Rosamunde's green gaze flicked over them—a hardbitten crew, as they had been at that other highwaymen's inn.

Harry nodded to the company, and one or two, showing a flicker of interest, nodded back. He turned to the landlord, who had bustled over.

"Is Will about?" he asked in a low voice.

"Upstairs." The landlord grunted. "He took a ball in the leg, and after the barber-surgeon cut it out, he preferred to lie abed and rest it for a spell. Room to your right."

"My young friend and I will dine upstairs with him then," said Harry. Ignoring Rosamunde, he tramped up the wooden stairs, leaving her to trail along after. She kept her head high and tried to swing her shoulders purposefully as Harry did, for there was curiosity in the eyes of that cutthroat pack below.

"You passed that test. Now we'll see if you pass this one," Harry muttered under his breath as they reached the top of the stairs and he knocked on a door.

"Who is it?" called a deep voice.

" 'Tis Harry, Will."

There was a limping sound on the other side of the door, the latch was lifted and the door swung inward to admit them.

"Harry, old friend!" A tall gaunt man, leaning heavily on a sheathed sword as if it were a cane, clapped Harry on the shoulder. "And who is this?" His gaze fixed on Rosamunde, who lounged nonchalantly into the room after Harry.

"Robbie." Harry turned to her. "This is Wily Will, and you'll be well advised to listen when he speaks."

"Robbie" inclined her head toward Will. "Your servant, sir," she said in as deep a voice as she could muster.

"Robbie." Will acknowledged the greeting. He latched the door again, limped back to his bed and got into it. His long craggy face was deeply scarred, she saw, and he looked puzzled. "It cannot be, Harry, that after all these years of riding alone ye've taken a partner?"

"Aye, Will, I've come to that." Harry straddled a chair, leaned his arms upon the back. Rosamunde, used to having chairs pulled up for her, remembered she was now a "boy" and quickly sat down. Harry's cold eyes turned to regard her. "It would seem I've grown old and need a staunch fellow at my back." There was an irony in his tone as he said this that brought a slight flush to Rosamunde's cheeks.

"A staunch fellow at your back," murmured Will, with lifted brows. "Faith, he's a pretty lad, Harry," he observed, eyeing Rosamunde. "And have ye been on the road long, young sir?"

Rosamunde looked to Harry for help—and found none. She rather thought he might be enjoying her discomfiture. "Nay, I'm but a raw beginner," she admitted hastily in

187

her throaty voice that could have been a lad's. "But I'm eager to learn."

"Ye've a soft voice, too," remarked Will. " 'Twill no doubt soothe the ladies as ye relieve them of their pearls!"

Rosamunde rose, twirled her chair around and straddled it jauntily in imitation of Harry. One boot swung idly. She did not feel that remark required an answer.

"Harry here won't rob a woman," said Will. "Did ye know that, Robbie?"

She hadn't known that, but it warmed her to hear it.

"I've no such compunction," she declared coolly. "All purses are the same to me. 'Tis the gold inside that counts."

"Can ye shoot?" asked Will, fascinated.

Rosamunde nodded.

"And ride?"

That she could! "I'll match my riding against any man," she declared ringingly.

"And handle a sword?"

"That not so well," she admitted.

Will turned to Harry. "I'm intrigued," he said slowly. "There must be more to this you have not told me."

Harry shrugged and turned his head at a knock on the door.

"Supper, gentlemen," called a rollicking female voice.

Harry unlatched the door, and trenchers of bread and meat were brought in for the newcomers, a great tart and large tankards of ale. All were set upon a wooden table dragged from a corner by a plump flirtatious serving girl who postured and giggled and shook her dark hair until Rosamunde was filled with disgust. The girl was obviously trying to entice Harry as well as Will. In sudden horror she realized that the girl was eyeing *her* as well. It was a relief when Will gave the girl's bottom a pinch and she gave a shouting laugh and left with a saucy flirt of her yellow petticoat.

Rosamunde, preoccupied with her irritation with the wench, realized tardily that Harry had already drawn up his chair to the table beside Will's bed. In haste she

188

joined him, and bent her head to her meat, hoping to escape notice.

"She's a hot wench, that Tillie," Will was saying.

"The girl who brought our supper? Ye've bedded her then?"

"Aye. A willing wench. She had eyes for you, Harry."

Rosamunde stiffened. She looked up over her meat to find Harry's gaze fixed on her pleasantly.

"I like my wenches a bit leaner," he murmured.

"Perhaps Robbie here would like to bed her then," suggested Will hopefully. " 'Twas plain Tillie had eyes for ye both."

Rosamunde choked.

Harry leaned over and patted her on the back in kindly fashion. "Ye eat too fast, Robbie," he chided. "Don't gulp your bread like that."

Rosamunde stifled a wild desire to protest. Plainly Harry was enjoying this. "She's—too fat for me also," she gasped.

Will sighed. "A bit buxom Tillie may be, but she's much to commend her," he insisted. "Being astride her is like being in a rocking chair."

Rosamunde's face was growing red. She looked quickly down at her plate.

"Reminds me of that barmaid—Nell, her name was. You remember her, Harry, at the old Hare and Hound outside Winchester?"

Rosamunde stiffened slightly. The Hare and Hound! That had been the name of that first inn to which Harry had taken her—and Nell was the name of the red-headed barmaid who'd been so obviously in love with Harry. She'd accused Harry of having Nell for a mistress. Old rocking chair indeed! She listened indignantly, unable to swallow, as Will rambled on.

"She bites your ear the same as Nell did and leaves clawmarks down your back—just like Nell. Ah, Nell." He sighed pensively. "She was mine before she was yours, Harry—and she'd be mine yet had she not decided she liked you better. Have ye seen her lately, Harry?"

189

"Not lately," said Harry in a very steady voice. He was looking at Rosamunde with some unease.

"Well, I saw her," said Will. "When I was down Winchester way a month ago."

"Is she still living with Dick Brue?" asked Harry absently.

"Off and on. When Dick's away she sleeps with a few old friends. I tell you, it was like old times bedding the lass again. She clawed me up proper!" Will smiled at the memory and took a deep draft of ale. "I asked her what it was about your style, Harry, that made her prefer you to me, and she said—"

Rosamunde would have liked to hear what it was about Harry's "style" that red-haired Nell preferred, but at the sound of hoofbeats below Harry interrupted. "Take a look out the window, Robbie," he said carelessly. "See what's about."

Knowing full well that Harry was trying to divert Will from this conversation about Nell, Rosamunde went to the window and stuck her head out. Behind her, Harry adroitly turned the conversation to other things.

So red-haired Nell *had* been his mistress! Ah, she'd thought so. She was glad to be sticking her head out the window, for indeed she felt the need of air to cool her anger. She gulped in large amounts of it, reminded herself grimly that this encounter with Will was a test she must pass and peered out into the night.

" 'Tis a lone rider on a white horse," she reported, remembering to make her voice throaty.

Harry joined her at the window. " 'Tis only John Dawes," he said.

From the bed Will was looking puzzled. "There is something about the way the youth moves that intrigues me," he murmured, and subsided, munching the great tart. For a while they ate in silence.

Then Tillie came up to clear the plates away. She gave Harry a bold wink, left and came back with a metal tub into which she poured hot water from a pitcher.

"I've ordered me a bath," said Will gloomily. "But
190

faith, with the way this wound pains me, I think I'll not take it. Either of ye are welcome to it. Robbie?"

Rosamunde flushed. "No, no," she said quickly. "I did but bathe this morning."

"Ah, let that not stop ye," said Will lazily. "Ye've been riding with Harry and he sets a hard pace. 'Twill relax ye and loosen your muscles a bit. Into the tub, Robbie."

Rosamunde shook her head, wondering why Harry did not move to save her from this. Her mind scurried about, seeking a way out.

"Thank you, no," she said politely. "Too much bathing can destroy the health," she added in a weak voice.

From the bed Will laughed. "I thought ye would not," he said slyly. "For ye be a wench, be ye not? And Harry here's a sly one passing ye off as a lad to an old friend like me!"

Harry sighed. "When did ye guess it, Will?"

Will pondered. "There's a sound to her voice that struck me at once—'twas too soft. And then the way her hips moved when she walked to the window. That and her lovely face. . . . What's your game with the wench, Harry? And what's her name?"

"Her name is Rosamunde," said Harry. "And she rides with me."

"Rosamunde," murmured Will, who in his youth had been taught Latin. "Rose of the World . . . the World's Rose. Ah, she's a wild rose indeed, Harry, but ride with ye? Never."

Harry sighed. "'Tis what I told her, Will, but she's stubborn."

"I fooled those men downstairs," said Rosamunde defiantly.

"Aye," agreed Will, nodding his head. "And most ye will fool. In your cloak, astride a horse perhaps. But not at close quarters—not for long."

"Nonetheless," said Harry calmly, "I have promised her she can ride with me, and I will keep my word."

"Ye'll die for it," predicted Will gloomily.

"Perhaps."

"But you could die from less attractive things, eh, Harry?" Will smote his knee and winced.

"I wanted you to know her, Will. We'll keep the secret of her sex as long as possible, though it will out eventually. But she might need a friend, and you're the best friend I've got."

Will's craggy face flushed with pleasure. "Ah, Harry, lad, a friend I've been to ye and will be to your lady. Faith, ye've ridden the roads too long alone. What say the three of us ride together?"

Harry looked relieved. "I was hoping ye'd suggest it, Will. Then should aught happen to either of us, the other could look after Rose here."

Will gave him a sharp look. "It's that way with you, is it?" he asked softly.

Harry nodded. "I fear it is, Will."

"Well, this is a mere knick in my leg that will soon be healed. Ye could stay here till I'm ready to ride and we'll go together."

Harry moved restively. "I've need of the yellow gold, Will."

"Ah, the shoe rubs, does it?"

Harry nodded, his face somber. "I had some plate, but Rose and I spent it lying over in Winchester. Think you you could look after my Rose for a night or two, Will? I'd take it as a kindness."

Rosamunde looked up sharply. He was leaving her?

"I thought she could sleep behind yon false wall," said Harry, and Rosamunde turned to stare at the wall. To show her, he went over and worked at a cupboard, which slid out, making a narrow opening. Wonderingly, she snatched up a candle and followed him inside, found there a decent pallet. The room, while hardly the size of a big closet, was aired by open chinks beneath the eaves. " 'Tis where we hide sometimes when the inn is searched," explained Harry to her questioning look. He turned to Will. "I'd kill the man who touched her," he said quietly. "So guard her well for me, Will."

Will's leathery countenance split into a grin. "Ah, I'd not poach on your territory, Harry, boy!"

192

" 'Twas not our agreement," insisted Rosamunde hotly, coming out of the "cupboard." "You promised me I'd ride with you, Harry."

"And so ye shall. But ye need seasoning, Rose. 'Twill be safer for you to learn with Will riding beside us." And to her rebellious look, he smiled whimsically. "Are ye bent on getting me killed, lass? For I'd have one eye out for you all the time and well might take a bullet for my inattention!"

She subsided at that.

"The inn's full," said Will. "So there'll be no remarking that the lad shares my room. And who's to know that she sleeps behind the wall?"

Harry nodded soberly. "That was my thought." He gave Rosamunde a yearning look which Will caught.

Will cleared his throat. "Though the inn be full, there's no reason to start out with a tired horse tonight, Harry, nor yet to sleep on a bench in the common room. I could stretch out my leg on yon pallet beyond the wall, while you and your lady share this bed."

Harry gave him a grateful look, and Rosamunde, touched by Will's generosity in the face of his injury, went in to plump up the pallet and make the little room as comfortable as she could while Harry went downstairs to make his arrangements with the landlord.

When he came back, Will was safely ensconced behind the wall and the cupboard door was innocently closed. It looked like any other cupboard.

By the light of the single candle Rosamunde undressed. She heaved a great sigh as she flung the hot padding that had given her a deep chest and wide shoulders from her, and signed again with relief as her bound-down breasts burst free. Harry's eyes lit at sight of them. Fond as a caress, his gaze traced the softly outthrusting mounds of her ripe young breasts, gleaming with perspiration in the heat, the gentle inward curve of her narrow waist.

He took an impulsive step toward her, and she stepped rapidly back, snatching up the chemise which she had carried wrapped across her stomach as extra padding. She gave him a defiant look and slipped into it—she'd

193

masqueraded as a boy long enough; it was a woman in skirts he'd bed tonight!

Harry's eyebrows elevated. "Faith, here's an unusual modesty," he murmured, amused, and turned to pour himself another tankard of wine from the bottle the serving girl had left.

Rosamunde ignored his levity. She let down her hair and ran her fingers through it. It poured like molten gold through her fingers in the candlelight. She was conscious of Harry's approving gaze.

"Will you be gone long?" she sighed, gracefully smoothing the chemise about her hips and sitting down on the edge of the bed.

"I'll be gone only long enough to get us money to live on until Will is able to ride," Harry assured her.

She leaned forward, and the leaping lamplight flowed along her bosom, touched the pearly tops of her young breasts. Harry wondered if she knew how the sight tempted him.

"Could we not have borrowed something from Will?" she whispered.

Harry frowned. "Had Will had it, he'd have offered." He downed his wine. "Will is my oldest friend. What I know of the road, he taught me. When I was a green young lad and very like to get myself killed."

"But—I thought we had plenty of money when you sold the plate!" she said plaintively.

"You are learning the real truths of the road now, Rose," he said in a sober voice, coming to stand over her. "Our money is soon gone, because a highwayman pays double, triple, for everything. The extra gold buys silence. 'Tis part of the price of being on the run."

She looked up at him, saw his bleak look, and realized that her dreams of taking a purse here or there and living on its contents for a long time were but smoke. The need for money and more money drove these men—drove them oftentimes to their death.

"I'll find us enough coin, Rose," Harry assured her, misunderstanding her concern. "We'll not starve."

Rosamunde flushed and bent her head, biting her lips.

194

The money he had got from the cache of plate he had spent on *her*—to outfit her like a fine young gentleman. She swore to herself she would break into the national treasury itself if necessary, to meet her bills. She would not have Harry risking his life for her like this!

"Come, Rose," he murmured, catching her rebellious look. "Ye asked to ride with me, and I consented, but I cannot change the world. We must take it as we find it."

She had to be content with that, but in a sudden burst of affection for him, she seized his hand and pressed it against her breast.

"I fear for you," she whispered.

"Rose." Harry's voice softened, and he cupped her breast in his warm hand and pressed a kiss onto the top of her golden head. He would have done more, but she pulled away. Throwing back the covers, she slid into the big enveloping bed and lay there and stretched. She smiled up at Harry. The candlelight caught her eyes, and they glimmered green at him with golden lights. Harry thought her the most beautiful sight in the world lying there, and the thought of taking her out and subjecting her to the dangers and hardships of the highway tore at his heart. Impatiently he tugged off his clothes, leaving a loaded pistol lying ready at the bedside in case of trouble. The door was latched, but a good kick might burst it open—in his trade one had to be ready for anything.

With a smile at the beauty on the bed, he blew out the candle and joined her, sinking deep with her into the drifting softness of the feather mattress. Her body seemed silken fire beside him as he raised himself on an elbow and smiled down at her. A white moon slanted in through the small-paned window set in the thick stone wall, and cast its pale-white light over her challenging upturned face and the great golden sweep of her carelessly tossed hair. That same moon glinted in Harry's gray eyes as he looked down at her. Rosamunde looked up into his dark face, so unmasked now and eager as a boy's and her breath caught in her throat for wanting him. Desire flowed between them like a river, and he bent his dark head to press a kiss upon her ardent lips, to thrust between them

195

with a probing tongue as they parted and she strained toward him. Big he seemed, and sturdy as the old trees of Sherwood Forest, as he gathered her to him. But while his body seemed hard as their trunks and his sinewy arms as strong as their branches, his touch was as silken as their shimmering leaves blowing in the summer wind. Gently his loving fingers traced down her body, leaving a trail of fire from shoulder to hip.

"Ye've no need of this, Rose," he murmured, seeking to relieve her of her chemise.

"Harry," she protested in an embarrassed whisper, for she was aware that through that false wall Will might be able to hear them "What if—what if somebody should knock on the door?"

"Why, then they'll wait till you dress," he said in a firm voice, and as firmly set about undressing her. She lay trembling as he tossed the offending chemise to the back of a chair.

"That's better." He clasped the sweet yielding length of her to his own naked body. Her body shivered with its own thrill at the contact with his hard muscular form, and she let herself relax in the big feather bed and lay back with a sigh of content as he swept a sinewy arm beneath her. His dark head rose above her, a dark shadow against the moon.

"Harry," she murmured. "Oh, Harry, I love you so."

His lips shut off her words, but the tenderness of his caress was its own answer. He had no need to say it—she *felt* his love for her in every loving gesture as he nuzzled her breasts till they tingled wildly and the nipples firmed to hardness beneath his touch, she felt his *need* for her as he stroked the satiny skin of her stomach and thighs and that golden-haired space between. Tantalizingly, lingeringly, his manly touch brought her yearning to flower. And when she was moaning softly in his arms, aflame with desire for him, he made a swift silken entrance that lifted her to the heights, fanning her passions with exquisite skill with every sure caressing movement.

"Sweet Rose," he murmured tenderly against her hair. And then more deeply, with a vibrant timbre, "My Rose."

With a caught breath, Rosamunde pressed her face into Harry's shoulder, dug her fingers into his muscled back and savored the beauty of those words and of this moment. *My Rose*. Ah, she was content to be his. Never would she desire more than this: to spend eternity—yes, a thousand eternities—here in his arms.

"Never leave me," she murmured, soft against his ear.

As if in answer, Harry's grip tightened convulsively, robbing her of breath. She clung to him, and their hot ignited passions flared up as one, making their bodies glow and tremble. The night seemed filled with magic as the ship of love on which they had embarked sought distant shores and faraway white beaches where night winds murmured of desire and the air was soft and perfumed. Clinging together in the stormy sea of their own emotions, their passion rose and fell in gusts, rippled tinglingly and towered into great waves that swept them irresistibly shoreward and crested at last into fulfillment in a moon-washed tide. The broken endearments Rosamunde whispered against Harry's dark cheek, the soft words of love he spoke to her, all were a part of the night and the moon-swept magic that washed them ashore in crashing fulfillment and left them limp and exhausted and content.

With her golden head nestled against the crook of Harry's arm, her hip touching his warm body, Rosamunde drifted off to dreamless sleep.

13   *Rosamunde woke groggily in the early-morning* light. Something had waked her, perhaps some clatter of pots and pans from the scullery below. Instinctively her arm reached out for Harry—and found him gone. She sat up, her gaze flying to the place where his weathered wide-topped leathern boots had stood the night before.

They too were gone.

Rosamunde sank back in the feather bed with a little shiver, despite the fact that the morning had dawned warm and gave promise of a sultry day. He had stolen away before cockcrow—without telling her goodbye. A great desolation seized her—and fear, too. For who knew against what odds Harry rode today? Hard Harry was known throughout England for his recklessness as well as his gallantry. She gave a swift earnest prayer to keep him safe and threw back the covers, dressed swiftly and struggled to open the cupboard doorway to Will's hiding-place.

Will himself put a shoulder to the cupboard on the other side of the wall and helped her. She heard his grunt as it came open.

" 'Tis a bit warped from the dampness lately," he commented, and then with a look at the striking lad Rosamunde's costume had made of her, he asked slyly, "Didst sleep well, Robbie, lad?"

Rosamunde flushed. "We are beholden to you for the loan of your room, Will."

Will grinned at her and hobbled forward. " 'Tis no more than Harry would do for me in like circumstances," he stated airily. But he seemed relieved when he reached the big bed and got into it with a sigh. Rosamunde guessed his cramped quarters had caused him some discomfort and offered eagerly to bring his breakfast herself. Will shook his head and patted the pistol that lay beneath the covers beside him.

"I'm in no condition to do running battle for you, lass," he sighed. "Please to stay near me until Harry's safe return. I'd like to hand you over to him in mint condition."

A knock on the door signaled breakfast, and over hot buttered buns and stewed apples and plump partridge, Rosamunde prodded Will about her principal interest—Harry.

"I guess ye could say I'm the next thing Harry's got to

a father," admitted Will. "When Harry took to the highways he was but a slight lad, unaccustomed to hardship. I took him under my wing, I did, and taught him the ways of the road. Ah, and what a pupil he's been!" He shook his head in admiration and then sighed. "Harry always preferred to work alone—as did I until lately. Perhaps 'tis the loneliness that disturbs me . . . perhaps 'tis the want of a lass like yourself to come back to. Even if I avoid the hangman's noose, someday I'll be cut down on the highway and they'll mount my head on the city gates. And what will it all have been for? I ask myself." He looked gloomy.

Rosamunde took the heavy trencher from Will's lap and piled it with her own outside the door. "Have you no wife then?" she ventured, tossing the remark over her shoulder as she latched the door.

"Wife? In my profession?" Will laughed shortly. "I had a wife once . . . but as to where she is today, I'd not be knowing. She spent all my money and ran off with a carter in the district, and no one's seen or heard from her since." There was an undertone of hurt in his gruff voice, and Rosamunde felt sorry for him. From the pride in his tone as he spoke of Harry, she guessed that Harry was the son Will had never had, and she warmed to the older man, lying gaunt in the big feather bed. "What of yourself?" Will asked sharply. "It must have been a hard decision for a gently bred lass like yourself to take to the road."

"I love him, Will," she said simply.

Will nodded and his face was sad. "Aye, Harry inspires love in his women. I never did. . . . "

She wondered if he was thinking of Nell, and was sorry for him—and somehow disturbed too, for red-haired Nell had once claimed Harry as her own, and on the road they well might meet her again. She hoped that for Harry at least the passion for Nell had burned out.

"Look not so pensive, lass. How did you and Harry meet?"

In terse sentences she told him her story. Will was silent for a while. Then, "So ye're as lost as we are," he said musingly. "I came from a good home myself and was

199

educated for the clergy. But the cloth sat not so well on me, and I fought a duel with the young squire over a farmer's daughter. It turned out she would not have me, and ran away with a tinker, but the young squire died of the wounds I gave him, my father turned his back on me—I'd no mind to rot in prison or swing from the gibbet, for it had been a fair fight. So I left at a gallop with no money, naught but the clothes I had on—and I've been on the road ever since. Ah well." He shrugged. "Life's an entertainment, they say, a repast. At least we sup at a better board than some."

With this cryptic remark, Will lay back and closed his eyes and left her to study his hard dissolute face and to wonder how Harry fared. Chafing at the inactivity, Rosamunde pulled off her boots and paced the floor barefoot, not to waken Will.

She found him a considerate host. When bathwater was brought, he ordered it left and hobbled back to the hiding place behind the cupboard. When buxom Tillie brought their supper and sidled over and nudged Will and slyly asked him if he or Robbie wouldn't like a bit of frivolity, Will gave her bottom a playful pinch.

"My wound pains me too much for wenching, Tillie. And Robbie here is mooning over a constable's daughter who'll like as not get him killed."

Tillie shrugged and left with a curious look at "Robbie." Rosamunde, who was sleeping in the small room behind the cupboard now, as Will considered it safer, while he slept in the big bed, guarding the entrance with his pistol, felt she was casting a blight over Will's social life.

"I can retire early," she offered. "So you and Tillie can . . . " She blushed uncomfortably.

"Nay, I've no coins left to give the lass." Will sighed. "We must both await Harry's return."

But buxom Tillie had no more than carried away their empty trenchers and tankards when there was a thunder of hooves down the road and downstairs the inn burst into activity.

"Look outside!" ordered Will, and Rosamunde, who had been sitting on the floor barefoot, learning to throw the dice according to Will's teaching, scrambled up and ran to the window.

Below in the summer dusk a body of men were surrounding the inn.

"Into the hidey-hole, lass," muttered Will. "And take your possessions with ye. The landlord will swear there's no one occupying this room."

"But my horse—Graylady!" Rosamunde had already snatched up her boots, grabbed her cloak and chemise from a chair, and tossed them all through the cupboard entrance Will had heaved open.

"The stableboy will have led some of the horses into the woods by now. For the rest, our landlord will claim he bought them at the Banbury fair." He grasped her arm as a shot rang out and there was a shout below.

"Wait!" Rosamunde pulled away and swiftly threw the coverlet over the bed, plumped up the pillow and ran to unlatch the door—it would be difficult for the landlord to explain how an unoccupied room was latched from the inside!

"Hurry," Will muttered, and she skittered across the room as boots pounded up the stairs. Between them, they pulled the cupboard closed and leaned against it tensely as the door of the room burst open and there was a shout: "There's no one in here! Search the other rooms!"

Rosamunde could feel the cold barrel of Will's pistol against her side. Her own pistol was ready in her hand, and her spine prickled as the heavy-footed search continued. She could hear the landlord's whine, the high keening rage of his slattern wife, and Tillie's indignant squawk, along with shouts, protests and surly talk. There was an overturning of kegs below, the crash of falling tankards, protesting creaks as cupboard doors were opened and peered into—and then suddenly the men departed as swiftly as they had come and hoofbeats thudded away into the night.

" 'Twas some tax collector was robbed upon the road," reported Tillie importantly when the men had gone and Rosamunde and Will had come out of their hiding place. " 'Twas he brought the constable's men down on us.

201

They're searching all the inns and taverns for miles around."

"And the highwayman?" asked Rosamunde, anxious for Harry.

"Got clean away." Tillie laughed. "Think you it could be Harry?"

"Not likely." Will shrugged. "He'd not lift a purse so close to his base."

"That be true," agreed Tillie. "Harry's not one to get a body into trouble who befriends him. But it did give us a scare. Slim Tom hid in the chimney, and he's downstairs cursing us all because he's all over soot. And Big Alf hid in the well—and the rope broke with his weight and they're still trying to get him out. He's down there hanging onto the bucket!"

Will laughed. "But none were taken?"

"Nay." Tillie shook her head. "I'd best go back downstairs. Such a mess the constable's men made! They overturned a keg of molasses, and everywhere you put your feet you stick to the floor!" She marched away.

"Do these things happen often?" wondered Rosamunde.

"Often enough," Will told her cheerfully. "I remember one time being surprised at an inn near Banbury when I was bouncing on the bed with—" He stopped, deeming the story unsuitable for her tender ears, but Rosamunde could well imagine his discomfiture if armed men interrupted his lovemaking.

On the third night Harry returned. He had jingling gold in his leather pouch and a reckless smile on his dark countenance. So silently had he approached the inn that none had heard him, but Rosamunde had looked up alertly at the sound of his step on the stair. She was ready to unlatch the door at the sound of his voice and swung the door wide to let him in. He came into the room with a swinging stride, and his light eyes danced as they fell on Rosamunde. He kicked the door shut and swung her up in his arms to give her a quick hug.

"Ye'd best latch the door, Harry," said Will from the bed.

Harry set Rosamunde down and latched the door. "Ye were ever cautious, Will." He grinned.

"From the look of ye, ye've been lucky," observed Will softly. "I was wishing ye'd find a bishop, Harry—churchmen are the best kind, they always carry money."

"Nay, 'twas a tax collector I chanced upon." Harry laughed. "As ye know, they're my favorites!"

"A tax collector?" cried Rosamunde. "But that's why they searched the inn last night—some tax collector had been robbed!"

Harry frowned at her. "But I led them eastward! I near wore out Nightwind setting them a merry chase." He turned to Will. "Why would they come here? Could it be they've wind where I'm staying?"

"Nay, they were searching everywhere, Harry," Will told him. " 'Twas the constable's men came here. They made but a cursory search and hurried on."

"Nonetheless, I like it not."

"Did ye make a rich haul then?"

"Nay, he'd not much gold as yet, but he had not much guard either—'twas an easy haul. But from the way he clung to it, I doubt it would ever have reached the treasury." He held up a pouch. " 'Tis enough to keep us all till ye're well healed, Will."

Will gave him back a wry look. "So ye guessed the state of my finances, did ye, Harry?"

Harry nodded. "When they told me ye'd tried to take a well-guarded coach alone, I figured you were desperate for money. And when I heard ye were shot and barely escaped with your hide, I guessed ye'd gotten none for your pains."

"That's the way of it. I'll pay ye back, Harry—once we're on the road again."

Harry nodded, but his eyes were all for Rosamunde. She blushed beneath the pressure of his hot gaze.

Will coughed. "I've need of some companionship other than a pair of calf-eyed lovers. Could you lend me a few coins and help me down into the common room, Harry? I'll see if I can win Tillie away from Big Alf—he was near drowned in the well hiding from the constable's men, and

I don't doubt me Tillie's been comforting him, for she always had an eye for him."

"Rest where you are, Will," said Harry absently, smiling at Rosamunde, who struck a challenging boyish pose and tossed her head airily. "The inn's near empty now, and I've taken a room for Rose and myself across the hall. I'll let Tillie know ye're fit again and seeking female companionship."

"Ye're a friend of the heart, Harry." Will sighed as Harry put a handful of coins on the table.

"Ye took care of Rose for me," Harry countered. "Come, Rose, see if ye like the room."

"It has no hidey-hole," Will reminded him. "If they search the inn again, come and join me behind the cupboard."

"Ye can count on it." Harry led the way across the hall and, looking for all the world like a slim young lad in her velvet doublet and boots, Rosamunde strolled along with him.

They went in—the room was almost identical with Will's but slightly smaller—and Harry latched the door behind them.

"I've missed you, Rose," he said huskily.

"And I you." She tried to keep the tremor out of her voice, but did not quite succeed.

"Ah, Rose, Rose." He took her face tenderly in both his big hands and smiled down at her. "You've a face that haunts my dreams. I wake to look for you in the crook of my arm and when you're not there it affrights me for a moment, thinking you've fled me."

Rosamunde wound both arms about his broad back and pressed her face against his doublet. "I'll not run away from you, Harry. More like," she added with asperity, "that you will run away from me!"

He laughed, holding her so close it interfered with her breathing. "If that's all you fear, then rest easy. I'd pursue you to hell, Rose. Ye'll ne'er escape me!"

Her thoughts swam happily and she hoped it was true, that she might never escape him, but spend her life wrapped in those strong sinewy arms. She looked up to
204

smile on Harry fondly as he swept her up and carried her over to the bed.

That room at the inn became their private heaven. They seldom left it during the next few days except to ride out and exercise their horses. Downstairs it was whispered that the fashionable young gentleman in green was Harry's younger brother and that Harry did not wish his brother "Robbie" to mingle with the likes of them. Black looks were cast at them as they came and went, but neither of them cared. They were young and in love, and once they left those walls and were on the road, each day might be their last. So they treasured their stolen moments and clung to them—breathlessly.

14   *Out they rode, the three of them, when Will was* well. Out across the wild byways to lie in wait at crossroads where travelers paused to make sure of their directions, and the tops of hills where horses drawing coaches must slow down to draw breath—and many were the rich purses that they shared.

But their first venture, the one in which Rosamunde was initiated into the trade, was unforgettable.

She wore a sword and baldric now—a light "dress" sword because Harry did not deem her strong enough to wield a heavy serviceable blade like his own. She guessed he was of the opinion that if it came to naked swordplay, he must rescue her or she would be lost. And although she practiced dutifully with him in a little woodland clearing near the inn, she was much of the same opinion herself. For although she was light of foot and skillful, Harry had the advantage of reach, and the very weight of his assault could drive her backward.

The guns were different. Harry bought her a brace of pistols from the landlord, who had had them from some other highwayman down on his luck. They were large for her hands to hold, but their aim was true, and she pleased Harry by proving the excellence of her marksmanship.

Pronounced ready by both Harry and Will, the three of them left the inn, telling the landlord they knew not whether they would be back or no. He nodded, for he was used to this sort of thing. Working highwaymen were often driven far afield, for they must needs kept ahead of their pursuers—sometimes those who rode out returned to the inn, sometimes not. Sometimes they never returned, for they were brought down by some musket ball or slash of a long sword, and their carcasses lay on the highway until hauled away in a cart, or were loaded over the back of a horse to be brought triumphantly into some market town and displayed. Some, of course, were taken alive and hanged; it was always an event of great public interest when a famous highwayman was hanged—people came from miles around, and the rogue himself made a short speech from the scaffold before the rope choked him off.

But Rosamunde's mind was not on the fate of highwaymen that day. She was blithe and excited as she and Harry and Will departed the inn, with Graylady stepping daintily between Nightwind and Will's big dappled gelding.

They journeyed some distance from the inn, lunched on apples and bread and cheese which they had brought along in their saddlebags, and washed it down with a bottle of wine that Will had thoughtfully provided. Then, having eaten, they stationed themselves on a low rise where, hidden by a stand of trees, they would have a long view of the road as it wound toward them through a long stretch of flower-strewn meadowland. Below them the road made a sharp turn as it skirted the low rise and passed beneath a bluff where there was a noisy waterfall and the road became rocky and wooded. There was noise from the water splashing over the rocks that anyone on that side would scarcely hear a commotion where they intended to take their prey.

Their plan was ingenious, for, the road being quite wide here until the sharp turn was reached, and relatively open, travelers would approach the turn without undue caution. And they had commandeered an old farm cart which was even now waiting just around that blind turn, for Will to push it into the road to block the way whenever Harry flashed his sword from the rise as a signal.

Atop the rise Harry and Rosamunde took turns watching the road for a likely target.

Harry was giving her final instructions:

"Understand me, Rose, if 'tis a coach, when I give the signal to Will, ye will ride in after me. Ye will keep out of my way lest ye be shot in a crossfire, but ye will keep your pistol leveled at the driver—at nobody else, the driver, do you hear? While Will and I relieve the passengers of their valuables. If 'tis another target, two horsemen or a litter perhaps—"

"Then I will take your instructions on the spot, as you told me." Rosamunde, who was leaning against a tree, nodded.

"And if—" Harry began, when his sharp eye spotted a movement far down the road. " 'Tis—yes, I think it is a coach." He squinted at the ribbon of road that led across the meadowland.

Rosamunde leaned forward and peered along with him. Horses were appearing now out of a cloud of dust. It was a coach.

"Remember what I said," Harry cautioned.

"I will remember," Rosamunde promised, checking her pistols as she prepared to mount Graylady.

"Wait—there is more than one coach." Harry's eyes were still trained on the road. "It is some sort of party, I believe, perhaps going to a wedding." His eyes narrowed, and she knew he was thinking there might be rich wedding gifts stowed aboard. He frowned and made his decision. "We'll take the last coach, Rose. They are far apart, so they do not scent danger. By the time the third coach rounds the turn below, the other two will have passed beyond the waterfall into the woods, and the ringing of their horses' hooves on the rocks and the rushing rapids and rustling leaves will cover any noise we make."

Again Rosamunde nodded. Her hands trembled a little as she tied a black kerchief around the lower part of her face—as she could see Harry was doing. And her heart was pounding in her chest. Although she was to play but a very small part in this operation—actually, she would only stand guard duty with her pistol trained on the driver and do Harry's bidding—she knew from the stories she had heard around the inn that much could go wrong with even the best-laid plans to seize a coach on the highway. It could spill out armed men, all with muskets at the ready, for instance.

She tensed as the first coach fled by them on the road below. The second coach was coming up fast, but the last was lagging far behind. Nervously she eased her mount a few steps farther down the slope so that she might be ready to sprint downward, and turned again to view the second coach.

It was painted yellow. She stiffened—*she knew that coach!* She knew the unusual lines of it and the matched black horses that drew it. It would have the Waverclay arms emblazoned on its side, and Lord Matthew Waverclay, if he still lived, should be inside it.

Rage blazed over Rosamunde at the memory of what she had suffered at Lord Matthew's hands. Her whole body quivered. *That* was the coach she wanted—and there was barely time!

"We will take the *second* coach!" she screamed at Harry. And even as she spoke she urged the gray mare on with her knee, and dragged her dress sword from its scabbard and flashed it in the sun for Will to see. Then she was off down the hill, careening through the trees at a dead run, bending low over Graylady's back to duck the low branches.

Harry, who had no reason to recognize Lord Matthew's coach, since he had never seen it before, thought her gone mad. He thought she must have cracked under the tension—as he had seen men do—and was hurling herself recklessly into danger. With a face gone suddenly ashen, he charged down the hill after her on his big black horse. Will, he knew, would have seen the signal of the flashing sword and would even now be dragging that long farm cart across the road to block the second coach's progress —but they would have two coaches now to deal with, for before they would be finished with this one, the next would be upon them. Before him, a flash of green velvet weaving through the trees, Rosamunde was flying into mortal danger—ah, the lass could get herself killed for her folly!

Cursing aloud, Harry thundered downhill after her and checked Nightwind so rapidly at the edge of the road that the horse reared up and, had he been less skillful a rider, would have unseated him. Before him he could see that Will had indeed done his duty. The farm cart solidly blocked the road, and Will himself, with drawn pistols and a handkerchief over half his face, waited astride the dappled gelding on the far side of the road. Rosamunde had sheathed her sword now and drawn her pistol. She was leaning forward tensely.

"Have ye taken leave of your senses?" Harry roared at her.

" 'Tis Lord Matthew's coach—I recognized it!" she cried impatiently over her shoulder.

Harry stiffened. Rosamunde had disobeyed his orders, and her folly might indeed cost them their lives, but— *Lord Matthew Waverclay!* For the life of him, he could not blame her.

Even as she spoke, the second coach was rounding the turn, and the shouting driver, seeing the road ahead of him blocked, began sawing desperately on the reins. The horses reared up, and the coach veered wildly on two wheels and shivered to a sickening halt.

"Hold the driver, Will!" cried Rosamunde, darting forward on Graylady. "For I've business with one of the passengers!"

Across the road, Will's eyes widened, but he kept his pistol aimed at the driver's head. The driver observed that and hastily dropped the reins and put up his hands.

Rosamunde, with Harry hot behind her, had reached

the coach door, and now she leaned over and wrenched it open, stuck a pistol inside.

"Out!" she shouted furiously. *"Out!"*

The occupants were still stunned by the violence with which the coach had been brought to a halt. Seen through the open coach door, they seemed but an unidentifiable jumble of periwigs knocked askew, and plumed hats smashed down, and gloved hands clawing desperately for purchase in a tangle of satin garments, as they tried to right themselves from the floor of the coach where they had landed.

But one shaky peach-gloved hand pushed back a plumed hat with a broken brim to reveal a tumble of fashionable black curls, and a woman's white face peered out.

"You will not hurt us?" she cried, flinching back from Rosamunde's pistol.

To her astonishment, Rosamunde saw that she was looking not at Lord Matthew, whom she had confidently expected, but into the wide horrified dark eyes of Louisa, wife to the earl of Kenwarren. And with Louisa, just now untangling themselves and trying to scramble up off the floor, were a satin-clad lady and a rotund gentleman in a plumed hat and pastel velvets.

"Out!" ordered Rosamunde in her newfound throaty voice. "Let me look at you."

The three occupants, with a shrinking Louisa in the lead, peered out uncertainly. Faced by this raging young highwayman brandishing a large pistol, they cringed back. But seeing another highwayman, much larger and more formidable, with hard gray eyes above his black kerchief, bestriding a black horse behind the first, they exchanged hopeless looks and tumbled out unceremoniously upon the road.

Louisa made the worst landing. Her foot encountered a stone, and she went down in an ignominious peach satin heap. "Reginald!" she cried in a voice of despair. "Do something—save us!"

The plumed gentleman gave her a wondering look. He made no rejoinder, but he was puffing as he helped peach-clad Louisa to her feet. She cowered against him, and his wife grasped his other arm. He tried to straighten up but he looked almost as alarmed as they did.

"Driver—off the coach. Come down!" cried Harry, for the other coach was fast thundering up. He forced passengers and driver to lie on their faces in the road—Rosamunde was delighted with that—and while she held a pistol on those prone figures, Harry and Will surged forward to take the next coach, which, even then, was swerving about in the road as its horrified driver tried to bring his horses to a halt before colliding with the coach ahead.

There were six passengers in this last coach, all servants. They had been jammed in like sardines, and they struggled out looking terrified. Now they stuck their arms in the air as stiff as pikes and waited, frozen, to see what would happen.

Harry promptly ordered them to join the group lying prone on the road.

"On your feet, sir." He turned abruptly to the rotund gentleman in the plumed hat.

This worthy struggled up after his second try to regain his feet. Fuming, he dusted off his mauve satin breeches and lavender silk stockings. "See here, sir!" he bellowed, red-faced. "I am Lord Reginald Paling and I resent this—this—" Words escaped him and he stood there mopping his face with a lace kerchief.

"I care not who you are," said Harry in a deadly tone. "But unless you choose to be the *late* Lord Reginald Paling, you will follow my instructions to the letter."

Lord Reginald paled and fell back a step.

"Do as he says, dear! Do as he says!" wailed his wife, lying flat on the road. She turned a frightened face up from her plumed hat as she scrabbled with creamy leather gloves in the dust of the roadway.

"You ladies need have no fear," said Harry sternly. He took angry Lord Reginald's purse and relieved him of a diamond stickpin that held the lace at his throat in shape, and a large gold watch with a heavy gold chain.

"*This* lady has reason to fear," said Rosamunde pleasantly. She had now dismounted and prodded Louisa's
211

prone rump with her foot. Louisa gave a little screech and groveled. "Stand up!" shouted Rosamunde. "What are you doing in Lord Matthew Waverclay's coach? Where is Lord Matthew?"

Spurred by this direct order, Louisa, trembling, gained her feet. It came to her that perhaps she was not the object of this young highwayman's rage—Lord Matthew was.

"He and my husband have ridden on ahead," she babbled. "Lord Matthew liked not the jolting of the coach, and he and the earl rode on ahead of us yesterday. We are all to a great party being held at Loseley House . . . "

She kept on talking, but Rosamunde was aware only of a dull disappointment that she could not take her revenge upon Lord Matthew's handsome body. But there was a pervasive feeling of relief as well: Harry had not killed Lord Matthew; at least they could not be charged with Lord Matthew's murder!

While Louisa babbled on, Harry and Will had swiftly checked the coach for valuables—and found none. The ladies' jewel boxes, if they had brought any along, must have gone ahead with the first coach, or were perhaps stuffed in the saddlebags of the servants attending the earl and Lord Matthew. Since Harry never robbed women and neither he nor Will would rob servants, who were poor men and could ill afford to lose the few coins they could garner, it was a poor haul indeed.

Rosamunde had no such qualms. She reached down and snatched the ruby earbobs from the plumed lady's ears. The lady screeched and clawed at her suddenly naked ears with dusty cream gloves.

Rosamunde turned to Louisa, who in her terror still had not recognized her. "You wear earbobs of price," she taunted, knowing full well they were not, for Louisa had always had a deadly fear of highwaymen and wore only the cheapest of glass earbobs when traveling. "What would you do to keep them?"

"Ah, I'd *give* you my jewels, young sir!" cried Louisa in a honeyed voice. Almost pitiable in her relief, she rested on her elbows in the dirt and tore the earbobs from her

212

ears. "If only you would let us go unharmed!" She held the earbobs out beseechingly.

Rosamunde laughed. She accepted the earbobs, tossed them in the air and caught them in a dexterous gauntlet-gloved hand. Her glittering green eyes were fixed on Louisa's white face. "I'll even give them back to you," she said grandly. And at Louisa's incredulously pleased expression, she added, "In return for the dress you are wearing."

Louisa gasped and recoiled.

"Get up," commanded Rosamunde. "I will have the dress."

Louisa staggered to her feet, and Will rolled his eyes at Harry, who sat his horse sternly, letting Rosamunde have her way.

"Take it off! Now!" Rosamunde shouted, brandishing the pistol in Louisa's face.

Louisa involuntarily retreated a step. She looked as if she would faint.

"Here, here!" Lord Reginald, who was again upon the ground, though this time in a seated position, essayed to rise. "I'll not have it! 'Tis indecent!" He was choked with indignation.

"Stay out of it, my lord," counseled Harry in a stern voice. " 'Tis between the two of them." But he too eyed Rosamunde in some alarm.

"Slow about it? Come, I will help you," said Rosamund insolently. She stepped forward and suddenly grasped Louisa's fashionable yellow-starched "falling band" that served as a great collar, and ripped it free. "Or shall I cut the dress off with my sword?" she mused aloud. "That might speed you."

At this new threat, Louisa fell back. "No, no, I will do it," she said hastily. Quickly she slipped out of her gold-embroidered overgown, stood anxiously in her peach satin dress.

"That too," instructed Rosamunde.

Louisa blanched, but when Rosamunde made a threatening movement she struggled out of the peach satin dress and stood trembling in a tight-fitting black silk chemise.

213

She looked very ripe with the tops of her large white breasts gleaming against the black lace, and shaking like large coconuts above her small waist, from her fright.

Will was supervising the rifling of the trunks, and he looked up, startled. He straightened up, forgetful of the trunks, for he thought Louisa a very handsome woman. He rather hoped Rosamunde would demand the chemise.

Harry hoped she would not. He gave Rosamunde an uneasy look.

Louisa, realizing that she was the center of all eyes, and observing the admiration in Will's gaze, bridled a little. "That is *my* trunk you're going through," she told the servant who was helping Will, with some asperity. "Use more care! You've thrown some of my dresses onto the highway!"

Rosamunde's eyes gleamed; she had not forgotten how Louisa loved her lavish wardrobe. "Bundle them all up," she commanded. "All the dresses that belong to this great lady. We will take them with us!"

"Oh, you will not take me!" wailed Louisa, not understanding. And the prone woman in the plumed hat set up a howl too.

"Not you, Louisa, just your clothes," said Rosamunde silkily.

"But—but I'll have nothing to wear!" blurted Louisa.

"Find a farthingale!" snapped Rosamunde, and Louisa gaped at her.

By now Will was having the drivers unhitch the horses. And once they were free, he set the servants to overturning both coaches, at which all three of the aristocratic passengers gave another wail. Righting those coaches would be more difficult than overturning them, they knew, and if they chanced to break a wheel in the process they might be here for the night.

In anguish, Louisa saw her beloved finery wadded up and tied in a great bulging bundle to Will's saddle. "Young sir," she cried in a pleading voice—for she still did not recognize Rosamunde in her masculine attire—"could we not discuss the theft of my clothes in—in private? Beyond—beyond those trees?"

Harry's brows elevated in amusement. But Rosamunde, in the act of mounting Graylady with the peach satin gown flung over her arm, paused and frowned at Louisa.

Louisa bridled and took a deep breath, boldly displaying her fine bustline for the young "highwayman's" approbation. Rosamunde surveyed her former guardian's wife in some amazement. Louisa was *offering* herself to her!

"You wish to trade me something for your clothes? A favor perhaps?" Her voice was ironic.

"Louisa!" cried the startled Lord Reginald from the ground. "Be not so forward with this young man! Can ye not see what he thinks ye mean? He will take ye beyond those trees and—"

He never finished his assessment of what she would do to Louisa, for Rosamunde trod upon his fingers and his remark ended in a painful yelp.

She smiled upon Louisa. "Toss me her bundle of clothes," she told Will, and Will untied the bundle and complied, watching her in fascination. Harry's shoulders jerked at her words. "Perhaps a kiss?" she suggested to Louisa. "Is that what you had in mind? Or perhaps something more?"

"Yes, yes, a kiss!" cried Louisa raggedly, giving Lord Reginald a hunted look. "A kiss in return for my gowns!" She leaned forward and pursed her lips and closed her eyes. Her white bosom rose and fell. Louisa had struck a seductive pose, and Rosamunde knew she was trying to look ravishing. "I'll kiss her for you," offered Will, and Rosamunde gave him a dark look. "Your lips don't please me," she told Louisa coldly. "But this does!" With a sudden pounce she forced her gloved hand into the bodice of Louisa's chemise and brought it away holding a small black silk pouch.

Louisa's eyes snapped open and she gave a screech of real fury as she clutched her bosom. "How did you know what I had concealed there? Who *are* you?" she cried and leaped forward, snatching the black silk kerchief from the young highwayman's smiling face. "Rosamunde!" she gasped, her lips ashen. And again in disbelief, "*Rosamunde!* You, a highwayman?" Her voice quavered.

Rosamunde stepped warily back, keeping control of the silk pouch. "I have chosen a better path than you would have led me down," she said coldly. "Tell Lord Matthew for me that I regret he was not here, for I would hve given him his ears—on a trencher."

Both the other passengers were staring up at the velvet-clad "youth" from the road. "Reginald," cried the lady in the plumed hat, "it is a *woman!*"

"It is my husband's ward," wailed Louisa, "who has lain in wait to rob me!"

"His ward no longer," corrected Rosamunde with a toss of her head. "I am my own woman." With a look of contempt at Louisa, she drew her sword.

"Oh—oh, you would not!" cried Louisa, cowering back.

"Rosamunde, have done," said Harry sternly, for while he could allow her to torment for a few moments this woman who had made her so miserable, he could not brook murder.

Smiling, Rosamunde drew back the blade, and Harry tensed, ready to leap forward and knock aside her arm, deflecting the blade. But then he divined her intent. While Louisa cringed, Rosamunde plunged the blade several times into the bundle of clothes that belonged to Louisa. "I am through playing with you, Louisa," she told the furious older woman. "You will find a few holes in some of your favorite gowns—think of me as you weep over them."

Her laughter floated back over her shoulder as she sprang to the gray mare's back, and the three of them shouted and drove away the coach horses. She looked back once and saw Lord Reginald holding his half-fainting lady. The drivers milled about, and Louisa stood in the road in her black chemise. Rosamunde's last glimpse was of Louisa wringing her peach-gloved hands while several servants attempted to dress her. She seemed to be rejecting each proffered gown—perhaps because of holes cut by Rosamunde's sword.

"We took not much gold there," worried Will. "But I know of a place where we can sell these horses if we can but get them there." He indicated the galloping coach horses they were driving before them.

" 'Tis a danger trying to transport so many horses," muttered Harry. "The cry for them will be out—perhaps ahead of us, for such matched horses are well known. Any passerby might recognize them."

Rosamunde laughed. "There'll be no need to sell the horses, and 'twas a rich haul!" She emptied the contents of the little black pouch, and something flowed like sparkling water into her gloved hand. " 'Tis Louisa's diamond necklace and diamond earbobs! She always carries them wedged between her breasts in a pouch when she travels. We can go to London with these and sell them there!"

Will was delighted. "What a lass ye have, Harry!" he cried, and slapped his thigh with a shouting laugh. "She'll earn her keep if she but cures ye of your nicety in not taking money from women!"

Flushed with triumph, Rosamunde turned to Harry. He gave her a level look. "Ye could have gotten us all killed back there, Rose," he said sternly. "Ye disobeyed me!"

"Ah, scold me not, Harry," sighed Rosamunde, stuffing the black pouch into her doublet. "I'll follow your orders next time. But if Lord Matthew should chance to cross my path . . . " Her careless shrug warned Harry she'd do the same again.

"If Lord Matthew crosses your path again, Rose, leave him to me," growled Harry. "I'll know much better what to do with him than you will, for we've some unfinished business together."

Rosamunde gazed at her lover through slanted lashes. The inference was plain. If Lord Matthew crossed her path again, Harry would kill him. She gave him a smile of pure contentment and began to daydream about what they would do with the proceeds of Louisa's diamonds.

Reluctantly, Will turned the horses loose in an empty

field where the grass was lush and there was a gushing spring with clear sweet water, which they all drank. Then they sped away up a rocky trout stream, the horses' hooves splashing through the cold water and frightening small darting fish that flashed away at their approach. They doubled back through a thick wood at dusk and took off—as Rosamunde had suggested—toward London.

Harry was not loath to show his Rose the sights of London. They put up at a respectable inn in Southwark and for two exciting weeks took in the sights. What happened on distant highroads was of little interest here; it was easy to lose themselves in the milling crowds of hawkers and litters and coaches and horsemen and weaving pedestrians that lined the city's twisting streets.

Rosamunde loved London. She loved the dark little shops with tinkling bells over the doorway to announce visitors. She loved the narrow alleys where the bulging wood-and-wattle houses, many dating from medieval times, almost met overhead. She loved London Bridge, the whole length of it lined with tall brick townhouses that pressed together so tightly coaches could not travel across it. Will told her proudly there was no such sight anywhere, and the three of them gaily crossed and recrossed the old bridge, making their way between crowded frowning houses that crouched on big stone arches above the Thames.

Here was fabled London, rich with history, and Rosamunde reveled in it.

But she was chilled by the sight of the Tower and the Yard where her father had unsuccessfully attempted to snatch Sir Walter Raleigh from the headsman's block. Harry too looked morose at sight of it, and she remembered that his father's head as well had fallen to the ax. Will, who had clean forgotten Harry's lineage, hastened them away to view the great guildhall, looming huge above the city. Rosamunde was enchanted by the guildhall—even to secretly wishing for a moment that Harry were a craftsman—and awed by the great bulk of St. Paul's Cathedral. The two buildings bulked enormously, dwarfing the uneven skyline.

218

They made no attempt at work—indeed, they might have been attending a fair. They bought savory food from street vendors, dined at famous inns, drank at taverns where Henry the Eighth had supped as a young man. And one night while Will attended a bearbaiting—Rosamunde had refused to accompany him; it made her heartsick to see the great beasts blinded and goaded to rage and tormented until they lashed out—she and Harry attended a play at Blackfriars. The play was Will Shakespeare's lively *As You Like It*. The women's parts were all played by handsome young boys dressed in female clothes, and when the words "And one man in his time plays many parts" were spoken, Rosamunde stole a look at Harry. Life had already given him three parts: the part of a son of wealth and power destined to command; that of a dispossessed youth driven from home and hearth; and now that of a hunted highwayman traveling with his doxy.

For Rosamunde saw herself in a hard clear light—she and Harry were married in their hearts but not in the eyes of men. She knew in the back of her mind that Harry planned for them a better life, and that he meant to marry her when that better life began.

But he did not mean to marry her now, and instinctively she knew why: Harry felt he might be cut down on the highway at any time, and her chances would be better as a single woman, still wearing her maiden name, than as his widow. Her loss of virginity would perhaps be waved aside by an eager suitor. Perhaps a beauty such as herself could even talk her way out of implication in his crimes, were he to die—but as his widow, never. The law would pounce on her and she would swing from the nearest gibbet—perhaps whipped toward it tied to the tail of a cart.

It was not a fate Harry wished for her.

And so they drifted on together, the lovers. And Will and Harry and Rosamunde enjoyed London—all on the proceeds of the necklace and the earbobs. For Rosamunde had changed into skirts and gone into a goldsmith's dark shop and posed as a certain "Lady Leffington" who must sell her family jewels to aid her husband, who lay

219

charged with treason in the Tower. That Lady Leffington's husband was imprisoned in the Tower was well known, for he had written seditious verses maligning the king. And it was rumored that his lady, known far and wide for her beauty, had ridden in from Bath to aid him by throwing herself on the king's mercy. The sympathetic goldsmith, smitten by Rosamunde's lovely face and moved to grief by her story, had given her a good price for the diamond necklace and the diamond earbobs, and the money kept them well.

And then their jolly London sojourn was over and they were on the road again.

15   *At first Harry was afraid Rosamunde would lose* her head again and go dashing into the fray, but soon he discovered that she had a cool head on her shoulders—she had become indeed the staunch fellow at his back she'd promised him to be.

The three of them roamed the countryside through the crisp fall weather, taking a purse here and there, working desultorily—for Harry knew each job held its dangers and was loath to take chances with his lady. Rosamunde would always remember those times: the fat bishop who gawked at her stupidly as if he could not believe his eyes; the coach-borne young dandy whose purse they gave back when he told them with tears in his eyes that his mother was dying in Oxford and this was her burial money (they were had there; the dandy was an Oxford student hastening back to the arms of his mistress, and she had a good laugh over the gullible soft-hearted highwaymen who had let him go so easily). Rosamunde remembered too with prickling skin the burly fellow who had come rolling out of his coach into Graylady's legs and caused the mare to throw her. Rosamunde had landed sprawling and the big fellow had been upon her. He might have broken her bones had not Harry's boot toe suddenly connected with the fellow's right ear and felled him like an ox. He had come to, cursing, to find that the strongbox of which he had custody—and which belonged to some loan sharks who'd been charging forty percent interest—was long gone.

The contents of that lucky strongbox had enabled them to winter in York—for English highroads were poor pickings in winter; those roads that were not thick with ice and snow became seas of mud which mired the horses and made travel almost impossible.

A devil's triumvirate they were: Wily Will, old and rugged; Hard Harry, lean and saturnine—and the graceful girl in men's clothing.

But Rosamunde's was a secret that could not long be kept. Hardly were they on the road a week before word was circulated among the "gentlemen of the road" that Will and Harry had teamed up with a beautiful woman who dressed like a man—and rode and shot like one.

Fair as a Rose, they said of her. And wild as Hard Harry. Someone overheard him call her Rose instead of Robbie and made a play on the name. "The Wild Rose" was the name they coined for her. Hard Harry's Wild Rose. And any man who desired her must first fight his way past Hard Harry.

Few tried. Those who did ended up on their faces on the white-scoured stones of out-of-the-way inns or the mud of the roadways.

The fame of the Wild Rose spread until even the earl of Kenwarren and Lord Matthew Waverclay—and their shared Louisa—heard of her exploits. They badgered the authorities to find and seize her, but the authorities had already tried to take the trio many times and failed. That unholy trio, they told a fuming Lord Matthew, rode like the wind and seldom lingered for more than one job in a particular locality. It would take the devil's own luck to

221

catch them, they assured him gloomily. But they would try, they insisted, electrified by the choleric rage that suffused his lordship's handsome countenance.

The three might have gone south with their strongbox, but an early snow caught them outside York and Will told them they'd find safe haven with a friend of his in the town. They rode in through heavy sleet, shivering in the freezing cold, for their cloaks were thin, and were relieved to find that Will's friend had not died or gone away, but was still in York and glad to offer them shelter.

Will's friend was a sturdy smiling butcher who had a shop in the Shambles, that narrow street where animals were slaughtered. Will found him at work in the butcher shop and brought Rosamunde and Harry there to meet him. The sights and sounds of that reeking street almost overpowered Rosamunde, and the smell made her sick, but she liked the butcher and thought he had an open honest face. She was glad when he brought them home to his "ample lodgings," which seemed small to her eyes, accustomed to the great rooms of Kenwarren House. But it was clean and neat, and he lived there happily with his pretty young wife and their two small children. He told Will grandly there was plenty of room, and the three of them crowded into space that seemed hardly sufficient for his family. They paid well for their lodgings, and the butcher and his wife were glad to have them. And since their faces were not known in York, they could come and go at will, riding out into the frozen countryside on clear days through the gates in York's thirteenth-century wall. There on the Micklegate Bar the head of the duke of York, defeated by the Lancastrians, had been impaled, the butcher told them cheerfully. Rosamunde shivered at this talk of heads impaled, and Harry put a comforting arm around her. She was brave and she was lovely and she was his—he would let no harm come to her while he lived.

Rosamunde knew this and was glad, warming herself by the warm glow of Harry's love for her. She might end up a famous woman of the road, but such fame meant nothing to her—only Harry's encircling arms.

222

But she was not so well known that first winter in York, where she wore skirts again and went by the name "Mistress Haversham" while Harry was "Mr. Haversham," her husband.

In York they celebrated Christmas, eating a jolly dinner in a tavern and joining the Christmas carolers in the icy streets. Warmed by ale and laughter, they made their way home through streets atinkle with falling icicles to warm their cold hands before the butcher's glowing hearth. The butcher's young wife had made enormous mincemeat pies, and Harry brought home a huge plum pudding and Will a goose, while Rosamunde contributed roasted chestnuts. They gave the children gifts trimmed with sprigs of holly and kissed beneath the mistletoe, and went skating on an icy pond with a great group of young people, and afterward warmed themselves before a bonfire on the bank and ate hot dripping sausages toasted on long sticks, and laughed and burned their fingers.

The whole twelve days of Christmas were joyful for them.

After Christmas they settled down to a snowy winter in York, and Harry and Rosamunde in their warm little room off the kitchen came as near to cottage life as a highwayman and his lady were ever likely to. They were part of the life of a family here, and there were laughing children playing about them, and a young wife with floury hands who let Rosamunde help her in the kitchen and taught her ways to economize in cooking. And if the butcher came home sometimes smelling rankly of blood, and the rooms were overcrowded and sometimes filled with smoke, they could walk out into the clear crisp air and drink wine at some likely tavern, or walk their horses sedately through the streets sightseeing, or hire a sleigh and ride over the fresh-fallen snow.

York was known for its cockfights, and Will spent much of his time attending them—he was a crafty bettor and oftentimes won—so Harry and Rosamunde had much of their time to themselves. Their sojourn in York lacked the lustrous wonder of their days at Locke Hall, but Rosamunde was more sure of herself now. She had chosen the road she meant to ride and she would ride it—even if it led in the end to the gibbet.

In midwinter Will found himself a doxy in York. Her name was Polly and he promptly moved in with her. After that the butcher's quarters were less crowded, though not as jolly, for Wily Will was good company, drunk or sober. They did not see much of Will after that for another reason: Rosamunde had taken an instant dislike to slatternly Polly, and the feeling was mutual. But Polly joined Will in frequenting the cockfights, and since she bet heavily and seldom won, she swiftly drained him of his money. It was because of Polly they left York, for Polly was overfond of drink and she became fiercely angry at Will one day when he did not bring her a bottle as promised. She slammed her door in his face and latched it, and as he left she rushed to her window and caterwauled down that he could go to perdition, even if he was a famous highwayman! People in the crowded street below pricked up their ears at that and turned to stare at Will, who jammed his hat down over his ears and hurried away. Worse, as he told Harry less than an hour later, when he arrived, fuming, at their quarters, in such a crush he could not be sure he was not followed. And Polly had been in such a passion that she well might scream out his name to the authorities.

"I may dance from a gibbet, they may mount my head on the city gates, but I'd rather it not be in York," said Will devoutly. "I'd prefer to postpone it for a time."

"So would we all." Harry grinned, for he was familiar with this gloomy streak of Will's. "Rose, 'tis time to pack. We're leaving York."

"Though it hurts me to leave." Will sighed. "For there's a good cockfight tomorrow and I'd thought to attend."

" 'Twill do ye little good if your head is mounted on the city gates in the meantime," joked Harry, and Will grimaced.

"I'd ne'er thought Polly would turn me out like that," he mourned.

Rosamunde and Harry exchanged looks. Will had little luck with women.

224

"We need a change anyway, Will," Rosamunde said quickly. She was already seizing their few belongings and stuffing them into their saddlebags, for she was ever mindful that since both Harry and Will had a price on their heads, disaster for one could mean disaster for the other.

As a hearty aroma filled the room, Will lifted his head. "What's that?"

"Our landlady has been baking kidney pies," explained Rosamunde. "Perchance we can purchase one to eat along the way."

With bulging saddlebags, they bade goodbye to the butcher and his family. They passed unchallenged through the city gates, where their horses shied at the clamor of a group of lepers who squatted there, leaping up to run with arms outstretched toward any passing rider. It was a kind of blackmail: give alms or be touched—and possibly infected! Rosamunde pitied them and tossed them so many coins that a wail of joy went up from that hooded throng.

"Ye've a soft heart, Rose," muttered Will. "But I think ye're sometimes mistaken. Thieves and cutpurses hide among the lepers, disguising themselves by the hoods the lepers wear."

Rosamunde shuddered. "There may be cutpurses among them, Will, as you say, but—*think of the others.*" Her green eyes were filled with horror.

Harry gave her a tender look.

Night found them riding down the road toward Lincoln. It was early spring and, though the roads were still soft, they were all tired of cramped smoky quarters and were not sorry to leave York behind them and venture out into the brisk summer air.

In the countryside around Lincoln they were lucky and took several good prizes before they rode on south. Which was fortunate, because, for such as they, the price of everything was trebled, and even a meager living must cost them dear. Even farmers who fed them no more than coarse brown bread and whey butter and curds must be well paid lest they tattle on who had supped there. It was one of the penalties of being on the road, but they paid it because they must. A hunted man would pay well for a chance to sleep safe, and the landlords who catered to their kind were hard-faced men who charged what the traffic would bear. No matter how well they fared, to Rosamunde they always seemed hard pressed for money and could never linger long in one spot but must be on to the next job.

But all spring they were successful. Nottingham, Leicester, Cambridge, Bedford—their luck held. And Rosamunde—with Will's cheerful applauding of her as an apt pupil—developed a slight swagger that made her look more than ever like a dashing youth.

She was now becoming known on the road—and she had discovered she liked it.

Inevitably so much success led to overconfidence. So smoothly did Harry and Will work together, so easy did their skill and expertise make each job seem, that Rosamunde began to believe that she could even work the road alone if necessary. Suppose Harry were hurt, suppose Will left to follow some doxy's flirting skirts (as he had been prone to do all his reckless life), suppose they needed money desperately? She could take a coach alone, if need be, she told herself sturdily.

Such thoughts were heady wine to her senses and sometimes made her forget that, while she was clever and quick, her strength when pitted against a strong man was not so very great.

This fact was brought home to her on a stormy summer night when they came out of a squishy bogged-down road and tethered their horses at a safe inn near the village of Olney. They had been en route from Bedford to Northampton, but the heavy downpour had prompted Harry to stop here, for a highwayman was ever dependent upon his mount, and their horses were tired from slogging through the mud. In spite of the driving rain, Rosamunde had halted her gray mare and looked wistfully at the Eleanor Cross near Olney—that cross which was one of three that King Edward the First had set up in memory of his wife, Eleanor of Castile, whose funeral procession had passed this way in the year 1290. Rosamunde had sat astride

Graylady with the rain running in rivulets down her face and stared at that cross. Edward had wanted his Eleanor to be remembered. She studied it soberly, and asked herself in a wicked moment of insight if—should she die some night on the highway—her memory would live on in any other heart but Harry's.

Abruptly she turned her face from the ancient cross and followed Harry, his head bent against the rain, slogging along astride Nightwind in the rain. It was enough, she told herself, for Harry to love her!

Her sagging spirits rose at sight of the yellow candlelight flickering from the small-paned windows of the inn that appeared before them through the trees. Rosamunde shook out her wet cloak and stamped her boots to knock off the raindrops while Harry took rooms for them. Then she carried her saddlebags upstairs while Harry and Will went out to the stable to look after the horses personally —they did not trust the stableboys at this inn, for the landlord, while safe, was known for his slovenly stables. Not so with the inn itself—his wife and daughters kept that clean and neat, though they went about glumly, looking like drabs.

Feeling that Rosamunde was tired after her rainy ride, Harry had sent her up to take her bath before the three of them dined downstairs in the common room. He and Will would drain a tankard downstairs after rubbing down the horses, and she would join them for supper in the common room.

Although Rosamunde usually insisted on doing her full share of the work, for once she was glad to be excused. She had surreptitiously purchased a new chemise and a green lawn dress and white petticoat at the last market town and was eager to change into them before she supped. This wearing of men's clothes was all very well, and she did indeed make a dashing youth, but—she tossed her head as she clattered up the stairs, booted and spurred—it was well known on the road by now that she was Harry's woman, and tonight she meant to dine in skirts. She would comb out her golden hair and let the lamplight play on her gleaming bosom and woo Harry's vision with the public sight of her as a woman.

No sooner had she tossed her wet cloak over a chair than she heard the sound of an altercation going on in the upstairs hallway outside her door. A woman was sobbing. "No, Nate, no!" she cried, and her young passionate treble voice was overborne by a man's heavy overtones. There was a sharp slap, a screech and the sound of a body falling.

Rosamunde, her hand instinctively going to her sword, flung open the door.

"What's this?" she cried sharply, for before her was an appalling sight.

The door across the hall stood open, as if the combatants had just surged through it into the hallway. Lying flat on her back on the floor was a flushed-faced plumpish young girl who could hardly have been more than thirteen. Her chestnut hair was wildly disheveled, and from her lips issued a series of hiccuping sobs and protests. Standing over her threateningly was a large bearded man dressed in colorful attire: scarlet doublet, green trousers festooned with yellow ribbons at the knee. His boots were caked with dried mud, and he was missing one festoon of yellow ribbons—it was clutched in the young girl's hand. At first glance, the scene looked weirdly as if the girl had stolen one of his garters and he was attempting to retrieve it, for he reached down to grab at her hand and she kicked at him desperately. Rosamunde noted that the girl had lost one shoe and a tuft of her chestnut hair, which was presently twined in the big man's fingers— and surmised that he must, unsuccessfully, have attempted to jerk the girl to her feet by her hair. Indignantly she observed that the girl's torn blue petticoat was riding up around her hips. It was an unequal struggle and could end only one way, but the girl was not ready to surrender. Her plump legs in their striped cotton stockings swung nimbly about kicking at the big man, who bent over her as if trying to decide how best to jerk her to her feet without getting jabbed by a solid heel.

At the sound of the door opening and Rosamunde's sharp question, they both turned their heads and gaped at her. The girl had a gamin's face, piquant—and dirty. Now her angry expression quickly turned to one of wild appeal.

" 'E's kidnappin' me, that 'e is!" she shrilled to Rosamunde. " 'E's carted me all the way from London and now 'e's—"

She never finished saying what he was trying to do to her, for she was interrupted by the big fellow. "Shut up, Lollie!" he roared. "This is betwixt you an' me!" He had a wild ginger beard and a coarse face that was almost as red with rage as his doublet, and now, with a curse, he lifted one large boot as if to stomp on the girl.

"No, Nate, no!" she screamed, and rolled over, away from him.

Fury overcame Rosamunde. Many bad things had she seen on the road, but this abduction of a child—and now to attempt to stamp on her! In a swift motion her sword left its scabbard and she leaped forward, brandishing it. Nate looked up to find the point of her blade pressing against his chest.

"Back!" she commanded furiously. "You'll not harm this child! Get up, Lollie."

Lollie's jaw dropped at this sudden turn of events. But she scrambled to her feet, tripping over the torn hem of her dirty blue petticoat. She stood in a kind of crouch, ready to spring in any direction, but she flashed Rosamunde a winsome smile that displayed a set of even white teeth.

"Who the devil may you be?" demanded Nate, staring down in amazement at the sword point, held by a stranger, that pressed against his scarlet doublet.

Rosamunde did not think it a good time to reveal the fact that she was a woman. "I ride with Hard Harry," she said menacingly.

Nate's features lit up. "You be the Wild Rose then?" He roared with laughter, and his barrel-like chest shook with it. "Ah, I've heard of ye—Harry's doxy!"

Lollie's jaw dropped still further and she leaned forward, perilously near to pitching forward on her face. She gave Rosamunde—in her man's clothing—a wild look.

"Doxy or no, you'll not harm this child." Rosamunde spoke through clenched teeth. She stepped forward, deliberately pressing the big man back toward the stairs. That stairway led down into the common room, deserted on this rainy night except for one of the innkeeper's drab daughters, who looked up indifferently from scrubbing a table and then returned to her work.

"I be goin', mistress, I be goin'," said Nate, hastily turning to start down the stairs. "Ye can have it your way, and a plague on ye both!"

Rosamunde watched him start down the top step and turned to Lollie. "Has he hurt you, Lollie? Are you all right?"

Lollie's eyes flew wide and her sudden screech gave Rosamunde warning. She whirled just in time to parry the long blade that sliced past her. Nate had swung about on the stairs and leaped back to the upstairs hallway. Now his little eyes gleamed as he bellowed, "Did ye think I'd let a wench best me?" The fury of his assault pushed her back as she brought up her sword to parry the blow.

The force of his sudden onslaught swept her backward, and she spun past Lollie, who had pressed her face against the inn wall and was screaming—great banshee wails that chilled the blood. Hard-pressed, Rosamunde still managed to parry his thrust, for her swordsmanship had improved now that she practiced often with both Harry and Will. Nate looked surprised that she did not immediately drop her sword and run to the shelter of her room, for his first blow, while heavy, had been meant to terrify but not to wound. Now he watched incredulously as Rosamunde presented to him a snaking naked blade and a grim lovely face.

She meant to fight him for Lollie!

With a big grin, Nate struck at his slim opponent—not too hard—and she parried the blow easily. Lollie had to draw breath between her wild screams, and in one of those choked interludes he laughed.

230

"They tell me ye wear a great weight of padding beneath that doublet," he said slyly. "Let's see if 'tis true!"

Before she guessed his intention, with a swift sidewise thrust the point of his blade had pinked her doublet, tearing the velvet and gouging into the padded undergarment she wore to help conceal her femininity—but it did not draw blood, and Rosamunde fell back hastily.

His nasty laugh made her see red. Reckless of the danger, she charged toward him, flailing with her sword—and Nate gave ground, warily, before the shimmering swiftness of that snaking blade. Her ears were still assaulted by Lollie's wild screams, for the girl never stopped screaming except to draw breath. Rosamunde wished she were barefoot, for her bootheels tended to skid on the smooth-worn boards of the hall floor. Blade clashed against blade, and the thought flicked through Rosamunde's mind that perhaps she was a better swordsman than she had believed, for was she not driving her opponent back to the top of the stairs? If he gave ground any farther he could miscalulate and topple down them. To that end she pressed her advantage with flashing blade.

It was this sight that met Harry's incredulous gaze as he swung open the door to the inn and charged through it. Will was right behind him, for from the stables they had heard a woman's screams and rushed back, thinking it to be Rosamunde. At the top of the stairs they could see big Nate's solid muscular back and—her doublet ripped and a look of desperation and perhaps even of fierce delight upon her lovely face—pressing Nate backward with her flashing blade was Rosamunde!

Harry took the stairs at two bounds, and even as Nate would have turned to face this new threat, Harry's long arm reached out, grasped Nate by his ginger beard and gave his head a sharp wrench that cost him his balance. Nate gave a strangled howl, and Harry's left hand struck Nate's head with a solid chopping blow that toppled him down the stairs. Will saw Nate falling toward him and leaped nimbly over the stair rail to let Nate crash by him to land in a slithering heap upon the clean-scoured stone floor.

Sword in hand, Harry dived past Will's brandishing blade and followed the body downstairs, arriving on his feet almost as fast as Nate had made it on his back. With a violent kick he knocked the blade—which Nate had held onto throughout his wild descent—from Nate's hand. He placed a heavy boot on Nate's chest and the point of his blade at Nate's throat.

"Harry!" Nate's eyes bulged in terror. "Your doxy attacked me! She leaped into the hall and came between me and Lollie!"

Rosamunde did not want to see Harry do murder—and she knew he was perilously close to murder at that moment. She leaned over the banister.

" 'Tis true," she called desperately. "I drew my sword and ordered him back—'twas *I* attacked *him*."

"He did not mark you, did he?" Harry demanded in a ferocious voice.

"No, Harry, he did not."

Nate, from the floor, thought he had never seen such a hellish face as was poised above him with a lock of dark hair swinging past a pair of murderous gray eyes.

"Rose's words give you back your life," Harry grated, raising the point of his sword an inch from Nate's throat. "But if ye touch my Rose again—if ye even *look* at her again—ye have my word I'll kill you!"

Nate gulped. He scooted on his back across the floor and regained his feet warily. His face was ashen.

Rosamunde had not wanted Harry to kill Nate, but neither did she want him to let Nate come back upstairs. "He abducted this girl, Harry!" she cried. "Lollie told me so herself!"

His blade swinging loosely from his arm, Harry brushed by Nate, who hastily gave ground, and came up the stairs three at a time. "See to the girl, Will," he called tonelessly over his shoulder. He went past cringing Lollie as if he did not see her and pushed Rosamunde through the open door of their bedroom and latched the door behind him. She sheathed her sword and would have walked away from him, for she did not like the look on his face, but he grasped her by the velvet of her doublet and swung her around. She had never seen him so angry.

"Now," he said between clenched teeth, "what demon possessed you to try your sword arm on a brute the size of Big Nate?"

"You know him?" asked Rosamunde, bewildered.

"Everybody knows him," said Harry heavily. "He has been on the road since he was fifteen, and 'tis estimated he has killed no fewer than eleven men with that sword you were so eager to match your skill against."

"I heard them fighting in the hall," defended Rosamunde. "Nate and this young girl—she can't be more than thirteen. She was sobbing and I heard him strike her and I rushed out. He had struck her down and she was lying on the floor kicking at him. She cried out to me that he had kidnapped her from London. He seemed about to stomp on her, and I drew my sword and stepped between them. The poor girl—"

"Stay here," ordered Harry. "I will see about this poor girl." As he opened the door, loud voices and a high keening whine erupted from below.

Rosamunde waited, pacing about. Her spurs had a loud jingle to her ears and her heels seemed to strike the floor noisily. Her heart was thudding in her chest and she anxiously fingered the padding of her specially made undergarment. She thought she could stitch it up neatly and it would not be much harmed. The doublet would have to be mended too, of course. She was fingering the green velvet nervously when Harry returned, striding into the room and slamming and latching the door behind him. His gray eyes glinted angrily.

"So you thought to come between a strapping fellow and his wench?" he said sarcastically, towering over her. "It did not occur to you to call me? Or Will? You thought to do battle yourself?"

Rosamunde was goaded by that scalding tone. "I was winning," she cried desperately, "when you inferfered! And what has happened to Lollie? I heard her call out just now."

Harry ignored the subject of Lollie, apparently leaving

233

that matter to Will. His eyebrows elevated. *"Winning!"* he said heavily. *"Winning*, you say? Did ye not know that Nate is a tricky swordsman? For all his weight, he's quick as a cat!"

No, of course she had not known that. It was unfair to expect her to! "How could I know that?" she demanded resentfully. "I'd never laid eyes on him before."

"But ye could see that he was twice your size and possessed of bulging muscles? Ye could see that! Ye could see that he had the advantage of reach on ye? And ye knew that since he was brawling with a woman *in this inn* that he was most likely a hardened veteran of the road? *Ye knew that, didn't ye?"*

His ringing voice was beginning to make her head hurt. She planted her feet. "Stop shouting at me, Harry. You could see for yourself I was driving him back."

"Driving him back!" Harry smote his forehead. He wrenched out his sword. "On guard!" he bellowed, and Rosamunde stepped back in alarm, for that long serviceable blade had whipped up and now it was pointed directly at her.

She looked at it wildly. "You mean I'm to—to duel with you?"

"Draw your sword!" thundered Harry.

Outside Will was pounding on the door.

Frightened now, Rosamunde drew her blade, stood looking uncertainly at Harry.

"Now drive me back," he roared. "Exactly as you did Nate!"

Rosamunde gave him an angry look. Harry had no right to talk to her like this—she had only been saving an innocent victim; he would have done the same himself! Biting her lips, she leaped forward, flashing her naked blade—and Harry gave ground just as Nate had.

And then suddenly—with a movement so swift she could hardly follow it—Harry's body had spun about and his sword had clashed against hers so violently that her own blade was torn from her grip and skittered across the floor.

"Harry, boy, what are ye doing?" cried Will in an

234

anguished voice from the hall. "Answer me or I'll kick this door down!"

"I'm teaching Rose a lesson in swordplay she'll never forget," called Harry as he looked down at his white-faced lady, staring appalled at the sword that had left her grasp and now reposed shining in a corner. "You were not winning, Rose. Nate was letting you push him back, luring you forward for just the right stroke—and then he would have been on you!"

Rosamunde gasped. "How could you know that?"

"I've watched him fight," said Harry grimly, "and that's his style. 'Tis a trick he's used over and over. I've spent a deal of time watching other men fight, Rose. 'Tis instructive, in case I have to fight them myself someday. Nate would have flicked your sword from your hand as easily as I did. And for your temerity, he'd have ripped your clothes off and no doubt taken you there on the floor, had I not interfered."

Rosamunde was shaking. *Nate had been playing with her!* "What a fool you must think me," she whispered.

"Yes," he said in a softer tone. "I do take you for a fool if you think you can match your blade with any burly stranger. Those clothes you're wearing, Rose, make you seem a pretty lad—but you'll do well to remember that they do not make a man of you nor give you a man's sinews."

It was easy now to see her folly. She need not have attempted to fight Nate herself. She could have run for Harry. Or Will. They would have come to Lollie's aid.

She stole a look at Harry. He still looked very fierce. She made an attempt to divert him. "I bought a dress in the last market town. I was going to wear it tonight—as a surprise for you."

Harry was not to be cajoled. He gave her a wintry look. "It is as well you put on the dress." He sheathed his sword. "Perhaps it will serve to remind you that you are a woman. I am back to the stables with Will, for we're not finished yet. Keep this door *latched*."

"Harry." Her voice followed him. "You will see about Lollie?"

"I will see about Lollie," he said heavily and went through the door, banging it behind him.

Hot bathwater in a tin tub was brought up by one of the landlord's slatternly daughters, who looked at Rosamunde with dull curiosity and plodded away. Rosamunde, very eager to look womanly this night after her violent brush with Harry, lingered over her bath, pouring the warm soapy water over her breasts and back with a sigh.

There was a knock on the door. " 'Tis Harry, Rose. Let me in."

Dripping wet, Rosamunde rose from the tub, seized a towel and made wet footsteps across the bare boards to the door, unlatched it and let him enter. He came in on muddy boots and frowned at her. Rosamunde tossed her head, dislodging a pinned-up gold curl, and went back to her bath, tossing the towel aside. She sat in the tub and tried to torment him by lifting a long white leg out of the water and soaping it carefully, pouring water from the pitcher over it to wash away the soap. Ordinarily this would have brought some comment from Harry, for he loved to lie back leisurely and watch her bathe, but tonight he was silent. With great concentration she washed the other leg. And then a dainty washing of her breasts that bounced them temptingly to Harry's view.

She looked up. Harry had thrown a leg over the end of the bed and was studying her, but he was still frowning.

Rosamunde flounced out of the tub, turned her back on him and toweled herself dry. In silence she dressed in her pretty new chemise, fastened her new white linen petticoat around her waist and slipped into the green lawn dress. Its sleeves were slashed to the elbow to reveal the snowy whiteness of the chemise below. The neck was cut low, and the bodice fit her lovely figure snugly. She had trouble reaching the hooks in the back, and Harry came up behind her and fastened them for her. She muttered a thank you but did not turn around. Instead she busied herself attaching a white cambric "falling band" around her neck, so that now a dazzling display of bosom could be glimpsed from the front. With a swift gesture, she

236

tucked up the green lawn dress to display her white petticoat, and sat down to dress her hair.

"Wear it combed out long, Rose," said Harry, drumming his fingers. "Will is waiting below."

It was the first time he had spoken to her, and since his
tone had softened, she laid down her comb without a word,
tossed back her long gleaming hair and accompanied him
downstairs. What matter that fashionable women were
wearing their hair flat across the top and puffed and rolled
with long curled sidepieces She would wear hers streaming down like a country girl. In this lonesome inn her new
dress and petticoat were enough to dazzle, her fair hair
could form a shining shawl about her shoulders.

Looking thus, she trailed pensively downstairs with
Harry. Two of the landlord's daughters were in the common room and they both stood and gawked at her beauty.

"Rose, you are a very vision!" said Will gallantly, leaping up to pull out a chair for her. "And we shall dine on
venison and kidney pie tonight—the landlord's best."

"Ah, but I forgot something, Will," sighed Rosamunde.
"I forgot to buy slippers!"

"I thought I heard a slight clanking of spurs as you
walked." Will laughed as he and Harry seated her with
some ceremony at the end of the long common board,
which was the only table in the room.

"Are we the only guests then?" asked Harry, turning to
look about the empty room. "What of Nate?"

"Nate has gone," said Will. "He rode out while you
were upstairs."

"In this weather?" Rosamunde was astonished.

Will laughed. "I think he feared Harry might have a
change of heart and run him through after all."

"But what of Lollie?" Rosamunde leaned forward anxiously. "Oh, Will, you did not let him take her with him?"

Will sighed. "Ye were wrong about Lollie, Rose. She's
a little street waif Nate picked up in a London whore-
house. She'd been there since she was eleven, and she was
eager for a taste of the road. She's his doxy, Rose. But
today he found her tumbling in the hay with a stableboy,

and they were fighting over *that*. When Lollie saw you, she thought to change partners—if you could best Nate."

Rosamunde was aghast. "She—she was *attracted* to me?" she faltered.

"She took ye for a lad, Rose—after all, ye were dressed like one and she got no very good look at you. Your clothes were rich, and she assumed you to be wealthy. When she discovered you were a woman, she began screaming with fright lest Nate beat her black and blue."

"But he won't, will he?"

"I don't know." Will shrugged. "When last I saw Lollie, she was running along after Nate in the mud, pleading with him to take her up on his saddle."

Rosamunde could not meet Harry's eyes. Red with mortification that she had so misjudged the situation, she sat silent while the venison was brought in on a big wooden trencher, and then the kidney pie. Will attacked his meal with gusto, and so did Harry, but Rosamunde only toyed with hers. She had no appetite, she felt lost in shame.

"Eat, Rose," commanded Harry gently. "The food here is good."

Still depressed that she had made such a fool of herself, Rosamunde forced down a few bites and then sat melancholy as Harry and Will pushed back their trenchers and took long drafts of ale.

"Your intentions were good, Rose," said Harry, when they had retired to their room and she had turned her back to him so that he might unfasten the hooks of her bodice. He sighed. " 'Tis your hot head makes you plunge forward before you think."

"Usually I'm cool," she protested sadly, stepping out of the green dress.

"When your emotions are not involved." Harry unbuckled his baldric and flung it and his sword aside. "Will was right—you looked a very vision tonight."

Rosamunde paused in removing her white petticoat and gave him a hopeful look. He was no longer angry with her then? She dropped her petticoat to the floor and stood surveying him in her chemise, wishing that she were not wearing those wide-topped leather boots, for they held out the long skirt of her chemise in an awkward manner. She sat down upon a chair and tugged off her boots, stood up barefoot and shook out her long hair. She looked very desirable, standing there in her chemise, caressed by the golden candlelight.

Harry was regarding her whimsically. "I was wrong to encourage you to wear the dress." He sighed. " 'Tis a joy to see you appear as a woman in all your beauty. But 'tis *safer,* Rose, that ye stay garbed as a man. Ye've a face and a body that inflames men, and I saw tonight that you do not want me to kill for you."

"No, I do not want that," she said in a stifled voice.

"Then 'tis best their eyes seek other vistas, Rose, than your sweet body. I am glad the inn was deserted when we supped, or I might have had to quell others besides Nate. You'd best put the dress away."

"I will," she said dully, staring down at the floor. "I'll give it away." Suddenly her head lifted and she gave him a tormented look. "Oh, Harry," she burst out, "what are we doing here? We should not be on the highways, you and I!"

Harry took her gently by her slender shoulders and drew her to him, held her comfortingly close. "Ah, Rose, Rose." He sighed. " 'Tis true we were not cast in this mold. We live in a world gone wrong."

"What has happened to us?" she whispered. "I thought —I thought it would be different, when we rode together."

"Naught has happened, Rose," Harry told her sadly, stroking her hair with gentle fingers. " 'Tis just that you are coming to realize the hard facts of the road—a life I tried to shield you from, you will remember." He swung her up in his arms and she lay there, the skirt of her chemise trailing down over his arm, her bright head nestled against his chest. Harry bent his dark head and his lips brushed gently over her closed eyelids, ruffling her long lashes, trailed down her peach-bloom cheek and found her mouth. "Rose," he whispered huskily, "I cannot give ye the life ye deserve. A home, an unblemished name, the protection of the law—I can give ye none of these."

Rosamunde twined her arms around his neck. "I do not need them, Harry," she told him in a low rich voice. "I have you."

He drew a ragged breath, and had she looked up at that moment, she would have seen a burning intensity in his gray eyes and a look of pain on his dark face that he could not give her more. His arms tightened about her. "We will keep the dress. Perhaps we'll go to Locke Hall this summer, Rose—you can wear it then."

But as things turned out they did not go to Locke Hall. Not that summer or ever again.

16   *All that reckless summer they pursued their call-ing.* Elusive as shadows, they struck and were on to the next place before pursuit could be well mounted. Their luck held and—although they did not go to Locke Hall, for they heard that Lord Penwether was still in residence there—there were other diversions: fairs where they could jostle about in the crowds, market towns where goods were offered and they could buy a length of Mechlin lace or have a bootheel repaired, pleasant stops at out-of-the-way inns, and perhaps best of all the camps they pitched by tinkling streams and slow-running rivers that mirrored the great overhanging trees—some of which dated from the Conqueror's time—and long nights when they lazed by their campfire beneath a slice of yellow moon and cold white stars.

Once, after they'd relieved three riders of a considerable sum of money, having pounced on them at the edge of a ravine where all the travelers' attention was concentrated on not falling over the edge, they took the chance of stopping at a strange inn. Confident that they had eluded pursuit, their spirits were high—and the place seemed quiet enough.

But by the time their supper was put before them, the excitement had gone, leaving Rosamunde feeling somehow forsaken. Silently she ate her fritters and partridge and curds, and afterward joined Will and Harry in a tankard as they sat at their ease in the inn's sparsely populated common room, feet propped up negligently and looking expansive. Will lifted his tankard to toast another successful job.

Rosamunde drank the toast, but her mood was pensive. "Do any ever leave this—this profession?" she asked.

Will banged down his empty tankard with a roar of laughter. "Aye—dangling from gibbets at Tyburn and other places!"

"Not so loud," muttered Harry, nudging Will with his elbow. "We know not that this inn be safe."

Will subsided and spoke to Rosamunde in a hoarse whisper. "If ye mean do they retire from it—and I take it ye do—there was one: Big Jim Balfour. Jim was a great hulk of a man who worked alone and always robbed women—if there were any women about to be robbed. The very opposite of Harry here, for as you know, Harry won't rob a woman."

Rosamunde knew and was perversely proud of him for it.

"Nay, Harry here prefers tax collectors and bishops with stout guards!" Will's raillery was affectionate. "Well, Big Jim Balfour happened to be working the Great North Road the night the duchess of Lyburn killed her husband and fled by coach, taking with her all the family jewels. By luck, Big Jim stopped the coach and relieved her of the jewels—all of them."

"What happened to the duchess?" asked Rosamunde breathlessly.

Will blinked. That was not the right question—she was supposed to ask what had happened to the *jewels*.

"She went to the block for her husband's murder," Harry said tersely.

"But Big Jim, he sailed for France with his loot and set himself up with a mansion in Paris and three mistresses."

So highwaymen did retire sometimes. . . . Rosamunde stared out over her tankard and saw distant vistas of a different life, a time when they would no longer be hunted.

"More ale?" asked Will.

Harry shook his head. His eyes were on Rosamunde. "Finish your story, Will." His voice was harsh.

"Of course, it did not last long," added Will. "The new duke of Lyburn, who'd inherited the jewels by right, sent agents to France, and they stabbed Big Jim to death in his bed and carried back to England what jewels they could find. All those Big Jim hadn't disposed of, that is. I was working the roads around Dover when the jewels came back, and I'd heard they were to be transported by coach, but they weren't. They came home, I'm told, under the hay of a big haycart nobody would bother with." He sighed.

Rosamunde smiled halfheartedly at Will. What he had told her, without realizing it, was that nobody retired from this game *successfully*.

"Come, Rose, cheer up." Harry gave her a look of silent understanding. "We took a good prize today and can take our time about picking a new target."

But his words did not cheer her. It was clear to her now that they were on a collision course with Death. Ah, they might cheat the Reaper for the moment, but he'd have them in the end.

She took a deep breath and drained her tankard. When she set it back down, her green eyes were steady—veiled. "Aye, Harry," she said in a cheerful voice. "A good prize."

But the words rang hollow in her ears.

She supposed it was because she had not quite given up the world she had lost. In her heart she was still Rosamunde Langley, who had had a genteel upbringing at vast Kenwarren House—Rosamunde Langley, who supped

242

with earls, whose hand was kissed deferentially by gentlemen who vied for her hand in marriage. . . .

That she had lost that world forever was borne in to her when they hied themselves to the home of a country squire by invitation, to sup and spend the night.

It had come about oddly. They'd been on their way to Banbury Fair, where rich pickings awaited. Being dusty and tired from their long ride, they had stopped at the first likely tavern, thinking to drain a glass and be on their way again. But as they entered the busy common room—entered it warily, for they were strangers here—a round-faced, pink-cheeked man in sky-blue silks rose up from one of the tables.

"Harry!" he cried. " 'Tis you!" And rushed toward them joyfully.

All three of them were instantly alert. Will's hand rested negligently on his sword hilt, while Rosamunde put one gauntlet-gloved hand inside her cloak seeking her pistol.

But Harry's dark face lit up with recognition. "Arthur!" he said, with pleasure in his voice. "Arthur Hallenby!" They wrung each other's hands, and Harry murmured, "Is the tavern safe for us, Arthur?"

"I had not thought . . . " stammered Arthur in confusion. "I had clean forgot your calling, Harry," he muttered sheepishly. "Come, there's a private room where we can be served." He called over his shoulder to the landlord, "Bates, these are old friends of mine. A bottle of your best wine. We'll drink it in private and reminisce about other days."

He shepherded them through the common room to a small room that opened off it and closed the door. That he was a man of some importance in the community Rosamunde surmised from the landlord's deferential treatment of him.

"If ye've forgot my calling, I am clean unaware of yours, Arthur," said Harry ironically, drawing off his gauntlets. "When last I saw you, you were trying your luck on the road, but that was some time ago."

"I've not forgot you saved my life on my first job, Harry," declared Arthur warmly.

243

"Ye were a bit inept." Harry smiled. "But perhaps ye've improved with time."

Arthur laughed ruefully. "No, I would never have improved. I gave it up. But who are these with ye, Harry? Can this be Wily Will of whom I've heard so much and the famous Wild Rose?"

"This is Will, right enough," said Harry, and Will took Arthur's outstretched hand in a bone-crunching grip. "And this is my lady, Mistress Rosamunde Langley. Rose, this is Arthur Hallenby. Our paths crossed long ago, but it seems Arthur has not forgot."

Rosamunde smiled winsomely at Arthur, and beneath the spell of that smile he made such a deep leg to her that the sandy curls of his great periwig nearly swept the floor.

"Ah, Harry, she is even fairer than they say," breathed Arthur when he had regained his balance. His tone was reverent. "To lead the life you do, Harry, and still to have such beauty at your side—" He paused as a bright-eyed serving wench brought in a bottle of fine Malmsey and four glasses which she handled with great care. Rosamunde suspected them of being the tavern's best.

Harry grinned as he raised his glass. "They treat ye well here, Arthur. We'll tarry for no more than one glass with you, lest we be recognized and you lose this reputation ye've no doubt carefully built up!"

Arthur laughed. "Times have indeed changed for me, Harry. My uncle died—the one who turned me out in the first place, saying he cared not whether I lived or died— as you'll remember I told you. He forgot to make out a will, and I inherited all his goods. I married an heiress and I'm now the local squire. My home and park lie but three leagues distant."

"Fortune has indeed smiled on ye, Arthur."

"Aye, since those days when I thought to make my way on the road. Lord, I was terrified, Harry, floundering about in the dark seeking to fall upon some likely coach." He shivered.

"Ye did it badly enough," Harry remembered dryly.

"And glad I am that those gloomy days are at an end,"

said Arthur devoutly. "But what brings ye to this part of the country, Harry?"

"The same as always. The likelihood of a good haul."

"Ah, don't do it in my district, Harry!"

Will grimaced and gave Rosamunde a jaded look.

"All right," said Harry slowly. "We'll make our way outside your district at once." He drained his glass and rose. " 'Twas good to see you again, Arthur. Consider I've bought you a drink for old times' sake. I'll pay the landlord for the wine on my way out."

"Ah, be not so stiff-necked, Harry. I only meant 'twould be awkward if ye were hauled into my court after everyone had seen me entertaining ye here. I'd thought to entertain ye at Hallenby Hall, for though my wife has two children now tugging at her skirts, she still claims 'tis a lonely place, and you'd be welcome guests."

"Your wife knows about your past misdeeds then?" said Harry wonderingly as he pulled on his gauntlets.

"Aye. My checkered career weighed in my favor with Eleanor, for she found her other swains dull."

Harry smiled, but would have been on his way nonetheless had not Rosamunde given his arm a sudden tug. He turned his dark visage to consider her and saw the wistful look in her green eyes. Suddenly it occurred to him how much she must miss the genteel life of the landed gentry in which she had been brought up. If they supped at Hallenby Hall, Rosamunde would have a chance to wear a lovely gown and sit at a long candlelit table drinking sociable toasts with the squire and his lady. She could forget for an evening that she was a woman with a price on her head. His face softened.

"Then we'll take ye up on your invitation, Arthur, if Will here is agreed."

"But the Banbury Fair's day after tomorrow!" exploded Will. "We've traveled a deal of a way, Harry, to let such an opportunity pass."

"Well, let that not deter you," said Arthur hastily, his pink cheeks growing even pinker with his earnestness. "Banbury's not in my district. Travel on to Banbury and

245

do what you must, but join me at Hallenby Hall for supper and the night three days hence. Are we agreed upon it?"

"Agreed." Harry shook Arthur's hand. " 'Twill be good for Rose here to dine at a gentleman's board again, for 'tis the manner of life she's used to."

" 'Tis obvious from the look of her," cried Arthur gallantly. "And my Eleanor will be overjoyed to have guests. She does naught but complain about the lonesomeness of the hall." He accompanied them to the inn door and waved as they left.

"Well, Rose, I'll buy ye a silk dress at Banbury with slippers to match." Harry smiled as they rode away.

Rosamunde gave him a sweet smile. She'd been thinking much the same herself. On the road, she enjoyed almost exclusively the company of men—for the only women she met were ignorant serving maids and bawds. She was lonesome for her kind. And she could play at being a lady again during her short stay at Hallenby Hall.

At Banbury she purchased a peach satin gown which reminded her of the one Louisa had worn when last they met, soft peach leather gloves, a petticoat of rustling apricot silk and a pair of cream satin slippers with apricot heels. She felt she would be the very last gasp of fashion, for these things had all been smuggled over from France and packed in to Banbury Fair in bulging saddlebags. And when Harry found for her a delicate chemise trimmed with creamy lace, her happiness was complete.

Will grumbled that neither of them was attending to business and spent his time roaming the fair, keeping a weather ear alert for conversations about wealthy persons who had journeyed here to enjoy the fair. He came back, excited.

"I've found us a lone traveler with money, Harry," he chortled. "One who's leaving tonight by the Oxford road."

"He has money now, you mean. By tonight he may have spent it on some wench."

"Not this man. He's here but for one reason—to fleece the fairgoers. He cheats at cards." Will smote his knee. "I watched him at play, Harry. 'Twas so baldfaced a cheat, ye'd hardly credit it. But he fooled the bumpkins
246

he was playing with and swaggered away with all their coin. I've been following him around, Harry. He has plans to sup this evening with a wealthy young student who's journeying home from Oxford and stopped by the fair on the way. He's been getting the lad drunk all afternoon, so 'tis easy to see what's afoot. He'll fleece the lad at cards, leave him in a drunken stupor and be gone." His eyes twinkled. "I even overheard him make arrangements for his horse to be brought to the tavern where he dines. 'Tis plain he plans to slip away in the night, before the lad knows he's been cheated. 'Twill be an easy haul."

And it was. The card cheat found himself cheated of his gains as three bold highwaymen left him afoot to find his horse, which they drove away after relieving him of his purse. Rosamunde and Harry had little compunction in robbing him, for they knew how he had come by his coin. They were laughing as they made the long ride to Hallenby Hall.

The hall was rather smaller than Rosamunde had expected, but it was charming and very old, of weathered pinkish brick festooned with ivy. It had enjoyed recent renovation, for the roof was new and there were other signs of money having been spent. Rosamunde remembered that Arthur Hallenby had mentioned that he had married an heiress and wondered if all this was her doing.

They reached the hall at dusk. Arthur rushed out to greet them, but his Eleanor was nowhere in sight. Rosamunde was rather glad she was not, for she preferred to greet her hostess in skirts rather than in her dusty boots and counterfeit man's attire.

A kindly servant girl escorted them to their rooms, and Rosamunde changed to the peach-and-apricot creation that had been smuggled in from France and put up her hair in the latest fashion. When she trailed down the long carved wooden stairway on Harry's arm, she felt indeed that she had returned to another life.

They were early and found only Will downstairs to greet them. Rosamunde remembered suddenly that she had left her fan—which Will had gallantly purchased for her at Banbury—upstairs on the bed.

"I'll get it for you," offered Harry, but Rosamunde thought it might have slipped off the edge of the coverlet. Harry might step on it by mistake.

"There's time, since we're the first down," she said. "I'll just run up and get it myself." She picked up her satin skirts and ran lightly back upstairs.

At the top of that long flight she paused for breath. From the room on her right a mutter of voices reached her.

"No, I will *not* come down!" said a woman's voice, atremble with rage. "What were you thinking of to bring these footpads here?"

Instinctively, Rosamunde stepped closer to that thick oaken door. Through it, plainly, she could hear the voice of her host.

"Eleanor, they are not common footpads. They are highwaymen, gentlemen of the road, as once I was—"

"And that doxy with them? Oh, I saw her ride up flaunting her men's clothing! I was standing behind the curtains peering out. Do you want your children . . ."

Rosamunde stepped cautiously back from the door. Her light-hearted expression had altered. Walking thoughtfully now, she retrieved her fan and went back downstairs. Her host and hostess were still nowhere to be seen.

"Harry," she said sighing, "I think we have made a mistake."

Before she could elaborate on that, Arthur Hallenby appeared at the door. His face was very flushed. He maintained a firm grasp on his wife's white-gloved hand, and Rosamunde suspected him of having dragged her down the stairs. Eleanor Hallenby was a handsome brunette, dressed, as nearly as Rosamunde could tell, in riding clothes. Her spurs jingled as she walked. Rosamunde guessed she had been out riding earlier and had obdurately refused to change for dinner. She greeted her guests in wooden fashion, nodded coldly at Rosamunde, while Arthur tried to cover for her by keeping up a stream of conversation, and they went in to dinner.

That cruel evening burned itself forever into Rosamunde's memory. Her hostess in violet sarsenet, hardly speaking, hardly eating. Her hard-pressed host, almost hysterically jovial. Will, ignoring his hostess' petulance, genial and telling droll stories. Harry, his dark face growing colder by the moment as he watched Rosamunde's discomfiture.

At last that terrible meal was ended. Rosamunde could not have told you anything she had eaten, for she had not tasted anything. It was time for the ladies to go into the withdrawing room while the gentlemen smoked or took snuff and drank their whisky.

The squire's wife rose. She had a determined look about her now, and Rosamunde accompanied her silently.

They went into one of the rooms that had obviously been recently renovated, for the red brocade hangings were new and almost matched the Turkey carpet on the floor. Eleanor did not ask Rosamunde to sit down. She stood stiffly in the center of the floor.

What she might have said, Rosamunde would never know, for suddenly a pretty little dark-haired girl dressed in a miniature version of the gown her mother was wearing toddled into the room from the hall. Behind her there was a scurry of footsteps coming down the stairs and a serving maid's voice calling, "Ellie! Ellie, where are you?"

The child gave a cooing laugh and started to run past Rosamunde, obviously intending to further elude the pursuing serving maid. But Rosamunde, who liked children, smiled and stepped forward to cut her off. She was bending down to pick up the little girl in her arms when her hostess' strained voice reached her like a whiplash.

"Don't touch my child!"

Rosamunde straightened up. The color had drained from her face. "Is it possible you are unaware of your husband's past activities? Or how Harry saved his life?"

"That was long ago," snapped Eleanor. "And has nothing to do with me." She warmed to her subject. "How dare you come here and endanger my children? If you were pursued here—and I doubt not you will be—do you not realize they could be shot?"

At this overdramatic statement, Rosamunde smiled— but it was a cold smile.

"Let us hope the constable's men take better aim, should that arise," she said dryly. She made a deep mock curtsy. "I thank you for your 'hospitality,' madam." She lingered sarcastically upon the word. "And I bid you remember," she added on a stern note, "that if you think to send the authorities after us when we are gone, and have us taken, that Harry may have some compunction about involving your husband—but I have no such compunction. I will describe to all who will listen—yes, even from the gallows—what friends we are, how I was entertained by you at Hallenby Hall. I will dwell upon the gifts I brought you—all of them stolen and you knew it —the dress you wore, made of material that I had sent you, the food you served, how very *happy* you were to have us at your table."

The squire's wife wrung her hands. "How horrible of Arthur to bring you here!" she wailed, and burst into tears as Rosamunde swung on her apricot heel and swept from the room.

She made her way swiftly up those stairs which she had trod so lightly on Harry's arm, changed to her green velvet doublet and trousers, bundled up her finery and clattered downstairs with spurs jingling.

"Harry," she said, swinging open the dining-room door, "it is time we left."

Harry took one look at her bleak expression, set down his glass of Madeira and rose. At the head of the long table Arthur sprang nimbly to his feet and seized Harry's arm. "I would not have had it this way, Harry," he cried almost tearfully. "But you know women!"

"Only too well," said Harry ironically. "My thanks for your hospitality, Arthur, and we'll be out of your district before the morning light."

Will showed no flicker of surprise. Rosamunde guessed from the jaded look of him that he had expected no less.

They rode for a long time in silence, through the park and into the woodlands, their progress followed by a white moon that winked at them through the trees.

"I am sorry, Rose," said Harry, coming up beside her when they paused to drink at a roadside spring and water

250

the horses. "I had thought you would enjoy a flutter back into the life you've known."

Rosamunde stood very still in the darkness, listening to the wild cry of a hunting owl, the scurrying night sounds. There were tears in her eyes. Lest he see them, she leaned over and splashed cold water over her hot face. " 'Tis no matter, Harry." Lithely she swung up into her saddle without assistance. "It has taught me a needed lesson. It taught me what I have become."

There was bitterness in her voice as she spoke. For until that moment she had never quite realized how far she had left the old life behind her . . . or that she could never go back.

That night Rosamunde became a highwayman—in heart as well as calling. There was a new hardness in her, forged by humiliation and disappointment. She told herself she did not care what the world thought of her. She had Harry and that was enough.

The peach-and-apricot garments she gave away to a ragged country lass in the first market town they came to.

17   *July passed, and August.*

And now with the coming of September, the tales of their many wild exploits on the road had spread, and the fame of the Wild Rose, who dressed and rode like a man but who was possessed of a stunning beauty, grew swiftly into a great renown. She became almost as famous as Hard Harry, the most successful highwayman of his day. And when craggy Will and lean sardonic Harry rode into some out-of-the-way safe inn with the fashionable "youth" between them, there were many who gave Rosamunde a greeting as well as Harry and Will.

And that gave Harry pause, for he realized that as Rosamunde's notoriety increased, her safety grew less. There was a price on her head now, put there by Lord Matthew Waverclay. Not "dead or alive"—he wanted her alive; at least Harry had that consolation. But fame brought danger. Rosamunde's was a striking face, hard for a man to forget. And conceal her slender body as she would in the stiff men's clothes of the day, it was hard to conceal that tempting bustline or the silken motion of her girlish hips. Friends told Harry privately she'd be the death of him—she'd be recognized someday as they passed heedless through some market town, and he'd swing for it. Harry heard them out in silence. It seemed futile to say that he would give his life a thousand times over just to ride by her side—or that he would cut to pieces without mercy anyone who threatened her.

But—inevitably—he fought for her once too often.

It happened at a hideaway inn frequented by rogues in the west of England. It was early September and the three of them had had a good night on the moonlit highway. They swept in laughing and jingling with yellow gold.

To be confronted by red-haired Nell, who dropped her empty tankards with a clatter at sight of them and stood stock still in the center of the common room.

"Hello, Nell." Harry inclined his head affably, and then his gaze left her to swing around the room, studying the company. There were several faces he recognized among those seated at the candlelit wooden tables, and nods were exchanged.

"Hello, Harry," Nell mumbled, bending down to pick up her armload of tankards.

"Why, Nell, are you working here now?" asked Will, surprised. "I thought you'd still be at Winchester."

"Winchester got too hot for us," said Nell, rising. "And so we come here. Don't care for it much, though." She sighed. "Would ye hand me that tankard, Will? It's rolled under that chair by your boot."

Will picked it up and handed it to her. " 'Tis good to see you again, Nell."

"Good to see you too, Will. Can I bring you some ale?"

"Aye, that you can, Nell," said Will heartily, and Rosa-munde saw that his eyes were agleam at seeing Nell again. "Three brimming tankards!" He would have said more, but Nell turned on her heel and hurried away through the crowded room to bring the ale.

Nell looked older, Rosamunde thought. More haggard. More *tarnished* than she had looked that night when Rosa-munde had come looking for a job at Harry's instigation. Nell had had a wild untamed look about her then. Now some of the gloss was gone. Rosamunde joined Harry and Will at a table in the corner—both men liked to have their backs to the wall—and tried to fathom this change in Nell. Certainly her hair was just as red, her torn satin dress—bright-pink this time—was just as blowzy. But her gaze had been sad as she considered the three of them, and now as she brought them their ale she gave Harry a look that was somehow bereft. Rosamunde felt sorry for her, because something in the way Nell looked at Harry told her that Nell loved him, had always loved him.

Harry seemed unaware that Nell had her heart in her eyes. He gave her a pleasant smile.

Will leaned forward. "I don't see Dick around, Nell. Has he gone off somewhere?"

"Dick's working tonight." Nell meant he was prowling the highways, looking for a purse to lift. "His luck's been terrible bad lately." She shook her head, as if such a run of bad luck went past understanding.

"Well, then, if he's working tonight," murmured Will, seizing her hand, "there's nothing to prevent you sharing a tankard with me, is there?"

Nell knew he meant more than a tankard. She gave him a haggard look and turned to Harry. "I've need of your advice, Harry."

Harry set down his tankard and considered her gravely. "Anytime, Nell."

"After you've supped, then?"

He nodded, and Rosamunde, who no longer felt the wild jealousy of Nell she once had, seeing her so sad and forlorn, wondered what trouble Nell was in that she

253

needed advice from Harry. Perhaps she needed money to get away from here. . . .

"Dick beats her," supplied Harry gloomily, and Rosamunde looked up in astonishment.

"Then why does she stay with him?"

Harry shrugged.

"Women are past comprehension," put in Will. "Nell's a good lass and a pretty one; she could have her pick of men. But she fancied the two ends of the stick—Harry, who didn't want her, and Dick, who won't treat her right."

Rosamunde's compassionate glance followed Nell, whose handsome satin shoulders drooped a little as she served the rowdy customers in the common room.

Harry disappeared after supper, leaving her with Will. Rosamunde knew he was with Nell, somewhere outside in the star-studded night, and felt a momentary prickling of the old jealousy. Nell had known him before she had, loved him before she had. . . . She told herself that was unworthy, Harry was true to her, but after a while she excused herself and strode restlessly to the doorway. And there in the moonlight she beheld a little pantomime that made her draw in her breath sharply.

In the shadow of a giant sycamore tree, dappled by moonlight, Nell sobbed against Harry's chest. He was patting her back and muttering. Rosamunde stood quietly watching them.

Not so the stranger who came around the corner of the stone building, walking silently on the soft earth. He too stood stock still, but he barked a single word into the night.

"Nell!"

Nell gave a compulsive jerk away from the shelter of Harry's arms and peered in the direction of the sound. "D—Dick?" she stammered. "I did not know you were back."

"So it appears," said Dick grimly. He strode forward, caught her by the arm and pulled her to him with such force that she collided against his chest. " 'Tis you, Harry?" He sounded surprised as Harry emerged from the semidarkness into the light.

254

"Aye, Dick." Harry's tone was nonchalant, but Rosamunde noted, with a prickle along her spine, that he kept his hand close to his sword hilt.

"And why are ye after my doxy when ye've one of your own?" Dick demanded bluntly. His long legs were planted wide apart, and he kept a firm grip on the struggling Nell.

"I'm not 'after her' as ye so nicely put it," said Harry. "She's wondering what she does that's so wrong that ye should beat her for it. Faith, I'm wondering myself!"

Dick gave red-haired Nell an impatient look. "I'll have the skin off her back if she hides under the trees with rogues like you!" He gave her a push. "Back inside, Nell. I can hear the innkeeper calling for you."

Nell whimpered and scurried away with her head bent. Harry lounged forward, past Dick, who stood glowering, looking after him, and brushed by Rosamunde in the doorway. "Get inside," he muttered. "Dick Brue's in an ugly mood this night, and poor Nell may pay for it."

"What did she want?" asked Rosamunde, when they had returned to their table.

"She wants to be shut of him, I don't doubt," divined Will, watching them cynically as he lifted his tankard.

Harry nodded. "She wants to return to her people in Dorset, but she has not the money. I gave her some," he said simply.

"Dick will take it, if he finds she's got any," warned Will in a gloomy voice. "He's done it before."

"Aye." Harry sighed. "That's not to be helped. She came to me for aid, and I gave her such help as I could. If she does not leave tonight, she probably won't go at all."

So Harry was assisting his discarded mistress to leave her new lover. . . . Rosamunde took a long swallow of ale. She had come to feel compassion for these women who followed the fortunes of highwaymen and roadside robbers. Too often their lovers took flight and deserted them. Too often their lovers were hanged. . . . She shivered.

"Are you cold?" asked Harry instantly, for he knew that she had not been feeling well of late.

255

She shook her head, but she saw that his gaze was not for her. It beamed over her shoulder through the crowd to the place where Dick Brue was now seated, drinking heavily with some rough-looking fellows from Lincolnshire. Nervously, Nell served them ale. Her eyes were red from crying.

"I think ye'll be having trouble with Dick before the evening's out, Harry," said Will evenly.

"I don't doubt it." Harry sighed. "It's been a long time brewing. Dick's jealous of Nell—for all he treats her badly—and she was my doxy before she was his."

"I know the weather's still hot, but have ye thought of the winter, Harry?" asked Will abruptly. "I'm thinking the West Country may have a hard winter—and we along with it, grubbing along the icy roads. Why do we not for London to spend the winter, Harry? Our Wild Rose here would like that, for she'd have a chance to wear women's clothes and see plays again."

Rosamunde brightened, remembering what a good time they had had in London last year on the proceeds of Louisa's diamonds.

"And perhaps," Will added wistfully, "Nell might decide to come with us. For she'll be tired of Dorset by then."

"All right," said Harry absently. "London it is, Will. But we'll have to finish off the fall strong, if we're to afford a whole winter in London. 'Tis an expensive place."

"All places are expensive for such as we." Will sighed.

And Rosamunde thought gloomily how true that was. She was staring down into her empty tankard and started as a long leg was suddenly flung over the bench beside her and Dick Brue, lean and smelling strongly of ale, pressed his thigh insinuatingly against hers.

"Ye've spent part of the evening with *my* doxy, Harry —I thought I'd end my evening with yours," he announced loudly.

There was a general silence. The whole room turned to watch.

Harry's hard gray eyes studied Dick. " 'Tis Rose's own choice whom she spends her evening with, Dick."

Dick flung a careless arm over Rosamunde's shoulders.

His whole pose was swaggering. "Any wench in her right senses would chose me! Am I not the better man, Rose?" he asked insolently.

Rosamunde sighed and disengaged his arm, edged away from his encroaching thigh. "Nell is watching," she muttered. "You'll hurt her feelings."

Dick laughed uproariously. "Hurt Nell's feelings? Ah, she's none left to hurt! She took up with her first man when she was eleven. Harry here was her tenth!"

"At least she kept count!" said Rosamunde through her teeth. She turned to see that Harry's frown had deepened dangerously. "Go away, Dick." She sighed. "Haven't you hurt poor Nell enough? She's watching." And Nell was. From across the room Rosamunde could see her anguished eyes, dark spots in her white face.

"Let her watch," said Dick indifferently. "Come, share a tankard with me, pretty Rose. Is it true you can slice a man's head off with that dainty blade you carry?"

There were open grins on many faces now as the rough men of the road edged forward to enjoy this baiting.

" 'Tis true I've sliced off none," said Rosamunde, remaining calm with an effort, for she still hoped to stave off a fight between Dick and Harry.

"Some ale here, Nell!" shouted Dick.

Nell stumbled miserably over. Her gaze on Dick was reproachful. "Another round for all?" she muttered.

"Two tankards only—for me and my new doxy here," said Dick in a thick voice. He leaned over and tried to kiss Rosamunde on the lips.

She ducked to avoid him, and the table creaked as Harry pushed it back. He reached over, grabbed Dick by the scruff and with a violent shove slid Dick farther down the bench. "Come over to the other side—beside Will here," he told Rosamunde tersely.

Dick, reeling backward from Harry's hard shove, had ended up banging into the shoulder of a rough-looking fellow who, mindful of Dick's reputation, growled something, picked up his tankard and moved across the room. Dick righted himself and brushed some spilled ale from his sleeve. "I take it amiss that ye'd treat a friend thus,

Harry," he cried. "Ye've shared my Nell—'tis only sporting I should share this Wild Rose with you!"

Green eyes flashing, Rosamunde stood her ground. "I am not a doxy to be shared," she said in a clear carrying voice. For emphasis she drew her blade and held it out before her, pointed at Dick's chest. "And if you lay hands on me again, Dick Brue, I'll test the edge of this blade on you!"

She hoped to make him back down by this show of bravado, but it did not work. Dick could see that her arm was extended to its full length; he could dive backward before she could more than pink him. Aware that he had an interested audience, he guffawed loudly.

"So your Wild Rose has thorns, Harry! Do ye bear her scars?"

People were nudging each other now. The whole room was agog, hoping for a fight between two such redoubtable highwaymen as Hard Harry and Dick Brue. Even more would they relish a skirmish between Dick and the beautiful Wild Rose, for none had seen her except in men's clothing, and they had no doubt that in any tussle Dick would manage to tear her clothes off.

Rosamunde trembled as Harry's hand clamped down on her shoulder. He drew her firmly back behind him. "Sheathe your sword, Rose. I'll deal with this," he said calmly. " 'Tis myself Dick wants. He itches for a fight."

"Nay, 'tis your doxy I want," taunted Dick, his voice rising so that all could hear. "And after I've bedded her, we'll *ask* her who's the better man!"

"Back off, Dick," warned Harry, half-rising in his chair. His dark face was intent, and he had a dangerous look to him. "We've known each other a long time, and I'll make due allowance for the fact that ye're drunk. But ye take your life in your hands when ye speak so of Rosamunde."

"Ah, say ye so? We'll let *her* decide, Harry!" Without warning, Dick suddenly launched himself at Harry, and from somewhere a dagger appeared in his hand. As Dick sprang, Will shot out an arm and jerked Rosamunde out of the way, for Harry was borne back against the wall by the suddenness of Dick's onslaught. His shoulder brought
258

up hard against the window casing, but he dodged by a hair's breadth the short length of steel that shot toward him. The point of that viciously driven short blade embedded itself in the window casing inches deep.

Cursing, Dick tried to wrench the dagger free. Their faces were almost nose to nose as Harry, with a rippling sinewy movement, threw Dick backward to land crashing among the tankards on the table top. Before Dick could rise, Harry grasped the heavy table, overturned it and sent Dick and the tankards crashing onto the hard stone floor. Like a cat, he leaped to his advantage, clearing the overturned table and fairly bestriding his opponent's chest, his strong hands closing about Dick's throat, throttling him.

"What devil came over you, Dick, to come at me with a knife?" he growled.

Dick gurgled something. His eyes were rolling balefully and he clutched convulsively at Harry's hands, trying to wrest them away from his throat.

"I could kill you easily," Harry said softly, pressing his fingers in deep. Dick's face was indeed turning blue as he wrestled with Harry for possession of his throat. His bloodshot eyes were popping and his chest heaved spasmodically. But he had courage. When Harry relaxed his grip only a little, Dick's gasping voice reached the silent watching company. "Then do so, Harry! Ye've the advantage."

"No, Harry!" Nell screamed.

Harry looked down into Dick's angry face, into which the color was now returning, with cold deliberation. "We were friends once, Dick. For that I give you your life —and because Nell would weep if you were dead. But so that it be a lesson to you . . . " His hard fist swung down into Dick's face in a quelling way; there was the crunch of bone when it landed.

For a moment Dick's body sagged; then, as Harry rose and stepped grimly aside, he stumbled up, gaining his feet amid raucous mocking laughter, for the assembled company were quick to cheer a victor—and quick to jeer a loser. With blood dripping from his sullen cut lip and holding his jaw, Dick stomped from the room.

Rosamunde had been on her feet, craning forward, wondering how to put a stop to this before murder was done. Now she expelled a deep shaky breath and sank back upon the bench, feeling weak.

As if such contests were an everyday occurrence with him, Harry nonchalantly righted the table and sat down again.

"Nell, we'll need more ale." He sighed. "For ours is spilled."

"Thank ye, Harry," muttered Nell. "For giving Dick his life."

Rosamunde watched with fascination as Nell hastily mopped up the spilled ale and retrieved the tankards, which had rolled about the room; she made no move to go after Dick, and Rosamunde thought perhaps she was afraid to. Unable to best Harry, Dick might vent his spleen on Nell. Around the room the wastrels and highwaymen and rakehells and their bawds settled down again to whatever they had been doing before. Fights were a common occurrence in these inns and served to lighten the day for these rough men.

"I think ye have made a mistake, Harry," said Will sternly. "Dick will not forget this night—nor forgive it, especially if Nell leaves him. He'll think she's gone to meet you somewhere."

"Let him think it." Harry shrugged. "Dick's changed with the years. He was once a good fellow, and many a tankard we shared together. I could not kill him as he lay there."

"You may wish you had," said Will with a moody look toward Nell, who looked very haggard.

"But Harry could not kill him in cold blood!" protested Rosamunde.

"Harry is too nice in his ways," muttered Will. " 'Twill get him killed in the long run."

Rosamunde looked around her at this rowdy crowd. Brass tankards were being clashed together noisily; someone was banging on a table top for emphasis and almost dislodging several pairs of boots, caked with mud, that reposed there. There was a loud altercation arising over a card game in one corner, where two fancily dressed bawds were helping cheat a newcomer at cards. On the stone floor at one end of the room a dice game was in progress, and Nell was having to step over the legs of the men who crouched around the coins and dice. One of the men reached up under Nell's skirts and pinched her bottom as she went by. She turned and kicked at him playfully, but her eyes were sad. She stepped out of the path of a reeling drunk and collided painfully with the spurs of a fellow who was sleeping it off on the floor and snoring loudly. Nell was limping a little as she brought them fresh tankards and another round of ale.

How many such scenes had she looked upon? Rosamunde asked herself. Life on the road was made up of lying in wait—often uncomfortably, in cramped positions, sometimes for hours; of dangerous clashes—usually with armed men, and often by night when, in a melee, it was hard to tell friend from foe; of long hard rides through any kind of weather pursued by men and dogs—and guns. And at the end their reward: evenings spent in a place like this.

She sighed and looked at Nell, who once had been Harry's mistress, and yet had come to this. Well, that was not the way she planned her life to be! Her hand shook a little as she passed it over her forehead.

Harry was instantly concerned. "Are you all right, Rose?"

"My head aches," she admitted. "I think 'tis the noise." She pushed back her ale.

" 'Tis indeed an infernal din," he agreed. "Why don't you go upstairs and rest awhile? Will and I have some talking to do."

She knew they wanted to consult with the landlord, whose name was Brill, and who was known to be able to put a man "onto a good thing" for a fat fee. They'd been arguing about it earlier. Harry had said he preferred to find his own targets, and Will maintained that Harry's attitude had cost them a good job near Southampton and another outside Newmarket; information was for sale, and unless they wanted to sit with their feet propped up on a tavern table until someone came to collect the reward on their heads, they'd best be buying it! Rosamunde had taken no part in this discussion, except to sigh and say she'd be glad to head back toward London. Harry had taken this to mean impatience, and had agreed that they'd talk to Brill and find out what he had to offer.

"Remember to latch your door, Rose," Harry cautioned in a low voice as she rose.

Rosamunde nodded and threaded her way through the noisy throng on her way upstairs, conscious that many eyes were on her. But nobody reached out to pinch *her*. And she knew it was not the light dress sword that swung from her leather baldric—it was the iron fist of Harry that kept them at bay. Otherwise they'd treat her as they treated poor Nell.

It was a sobering thought.

She had other things to think about too: worrying things. She had skipped two periods and was almost sure she was pregnant. To bear a child under these conditions! She shrank from the thought. And yet . . . she longed to hold Harry's child in her arms, to shield him, to love him, to watch him grow up. Long were her thoughts that night.

Eventually Harry came upstairs and she got up and unlatched the door, for guests were unruly in these inns and it would not do to leave one's door unlatched.

"Did you learn anything from the landlord?" she asked.

"No. We'll leave here tomorrow, Rose. I know you don't like it here." He sat down and tugged off his boots. "Where would you like to go, Rose?"

Rosamunde had thought long about that. "By easy stages to London," she said. "And winter there." In London she would tell him that she was pregnant; perhaps he would find some kind of work to be near her, perhaps even—ah, these were but dreams—he would find a way to take them to the Colonies. "We could go by way of Dorset," she pursued. "And give Nell safe conduct there—if we are not taken and she is hanged with us," she added dryly.

"Yes, Will would like that. He has always wanted her."

"I know." She was no longer jealous of Nell, who was well started on a long downhill road. But she was glad in her heart that they were leaving, for Harry was right; she did not like it here. She did not like any of these safe inns with their rowdy swaggering rogues and feverish-eyed bawds. But she need not think about that, for they would be going to London, where she had been so happy. And there, perhaps at Christmastime, she would tell Harry that she was to bear his child. And hope the news would be accepted as a gift.

Dreaming these dreams, she watched Harry undress, blow out the candle. The bed creaked as he joined her and she went into his arms with a contented sigh, letting the warm competent feel of him erase her troubles from her mind.

"Rose." He fondled her neck and pressed kisses into her bright hair, while his other hand stroked her trembling body that always melted to fire at his touch. "Ah, Rose, you do not know what it has meant to me to have you beside me." He spoke humbly, and she was shaken by the deep emotion in his timbred voice.

"I am where I want to be, Harry," she whispered. "In your arms."

He slipped an arm beneath her, cradling her back. "You could have chosen another path, Rose. An easier path."

She gave a soft whimsical laugh. "Oh, yes, I could have been Lord Matthew's mistress—or perhaps an inept dairymaid being kicked across the barn every time I milked the cow!"

His lips brushed her ear and his lean naked body insinuated itself against hers, and talk was forgotten as they strained together as lovers, kissing, touching, letting their shared emotions wash over them like waves, letting their passions build into a sweet madness and sweep them downstream on an irresistible river of wanting, loving, having.

But the next morning Will brought evil tidings. Dick Brue, it seemed, had teamed up with Big Nate—the man whose doxy, Lollie, Rosamunde had attempted to "save." The rumor was they had sworn to "get" Harry.

Rosamunde had not even known Big Nate was staying at the inn; he must have arrived after she had gone upstairs last night. She wondered if plump Lollie was still with him, or if he had abandoned her for some other wench.

But Harry was drumming his fingers.

"That's ill news indeed, Will," he said thoughtfully.

Will's face was a thundercloud. "We'll have to kill them both now. Ye should not have been so merciful, Harry."

"Think you they will lie in wait for us on the road to Dorset?" wondered Rosamunde. She lowered her voice, for they were seated in the nearly deserted common room having a late breakfast, and she did not want the one or two idlers to overhear their destination.

"They will not have to," said Harry, taking a large helping of kidney pie. "Put out the word, Will, that I'll wait for them here. That should bring matters to a head."

Will shook his head, but he acquiesced gloomily and left. They ate the rest of their meal in comparative silence, although Harry was cheerful. Rosamunde looked down at her trencher and toyed with the food on it. She hardly tasted what little she ate. It had come to her chillingly that Harry had indeed made a mistake in not killing Dick Brue.

18 *The morning of the worst day of her life dawned* hot and murky for Rosamunde. She had tossed and turned through the night—she was sure she had kept Harry awake, but she could not help it. Now with the morning her stomach was queasy and the room tended to whirl around when she sat up.

Oh, no! she thought. *Morning sickness!* Holding onto her head and hoping her stomach would stop doing tricks, she wavered, not quite willing to get out of bed, and fell back with a slight groan.

Harry, already up and buckling on his baldric, said, "You're not to come with us, Rose. You aren't well enough. Will and I can handle this easily."

Usually that would be very true, but maybe this was the day it would not be true. Maybe Harry would need her today—desperately. That thought was always in the back of her mind. She struggled to a sitting position and the black nausea overcame her again. She sank back, trying not to retch.

"It will go away," she said weakly. "If you'll just wait for a minute."

"*No.*" Harry's voice was firm. "We'll be back when it's over, and we'll all ride for Dorset."

All but Nell, she thought. For Nell had decided not to go. God alone knew why, for Dick Brue had blacked her eye that night after Harry had bested him.

"Stay abed, Rose. We'll be back when it's over." Harry bent down and gave her a tender kiss, and she held onto him for a luminous moment, wishing in an unhappy bittersweet way that he did not have to leave her.

"Suppose things go wrong?" she asked wearily.

"Should anything go wrong, I'll send word. If I'm late, if you feel endangered here at the inn, ride for the coast. Hide there—I'll find you. But nothing will go wrong, Rose. Remember to latch this door after I'm gone."

She sat up in her chemise, her hair disheveled. The room seemed to be rocking about her as she watched the door close. Unsteadily she got to her feet and stumbled to the door, latched it and went back and collapsed on the creaking bed with a groan. A real blackness had come over her as the latch slipped into place, and she was glad to fall back onto the bed.

After a while she sat up, a little cheered. Tonight they

would leave this place—and hardly soon enough to suit her! She supposed she should go downstairs and eat breakfast, to be there in case Harry should send her word, but she was reluctant to go down. For downstairs in the common room snoring drunks would be lying about, sleeping off last night's revelry, a couple of half-dressed bawds among them, snoring as loudly as the others. The room would be filled with the odor of pipe smoke and stale beer. She hated mornings in these places.

Three days had passed since Dick Brue had rushed out of the inn swearing vengeance. And in those three days, while Harry waited for a confrontation with Dick and his new partner in crime, Big Nate, Brill the landlord had happened onto a "good thing" for them. John Snively, one of the men who kept an eye out for good things, had brought in word of something just right, and Brill had passed the deal on to Will and Harry—for a cut of the loot, of course.

Harry had outlined the plan to Rosamunde.

They were a hard day's ride from the coast, and one of the smugglers who frequented the coves of that coast was due in tonight with a load of French brandy for thirsty Cornwall. The constable of a nearby village—who always dealt with him; in his district the importing of brandy was his little monopoly—would be riding to the coast carrying jingling gold to pay for the shipment, for smugglers dealt in cash. There would be two men accompanying the constable, but neither was much force. Nor would they put up a fight, for the constable was known to be cowardly, and to rely more on arrests by night than confrontations by day. John Snively had a sister who worked in the constable's household and while doing her dusting frequently heard his plans. She had reported to Snively the route they would take. Harry and Will could lie comfortably in wait at a narrow place in the road where it passed through a grove of trees. At midmorning the constable would pass their hiding place. They would step out and take the gold.

It was simple enough. As Harry said, they would not need her.

Still, worry plagued at Rosamunde. They had had such a long run of good luck. Will had marveled at it. Coaches and stage wagons had fallen into their laps with regularity. Always they had struck at the right time, the right place. The gods had smiled on them.

She told herself it was because she was feeling unwell that she had these forebodings.

She got up and dressed. She was feeling better now; the sickness had gone. She went to the open window and looked out, feeling her hair sticking to her neck in the oppressive heat of that September morning. The gold of the sun had been dimmed by soft gray clouds that scudded across the azure sky. Perhaps it would rain. That would cool things off, and if Will and Harry made it back before the rain stopped, they could be away with the rain to obscure their tracks. She had met Harry on a rainy night. Somehow she felt that rain was lucky for them.

She had finished dressing and had just adjusted her baldric and sword over her doublet when there was a scurry of feet up the stairs and a pounding on the door.

"Let me in, Harry! Let me in!" Nell's voice, shrill and excited.

Rosamunde threw open the door and Nell burst in. She was sporting two black eyes and a cut lip. The sleeve was torn out of her satin dress, and from the dirt on her petticoat, she looked to have been dragged down the road for some distance. "Where's Harry?" she cried, looking wildly around her.

"Gone with Will," said Rosamunde.

"'Tis a trap!" wailed Nell. "Nate and Dick promised John Snively half what they take on their next job if he'd set this up. He was to tell the landlord some story about a smuggler—"

"A constable who deals with a smuggler," corrected Rosamunde in alarm. She listened with fierce concentration as Nell went on.

"Aye, but 'tis not true, Rose. Brill believed Snively because Snively's sister *does* work in the constable's household. But she knows naught about it; 'tis all a lie to trap Harry. This particular constable don't deal with
267

smugglers. But Snively's alerted him that Will and Harry will be waiting, and the constable will come through with two men—*but there'll be a larger party following.*"

Rosamunde felt the blood drain away from her face. She seized Nell by the shoulders. "Nell, *is this true?*"

Nell bobbed her disheveled head. "True as Gospel—and you know I wouldn't lie about it, because of the way I feel about Harry."

"How did you learn it?"

"I overheard Dick braggin' to that wench of Nate's—Lollie—about it. Dick's after *her* now." She touched her bruised face. "He give me this for sayin' Lollie would have his coin and leave him for a better man. And I guess he'll kill me for lettin' the cat out o' the bag about today's dirty work—but I don't care none. I couldn't see 'em ambush Harry! Rose, you got to go and warn him! I'd have gone but I didn't have no horse. Dick and Nate is camped near here. I ran all the way."

No wonder Nell had arrived out of breath!

"Does Dick know you've come here?" asked Rosamunde sharply.

Nell shook her head. "He don't know. He and Lollie were out in the bushes when I left—I could hear Nate callin' 'em."

"You can hide here, Nell. We'll take you to Dorset, where you'll be safe."

"Remember, 'tis but a little ways from the fork in the road," Nell told her earnestly. "The road to your left ends a little ways on, but the road to your right—'tis barely more than a cart track, Dick says—is the road ye must take. That is the road that leads down to the coast, and Will and Harry will be waiting there for the constable to pass by."

Rosamunde stuck her pistols in her belt. "Don't worry, Nell. I'll find them."

They both paused at the sound of hoofbeats below. Nell rushed to the window. "Oh, my God," she groaned. "There's Dick now—and Nate's with him. Dick'll kill me sure!"

Rosamunde plucked one of the pistols from her belt and tossed it to Nell. "Don't let him," she advised tersely.

Nell caught the pistol with a thankful look. "You'll have to go out over the roof, Rose," she muttered. "They're coming in."

Rosamunde had no intention of going out over the roof and risking a broken leg—that would seal Harry's fate for certain.

"I'm going down the stairs," she said tensely. "Do you want to come along, Nell? If we hurry, we can rush past them and be away before they can catch us—on *their* horses!"

Nell studied Rosamunde in wonderment. "I guess I see why Harry loves you," she said with reluctant admiration. "I'm afeared, but I do reckon if you can do it, I can —I do reckon."

But they were not to get the chance. Already footsteps were pounding up the stairs.

"They're comin' for us, Rose!" cried Nell on a high keening note of excitement.

"Let them," said Rosamunde grimly. She cocked her pistol.

"Nell!" Dick Brue's menacing voice. "Are you in there?"

Nell gave Rosamunde a frightened look. Rosamunde nodded.

"Yes," said Nell sullenly. "What about it?"

"Come out!"

"No. I'm stayin' in here, Dick."

Dick gave the door a lusty kick. It shuddered but it held. With the next kick it burst open, and Dick Brue spilled into the room with Big Nate just behind him.

Nell stood facing the entrance with pistol drawn. She did not wait. She fired. Dick went down with an expression of disbelief on his face, mouth open, eyes staring. Nell screamed as the blood splashed over his chest. She tossed away the pistol and ran toward him.

"Oh, Dick, Dick," she blubbered. "What have you made me do?"

But for Rosamunde the problem was Big Nate. With

his girth, a ball that did not strike a vital spot might not stop him. And then Harry and Will would be lost.

She was white to the lips, for she had never killed a man before, and now, if need be, she was going to. But her voice was level and cold. "Get out of my way, Nate."

Nate too ignored Dick's prostrate form and Nell's sobbing body bending over him, cradling him in her arms as he tried to gasp out his last words. He gave a crafty laugh. "Would you like to try your sword on me again?"

"Not this time, Nate. This time I'm going to kill you if you don't get out of my way."

Nate took a step toward her.

Rosamunde lowered the pistol a bit and aimed at his groin. Nate saw that and glowered. "You wouldn't do that, would you, Rose?" he asked softly, stepping to the side. "Blow a man's head off, yes, but not his . . . "

Rosamunde saw what he was going to do—step to the side and then leap on her as she tried to pass by. And there were people in the hallway now, ogling watchers who had run up the stairs at the sound of Nell's shot and scream. She couldn't tell whose side they were on, so she dared not edge out and then back into them. They might not let her through; they might seize her from behind.

She took careful aim and fired.

Nate tried to dodge, but he didn't make it quite far enough. The bullet hit him near the hipbone and dropped him to the floor. Rosamunde didn't wait to see if he would regain his feet. With smoking pistol, she ran out past the little group, who parted to let her by.

As she passed, a downhill bawd shrilled resentfully, "Did you see that? Aimed at his balls, she did!" And a man's whisky-roughened voice said, "Harry would have aimed at his heart. Nate got off cheap!"

Then she was past them and her boots were clattering down the wooden stairs, spurs ajingle. She ran through the inn door and stared for a moment at the horses Nate and Dick had ridden up on: poor horseflesh indeed. One looked half-starved with all his ribs showing; the other was so winded his head hung down. Better by far to ride Graylady!

She dashed to the stable, and grimly loaded her pistol while the astonished stableboy saddled the gray mare. And was out the stable door, bending low lest she be brushed off, and down the road at a gallop.

She knew the place where Harry and Will would wait, for she had listened closely as they made their plans—after all, she had expected to be waiting there with them in the place John Snively had suggested. But that Nell had known too was added proof of the truth of her story.

She didn't think she was too late—and she prayed she would not be. Fast she rode, looking alertly about her for signs of trouble.

There were no such signs.

The azure brightness of the early morning had departed entirely now, leaving only scudding gray clouds that darkened with the promise of rain. It was not so far from the inn, the place where they would be waiting. She had reached the fork in the road now and confidently turned down the right fork that led toward the coast. Anxiously she scanned the road ahead for sight of them, but there were only the trees and the waving grasses, already turning to the gold of autumn.

A few raindrops fell, spattering her face and the gray mare's mane. She scanned the sky anxiously. Heavy rain now would delay their flight, for it would turn this dusty road to mire. Nightwind could slog through it, as could Will's big gelding, but Graylady, while fast, was not strong enough to plow through mud for long—and she had no doubt they would have to run for it, and run fast, for the constable and his men could not be far away.

Anxiously her eyes combed the road ahead for sight of Harry or Will. She knew she must look for a heavy clump of trees, a place where the road narrowed sharply. Faith, it had been narrow enough all the way, a mere cart track!

Some twigs snapped in the trees over to her right, and Graylady shied and reared up. Rosamunde studied those trees fearfully—did they shelter armed men? Men who might stop her from her mission? But there was only silence, now broken by the patter of a few raindrops.

She shivered and rode on.

She topped a slight rise where the clouds seemed to press down upon the road—and there she saw them, below her where the trees grew thick and the road narrowed to passage for a single cart. Harry was there, and Will, and— her heart almost stopped—three other men, whom Harry was holding at gunpoint while Will searched their saddlebags. She urged the gray mare forward with her knee and her voice carried down the road.

"Harry!" she screamed. " 'Tis a trap!"

Both Harry and Will looked up as she spoke, and one of the three constable's men, a fellow garbed in scarlet, leaped forward suddenly and struck Harry's gun away. Will turned and shot him and he rolled in a writhing scarlet heap in the dust of the road.

Rosamunde's pistol was out now and she was racing forward down the low hill, but she was still too far away to get in a good shot. Below her another of the men—who looked to be the constable himself, for he was the most richly dressed—had leaped upon Will's back and borne him to the ground. The other burly fellow had dived for Harry's pistol and Harry's boot had crashed onto his hand, but he had grasped Harry's leg with his free hand and Harry had gone down to the ground as well. As Rosamunde flew toward them on Graylady's back, she could see only a tangle of arms and legs, for all four of them were down in a flailing heap.

From the shelter of the trees suddenly thundered a group of armed men. They were shouting as they rode forward, and there were musket balls flying round her head now. Graylady had carried her almost to the place where the action was taking place, and at the spatter of gunfire, the shouts of the men who had burst from the cover of the trees, she became terrified. She leaped forward, refusing to halt. She almost collided with Nightwind, who neighed and reared up and crashed back against Will's gelding. Their combined weight broke a sapling and took them out of Graylady's terrified path.

272

Not so the men. They were directly ahead in a struggling heap. White-faced, Rosamunde realized she could not bring the terrified horse to a halt. And she was on a collision course with that jumble of men in the road. There was only one way now—over!

Even as she let Graylady have her head, she saw the constable from somewhere produce a gun and fire it directly into Will's face—and Will's face disappeared in a sudden gush of blood.

Then she was aloft, borne into the air as the frightened mare took a great leap into the air and cleared the men in her path. Rosamunde took a quick shot at Harry's attacker—and missed as Graylady's forelegs rose into the air at the beginning of her leap. As she was swept past, she heard Harry's hoarse, desperate cry: "Ride, Rose, ride! Away!"

Graylady landed in the dusty roadway and went down almost to her knees. Rosamunde was hard put to keep her seat in the saddle. As the horse staggered up, trembling, and shot away again, she turned her head to see how Harry fared. And that saved her life, for a musket ball that would have struck just below her left ear whistled harmlessly by.

Rosamunde was hardly aware of it. Her agonized gaze was riveted on the scene behind her.

The armed men who had burst from the bushes had reached that struggling group by now. Harry had just gotten the advantage of his attacker, had struck him a great blow that had felled him. But as he sprang to his feet she saw in horror the lead rider of the attacking party reverse his smoking pistol, and grasp it by the barrel. She screamed as she saw him lift it, saw him—as his horse plunged into the group—bring that pistol butt down upon Harry's dark head with smashing force. Saw Harry's tall form buckle and drop to the ground as if struck by lightning.

And then he disappeared from her view beneath the horses' hooves and the boots of the dismounting men as his pursuers crashed to a halt to surround their prey.

But the frightened mare had carried her past the battle,

was carrying her fast away. And from somewhere, loudly, rang Harry's voice, pealing down the corridors of her mind: *If I should fall . . . promise me, Rosamunde.* And her own reluctant voice: *I swear.*

She had taken an oath that if he fell, she would ride on. Now, with sobs choking her throat and tears blurring her vision, she honored that oath. For there was someone else now to think of—not only Harry and herself. There was her unborn child.

And for the sake of that child, her old craftiness came back to her. She would go back for Harry—ah, she would go back for him later. And somehow she would save him—no matter where they had taken him. Even in hell she would find him! He must be badly hurt to have fallen like that. But she would nurse him back to health. Ah, she would do it!

And with that hard resolve, she dashed the tears from her eyes and looked back.

With grim satisfaction, she saw that only two of the knot of men around the fallen highwaymen had broken away to follow her. They were leaning low over their horses' heads urging them on, but their mounts were not so fast as Graylady and they were falling behind.

Graylady was slowing her breakneck pace now, gaining confidence now that the shouts and the bullets lay well behind her. At a bend in the road, Rosamunde veered her into the trees, and when her pursuers rounded that bend, she seemed to have disappeared. They stopped, dismayed for a moment, then took off through the trees after her.

Rosamunde had been well schooled. She lost them easily. She waited awhile, and then she doubled back. By now Harry and Will would have been taken away, Harry swaying in Nightwind's saddle, and Will—who must be dead, for she had seen his face ripped away—would have been thrown across the back of the big gelding, a limp burden, for his last ride to—where? At least she could track them from there, for the rain had held off and the hoofprints of such a body of men would be easy to follow.

If she did not find them, she could return to the inn.

At nightfall, that would be the best time. There might be constable's men looking for her there, but she would have to chance it. She would find Nell. Nell would help her learn where they had taken Harry.

That Nell might be in deep trouble herself she refused to consider. She had seen hasty burials in innyards before, for these highwaymen's haunts were loath to bring in the authorities. She guessed that Dick Brue was safely under the sod by now, perhaps behind the stable, while Lollie would be nursing a sullen Nate back to health. Nell, if things went true to form, should be back serving ale by now and waiting to hear from them.

But she could not be sure that all the men were gone yet. So she left the mare a short distance from the road and walked, bent down, through the trees to the place where it had all happened.

She approached cautiously, making hardly a sound, the way Harry had taught her.

It was a shock to see that both Harry and Will still lay supine in the roadway, Harry, she noted in fright, lay as still as Will. Her heart beating wildly, she slipped up as close through the brush as she dared. There were two men seated on horseback, guarding them. She was closer now, and she could see better. Will lay nearer her and—for a moment she closed her eyes—there were flies buzzing over his bloody face. Harry lay face down, but she could see the blood clotted in his dark hair. She fingered her loaded pistol, automatically reached for a second one—and remembered that she had given her other pistol to Nell. Even with a lucky shot, at best she could drop only one of these men. Before she could reload the other would be on her, and Harry had taught her that she was no match for a strong determined man with a sword.

They were talking, and their words carried to her clearly.

"Two of 'em done for," ruminated one, spitting on the dusty road. "And both of 'em alive and full of fight just a bit ago!"

275

Done for! But it could not be true! Rosamunde grasped the bole of a tree to keep from falling. She felt sick.

"Aye," said the other thoughtfully, bestirring Will's body with his whip. "They give up plenty of trouble, this pair—but they won't no more. Think ye they've captured the Wild Rose by now?"

"Aye, and probably all had her by now in some likely spot beneath the trees. I would I were there." He sighed, brightened. "Mayhap we'll yet get our chance, Aaron, if they bring her by this way. Ah, she looked to be a hot piece, did she not? Riding into the fight like a very devil, leaping her horse over them and turning to fire in our faces! Have ye ever had a woman like that, Aaron?"

"There are no women like that," said Aaron dryly. "There be only the Wild Rose."

"Well, they'll have her pleading for mercy by now," predicted his companion, "and promising to warm all their beds for a fortnight if they'll but let her go!"

"I doubt she will plead." Aaron spat again. "I for one was glad to see her escape."

"Perhaps if we arrange it right, the jailer will let us into her cell tonight. How much coin have ye, Aaron?"

"Not enough. There'll be others ahead of ye, Bob, itchin' for a chance at the famous Wild Rose. The jailer will grow rich if he can but get the hangin' postponed."

Bob sighed. "It be a pity to hang such a woman." Morosely he stirred Harry's still form with his musket. "Ah, she'd have danced to our tune if we'd taken Hard Harry alive and hurt him a bit to encourage her!"

"Harry was a lucky devil while he lived. He had *her*," said Aaron softly.

Lucky! Rosamunde sagged against the tree bole. Lucky to have had her? But she had brought him death with her prodding him to go to London. Harry had never bought information before. Nor would he have this time had not Will urged him and she insisted she was eager to leave, to try London again. She brought no man luck! Not even Harry, whom she had loved with all her heart.

"Think you the constable has forgot us?" demanded Bob fretfully. " 'Tis going to pour down rain anytime and
276

you and me here with a couple of dead ones on our hands."

"If he has the Wild Rose in his arms, he's forgot us." Aaron shrugged. "But more like, he's had trouble finding a cart. He'll be wanting to exhibit this pretty pair of rogues—mount their heads on the city gates somewheres most likely."

Rosamunde felt her breakfast rise up in her throat. *Harry's head displayed on a city gate!* She clung to the tree bole, dizzily.

Wild thoughts coursed through her mind—that she should have managed to warn them sooner, or failing that, she should have wheeled Graylady about and come back to fight. But that would have done no good, for Harry had been killed when that heavy pistol had crashed into his skull—she had seen him die. Had she come charging back, they would only have shot her down. Or else taken her alive. And that conjured up a terrible picture, for to avoid hanging she must needs plead her belly, and her baby would be born in jail—and *then* they would take her out and hang her, and what would happen to her child?

Some semblance of coherence came back to her disordered thoughts.

What to do now? She could not stay here, for she had left Graylady untethered. The horse might wander away. Worse, she might whinny for Rosamunde, and this pair left on guard might discover her. Her flesh crawled at the memory of the things they had said.

But she could not just leave Harry lying here. Someone must bury him. Even if . . . even if the constable's men slashed off his head and took only *that* away, his body must be buried. Hot tears stung her eyes—Harry and Will deserved better. Her delicate jaw clenched. They would *have* better!

Still dazed, her eyes hot with scorching tears—though she could hardly comprehend it yet, hardly take in that Harry would never ride with her again, never love her again—she stumbled back toward the gray mare, dragged herself up on that sleek gray back and rode south for a

277

short distance. Then she turned and rode roughly parallel with the road she had followed from the inn. She would intersect this road farther along, and lie in wait for a while. When the cart lumbered by carrying Harry and Will, she would follow it. She would follow his body and somehow get possession of it. She would see Harry and Will decently buried in some churchyard even if she dug the graves herself by night!

She passed a little spring, and Graylady reared up, danced on her hooves and turned her head toward her rider with a reproachful look. Rosamunde started guiltily. Graylady needed water.

She dismounted and let the mare drink thirstily from the small clear spring, patted that silky gray side affectionately. Graylady . . . Harry's gift to her. How often had the gray mare danced alongside Nightwind on some nocturnal errand. . . .

Sadly Rosamunde remounted a now refreshed Graylady and rode on. Her senses were dulled by grief, and she promptly blundered into a small party of men camped around the dead coals of last night's fire.

They gaped at this apparition that had appeared so suddenly in their midst. But one, more alert than the rest, cried, " 'Tis her! 'Tis the Wild Rose! 'Tis her they seek!" He leaped for her bridle, and she kicked away his hand with the toe of her boot. Graylady cleared the dead embers of their campfire in one leap and thundered away. Behind her, Rosamunde could hear excited shouts as the men hastily mounted to give chase, and she cursed herself for her inattention. She could not go back to the road now, for this wild pursuit would alert the constable's men that she was still in the area. Though her heart rebelled against it, reason bade her wait until tomorrow.

As if the heavens shared her grief, the sky opened up and rain pelted down. For hours she rode in the pouring rain, a rain that mingled with the tears that streamed down her cheeks. Gone . . . gone . . . all was gone. She had found her love and held him in her arms for but a single year. And now he was dead and she must live on memories.

Those memories flooded back to her in a sweet warm painful rush: Harry's dark smiling face close to hers, the fierce excitement of riding beside the lean highwayman, sharing his dangers, the wild remembered thrill that went through her as he pulled her naked body to him in so many strange beds, beside so many hasty campfires.

Her slender shoulders shook with the agony of it, and when finally she sought shelter for her winded horse in a deserted outbuilding, she rubbed the mare down and collapsed onto a pile of moldy hay in one corner and cried as if her very heart would break.

Morning found the rain gone. Morning found her dry-eyed and determined. She must go back, she must find Harry, help him to his last resting place . . . beneath sod that she would water with her tears.

She watered Graylady at a little stream edged by fresh tall grass, and while the mare grazed, Rosamunde took stock of her situation. The pursuit had driven her far south into strange country. But there was a road nearby—muddy but clear of carts and men. At a sedate pace, not to attract attention if she should pass a hut or walking farmer, she walked Graylady down that road debating whether to try for the inn cross-country or by the roads.

She peered ahead: a crossroads. That at least would give her a chance to head north by other than sodden fields.

But as she approached the gray crossroads marker there came a shout. Riders broke from the bush and thundered toward her. She had been seen, identified. Her heels dug into the mare's gray sides, and Graylady lifted her head and dashed away like the wind, down the road she had come.

Suddenly the folly of her behavior crashed in on Rosamunde. Harry would not want it this way. Harry had not known about the child. *She was risking Harry's unborn child* by her determination, born of her wild grief, to go back and bury him.

Harry's stern voice came back to her: *If I should fall . . . promise me, Rosamunde . . .* He had meant for her to ride on, to save herself, not to return for him. She

279

was violating the very spirit of her oath by trying to re-turn.

Ah, but Harry, I cannot entirely keep that promise, she whispered to herself. *I cannot let your body be thrown to the winds.*

But what of her baby? What of the small son or daughter she carried within her? What of her loyalty to Harry's child? Her face was haggard as she made her great decision.

She must not let them take her. Her first duty was to save her baby.

What did Harry counsel? she asked herself wildly, for she was being driven deeper into strange territory and she knew not what pitfalls lay ahead. *Ride for the coast!* he had said. And good advice, for there were coves there, caves in the rocks, little fishing smacks on which she might hide under cover of darkness. Many fishermen obeyed the laws of the sea and cared but little for the laws of the land. Perhaps she could find a smuggler's boat to take her to France. She had a little money. Perhaps she could hide awhile and arrange with some fisherman's wife or farmwife to lie in and have her baby there.

Past that point she did not dare to think.

Ride for the coast! She glanced up at the sun. The coast lay to the west—it was that way! She wheeled the mare's head around, left the road at an angle and set off on a broken path through some trees.

All day her pursuers played hide-and-seek with her. She circled, edging ever westward; she brought the mare through water. She hid and rested the tired animal. But still, when a north-south road intersected her journey west-ward, again she heard a shout. Again she careened into the woods and again those thudding hooves pursued her. They must be watching the roads everywhere, determined not to let her slip through their fingers!

She could not know that half the countryside was out pursuing the Wild Rose, more for sport than anything else—yet if they caught her, they would turn her in to stand trial. But she had some glimmering of the great body of men following her, for thrice she had tried to turn and break through their unseen line, but each time there had been a shout and poor Graylady had had to sprint again.

She knew now how the fox felt before the hunters, as the body of men who followed her closed their net and herded her relentlessly forward. Dusk fell, and with it she lost her sense of direction, blundering forward hopelessly. Gallantly, Graylady kept on going.

The dusk deepened, night fell as she rode, and a low-hanging white moon looked down upon a tired woman, swaying in the saddle, and a winded horse whose faltering hooves made little sound on the soft damp sod.

That soft sod could well be treacherous. In the morning they would probably be able to track her by the imprints of Graylady's hooves.

She was too tired to care.

They were plodding up a little rise now and suddenly Graylady lifted her head and sniffed. Tired as she was, Rosamunde's spirits rose a little. She could smell the sea!

At the crest of that rise was a stand of windswept gnarled pines, and Rosamunde headed for them eagerly. She knew not what part of the Cornish coast she had found when she reached the grove of pines. She rode through them and brought Graylady to a halt on the edge of a cliff.

Together they stared out across the boundless sea.

Behind her in the distance she could hear her pursuers. They were shouting to each other, and the sound reached her chillingly, coming from the north and east. They would be here soon; she dare not tarry.

At another distant cry, she whirled about. That cry had come from the south! Pursuit was coming from all directions now. Having herded her to the coast, they were going to close in on her from everywhere. The sea, which she had struggled so hard to reach, had proved a trap.

She closed her eyes. How they would enjoy taking her, exhibiting her, dragging her through the public streets, raping her—hanging her! A female highwayman—ah, the crowd at her execution would love that. She pushed such thoughts away and instead breathed a small prayer for her unborn child.

"Harry," she whispered into the sea wind. "I did as you told me. I rode for the coast. And I have reached it."

What lay ahead, only God could foretell.

2

The Spaniard's Captive

1621

19   *Graylady was nearly done. She stood on trem-*
bling legs, her arched neck drooping. To drive the poor
horse further would only be to kill her. Rosamunde dismounted and looked about her.

Below in the moonlight sparkled a small cove, one of
the many that split the broken cliffs of Cornwall. Nestled
on its shore was a tiny village, a scattering of huts. The
shoreline was dotted with tiny fishing boats. Rosamunde's eyes narrowed. If she could reach one of those—!
She cast her glance farther out. Anchored well offshore
where the water was deeper rode a single tall ship, sails
furled, rolling slightly with the breeze. Rosamunde knew
little about ships, but it looked to be a galleon. The land
sloped down dishlike to the little fishing village and rose
again sharply on either side, culminating in rocky cliffs
that jutted out to sea, making a small natural harbor,
horseshoe-shaped. Across from her on the opposite promontory, a gloomy but imposing pile in the moonlight, rose
the stone walls of a castle—one of dozens that had
guarded these shores against invaders who came by sea.

Her gaze passed beyond the castle. There was little
help for her there—even if she could reach it. She, a
hunted highwayman living beyond the law, could expect
short shrift from the lord of that fortress or his highborn
lady. Nor could she stay where she was. The open point
of land on which she stood was one end of the horseshoe
of land that encircled the bay, a promontory that gave
her a broad view but only two avenues of retreat: back
through the woods whence she had come, or down to the
fishing village below.

She could not go back through the woods. They would be beating those woods for her in minutes. Soon her pursuers would break through that strip of woodland behind her and out into the open. She would be fair game for them then, her choice a clear one: to hurl herself over the cliffs upon the foam-splashed rocks below, or to be taken.

For a treacherous moment she considered cheating them, those boisterous men who pursued her as if it were some blood sport they enjoyed. Considered mounting Graylady again, tossing her cloak over the horse's eyes and riding her full tilt over the cliff into the sea and oblivion.

But . . . she could not do it. Not while there was a chance left to her.

And in that village below she might find that chance. She peered down at the cluster of huts, some of their windows winking with the light of a single candle. That larger building among the low huts might be an inn; she would have to chance it.

The tired mare looked at her with mournful eyes, and she patted her great neck and gently smoothed back her tumbling mane. "Graylady," she said softly. "You'll have food and rest and currying this night."

Even though I am taken, she finished silently. For once in the village there would be no way out, and now she doubted that she could escape by sea, unless some smuggler who cared not for English law were about to up anchor. She would have to trust to luck.

Some of her near-spent strength came back to her, and all of her courage. She would go in boldly. Perhaps she could yet slip through the net.

Seizing Graylady's bridle, she urged the horse down the rocky path that led to the hamlet below. It was narrow and treacherous. She had to encourage Graylady with every step, for the tired horse slipped and slid and twice nearly fell.

Once they reached the village she remounted. For the last time she vaulted to the gray mare's saddle and rode along the muddy track that led to the larger building.

She had been right; it was an inn. A dilapidated sign

announced it nautically as the Sail and Star. Into the muddy courtyard she rode, and a tow-haired stableboy, seeing what looked to his startled eyes like a young gentleman of fashion, sprang forward and eagerly seized Graylady's bridle.

Rosamunde dismounted, gave the mare a last pat and fixed the boy with a stern eye. "Curry her well, lad. See that she has both hay and grain in plenty—and ample water, for she is thirsty. And a good place to sleep." She gave him a gold piece, though a copper would have been sufficient, and watched his eyes bulge. But then, she reasoned, she could afford to be carefree with her coins; the odds were a thousand to one they would all be wrested away from her before morning. "There will be another gold piece for you tomorrow if I am pleased with the mare's condition," she added.

The boy nodded energetically and led the gray mare away to the stable that adjoined the inn. Rosamunde stood a moment watching them go, Graylady so tired and grateful for the sight of the stable, the boy surreptitiously biting the coin she had given him to make sure it was gold. She hoped the boy would be good to the gray mare. Tomorrow—well, if she had any gold pieces left by the morrow, she would keep her promise to the boy. If not, perhaps he'd like her gauntlet gloves; they were very fancy, he could give them to his sweetheart. She decided if Graylady looked refreshed and she had the chance to do it, she'd give the boy her gloves.

Careful not to hurry too much, lest hidden eyes be watching, she strolled across the empty courtyard to the door of the inn. There she paused for a moment. She would enter this place a free woman, but how would she come out of it?

She took a deep breath of the salt air and swung open the battered wooden door of the inn.

It was surprisingly crowded and smoky inside. She would not have dreamed the town held so many men. For the smoke she was grateful, although she had to struggle to control a cough—at least the murk and the scarcity of candles obscured her face should any know it. A plump
286

barmaid bustled by carrying a huge baked fish on a charger, and the crisp appetizing odor reminded Rosamunde that she had not eaten in the past two days. A large man in seaman's garb jostled her as she entered, and she stepped back into the shadows to avoid being stepped on by the milling crowd.

She was still standing there, getting her bearings in the gloom as she toyed arrogantly with her gauntlet gloves, when she heard the fellow just ahead mutter, "Her ladyship do be goin' to put the Spaniard in chains this night; the boats be takin' off at midnight for the Spanish ship, lad—don't be late. There'll be Spanish blood and Spanish gold for all!"

Rosamunde, alert for anything that might assist her in her desperate plight, frowned. Spanish gold? The galleon anchored in the bay was a Spaniard, then . . . and some of the local gentry were planning to raid it?

"His lordship will not like it," came the muttered reply. "Her doin' this while he's gone."

"Shut up, lad, and get ye gone. Ye've got to alert the forest folk. We'll need them for this night's work. Tell them the ship's laden with wine and spirits—that'll bring 'em!"

The youth's voice rose high and squeaky with excitement. "But what if the Spanish captain—"

"Quiet!" The word was hissed. "Do ye want him to hear ye? He's right upstairs, so keep your voice down." His own voice died away as he turned and saw Rosamunde, standing and looking about her with all the arrogance of a young lord. "Away with ye, lad," he muttered, and over the heads of the crowd he beckoned to a large man and nodded at Rosamunde.

Rosamunde guessed it might be the innkeeper he was beckoning. She did not hesitate. She brushed by the large man with a slight swagger and met the approaching fellow halfway. His curious blue eyes hardened at sight of her, and he cast a quick glance at the large fellow. Rosamunde guessed he must know about the raid—was probably in on it.

"D'ye keep this inn?" she demanded in a bored voice.

"Aye. What's your pleasure, young sir?"

For a terrible moment Rosamunde had almost forgotten that she was attired as a man. "I seek lodgings for the night," she said throatily, stifling a yawn—and that illusion of boredom cost her a deal, for she was tense as a drawn bowstring.

The innkeeper hesitated. She realized with a cold prickling feeling that with tonight's plans afoot he might not want a stranger upstairs who might possibly alert the Spaniard.

"Come, come," she said testily. "I have traveled a long way and am tired." She leaned forward, thrusting her face almost into the innkeeper's speculative countenance, and spoke in a hoarse conspiratorial whisper. "I seek the best accommodations you have, and the room must be private, as I am to meet a lady here—the Lady Anne Chester, of whom you may have heard?"

The innkeeper had not. His gaze was blank.

"But she is famous for her beauty!" protested Rosamunde with apparent chagrin. "God's teeth, I thought all in the West Country had heard of her! She'll arrive before morning and I'll be needing the room until"—she smiled lecherously—"until late in the day. I will tell you in strictest confidence that we are fleeing her father, for we are betrothed against his wishes, so we'll wish on no account to be disturbed."

The innkeeper, who, when beckoned, had leaped forward suspecting this well-dressed youth might have come to warn the Spanish captain upstairs of tonight's plans, now broke into a broad friendly smile. By custom, marriages among the well-to-do were usually arranged by the parents without the bride's consent—often without the groom's as well—and many were the headlong flights of couples who rushed out into the night with angry fathers pursuing.

"Ye can have the room to your left, young sir," he said graciously. "Upstairs. The room to your right be taken."

"You will call me the moment she arrives?"

"So few people arrive here," grunted the landlord

sardonically, "that any new arrival causes comment. I'll call ye."

Rosamunde thought-grimly that a great many people were going to arrive, and very suddenly—seeking her. But she must be careful to give no appearance of haste. She inclined her head languidly. "I've told the boy to stable my horse," she declared in a regal voice. "She's a good horse—I hold you accountable that she be treated well." It was all she could do for Graylady. Carelessly she pulled out several gold coins, and the landlord's eyes widened. "That's for the room, the stabling—and your silence."

Eyes twinkling, the landlord took the coins. "Will ye be wanting supper sent up?"

"No, I'll be down to sup."

The landlord gave the handsomely dressed lad a look of approval. Heavily armed, he noted, but then perhaps he'd come through wild country. The roads were thick with highwaymen, he'd heard. A likely lad and dashing —off to wed his sweetheart and devil take the kinsmen! Smiling, he turned away and nodded to the big man who was watching that it was all right; this had naught to do with the Spaniard.

It had been easier than Rosamunde had expected. The common room continued to seethe with activity, and none seemed to remark her stroll up the stairs. It was a small inn with only two doors at the top of the steps—one to the left, which was hers, and one to the right, which must be the Spanish captain's. And so dim was it up here, what with the smoke from cooking and the pipes in everybody's mouths, that she doubted they could see which way she went. In case they were peering at her through the smoke, she quickly opened the door to the left and went in, closing it smartly.

A moment later she opened it quietly and closed it again behind her—silently.

Without hesitation, though her heart was beating doubletime, she knocked softly on the door across the hall.

From within the room, Don Rodrigue Avilo, captain of the galleon *Santa Cecilia,* heard a light tap on the door.

289

Don Rodrigue was dark and capable and in his thirties. In build he was narrow and lean, in disposition volatile. A Majorcan, he had been *el capitán* of the *Santa Cecilia* for over four years now, and he would never have put into this damned English port save that he'd had no choice. The blustery storm winds had blown him far off course and damaged his ship. He'd limped into this tiny cove on the Cornish coast, short of food and out of water. He was tired from a day of overseeing the provisioning and the filling and storing of water casks aboard, irritated that the caulking and repairs had proceeded no faster, and at the moment Rosamunde knocked he was lying flat on his back on the lumpy bed with his boots on. Expecting his supper—for he had no heart tonight for that lot of wolf-faced Englishmen thirsting for his blood in the common room downstairs—he bade the knocker make entry.

The door opened and as soon as the caller was in, was instantly latched. At this novel gesture, Don Rodrigue's boot heels banged upon the floor and he was instantly on his feet and reaching for his basket-hilted sword. Before him he saw a pretty youth, wearing a sweeping plumed hat and gauntleted leather gloves. The youth was slender and not so tall, and his entrance had been exceedingly graceful. He must be very young, thought Don Rodrigue, for his cheek was as smooth as a babe's and slightly pink. A girl might have enjoyed that complexion.

This newcomer had a very appealing smile that lit her face, although the green eyes were grave and steady and tired and had a look of suffering about them. A neat boot of fine Cordovan leather was thrust forward as the young stranger, making an impatient gesture for Don Rodrigue to put his sword away, came forward into the room.

The newcomer spoke impatiently. "Are you the Spanish captain? Do you speak English?"

Don Rodrigue nodded a grim yes to both questions.

"Then, captain," said that soft throaty voice to the frowning man who stood with feet planted and naked blade in hand, "you'd best away. The lady in yon castle" —here the plumed hat nodded lazily toward the window with its view of a frowning castle etched in moonlight on

290

the promontory above the sea—"is up to mischief this night. Her lord's away and she's thought to bring him a rich prize: *your ship*."

Don Rodrigue stared at his youthful informer, all his battle-trained senses coming alert. Aye, he'd sensed treachery ever since the unfortunate wind had swept him into this English hellhole!

"Her method?" he asked tersely.

"I heard not so much downstairs. But I think you've time to cast anchor before they board you. Midnight, they said. Is your crew aboard?"

Don Rodrigue nodded grimly. He reached for his velvet purse. "Your price for this bit of news?"

A sad smile answered him. "To be taken along. By trade, I'm a highwayman. Those horses you hear pounding up to the front door of the inn are the king's men looking for me. If I'm found, it's the gibbet."

Putting away his purse, Don Rodrigue nodded. Though he'd no love for highwaymen, any man who saved your life—yes, and your ship too—was a friend.

Sword in hand, he strode for the door, but a gesture from his young friend stayed him. "I think the window is best, captain. We can slide down the roof and run down to the waterfront. Stealing a boat there should not be so difficult."

Don Rodrigue's dark face split in a smile. The lad was heavily armed. A pistol he'd noted, and a sword as well. Though slight, the boy might do in a fight. As for himself, he was known as a good blade. The lad was having trouble with the window, which was stuck. Don Rodrigue reached over the lad's shoulder and opened it—and a familiar pain gripped his stomach, bent him double and put beads of sweat on his brow.

"What is it?" Rosamunde asked anxiously.

"Nothing," gasped Don Rodrigue. "The result of a wound I sustained recently in Lisbon." He did not think it necessary to add it had been a fight over a hot wench at a tavern. "It will go away presently."

After a moment he straightened up, saw the green eyes looking at him with some concern. Downstairs there was a commotion now, and Rosamunde guessed there would be some confusion too, for the arrival of a strange group of armed men would be certain to be interpreted by those below as aid come to assist the Spaniard. She hoped the Cornishmen would argue long enough to allow them to make their escape.

Don Rodrigue motioned to the lad to go first and watched him slide down the roof, leap lightly to the pile of straw below. In a moment he followed, landing with a slight groan, and together they slipped through the night, finding patches of darkness in the shadow of thatched roofs as they hurried toward the waterfront.

"That one!" Don Rodrigue swiftly chose the boat they would take: a shallow-draft boat with oars, one that would skim across the water.

Behind them they could hear shouts and curses. There was fighting at the inn door now. Rosamunde smiled grimly. The Cornishmen had misunderstood—they had thought these armed men had come to take *them* into custody.

"I'll row," she offered.

"You'll not," corrected Don Rodrigue sternly, flexing his strong shoulder muscles.

"But your wound!" she protested.

"We'll get there more speedily if I do it."

Submissive, the plumed hat nodded, and Don Rodrigue bent to the oars. Strong and wiry he was, and a practiced oarsman, moving rhythmically. Their shallow boat sped fast over the smooth water, unnoticed by the brawling men back at the inn.

Fighting must interest his companion, thought Don Rodrigue, for the lad was not watching for the galleon looming up ahead—all the way to the ship he kept his brooding eyes on the shore. Don Rodrigue wondered what the young highwayman was thinking.

He'd no time to find out, for all was bustle as they came aboard and he busied himself with getting the great ship underway. Men, already in their bunks for the night, rushed up topside. A sailor's plaintive ditty from below was interrupted in mid-note as the singer tossed aside his *viola da gamba* and hurried up to climb the rigging.

Rosamunde was no sailor, and the deck of the ship seemed strange to her land-based feet. Don Rodrigue barked his orders and the crew raced about, paying scant attention to the well-dressed English lad *el capitán* had brought aboard. The great sails were unfurled but drooped for lack of wind.

Rosamunde studied those drooping sails with almost detached interest. On a breath of wind her life depended —hers and the lives of all on board. For the lady of the castle, if she dared to instigate such a raid on a passing merchantman, would hardly leave captain and crew alive to tell the tale and bring reprisals from the king of Spain.

She heard the groaning creak as the anchor was hoisted, jumped back as a sailor dashed past her crying out hoarsely some nautical message she did not understand. Fighting physical exhaustion, she leaned against the rail. From the shore there was a sudden outcry and the sight of lanterns swinging. Ah, they had resolved their differences and someone had looked out to sea, noticed the activity on board the galleon. She could see men piling into little boats; moonlight glinted on swords and muskets. With a sigh she loosened her own sword in its scabbard. Strange that she should end her life on a foreign ship fighting her own countrymen, but when the moment arrived and her pistol was smoking and empty, she meant to sell her life dear with cold steel. For this was the Wild Rose who leaned upon the rail, watching that fleet of small boats leave the shore with cold green eyes. She was a far cry from the well-bred girl who had shrunk from Lord Matthew Waverclay's advances in Kenwarren House.

Rosamunde Langley had come a long way.

But God was with the Spaniard that night. On board the galleon there was a sudden joyful shout as the wind came up. The great ship shuddered as her white sails billowed out. From the fleet of pursuing small boats came a rattle of musketry—harmless at this range—and angry shouts. Don Rodrigue smiled grimly. The anchor had been raised, the tide was flowing out, and as if to aid the captain from Majorca to see his homeland once again, a sudden fierce wind blew toward the Atlantic. The sails took it and the galleon seemed fairly to leap forward, running with the tide away from the inhospitable English coast.

As they reached the narrow end of the horseshoe, where the bay spilled into the open ocean, the castle guns boomed ineffectually, and while they were still in range boomed once again. But their marksmanship was bad. The first shot struck the water so far from the ship that Don Rodrigue sneered; the second only sent a light plume of spray over the starboard rail. Don Rodrigue did not even bother to return the fire. He was short of ammunition and well might need it later.

As his frowning eyes watched the Cornish cliffs recede in the moonlight, Don Rodrigue had reason to be thankful that there were no craft of any consequence in the harbor that night to follow him. Grimly he looked about him at his storm-battered ship. For all that the moon was bright and the stars were out, there was a darkness to the south he did not like. Tomorrow they'd work again at the caulking. God willing, they'd have all the leaks plugged before they had to weather another squall.

His gaze swung to his young companion of the night. By the rail the lad stood, his brooding eyes watching that distant coast grow smaller. Highwayman or not, Don Rodrigue's sympathy went out to the boy. A sad wrench it must be to leave one's own country with the hooves of the law pounding after you, to seek unknown shores. For himself it was different. He was a wanderer by nature. Others weren't.

Take his brother in Majorca: Don Ignacio Avilo had no desire to roam—his only desire was to drink the wine of the country and roister the night away with his many whores. What his wife, Doña Margarita, must think about that! Don Rodrigue's jaws closed with a snap. He'd loved Margarita himself, and he'd thought that—shyly behind her fan—she'd returned his affections. But no, it was the elder brother who had been chosen for her—and she'd gone to his arms without a murmur of protest. It was still

294

a knife in the heart to Rodrigue, how happy his Margarita had been to marry Ignacio—a man whose shallow nature Rodrigue knew all too well. That Doña Margarita was also of a shallow nature and had gotten only what she deserved had never occurred to him. But being in the same house with the dark-eyed Margarita—for Ignacio had brought her home to Majorca—knowing her wed to his brother, had been too much for Rodrigue. She was the real reason he had taken so wholeheartedly to the sea. Henceforth his life would be lived on ships with only occasional hurtful journeys home.

He frowned. Reminiscing was painful. He'd dismiss Majorca and Margarita from his mind and learn more about the young dandy in green velvet who had saved his life.

He beckoned to the slight figure by the rail, and Rosamunde joined him on the poop deck. Beside him she leaned on the taffrail and watched the coast of England disappear. All that she had ever loved was lost to her now—Harry, England, the life she knew. She had set out with a stranger on a Spanish ship dressed as a man. What her future would be, God alone knew.

She roused herself, for the Spanish captain was speaking to her. He was inviting her to sup with him in his cabin.

20   *On that Cornish road where Harry and Will lay,* Rosamunde had hardly stumbled away with tear-blurred eyes toward Graylady and her long ride for the coast when another watcher, who had been crouched silently behind berry bushes watching the whole thing, lifted his head.

He was Rafe Thatcher, a hawk-eyed crofter with a weathered face—a huge, barrel-chested man whose heavy-muscled shoulders and back and giant forearms were used to lifting huge sheaves and barrels of grain. He'd had practice—he'd been lifting sheaves all his life. Hot and perspiring from his work, and thirsty—he'd been in the fields since sunup—he had left his horse and loaded wagon some distance away in the woods and had made his way through the tangle of berry bushes and shrub beneath the trees to a wet-weather spring that bubbled up near the road. There he had stooped to quench his thirst when Harry and Will rode up.

Silently he had watched them, from his crouched position by the spring. From the way they loosened their swords in their scabbards and inspected their pistols, he'd known something was afoot.

But nothing had happened, and he had been about to steal away when the constable and his men had ridden up and been promptly pounced upon by the two highwaymen.

Rafe had watched with interest. He had no love for the constable, an overbearing man who had cheated him on some grain he had brought to market. The constable was used to walking over people; he would not remember Rafe if he saw him again. But Rafe remembered the constable, and the memory still rankled.

Now that memory kept him from giving what aid he might and cast his sympathies with the two lean highwaymen who held the constable and his men at bay at gunpoint.

Rafe had been riveted when Rosamunde had suddenly shouted from the top of the hill and made her wild charge into the fray, followed by the body of armed men, one of whom had struck Harry down. Rafe had watched the exciting scene that followed and had lain in wait ever since, mainly in the hope of seeing the reckless beauty again if they caught her and brought her back.

He had lain there, still as some woodland creature, and watched her sad return, had held his breath as she slipped up soft-footed and peered through the underbrush at the doleful scene.

From the babble of voices on the road, he had learned who they all were. He knew it was the famous highwaymen Hard Harry and Wily Will who lay stretched out dead in the dirt, while the lithe figure in men's clothing who had come charging down the hill was the most famous highwayman's doxy of them all—the fabled Wild Rose herself.

He had been doubly thrilled to see her come stealing back, for in his impoverished youth he had toyed with the idea of taking to the road himself—and his youthful dreams had included a wonderful doxy like her. But that was before he had married a bonny serving maid from one of the district's big farms, brought her to his tiny croft and sired six children by her. He had buried her in the churchyard last autumn, poor lass, but the day did not go by that he did not miss her, and he had seen something of her quick light-hearted charm as a girl in the fair-haired lass dressed as a lad, whose face was wet with tears as she stared bleakly toward the road.

Indeed, had the Wild Rose not been so preoccupied with that sight, he told himself, she'd have seen him and perhaps in fright emptied her pistol into him! But—the lass had looked so sad.

He was slow-witted, but it seemed to him she must have known the pair who lay in the road were dead and past her aid. Obviously she had made her escape from the constable's men and could have been far from here by now. But Harry was her lover, as all England knew, and she had returned, braving great danger as he had seen wild creatures do, to mourn over her beloved . . . and found him too well guarded to reach. It hurt Rafe's heart that such a woman had not been able to say a last goodbye.

He glowered at the pair of guards on the road, who by now had dismounted and were lolling by the roadside, gloomily watching the sky, which looked about to shed rain on them. *Bad luck to them!* he thought, remembering angrily the things they'd said about the girl—and her so lovely, and fresh as the Wild Rose for which she was named!

He was about to take his leave, edging cautiously away, when a horseman came thundering up.

"Quick, you two, mount up!" he cried. "We think we've picked up the Wild Rose's trail. The constable says he'll get her if he has to raise every man in the district!"

Both men rose from their sprawled positions by the roadside.

"But what of these two?" wondered Aaron, nodding at the two prone bodies.

"Leave them—we can collect them later. They're dead —they won't run away!" Aaron gave the bodies a doubtful look, but the newcomer waved his arm impatiently. "Mount up and ride, lads! If we take the Wild Rose, we'll pass her around among us this night!"

At this inspiring suggestion both guards leaped on their horses and thundered away after the man who had been sent to get them.

The watching crofter scratched his head and followed their departure with a resentful look. Men—even highwaymen—ought not to be left in the road like carrion for the vultures. He'd a cart nearby—he'd unload the wood he'd been hauling and give those fellows decent burial on his own land. The constable would send men back for the bodies to put them on exhibit—and find them gone. Rafe smiled grimly—it would be fitting justice for a man who had cheated him in a grain deal!

Moving swiftly—for this was the most interesting day he had had all year—he unloaded his wagon. Cannily, he did not bring it crashing through the woods, breaking down branches, but reached the main road via a little-used cart track. When he reached the bodies, no one had disturbed them. He had lifted the closest body—which was Harry's—up to deposit it on the cart when he heard a faint groan, and his big shoulders jerked in surprise. What, wasn't the fellow dead after all? He leaned over and pressed his head to Harry's chest. A weak uncertain beat there . . . but still a heartbeat.

Not dead! Well, that changed things. He squinted down at the highwayman, uncertain now what to do.

Harry's weight being considerable, he deposited him on the bed of the wagon.

As he stood there considering, there was a pounding of hooves and a woman in a torn pink satin dress, and riding a horse so thin all its ribs showed, came to a wild halt beside him.

"Are they dead?" she cried tearfully, seeing Will's body sprawled on the road and Harry lying on the wagon bed.

It was Nell, looking worse than ever, with her bruised eyes swollen with tears and her cut lip swollen up.

The crofter was taken aback by this apparition. "Nay, mistress, this one's alive." He nodded doubtfully at Harry.

"Oh, thank God!" cried Nell. And then fearfully, "But where's to go? We'll have to hide him!"

The crofter stepped back and took a look at Nell. Her face was bunged up and she'd been crying, but she had a fine figure and satin-smooth fair skin—and a lot of it was showing where her sleeve had been ripped off. *This* wild-looking red-haired woman was the kind of doxy he'd thought to have in the days when he'd dreamed of jauntily riding the highways, taking a purse here and there for his living.

He turned and squinted down at the lean highwayman. Alive—but barely. It was said fellows like this had pots of gold stashed away here and there against a bad season on the road. If he nursed this one back to life, perhaps he'd share a pot of gold with him.

Nell gave him a beseeching look, and he'd have done it if Harry hadn't so much as a copper penny. It had been a long time since a woman had looked at him like that— meltingly, with her very heart in her eyes.

" 'Tis a chance I'd be taking," he grumbled. "For if 'twere known I'd sheltered a highwayman—"

"Oh, please! Please do it!" Nell leaned enchantingly nearer and he could smell her cheap perfume—a heady fragrance for a man who was mainly used to smelling barnyard manure.

"I couldn't nurse him myself, and my children are all needed at their chores."

"*I'd* nurse him," breathed Nell.

He frowned. "But this be Hard Harry, and the Wild Rose be his doxy. She come back but they was guarding him, so she left."

"Please." Nell caught at his arm. Her hands were rough by London standards, from her work at the inn. But Rafe thought her touch was like gossamer on his thick-muscled forearm. "I'd do anything for Harry," she added tearfully.

About to grant her wish, Rafe stiffened. So she'd do anything for Harry. . . . His face hardened. It wasn't fair that men like Hard Harry had all the women after them, while he, an honest widower, slept alone. He studied her for a moment, noting with desire how plump and rounded and womanly were her breasts and hips. She moved restively, and he yearned to touch her.

"And would ye be proper grateful?" he asked in a voice rough with fear that she'd turn him down.

Nell took his meaning. She had known what men wanted of her since the day she'd turned eleven. "I'd be proper grateful," she promised earnestly. "Only do take him away from here before somebody comes!"

"This other one—" Rafe began, looking at Will.

"Oh, leave him, leave him!" begged Nell. "He's dead, you said?"

"Aye."

"Then hurry." Nell swung her skeleton-thin horse around and followed Rafe's wagon. She left the scene with never a look back at Will, who'd have died twice if only he could have pleased her.

When the first ambush had failed—Rosamunde having got away by virtue of Graylady's speed—the pursuit had broken up, some heading for the coast to waylay her there, others recruiting men with fresh horses to aid in the chase. But one little group had gone back with a cart to collect the fallen highwaymen and cart them to Barnstaple, where a great fair was being held. They were startled to find only one body. A driving rain had washed away the cart tracks, and a search of the neighborhood revealed nothing.

"Think ye Hard Harry could have fooled us? That he

was alive all the time and got up and walked away?" demanded the puzzled constable when the search had failed.

"Naw, he were dead." The heavy-set fellow beside him spat. "Some animal must have dragged him off."

The constable drummed his fingers.

"We'll all swear under oath that he were dead—ye'll collect the reward."

The constable had friends in high places—even without a corpse, the reward on Harry's head was paid.

At the safe inn where Nell had worked, it was assumed by the knowing that Nell had gone for Harry's body riding Dick Brue's horse—for both Nell and the horse had disappeared. They believed she had buried Harry somewhere and gone to her people in Dorset. She'd be back, they predicted confidently. But being what they were, they confided none of this to the constable's men when they came prowling about.

Will's body was taken to Barnstaple on the River Taw and displayed to the curious at the fair being held there. Then his head was mounted on the city gates as a warning to those who might seek a living on the highroads. High above the gaping onlookers, his sightless eyes looked—not back toward England and Nell, who had never loved him, but out toward the wild sea where Rosamunde had gone.

Will's gloomy prediction had come true. He had ended his life on the highway and his head had been mounted on the city gates.

The reward being paid, Hard Harry was accounted dead. And indeed he seemed more dead than alive those first days in the loft of the farmer's tiny cottage. Nell took tender care of him. She was a born nurse who had missed her calling, and now she gave to Harry all the skill and patience and kindness of which she was capable. She hardly slept, but when she ate, or on those occasions when she fell asleep in her chair, she was aided by the crofter's two eldest daughters, who slunk in silently and bathed the hot forehead of the man lying in the bed and spooned broth into his mouth. It was an exciting time for the crofter's children: a lady in a torn satin dress had come

301

into their house, a lady with a face that showed she'd been beaten, and a man near dead! Nothing so exciting had ever happened in their drab lives, and all the children went around looking big-eyed and important—all sworn to secrecy about the man in the loft. Fortunately the tiny croft was surrounded by larger holdings, and the crofter—who was considered a poacher by his neighbors—had few visitors.

When, inevitably, the constable's men came looking for Harry, it was a great game for the children to help hide him. The constable's men searched the downstairs and the outbuildings thoroughly, but they made only a cursory search of the loft—and none at all of the pile of straw and blankets where the two youngest children lay, their eyes fever-bright, coughing incessantly. In part the searchers were intimidated by Nell, who, in her homespun gown—it had belonged to Alice—they believed to be the crofter's wife. Nell had shooed them out of her "children's" sickroom and had a few strident comments on "great booted men who came botherin' a body who was tendin' her poor little ones!"

When the crofter reported the searchers were gone, the children jumped off the pile of straw beneath which Harry lay, and Nell threw back the coverlet that was over his face and anxiously assured herself that he still lived.

That night she did what she had not done in years—she went down on her knees and prayed.

At last, too weak even to raise his head, Harry opened his eyes and blinked as he saw a blurry square of blue sky showing through the loft's small unglazed window. He managed to focus his eyes and saw a hawk winging lazily by.

"Where am I?" he asked feebly.

"Safe," said Nell instantly, and a feeling of triumph washed over her. It had been touch and go with Harry. There had been times when she'd thought he'd not make it, that he would never open his eyes or look at her again. She was thinner and her face showed the strain of her long battle, but—she had won! Harry would live!

302

"Nell?" Harry's eyes focused on her briefly, flickered shut again.

"Aye, Harry. I'm here."

"Rose?" he asked weakly, opening his eyes again with an effort. He tried to lift his head. "What of Rose?"

Nell pressed a wet cloth to his forehead with competent fingers. "She's safe, Harry. Rose is safe." She gave him a tormented look; she had no idea whether Rose was safe or not, only that she was gone.

"And Will?"

"She's with him," lied Nell.

Harry gave a great sigh and sank back. *Will would look after Rose* was his last conscious thought.

He did not raise his head again for a fortnight.

21   *But Nell had given Harry a long tender look. She* got up, stretched, and took a turn around the room. Then she called the crofter's eldest daughter to keep an eye on Harry, climbed down the ladder that was stuck through the trapdoor of the loft and went out and found the crofter. It was noon on a crisp sunshiny day, and the hay he was forking smelled sweet.

Rafe looked up, surprised to see her out here; she had been such a faithful nurse, seldom leaving the room where the injured man lay.

"Is he worse, then?" he inquired alertly.

"No. He's better." Nell smiled.

Rafe smiled back at her. She looked grand, he thought. She was thinner, but that only made her homespun dress fit her better—it had been too tight at first. He could not know that she looked more like the young girl she had once been than she had in years, but he knew he wanted to please her.

"See?" he said proudly. "How does he look to you?"

Nell looked where he was pointing. In a corner of the barn, a dappled gray horse was contentedly munching hay.

"But—that can't be Dick's horse!" She gasped. "I've never seen him look so good! Why, all his ribs used to show!"

"He was half-starved."

"He was? Dick always said he just wouldn't eat, was the reason he looked like that." She went over and patted the horse's side. "He's *fat!*"

Rafe beamed on her expansively. The horse wasn't fat, not yet. But he was beginning to look like a horse again, instead of a mistreated animal on his last legs.

"I'll show you around," Rafe offered.

Nell gave him an arch look. "This place reminds me of—" She was about to say, "This place reminds me of the farm in Dorset where I grew up," but she checked herself. She'd lied about having people in Dorset. She had no people in Dorset; she'd grown up in a London slum. Her father was dead of drink before she was born; her brothers were scattered to the waterfronts of the world. Her mother had died five years ago, coughing out her life in a London workhouse. Rafe had been good to her; he deserved better than lies.

She gave him a steady look. "I've come to make good my bargain with you, Rafe," she said simply.

Rafe looked at her and straightened. He hadn't had the heart to pry her away from the injured man, but he had hankered for her every time he'd seen her climb down that ladder from the loft, her buttocks round and saucy in her borrowed homespun, and her skirt drawn up a shade higher than was necessary to make a safe descent. Ah, she was a woman to stir a man's blood, was Nell—ripe and round, and now that her bruises were fading and her lip was healed, she had a warm sunny smile that made him remember what it had been to love the woman who lay buried in the churchyard.

But he had watched her nurse the injured highwayman,
304

seen how tenderly she'd handled him, how unstintingly she gave of herself. For Nell was tireless, never asking for rest, only dropping to sleep from sheer exhaustion. Watching her, he had marveled. Not since his Alice had he seen such devotion. Watching Nell reminded him of the way Alice had nursed the children through whooping cough. . . .

He had come to respect this woman Nell, whatever her past had been—and now he couldn't go through with it, he couldn't make her yield to him just because he'd done what any decent man should do and helped a dying man on the road.

But his lips hated to form the words.

"I don't hold you to your bargain, Mistress Nell," he mumbled, leaning on his pitchfork. "It weren't a bargain I should ever have made. I'm not proud of it."

Nell looked at Rafe in astonishment. Not in all her life had any man refused her charms through shame.

"Don't you—want me?" she managed to get out.

"Ah, I do, Mistress Nell." His yearning looked through his blue eyes, spoke to her through his hesitant voice. "I do." He breathed a deep gusty sigh. "But I wouldn't ask ye to have me—since ye don't fancy me."

Nell sank down on a pile of hay and stared up at him. This was something new in her blowzy life. The men she'd known—except for Harry—hadn't asked, they'd just taken.

"How will I know I don't fancy ye, if I don't try ye out?" she wondered archly.

Rafe was startled by that answer. It made sense to him, of course, but . . . He hitched up his breeches and swallowed. His weathered face was growing red.

"Ye mean ye'd like to try me, Mistress Nell?"

Nell nodded, a bright smile breaking like sunshine across her still-battered face.

Rafe gave her a sweet smile of his own and—swaggering only a little—led her up into the barn loft. Some barn swallows who made their nests there and lived on the meadow insects took wing as Rafe and Nell climbed the wooden ladder into the hayloft, and there were soft rustlings from a couple of nesting females who hadn't wanted to leave their eggs.

Silently Rafe indicated a big soft pile of new hay he'd just pitched in there this morning. Her bright eyes never leaving his face, Nell lay down upon it, calmly hitched up her skirts and watched as he took down his breeches. She seemed to like what she saw.

Rafe had remembered to pull the ladder up—wouldn't do to have one of the children running up here playing hide-and-seek! And now he came over and lay down beside her. He felt unaccountably shy.

Nell turned and gave him a puzzled look. And suddenly she understood how he felt. It had been long since Rafe had had a woman, and she knew he stood in awe of her. Why, this was going to be for him like—like her first time. Lor, how scared she'd been! Some big drunken lout from the tavern where her mother worked as a barmaid had cornered her in her dark upstairs room. He'd thrown her down and pierced her maidenhead even with her mother beating on his head with a bottle—for Nell's screams had brought her running upstairs.

But afterward her mother had taken it in good part, for she was a downhill bawd like the rest of them. She'd thrown away the bottle, accepted the coins the drunk with a trickle of blood running down his face had sheepishly given her, and shrugged. "Oh, well, 'tis a little early but perhaps 'tis good to get broke in early, Nell, for ye stand a better chance when ye're young—ye're worth more."

Sobbing Nell, crouched trembling in the corner, hadn't understood what she meant then, but it had all come clear to her when her mother started sending men up to her room regularly, for Nell and her mother lived in a loft over the tavern and reached their quarters at night by means of a ladder. Instead of letting Nell take the ladder up with her, Nell's mother now kept the ladder downstairs, and anyone she liked the looks of, she'd go and get the ladder and push it toward him—if he had the price, which was often only to stand her for another tankard. For she had an insatiable thirst, did Nell's mother.

Nell had grown tired of the constant scraping of that

ladder and had run away with a sailor, who'd deserted her in Plymouth and taken ship for the Indies. She might have drifted all the way down to the gutter after that, but she fell in with a young highwayman, who'd taken her out of Plymouth, dressed her in new clothes and treated her like a lady.

His name was Harry.

Nell adored him.

And now this blue-eyed crofter was treating her like a lady too—afraid to touch her, he was. It was comical but—it was nice.

Nell laughed, deep in her throat, and lifted a lazy leg and pulled him over onto her. The big crofter eased his body onto her eagerly enough—and marveled at the womanly softness of her, for it had been a long long time since he had held a woman in his arms. Nell threw a husky pair of white arms around his neck and laughed and raked her nails lightly down his back. Rafe jumped, startled, and then decided he liked it, and soon he was seesawing above her for all the world as if he were in a rocking chair.

Rafe clung to this prize he felt he didn't deserve, and Nell giggled and bounced. She chewed at his ear and nipped his lower lip and playfully tried to buck him off. But once embarked on the venture, Rafe was a determined lover; he clung to her soft body like bark to a tree. Forgetful of his children, who might be listening, he let out a rumbling roar of pleasure. Nell was pleased at this response; she redoubled her efforts, swearing to herself this would be the best time he had ever had. Unused to such fiery assaults, Rafe was transported. He did his best by Nell, and his heart beat with joy when she wouldn't let him go until he'd made love to her all over again.

When Rafe finally rolled off her, he felt like that new young bull in the pasture who'd been walking around in a daze ever since he'd had his first heifer.

He was bowled over.

He felt somehow he ought to grovel into the hay and thank her. Humbly. For nothing so exciting had ever

307

happened to him as to be grasped and playfully mauled and roughly handled by this big good-natured woman.

"Rafe," Nell was asking him lazily, "where do you sleep?"

Rafe's blue eyes widened. She was asking him where he slept! That must mean she wanted more! He'd never expected to have her more than once—a beautiful woman like her! He turned and gave her a cautious look. "In the corner opposite the hearth," he said, for his cottage had only one large room and a loft. "The children sleep near the hearth, where it's warmer."

"It won't do, you know." Nell smiled. "Unless you want to give the children a liberal education!"

Rafe took a deep glowing breath. "Well," he said carelessly, "the weather's still fine. We could sleep up here till the stranger's gone." He couldn't bring himself to call the man "Harry," for he knew in his bones the stranger had had Nell. "And then, we could move into the loft ourselves."

Nell gave him a loving look and dragged a handful of scratchy hay over his stomach, tangled it in the sandy tuft of hair at his groin and laughed. "That'd be nice," she said. And swished down her skirts and got up and put the ladder back and descended it.

Nell went back to the cottage with her red head held high and a new sense of confidence. She felt very pleased with herself. Rafe's obvious infatuation was not only flattering, it gave her a sense of power she hadn't known in a long time, for she didn't realize how much her spirit had been crushed by men like Dick Brue. And she'd been surprised how much she'd liked being held in Rafe's big muscular arms. Next to Harry he was the nicest thing that had ever happened to her. She sighed. Next to Harry . . .

At supper Rafe kept looking at Nell to see if there was some sign that she felt as he did—alight with the fires of spring. But the flickering rushlight only showed a placid still-pretty face that told him nothing extraordinary had happened. He was so worried he hadn't made an impression on her that he could hardly swallow his cold mutton.

But after supper, after she'd checked on Harry, reported him sleeping nicely, after she'd helped the older girls clear up and given the youngest toddler a kiss and an affectionate swat on the bottom, she turned to Rafe and said in a casual tone, " 'Tis a nice night."

"Aye," he agreed, looking up at the big yellow moon just rising like a gold doubloon over the dark shape of the hill where he'd fallen on his knees and wept the night his Alice died.

"I'm one to keep my bargains," said Nell pointedly, and stalked away to the barn.

It didn't take Rafe long to follow her.

Amid smothered laughter, in the sweet-smelling hay of the dark loft, they indulged in happy roguish horseplay—he tumbling her about, she scuttling away in a burst of giggles. They played cat-and-mouse—she would creep through the rustling hay and he would stalk her and pounce, sending them both deep into the hay, while she tried playfully to topple him off. And then of a sudden her body tensed and she clutched him to her and her nails tore at his back as she writhed and moaned.

She likes me! thought Rafe, lost in joy. And the scratches down his muscular back burned less than the fire Nell lighted in his racing blood.

And afterward, when he lay panting and spent beside her with a pulse throbbing in his temple and inertia spreading blissfully over his whole body, Nell leaned over and nipped his ear and said affectionately, "I'm glad I come here, Rafe. I'm glad we made our bargain."

Sweet words to hear! Rafe mumbled something gruff to hide his feelings and kept his eyes closed out of embarrassment lest the moonlight show her that they had filled with tears. But even with his eyes tight shut, the dark hayloft sparkled for him brighter than the biggest galaxy of stars.

And then Nell sat up and began to fasten up her clothes, to tuck in her big white breasts and smooth her homespun skirts down over her big moonwashed legs. Rafe lay there enjoying the miracle of her. She was—she was *town,* he thought reverently. For him Nell had all the glamour of a court lady.

309

"Well," Nell laughed. "I'm actin' like I have to get up and go, but Harry can get through the night without me. Reckon I'll stay here!" She gave Rafe an impish look. "Who knows, it might turn cold before morning and I'd need a body to warm me!"

Rafe hadn't slept so well in months. He waked at cockcrow to find himself looking up into Nell's laughing face.

"I think there's time before breakfast, don't you?" she asked slyly, running her hand wickedly down his groin and causing his muscles to contract so that his body lurched.

"There's always time for you, Nell," he said huskily. "Always."

After that he was jealous of Nell, and his palms grew damp with fear every time she went up into the cottage loft to nurse the highwayman. He no longer thought of the gold a grateful highwayman, snatched from death, might bestow on him and his family. Instead he lived in bright terror lest a fully recovered Harry take Nell away with him. Nell had come into his lonely heart as a longed-for gift, and he wanted desperately to keep her. He prayed that Harry would recover swiftly and ride away forever, and he was upset every time he saw Nell mount the ladder to the loft where Harry lay. For the lean highwayman was mending now, and Rafe lived in deathly fear that Nell would crawl onto the straw pallet and wind her big legs around the highwayman as she had him, and claw *his* back. He had to keep his rough homespun shirt on these days lest the children see and wonder. He'd already explained to his youngest son that the old rooster had raked him when he bent down gathering eggs, and again that the cat had clawed him. He was running out of explanations.

But Rafe need not have worried. Nell's love for Harry had a bittersweet tang. In a treasured corner of her heart she would always love the lean highwayman. But she wasn't going to crawl back into his bed again—not unless he asked her.

Soon Harry was rousing for short periods and asking
310

questions, pressing Nell: Where had Will taken Rose? Had she heard anything?

Nell, happy that she could share this little time with Harry, shook her head. She didn't know where they'd gone, she told him gently, but they'd made it safe away —of that she was sure.

And then came the day when he would be put off no longer.

He sat up on the pallet, pressed his hands to his forehead and tried to remember. He could remember the beginning of the fight, Rosamunde riding toward him and screaming that it was a trap. Then she had leaped her horse over them. After that all he remembered was a blow like the kick of a horse and how the dusty road had come up to meet him. It worried him that Nell insisted she knew nothing. There should be word by now—Will would know he was worried. Alarmed, he decided he'd best go looking for them, and tried to rise. He was so rickety on his feet he almost fell back onto the pallet, but he caught hold of a beam and was still holding onto it, swaying, when Nell came through the trapdoor.

"Nell," he muttered. "I've got to find Rose."

" 'Tis no good seeking them, Harry," Nell sighed. She had decided it was time to tell him. "Will's dead."

Harry turned and gave Nell a long look. "And Rose?"

"She run away. She saw them kill Will and strike you down. No one knows where she is."

"Then I'd best find her." He tried to reach his baldric, lost his grip on the beam. His head wasn't clear, he felt dizzy. The floor came up to meet him.

"Harry, Harry," pleaded Nell, when finally she got him back to the pallet and he opened his eyes. "You're not fit to travel, and you know it. Rose is holed up somewheres safe, she's a smart lass. If you go out on the road like this, you can't fight—you'll be taken, and then where will Rose be?"

It made sense in a kind of terrible way.

A week later he was mended enough to go out looking for Rosamunde.

Nell rode along with him for a way, over the almost

indiscernible track that led back to the crofter's tiny cottage. The horse Nell had brought with her had stepped on a stone and gone lame. So they had borrowed the crofter's horse and rode companionably double, Nell astride behind Harry, with her arms around his waist. She lolled there, leaning against him, her head on his shoulder. A deep pain surged through Rafe at the sight of them thus together. He turned convulsively and began to work as if impelled by demons.

Nell rode as far as the main road with Harry. There he dismounted, gave her a quick kiss and trudged away. Nell sat the horse and watched his lean body till he disappeared over the brow of a hill. Then she rode leisurely back. She had decided to stay with Rafe. He was a good man and he'd shown her a good clean way of life. She'd taken to it, too—learned to milk the cow and slop the hogs, to gather eggs and candle them. She'd even learned to make butter in the round wooden churn. To Nell—a product of the London streets who'd never lived on a farm before—every day brought new marvels. And it was nice to be treated with respect—like a real lady. Of all the men she'd known before Rafe, only Harry had ever treated her that way, which was part of the reason why she loved him so much. But Rafe, though gruff, was always polite. He made his children mind her, and she enjoyed bossing them. Now they were coming to trust her, bringing her their small wounds to be dressed, asking her to settle arguments, confiding in her. Someday, she promised herself, they would come to love her. And be like her own children. For Nell knew she could have no children herself—not after what that old slut in Cheapside had done to her with that long iron spoon. She shuddered. It had brought the baby before its time, all right, but she had near died of it.

But now life had opened its arms to her once again, and she meant to embrace it. She rode back, and it made her feel good to see the neat little cottage appear out of the trees and know that this was hers. Would always be hers. Nothing like this had *ever* come her way before. And now Rafe had even offered to take her to the church! She was going to do it, too! She'd wed him and she'd be the best

312

wife he ever had, she'd make him forget the first one who slumbered in the churchyard—oh, she'd make him forget!

She rode up and saw Rafe standing in the barnyard looking worried for he'd half-expected her to keep riding and that he'd never see her nor Harry nor the horse again —but she'd come back! A big smile split his weathered face and he hurried forward to lift her down from the saddle.

"Did you think I wasn't coming back, Rafe?" she teased. "Just try to get rid of me—just you try!"

Rafe held her fast in those big bulging arms that could pitchfork hay tirelessly all day, or strain for hours following the horse with the plow through the hard-packed earth. And thanked God for giving him a second chance at happiness.

Harry walked along the road until he came to a small village. There he hid in a clump of beech trees until dark and then slipped into the vicarage stable and led out the vicar's pride—a roan stallion. He was miles away before the vicar's servants discovered the loss. Since the horse had no distinguishing marks, and since Harry stole a saddle and a cloak elsewhere, he was soon safe enough from pursuit.

It was then he went in search of Rosamunde, seeking for her in all the likely places. He mourned for Will, but he was actively alarmed for Rosamunde. She was so brave and sometimes so reckless. He had no doubt she'd make decisions, lots of them—but would they be the right ones, or would they land her in trouble?

But for all the worry, his blood sang in his veins. He would find Rosamunde! Doubtless she thought him dead, since all the rest of the country did. Ah, what a reunion they would have!

He combed the countryside for her. He had to search carefully, for he did not wish to endanger her, nor yet did he wish to give himself away, for it was very convenient in his profession to be accounted dead, and he had assumed a whole new identity, calling himself John Howard.

313

He shunned his former haunts, took purses only when he had to in order to live, stayed openly at regular inns and innocently discussed the price of corn and wool with all comers. A country gentleman he! If only he could find his Rosamunde. . . .

It was a long time before he found the village on the Cornish coast where Rosamunde had departed on a Spanish ship—and that only because he chanced to recognize the horse, Graylady, as she stood patiently tied to a hitching post outside an apothecary's shop in Falmouth. Graylady was wearing a very handsome saddle and looked sleek and well fed. As Harry approached, she gave him a sudden look of recognition and leaned forward to nuzzle him. Harry stroked that soft nose and remembered the gallant girl who had ridden her all across England.

"She's very gentle," observed a cool female voice, and Harry turned to find himself looking at a lady in a riding costume of violet silk with a wealth of lavender plumes on her hat.

Harry made a sweeping leg to the lady, and his smile flashed in his dark face. "So gentle I've a mind to buy her for my niece's birthday. Do you know who the owner is?"

"I am the owner," said the violet-clad lady with composure. "And she is not for sale. Would you step aside so I can mount?"

Harry promptly stepped aside, offered his cupped hands to assist her in mounting, but his words stayed her departure.

" 'Tis strange," he frowned. "As you can see, the horse knows me. I would swear she is Lord Aylesford's favorite mare . . . would you happen to know if she once belonged to Lord Aylesford of Southampton?"

"I know not to whom she once belonged." The lady laughed. "But I bought her at a public sale. She had been left behind by a female highwayman who escaped from some fishing village in a large Spanish vessel. Remarkable!"

Harry frowned. Rose was not in England, then.

"Yes—remarkable," he murmured. "I seem to re-

314

member the incident. Were there not several highwaymen taken at the time?"

"Yes, there was talk of it at the sale."

"Lord Aylesford had a great black stallion that was stolen. Were the other highwaymen's horses sold at the sale of which you speak?"

She looked at him in surprise. "Yes, there was a big black stallion. It brought the highest price of the sale."

"D'you remember who bought him?"

Her eyes danced. "If Lord Aylesford hopes to get his stock back, tell him to abandon hope! The stallion was purchased by an agent on the lookout for breeding stock for Sir Wilfred Keyes in Surrey. Sir Wilfred is a famous horse breeder. The stallion will be on Sir Wilfred's estate, siring fine foals—he'll not sell him back to Lord Aylesford."

Harry believed Nightwind might like his new occupation. But the thought that he would not see again his old friend who had carried him on so many dangerous journeys saddened him.

He helped the lady in violet to mount Graylady and went to comb the coast for word of Rosamunde. And learned at last that she had departed in a wild blast of gunfire aboard a Spanish ship, the *Santa Cecilia*.

At last, he had something concrete to go on. He made careful inquiries, learned the *Santa Cecilia* was out of Barcelona, her captain one Don Rodrigue Avilo. A storm had driven her upon the Cornish coast, but as to whether she had returned to Barcelona no one knew. England was not on friendly terms with Spain. Inquiries took time. Perhaps in London he might learn.

Harry went to London and there made inquiries. It would be expensive, but word would eventually filter back to him, he was told.

He knew that he must wait for news, but he chafed, waiting. He worked the road, and when he took a large purse he rode back to the little cottage in southwest England where he had been nursed back to life. Nell was still there—he guessed she would always be there. She was

315

smiling and looked content, as did Rafe. They were married now.

Harry, who always paid his debts, handed sturdy Rafe a velvet purse. "I promised I would come your way again." He smiled.

Rafe hefted the purse—it was heavy—and looked surprised. Once Harry was gone he had never expected to see him again—and Nell was gift enough. Rafe would always be thankful for the day she had chanced into his life. But when he opened the purse and poured out the coins in a steady stream into his hand, he could not believe it—more gold than he had ever seen gathered together in one place in his life. Enough to give his two oldest daughters a dowry and buy another plowhorse!

"I thank ye," he muttered.

" 'Tis I who thank you." Harry pulled from his saddlebag a bright-red satin dress garnished with black lace. "For you, Nell." He smiled at the round O her mouth made. "Ye always liked bright-colored things."

Joyfully Nell grasped the dress and gave Harry a big noisy kiss. This time Rafe did not mind.

After that, Harry did a characteristic thing—he went to Surrey to look for Nightwind.

The estate of Sir Wilfred Keyes was not hard to find, for Sir Wilfred was indeed a famous horse breeder and had, Harry was told by a loquacious blacksmith, scoured the country for the finest brood mares to match to his great stallions. His estate was named Chatsbury—the house was nothing so much, but it had the finest barns and pastures in the county. It was located near the little hamlet of Wentworth-Hastings.

Harry digested this information and moved the discussion smoothly to the advantages of the Arab strain in horses, but the next night found him skirting the pasture fence of Chatsbury, looking for the gate.

He found it—in sight of the big stone barn in the distance. There were deep ruts around it, for this was the gate the lumbering farm carts used to bring hay from the meadows to the barn. Harry got down and opened it carefully lest its great iron hinges creak, led the big roan

316

through and closed it again. Holding the reins, he walked down the moonlit pasture studying the mares—tame and sleek and not at all disquieted by horse and man walking quietly by.

He had half-expected a shout from the barn, but on Sir Wilfred's estate the help in barn and stable slept as soundly as those in the manor house, so there was never a hail or shot to stop Harry in his design. He went slowly through the pasture—and then he saw him, a big black shape, standing alert at the sight of intruders in his territory.

A step closer Harry came, and he could see in the moonlight that Nightwind was in top condition and suited to his new occupation. Sidling around him and strolling by at a modest distance were several mares, who gave the big black horse sleepy sidewise looks. Harry grinned to see him there, looking so fit. At sight of Harry the black stallion lifted his head and whinnied. He galloped over joyfully, and Harry hugged his neck and allowed himself to be nuzzled.

"Together again, old friend." He chuckled. "I see ye've been spending your days in light frivolity without me!"

By now Nightwind and the roan were studying each other suspiciously. Nightwind circled the roan, showing his teeth. The roan rolled his eyes, and Harry was hard put to steady the horse sufficiently to remove his saddle and bridle. "Easy, Nightwind, easy," Harry muttered as the roan wandered away, eyeing the mares, who galloped away from this new male in skittish fashion.

Harry saddled up Nightwind, and the big horse pawed the earth gently with his forefeet and seemed eager to be off. He left the roan in the pasture in gratitude for the good condition in which he found his horse and, scorning the gate, cleared the pasture fence on Nightwind.

Together these two old campaigners rode back to London, where news of the *Santa Cecilia*'s whereabouts was supposed to filter back through a certain Mr. Desmond, who made a handsome profit as a link between the world of highwaymen and smugglers and the world of traders and merchants.

Mr. Desmond had nothing to report, and Harry decided not to linger in London. Restlessly he sought the roads once more. He returned to London at regular intervals to inquire of Mr. Desmond as to the *Santa Cecilia*'s whereabouts, but there was never any news.

Not till his third fruitless trip to London was it borne in upon Harry that Rosamunde was really gone, that he might never find her. She had always seemed just around the corner; he would chance upon her presently. But now he faced the enormity of life without her, and it staggered him.

News would come, he told himself uneasily. And it would be good news, she would be safe somewhere and he could go to her. In the meantime, he faced the bleak fact that his Rosamunde seemed to have been swallowed up by the wild sea.

22   *In her haste to leave England on any terms,* Rosamunde had not considered the difficulty of posing as a man on board a ship. She would encounter many such difficulties in the days to come, but on that first evening she was hard-pressed to fabricate a suitable background as she sat at her ease in the *Santa Cecilia*'s great cabin drinking Malaga from a silver goblet.

The great cabin was richly appointed. Large maps adorned the walls, and the furnishings were of dark carved wood. Plainly Don Rodrigue Avilo had a taste for luxury. And he matched his surroundings, dressed in rich black as was the Spanish fashion, a gold chain resting against a doublet shot with gold threads, a large ruby flashing from his finger. That the lean captain was fast developing a liking for her she could readily see. He leaned back expansively, crossed legs booted in fine Cordovan leather, and pressed more wine upon her. He urged her to talk, he waxed voluble on his own background.

Exhausted from her experiences of the last two days, Rosamunde smiled wanly and sat and listened.

Don Rodrigue was from the town of San Telmo on the island of Majorca in the Balearics, which Rosamunde knew vaguely lay in the Mediterranean somewhere between North Africa and Spain. Majorca, he explained, was Spanish territory, and Spain was under harsh Castilian rule.

"But—are you not Spanish?" asked Rosamunde hesitantly.

He smiled. "Catalan. My family is from Barcelona. We have easy Catalonian ways—though we have been long in Majorca." He sighed and explained that when Ferdinand had married Isabella, and Castile and Aragon had been united, all had changed for Majorca. The stiffer ways had come in, a more rigid government and manners. Don Rodrigue was unhappy about that, for although it had happened a long time ago and he had never known those days, his merry heart was Catalonian still. More wine, perhaps?

Rosamunde shook her head, toying with her glass. It occurred to her to wonder where she was to sleep. She hoped the innkeeper at the inn she had left so precipitately would be good to Graylady, the gallant mare. She hoped —no, she must not think of Harry. If she did, she would surely cry, and that would bring explanations and perhaps exposure. She fought back her fatigue and forced herself to listen.

Don Rodrigue was grumbling that he did not like these waters. He wanted no part of the treacherous Irish Sea nor St. George's Channel nor indeed the rocky coast of Ireland. His father had sailed with the Great Armada which had been defeated by Drake and Howard. On the return voyage, his battered carrack had broken up in a storm on the rocks of the Irish coast. Rodrigue's father had been one of the few survivors. The Irishmen who

319

found him—more dead than alive—had fed him and sheltered him, and he had at last got home by way of Scotland. But so terrible had been his privations that his health had never been the same since. As a boy he remembered . . . Don Rodrigue's voice trailed off.

"You remembered—?" wondered Rosamunde politely.

"I remember his nightmares," said Don Rodrigue shortly. "I remember how he tossed in his sleep, how he shouted that great seas were breaking over the bows, the masts were splintering, the taffrail was shattered. I remember how he cried out in despair that the ship was sinking, broken bodies lay all about. I saw it all through his eyes." He stared into his glass with a morose expression on his dark face. "It was so vivid to me that all through my childhood, I believed that was the way I would die—dashed onto the rocks of the Irish coast."

"You were always a sailor, then?"

"Not always, although I was trained to the sea." He hesitated, wondering why he should feel such an urge to confide in the slender velvet-clad lad who lounged opposite him. "Mine was a rebellious nature. Always I had resisted the arranged marriages my parents espoused. At last my father, in despair of having a grandchild, sent me to Barcelona. 'Find a wife who pleases you,' he told me. 'And bring her home to Majorca.' "

"And did you find a wife there?"

"I found a beautiful lady of Castile who was visiting cousins in Barcelona." His dark face grew even darker. "She hated the sea. I promised her I would keep to the land if she would come to Majorca as my bride." He downed his drink and set the goblet down rather hard.

Rosamunde gave him a questioning look.

"She came to Majorca," he said grimly. "She married my brother."

Rosamunde sat back, digesting that bit of information. "You are not married, then?" she ventured.

He shook his dark head with great firmness and his eyes flashed. "Nor likely to be." He did not tell her that every night he saw Margarita's arrogant Castilian face, heard her sensuous voice teasing him, felt the gossamer
320

touch of her pale hands as she brushed him accidentally, heard the sinuous rustle of her skirts moving ever away from him. . . . "I've developed wandering ways," he added lightly. He poured more wine, sipped it, studying his guest. It occurred to him suddenly that this English lad had the longest eyelashes he had ever seen—a thick dark fringe that shadowed eyes of brilliant iridescent green. He felt suddenly restive under their calm inspection, as if part of his soul were bared to their view. He had spoken so frankly, said so much. . . .

But when Rosamunde spoke, it was not to ask him anything personal.

"I did not ask you where we are bound."

He smiled at her. "This ship belongs to my father, but the cargo is a joint venture between myself and three other Catalans, all of Barcelona. We carry wine for Holland."

Rosamunde was surprised. "But I thought Holland was at war with Spain."

Don Rodrigue shrugged. "There has been for twelve years now a truce of sorts, and we have become used to trading with Holland. All on the ship are Catalans. They will not spread the word that we have been to Holland—even my father does not know of it, for he lets me have the use of his ship for a share of the cargo. The length of our voyage will be passed off as due to bad weather. But"—his dark eyes danced—"when we sail into Amsterdam you will note that we will be flying the Dutch flag and the name *Margheretha* will be painted on the *Santa Cecilia*'s side! That will be done when we leave the Spanish Netherlands at Ostend for our short run to Amsterdam in Holland. The ship's name will be changed to *Santa Cecilia* again once we leave Dutch waters, and we will again fly the Spanish flag. Had I had the forethought to raise the Dutch flag when I limped into port in Cornwall, the English might have made no plans to attack me —had I been able to keep my crew silent. For I speak Dutch fluently."

Dutch flag? Spanish flag? What game was this? To the long-lashed lad across from him, Don Rodrigue continued to explain. "The king of Spain oppresses Catalonia—he would reshape our province into another harsh Castile. Majorca is Catalan, we have no wish for Castilian rule—and on behalf of my people I resent the invasion of our national rights."

So this was what he had meant when he had explained that when Isabella of Castile had married Ferdinand, and Catalonia had gone willy-nilly into the bargain, the Catalans had been unhappy . . . and they remained unhappy under the inflexibly Castilian rule of Spain. She began to understand.

So it would be a long voyage, with many chances to leave the ship on the way. . . .

"Your wound," she wondered. "Does it trouble you much?"

Don Rodrigue gave her a surprised look. "Not much. Wounds heal. This one has been troublesome—but it will mend." He was touched that this soft-voiced lad had asked him that, and now he considered his likely young guest. Too pretty, of course, but time would doubtless alter and coarsen that appealing face as the lad grew into maturity. No razor needed for that velvet cheek as yet. A pity the lad had been driven from his homeland; Don Rodrigue knew the feeling. Not in a long time had he taken such a liking to anyone as he had for this stripling in velvet. He could not know that it was the instinctive warmth a man feels toward a beautiful feminine woman that stirred him. "Have you given thought to your future now that you have left the highways of England in other hands?"

Rosamunde sensed the irony in his tone and stiffened a little. "I was not always a highwayman," she said defensively. "I was gently bred. My grandfather's holdings lie northwest of Nottingham on the River Trent. My father married against his wishes and spent his life as a soldier of fortune in foreign wars. In his youth he served under Drake at Cádiz when he—" She stopped abruptly, for she had just remembered that Captain Rodrigue Avilo was a Spaniard.

"Perhaps you were about to add, 'when he destroyed the Spanish fleet,' " he suggested softly.

Rosamunde nodded.

"A brave family," approved Rodrigue. "Is your father living?"

"No. His death broke my mother's heart. I think she had no will to live after that. She was killed when her new hunter refused a jump and threw her into a stone wall. After that my—my guardian and I disagreed. My only course was to leave—and without money, little was open to me."

"Except the highroads."

"Except the highroads, yes."

He studied her. "I am curious. You are of a slight build and your reach is short. Does it not hamper your swordsmanship?"

"I am a good shot," said Rosamunde grimly.

He nodded and sighed. "Many prefer firearms. For myself, I prefer the blade."

You would, she thought, studying that long sinewy arm, that hard lean body clad in the dark well-fitting Spanish fashion that so became him. Sunk in fatigue, she snapped suddenly to attention. The captain was speaking to her.

"You took to the road alone?"

"No. I had the best teacher in all England. A gentleman's son, unfairly dispossessed of his patrimony. His name was Harry." Her voice rang with pride. "You may have heard of him."

Don Rodrigue's lips twitched at this innocence of the size of the world. "I have not such knowledge of your country," he admitted wryly. "My command of the language comes from a homesick English pilot who taught me your tongue. Languages come easily to me."

"Harry was the most famous highwayman in England," said Rosamunde, following her own somber thoughts.

"Was?"

"He is dead," she said, and her voice broke. "He saved my life—so many times."

Rodrigue's dark brows lifted at the wave of emotion in her voice. The lad was loyal! He raised his silver goblet. "Such a comrade deserves our admiration. I drink to your Harry."

323

Silently Rosamunde lifted her own goblet. Tears glimmered unashamed on her long lashes. *I drink to Harry too*, she thought. *Forever my love.* . . . She drained her goblet and brushed the tears from her eyes with her knuckles and looked away, seeing not the great cabin or the lean Spaniard who watched her, but only Harry.

Rodrigue was touched. "Here, lad," he said gruffly. " 'Tis no shame to weep for a fallen comrade. I have myself at times. Another goblet of wine will aid you."

Rosamunde shook her head. Her face was very pale. "I am very tired," she admitted. "The king's men harried me for two days. My horse was near done when I reached the coast."

"Of course," he said, his heart going out to one so young and so troubled. "I am not being a good host to one who saved my life at no small risk."

"No risk," Rosamunde told him in a rueful voice. "They would have hanged me anyway, had they caught me. It put me in no greater danger to help you."

He smiled. "Nevertheless I am grateful to you, Don— what is your given name? I cannot call you 'Langley.' "

"Ro—" She had almost said "Rosamunde"! "Robert," she choked. "My friends call me Robbie."

"Our ship is crowded, Robbie. You may bunk in here with me." He indicated a bunk across the room from his own large one.

Rosamunde swallowed and her eyes widened. She had not thought of that! She would be sleeping in the same room with this Spanish captain. "I—I am most grateful, Captain Avilo," she stammered. "But will it not be a great inconvenience to you?"

"Oh, no. This great cabin is the most commodious on the ship—and thanks to you I still enjoy it. After all, I could not enjoy it in heaven," he added gaily. "Assuming I were fortunate enough to reach there! Since you saved me from my just deserts, it is fitting, I think, that you share this cabin with me."

She knew she must seem grateful for his courtesy, but this new state of affairs only increased her alarm. How would she manage undressing before him?

"Excuse me, Robbie. I must see to the watch." Rodrigue rose with a slight bow and walked out.

Rosamunde stripped down to her flowing shirt and undergarments. Her heart was beating triphammer blows as she hastily plunged into her bunk and pulled the coverlet up over her. She would find some excuse not to dress before Captain Avilo. She would manage to bathe, to do anything that would compromise her disguise, when he was occupied elsewhere. She did not realize that this knotty problem was in itself a godsend, for otherwise her grief would have overwhelmed her. As it was, she was forced of necessity to think of other things.

When the captain returned, she pretended to be asleep. She could hear him divesting himself of his clothes and kept her eyes tight shut. And then, with the great ship creaking a lullaby around her, she fell asleep.

And dreamed of Harry and the lovely ruined estate where he had taken her and which had seemed for a wonderful misty time their very own . . . Locke Hall, that seat of Harry Waring's lost birthright. There were tears on her lashes as she tossed and turned in the moonlight, and Don Rodrigue, arising at a sound he did not like, which he thought might come from the rudder, noted them. He came back soft-footed so as not to disturb his young guest, saw the tearstains on that pale exhausted young face as she lay asleep, and was moved by them. He knew not why he had taken such a fondness for the English lad, but as he went to bed a second time his mind was filled with thoughts of the boy's brave stance and the undoubted troubles that had forced him into the reckless life he led.

Perhaps the lad would take to the seafaring life, he mused, and for the first time in years he went to sleep without once thinking of Margarita—beautiful treacherous Margarita, asleep in Majorca in the arms of his brother. . . .

It was Rodrigue's custom to rise early, and in the morning he briskly offered his young guest the use of his razor. The offer was somewhat ironic for a beardless

325

boy, and he made it in some amusement, using it as an excuse to rouse the lad.

Rosamunde woke, startled, stared up at Rodrigue wild-eyed for a moment—and then remembered where she was. "My beard is not yet a trouble to me," she muttered.

"So I perceive," said Don Rodrigue lightly, and she was left to wonder about that remark, and if this Spanish captain suspected that beneath her men's clothing was a woman's body.

Once he had gone, she leaped up. She managed to dress hurriedly, in privacy, swallowed the breakfast that was brought her, and went up on deck and joined Don Rodrigue on the poop.

The wind had changed, she noted. It now drove steadily from the north under a cloudless sky.

"The wind favors us," Rodrigue told Rosamunde. He looked very fit this morning, she thought. Strong and alert and arrogant, as became a gentleman of Spain and the captain of a great ship. "Late last night the sails flapped idly, but morning has brought us a strong wind to the south, and now we run before her. We are far from your Cornish friends by now. And if the winds continue to favor us, we should make a fast voyage and have more than enough water and provisions to reach our destination."

She cast a quick look at the virile black-clad figure beside her. "You did not have time to secure all the supplies you needed ashore?"

"No, nor to do all the caulking and repairs of the damage we suffered from the sudden squall that drove us onto that infernal coast." His dark face broke into a smile. "I am sorry, Robbie. I had forgotten that I was speaking of your homeland."

Rosamunde refused to take affront. "Doubtless opinions differ," she said soberly. "But I love England, Captain Avilo. It is terrible to think that it is lost to me."

"There are other lands," he said carelessly.

Ah, but none so fair to me . . . and none where I loved Harry.

"Homesickness," he observed, watching her sad face,

326

"is a malady of the heart that tends to recede with time. Have you thought of following the sea as a profession?"

Rosamunde's head jerked up and she looked at the Spanish captain sharply. He was on the verge of making her an offer, she felt, and a generous one. He could not know that before she could learn the lore of the sea she would already have become a mother. "I—I had not thought of it," she faltered. "I know not if I have the sea legs to consider such a thing."

Rodrigue laughed. "You will have time on this voyage to consider. If you choose to follow the sea, Robbie, you are welcome to sail with me. But I will not press you."

She gave him a troubled look. She liked this captain from Majorca. He seemed trustworthy, and she hated deceiving him. But she dared not tell him that she was a woman.

Instead she spoke of something else that was troubling her. "Captain Avilo," she said hesitantly, "I am aware that Spain is a Catholic country. My faith is Church of England. Will that make a difference?"

"Not aboard this ship," Rodrigue replied promptly. "We Catalans"—she noticed that he spoke of himself always as a Catalan although he lived on Majorca— "allow men to worship God as they please. But were we in Spain, or in Majorca, which lies prone beneath the boot of Spain . . ." He shrugged, and Rosamunde nodded in uneasy understanding. The fires of the Inquisition burned bright in the back of her mind.

"I ordered breakfast brought to you in my cabin. Did you find it sufficient? I care little for breakfast myself and eat but a crust, but tonight you will sup with my officers and meet all of them—they are very busy just now, for we are still occupied with repairs, and we must make the most of this good wind. Autumn is a season of storms. You will excuse me—I have matters to attend to. Make yourself free of the deck in my absence."

He bowed slightly and left her. A handsome man, Captain Rodrigue Avilo, she thought, watching him go. Not in the way Harry had been handsome, of course. There'd been more breadth of shoulder in Harry, a more

327

determined jaw, colder eyes that had . . . softened for her. A sob caught in her throat and she forced her unhappy thoughts back to the captain from Majorca. Don Rodrigue had a wiry grace; she suspected that almost-too-lean body of being hard as steel. His dark eyes were unfathomable, but his smile was merry and gentle—a flash of white teeth in a dark narrow face.

Then—still to avoid thinking of Harry, and mourning for him—she bethought herself of her own future. At some foreign port she would go ashore—though heaven only knew what she would do there, for she spoke no foreign tongues and had no profession save that of the road. She was still puzzling over that when Rodrigue returned and showed her around the ship.

It was a fat-bodied, three-masted ship and not especially luxurious, save for its great cabin. Its main distinction seemed to be the figurehead that nosed out to sea from the prow—a gilded horse's head with a tossing mane. Rosa-munde commented on it.

"Ah, the figurehead," said Rodrigue, smiling. "'Tis modeled after an Arab stallion. His name was Hassim, and he was the pride of Don Esteban Sanchez, who owned this vessel before my father bought her. Don Esteban bred fighting bulls, and one day he dismounted in his pasture to study a plant growing wild—Don Esteban is fond of plants. It was a near-fatal mistake, for he was charged by a bull. His valiant horse, Hassim, sprang between them and took the bull's horns, allowing Don Esteban to escape with his life. Don Esteban has since put a horse's head over the entrance to his *estancia*, on his door knocker, engraved on his silver, embroidered on his table linens —all as a memorial to Hassim."

Rosamunde smiled. That wild tossing mane, that noble head, reminded her of Nightwind. But wilder than the horse had been the rider—and there was only herself to mourn him. "A lovely reminder," she said in a flat voice, and followed the captain as he continued to show her around. She was always welcome on the poop deck, he assured her affably, and he would be glad to translate for her any instructions she wished to give the cabin boy.

He also translated for her when she met the ship's officers—and by suppertime she had met all of them. She was a bit confused as to their rank, only being able to separate out the first officer, a huge efficient-looking man in his forties, whose name was Don Rios de Guzman. Then there was Don Alberto, tall and gaunt; Don Tomás, short and fat; Don Felipe, swarthiest of all and with a merry smile; and others whose names she could not remember, but these first seemed to her the most senior. None of them spoke any English, she learned to her chagrin, and although they were unfailingly courteous, they looked at her curiously. They spoke to one another in musical Catalan, and occasionally Don Rodrigue translated a remark aimed at her and again translated her reply. She gathered from the tone of the conversation that he had not told them she was by profession a highwayman, and during a lull in the conversation at supper she asked him if he had.

Rodrigue laughed. "No, I told them you were affronted that innocent strangers cast upon your shores should be attacked and butchered by stealth in the night—and that you gave us warning for that reason."

"How noble of me," said Rosamunde dryly. "Then you did not tell them why I fled with you?"

"I told them you were seen ascending the stairs to my room at the English inn, and would undoubtedly have been killed had you remained in England. They are full of sympathy."

Rosamunde felt a bit subdued. She had been thinking at the time not so much of the unfortunate Spaniards, driven into an unfriendly port by a storm, as of herself. She straightened. No, that was not entirely true. Back on the road where Harry had been struck down, in blind grief she might have ridden back, fired at his assailants, and thrown her life away . . . had she not been convinced she was pregnant. She had ridden away from his prone body when ever nerve screamed at her to go back—because of the child. She had alerted the Spaniard for the same reason . . . and because when she reached the coast she had lost her thirst for dying and wanted to

329

live. But the treachery had angered her—indeed, she might have warned him anyway. Her green eyes were shadowed. She would never know that much about herself, whether she would have done it or not.

She looked up from her food. Don Rodrigue was speaking to her. "We are discussing our habit, when we are becalmed, of bathing in the sea beside the ship. Are you fond of swimming?"

Swimming! In the nude with all these men naked also! She could scarce restrain a shudder. "I do not swim," she said hastily.

Don Rodrigue sighed, remembering his childhood days spent plunging through the wild surf that broke on Majorca's white beaches, swimming out strongly through the warm azure water. "I will teach you," he said kindly. "Should we encounter a calm."

Rosamunde sat straighter and prayed for a strong wind all the way to port.

But the wind did not hold. It was fitful, capricious, as—standing well out to sea, for Don Rodrigue no longer trusted what he called "that cursed shore"—they beat their way past Lands End. Rosamunde was fascinated by the way the pilots heaved the lead to check the depth in fathoms to the bottom. Carefully they studied the shell and sand they had dredged from the bottom and reported their position as some seventy leagues south of the Scilly Isles. The next morning Lizard Head was sighted, and Rosamunde knew this meant they would be sailing up the English Channel. As they neared Plymouth they passed a number of sailing sloops and several tall white ships, for Plymouth was a busy harbor. On past Start Point the great ship drove until a sudden brief squall obscured the dying sun. And as the *Santa Cecilia* lunged about that evening in the choppy Channel waters off England's south coast, Don Rodrigue Avilo, at ease in the great cabin, drew out a pack of cards and suggested they have a game.

Rosamunde had played cards frequently with the elderly earl of Kenwarren, for Louisa had not had the patience. And Will and Harry, on idle evenings in safe highwaymen's inns, had amused themselves by teaching her how to detect a cheat. So Rosamunde felt on firm ground at last and shuffled the deck with confidence.

Rodrigue was a tricky player, but she very nearly beat him. Indeed she might have beaten him, save that as they played he distracted her by telling her about the doomed Armada that had come this way and fought its first great battle with Drake and Howard off the Eddystone—somewhere north of them in the gloom. So diverted was she by his vivid description of the blowing up of the *San Salvador* and the abandonment of the wallowing *Rosario* that she almost forgot to play her hand.

But she was edgy as the game ended and Rodrigue yawned, for she was afraid that her Spanish captain would suddenly announce for bed and she would be hard put to undress before him. But to her great relief he excused himself to have a look around deck before retiring (she was to learn, gratefully, that such was his habit), and this gave her time to make swift preparations for bed and be well tucked in when he returned.

When Rodrigue returned, Rosamunde was still awake. But she let her long dark lashes rest on her cheeks and lay silent lest this tireless Spanish captain notice her wakefulness and politely suggest another game, which would of course require her to arise in her undergarments. It was with a sigh of relief that she heard his sword scrape the chair as he tossed it aside, heard the clunk of his boots dropping, the slight creak as he threw himself into his bunk, and then his regular even breathing as he sank into sleep.

Not till then did she turn over and sleep herself.

The *Santa Cecilia* drove on, past Start Point, on to Portland Bill. The officers and men were used to Rosamunde now and paid her no attention as she strolled about the deck or leaned upon the rail. She might have been some diplomatic passenger of minor rank, so courteous and reserved was the Catalonians' treatment of her. Sometimes she heard the crew singing down below, sad melodious songs of their country, and once she was roused from her reverie at the taffrail by a raucous stamping dance upon the deck, which was soon quieted as a ship's officer strolled by.

Before freshening winds they passed Portland Bill on England's south coast and sped through choppy water toward Calais Roads, almost a hundred and seventy miles away. Rodrigue had been telling her somberly, as they sailed, of each catastrophe that had beset the Great Armada that had sailed so confidently from Spain. Here the huge but disabled forty-six gun *Rosario* had been taken by Drake, here the mighty Armada had drawn up in crescent formation to await the English advance . . . Listening to Rodrigue's rich hypnotic voice, Rosamunde could almost feel she was on board a ship of that doomed Armada, rather than a privately owned Spanish merchantman out of Barcelona whose Catalan joint venturers were sorely in need of the fruits of this voyage—for so Rodrigue had assured her in a moment of confidence. When, made curious, she had asked him, he had admitted that much of his own private fortune as well was invested in the cargo of wines, so a swift and successful voyage was as important to him as it was to the other Catalans. "I live beyond my means," he had admitted ruefully, and went on to tell her more about the Armada.

Rosamunde was beginning to feel a very un-English sympathy for the men of those proud ships of the Spanish Armada, sailing toward a hostile shore in tall ships that rose like wooden castles from the sea. She winced at their chagrin at finding themselves outnumbered and outgunned, their brave tradition of grappling and boarding the enemy and fighting with cold steel on slippery decks made impossible by the swift maneuverable English ships that could almost sail circles around them. She—who was English to the core—saw how terrible it must have been for the bold Spaniards, pounded by English broadsides, to realize that they were far from home, short of ammunition—and losing. Almost she wept for them.

Not only had she fallen under the spell of that warm musical Majorcan voice, Rosamunde had begun to rely on the captain's punctual habits. She had been so yearning for a long soaking bath—so different from the brief sur-

332

reptitious scrubs when Don Rodrigue was mercifully absent from the great cabin. Finally she decided that if she timed it well enough, she would have time to bathe in leisurely fashion while Don Rodrigue was on deck battening down things for the night. He was gone long enough ordinarily, and this was a squally night which would keep him even longer, she reasoned.

That night her yearning for a hot bath had at last outweighed her caution. Casually she ordered the metal tub and the hot water, telling the boy who brought it just to leave it—a command hastily translated by Don Rodrigue. Don Rodrigue, who was playing cards with her, would have put away the deck at that point, saying she should plunge in while the water was hot; he would have the boy come back with water to rinse her off. Since he showed no disposition to go on deck—as she had confidently expected him to—Rosamunde quickly laughed and said she would play one more hand; he had beaten her twice and she sought revenge! Rodrigue smiled and sat back in his chair as they played another hand. Rosamunde won, and gave him a smile of triumph. Now there was no longer any excuse for staying out of the tub. She strolled over to her bunk and made a great thing of getting her boots off, expecting Rodrigue to leave at any minute.

Instead, believing she was having trouble with the boots, Rodrigue stayed to help her with them. He crossed the room and pulled them with ease from her pretty calves. Rosamunde gave him a bright worried smile and bent to toy with her lace-edged boothose. She was inwardly cursing herself for her stupid decision to take a "real" bath when Rodrigue announced he must see to his ship before retiring. When she looked up, the cabin door had closed behind him.

Weak with relief, Rosamunde pinned up her hair with flying fingers and quickly stripped. Leaving her clothes in a pile on the cabin floor, she jumped into the still-warm tub and sank down into the water in a sitting position with her bent knees almost touching her nipples, for that was all the leeway the tub's small size allowed.

She had the soap poised in her right hand to lather her

left shoulder when the door swung open and Rodrigue stepped back into the cabin.

He had forgotten his glass, which he now wanted to see if he could discern the nationality of a passing ship, illuminated by a swinging ship's lantern.

And he forgot his glass again in his instant stupefaction at the sight that met his gaze.

Rosamunde, her pink-and-white skin gilded by the lamplight, her pale hair pinned up and haloed by the soft golden light, sat naked in the tub. For a horrified moment she went rigid, holding the soap aloft, and stared at Rodrigue with dilated green eyes. Her white arms were wet and gleaming, her wet knees silvery. And her whiter breasts were pearly mounds, pink-tipped and suddenly shaken by her swift indrawn breath.

The moment she had dreaded was upon her.

23

Abruptly Rodrigue banged the door shut behind him and leaned against it, his astonished face almost as white as her own. Now he understood his strangely protective feeling toward the lad, now he understood that odd mixture of feelings that churned in his chest when he looked at her, the reluctant way he had noted her beauty —*not a lad but a woman!* And a desirable one.

Instinctively Rosamunde dropped the soap and covered her round breasts with her crossed arms. Her white knees, silvery and wet, made a silken barrier to his silent gaze.

"Captain Avilo—" she began desperately, her words fading away as she saw that the Spanish captain had bent and was pulling a heavy chest over to block the door, which had no latch. She watched him uneasily.

"Now." Rodrigue straightened up. He loomed tall in his rich black clothing, and his expression was more dour than she could have imagined it. "I think we will have some explanation."

"Now?" she said unhappily. "Couldn't it wait until after I have had my bath?" She cast an anxious look at her clothes, too far away to reach, and her voice grew plaintive. "You can't—you *can't* just stand there and watch me!"

Coolly, the Spanish captain sat down on the edge of his bunk. One booted leg swung. He looked alert and quite dangerous.

"We will talk *now*," he said pleasantly. "Before you have had a chance to fabricate more lies. Who are you?"

Rosamunde flushed at that accusation, and the soft color suffused her face and neck, her shoulders and breast. Rodrigue fought to keep his face stern—it was difficult in the face of such appealing beauty.

"I am Rosamunde Langley, granddaughter of the earl of Arne."

Rodrigue snapped to attention. He had heard of the earl of Arne—a noble name!

"You will have heard of my father, I think," she said softly. "Jonathan Langley. He was beheaded some three years ago on Tower Green."

Ah, that was where he had heard of the noble earl—in connection with some plot against the English king. "And that is how you took to the road?"

"No." She hesitated. "I was being forced into a loveless marriage by my guardian, and I"—she smiled a little sadly—"I bolted."

Bolted! And wild as a young colt she was—one with a tossing mane that had never known bridle or spur! "You could not go back?" he mused.

She shook her head, remembering that moonlit night when she had held the earl and Lord Matthew at bay with Harry's pistol. "I—I left in an odd fashion," she said faintly.

Rodrigue studied her narrowly, wondering if the rest of the story she had told him was all lies. "The man?" he asked steadily. "You'll not tell me you've been riding the night roads of England unattended?"

Rosamunde shot him an uneasy look. "Yes, there was a man. But he lies dead a day's ride from the Cornish coast where I found you. 'Twas he who rescued me from my plight, and—and we took to the road together. 'Twas his profession, you see."

Rodrigue smiled grimly at this lad-turned-lass. Highwaymen were a lucky lot, chancing on all sorts of treasures.

"So the rest of what you told me is true?"

"Basically. My horse was near gone; I'd been harried all the way to the inn. I was sure I was spent and had loosened my sword in its scabbard, intending to sell my life dearly. But I chanced to hear some talk in the inn, not meant for my ears, about the Spanish captain upstairs and how her ladyship at the castle planned to take his ship by stealth. I brazened my way upstairs and—'twas an easy thing to throw in my lot with you." Her voice faltered. "Does—does my being a woman make such a difference?"

He frowned. "Yes, it does." He studied her intently. She was growing tired of that inspection.

"Turn your back, Captain Avilo," she said crisply. "I intend to finish my bath. Remember I saved your life. You can put me ashore at the first port, and I'll go my way and trouble you no further."

He was even more astonished, and his dark brows shot up. Go her way? A woman, friendless, without funds, wanted by the law in her own country? He turned his back.

Rosamunde continued to bathe, cursing her luck that he had felt it necessary to return. "Are you not needed on deck?" she demanded bitterly. "To put this ship to bed?"

He turned angrily. "I cannot leave you naked in a cabin with an unlatched door—"

"Turn about, Rodrigue," she said fiercely. No more "Don Rodrigue" or "Captain Avilo" for her. She was a

336

woman, sternly ordering a man to turn his back while she was in her bath.

Hastily, Rodrigue obeyed this peremptory summons and turned his back again. "I doubt anyone suspects," he muttered.

"Obviously not, since *you* did not," she flung at him.

"Why are *you* angry?" he demanded, amazed. "It seems to me that if anyone is angry, *I* should be the one!"

"Indeed?" Her voice was cold. "The predicament is mine, not yours, Rodrigue."

He whirled, annoyed that he had lost command of the situation. "I have not given you leave to call me by my given name," he declared with hauteur, lifting his head to an arrogant height.

"What?" she cried waspishly. "We are trapped in this cabin together, have been so for days—and we are not yet on a first-name basis? *Turn your back!*"

Goaded by her tone, Rodrigue complied. And Rosamunde, having finished bathing, rose dripping from the tub and reached for a large square of white linen to towel herself dry.

It had come to Rodrigue how ridiculous was the situation. "I apologize," he said abruptly, turning about—and stopped as he was met by the sight of the full beautiful naked length of her.

Wrathfully, Rosamunde threw the soap at him, and he ducked. A moment later she had wrapped the white linen square about her torso and stepped out of the tub on long graceful white legs, bracing her wet feet against the roll of the ship. "You must stop this staring at my body!" she cried in outrage.

Her captain was about to give her a heated reply when there was a knock and the voice of the cabin boy asking if he could bring in the rinse water.

Rodrigue answered hastily in Catalan, ordering the boy to set the pitcher down and depart. Mystified, the boy did so, and Rodrigue—once he was gone—pulled aside the chest, snatched up the pitcher, hastily closed the door and pushed the chest back into position again.

"What are you going to do with that pitcher?" asked

337

Rosamunde warily, for although he had sloshed out some of the water as he moved the chest, he had not set the pitcher down. She had watched this maneuver with fascination.

"I am going to rinse you," he said in a tart voice. "Since obviously the cabin boy cannot. I do not know how you have managed thus far."

She reached out to snatch the pitcher. "I will rinse myself—*if you will please leave!*"

Overcome with fury at the wench's audacity—to a captain on his own ship, indeed in his own cabin—Rodrigue surrendered the pitcher, kicked aside the chest and flung out, banging the cabin door shut behind him.

Green eyes snapping, Rosamunde threw aside the soapy linen towel and rinsed herself with the warm pleasant water. She dried herself with a fresh towel, washed out her underwear in the tub, hung it defiantly on a line she strung across the cabin. Then she wrapped herself in a large clean towel and climbed into bed, pulling the coverlet up to her neck.

Her gaze was still baleful when Rodrigue returned. He fell back in shock at the sight of the clean wet undergarments strung across his cabin, dripping onto the floor.

"Are you gone mad?" He snatched them down, tossed them into a corner. "Your laundry will be done as ours is —by washerwomen when we arrive on shore!"

She would have scrambled up in fury, but remembered in time that she was wearing only a linen square which in any tussle would promptly come off. "I must wear clean underthings!" she shouted.

"Keep your voice down," commanded Rodrigue in a dangerous tone. "Else I will have you chained!"

She flinched before this threat, gave him back a mutinous look. "This is your thanks?" she asked bitterly.

But he was already rummaging through a large chest. "Clean linen, is it? Clean linen you shall have! Here!" He strode toward her, thrust an armload of fresh underwear at her. "Put them on!"

"With you here?" Her brows shot up. "Certainly not!"

"Ships are subject to emergency," he said coldly. "I cannot have you tumbling out in the night in your bare skin—it would demoralize my men."

Demoralize his men! She gasped at the hypocrisy of that remark. "I'll not!" she declared, turning her head away from him and thumping the pillow for emphasis.

She heard him step forward and turned her head quickly to face him. Before she could divine his intention, his hand shot out and he seized her by the wrist. One jerk and she was propelled from the bunk, landing perilously on the cabin floor in her bare feet with the bedclothes streaming behind her and the towel departed her body—for she had made the mistake of grabbing at the edge of the bunk with her free hand, instead of the towel.

"Put them on!" Rodrigue thundered, waving the clean linens in her face.

Rosamunde was flushed with indignation and trembling. Her whole lovely body was suffused with rosy pink. Muttering, she snatched at the underdrawers he proffered, stepped into them, and even accepted his aid in slipping the undershirt over her head and arms.

"Now are you satisfied?" she flashed. Green eyes blazing, she stood there barefoot in linen underdrawers far too long for her and a billowing shirt. Tendrils of her fair hair had come unpinned from being shaken about. She looked very wild.

"That is much better," said Rodrigue mildly. He took a couple of steps away from her. The sight of her lovely flushed body, the rosy-nippled breasts and softly rounded hips, the creamy white legs, had unsteadied him. He thought it best to put some distance between them. "You must understand," he added in what he meant to be a placating tone, "that I am in command here."

"Not only in command—you are bullying me!"

"I did not so intend it," he said seriously. "It is necessary that you continue this masquerade until I can get you safe ashore—now that we have begun it; otherwise you would be subject perhaps to lewd suggestions, for it is well known you have slept in my cabin all these nights."

In the act of returning to bed, she stopped short and her eyes widened. The crew would think—of course they would assume her to be his mistress, hidden in boy's clothing! What else could they think?

"I see that you are beginning to realize the implications," he said quietly. "There are men of blood on this vessel besides myself."

"I think you should assign me a private cabin," she told him with a level look.

He frowned and ran a hand through his dark hair. "I do not consider it wise to make a change now," he said shortly. "You saw the situation with the cabin boy and the bath just now? How would you have handled it were you in a private cabin?"

"The same way you did. I'd have told him to leave the pitcher on the floor and go."

"Ah, but you speak no Catalan. And he speaks no English."

Rosamunde sat down suddenly upon the bunk as that sank in on her. She had forgotten that she could not give even the smallest commands on board this ship, for she did not know the language. Nor would she learn it overnight.

She *needed* this captain who had pulled her naked and protesting from her bed!

She sighed. "I suppose you are right."

"I am glad you agree." His voice was wry. "As to what to do with you, I will give the matter thought. In the meantime, I begin to realize what a strain this journey must so far have been on you."

Rosamunde gave him a wan nod.

"I will see that you have privacy for such personal matters as bathing and dressing and—other things."

Relief drained her anger away. "Thank you, Captain Avilo. I am indeed grateful."

He smiled at her; it was an extremely sunny smile. "I think in private you might call me Rodrigue, and I will call you . . . Rosamunde."

Thoughtfully she nodded and lay down in her bunk, resting her head on one arm, with the coverlet thrown over her, considering him from this distance. A strange man, this Spanish captain, she thought. Peppery—but not bad.

340

He could so easily have pursued his advantage when he had found her naked in her bath. Yet he had not. And he had dragged her from her bed and forced his underdrawers and undershirt upon her not to bully her but because he feared for her safety if—in the event of accident at sea— she should be forced half-clothed onto the deck. A complex man, she told herself ruefully, studying the lean Spaniard, who walked restlessly about, now ruffling through his chests, now pouring himself a goblet of wine. Complex, fierce—yet gallant. . . .

Rodrigue was aware that Rosamunde's eyes were following him as he moved restlessly about the cabin. Her steady stare made him nervous. What was the wench thinking, with her luminous green eyes focused on him so unblinkingly? Had she noticed how the very sight of her white body heated him up? Ah, the wench had the power to sway him! Noble lady she might be, as she claimed—but she was also a vixen!

Why did she lie there on her arm, studying him in that dispassionate way? As if she were some luxury-loving feline and he a large rat that she had cornered and would dispose of at her leisure? He must get that gaze off of him before he melted under her cool green stare and was reduced to begging for her favors!

"I wish to make ready for bed, Rosamunde," he said irritably, determined not to undress before that bright surveillance and exhibit concrete evidence of her power to move him.

"And I am not to watch *you?*" she said in some amusement.

Rodrigue glared at her, and she turned over on her back chuckling and was soon asleep.

But this new knowledge had erected an invisible wall between them. It was one thing for Captain Avilo to share his cabin with "Robbie," a young highwayman who had befriended him—and quite another to share that cabin with beautiful Rosamunde Langley, a woman whose very presence heated up his hot Majorcan blood. No longer did he relax so much in her presence, nor did he touch her so familiarly. He treated her with a new diffidence that was hard for her to fathom. She might almost have thought he was afraid of her.

One consequence of his discovery that she was a woman was a new latch on his cabin door. He, who had never felt the need of a latch on his door before, installed one at once. If his officers or crew noted this, they made no comment—at least not in their hot-headed *capitán's* presence.

Indeed Rodrigue now treated Rosamunde with such an extreme of courtesy that she feared his changed manner would be marked by the ship's officers. He was very protective. At supper when one of the younger officers, having noted Rosamunde's sword, suggested they have a go at fencing on deck, Rodrigue grew quite pale beneath his dark tan. He said rather sharply that his young guest had strained his back in aiding his escape from the inn as they went across the roof, and that it would be hardly hospitable to press a guest into worsening an injury. The young Catalan officer, who had heard nothing heretofore about a bad back, withdrew his offer in some confusion.

Rosamunde, who had not understood a word of this fast exchange of Catalan, promptly made matters worse by lifting her own heavy chair and setting it back from the table as they rose.

"What was that all about?" she asked Rodrigue when they were back at the cabin. "Everyone looked at me as if I'd done something monstrous wrong when I pushed back my chair."

Rodrigue explained his fabrication about a back injury, and she stared at him.

"But that's preposterous," she objected. "Everyone on board has seen me dashing about—I even climbed the rigging once! 'Tis true I handle a sword only indifferently well, but he was not challenging me to a duel, only a fencing match. Why did you not let me meet him?"

"I will not have you hurt," said Rodrigue harshly. "You are a woman—I might leap for the throat of a man I saw strike you down!"

There was a controlled violence in his tone that surprised her.

342

"I will endeavor to give you no cause to leap for the throats of your officers," she said mildly. And to his smouldering look, "Would you like a game of cards?"

He assented, but while they played, as if unable to express what he wanted to say to her, he fell back on describing the doomed Armada. For the *Santa Cecilia* had now reached the neighborhood of Calais—and that was where eight British fireships set ablaze had sailed like bursting bombs into that tall and formidable wall of Spanish ships, drawn up for battle in their famous half-moon formation—and broken that fearsome line and sent them scattering. And in the resultant bloody battle the Armada had taken such a pounding as had sent her, broken and bleeding, home to Spain. Rosamunde listened, spellbound, as he told how the hard-pressed galleons, being torn to pieces by heavy shot, had struggled to come to grips with faster British ships, hoping to clamber aboard and meet cold steel with steel. But the brave men of Spain had died aboard their galleons, their sabers spattered only with their own blood and that of their horses. Out of ammunition, far from home, with their big guns silent, gallantly firing at cannon with their sidearms . . . it brought tears to Rosamunde's eyes, for she had never heard this version of the great battle—only the glory of the English victory. Now she saw the battle through Rodrigue's eyes, saw the mighty galleons and carracks caving in under heavy broadsides, masts splintered, blood spilling out of their scuppers, their decks a slippery hell—and felt sorrow for these brave and bitter Spaniards who had never had a chance even to strike a blow at Drake for his attack the year before on Cádiz.

Even though her own father and Sir Walter Raleigh had fought at Cádiz under Drake—and won—Rosamunde, from the depths of her English heart, sympathized with Spain as she listened to this strange contradictory man with the dark liquid eyes tell in bitter words how his father had fared on the great carrack on which he had been so proud to sail . . . and she grieved with him as he told her gloomily how the shattered Armada, bloody

343

and battered, re-formed to fight—and beaten, defiantly drew up in battle line once again.

There were tears glimmering on her long lashes when Rodrigue finished his story of the battle—and of the losers beating their way home on dying ships. Rodrigue looked into luminous green eyes swimming with tears and was startled. Though he had felt an urge to tell her these things, somehow he had not expected this English girl —daughter of the victors in that battle—to share his feelings and grieve for those who had lost. And that she could made him somehow humble.

"I have been—brusque with you on this voyage," he said huskily. "For this I beg your pardon."

"You have been kindness itself," protested Rosamunde in a burst of gratitude. "It is I who have been difficult. I was—I was exasperated with the situation. It seemed so—so bizarre to be pretending—"

"I understand." Rodrigue's darkly tanned hand closed over her own, and Rosamunde felt a slight thrill go through her at his touch.

Carefully, she removed her hand. "I see you have beaten me for two games," she said. "Come, we will play another hand and I promise *I* will beat *you!*"

"Why not?" murmured Rodrigue. "It would seem to be an English habit!"

But his irony was lost on Rosamunde, who concentrated intently on her cards. And if he noted that her color was high, he made no comment.

That night Rosamunde went to bed feeling unaccountably guilty. And wept silently for Harry, with her face smothered in her pillow, while the moon shone down on nearby Calais. And across from her the Spanish captain, unable to sleep, rose and strode up and down the moonlit deck and tried not to think about the English girl in his cabin, or what she was beginning to mean to him. . . .

Morning found him even more protective. When Rosamunde, standing by the rail, made a jest about being a man by day, a woman by night, Rodrigue suddenly shut her off. She looked up and saw that Don Tomás, one of the ship's officers, was strolling by.

"But he speaks no English," she murmured after the man had gone.

"Perhaps . . . perhaps not," said Rodrigue, following Don Tomás with an uneasy glance. "He may not speak English, but he has certainly heard it spoken many times. Perhaps he—and the others as well—understand more English than they pretend. I prefer to take no chances with you, Rosamunde. It would not be a fitting repayment for saving my life."

Rosamunde gave him an odd look. There was a richness to his voice that she had heard before . . . when Harry spoke to her.

This love feast between captain and unwilling guest did not endure for long. Though the loss of Harry was still a bright ache in her breast, the morning sickness had not returned during the voyage; now that Rodrigue knew her for what she was, she could at least relax on that score, and in spite of her grief she felt strong and quite able to tackle a new life—for her and her child to be. When the *Santa Cecilia* put in at Ostend in the Spanish Netherlands (a feint: for a small bribe the Spanish authorities would certify the ship had unloaded at Ostend, whereas her real destination was Amsterdam, a city beyond the control of Spain) and took on fresh water and provisions, Rosamunde announced she would leave the ship. Rodrigue would not hear of it. Ostend was governed by Spain; she would not like it. Amsterdam would suit her much better, he insisted. It was full of Protestants and besides was a thriving city where she could gain employment. She would like Amsterdam. No, no, he would not hear of her leaving the ship at Ostend. She must abide by his decision in this matter!

Surprised, Rosamunde desisted, for she had thought that while attracted to her, Rodrigue would have been glad to rid himself of her at the first opportunity, lest his Catalonian officers discover he was harboring a woman—and an English one at that—in his great cabin.

But having held forth at length on the desirability of Amsterdam all the time they were in Ostend, once they cleared the harbor Rodrigue seemed to forget all about it.

He had become morose, watching her with smoldering eyes. Her attempts at making small talk with him died away.

Once she thought she had found the reason for his attitude.

It was a bright sunshiny day and a fair wind was blowing them toward Holland—and Amsterdam. Rosamunde had joined Rodrigue on the poop deck, but found him taciturn. She was growing used to his mercurial moods and amused herself by watching the screaming gulls that circled, white as the billowing shrouds, overhead.

Beside her, leaning on the taffrail, a rigid figure in his somber black, Rodrigue stared fiercely away from her, apparently intent on the rolling sea.

"That—highwayman you spoke of," he muttered, enunciating the words with some difficulty as if he hated himself for speaking of it. "He was more than a comrade of the road. You lived with him?"

"Yes," said Rosamunde crisply. "His name was Harry."

Without a word, Rodrigue turned on his heel and left her. Rosamunde stayed by the rail, staring out at the blue water running by and remembering . . . remembering . . .

A little later Rodrigue was back, his mood completely changed. "I have a surprise for you tonight," he said merrily. "A feast to be served in our cabin." She noted uneasily his use of the word "our."

"Will not your officers miss us at supper?" she demurred. "We always sup with them."

Rodrigue shrugged and made an expansive gesture. "Tonight we will sup alone—the two of us."

The blitheness of his tone made Rosamunde wary. But Rodrigue was her host—and by necessity roommate as well—so she did not protest, but accompanied him back to his cabin at suppertime.

The meal seemed a long time in coming, and she made small talk to hide her nervousness. She watched with foreboding as an excellent repast—surely the best of what they had been able to purchase in Ostend—was piled upon the table. It was a fine night. A fair wind was blowing,

346

above the deck the great white sails billowed white against a dark blue sky, and the moon was full and golden and poured a silver light through the open windows of the great cabin.

Rodrigue had dressed in his best for the occasion. A rich black brocade doublet with a gold chain carrying his family crest swung from his throat past a burst of white Mechlin; his lean legs were encased in black velvet breeches with black grosgrain rosettes. It was his habit to wear fresh linens, but today even his point-edged lace boothose were a frosty white above his polished boots. As was the fashion indoors, he was wearing his hat—a great plumed hat, wide-brimmed and trimmed with a sapphire whose blue fire offset the somber hue of the ebony plumes.

"I wish that you could be wearing a dress of fine black silk," he said, "with polished jet and pearls to offset your fair skin. There would not be a lady in Spain to match you!" With a flourish he poured her some wine. Rosamunde, also wearing her hat—for it had managed to survive the journey—and gloves as well, for fashionable people dined in gloves, accepted the silver goblet and took a sip, staring soberly at her host.

Over breast of capon simmered in orange sauce, he told her of Majorca—ah, the unearthly beauty of its jeweled bays, its sparkling coves, its wave-lashed cliffs, the wooded heights that rose above the sea. She should see the ancient twisted olive trees, the holm oaks and mastic trees and stone pines. In January the almond trees burst into bloom. In Majorca even the wastelands were wondrous places, for among the broken stones as a boy he had found brilliant remnants of Moorish and Roman pottery, and once or twice the slingstones of those remote catapulters for whom the island was named—ah, she had not known Majorca was named for the ancients who had used catapults?

Rosamunde toyed with her orange capon and admitted that she had not.

Rodrigue leaned back, as uninterested in the excellent dinner as she, and waxed even more expansive. Of scented orange trees, blossoming and fruiting at the same time against a background of dark green satin leaves, he told her. Of the salt which was sprayed up by the waves breaking against the ancient cliffs, which collected in glistening white crystals in the hollows between the rocks. Of joy and laughter, of pomegranates and the song of nightingales, he told her.

She knew beyond doubt that she was being wooed.

And when their largely untouched meal was finished and they had sat in silence while the cabin boy cleared it away, when Rodrigue had predictably latched the door and poured her another goblet of wine and blown out the lamp "because the moon was so bright," and beckoned her to the window to see "a great ship sailing by—a Portuguese carrack, I think," Rosamunde stood beside him at the open windows with the sea wind cooling her hot cheeks and waited silently for him to make some declaration.

But Rodrigue was in no hurry.

"Take off your hat," he said, and tossed his own carelessly to a chair. "I would see your eyes."

Rosamunde, who until now had kept her hat firmly clapped on her head indoors as was the custom, sighed and turned to face him. Her soft mouth was enticing in the moonlight, but her eyes were shadowed by her hat's wide brim. The hat he smilingly removed, sailing it to the chair to join his own. But when he would have looked deep into her eyes, he found them shadowed by her thick dark lashes.

"Rodrigue," she murmured, troubled by this turn of events.

"Hush," he said, looking down at her raptly. "In this light your eyes are not green but silver, and deep as the sea itself. A man could lose himself in those eyes, Rosamunde."

He seized her hand and she stiffened slightly, reached out to set down her goblet. "No, Rodrigue, I—"

"In Majorca we have named the winds," his rich voice interrupted her. He reached out and pushed back a tendril of her hair, and she flinched. "There are eight winds that
348

blow for us in Majorca, and all are different. To me you are the *mitjorn*, Rosamunde."

"*Mitjorn?*"

"It is the name we give to the south wind—the hot and sultry wind that blows from Africa. To me you are like that wind." He bent down to kiss her, but she turned her head to avoid his lips. Undeterred, his warm mouth pressed against her jaw, trailed down her neck, and would have gone farther, for already he was pushing aside the lace at her throat and working at the fastenings of her shirt, when she pushed him back—very firmly, with both hands flat against his chest.

"Rodrigue," she said in a clear level voice. "Listen to me. I know you think that because I am not a virgin I am any man's prey—"

"No, never that," he protested. "I have only respect for you, Rosamunde. And desire."

The desire was very evident, for he reached for her again, his dark eyes glowing in a face cast in shadow as he stood with his back toward the silver sea. Swiftly Rosamunde eluded him, taking a step backward. Her face loomed up pale and lovely in the moonlight above the froth of lace at her throat.

"I gave myself to Harry of my own free will," she said steadily. "I would have done so no matter what the cost." She thought he winced at that, but she kept on talking—because she felt it must be said. "You must not think me a cheap woman because of that, Rodrigue. To me it was a marriage, although we could not solemnize it in a church, for Harry had sworn that his real name would never again pass his lips until he was restored to his lands, and there were those who would have dragged me back to a life of shame had my own name been known."

"You do not have to tell me these things," he broke in hastily.

"I *want* to tell you, Rodrigue. So that you will understand. Harry was my only lover, and I will never cease to love him. I do not love you, Rodrigue, and I cannot accept your offer."

"I have not offered you anything," he said, nettled.

"No, but you are about to."

He leaned forward, his voice low and urgent. "I ask only, do you not feel the life of this ship as she surges forward, the beat of the wind against your breast? Have you not known all along the passion you aroused in me? You trembled just now when I touched you. Did not your heart beat faster? Are you made of marble, Englishwoman, or of flesh? Do you not feel these things?"

Rosamunde sighed, for the fervor of this Catalan captain was very real to her. She could feel almost as an overwhelming physical force the strength of his pent-up desire, the power of his will attempting to bend her to his design. He would have taken her by the shoulders, but she pushed him away with shaking hands.

"For me there must be more, Rodrigue. I must love the man who holds me in his arms—and *I* must make the choice. I alone."

"That I desire you counts for nothing?" he demanded in a rough voice.

"Nothing," she said faintly. "It does not count with me at all."

"Then I was wrong," he said harshly. "You are not the sun-warmed *mitjorn*, but the treacherous *tramontana*—the cold north wind which brings us snow in winter." He turned away from her with a bitter expression. "Go to bed. Do not think that I will look at you! I am going on deck. Even the empty sea is better company!"

He flung out. Rosamunde looked after him hopelessly and winced as the cabin door slammed shut. She had felt—no, perhaps she had *known* it would come to this, but she had hoped so desperately that it would not. Rodrigue was kind, he was attractive in his lean debonair Spanish way, she had become very fond of him during this voyage, but . . . the loss of Harry was too near, too close, too hurtful. She carried Harry's child within her; she could not bring herself to take a lover.

Perhaps, she thought bleakly, she could never take a lover . . . never again. Perhaps all the sweet bright fires of loving had been extinguished for her, burned to ashes

350

on a lonely road in Cornwall where a highwayman named Harry lay in his blood. . . .

Rosamunde pressed her anguished face into her pillow and wept for a love that was gone.

24   *Rodrigue pointedly ignored Rosamunde all the* rest of the way to Amsterdam. Rosamunde was sorry for that, because she was to leave the ship there and try to make her own way in the big trading city of the hospitable Dutch. Rodrigue had helped her through the first terrible days of her grief, had made living bearable. Indeed, she had grown truly fond of the dark-haired captain from Majorca and hated to leave him smoldering. But she told herself it was only Rodrigue's pride that had suffered— not his heart. She spent most of her time on deck, thankful that she had not succumbed to seasickness, and admitted to herself that she missed Rodrigue's conversation, which was tangy as the salt sea air. And although she would never have admitted it, she could have used some encouragement on the road that lay ahead, for she was facing a new and foreign world, friendless and pregnant.

After leaving Ostend, as Rodrigue had predicted, the name *Santa Cecilia* was changed to *Margheretha*, the Spanish flag was lowered and the Dutch flag raised. So it was aboard the merchantman *Margheretha*, with the gilded figurehead of the gallant horse Hassim on her prow, that Rosamunde sailed at last into Amsterdam, and viewed with a catch of her breath its thrusting skyline, full of tall buildings with step gables and handsome weathervanes and hundreds of tall chimneys reaching for the sky.

Cold and distant now, but faultlessly correct, in Amsterdam Rodrigue took her in tow. He found a room for her in the same inn where he secured lodgings for himself. Rosamunde was grateful, for she spoke no Dutch and would have been at a disadvantage in making her own arrangements. Also, since she had very little money, she hoped to secure a job before her lodging bill must be paid. To her surprise—for she had expected to be dropped at that point—once Rodrigue had arranged for his ship to be unloaded in the busy harbor, he volunteered to escort her around Amsterdam, that great port city situated on the Zuider Zee.

"We will see what disposal can be made of you," he said grimly, as if to show her that he did not do this to please her or to woo her, but because he had a responsibility to see her safely settled in her new home.

She accepted his comment meekly, feeling it was perhaps deserved, and brightened as Rodrigue told her the city's intriguing name came from the River Amstel that flowed through it and the Dam—thus, Amsterdam.

"I saw none of the ship's officers at breakfast," she remarked, matching her stride to his long one as they walked along. "Are none of them staying at the inn?"

"Don Rios stays aboard ship in my stead. Don Alberto has a wife and six children at home—he will not part with a single coin for lodgings if he can avoid it. Don Felipe has a mistress in Amsterdam with whom he will stay, and Don Tomás will spend the entire time whor—" He stopped, remembering he was talking to a woman. "We will see neither of them until we are ready to sail. As for the other officers, they are too poor to take lodgings in the town and must needs stay aboard like the men."

So it was unlikely they would be running into the ship's officers. . . .

"It is kind of you to show me about, Rodrigue."

"We will take our meals together when possible," he told her more kindly. "I am sure it is difficult for you since you speak no Dutch."

Rosamunde gave him a grateful look and gazed about eagerly, enjoying the sightseeing. Amsterdam was a boom town being erected on the bones of an old medieval city. The entire place delighted her. It was bisected by canals, laced with beautiful bridges. The buildings were tall and steep-gabled and crowded together and reminded her of

353

London, where the buildings were jammed together. Her face grew pensive. London . . . she had been so happy there with Harry.

She stepped hastily aside as a couple of chimney sweeps hurried by, their hands and faces grimed by the soot of their profession. Then they were crossing the street to avoid a little group of lepers being herded along by an officer, who kept a wary distance from his hooded charges.

"So *many* of them," Rosamunde gave the unfortunates a shadowed look. "You see them everywhere!"

"Indeed they *are* everywhere," agreed Rodrigue in a brooding voice. "There's not a town in Europe but has a leprosarium on its outskirts. My old nurse has come down with leprosy," he added gloomily. "She cared for me as a child, but after I became a young man she went back to live with her daughter in Barcelona. I often visited her there on my voyages. The last time, her daughter told me that she had been sent to a leprosarium, that she had been concealing her disease for years."

"And the daughter turned her out?"

"Yes—as soon as she suspected. It was terrible for her. For 'tis said that if one lives with a leper, one is sure to contract the disease—that even a touch can mean death. Now her neighbors shun her, knowing that her mother is in a leprosarium."

Rosamunde turned and gave him a level look from scornful green eyes. "Had *I* been her daughter, I'd not have turned her out!" she declared recklessly.

"You do not know what you are saying," Rodrigue hushed her roughly. " 'Tis a terrible disease. I saw a leper raise his hood once to drink from a well. His face was eaten away."

Rosamunde felt suffocated. "What is that building?" she asked, desperate to change the subject.

"That? 'Tis the Waag. Its walls are five feet thick. A fortress built to withstand attack from the east, I am told, but today it is used for more mundane purposes. It houses the guild chambers of barber-surgeons and painters and such like."

Rosamunde looked with curiosity at the old fort, glad

to forget the lepers. A trio of laughing women parted to let them pass. Their brown overskirts were tucked up, and Rosamunde admired their frosty starched lace caps and was fascinated by their wooden shoes. On their arms they all carried market baskets full of live ducks with bright-yellow bills. Still looking at them, she brushed the sleeve of an old man in a long sweeping velvet cloak that reminded her of the cloak her guardian, the earl of Kenwarren, had worn when last she saw him—the man could easily be a banker, for many dressed that way. And then they were into a medley of rakish foreign sailors who broke like the sea to let them through. Their dark faces beamed at them. She thought they were speaking French. And what they said must have been lewd, for Rodrigue hurried her away.

Past stalls full of merchandise and surrounded by haggling people they walked, while overhead the noisy sea birds wheeled. Rodrigue's dark mood had lightened. He looked down at her.

"Do not be deceived by Amsterdam," he cautioned, his narrow face breaking into a smile. "This is a trading city, a marketplace—but Holland is a rural land of windmills and dikes and wooden shoes."

"And flowers and fat cattle." *Like England*, she thought.

"That too." He inclined his head.

"I fit this land," she murmured thoughtfully. "For there are many women here with wheat-colored hair as light as mine, and men too."

Rodrigue gave her a critical look. "But not with eyes so green," he demurred. "Look around you—this is a blue-eyed city."

Rosamunde laughed. "Perhaps they will accept a green-eyed woman to help out in a shop or—or perhaps work as a scribe."

"The guilds are very fierce here," he cautioned. "I am sure you would have to be apprenticed to a shopkeeper, just as you would in your own great city of London."

Rosamunde's green eyes opened wider that Rodrigue should know so much about England.

They strolled along the Dam, and Rosamunde, looking

355

westward, saw the handsome but not yet completed town hall, which, Rodrigue told her, had been built on some fourteen thousand piles—a veritable forest of wood below a mountain of stone. But mainly the houses of this water city, laced by *grachts* or canals, were built of brick fired from the river clay, for natural building stone was not to be found on Dutch soil. It was a busy commercial city of perhaps 200,000 souls, and Rosamunde was enchanted by the high tower of the Westerkerk, the West Church, which was topped with a crown. Everywhere there were towers; they rose strikingly from the flat marshy country-side. And atop the towers perched handsome weather-vanes. Steep step gables and tall chimneys were reflected in the smooth waters of the canals. A new city, Amsterdam seemed to her, for so much was under construction and workmen bustled about everywhere.

"All of Amsterdam is built on wooden pilings, else it would sink," Rodrigue told her critically. "A forest of pilings underneath each house. In Majorca we build on stone."

His voice rang with national pride and was haughtily critical of the hard-working Dutch. But Rosamunde forgave him that bit of hauteur—everyone loved the ways of his own country best. But she looked around her curiously, for this strange canal-city built on an underground wooden jungle was to be *her* city; her child would be born here.

They stopped at a sugar-bread bakery with a front of warm orange-colored brick, and Rodrigue bought buns, which they munched as they strolled. The damp breeze blew their cloaks as they walked. And it seemed to Rosamunde that every language must be spoken by the people who hurried by, flowing past them like a tide. Rodrigue told her this was not only because Amsterdam was a great trading center, but because the city had opened its arms to religious refugees—Walloons and Anglicans, German Lutherans, and Jews from Portugal and Spain.

"A kindly city," she murmured. "I think I will like it here, Rodrigue."

356

"You will not like it so well when the guilds refuse to let you work," he told her crisply.

"I will find a way." She set her jaw stubbornly and then was silent, munching her sweet bun.

But Rodrigue's snub did not depress her for long. Hers was an optimistic nature—things would work out all right.

Rodrigue gave her a look of longing that she did not see, for now she was admiring the Oude Kerk with its medieval church tower. And now the marvelous construction of the brick facades of the row houses.

"These merchants are very rich," he told her soberly. "They employ the best of master builders; you can see how fine the work is. And all these tall houses that line the canals have gardens at the back and summer houses which back on coach houses."

Rosamunde admired them, seeing that they were entered from flights of steps and had elegant gables.

"What is that?" she asked curiously, peering up at a gable.

"A hoisting beam. Every house has one. The goods arrive by water and must be stored in the attics. See, there is a wooden shaft there by the attic window and a rope. Some of them are very decorative—see that one?"

"No."

"It is hidden in that carved lion's head."

Rosamunde smiled up at the lion's head. "I am glad I did not stay at Ostend—it could not be so interesting as this."

Rodrigue gave her an unhappy look. His desire for this woman had grown very intense—whetted by her steadfast refusal to consider him as a lover. It was difficult for him to understand her refusal, for he had—except for Margarita—been very successful with women, and he knew that this one was not indifferent to him. Too, she was alone, without prospects . . . no, he did not understand this straight-backed English girl with her steady eyes and faintly smiling mouth. She seemed willing to press ahead on her own. To his Spanish-oriented mind—and in Spain women were little more than chattels; a man in Madrid had stabbed his wife for allowing her foot to be seen on a

357

public street—this was unthinkable madness. He started —she was speaking to him.

"If I must," she said quietly, "I will go into domestic service. I would perhaps make a good lady's maid," she added reluctantly.

"For that you would have to be apprenticed also," he reminded her. "Also"—his tone was cool—"you have not the temper for a long apprenticeship. You would become insolent and you would be whipped."

"What then is left for me?" she asked hopelessly.

They were walking through a more run-down district now, crowded and full of hawkers crying their wares. Carts and children ran about. Rodrigue seemed lost in thought. Rosamunde, looking up, saw large-breasted women leaning out of the windows. They waved to Rodrigue—and to Rosamunde too in her boy's clothes—they whistled, they called out to them in sultry Dutch. One of them with long yellow braids and languishing blue eyes even pulled down her bodice impudently so that her dark rosy nipples showed. Rosamunde reddened. Such things had happened to her before, of course, at strange inns in Harry's company when she had been dressed as a man. But she could never become used to them.

Rodrigue had not answered her "What then is left for me?" He was staring around him as if he had never seen such a district before. Which was indeed strange, because he had frequented many such districts in his seafaring life. His expression was, Rosamunde thought, rather wild. She could not know that he felt he was seeing her probable future. In his mind he envisioned her apprenticed as a servant in some wealthy merchant's house. He could imagine the master—or perchance the master's son— reeling home drunk from a tavern and falling upon her on the stairs, stifling her screams and having his fill of enjoyment of her luscious body, leaving her weeping and spent, to drag herself back to her tiny room. He could see her swift departure in the night, her brave but futile efforts to find employment in a town where guilds were everything and almost every field of employment was jealously guarded. He could see her being forced down into a district like this one, full of bawds and brothels, could see her finally and at last, her green eyes dimmed of their lovely light, leaning out of one of these windows and calling down to passersby to come and enjoy her body for a few coins. In horror he looked down at the stripling in velvet by his side and was struck again by the cool beauty of her face. No, she would not come to that, this English girl. Proud and starving, she would be found floating dead one morning in some canal.

He was white to the lips from these imaginings.

"Come away," he said quickly. "It is clear to me that Amsterdam will not do either."

Rosamunde blinked at this sudden about-face. But she was glad to leave the women's district and return to the inn, where Rodrigue ordered them a good dinner served in a cozy corner of the common room and addressed himself to her with great seriousness.

"You must not even consider staying here," he said. "It would be a great mistake. There will be no future for you here, I can see that. Remember that we must stop for provisions and water on the return voyage. I will think about it on the journey and decide which port would be best for you."

Rosamunde thought of the pretty tall-gabled houses, the fair-haired people with their smiling faces. She told herself she would learn the language soon enough and she would get a job too. Somehow.

"Rodrigue," she said gravely, leaning forward and laying down her knife. "I must go *somewhere*. I cannot live aboard the *Santa Cecilia* on your charity—nor do I wish to spend the rest of my life in men's clothing. Suppose your ship's officers were to realize suddenly that I was a woman? Would there not be a scandal that would reach all the way to your father's house in Majorca?"

"I ask only that you do nothing precipitous. Allow me time to make inquiries and find you a place."

"Amsterdam is a large city," she insisted. "There is sure to be a place for me here. It would be better if you did not even consider other places."

"I will think about it," he promised. "But you must
359

abide by my judgment in the matter. There, you are not drinking your wine, and it is a good vintage."

She gave him a rueful look as, preoccupied and thoughtful, he escorted her to her room after dinner and gave her a brusque goodnight. For regardless of Rodrigue's decision, she meant to stay in Amsterdam.

The next day, while Rodrigue was supervising the unloading of his ship, Rosamunde went out on her own into the town. Looking like a remarkably handsome youth, she strolled about in her wide-topped boots and jaunty short cloak and lace-trimmed cuffs and plumed hat.

In walking with Rodrigue she had noticed that there were excellent markets located on the water side of some of the streets along the canals. She walked briskly, getting her bearings—ah, there was the great weigh-house which had served as the city gate in medieval times. Now she was looking up at the yellow brick Tower of Tears, which was the point of departure for great voyages of discovery. It had been so named because it was here the women bade their men tearful goodbyes—for many never held them in their arms again. As Harry would never hold her again . . .

Sobered, she found herself passing markets without seeing them and roused herself. That market she was approaching should have what she wanted. Ah, there it was—bolts of cloth, with two stout *vrouwen* selling the goods. Rosamunde fingered the cloth, ignoring the handsome velvets, the silk damasks the *vrouwen* would have urged on her, for she knew she could not afford them. Her small remaining store of coins might not even be enough to purchase what she needed. At last she selected a length of sky-blue linen, spun from fine Flanders flax, and held it around her waist to estimate the length she would need. The *vrouwen* laughed, their fat sides jiggling with mirth, and one shook her head and used the word *bree*. Rosamunde looked at her, mystified.

"Is it enough to make a dress?" she inquired in careful English, indicating the length of linen.

"More than enough," said a female voice behind her in English. "*Bree* means 'wide'. She is saying it is not enough if the woman for whom you purchase it is very *bree*."

Rosamunde turned to smile at the speaker. She was looking at a slender wiry woman of uncertain age but with a worldly face and bright-red hair. "No, not very *bree*," she told the woman. "Slender like"—she hesitated—"like me. Do you know how much I should pay for it?" She held out her coins, and the red-haired woman selected two, haggled for a moment, and the cloth was Rosamunde's.

"Do you live in Amsterdam?" asked Rosamunde, as one of the *vrouwen* handed her the length of blue linen.

The slender woman shrugged. "I do now. Here I am called Wilhelmina. But I'm from London."

"I will need some of that white cambric, too—enough for a chemise and petticoat," Rosamunde told Wilhelmina. "And hooks and thread and a needle—and yes, shoes and stockings."

Wilhelmina seemed amused. She strolled about the stalls with Rosamunde and helped her bargain for all her purchases, including a pair of white cotton hose and dainty blue leather shoes with high heels. "Since you're outfitting your young lady from head to toe, you'll need a falling band too," she pointed out to Rosamunde, indicating some lawn collars at another stall. "They're very fashionable now."

Rosamunde hesitated, but she *would* need a collar. She offered the last of her coins to Wilhelmina and hoped they would be enough. They were. She came away with a falling band.

But she had not missed Wilhelmina's careless remark about "your young lady." In a burst of honesty, she explained, "The dress is really for myself. You see, I am not really a man—I am a woman."

She would have said more, but Wilhelmina's lip curled. She looked at Rosamunde in deepest scorn. "I can surely pick 'em!" she cried in disgust. "Now I'm mistaking wenches for gallants! How's a girl to make an honest living?" She flounced away, disappearing in the crowd among the stalls.

That was the first hint Rosamunde had had that she'd

been talking to a prostitute—one of that vast international sisterhood that frequented great cities such as Amsterdam.

Disappointed—for she had liked breezy Wilhelmina—she carried her purchases back to the inn and at once set about making herself a dress—for she could not afford to hire a seamstress. When Rodrigue asked her that evening what she had done with herself while he was gone, she replied evasively that she had walked about a little, but had spent most of the time in her room. He seemed pleased. She guessed shrewdly that he did not really like for her to walk about Amsterdam unchaperoned. Life must be very different for women in Spain, she realized—cloistered.

It took Rosamunde three whole days to make the dress, for she was no hand with a needle. Although it was of necessity of simple design, it was trim and fashionable. Below a U-shaped neckline its tight bodice ended in a slight point. The full blue linen skirt swished over a white cambric petticoat, and the huge puffed sleeves that ended at the elbow showed the ruffled undersleeves of a plain white cambric chemise. One of those puffed sleeves was a little less huge than the other and the hem was not quite straight and showed more white petticoat than she had intended, but it was as good a job as Rosamunde could do. When at last it was finished, she dressed and arranged her hair carefully. She was chagrined that she had forgotten to buy garters and now had no money left to purchase any, but she tied up her white stockings any old way with strips of knotted left-over white cambric, and waited anxiously for Rodrigue's inspection at supper.

When he knocked on her door to take her down to the common room—for Rosamunde had from the first rejected the idea of a private room, saying she must learn Dutch, and how could she if she never heard it spoken?—she flung the door wide and sank almost to the floor in a deep curtsy. Rodrigue looked in astonishment at her sky-blue linen gown and immediately hurried into the room and closed the door behind him.

"Are you sure it is wise for you to go about garbed as a woman?" he demanded anxiously.

"Certainly. You can't imagine that I would go through

362

life garbed as a man! Do you like it?" Rosamunde turned about so that her wide skirts swirled. "Tell me, is the skirt too *bree*? What do you think of the color? I hoped it would turn my green eyes blue."

Rodrigue laughed at that, and his face, which had been very tense, relaxed. She guessed he was thinking of the scandal if some of his ship's officers saw her in her blue gown and said lightly, "Who would know me, Rodrigue? With my hair fixed like this?" She indicated her fashionable hairdo with her hair piled up and long pale-gold curls dangling about her ears.

Rodrigue stared at her with mixed emotions. She looked enchanting—fresh and young and lovely, and as if she had not a farthing in the world. In an age of beautiful lace, there was none to trim her plain lawn falling band or her chemise. In an age of flashing jewels, her lovely white neck was bare. And yet . . . he swallowed.

"You are very beautiful, Rosamunde," he murmured, and added something in Majorcan which she guessed was a term of endearment.

Feeling her effort as a seamstress was a success, she accompanied him downstairs.

Nobody recognized her.

Rodrigue looked relieved, and he escorted her back to her room after supper with a rather courtly air, kissed her hand, looked longingly into her green eyes, and allowed the door—as usual—to be closed firmly in his face.

Rosamunde undressed that night thinking that Rodrigue was like an impetuous child, full of tempers but generous and warm-hearted.

The next morning he made arrangements for the day's unloading to be overseen without him and after breakfast, scowling, took her into the town to find employment.

The entire morning was a disaster. Rodrigue, with his facility for languages, spoke fluent enough Dutch. But with his scowling face and proprietary manner, he managed to antagonize every shopkeeper with whom he talked. Always he ended in a rage and jerked Rosamunde peremptorily through the shop door, banging it behind him.

363

By noon she realized that she would never find a job in Rodrigue's company.

"Rodrigue," she accused, planting her blue-shod feet on the bricks before the entrance to a cellar shop that jutted out from an orange brick facade at street level, "you are hindering me. Everyone is afraid of you—you look about to run them through with that Toledo blade you carry. How will I ever find work if you frighten my prospective employers by flying into rages?"

"It is true," he muttered, "that I am of no temper to help you. I fear each so-called 'position' will prove to be a trap."

Rosamunde sighed. "I had best try my luck alone."

His back stiffened in its black brocade doublet. "I will escort you back to the inn," he said in a formal tone. "I am occupied with other matters this afternoon, and you need rest from this fatiguing business. Tomorrow we will return to the search."

He was telling her what to do again! Rosamunde bit back a retort that she would continue her search right now without him, and accompanied him back to the inn. But she *was* tired, for she had spent long hours by candlelight working stitch by painstaking stitch on her new blue dress. Meaning to rest only a moment, she threw herself across the bed and slept until suppertime, when he knocked on her door.

Sleepily, she went to the door, and Rodrigue gave her a big smile and handed her a large wrapped bundle. "You will find this more suitable for dining with me," he said mysteriously. "I will return when you are dressed."

Jolted awake by that remark, Rosamunde accepted the parcel. Her eyes widened as she inspected its contents. Rodrigue must have spent the afternoon shopping for her! She spread his purchases out on her bed. A beautiful dress of silk velvet in a deep viridian green, with handsome slashed sleeves lined in red satin. A rustling red silk petticoat with a lustrous shimmer. A delicate white lawn chemise which would spill a froth of creamy lace about her arms. Green satin slippers with high red heels and green silk stockings. Rodrigue had forgotten nothing, she thought, touched. There were even gloves of soft green leather, a green velvet purse, and garters with rosettes of red satin ribbon—and a wide-brimmed green hat with waving scarlet plumes.

Tears stung her eyes. She had been unpleasant to him this morning because he was overzealous in screening her employers, had even considered flinging away from him, and he had spent his afternoon buying her—all this.

Of course these handsome garments would never do to wear when she went to look for a job. They would mark her as a great lady, and employers, she divined, were not looking for condescension in their employees. But she would not upset generous Rodrigue by refusing his gift. She would wear these lovely clothes as he had requested—tonight, to sup with him.

When she had dressed, even she could not believe how she looked in the mirror. The deep U-neckline revealed an expanse of pearly white bosom and the tops of her round breasts. The gleaming deep green of the velvet skirt moved sensuously as she moved. The red silk petticoat rustled and rasped delicately against her green silk stockings. Even the shoes fit! What an eye for size Rodrigue must have!

He looked quite dazzled when she ran to his room and knocked, whirled in with her scarlet plumes atremble on her hat, and turned about before him, dangling her purse from one green-gloved hand.

"The color is better," he said gruffly. "Green to set off the green of your eyes."

She laughed. "It is a wonderful costume, Rodrigue—and oh, I do thank you. I do not know how you managed to assemble it all in one afternoon!"

Rodrigue gave her a lazy smile. "I have friends in Amsterdam," he murmured.

She gave him a sharp look. None of those "friends" had been trotted out to give her a job! But her heart softened again at the wonderful feel of these luxurious new clothes. For tonight she could be Rosamunde Langley of Kenwarren House once again. She could play at being a great lady—even if tomorrow might see her embarked upon a career as a slavey in a scullery or a dairy.

Rodrigue marched down proudly beside her, his boots clomping on the stairs. Rosamunde accompanied him airily. It pleased her that conversation stopped and every head turned at their entrance into the common room.

"I should have engaged a private room," Rodrigue muttered, looking about him restlessly at pipes poised halfway to mouths and tankards held rigidly as everyone gawked at Rosamunde.

"You should not indeed!" Rosamunde corrected him lightly. "I am enjoying my new notoriety!"

It was the wrong word to have used. It reminded him of her background on the English highroads. He scowled for a moment and then decided to play along with her. "A bottle of wine," he told the barmaid. "I shall drink tonight to the most beautiful lady in the room."

And the only lady in the room, thought Rosamunde wryly, *unless you count the two husky barmaids who work here, neither of whom look remotely like ladies.* One of them brought their wine, and she wondered as Rodrigue drained his glass and poured himself another from the tall bottle beside him if she herself would end up as a barmaid at an inn.

She suggested the possibility, and Rodrigue paled beneath his tan. *"Never!"* he cried. His glass crashed down upon the table, spilling his drink, and he leaned forward, eyes blazing. For a moment he glared at her, then got control of himself and muttered, "You must never consider such a thing, Rosamunde. 'Tis only one step removed from—"

"I know," she said ironically. "From the brothel."

"From the street," Rodrigue said heavily. And as their supper was served, "Attend your food. Eat while it is hot. This fish is very good."

"Zeevrugt," she said, trying to cajole him into a better humor. "That means 'sea fruit.' I heard that word today. You see, I am learning Dutch."

He laughed. "So your green eyes will turn blue at last?"
366

"Perhaps." She smiled. "Is this not a lovely city, Rodrigue?"

"I think," he said slowly, watching her from beneath lowering dark brows, "that you have fallen in love with Amsterdam. It is a mistake. The weather here is unpredictable; there is much rain and mist."

"I come from a land of unpredictable weather," she reminded him.

"You would like a hot country much better." He sulked.

Rosamunde burst out laughing. He was trying to lure her to Majorca! "Rodrigue," she said, "you are a seafaring man. You have told me you come often to Amsterdam. I will await your visits and sup with you at this inn wearing this very dress!

"You will wait for me?"

"Of course," she teased him. "When you sail into the harbor, I will leave my drudgery and we will spend a whole merry evening together—unless you are busy and forget that I am in Amsterdam."

"Unless I forget . . ." he murmured, and she could not read the look in his eyes. But at least the rest of the meal was uneventful—except when a young Dutchman in his cups lurched toward them drunkenly, stumbled and caught himself with his hands on the edge of their table. He stood foolishly beaming down into Rosamunde's face, murmuring in Dutch.

Rodrigue put his hand on his sword and half-rose from his chair, but Rosamunde stopped him with a hand on his arm. "He is drunk, Rodrigue," she cried. "And he is but a boy. There is no honor in a grown man butchering a boy!"

The young Dutchman's friends dragged him away apologetically, and Rodrigue gave her an uncertain look and sat back down. "You did not hear what he said to you!" he muttered.

"And since I could not understand a word, how could it matter?" She shrugged. She guessed Rodrigue was the veteran of many a tavern brawl, and this would have been but one more. He still looked quite fiery and hurried through his meal as if running from his own rage. Rosamunde sat back and smiled at him across the table, and after a while this warm scrutiny seemed to placate him.

He began to talk once again, this time of Majorca and its myriad beauties. Rosamunde realized for a poignant moment how much Rodrigue had helped in getting her through her first wild grief at Harry's loss. His ready wit, his laughter, his generosity, even his peppery temper—all were diverting.

The next day—chill and misty as Rodrigue had prophesied—she went out early and tried to find work on her own. Not in the new finery Rodrigue had purchased for her—that reposed carefully in the great chest in her room —but in the sky-blue linen she had made herself and which looked more suitable for domestic service. She was cold, but she thought she looked better without her cloak, so she walked the windy canalsides and shivered.

Her search was difficult, for with the few words of Dutch she had picked up, she could not make herself well understood. Those shopkeepers who did understand that this green-eyed beauty wanted something from them often misconstrued what it was she sought. They offered her various wares in their shops—and sometimes, themselves.

It made her blush.

Rodrigue had run into troubles with the unloading and was occupied on the docks, so she had her time free. Four days later she found an English-speaking Dutch merchant who said thoughtfully that perhaps he could use her in his household—they had just lost their upstairs maid to marriage. Rosamunde did not quite like the lascivious look on his dark face as he said that, or the way he twitched his dark pointed beard, but she was growing desperate, for with the purchase of her dress material and slippers her money had run out, and her bill at the inn was mounting.

When she reached the merchant's handsome brick house, she paused to admire its steep step gable and then banged the iron griffin's head knocker. A homely servant girl with a long sad face and stooped shoulders let her in— but she did not stay for long. A large bewigged *vrouw* with a great yellow-starched ruff and stiff brocade gown promptly sailed into the room and turned her out with a torrent of abusive Dutch.

Rosamunde reached the steps just as the merchant himself trotted up them, and the *vrouw* unloosed a tirade at him and threw several expensive blue-and-white Delft plates at his head for good measure. The merchant dodged nimbly and ran down the street loudly bemoaning the loss of the plates, and Rosamunde retreated ruefully to her inn.

She was afraid to tell Rodrigue about that adventure, for he would certainly have said, "Did I not tell you how it would be?"

25   On the fifth day Rosamunde found work of a lowly nature in a butcher shop, scouring the rendering caldrons and pots. The sights and sounds and smells were enough to make a stout heart quail, but she was desperate for a job now and agreed to go to work the next day. That night at supper she told Rodrigue about it. He had been growing increasingly reserved as she spoke, and now he began to scowl.

"Your heart is too soft for butchering," he said bluntly.

"If I can fight a man with a sword, I can carve a dead pig with a cleaver," Rosamunde countered, although in her heart she feared he was right. "Anyway, I am not to do the butchering, but to scrub the pots and caldrons."

"Where is this place?" cried Rodrigue. "I will go have a look at it!"

She told him, bewildered, and he abandoned his supper and stomped off even though the hour was late. Rosamunde finished her meal alone. She wondered what on earth he sought to accomplish by rushing off like that and went up to bed before he returned.

He must have made some sort of trouble, for when she reported for work the next day, the butcher was apologetic. Rubbing bloody hands on his greasy apron, he explained vaguely that he had forgotten the guilds—the guilds would object, he could not hire her.

Disappointed and certain that Rodrigue had somehow offended the man, Rosamunde returned to her inn. Next time she found a job she would not tell Rodrigue about it until after she had entered on her duties! In any case he would be gone soon, for the ship had been swiftly unloaded—space was at a premium in the busy harbor—and the new cargo was being taken on at a great rate; Rodrigue was very encouraged with his progress.

But after the fiasco of the butcher shop, Rosamunde had little luck in her pursuit of employment. Nor was Rodrigue any help to her.

Three days later she rose early as was her custom and knocked on Rodrigue's door to rouse him for breakfast. Though she knocked three times, he did not answer. Puzzled—for Rodrigue always made a point of breakfasting with her and warning her anew about the evils of Amsterdam—she went down to inquire of the innkeeper if Captain Avilo had left some message for her.

The innkeeper's English was very bad. While he was struggling with her request, a stranger—a large man with brown-gold hair and extremely wide-topped fashionable boots—lounged forward. His big body was encased in worn russet velvet and seemed to break in half as he bowed so low the ragged plumes of his hat nearly swept the floor.

"My name is Van Hoorn," he said in excellent English. "Could I be of assistance in this matter?"

Rosamunde breathed a sigh of relief. "Indeed you could," she said, and Van Hoorn translated her message to the innkeeper, who replied that Captain Avilo had left word he would return shortly.

The gentleman in russet velvet then tweaked his drooping brown-gold mustache, caressed his brown-gold Van Dyke beard thoughtfully for a moment, and inquired if she would have a glass of cider with him. Rosamunde,
370

eagerly sensing that here was a source of information about employment, agreed and swished her blue linen skirt beside him to a table by the small-paned window. She was fully aware of how strongly Rodrigue would have disapproved of this chance meeting, but at the moment she did not care. Van Hoorn pulled back her chair and lounged gracefully into the chair across from her and ordered cider. By the time it was brought, Rosamunde had discovered that Van Hoorn lived in Haarlem but now spent much of his time in Amsterdam.

That was wonderful! She overwhelmed him with questions, about the city, about jobs—so many that he held up his hand to ward them off, but his answer was meditative.

"You say you have had no success in seeking employment? Amsterdam is a busy city, and there is perhaps a coldness toward strangers . . . have you no relatives or friends to whom you could turn for advice?"

"None."

Van Hoorn put his fingertips together pontifically and appeared to be thinking. "Would you allow me to make some inquiries? I am well connected here."

She was so grateful she did not pause to wonder why a man who was so well connected also had frayed cuffs and worn boots.

"Have you had any special training?" he wondered. "Any skills?"

For a moment Rosamunde was tempted to tell him she could shoot off a man's hat at full gallop at a distance of twenty paces, but she forbore. "I read and write English passably well," she volunteered.

"That would perhaps be useful," he agreed gravely. "You could tutor in English—but not, of course, until you have learned Dutch. Do you speak other languages or have skill with a needle?"

Rosamunde shook her head regretfully. "I ride well and am considered a good judge of horseflesh."

She meant that perhaps she could be of use to a gentleman purchasing breeding stock for his stables, or racing stock, but Van Hoorn put the wrong construction on it. "As you can see," he explained with a twinkle in his blue

371

eyes, "here we go about mainly by boat—although there are squares at the city gates for horses to be unharnessed. Female coachmen and footmen," he added dryly, "are not in great demand here—nor female grooms."

Rosamunde flushed and bit her lip. "I could—enter domestic service," she said reluctantly. "I was gently brought up and know what is required of good servants."

Van Hoorn again caressed his gold-brown beard; it was a characteristic gesture. "It may be that is the answer. I have business in the city today, but I will make inquires." He rose and bowed very genteelly. "I will let you know tomorrow. Or perhaps tonight? Might we not sup together tonight and discuss it? I am also staying here at the inn."

Rosamunde thought of Rodrigue's wild jealousy and was about to say no—but she had her future to think of: she could not afford to put it off. "I—yes," she decided defiantly. "I would like that very much, Mynheer Van Hoorn."

"Good. I will engage a private room for us then." He was watching her alertly, and at her sudden frown he added hastily, "For we will have much to discuss and the clamor of the common room at night is"—he smiled—"uncommon loud."

Her set face relaxed. He did not mean to seduce her after all!

Bright-eyed, she thanked him for the cider and bade him goodbye. She was still sitting there, staring into her empty glass and wondering what position Van Hoorn would find for her, when Rodrigue strode in, looking for her.

She thought it best to tell him about Van Hoorn at once—lest the innkeeper whisper it and make trouble. "Rodrigue," she said in an excited tone, "I have met a gentleman who believes he can find a position for me—his name is Mynheer Van Hoorn and he has excellent connections in Amsterdam!"

Rodrigue was in one of his moods. "I have no time to discuss this mynheer," he told her crisply. "Will you come upstairs, Rosamunde? I have something to say to you."

Wondering uneasily what could be the matter, for his manner was threatening, she accompanied him up the stairs to his room and followed him in. His stout wooden sea chest, she saw, was packed. She turned to him with a question in her green eyes.

"Yes," he said. "I am leaving, Rosamunde. The *Margheretha*'s cargo is loaded, there is nothing here to detain me. I sail with the morning tide."

She had not realized until then how much this man's passions and tempests and sparkling humor had come to fill her life. Sometimes he was lightly diverting, sometimes annoying—but always he was interesting. She would miss volatile Rodrigue Avilo.

"I—I did not know you were leaving so soon," she stammered, thinking that if this was his last night in Amsterdam, she should not hurt him by supping with Van Hoorn.

The frown suddenly left his face, leaving it intent and earnest. "Ah, Rosamunde," he cried eagerly, "come with me! There are other cities—better than this one. Why stay here where there is nothing for you?"

It was a tempting offer. Rosamunde sighed. "Rodrigue, if I were to leave Amsterdam with you now. . . ." She hesitated.

His keen dark eyes searched her face. "You would become my mistress," he supplied bluntly. "Is that what bothers you?"

She nodded soberly. "Yes. I cannot do that."

"And why can you not?" he shot at her. "For I am aware that you are not indifferent to me!"

"Because . . ." She did not want to tell him about the child, and she could not meet his eyes. "Because I am loyal to Harry still, Rodrigue."

"Pish! You cannot go on being loyal to a dead man! He would not expect such a sacrifice."

"No," she said bleakly. "Harry would ask nothing, expect nothing. Nevertheless I will be true to him."

Shutters closed down over the dark eyes that had seemed so open and yearning a moment before. "Very
373

well. Then this is goodbye, Rosamunde." He moved toward his sea chest.

"But you—Rodrigue, you aren't going now?" she cried, appalled that they should part on such a bitter note.

"Since we set sail early tomorrow, and since we have nothing to say to each other, I will spend the night on board my ship."

He lifted the small sea chest, heaved it to his shoulder and would have swung away from her but she ran forward and placed detaining fingers on his arm. "Rodrigue." Her voice was wistful. "I had hoped we could part as friends."

A quiver went through his lean body, but he turned on her a look almost of hatred. "There can be no friendship between a man and a woman," he declared passionately. "There can be only love—or indifference." He shook off her arm.

"I was Harry's friend," she said steadily, stepping back.

"You were Harry's mistress," he corrected in a fierce voice.

"That too. But I was also his friend."

"Allow me to doubt it!" He jammed his broad-brimmed hat more firmly on his head. "Since you have found no gainful employ and I am of no temper to help you, I hope that this—Van Hoorn, is it?—will be of aid. Remember that you are a woman alone, and try not to become ensnared into some brothel!"

She was speechless with rage.

"I will look after my own affairs!" she flashed. "Goodbye and good journey!"

Rodrigue gave her a wintry look and stalked out. He did not even say goodbye. Her eyes were filled with angry tears as she watched him go. Rodrigue was impossible! Jealous, overbearing—and yet, it was terrible that he should leave her on such a note as this.

The encounter upset her, for she had grown genuinely fond of Rodrigue. She considered going after him but decided against it—they would only clash again. Instead she returned to her room and found a maid cleaning up. This maid spoke a little English, and Rosamunde finally managed to make her understand that she was looking for work. Was help needed here at the inn?

A decided negative shake of the head greeted this inquiry, but the woman, who was middle-aged and heavy-set and stolid, thought for a moment. She wiped her hands on her gray apron. "Have you—asked church?" she asked in a guttural accent.

Rosamunde, who felt her late relationship with Harry had put her outside the church, said evasively, "I—I have not been to church lately."

The older woman gave her a disapproving look. She shrugged and turned away, picking up the wooden pail she had set down to consider Rosamunde's question.

Restless and uneasy, for now that Rodrigue was gone, the landlord might well demand she pay the bill for her lodgings, Rosamunde passed the remainder of the day in walking fruitlessly about the town. Now that she was wearing skirts, as a woman alone her beauty excited admiring glances from passing workmen, who nudged one another, and from bored-looking gentlemen in plumed hats, who came to life at the sight of her. More than once she had to move on quickly to avoid unwelcome attentions, yet the shopkeepers seemed more obdurate than ever about hiring her. She came home late—already the candles were being lit—and still no work.

She determined that if Van Hoorn had turned up no prospects for her, she would try the taverns—although her memory of that one evening she had spent in England working as a barmaid still filled her with distaste.

There was plenty of time, so she bathed leisurely, arranged her hair in fashionable style, and was already dressed in the green velvet gown Rodrigue had bought for her when a faint knock and a small piping voice announced the innkeeper's small daughter, Geertje. The child curtsied and delivered a stilted message, the only words of which Rosamunde understood were "Mynheer Van Hoorn."

Rosamunde smiled at the child, gave her blonde coiffure a last pat and went out into the hall. It occurred to her suddenly that the private room might well turn out to

375

be a bedroom and that Van Hoorn was a very large man . . . she might have trouble with him. With a sigh she went back into her room, plucked her pistol from the chest in the corner where she kept it, loaded it, and stuck it into the commodious pocket she had fashioned at the side of her petticoat. For the sobering thought had long since occurred to her that she was a woman alone in a strange city and might one day need to protect herself at gunpoint.

Along the hall and down a half-stairway she followed the little girl, who opened a creaking door, curtsied again and left. Rosamunde was relieved to find herself in a small cozy sitting room with windows that looked out on the canal. From his seat at a wooden table in the center of the room, Van Hoorn rose to his considerable height. If he was startled at the transformation that her fine clothes had wrought in her, from simple country girl to great lady, he did not show it other than by a deep bow so sweeping that his wavy brown-gold hair cascaded over his coat. "You do me honor!" he cried enthusiastically, hastening to pull back a chair for her.

Rosamunde extended a green-gloved hand and greeted her host. Van Hoorn lingered over the kissing of that hand. "You are too lovely to drudge your life away," he told her gallantly.

Rosamunde smiled and seated herself gracefully across the table from him. "Do not be deceived, Mynheer Van Hoorn. I have fine clothes—but an empty purse."

"It is hard to believe," he murmured. "You look a very queen!" He shook his head as if to clear away cobwebs. "As you can see"—his expansive gesture indicated the pair of goblets and two bottles already on the table—"I have ordered wine for you, brandy for me." She saw that he had already been at the brandy, but now he poured a brimming goblet of wine for her.

"So much?" she murmured humorously. "You will get me drunk, mynheer!" She toyed with the idea that that might be his intention. She must have seemed to him very naive in her homemade gown this morning . . . perhaps he thought her quite unused to strong wine.

376

"Large goblets for long evenings." He laughed, pouring himself another large brandy. "I have much to tell you."

From across the table Rosamunde's steady green eyes smiled into his. Hers was a bold nature, hers a cool resolve. He was too bluff tonight, she thought. It occurred to her that Mynheer Van Hoorn might not be trying to get her a job after all. "I am glad to hear it," she said cautiously.

"Oh, 'tis an excellent position. I think you will like it."

She sipped her wine thoughtfully. Once again he had sounded too offhand. "Perhaps you will tell me about it, mynheer?" she suggested gently.

Van Hoorn studied her in the candlelight, his gaze caressing the radiant sheen of her skin, the pale gleam of her fashionable curls as they touched her white neck. A magnificent woman. Suddenly he leaned forward, blue eyes recklessly agleam. His voice was husky. "I would rather you would fly away with me. Now."

To keep the conversation on the right note, she pretended to misunderstand him. "I am sure you would find me a good position in Haarlem, Mynheer Van Hoorn," she said politely. "But I find that I have fallen in love with Amsterdam."

For a moment Van Hoorn's expression was filled with chagrin that one so beautiful should be so obtuse. "Englishwomen are very beautiful." He sighed. "Let us drain our glasses to the land that bred them. To your home land!" He held out his goblet, touched it to hers.

Rosamunde laughed inwardly. Did Van Hoorn think he could make her drunk, she who had learned to drink strong brandy at the haunts of highwaymen?

"To England!" she echoed, and drained her glass, calmly held it out for a refill.

She thought he looked a bit daunted at that, but he reached quickly for the wine bottle. Too quickly. His arm awkwardly knocked it from the table, breaking it. The wine splashed over her velvet skirt and on Van Hoorn's worn boots. With an exasperated cry, he sprang forward, hastily wiping the wine from her skirt with a linen napkin.

" 'Tis no matter," said Rosamunde, ruefully thinking that this was her only good dress and now it smelled strongly of wine. Van Hoorn's hand was resting on her knee, and she gestured him away before he began to show too much interest in what lay beneath the velvet.

Van Hoorn made a show of finishing his dabbling, smiled up at her. "I must apologize for my clumsiness. Our supper will be along shortly and I will order another bottle then."

She nodded pleasantly. "In the meantime, could you satisfy my curiosity? What is this position you have found for me?"

Van Hoorn resumed his seat. He sat watching her with a bland expression. His voice flowed like cream. "It is with the family Van den Vondel," he said carelessly. "Joost Van den Vondel is a friend of mine."

Van den Vondel . . . it had a nice ring. Too nice. She was sure he had made it all up. She toyed with her empty goblet, reflecting whether to interrogate him further or simply let the evening degenerate.

She decided that having let herself in for this, she should see it through—and besides, there was a slim chance that he was telling the truth. "I will have a dash of that brandy, mynheer, if you please." She held out her goblet.

If Van Hoorn was surprised, he concealed it well. "Certainly. I had not thought you would care for such strong spirits." He splashed some brandy into her goblet. "There is but one thing. . . ." He coughed.

She waited. Now he would suggest a liaison. She took a stiff drink of the brandy to bolster her. Her head began to hum. She wondered if it had been a bad idea to combine wine with brandy and set down her glass.

"Joost will be sure to discover that a Spanish captain brought you to this inn," he said delicately.

Ah, he was subtle, this Dutchman! He had made inquiries about her from the innkeeper! She watched him in silence, listening to the hum in her head.

He coughed. "Could one inquire as to your relationship with this Captain Avilo?" He leaned forward as if her answer might be too faint to hear.

378

"Captain Avilo is a friend," she said firmly.

"Yet he brings you here attired as a man, he pays the bill for your lodgings."

Rosamunde's eyes widened. "I—I did not know Rodrigue had paid my bill," she murmured. "I must find some way to repay him."

"No doubt you will," he said kindly.

She rose. She felt light-headed, as if she might faint. Her pregnancy must be playing tricks on her. "I must ask you to excuse me, mynheer," she said in a slurred voice. "I do not feel well."

Van Hoorn jumped up, eased her back down into her chair. "If you don't feel well, then 'tis best you don't walk about. Perhaps some food—have you eaten?"

"Not since breakfast, but—"

"Ah, then that is what is the matter."

His golden-bearded face was wavering before her. She made a great effort to rise. "I think—I think I had best go to my room, Mynheer Van Hoorn."

"Ah, that I cannot allow." His face swooped down suddenly very close, and his blue eyes, she noticed swimmingly, had a cruel light. She gained her feet, but the room seemed aslant. It rocked and shimmered, and the floor billowed up like the sea. Unable to keep her balance, she swayed against Van Hoorn's arm.

The wine! The bottles had been there when she arrived, he would have had plenty of time to tamper with the contents. And Van Hoorn had drunk none of the wine, only brandy. Indeed he had made sure—by the simple expedient of knocking over the bottle—that she drank but one glass.

She had been drugged!

She staggered away from him, dragging out her pistol, her movements slowed by the effects of the drug. Van Hoorn pounced on it, wrested it away from her.

"I was told you were dangerous," he murmured pleasantly.

She opened her mouth to scream, and Van Hoorn smothered that scream with a kiss. His mouth was hot and moist and urgent, and his thick gold-brown mustache

379

and beard pressed against her face and neck like a smothering fur. She struggled in his arms as her senses reeled. Then there was a loud noise—perhaps a hammering on the door—and she was suddenly flung away from him, landing sprawled on the floor, her progress arrested by the wooden table leg.

She was lying face down and she thought she heard the door kicked open. She thought she heard the crack of bone against bone. She thought she heard Van Hoorn howl.

Then there was only blackness.

26   *Rosamunde awoke feeling the familiar roll of a* ship beneath her, hearing the protesting creak of its timbers. She moved her arm, groaned, touched wood and realized that she was lying in a ship's bunk.

Not in Amsterdam, then!

Her eyes snapped open and she saw that she was back in the great cabin of the *Santa Cecilia.*

Dizzily the events of the night before came back to her—in bits and pieces: Van Hoorn . . . the private dining room . . . the wine . . . being drugged . . . some kind of a fight . . . passing out.

She looked around, half-expecting to see Van Hoorn staring at her from those crafty blue eyes.

Instead she saw Rodrigue, handsomely dressed in his best black velvet doublet, adorned with his heavy gold chain. He stood with his legs wide apart, arms folded, in the center of the room, considering her.

Rosamunde sat up, leaning on one elbow. A pain shot through her head and she winced. "Rodrigue! What—what is going on? Why am I here? Where is Mynheer Van Hoorn?"

Rodrigue moved toward her with a slight swagger that emphasized the narrowness of his hips. His tone was scathing. "I came back in time to save you from being carted off to a brothel. Doubtless Van Hoorn told you he had made arrangements for your employment—and indeed he had; he had made arrangements to sell you to a brothel. I throttled the truth from him. His 'sister' was about to appear—indeed, she was no sister at all, but a famous madam known to the police of three continents. It was Van Hoorn's intention to tell the innkeeper you had had too much wine and that his 'sister' would take you to her home. That would have been the end of you!"

"Thank you, Rodrigue." Rosamunde shivered and sat up, holding onto her aching head. She realized suddenly that she was wearing only her thin chemise and looked down in alarm. "I—who undressed me?"

"I did. And brought you here wrapped in a blanket. You will be good enough to put on the man's clothing you wore when you came aboard. I do not believe any of my ship's officers or men saw you wearing woman's clothes in Amsterdam—at least none have remarked it."

She shook her head to clear it. The pain was very real. "Rodrigue," she gasped. "I cannot go with you on this voyage. You must set me ashore. Any small boat will do—I can row myself ashore."

Rodrigue's face clouded up. "Is it not clear to you by now that you need me?" he rasped. "Are you still under the impression that you can survive in Amsterdam or some other foreign city alone?"

"I will have to," she insisted. She threw her legs over the side of the bunk and would have risen, but that he surged forward and pushed her back to a sitting position.

"No, you will not!" he shouted. "First Wilhelm Van Hoorn, and then how many others? Have you not learned your lesson?"

Rosamunde gave him an odd look. "I never told you his name was Wilhelm. Indeed, I did not know it. I knew him only as Mynheer Van Hoorn."

Rodrigue gave a sulky shrug. "One hears first names —who knows where I heard it?"

A great light burst over Rosamunde.

"I will tell you where you heard it," she said, leaning forward tensely and fixing him with her angry green gaze. "You heard it when you hired him to drug me and bring me back aboard! I am sure you told everyone you had found poor 'Robbie' the worse for drink and minus his clothes in some sporting house, and that you were bringing the poor lad back aboard before something worse happened to him!"

He did not bother to deny it. "That is of no importance," he said heavily, sweeping aside his lies with an impatient wave of his hand. "Can you not see that I merely forestalled what would have happened to you—if not tonight, tomorrow? When I arrived at the inn, I found your pistol lying on the floor and Van Hoorn was smothering you with kisses—is that not proof enough of what your fate would have been in Amsterdam? Another moment and he would have had your skirts up and taken you there on the floor like any harlot." His voice rose with indignation. "You should be happy that you have been saved from so ugly a fate!"

Saved! He had kidnapped her, lied to her—and now he had the gall to think she should be pleased about it! She leaped up, shaking with rage, her fists balled. "Set me ashore!" she shouted.

"I could not, even if I would," Rodrigue told her coldly. "We have been at sea for some hours. It is now afternoon."

"Then turn this ship around and take me back to Amsterdam!"

His reply was a taunting laugh as he left the great cabin.

The slam of the cabin door made a further pain shoot through Rosamunde's aching head, and she sank back on the bunk with a moan, her fingers pressed to her throbbing temples. But she was too angry to sit still. She sprang up and took a quick drink of water from the carafe beside the bunk and choked. *Damn Rodrigue!* How dare he abduct her in this high-handed fashion?

382

She knew there was no question of turning the ship around, no question of a boat putting in to shore. Rodrigue was determined to drag her with him—perhaps all the way to Barcelona, where he was taking his cargo of hides! She smoldered. It would be worse to be a woman alone in Barcelona than it ever could be in Amsterdam, for in Barcelona—as in all of Spain—the Inquisition still held sway.

Stonily she contemplated revenging herself on Rodrigue. As her headache abated, a thought came to her and her green eyes sparkled with malice. She rather thought Rodrigue would stay away from her for a time to let her temper cool. Indeed, she was right—the cabin boy came, bringing her supper on a tray. She gave him a sweet smile and waved him away.

With a black look at the tray of food, she dressed swiftly in the handsome green velvet dress and red silk petticoat Rodrigue had bought for her. A quick search had located them stashed away in his sea chest. She had not thought he would leave such valuable garments behind —he had even brought along the blue linen she had made herself! She had no time for a truly elaborate hairdo, but she did arrange her blond hair in a fetchingly feminine fashion, piling it up and allowing it to cascade down over one shoulder. With her legs encased in the green silk stockings and her feet in dainty green shoes with red heels, she smoothed down the rustling red silk petticoat, tossed back her head in its plumed hat and swept down to the officers' mess.

A brave man would have quailed at the light in her eye.

On the way she passed an astonished sailor, who gaped at her as if he had seen a ghost. On past him she marched, flung wide the door and stood for a dramatic moment in the entrance, surveying the assembled ship's officers with a sardonic gaze, as they sat at table.

Conversation ceased, hung suspended in midsentence as every eye in the room turned to regard her. It was clear they did not at first recognize her as "Robbie," but they recognized her as a woman and a beauty. As one man, they sprang hastily to their feet.

Rosamunde took a deep breath that strained the material of her low-cut gown and focused all those masculine eyes, fascinated, upon the swelling beauty of the tops of her white breasts. With the aplomb of a duchess, she swept them all a deep ironic curtsy and advanced on Rodrigue. Her smile was bright and dangerous.

"It is time you informed these good gentlemen that I am Mistress Rosamunde Langley and not some bright lad you are making into a sailor," she told Rodrigue in a cold voice.

She saw that he was white to the lips, and perhaps past speech. But he bowed with icy formality. His heavy gold chain swung away from his black velvet doublet and clashed with an angry sound against one of the pewter trenchers as he seated her with much ceremony. Standing erect and fierce, his eyes flashing about him as if daring any of his officers to challenge him, he then spoke for some time in Catalan. Rosamunde waited, stony-faced, during this recital. She would have given much to have understood what he said, for all their faces remained puzzled when he had finished.

"What did you say to them?" she demanded haughtily.

Rodrigue flashed her a look of pure hatred. "I told them that you were my affianced bride, and therefore under my protection," he growled.

Rosamunde gave a contemptuous laugh and tossed back a lock of her hair with a green-gloved hand, a gesture that caused her daintily molded breasts to ripple beneath her green velvet bodice and brought the fascinated gaze of the ship's officers back to her pearly flesh.

"How ridiculous!" she jeered. "They must remember how I was brought on board—seized from my inn, carried onto the ship in a blanket, *kidnapped* by you!"

If possible, Rodrigue's tense face went a shade paler. "Rosamunde, you will be silent," he commanded in a shaking voice.

"Certainly," she agreed, tossing her head so that the plumes of her wide-brimmed hat danced. "I will be ex-
384

ceedingly silent. It is my intention not to speak to you—not another word after I leave this table—for the remainder of the voyage." She turned to de Guzman, huge, frowning and correct, who sat stiff with embarrassment beside her. "Are you uncomfortable because you suspect I am your captain's mistress?" she asked him sweetly. "Ah, but don't be! Just consider what a lovely story you will have to tell back in Barcelona or wherever you are going. All about the captain who brought a man aboard from Cornwall and turned her into a woman and then—remarkably—claimed her for his affianced bride!"

De Guzman gave her a mystified look, for like the rest he spoke no English. Rosamunde lifted her glass and smiled down the table with a flash of her pretty even teeth, and the ship's officers gallantly lifted their glasses too and smiled with her, quite unaware of what she was saying.

"If you are not silent, I will punish you," warned Rodrigue in a low dangerous tone, and she knew he was in agony that his officers might understand a chance phrase here and there, and piece it together by comparing notes.

"You have already punished me," she retorted, setting down her glass and biting into a biscuit with a snap of her white teeth. "For you have dragged me back aboard your ship. But I will not spend my life in trousers even though you desire it!"

She thought Rodrigue might have a stroke, but he took several deep breaths and subsided. The men at the table were edgy, and they gave each other uneasy glances. She guessed they were expecting anything to happen, for their volatile captain looked about to explode.

Down the table one of the younger officers was looking at this sumptuous velvet-clad lady who had joined them, in dawning horror.

"What is the matter with him?" she asked Rodrigue crossly. "One would think I had just swallowed my knife from the look on his face!"

"He is doubtless remembering how he asked you to cross swords with him and imagining that he could have

385

wounded you had I not forbidden the engagement," said Rodrigue in a terse voice.

"Doubtless that is what ails him," she agreed indifferently. She looked up, eyes alight. "Could I not cross swords with him yet? Barefoot on the deck? Why not this very evening? It is a moonlit night. I could tuck up my skirts—indeed, he will discover that I am a good blade!"

"No!" snarled Rodrigue, and her mocking laugh pealed. Rodrigue's hands clenched, and for a savage moment he envisioned her lily-white throat caught between them. Then some other emotion clouded his vision and he returned stormily to his food. He cursed the day he had seen her, and yet—she sat there, a very temptress, and he was eaten up with desire for her. Savagely he forced himself to eat, crunching down so vindictively that at one point he bit his tongue and was hard put to repress a howl of pain.

Beside him, Rosamunde was maliciously aware of his distress.

"Perhaps," she mused aloud to further torment him, "since you are so set against swordplay, I should instead teach your officers the latest English dances after supper. I must find some way to amuse myself!"

Rodrigue choked on his wine. The thought of Rosamunde dancing and flirting with his ship's officers almost overcame him. He fought for air. "There will be no dancing," he told her sternly, when he had recovered himself.

Rosamunde sighed and addressed herself to her food. Now that the initial excitement of this confrontation was over, she had discovered that she was quite hungry—after all, she had not eaten since yesterday morning. What a pity none of these Spanish officers spoke English, she told herself, aggrieved. Ah, she could have had a merry time if they had spoken it—and wreaked a suitable revenge on Rodrigue for kidnapping her!

Down the table swarthy Don Felipe, his composure regained, lifted his glass. His white teeth flashed in a smile as he said something which must have been complimentary to her, for all of them turned to her, smiling.

She gave Rodrigue a questioning look.

"They are drinking a toast to you," Rodrigue told her through clenched teeth. "Although *I* am considering hurling you overboard."

"I would you had done so in Amsterdam harbor, for then I could have swum ashore and been done with you," retorted Rosamunde coolly, acknowledging Don Felipe's toast with a charming smile.

Rodrigue also bared his teeth in a smile, although the effort it cost him nearly wrenched him apart. "We will have words later in our cabin!"

Rosamunde turned her sunny smile on her captain, but her tone was biting. "A cabin of my own, if you please, sirrah! Now that it is known I am a woman, I'll not share your quarters. Consider, Rodrigue, my reputation! If you try to invade my privacy, you'll find the cabin door latched against you."

Rodrigue set down his knife; he had lost all appetite. Abruptly he signaled to a cabin boy who hovered nearby. He leaned over and muttered something in the boy's ear. The boy nodded and left the room at a trot. Rosamunde was vaguely aware of a distant hammering as she ate. After a time the cabin boy returned and handed Rodrigue a large key.

Rosamunde did not see the key for, happily conscious of the havoc she had caused, she was eating hungrily. Down the table Don Alberto inclined his gray head toward Don Tomás, who rocked in his fat with laughter at something Don Alberto said. Soon there was a general conversation about the table which had in it a kind of desperation and a strong sense of relief. Rosamunde, looking up from her trencher, realized that things were normalizing. These men were accepting the fact that their captain had a lady —be she affianced bride or mistress—and that the lady, for whatever reason, had sat at table with them for some time disguised as a man. They might mull over this strange behavior privately, they might mutter about it later, but for now, on the surface at least, all was serene.

Except in the great cabin of the *Santa Cecilia*, where Rosamunde faced a furious Rodrigue after supper. Now she understood the reason for the sounds of hammering she had heard and ignored during supper. A very large lock had appeared on the cabin door.

"If you think to lock me in, Rodrigue," she told him menacingly, "it will not work. I will find a way to escape you!"

The lock had been placed there for her safety. Rodrigue well knew the temper of men on long voyages, and it had come to him in a burst of fear that she might forget to latch the door when he was on deck, and some woman-starved member of the crew might burst in, inflamed by the sight of her loveliness. It had been done for *her*.

But now, pressed to the boiling point, by this new and unjustified accusation, he suddenly saw this cool and lustrous object of his desire in a red blur. He advanced upon her with a savage snarl, and she gave ground before him warily.

"Rodrigue!" she cried on a note of warning, for she realized her danger. "Get hold of yourself."

Instead he got hold of *her*. In a flash he had pounced on her, seized her wrists even as she brought her hands up to defend herself. She found herself irresistibly forced back upon the bunk, her wrists held cruelly tight. Too late panic seized her. She had driven this strange wild Spaniard too far. With an angry scream, she kicked at him, but he gave her body a twist. Simultaneously one of his legs came up sharply behind her knees, jackknifed them and toppled her backward onto the bunk. Her hat came off and skittered across the floor, and her hair came loose as she went down.

Landing on her back in the bedclothes, Rosamunde screamed again. As she fell she managed to wrest one wrist free and aimed a hard blow at his face. Easily he struck her hand away, captured it again as, pressing his advantage, he bent over her, one knee on the bunk, one booted foot firmly on the floor and fought to subdue her.

His dark face was very close, his hot breath—for like herself he was breathing hard—seemed to scorch her face.

"No, Rodrigue, no!" she shouted.

Outside, Rosamunde's furious screams had carried to

other parts of the ship. The officers looked at each other significantly. The captain's lady—be she affianced bride or no—was in a rebellious mood tonight. That much had been evident from her stance at dinner and from Rodrigue's evident displeasure.

They exchanged uneasy glances as the screams continued. One or two of them might even have intervened, but, passing herself off as a man, all this time she had been sleeping in Rodrigue's cabin. None of them now had any doubts as to what had gone on there. She had been carried aboard drunk and had descended on them all, flashing-eyed, at supper. Who knew what kind of falling-out the captain and his lady had had in Amsterdam? Perhaps she had cast her eyes at some other man there . . . and if the Captain wanted to punish her now—well, they could only hope he would not beat her too hard. A pity to mar such beauty. But her prior conduct had put her beyond their aid, even had they wanted to shorten their lives by confronting their angry captain. They shrugged and resumed whatever they were doing as the sounds of her screaming died away in the night.

Rosamunde's screams had been muffled because Rodrigue's warm determined mouth had been clamped firmly over her own, stifling them. Now his hot breath seemed to fill her whole being as his tongue began an eager exploration. Her own breath sobbed in her throat and she writhed in that viselike grip. He was wild, unbridled; in her anger she had driven him too far—and now she would pay for it.

He took her with wild eagerness and flaming passion. As if she were some wild creature who must be held firmly to have its fur stroked, else one would be bitten. He held her immobilized—or as nearly immobilized as a struggling furious woman can be held. The hooks of her velvet bodice were wrenched open, her falling band was snatched from her throat with a rip, her dress and chemise were jerked down about her shoulders, effectively pinioning her upper arms—and her warm full bouncing breasts were set free, pale and pink-tipped and tempting in his groping hands. Deliberately he played with them, inciting her to passion, kneading, stroking.

389

Under that soft assault, Rosamunde felt a sudden lurching of the senses, as if she had been running hard from a strong adversary; hotly pursued, she had suddenly found herself fenced in, jammed up against a locked gate with no alternative but to turn and fight. She had not thought it would come to this. She had never really been afraid of Rodrigue, whose life she had saved, and on whose courtesy she had relied. Now sparks went through her and she cursed him roundly as his lips left her mouth and descended impudently to worry her nipples.

"You'll not, you bastard!" she cried. "I won't let—" Her remark ended in choking fury, like a spitting cat. For now—now his free hand was fumbling at her silk-stockinged legs, pulling her skirts up so that they would ride about her hips.

This new assault brought renewed struggles from Rosamunde. She lay trapped in a sea of velvet, which as she writhed rose and fell in green waves, edged by the white froth of her delicate chemise. Her pearly breasts rose mermaidlike from the lacy foam of her torn chemise, and her green silken legs in the lamplight glimmered as if they had just risen from the wet depths. She tried to kick at him again and her shoe came off, tangled in the bedclothes. Rodrigue held her easily.

With his blood throbbing in his temples, his whole body tense and hard with desire, Rodrigue lifted his head for a moment to survey this wild beauty in his grasp. His eyes were wicked—but he was smiling, as his dark head swooped down again to nuzzle her quivering breasts.

Smiling!

Such rage swept over Rosamunde at the impudence of that smile that she made a last violent effort to break free. In fury that he would dare to violate her—and *smile* about it!—she managed, as he lifted his lips from her trembling breasts, to turn her head and bite him savagely in the hand. She tasted blood, she felt him wince. Then her head snapped back against the pillow as he gave her a stinging slap that left the side of her face feeling numb.

"Devil woman!" His voice was low and fierce. "You are mine—resign yourself to it!"

390

Resign herself! She twisted so fiercely in his grasp she almost got away. "Damn you, damn you!" she sobbed, on the wisps of breath left her from her struggles.

But his progress was inexorable. Even now he had parted her legs with a bleeding hand, even now he had torn free his own garments and descended upon her in a rush. His fierce masculinity bored in on her and she felt a great tremor go through her limbs, through her whole pulsating body, as the lean Spaniard took her—and made her his own.

Against her will she relaxed in his arms, against her will she responded to the wild thrusts of his passion. Against her will she melted against him and knew a wild exultation that equaled—perhaps exceeded—his own. It had been so long since a man's strong arms had held her—and hers was a woman's body, fashioned for love.

Her defenses shattered, she returned his passion with a consuming ardor. Her pliant body arched toward his, and a gentle moan rose in her throat. His hands rasped softly against the silken skin of her hips and buttocks, his lips found her breasts again. And Rosamunde, the world and her anger all forgotten, seemed to be soaring through deep-blue space, like the sea birds that wheeled above the ship. No longer Rosamunde Langley but some other woman, a woman with no identity whose need for love was like a primal scream.

And so this new Rosamunde of unplumbed depths went limp and her arms locked fiercely about her Spanish captain, as if to hold him against all the world—she who had fought him so viciously but a few short moments before.

With shock it came to Rodrigue that she no longer sought escape—indeed, she was hanging onto him!

"Rosamunde," he murmured huskily as the shattering delight of her surrender was borne in upon him. "Ah, Rosamunde!"

Rosamunde scarce heard him, so carried away was she. But her body heard him. Her body moved deliciously beneath his own, savored his caresses, reveled in rapture, returned each new assault with an assault of her own.

As waves lash a ship, so the green velvet rose and sub-

391

sided and rose again. And then, as if driven forward by whipping storm winds that would not be denied, their bodies—held so tinglingly close they seemed lashed together—burst forth frenziedly into a maelstrom of endeavor. Driven by the fierce winds of their own desires, they crested each wave to rise again to new heights. Whispering, murmuring, touching, yielding themselves, they reached at last the surging crest of a giant wave that burst over them thunderously in a wild fulfillment, then toppled them down and down into the bright shallows, where emotions rippled and teased—and promised new wonders when next the great seas ran.

After a long shuddering moment of shared delight and sensual pleasure, Rodrigue drew away from her. Although his long legs still pinioned her pulsing body, he thrust his face into the pillow beside her and lay thus face down in a spent exhaustion of mind and body.

Rosamunde, fresh from her soul-shattering experience, was brought back to earth as if she had been struck down by a mallet. She had cascaded down from the heights and now she lay with the Spaniard's lean body flung across her, listening to his heavy breathing.

Her face went gray—oh, God, she had betrayed Harry's memory! She had let another man seize her, arouse her, have her! Had Rodrigue taken her merely by force, roughly bending her to his will, she could have absolved herself, but after that first wild joining she had welcomed him, had trembled beneath him. Hot shame washed over her face at the memory of her rich response, of the shock she had felt go through him as he realized the depth and passion of her response to him, the husky way he had murmured her name as, legs twined and bodies locked in a silken torment of rhythmic motion, he had brought her at last to fulfillment.

Ah, she was a very harlot! That she could so forget Harry's memory. Her hands clenched until the nails bit into the flesh, and tears stung her eyes as she flayed herself with regrets.

And with these self-accusations came a cold fury at

the man whose caresses had seduced her away from her cherished memories.

Rodrigue was to blame! He had known she was Harry's woman, would always be Harry's woman—why had he not let her alone? Why must he kidnap her, force himself upon her? Anger pounded in her temples, for he had degraded her in her own sight. But he would not get off scot-free —she would make him pay for it!

Rigid with rage, she turned her head away from him when he stirred. He reached out a lazy hand to fondle her naked breast, but she struck his hand away petulantly. Rodrigue removed his hand at once. He got up quietly, and she could hear him adjusting his clothes, walking restlessly about.

Only then, when she felt he might be about to leave the cabin—and before he left she meant to have her say!— did she turn toward him.

She sat up, dragging her white lace-trimmed chemise over her bare breasts to shield them from his view. And leaned almost casually on one bare arm in the bunk, for in the first fury of their encounter her sleeve had been wrested from her. She lifted her head and looked at him through a tangle of blond hair. A defiant woman, thoroughly aroused—but not to love.

He stood, proud and tall and narrow as the Toledo blade he carried, and faced her. There was arrogance in that stance, but his face was somehow vulnerable.

Her cold merciless gaze raked over him. "So this is how you repay me for saving your life, Rodrigue?" she mocked.

A tremor went through that lean black-clad body. She hoped it was pain. She wanted to hurt him. "Pray do not tell me that you saved mine as well. Doubtless I could have paid for my life in England in the same coin as tonight."

Her lazy voice, cutting as a sharp blade, went through him, and he drew a deep ragged breath. His face had gone haggard. "*Madre de Dios*, you drove me too far, Rosamunde! I am not made of iron!"

She gave a contemptuous laugh. "There is a name for what you are!"

Rodrigue glared at her fiercely, his proud temperament torn between desire and anger. Suddenly he rushed to the bunk, went down on one knee and turned on her a tortured countenance. "Rosamunde," he begged hoarsely. "*Love me. Desire me as I desire you.* Ah, tell me that I was not wrong—that you feel for me as I for you."

Even though he had ravished her, and her blood still sang in her veins in guilty memory that she had enjoyed it, even though she was punishing him now for that enjoyment, she could feel a rushing pity for him steal over her. It was not honest marriage he was offering her, but so scalding a passion that she could feel the heat from this distance.

Still, he had taken her against her will, and she wanted to hurt him. She leaned forward and her voice was scornful. She chose her words carefully.

"Do not be deceived by my seeming heat, Rodrigue. I am a hot-blooded woman—indeed, I might have ended up in the Dutchman's arms for an evening. But hear me well." (It was not true, but she knew it would hurt him.) *"I do not desire you, Rodrigue!"*

He quivered as if she had run him through with a blade. For a tormented moment he stared at her with all his heart, all his longing, reflected in his dark eyes. She turned away, suddenly unable to bear the pressure of that look, and he rose in silence and flung out of the cabin. At the door he turned. His voice was flat, defeated.

"I will put you ashore at the first port, Rosamunde."

Her head swung around in surprise, but he was gone. She heard a key turn in the new heavy lock.

That is how it will be on this voyage, she told herself dully, running a distracted hand through her blond hair. *Locked in, prey to this man's gusting passions, his ever-changing moods*. She pushed away the thought that she would also be prey to her own wild passions.

As to whether he would keep his promise to set her ashore, she had no idea. He was a strange mercurial man. He might decide to keep her!

She drew a ragged breath and forced her mind back to

Harry. Then with narrowed eyes she got up and went over and inspected the array of weapons displayed in this cabin. There were plenty of them, but she preferred the gun Harry had given her.

When Rodrigue came back she had bathed with water from the basin, and had mended her chemise and was wearing it, for she had now prepared for bed. She had combed out her pale-gold hair and composed herself and was sitting on the edge of her bunk when the key turned in the lock.

Rodrigue came in, and the swinging ship's lamp revealed to him a strange scene.

Rosamunde was sitting on the edge of her bunk wearing both her chemise and a calm expression. She was holding a large pistol pointed steadily at his heart.

"Your cabin is full of weapons," she said coldly. "If you attack me again on this voyage it is my intention to kill you."

Rodrigue gave her a long sad look and turned to the business of locking the door. "Put the pistol down or shoot—as you choose," he said in a tired voice. "But you have my word as a Spanish gentleman that I will not touch you again on this voyage without your consent."

Rosamunde set the pistol down and surveyed him warily. Rodrigue was a man of hot temper and mercurial moods. He meant what he said for now—but would he mean it later?

She sat there considering him, and he gave her an almost whimsical look as he undressed for bed. "It would be wise for you to remember"—and there was a cool note of warning in his tone—"that I am all that stands between you and my crew. If you were to kill me, they would consider you their legitimate prey—before they hanged you. Not even my officers could stop them. I doubt you would like it."

The thought chilled her. She thought of those men with their hungry eyes, men without women, long at sea. Many had had no money for the whorehouses of Amsterdam.

What indeed would they do to a woman they found at their mercy and toward whom they felt vengeful?

Without a word she laid the pistol down beside her within easy reach and watched Rodrigue with large steady green eyes until he put out the lamp. Even then she stared into the darkness until his regular breathing told her he was asleep.

But Rosamunde did not sleep. She lay there with her eyes turned up to the cabin's dark ceiling until the gray dawn made it visible at last—then turned her face to the wall lest Rodrigue, rising, should see her ravaged face. Too many questions had occurred to her during the long night, and she was not ready to answer any of them.

But foremost among them was how she felt—how she *really* felt—about this Spanish captain.

27   *The winds, as they sailed away from Amsterdam* into the Zee, had been light and variable, with the *Santa Cecilia* making hardly any progress on her return journey laden with hides for Barcelona's skillful leatherworkers. But once in the North Sea, a sudden violent squall overtook them and stripped half the rigging from the ship. Rodrigue Avilo cursed as he saw the tangle of broken wood and tumbled sail and rope that littered the decks.

Repairs were hastily made. Rosamunde marveled at the brisk efficiency of these dark Catalan sailors, at their hardihood and stoic acceptance of whatever ills the sea and the weather brought them.

The swift squall having blown on to other waters, the *Santa Cecilia* rode on the great swells the storm had left.

Rodrigue came and went glumly, with little to say to Rosamunde. She gathered he was repenting his sins and wondered grimly what he would be like when he had done with repentance.

That night she was thrown from her bunk as the great ship lurched and shuddered from end to end. She thought at first they had run aground and dressed hurriedly and came on deck.

One of the crew members, running by, almost barged into her as she emerged on the deck. He stopped abruptly and for a moment she thought she saw fear in his dark eyes. Then he dodged around her and ran on down toward a tangle of rigging.

The moonlight illuminated a scene of hurrying men. Rosamunde stood, uncertain what to do. The wind was blowing hard, and her fair hair—it had been growing longer since last she had cut it in England, and she had not troubled to put it up—kept flying into her eyes. At first she did not perceive what was the matter, but she noticed that the deck seemed slightly slanted.

Then she saw it. Sticking up from the water, the prow of a great ship, ominous in the night. She stared at it, appalled. Had they struck another ship? Had they sunk her?

Rodrigue's dark face loomed up before her, looking drawn and tired.

"What is it?" she cried. "Have we collided with another vessel?"

"We were fighting for sea room to keep from going aground on the Zeeland sands, when this hulk—loosened by the great seas we have been having, no doubt—spewed up out of the water." He indicated the prow of the hulk pointed toward the moon.

"You mean a ship came up from the bottom?" she cried incredulously.

"Half a wrecked ship," he said. "It must have worked loose from the sand in the rough seas. In coming about, we struck her, fouled our rudder and drove her into the sand. Now we must get free of her or the next tide will grind us to pieces."

"Is there anything I can do to help?"

He gave her a look of astonishment. Then, "Yes," he said dryly. "You can stay out of the way. The men know what to do. But if we have broken a rudder . . . " He glanced toward the south and she followed his gaze. There the stars were blotted out in blackness.

She understood then. It was a race against time. Straining men against the elements. They must break free of this hulk before the storm driving up from the south overtook them.

But nature's armies were more powerful than striving men on wooden ships. The wind from the south hit them suddenly as a hammer blow, and the rising water lifted them clear of the dragging hulk and sent them staggering with a broken rudder, almost heeled over, deep into the wilds of the North Sea.

Rosamunde could hear the shouts as the seamen leaped forward to right the ship, and she herself was propelled forward, stumbling, lashed by the storm's sudden violence. Bent double against the whistling wind, soaked with spray, she made her way back to the great cabin.

Rosamunde hardly saw Rodrigue in the storm-lashed days that followed. He would come to his cabin, exhausted, to sleep for short intervals before he hurried back to the pitching deck.

Once he turned to her with a grave face, speaking gently, as though to a child. "You are not to worry," he told her. "The ship is very weatherly."

She was touched that he should try to comfort her, for she had not grown up with ships as he had and her anxiety for their safety on this wooden ship was very real.

Chastened now from her anger, she began to talk to Rodrigue again. But he was reserved and wary with her. How much of this wariness was due to fatigue, how much to other causes, she could only guess.

Sometimes she asked him their position. They had passed the Firth of Forth. Scotland was flying by them to the west. This storm was carrying them into the Sea of Norway.

"The storm is very fierce," he told her once in a monotone. "We are being blown far off course. I am needed on deck. You had best remain in the cabin, for the wind is cold."

She watched him go. He was a complex violent man—a man to fear, a man to love. And that he had stirred in her fierce emotions she had thought all but dead, she could not deny. But her heart belonged to Harry still, and no matter how tempting the offer, she would not accompany this wild Majorcan captain on his far-flung voyages. For such, she divined, was what Rodrigue intended. A companion by day, a mistress by night.

She was almost sorry.

But . . . she grimaced. It could not have gone on for long in any event. Her pregnancy would soon become noticeable even in the heavy velvets she wore.

The weather worsened. On the few occasions when she struggled onto the deck—to be immediately deluged with slanting sheets of rain and almost swept back to her cabin by the wind—the crew members looked at her with dull hatred in their storm-wet faces. Once one of them crossed himself. Others turned away and spat.

Rosamunde was astonished at these manifestations of dislike.

"What is the matter with the crew?" she demanded of Rodrigue, when he sloshed down, wet and exhausted, to the great cabin. "They did not dislike me when I wore trousers!"

Rodrigue hesitated. "Nothing is the matter," he said. "Stay belowdecks until the storm passes."

Rosamunde was combing out her hair, and now she threw down her comb in exasperation and her voice rose. "It is certainly apparent that they despise me! The question is—why?"

Rodrigue was too tired to argue. He sat down and struggled to pull off his wet boots. "They are ignorant superstitious men," he explained. "They believe you are a devil come out of England to plague our ship. De Guzman told me there were mutterings in the crew's quarters about how you had changed magically from a man into a woman, and that the night the storm blew us into the North Sea you were seen flying about in the shrouds, directing the winds. It is all nonsense, but best you stay below."

"But I—I saved their lives, all your lives, by telling you about the planned attack in Cornwall!"

"Men have short memories," he said bitterly. "And the crew is frightened. They are brave men ordinarily, but this storm for duration and strength passes their experience. They consider it unnatural and seek a reason. One must bear with them."

"Bear with them!" Rosamunde was filled with indignation, and her voice showed it. "I'll not bear such lies another instant—nor should you! Let me talk to them, Rodrigue—translate for me."

Rodrigue jerked off a sodden boot with a grunt. The boot slid away from him in the pitching cabin and journeyed across the floor toward Rosamunde. His voice was almost as menacing as the roar of the wind and water outside. "You will stay away from the men, do you hear me? These wild stories are the result of your folly in suddenly appearing before them garbed as a woman. They do not understand; they believe you to be a Jonah. De Guzman says they mutter to each other that the wind would turn favorable and the sea would grow calm if they were to throw you overboard. Keep the cabin door locked and stay out of their sight."

A Jonah! Throw her overboard to be drowned in this wild sea! She shrank back, laid down the comb with nerveless fingers. "It was an ill day you dragged me back aboard your ship in Amsterdam," she said bitterly. "And we are both paying a price for it. Now I have come between you and your men."

"All will right itself when the storm is over," he said harshly. "A few rays of sunshine will rout these dark thoughts." Exhausted, he threw himself in his wet clothes onto the bunk and slept until he was called back to the deck.

Rosamunde lay sleepless, tossing on her bunk. She felt more vulnerable aboard this ship than ever she had on the highroads of England. A Jonah! She pressed her knuckles against her closed eyes and tried fiercely to

400

think. Should Rodrigue lose control of his surly crew, should they decide to mutiny and take matters into their own superstitious hands ... Chill fingers prickled down her spine, and abruptly she got up and loaded the pistol she had been wearing when first she boarded the *Santa Cecilia.* She had abandoned it for a while during the storm. But from now on she would sleep fully dressed with a loaded pistol beside her—not from fear of Rodrigue, but from fear of his superstitious men. If they came, assaulting the cabin door, they would find her ready!

So a new fear was added to the inhuman howling of the elements outside—a fear of ignorant men, running savagely amok.

Rosamunde no longer took her meals in the officers' mess. Rodrigue did not think it safe for her to move about the ship, so trays were brought to her in the great cabin.

"You can come up on deck when the storm blows over," was his inexorable reply when she protested at the confinement. "It will be safe then. In the meantime, stay below—for your safety."

But the night a great blow rocked the ship from stem to stern and Rosamunde was thrown from her bunk to land sprawling on the floor, she forgot this good advice. Her first thought was that they had collided with another ship in the darkness and were sinking—she would drown locked in here, the water would rush in and trap her!

Snatching up the key, she ran toward the cabin door—and a sudden roll of the ship caused her to stumble and drop the key. She clawed for it on the slanting floor, found it, tumbled out of the door and up onto the deck.

The sight that met her eyes was bizarre. A huge piece of floating timber—perhaps wreckage from some other merchant vessel that had foundered in the storm—had rammed their ship, and when the *Santa Cecilia* heeled over in the wind, had become fouled in her rigging. Now this great weight was threatening to bring down the mainmast, and the ship, pounded by heavy seas, was listing dangerously. They could capsize! Between gusts of rain she could see Rodrigue high up in the rigging, directing the swarming men in cutting them loose from this ominous wooden monster that had charged into them out of the wild sea.

But Rosamunde had not emerged on deck unobserved.

"Jonah! Jonah!" roared a voice nearby, and Rosamunde turned to see a huge hulking Majorcan seaman named Pancho, who had always crossed himself and spat whenever she passed.

She stepped back and would have run, but Pancho lunged at her, grasped her around the body and hauled her over his shoulder. To no avail, Rosamunde pummeled his ropy back muscles and kicked at him. She was being carried inexorably forward, and now, icily, she guessed his intention—he was going to hurl her into that raging sea!

She could not free herself. No one was near. Of those on deck, all eyes were concentrated anxiously on the menacing wooden thing trapped in the rigging.

"Rodrigue," she screamed desperately, her voice lost in the howling wind. "Rodrigue, throw me your sword! *Rodrigue!*"

From the rigging—for he could not hear her—some inner voice told Rodrigue to turn and look down. He was appalled to see below him on the deck Rosamunde struggling in the arms of the giant crewman. Even as his horrified eyes took in the scene, the man below lifted Rosamunde high over his head to dash her into the sea—but a huge wave breaking green across the deck just then drove him staggering back.

There was not time to reach them! And a lightning look told Rodrigue there were no ship's officers nearby. In the halflight, Rodrigue saw a white arm reach out to him appealingly, and as if he had heard her desperate cry, he drew his sword from its scabbard and tossed it down to her.

It was a desperate move, and the odds were against her catching it. But by some miracle she reached out and caught it—although it was immediately almost wrenched from her hand by the roaring wind. Her wrist felt numb, but hers was the strength of necessity—for now the wave

402

had subsided and the big seaman held her high in his arms again and surged toward the ship's rail.

"Jonah!" he roared in his guttural voice. "Jonah!"

Rosamunde raised the sword with a silent prayer. From the rigging Rodrigue watched like a man paralyzed. Almost any slash Rosamunde made at that moment would merely have sealed her fate—for the fury of Pancho's charge was sufficient to send them both crashing into the sea. But Rosamunde chose her target well—she slashed downward and cut the muscles just behind his knees. A clean sharp stroke through his ragged trousers and the big man's heavy muscled legs buckled under him. He went down just as he reached the rail. Rosamunde might have catapulted over his head into the ocean, but in his surprise at the sharp pain and his legs giving way beneath him, he released his grip on her involuntarily and tried to catch hold of the rail for support. But he was too late—a great wave caught him and with a howl he disappeared into the green water.

Rosamunde too would have been washed overboard, for when Pancho let her go, the water struck her and she was hurled helplessly backward—but she was lucky. Her wild progress across the deck was arrested by a snarl of fallen ratlines, which entangled her foot. Instinctively she seized it and held on, half-drowning, until the water subsided.

From his high perch Rodrigue saw the huge seaman swept overboard, saw Rosamunde disappear into that green water—and his heart seemed to stop in his chest. Then as the wave subsided, he saw that she was lying on her back, tangled in the fallen ratlines—and that she still gamely held onto her sword in challenge to any other enemies.

With a lurch, his heart began to beat again. He roared to de Guzman to help her, but de Guzman's back was turned, and Rodrigue's voice was lost in the wind. She was still lying thus, clinging to the fallen ropes, but her right arm free to fight for her life, when Rodrigue scrambled down from topside. Through waist-deep seas, he fought his way toward her.

Rosamunde saw him coming. His face, she thought, was whiter than the foam that crested the waves.

And then he was dragging her back to her cabin.

"You will kill us all," he gasped, pushing her through the door with a sodden arm. "Can you not stay below? Must I lock you in? Now you have cost us Pancho's life and we could ill afford to lose his strength!"

Rosamunde shook back her wet hair and in silence proffered him his sword.

"Thank you for throwing me your sword, Rodrigue. I did not think you could hear me call out for it in the storm."

He gave her an odd look, his wet face puzzled. "But I did not hear you," he insisted. "Or perhaps I did . . . in my heart." He looked at her in surprise as she stood in her soaking velvet dress, already making a pool of water on the cabin floor. Was his rapport with this woman such that he could hear her very thoughts?

Now that it was over, Rosamunde's knees were trembling. Her close call with being a human sacrifice to the elements had frightened her. "I thought we had struck a rock and were foundering," she told Rodrigue in a shaky voice. "I promise you, Rodrigue, that I will lock the door when you leave—and that I will keep it locked."

He nodded grimly. "They say you are a witch—perhaps you are. . . . Certainly catching that sword and bringing Pancho down with it was devilish good work. I thought you were done for. But at least ye're a thoughtful witch—for the sea that washed big Pancho overboard has saved me the trouble of hanging him from the yardarm, as I'd have been bound to do—and which would have caused trouble among the men. Well, I must get back before we are dismasted by that great timber that has fouled our rigging." He paused at the door, and his hoarse voice softened. "Do not be too dismayed by all this, Rosamunde. Pancho was always half mad, but as to the others—these are storm thoughts, storm rumblings, that attend us. When the weather clears, the men will forget and think of other things."

Rosamunde sincerely hoped so. Wet and shivering, she
404

watched Rodrigue go, rushed to lock the heavy door. It had been brought in on her stabbingly what it was like to be a cringing human sacrifice. She feared the crew now, and that fear made her edgy and irritable with Rodrigue, when he came down to tell her the crisis was over, the ship had been freed of that great dangling timber. For she, who would match herself bravely against any man, had a horror of the onrushing mob.

That night she dreamed not of any menace that came from the crashing seas outside but of howling half-human faces that leered up out of the darkness and were on her in a pack. She awoke in terror and lay shuddering in the cold dark cabin.

A pack . . . a half-mad human pack . . .

28   *The trouble, when it came, was very different—* and neither Rosamunde nor Rodrigue was prepared to meet it.

The wind had blown itself out. A great calm lay over the swollen sea. The sea rolled in high rounded mountains in the wake of the storm, but there was no wind to flap the drooping sails. An eerie clean-washed silence prevailed—and it had grown very cold.

Rosamunde, feeling the worst was over, came up to the deck wrapped in her short cloak. The world about her seemed misty and unreal, and she shivered as she watched the men working like furious ants on an anthill, rushing about trying to repair the damage the storm had done them. The rigging was a tangled mass out of which order was slowly coming, but worst of all, the rudder had been damaged as they fought to free themselves from the great timber.

"Will you be able to repair the rudder?" she asked Rodrigue, knowing how crucial that was to their making land safely.

"We are trying," he said wearily. "At worst we can lash it together."

In the end that was what they did, but the ship handled badly, and they bobbed about like a cork in the swift-running sea.

"Where are we?" she asked.

"We are in the Norway Channel," he told her. "Our course will miss the Shetlands. We will try for a port on the coast of Norway."

So they would sail on into the cold northern mists. . . . Something of the fear the ancient mariners must have known on long gloomy voyages into the unknown came to her. Reluctantly, she began to understand why the superstitious sailors—indifferent to her now that the storm had passed—had wanted to cast her overboard at the height of the storm. They *wanted* to believe in sea gods and demons who, if appeased, might save them. They *needed* some belief to hold onto in this trackless waste, some water god to steer them safely home to port. . . .

But her recent experience had been a shattering one. It had shaken a little her belief in herself. She shivered, and Rodrigue, as if to comfort a child, put an arm around her shoulders.

Rosamunde stiffened. He had brought her to this! She would not be aboard this ship if he had not abducted her! Pettishly she pushed him away. His face whitened under its tan.

"I will set you ashore in Norway!" he cried in a strangled voice. "I will be rid of you!"

"Good!" shouted Rosamunde, for her nerves were taut as a drawn bowstring. "I would welcome any port without you!"

For a moment blind anger boiled up in Rodrigue and he might have struck at that beautiful rebellious face so near his own. But his attention was diverted, for almost as she spoke the wind changed. It swung around wildly, blowing from the east almost at gale force, sweeping them west into the broad reaches of the North Atlantic.

Rodrigue leaped forward with a shout and took over the steering of the ship. Rosamunde clung to the rail, and even the hardy seamen looked startled to see the great ship suddnly cease her wallowing, lift her billowing sails and run west before the wind.

One of the sailors, barefoot and sturdy, caught sight of Rosamunde, and his dark face took on a kind of ashen terror. He turned to his companions, and she could guess what he muttered to them, for all turned sullen faces toward her: *She is here, the witch. . . . See, she has made the wind to blow! She mocks the captain, blowing the ship in the opposite direction from the way that he would steer!*

But Rosamunde understood them better now. They might mutter, but they would not attack her. That attack had been born of the hysteria and terror that had grown out of the storm. Pale and resolute, for she was forcing herself to get over her fear of them, she stayed where she was, hanging onto the ship's rail with the cold salt spray striking her face, wetting her hair and clothes. After a while Rodrigue came back to her, his anger abated.

"For the time, the wind has decided our course," he said grimly. "We cannot beat our way to Norway against it in a disabled vessel."

So he would not be setting her ashore on the coast of Norway. . . .

"Any port will do," she muttered sullenly, eyeing the crew with distrust.

He gave her a long slow look. Then, "I am sorry, Rosamunde," he said thickly, and flung away from her.

Puzzled, she stood watching his retreating figure. His shoulders were bent in despondency. Was it possible Rodrigue was in love with her? No, she told herself, he desired her—nothing more. And there was a whole trackless ocean between desire and love. Love was what she had known with Harry—not the hot feverish ecstasy she had felt when Rodrigue held her in his arms.

Shivering with cold in the biting wind, she went below to meditate and wonder what lay ahead.

The Catalan seamen too wondered what lay ahead. For the weather was strange. Gray glancing sheets of rain struck the wooden hull like broadsides. Once a light hail fell, crackling against the clean-scoured deck. Then it grew very cold and began to snow. And always the wind pushed them west.

In this turbulence an anxious council was held in the great cabin of the *Santa Cecilia*. They were being driven far off course, the jerry-rigged rudder was causing great uneasiness. Had they best not try for the Norwegian coast at all but sail around Ireland and so reach a Spanish port? De Guzman was for this course and was supported in his stand by Don Tomás, whose fat jowls shook as he nodded his head vigorously. Gaunt Don Alberto in his threadbare clothes was for beating their way back and putting in to some Norwegian port for repairs and a fresh water supply, while swarthy Don Felipe, who had lost his merry smile and now looked as gloomy as the rest, shrugged and said he had no opinion, either course would suit him.

Rosamunde sat quietly on the edge of her bunk, as far from the table around which were grouped the ship's officers as Rodrigue could place her. She heard the excited murmur of voices that rose and fell as they poured over the charts, pointed out this and that. Although she understood not a word of the conversation, she could see the set look on Rodrigue's face as the council reached their decision, saw the pallor underneath his tan. He had listened silently, and from his obvious reluctance, she gathered that he had at last bowed to the will of his officers, who at the end of the discussion all seemed agreed as to the best course. The wind had abated, and now in a showery mist the *Santa Cecilia* changed course, close-hauled on the port tack and headed southward.

After the conference of the officers, everyone left in a group. Rosamunde followed and joined Rodrigue on the poop deck. They were unfailingly civil to each other now, polite as if they had been strangers after their wild encounter in her bunk, and the harsh eventful days that had followed.

Rodrigue was leaning on the taffrail, staring into the mist that lay ahead. As Rosamunde appeared out of the drifting fog, he straightened and made her a small ironic bow.

"We have changed course, Rodrigue. Why? Where are we going?"

"My officers were as one that since we are well provisioned, we should route ourselves around Ireland and so seek a Spanish port. We were being driven away from the Norwegian coast by the wind, and they had no desire to seek a Scottish port after their experience in England. I have agreed to their desires. We sail south."

"But it troubles you, does it not?"

A long sigh heaved from the Spanish captain's chest. "Ever since we left the Zeeland sands we have followed the route my father's carrack took . . . and now we go a further leg on that journey."

She understood at last the reason for the shadowed fear in Rodrigue's eyes. They were following the route of the doomed Armada.

As if fate were a wicked child who played evil games with them and laughed at their sufferings, they were buffeted this way and that, battered by constant squalls and swept far off course into the watery wastes of the North Atlantic as they tried desperately to beat their way south. Rodrigue grew grimmer day by day. He had lost weight and was whipcord-lean.

Once when he came down to the great cabin for his cloak, he told her shortly that there would be no more baths. All the water must be saved for drinking. To Rosamunde's startled protest he added grimly, "God willing, our food and water casks will hold until we touch a Spanish port, for in these storms we have made little progress."

Rosamunde, who had retreated from the cold deck when it had begun to snow again, was thoughtful. "Could we not put into some Irish port?" she wondered. "At least for water, if we run too low?"

"God protect us from the necessity. But if the need is too great, we may be forced to try it."

She remembered that his father, returning home with the beaten Armada, had been shipwrecked on the wild coast of Ireland. And Rodrigue's wild nightmares had told her that since he was a child he had believed that was the way he himself would someday end his life—with his ship dashed to pieces against some formidable Irish cliff. She had heard him cry out in his sleep, sometimes in Catalan or Majorcan, but sometimes in English, and she had managed to piece together the broken bits and made a whole of it. Rodrigue lived in sweaty terror of the western coast of Ireland that they must pass. He had communicated to her some of the inner dread that gnawed at him, and she had begun to feel deeply sorry for him. In spite of his rough taking of her, she now spoke to him with a new gentleness. He seemed not to notice.

Battered and shaken by great waves and the wild and variable winds—some that blew from the north, frosting the deck with snow and nearly freezing the fingers of the agile men who climbed the rigging—the *Santa Cecilia* limped south like a crippled bird, at the mercy of the wild wind. It was too cold to stay long on deck, even had she desired to do so, and Rosamunde spent her days huddled in the damp cabin wrapped in everything she owned.

They were almost out of drinking water now, but still they limped on. Rodrigue was gambling desperately with their lives in his attempt to get them by Ireland without making port.

He was very gaunt now. When he came into the cabin shivering from the cold, Rosamunde gave him a look of sympathy.

Proud Rodrigue hated sympathy. He gave her a haggard look and flung away from her.

He had not attempted to touch her since the night she had worn her green velvet dress and created a sensation among his officers.

In the high rolling aftermath of the latest storm, a piece of floating debris slammed into them and fouled their jerry-built rudder. As they tried to free themselves of it, the rudder broke. Rodrigue was livid. He smote the taffrail with a blow almost hard enough to splinter it and shook his fist at the sky. Rosamunde guessed he was having a confrontation with God.

They repaired the rudder as best they could and limped on. It was horribly cold and the ship was barely maneuverable. Rodrigue kept watching the sky anxiously, and when a great darkness appeared from the west in the wake of a pale watery dawn, his jaw hardened. He piled on all the canvas the *Santa Cecilia* would carry and tried desperately to beat his way south. But the wind had deserted him. Above his head the sails flapped disconsolately, limp useless things.

For half a day they floated thus over a glassy ocean, while the darkness to the west increased and assumed a strange greenish hue. Rodrigue watched it uneasily.

"We must find a sheltered bay," he muttered when he came down to the great cabin and found Rosamunde shivering in her bunk. "The ship cannot stand another pounding. A bad storm now could drive us into whatever is out there on that cursed coast—rocks or cliffs."

"Or bays," said Rosamunde steadily, from her bunk. "Harbors."

His dark eyes softened. "You are optimistic."

"No," she said. "But we have had so much bad weather, it is only reasonable that we will get some break in it."

He did not tell her that the homeward-bound Armada following this same track had been buffeted by one gale after another, so that the great ships—those that had not sunk into the ocean, one by one, or been dashed onto the rocks and lost, often with all hands—had limped in with dying crews; some had gone aground in sight of home because there were no able-bodied men left to throw out the anchors. Many of the exhausted sailors who had gone without food and water for so long had reached home only to die in port. . . .

So, Rodrigue felt in his fatalistic Catalan bones, it would be with them. But he did not say so to this brave English girl who watched him so steadily from her bunk. He tried to keep a good face on it for her, even in view of this monster storm moving inexorably upon them from the west.

But there was no longer any choice. He must make port—somewhere.

At the first wind that sprang up, he headed for the distant coast of Ireland that he knew was there.

The first sight of that coast was not reassuring. A line of jutting rocks appeared, shoals and white water rushing about over jagged black sawteeth that stuck up from the ocean.

The *Santa Cecilia* sheered off, seeking a sheltered bay. But her captain cast another uneasy glance at the huge yellow-green blackness, now lit by lacelike forks of lightning, that was steadily gaining on them.

On deck for air, Rosamunde watched his face. She read bitterness there and perhaps an underlying panic.

Almost without warning the wind struck them a solid blow and began to howl in loud banshee wails. It blew with a fierceness that bent the *Santa Cecilia*'s masts and brought the water up in great waves to break green across the deck. Rosamunde, caught unaware, clung to the taffrail and watched what seemed to be a mountain of water pouring over the wallowing ship.

"You had best get below," Rodrigue shouted at her.

"I can die as well here," she gasped, water streaming from her hair and over her eyes. For an overwhelming sense of calamity had seized her. That towering lightning-laced blackness, this sudden death knell of a wind, the booming of the surf on that treacherous distant shoreline —all had combined to make her view the scene as Rodrigue saw it.

For Rodrigue's long-ago nightmare, she felt, was coming true. They were following in the doomed Armada's footsteps, and now they would pile up, shattered to kindling, on the coast of Ireland.

Rosamunde watched as the ship fought for sea room, watched as they were inexorably drawn toward those jutting rocky promontories. They were south of the first line of rocks now, and tall cliffs loomed up like giants' castles rising from the foam.

But now at last she could see a cove—at least she thought it was a cove, a place where the tall cliffs seemed
412

to part. Rodrigue and the pilot saw it too. She could tell by the way they tried to bring the ship about and head for it.

They almost made it, through the narrow mouth of that bay into a sheltered cove between the cliffs.

And then a mountainous wave smashed over the ship. It broke the *Santa Cecilia*'s much-mended rudder. The disabled ship veered wildly and turned sideways, floundering. Rosamunde clung to the taffrail, watching the sky race by at a crazy angle as the ship flopped over almost on its side, then as if by some gigantic effort, seemed to lift its shoulders and right itself.

Rosamunde had lost her footing and her feet were scrambling for purchase on the slippery deck when they were lifted up by yet another great wave. Amid the wind's inhuman howling that assaulted her ears like a living thing, amid the deep pulsing thunder of the breakers smashing against the cliff's gray sides, through the salt spray that burned her eyes, she could see them seem to ride that mountainous crest. Eerily, as if they towered over the world. She wrapped her arms around the taffrail and prayed.

For moments the ship wavered as if she would take wing. Then down she plunged into a deep green watery valley. It was as if the *Santa Cecilia* had suddenly dropped off a cliff into the sea—the whole ship shuddered. The shock of their fall almost tore loose Rosamunde's grip from the taffrail, and she again lost her footing, came up bruised and gasping. If only they could make their way between the cliffs, they would be out of this living nightmare!

The next wave snapped the masts, and Rosamunde could hear even above the inhuman shriek of wind and ocean the screams of dying men, broken and entangled in the fallen timbers and rigging. They were past her aid, for there was no hope that she could keep her footing on that slippery careening deck. She could only hang on and hope.

Then, dead ahead, she saw it.

A huge black rock rising dark and foam-shrouded as if

from a steaming caldron. A great dark tower that blocked their way—certain death.

It was so huge she could not believe it. She closed her eyes, but when she opened them again it was still there—and looming larger.

Rosamunde screamed as the ship struck. She heard the unearthly grinding as its wooden belly was pierced, its entrails scourged and strewn about. For a moment the *Santa Cecilia*, with her deck at a crazy angle, stayed perched where she was, trembling like a living thing suddenly speared. And then the tilt of that slippery deck increased as the ship angled up crazily and men and wreckage slid down it in a helpless tangle.

The next wave swept the deck clear and broke the ship into a thousand pieces. As if fighting valiantly for life, the gilded horse's head on the *Santa Cecilia*'s prow reared up once and seemed to shake itself, sending off a golden spray. Then the gilded figurehead went down forever, along with the broken masts and shattered hull, and dead seamen tangled in the fallen rigging, to lie beneath the foam on the ocean's restless floor.

Rodrigue's darkest nightmare had come true. His ship had broken up on the rocky coast of Ireland.

29   *Rosamunde, clinging to the taffrail like a burr* to a saddle, felt her hands torn free as the wave struck her. She was lifted up by the onrushing water and thrown clear of the deck. Borne irresistibly forward on the crest of that wave, she seemed to rise up and up that towering rock wall before she reached it—and then she was dashed against it and the world went dark. Like a broken doll she relaxed and slid away down the cliff's bleak face into the churning sea.

Rodrigue too was washed overboard by the wave. He saw Rosamunde thrown free of the taffrail, saw her borne upward, saw her strike that black rock and slide into the sea. As much at home as a fish in the water, he had seized a floating timber and managed to let it take the main shock as it struck the cliff. Now as the wave retreated he went under, surfaced, fought his way through the water toward her. A vagrant current, knifing through a hole in the cliff face, caught him and flipped him end over end, but he managed to grasp her shoulder-length fair hair. It was a good grip he got, and with the next wave he took the shock with his shoulder, winced at the blinding pain that went through his arm—but he kept his hold on Rosamunde's limp form and managed to keep her from being dashed again against the rocks. As the wave retreated he struggled toward a break in the rocks, and the next wave took him through it. They plummeted through as if in a spillway and out the other side—and there he found himself swirled about in the churning waters of the small bay where he had sought to bring his crippled *Santa Cecilia*.

He gritted his teeth against the pain in his half-numbed arm. Ahead lay the shore—he could make it, he *would* make it! With what was left of his strength, this powerful swimmer who had spent half the days of his youth fighting the powerful currents off Majorca gripped his woman by the hair and managed to beach her. Crawling up out of the waves that tore at him and tried to suck him back into the bay, he dragged her along with him until he sprawled exhausted, spread-eagled on the spray-wet rocks.

Not till he had beached her did his grip relax. For long minutes he lay there like a dead man, freed at last of the grip of the sea, but still buffeted by the snarling wind.

After a while he raised his head and flexed his arm. The pain had lessened a bit; he could move it better now. He raised himself up on both arms and looked down wearily at the woman beside him. She lay sprawled out, her green velvet dress—that dress, wet, had almost drowned them both—a dark sodden mass on the glistening rocks. One arm was flung out like a sleeping child's, and her wet fair hair streamed out about her like a mermaid's. Her eyes were closed, dark lashes resting on pale wet cheeks, and the top of her dress was rent so that a white shoulder and all but the nipples of her pearly breasts lay exposed.

She lay so still . . . for a terrible moment he thought she must be dead, that he had brought her through all this only to have her die at the end. He held his breath, leaned down until his face touched the softness of those pale gleaming breasts. She was breathing! A deep consuming tenderness swept over Rodrigue. He pressed a thankful kiss upon that wet white flesh, tasted seawater, and dragged the soggy material of her torn bodice over her tenderly to cover her up.

Then and only then did he cast his eyes along the rocky slope that rose from the bay, where the spray flung itself up in a white shower.

It was an evil sight that met his eyes.

416

Several men from the *Santa Cecilia* lay sprawled at the water's edge. De Guzman was dead—he could tell that from here by the position of the man's broken body. Gray-haired Don Alberto's long form was struggling feebly away from the surf that licked and tore at his thin legs. Rodrigue struggled to his feet and staggered down the slippery rocks toward him. He saw a deep gash in the man's throat from which the blood flowed heavily. Don Alberto was dying.

"Rodrigue!" Don Alberto clutched at him, and the two men sank to the rocks.

"Easy, Alberto, easy." Rodrigue eased that gaunt body gently down, knelt beside him.

"Tell my Maria—" Don Alberto choked. "Tell her—" He could not get out the words.

"I will tell her," cried Rodrigue. "I know what to say, Alberto."

He thought he saw a look of gratitude pass over Don Alberto's gaunt face before his eyes glazed and his wet head sagged to the rocks' hard surface.

Rodrigue swallowed hard, for he had sailed with Don Alberto longer than any of the others. He would tell Maria that her husband had died a hero's death, that he had dragged his captain ashore. That much he could do for Don Alberto.

He lifted his head. Beyond, head down, two of the crew washed about in the surf. Mechanically, Rodrigue pulled them onto the shore, knowing he was too late.

He turned at a cry. Fat Don Tomás came reeling around a boulder, clinging to the rocks. Rodrigue saw that he was dragging his right leg behind him, and that it was nearly severed at the hip. Rodrigue felt sick.

"Tomás!" He hurried toward him, reached him as he fell, helped him to a position where he could lean against the rocks.

Don Tomás' face was contorted with pain. "The others," he gasped. "What of the others?"

"I am trying to find them. De Guzman is dead—and Don Alberto. But there may be others alive." He tore

417

off a piece of his shirt and was trying to bind up Don Tomás' wound as he spoke.

"Leave me," panted Don Tomás. "I can finish that. There may be others worse off. You must go and find them."

Swallowing, Rodrigue left his friend and hurried away. But he found only the dead.

On Don Felipe's lifeless battered body he found a sword and baldric. Doubtless their weight had helped to drown Don Felipe and sealed his fate, but Rodrigue was glad to see the weapon. His own sword he had torn off and tossed away when he saw the ship was lost and they must swim for it. Swiftly he buckled on Don Felipe's sword and baldric, and cast an uneasy look about him under the sickly clearing sky. Dawn was breaking over the Irish coast, a gray lifeless dawn that could herald new dangers.

As a boy Rodrigue had listened breathlessly to the stories the Armada's survivors had brought back from Ireland. His father had been one of the lucky ones, but there had been those less lucky. His childhood had been haunted by hair-raising tales of half-drowned Spanish sailors clubbed to death as they lay insensible in the Irish surf, of shipwrecked Spanish seamen hunted down like wild animals as they fled weaponless and starving through bogs and bracken, of proud officers of the lost Armada summarily turned over by Irish peasants to English overlords for speedy execution. All his life Rodrigue had nurtured a fear of this land and its wild half-tamed people. Even more than for himself, he feared for Rosamunde, whose lightsome beauty made all men desire her. Grimly he stalked back to the place where he had left her, taking some comfort from the sword that now swung against his lean leg.

Rosamunde was rising unsteadily as he returned. He saw her sweep back her fair hair, wince as she shook it out and a pain went through her head. In the pale dawn she seemed to him again like some lovely mermaid of unearthly beauty risen from the foam.

But he took no time to admire her. Instead he beckoned her to where Don Tomás lay, pale and suffering, his short body propped against the rocks. With a little cry, Rosamunde knelt and gently rebandaged the wound, using a strip torn from her chemise. Don Tomás gave her a painful smile and muttered something, and she knew that he was thanking her in his native Catalan.

Rodrigue gave his friend a bleak look. There was no stanching that wound. Don Tomás was losing too much blood. He had seen men die like that before. But—they would all die if they did not find shelter and water and food.

He sighed. "We must win to the heights. I think I see a ruined tower up there. Where there are buildings there is fresh water."

Rosamunde, who was full of sea salt and very thirsty, nodded. "I can help you with Don Tomás."

He gave her a grateful look, and together they lugged a half-fainting Don Tomás up a slippery stone path that led up the cliff. In places it looked as if axes had hammered rude steps into the stone, and Rosamunde guessed that whoever had lived in that broken round tower that loomed overhead had used this path to go down to the sea to fish.

To their disappointment the tower was indeed a ruin, unroofed, with walls that streamed with water. But there was a spring, and all of them drank deep of the cold water.

"I will go back." Rodrigue sighed. "Perhaps I can salvage something useful from the wreck."

"I will go with you," said Rosamunde sturdily.

Rodrigue turned and spoke to Don Tomás, who answered feebly and waved them away.

By the end of the day they had salvaged a cask of biscuit, unhurt by seawater, half a cheese and enough canvas and rope to construct a roof shelter over a corner of the ruined walls.

"This tower has been deserted for a long time," said Rosamunde as she helped Rodrigue stretch the canvas across the stones.

"Yes. I suspect it was last used to watch for the Danes who came raiding this coast."

She was silent, for she knew there was Danish blood in her own heritage. Ah, well, that was long ago. She was not to blame for their depredations! Indeed this Spanish captain had carried her off in much the same fashion as those long-ago Danes had abducted their women! Quietly she munched her biscuit and salty cheese, washed them down with the cold spring water, and warmed herself at the smoky fire Rodrigue had been able to make of dung and driftwood.

"Do you know where we are?" she asked.

"Far from any town, if my last calculations were right. There is a long stretch of coast here that is almost uninhabited. But we will reach a village."

Rosamunde cast a worried look at the injured man, his head slumped over in exhausted sleep.

"But what of Don Tomás?" she murmured.

"We will stay with him while he lives," Rodrigue told her in an undertone. "But there is little chance he will accompany us."

Rodrigue's prediction was right. In spite of all they could do, on the third day Don Tomás died. Throughout, the gallant Spaniard had never complained; indeed, he had seemed a little better at the end. He had looked up at Rosamunde with a sweet smile. He had muttered the word "angel" in the Majorcan tongue—and then he had died very quietly.

Rosamunde mourned him along with Rodrigue, for Don Tomás had been courageous and cheerful to the end. They wrapped his short body in salvaged ship's canvas. They scratched out a shallow grave for him as they had for the others, lowered him into it, and marked his resting place with a sturdy piece of wood salvaged from the ship, on which they crudely scratched his name.

It was all they could do for Don Tomás.

The days that followed were grim ones. They wrapped what food they had left in torn bits of canvas and headed south. Starving and exhausted, they won at last to a ruined unroofed abbey perched high on the grim gray cliffs. And by then Rodrigue had discovered a truth that grew more obvious every day. He had known it for certain when
420

he had by accident chanced on Rosamunde as she bathed in a clear brook that ran down to the sea. The impudent shell-pink nipples that crested her round breasts had turned a deeper rose. Rosamunde was with child. Not his child . . . it would have been too soon for that.

Rodrigue kept his silence about this discovery, but the knowledge sobered him, for her condition had made their plight all the more desperate. He was glad when they found the abbey.

Living in a corner of the ruined abbey they found two brothers who had fled the fishing village located on a small bay down the coast. Although they looked as alike as two peas, both being short dark stocky men with twinkling blue eyes, their callings differed. One, Father Paul, was a priest, and the other, Patrick O'Toole, a thatcher. Practice of his religion being at that time forbidden in Ireland, brother Patrick had hidden Father Paul in his cottage, and when it was discovered that he was hiding a priest, both brothers had had to flee. They had remembered this moldering ruin and had come here to eke out a bare living by fishing, making up for their lack from the "gifts" of food and wine given to Father Paul by villagers, when he slipped down at night to give last rites or hear a confession. Their presence in the abbey was a tight-lipped secret in the village.

The brothers were nervous at first of these newcomers who had straggled down from the north, but Rodrigue was overjoyed to find them. Though Patrick spoke only Gaelic, Rodrigue could converse with Father Paul in Latin, for he had been schooled in Latin as a child in Majorca—indeed, at one time his father had wanted him to take holy orders.

The brothers listened to his tale of shipwreck with sympathy, but they could do little to help him. This land was ruled by the English, and who knew what attitude the English law would take toward a 'Spanish captain who had departed the English coast under such uneasy circumstances? Rodrigue and Rosamunde faced each other with anxiety glowing in their eyes. Plainly they dared not go down to the fishing village which lay before them down

421

the coast, and the lands to the east, they were told, were wild and dangerous.

But the brothers were hospitable. They fed the newcomers, generously sharing what little they had. They could do little more, for they were poor men, but they indicated these wanderers could stay with them as long as they liked. Indeed, Rodrigue could help them with their fishing.

Rodrigue was glad to be of help. And one day when Father Paul had made a nocturnal visit to the village for a christening, he came back lugging several skins of wine and gave one to Rodrigue. The next day the brothers spent mending their nets—something for which neither Rodrigue nor Rosamunde had any skill. So Rodrigue and his lady wandered off and shared a loaf and a skin of wine on the high cliffs together. Rosamunde's green eyes were sad as she looked out to sea, and Rodrigue guessed that she was thinking of England and all that she had lost, perhaps sorrowing for the lover whose child she carried in her body. Watching her sad beautiful face, he knew a wild rending jealousy and a compassion of which he had not known he was capable—and overall a surpassing tenderness.

"Rosamunde." He leaned over and lifted a tendril of her fair hair. " 'Tis a lovely name."

"My father read Latin," she said. "When I was born he told my mother I was fairer than a rose—and then he laughed and said that they should call me Rosamunde, which means the World's Rose."

"Rose of the world," he murmured.

"Worldly Rose." She sighed.

"No, never that," he murmured. For he saw her as young and untried in spite of the fact that before many months had passed she would bear another man's child.

"I was called the Wild Rose," she remembered, "when I rode the highways of England, taking a purse where I could."

It was all Rodrigue could do not to gather her into his arms. His whole body ached for her. "I am sorry, Rosamunde," he said somberly, looking not at her but out at the wild ocean, "that I took you against your will."

"You are forgiven," said Rosamunde, choosing to misunderstand him. Her voice was rueful. "For you took me from the shores of Cornwall, where at best I'd have met the hangman—and now you have saved my life again, for you dragged me from the sea."

"Had I left you in Holland, you would be safe now," he reminded her.

"Perhaps not," she said flippantly. "Perhaps I'd have ended as badly as you predicted—in a brothel."

He turned and gave the unflinching beauty beside him a steady look from his dark expressive eyes. "I think not," he said in a quiet voice. "I think you would have won through to something better." She gave him a grateful look, but his brow was furrowed. "Do you know, Rosamunde, I used to dream of Margarita every night? For years I thought of no other woman. But since you came into my life I have not dreamed of her even once. It is a blessed release," he added bitterly, "for she is wed to my brother and forever beyond my reach."

Rosamunde rose, beating down her skirts against the strong west wind that blew in from the sea. "Let us not recall the past, Rodrigue," she said unsteadily, for the timbre in his voice had made her think of Harry, and she ached to have him here beside her—Harry, whom she would never see again. "It does neither of us any good to relive the past. We must collect ourselves and look to the future."

"Yes," he agreed thoughtfully. "To the future."

30   *Rodrigue shouldered the empty wineskin, and* together they walked back to the ruined abbey. Past tall Celtic stone crosses that were there when the Vikings had come, moving toward the spot on the other side of the abbey where Patrick and Father Paul would be mending the nets. Their way led them past the well, and at that well stood a newcomer—not a priest or a thatcher this time, but a huge wild-looking warrior in a coarse woolen cloak that might once have been red but was weathered to russet. His tangled beard blew red, and as he rose from drinking the water he set the wooden bucket down with a thump on the well's stone rim. The wind from the sea rippled his thick shoulder-length red hair and blew back his cloak, showing that his clothing was made mainly of animal skins, carelessly sewn. It showed also that he carried a large broadsword. He had a fierce stance.

Noting the heavy shoulder muscles of this red-bearded giant, his lightness of foot as he stepped backward from the well, Rodrigue loosened the sword in his baldric. "I will speak for us both, Rosamunde," he muttered sternly to the woman in tattered velvet beside him. "Deny nothing that I say."

Rosamunde nodded and trailed him to the well, where the giant, feet planted and green eyes glinting, studied them both. Rodrigue tried speaking to the man in Spanish, in Majorcan, even in Latin, but without success.

"He does not understand what you are saying, Rodrigue," sighed Rosamunde, and the giant swung on her in surprise.

"You are English?" he asked in a deep, almost guttural, voice.

It was Rosamunde's turn to look startled. In the tension of the moment she had forgotten that in Ireland the lords of the land were English.

But Rodrigue had correctly guessed the cold gleam that lit up the other man's eyes. This huge newcomer was identifying Rosamunde as a woman of the enemy camp—and that would be dangerous. Swiftly Rodrigue motioned Rosamunde to be silent and spoke in English.

"I am from Majorca," he interposed swiftly. "Captain of the *Santa Cecilia*, which was wrecked on the coast north of here some days ago. But before that my ship was blown onto the Cornish coast, and there my men and I would have been butchered by the English"—ah, he was right, the giant's face hardened and he nodded his head in brusque sympathy—"but for this lady, who was fleeing a great body of mounted men—"

"Why did they seek her?" queried that deep voice.

"She had killed the king's tax collector, who had raped her."

Rosamunde's shoulders jerked slightly at this bald-faced lie. But she swallowed her protest when she realized that above that red beard a pair of hard green eyes gazed at her in commiseration.

"She told me of the plot to seize my ship and kill my men, and when we made our escape, we took her with us. Storms drove us to this coast, and when our ship struck, she and I were the only survivors."

A huge hairy hand was thrust forward, gripped by Rodrigue and shaken. "The brothers told me of you," said the deep voice laconically. "But they are simple trusting men, and I wanted to hear your story from your own lips. Nor had they told me the woman was English." (*They were afraid to!* thought Rosamunde, studying that wild face. *They must have thought you would kill us out of hand!*) The red-bearded face split in a smile that showed large even white teeth. "My name is O'Lear. Welcome to Ireland!" He wrung Rodrigue's hand until Rodrigue winced, and then with a careless nod toward the ruined abbey, added, "Like me, the brothers live outside the law of this land. I have brought them a sheep I lifted from the English—for Father Paul's blessing. Sure, 'twill taste the better for it. Come, 'tis being prepared now. We will eat it."

Silently Rodrigue and Rosamunde accompanied the giant as he moved, sure-footed, through the ruined building. A wisp of smoke told them where the sheep was being cooked. They found its carcass being turned on a spit above the flames and both brothers looking alternately pleased and apprehensive. She gathered they were afraid of O'Lear and the trouble he might bring down on them, even though they were willing enough to accept his largess.

Later they ate, seated on stones around the fire, and Rosamunde studied the giant Irishman. He spoke English well—he had learned the cursed tongue in an English jail, he told them carelessly. And his strong white teeth tore great bites from the leg of mutton he held in one huge hairy hand. His unkempt red hair tumbled over his eyes as he ate, and those brilliant green eyes glinted at her through that forest of hair like an animal's reflecting the glow of a campfire in the night. He spoke Gaelic to the brothers and seemed friendly enough, but the way he watched her made Rosamunde nervous. She sensed in this giant an unbridled dangerous man who would take what he wanted—in every sense—just as it pleased him, and would only be deterred in his purpose by the long bright edge of a blade or a musket ball.

"Had ye no brothers in England to defend ye?" he asked on a note of sudden contempt. "That they let ye be hunted like a deer through the forest?"

"I have no brothers at all," said Rosamunde truthfully.

"A father then?"

"My father was taken when he sought to snatch a friend from the king's executioners, and fell to the headsman's ax."

The big head opposite her came up alertly. "So the tax collector took ye from your father's house?"

Somehow it stuck in Rosamunde's throat, lying to

O'Lear. He was rough, he was dangerous—but there was honesty in him. It called out to her.

"There was no tax collector," she said quietly. "And he did not rape me."

A silence fell upon the meal as O'Lear's big head turned toward Rodrigue, whose face had whitened at this revelation.

"I was in the care of a guardian, who would have forced on me a noble lord I hated. I escaped in the company of a highwayman and for a time we harried the roads together. I was his doxy. When he was killed I fled to the coast—and was pursued by a large body of mounted men. The rest is as Rodrigue told you." She leaned forward earnestly. "Rodrigue told you about the tax collector in an attempt to save my reputation. He thought it unseemly that a woman should roam the highways."

O'Lear's face split in a genial smile. "I find it seemly enough," he observed. "Though ye're built a bit light for the work," he added critically, his green gaze raking up and down her body in the tattered velvet gown.

"I'm a good shot," protested Rosamunde. "And those I rode with were built strong enough. My Harry was the most famous highwayman in all England." Her voice rang with pride. Had she been looking at Rodrigue at that moment, she would have seen a shadow of pain cross his face.

"Was he now? The most famous in all England?" O'Lear digested that. "Ye'll be mourning him then?" he shot at her.

"Yes," said Rosamunde, and her bleak face spoke more eloquently than any words. "I mourn him."

"Ah, 'tis the way it should be," said O'Lear with satisfaction. "A good man should be mourned." He tossed aside the mutton bone and wiped a hand across his mouth. "And how do you like Ireland?"

"It has given us shelter, and the brothers are kind." Rosamunde chose her words carefully lest she offend this man. "But the weather is cold and damp."

"Ye need a warm cloak. I will see to it."

Rosamunde looked at him in surprise. He turned and

427

spoke to the brothers in Gaelic, and they burst into an excited chatter, seemingly entreating him not to do something. Rodrigue, speaking Latin, learned from Father Paul that Brian O'Lear proposed to lift a handsome lady's cloak from the nearest castle, and they were begging him not to do so, having a lively fear of English hounds and English law.

When Rodrigue told her this, Rosamunde turned to O'Lear and said with dignity, "I am well enough. Please do not endanger these good brothers who have given us shelter."

Even as she spoke, both brothers erupted with a torrent of words. Father Paul even seized O'Lear by the arm.

"What are they saying?" she asked.

O'Lear turned to her. "Since I am set on bringing you a cloak, they are urging me to bring you some lesser one. A cloak that is not fur-trimmed or of such fine material that it will be identified on sight and bring the English down on everyone's head."

"And they are right!"

Brian O'Lear looked amused. "I will please myself," he said, looking her boldly in the eyes. "And it pleases me to cloak you. The choice will be mine. But 'twill not be for a week or two, for I've a journey to make." A smile played about his wide mouth. "Would you not like to go along—and see Ireland?"

Beside her Rodrigue stiffened. Rosamunde laid a light cautioning hand on his—which, she guessed, ached to go for his sword. " 'Tis a bad time for me to travel," she told O'Lear frankly. "For I will bear a child in the spring. The child of the highwayman I mourn." She had thought her words might shock Rodrigue, but they did not. He was watching O'Lear.

The green eyes grew murky and a frown furrowed O'Lear's wide brow. For a time he drummed his fingers, and Rosamunde wondered nervously what he was thinking. Then, "I'm for sleeping," he said, and strode over to a sheltered spot by the wall. He wrapped himself in his russet cloak and was instantly asleep. Rosamunde watched him soberly. She saw that he had chosen a point from which he could, if he lifted his head, watch the approach to the monastery on three sides. A fighting man, Brian O'Lear—and she was afraid of the unbridled wildness she saw in him. Afraid that on a sudden reckless impulse he might "lift" her as he had "lifted" the English sheep, knock Rodrigue in the head and carry her off into the wilds of Ireland.

"You answered him well," muttered Rodrigue, as they made ready for bed in the sheltered place the brothers had fashioned for them. It was little better than a ruined cell, but there was a pile of clean grasses for Rosamunde to lie on. As usual Rodrigue stretched himself across the entrance, but neither he nor Rosamunde slept till morning.

They awoke to find O'Lear gone. Where? They asked the brothers and were answered by indifferent shakes of the head. Who knew where O'Lear went? He was driven like the fierce winds that tore at these cliffs. A restless man, a wanderer. Did he have a woman? asked Rosamunde. Sometimes, was the reply. Women could not keep up with such a man—they faltered, they fell. The last had died in childbirth, the one before of a distemper of the lungs. . . . Rosamunde, who had watched that long eager stride, those great bunching muscles, did not doubt that women had difficulty keeping up with O'Lear.

She herself had no mind to try it!

That morning Rodrigue and the brothers held anxious counsel, and it was decided that for everyone's sake Rosamunde had best away. Before O'Lear came back, possibly with English pursuit hard at his heels. Father Paul guided them to a shepherd's hut, high up, near the cliffs that overlooked the sea. It was a one-room stone affair with a rakish thatched roof, and when the cold sea gales sang through its rafters, the tiny peat fire hardly warmed it. To their surprise, the hut was occupied—by a woman.

Her name was Meara. She was as tall as Rodrigue, big-boned and gaunt. She grasped a wooden staff and walked toward them frowning. But she greeted Father Paul warmly and studied Rosamunde with wide-eyed curiosity. Meara would have been pretty except that she had a great gashing scar across her face that had twisted up the corner of her mouth and pulled down one eye. Her hair was thick and wild and black and her eyes a dark sapphire blue, startling against her black lashes and fair skin. Rosamunde guessed her thinness came from starvation, and saw that her clothes were mere rags of homespun. But they were clean-washed, and the tiny hut, though almost barren of furniture, was clean too, with a pile of fresh grasses in the corner for her bed. She was neat, too, for she took the staff indoors and stood it carefully in the corner by her bed.

She frowned and drew back when Father Paul told her Rosamunde was English, but was all sympathy when he explained that her father had been beheaded on the king's orders, and Rosamunde had fled the country lest she be hanged.

" 'Twas much the same with me," Meara burst out in English, turning to Rosamunde—and this was the first inkling Rosamunde had had that Meara knew the language. "I was bound in service to an English family in Cork and was raped by the master of the house one night when he was in his cups. He was a great broth of a man—I could not throw him off me. His wife heard us scuffling and burst in. She was very jealous; she ordered her servants to hold me and she came at me with a large kitchen knife. She slashed my face"—here Meara indicated her scars with a careless gesture—"and I think she might have killed me but that I tore free and fled. Pursued by hounds I was, for she did tell the law that I had stolen the silver! And when at last the dogs lost my trail in the bracken, I was lost. I wandered about and nearly starved. But at last by good fortune I made my way to the abbey and Father Paul led me to this shepherd's hut, which was deserted, for the shepherd had died." Here she lived by grubbing out a miserable plot and by fishing in the sea—at which, she admitted ruefully, she was not very expert. She nodded significantly at a fishing spear and some nets that were hung up to dry.
430

"In that I can help," said Rodrigue. "For I am a great fisherman."

Meara showed him the boat the brothers had found for her, and Rodrigue grunted and said he would improve it. They were very friendly by the time Father Paul left, and Rodrigue plunged immediately into his duties as fisherman. Soon there was plenty of fish for the table, and Meara, who was a tall strong woman, began to fill out, her looks improved.

Rosamunde, in her mended velvet gown, was always cold. It was the season of storms, Meara explained, but with spring and better weather there would be ships calling down at the bay—she nodded her head toward the fishing village, several hours' walk away. Eventually a ship would come that would carry them back to Spain, for the brothers had sent word to friends in the fishing village about the Majorcan captain's shipwreck.

In the meantime, Rosamunde was growing big with child and walked more heavily as she helped prepare their plain meals, setting wooden bowls upon a rude table, plaiting straw into a primitive basket to hold their coarse bread, cleaning fish, mending nets.

Sometimes she walked to the windy cliff edge and sat there with her legs dangling over, combing her fair hair with the crude wooden comb Rodrigue had carved for her—he had carved one for Meara too and brought a sparkling light to her blue eyes. She would sit there and watch Rodrigue and Meara in the little fishing boat far below, throwing out their nets and lines. Rosamunde would sit there moodily, combing out her hair that blew about her in a bright shower, and look out across the wild reaches of the North Atlantic—and try not to think about Harry and her shattered life.

It was on such a day that O'Lear found her.

She sensed his arrival rather than actually hearing him come up. She turned with a start and there he was, his big body seeming to fill the sky as he stared down at her. It had been six weeks since he had promised to bring her a cloak, and she thought they had seen the last of him. It

431

was a shock to see him standing there, a woolen cloak thrown across his muscular arm.

"Brian!" she exclaimed, startled.

His bearded face broke into a smile. "You see, I have not forgot. I have brought you the cloak I promised. A bit late, but 'tis still cold and damp—and 'tis like to remain so." His keen green eyes beneath their heavy brows were studying her thickened figure, and he reached down and pulled her to her feet with a big hand and draped the woolen cloak about her shoulders.

There was nothing for it but to accept the gift he so gallantly offered. "It's lovely, Brian," she said helplessly, fingering the warm material of a neutral buff color. "I'd thought to pass the winter in Rodrigue's cloak—leaving him to bear the weather."

She had brought in Rodrigue's name deliberately, and O'Lear frowned and studied her for a minute. Then, " 'Tis a good cloak. 'Tis not the fine fur-trimmed cloak I promised ye—but ye were right, that one might have brought trouble down on ye, and ye're in no condition to run."

How right he is! she thought ruefully. "Then you did not get it at the castle?"

"Nay. From a country house far from here. The Englishwoman from whom I lifted it had many others to keep her warm," he added lightly. "Bought by gold she'd gulled the Irish of, no doubt."

His tone was so scathing that Rosamunde's head lifted. "*I* am an Englishwoman, Brian," she reminded him in a steady voice.

"Ah, that's your misfortune." He grinned. " 'Tis better to be Irish, you'll find. 'Tis better to sleep beside an Irishman."

Ah, so that was what she'd find, was it? Slowly Rosamunde drew the cloak from her shoulders and held it out to him. "The price is too high," she said dryly.

O'Lear stiffened as if she had struck him. "I pay no price for any woman," he said in a voice gone suddenly fierce. "They come to me of their own free will or not at all!" He pushed the cloak back to her. "You will accept my gift," he said menacingly. "For it has cost me dear.
432

I near lost a leg when I fled with it and they set the hounds after me."

Only then did she realize that his left leg was bound up in dirty rags and that he favored it. She exclaimed, and offered to dress the wound, but he brushed her words aside. " 'Tis near well now. But 'twas the reason I was late." He reached out, calmly took possession of her right hand in his huge warm one, smiled down at it and suddenly bent and kissed it. He kissed her palm, her wrist, her arm.

Rosamunde drew back with a hopeless look and he released her gently. She kept the cloak bundled up between them and cast a hunted look around her. This vast Irish giant was wooing her—and she hardly knew how to fend him off.

"There is no need to fear," he said calmly. "I respect your condition. But after the babe is born, I will be back —and *then* I will take you with me and show you Ireland."

"No," Rosamunde insisted. "Understand me, Brian. I cannot go with you. A small baby cannot safely be dragged about—"

O'Lear gave her a look so fierce she fell silent. "I say that I will be back for you," he rumbled. "Depend upon it." He mouthed an oath in Gaelic and smote one hand with the other. Rosamunde, fearing for Rodrigue, held her peace. "Come," he said. "I will walk you back to the hut."

Again he draped the woolen cloak about her shoulders, and in silence Rosamunde accompanied him. At a bend in the path they met Meara and Rodrigue returning home tired and cold from a fruitless day's fishing. Meara stopped dead at sight of O'Lear and almost dropped her fishing spear. Her pale face grew even paler.

" 'Tis yourself, Brian," she said tonelessly.

"Aye." The giant nodded in a taciturn manner. "How fare you, Meara?" He ignored Rodrigue, who gave him a curt nod and passed on to speak to Rosamunde. Meara stepped forward and took her place beside O'Lear, while Rodrigue fell in beside Rosamunde as they approached the hut.

"How long has O'Lear been here?" he asked in a low tone.

"A few minutes, no more."

Rodrigue looked relieved. "I suppose he frightened the brothers into telling him where you were. We might have expected it, but I will be glad when he leaves."

So would Rosamunde, for she thought the giant Irishman, in the full flower of his anger, might well be able to subdue them all. It would be dangerous to thwart him. O'Lear was still surly at dinner, which was leftover hare stew, for the fishing had been bad lately. He ate sparingly and hardly spoke. Rosamunde guessed he did not desire to reduce their meager larder.

Meara noticed his lack of appetite and glared at him fiercely. "And will ye not eat at my table, Brian O'Lear? Is my food not good enough for you?"

O'Lear gave her a tired look. "I will bring ye a sheep," he said mildly. "Next time I lift one."

Meara jumped up and began knocking the wooden bowls about. Rosamunde had never seen her display so much temper, for ordinarily she was a calm resolute woman. O'Lear ignored Meara's petulance and watched Rosamunde from beneath brooding brows.

Rosamunde squirmed under that penetrating gaze, and looked up to see Meara watching them both with tears in her eyes. It came to her with a shock that poor Meara was in love with Brian O'Lear. And he—perhaps because of her scarred face—never noticed Meara at all. Rosamunde felt suddenly unhappy that she herself should be possessed of so much beauty. She had not meant to flaunt her good fortune before one so much less fortunate. Would she had smudged her face with ashes from the fire, on the pretext of cleaning the hearth!

Now, dawdling over her bowl, Rosamunde studied gaunt Meara and the giant Irishman. Meara was so right for him. Irish—as he was. Beyond the law—as he was. Strong and resourceful—though never so strong and resourceful as he. The determined Meara, who had made her way, injured and alone, through strange wild country,

434

who had lost her pursuers and their dogs and won through to this hut, was surely a fit mate for the mighty Brian!

It was too bad, Rosamunde thought, that Brian did not realize it as Meara did. For a long time she pondered on the wickedness of fate that would make a man desire a woman who did not want him, who would never want him, while right under his nose was a woman who would suit him admirably—and who desired him with all her heart.

She saw Meara pass a surreptitious hand across her blue eyes to brush away the bright tears that glittered there, saw her lean earnestly above the pot of hare stew, stirring the steaming watery broth.

Poor Meara . . . if she yearned for a kind word from her hero, she received none. Dinner over, O'Lear retired with a grunt to a cold corner of the hut, wrapped his cloak about him and slept. He was gone with the dawn. Although Rodrigue, worried about Rosamunde, made excuses to stay home from fishing for several days, O'Lear did not return.

Meara spoke of him several times to Rosamunde. "Ah, he is a great broth of a man," she declared gloomily. "And knows not his own heart. 'Tis a wonder the English do not catch him and kill him, for I do think his great head is put on backward."

Rosamunde smiled at that. It was Meara's way of saying that O'Lear was looking in the wrong direction for his light of love. "Do you think he would make a good husband, Meara?" she ventured.

Meara planted both feet and shot Rosamunde a dark look. With both hands on her hips she looked very formidable.

"For yourself," amended Rosamunde hastily. "Not for me."

"I do not know," mumbled Meara, her face suddenly suffusing with color. She turned and began vigorously to brush the hearth. But later that day she boasted to Rosamunde, "Brian is a great man. The English will never catch him. He comes here but seldom, for his favorite haunts are farther south." She fixed Rosamunde with a

435

stern look. "I think," she said, "that he came only to see you."

"He came of his kindness to bring me a cloak because I was cold."

"We are all cold."

"True, but O'Lear respects my condition. He knows that in England I was a highwayman's doxy. 'Tis his child I carry in my body. When he was killed on the highway, I fled. And I was pursued to the coast by half the country-side, for the noble lord my guardian would have forced on me had put a price on my head. In England my Harry had as great a reputation as Brian has in Ireland. Brian knows that I mourn him. He believes a good man should be mourned. He said so."

"Aye," agreed Meara reluctantly. "Brian believes that."

"So you see I am not like to become his woman, Meara. Although I hear he has had several."

"Aye." Meara nodded, and Rosamunde divined that this subject was one of consummate interest to her. "There have been three altogether. One fell from a high crag to her death. One died in childbirth—and one of a distemper of the lungs. Myself, I climb like a goat," she added in a disheartened tone. "And I am very healthy."

Rosamunde felt compassion for her. "Perhaps he will turn to you, Meara," she pointed out gently.

"How can he when he has eyes only for your pretty face?" snapped Meara and stalked away.

Rosamunde sighed and looked at her hands. Because of her, kind Meara was unhappy, for what she had said of O'Lear was true. Because of her, Rodrigue was un-happy, for he feared the giant Irishman would try to claim her. She leaned her head pensively in her hands and watched through the hut's single window some great hawks soaring overhead, their wings dark against the cloudy sky. If only she could leave this place!

A fortnight later O'Lear came by again. He was leading a blind harper by the hand. Over his shoulder he carried the man's harp along with a strange-looking instrument which Meara called a *piopai*—a kind of bagpipe.

Jauntily the giant Irishman greeted them. He found the
436

blind harper—whom he introduced merely as Shawn—
a seat on one of the big stones outside the hut. Then he
grasped the *piopai* and himself struck up so wild a tune
that the sea birds shrieked away in fright. Meara stared
at him in open-mouthed wonder. But it was before Rosamunde he stood as he played, watching her with bright
devilish eyes.

The two of them stayed for supper, and after they
had supped, the blind harper sang Irish songs in Gaelic,
no word of which Rosamunde could understand, but the
sadness of his mellow voice and the wailing music brought
tears to her eyes. Meara sat with her arms hugging her
knees, staring at O'Lear as if to memorize his features.
Her scars were all too apparent tonight, and she made no
attempt to hide them, as if scorning any dissembling. She
too looked sad.

Rodrigue, carried away like the rest of them, picked up
the harp while the blind man drank the wine that Meara
brought him. He ran his olive-skinned fingers across the
strings and picked out a tune, sang it softly into the damp
night air. A Majorcan love song, plaintive and lovely.
Rosamunde felt her heart would break.

O'Lear gave her an impatient look. With Rodrigue's
last note he leaped to his feet, and the hut rang and the
very cliffs echoed with the wild sound of his bagpipes.
His lungs drew in huge quantities of air and the wild music
boomed and shrieked and howled eerily. The noise gave
Rosamunde a headache, but Meara was on her feet. Dancing and clapping her hands, she laughed as she circled
about O'Lear, who kept his gaze fixed with frightening
intensity on the seated Rosamunde.

"Where did you find the harper?" Rosamunde asked,
when O'Lear had near blown his lungs out and sat down,

"I found Shawn on the way here. He had lost his way.
I promised to guide him to his destination if he would
but stop here and play his harp for you." His green eyes
smiled into hers, and she knew, uneasily, that she was
being serenaded.

Meara, who had flung herself down on a bench after

her wild gyrations, cut in. "Ye've a way with the pipes, Brian—'tis a pity ye've no voice for singing!" she jibed.

O'Lear gave her an impatient look. "If your stew was as good as your tongue, Meara, 'tis the finest cook in the land ye would be!"

She subsided, watching him from her deep-blue eyes shadowed by their dark lashes. Rosamunde wished impatiently that Meara would lean her face upon her left hand instead of her right, so she would hide her ugly scars and show O'Lear the beauty that was hers. But Meara had no thought of that.

"The O'Lear is long o' the tongue tonight," she observed, deliberately goading him. "But perhaps he has lost his touch. 'Tis the pipes he is lifting now—not some good sheep or English purse! Perhaps ye've no longer any heart for the work, Brian? Faith and ye'll starve while ye blow your lungs out with a stolen *piopai!*"

Rosamunde shuddered as O'Lear turned his heavy frown on Meara. It was madness to bait him! This huge half-wild creature, driven to rage, might well demolish everything in the hut—or take them all prisoner and drag them into the depths of this savage land. But O'Lear only shrugged. "The *piopai* is my own," he stated coldly. "And as for having no heart for the work, I've cut men in half for saying less!"

"I've no doubt ye have," Meara rallied him. "But ye'll find women are nimble and harder to catch!" She stuck out her jaw and displayed her scars mockingly. "It took five men to catch *me!*" she taunted. "And to hold me while *she* gave me this!" She tossed her dark head as if to say, *Match this if you can!*

"Five men?" O'Lear regarded her in amusement. "Five to hold you, you say? One for each arm and leg and one for your tongue, no doubt!" He roared with laughter at his own sally, and Meara, flushed red with fury, suddenly grabbed a heavy iron pot and hurled it at his head.

Rodrigue cried a warning and the harp strings twanged discordantly as Rosamunde hastily pulled the harper out of the line of fire. But the giant Irishman ducked the pot neatly and caught it too, although his low bench went
438

over backward as his big arms swept up to catch the pot. He crashed to the floor, almost in the hearth, and Meara, with a swiftness surprising in such a big woman, darted around the table and kicked away the embers lest they burn him. "You're not hurt?" she asked him sharply.

"No, but 'tis no fault of yours that this big pot did not smash my nose!" O'Lear rose, towering over her, and his big voice rumbled a warning. "Ye'd best mind your manners, colleen, or I'll return this pot to ye the same way ye sent it!"

Meara sniffed, but she kept a wary eye on O'Lear until he had thumped the pot down upon the table.

"D'ye know the best way to keep a lass like Meara dutiful and sweet-tongued?" O'Lear resumed his seat and turned to Rodrigue. " 'Tis by lifting her wide skirts and turning her across your knee each morning and paddling her bare backside with a wee shillelagh till 'tis pink as a rose. Have ye not found that method useful?"

"I've not had to resort to it." Rodrigue grinned, for once in total sympathy with the big Irishman. "But I can see it would have its uses. Someday I may try it."

Rosamunde and Meara exchanged smoldering glances.

"I'd not take a spanking from any man," declared Rosamunde hotly.

"Ah, ye're with child and that saves ye," pointed out O'Lear.

"*I'd* flay the bejesus out of any man who laid hands on *me!*" flashed Meara.

"*If* he let you," finished O'Lear with heavy irony.

Meara was livid. Her fists balled up, and Rosamunde felt uneasily that at any moment Meara might spring upon this vexing giant and belabor him with her fists.

Beside her the harper muttered some plaintive words in Gaelic, and Rosamunde gave a guilty start. She had forgotten the harper. They had *all* forgotten the blind harper spoke no English. How frightened and confused he must be by all this bombast!

"Shawn doesn't know what we're saying," she said sharply. "You should translate for him, Brian."

Thus commanded by his lady, O'Lear turned and spoke

in rapid Gaelic. The harper laughed and groped for his harp, which O'Lear reached over and politely handed to him. He strummed it and broke into a light-hearted tune, singing in Gaelic. Meara grew red-faced again and O'Lear laughed uproariously.

"What's he saying?" demanded Rosamunde, alarmed at the effect the song was having on Meara.

"He's singing about a woman whose husband cut the back out of her petticoat that he might spank her the better!" cried Meara indignantly. "O'Lear, you put him up to this!"

O'Lear made a ribald retort, and they argued animatedly while Shawn finished his song. Rosamunde watched them. Ill-mannered and boisterous they might be, but they had an elemental strength and violence and exuberance that *matched*. The pity was that O'Lear didn't see it.

In an attempt to stop their bickering, Rosamunde suggested that O'Lear join the harper in a song. Meara hooted at that, but O'Lear flashed his even white teeth at Rosamunde and bellowed unmusically in a way that made the harper wince. But the last notes of the song had scarcely died away before Meara was sniping at O'Lear again.

O'Lear, flushed with pride at the carrying power of his voice, which he accounted nothing short of miraculous, grumbled, "Keep watch o'er your tongue, Meara, or I'll take ye with me to the peak of Carran Tual and leave ye there!"

"Is that where you're going, Brian?" gasped Meara, for the Carran Tual was the highest peak in Ireland.

"Only to the western slope to find the dwelling of Shawn's sister." O'Lear nodded at the harper. "She's said to be ailing bad, and Shawn's of a mind to see her again before she passes on."

Meara nodded, her impudence quenched. She cast a look of pity at the blind man. "I can scarce remember my own family," she said gruffly. "I was bound out before I was ten years old." She poured out the last of the wine and gave it to Shawn.

The blind harper smiled and drank the wine. Then he took up his harp again and played softly. He seemed never to tire of playing, and when at last by rushlight they made ready for bed he still strummed on, singing half to himself, the old sad songs of a beautiful and tragic land. Rosamunde lay on her pallet of straw and listened—and wished she could be with Harry tonight. As the melody wailed on, she pressed her face into her cloak and wept silently—for Harry, for England, for a way of life that she would never know again.

31 *When Rosamunde awoke the hut was deserted.* She went out, hugging her cloak around her against the sharp wind. In the distance she could see Rodrigue striding toward the cliffs and the fishing boat. O'Lear and the harper were gone. But where was Meara?

She heard a sound like an animal snuffling and rounded the corner of the hut warily. There was Meara, standing in her worn homespun dress, with her face and arms pressed against the cold stone wall of the hut, crying as if her heart would break.

Rosamunde retreated silently. She had no need to ask why Meara was weeping. Meara loved the big Irishman, O'Lear—and he had eyes only for the English girl fate had washed upon these shores.

She stood for a while shivering in front of the hut. Overhead the gulls screamed and circled. The air was damp and smelled of rain. Rosamunde sighed. In Ireland it always seemed to be raining. Presently Meara rounded the corner of the hut and walked past her with only a brusque nod.

Meara knew who her rival was. And resented it.

"Meara." Rosamunde's voice stayed her. The taller woman turned, scowling at Rosamunde from a tear-stained face. Rosamunde chose her words carefully. "When I am gone, O'Lear will forget me. He wants me only because he cannot have me. 'Tis a challenge to his manhood, I suppose."

"Who says he cannot have you?" demanded Meara harshly. "If he wants you, he will take you! And he wants you because you are beautiful," she mumbled, unconsciously touching her own scarred cheek.

Rosamunde sighed. "Meara, how can Brian think me beautiful? My body is as big as a washtub!"

"Brian knows you will soon be slender again," said Meara significantly, and Rosamunde had no answer for that.

She got up and went inside, to breakfast on watery broth and oatcakes, and to wonder what drove O'Lear. Hot-tempered, kind, for the most part insensitive. She guessed he had loved many women—and stayed with none.

When she asked Meara about that—for Meara had followed her inside—Meara was rude to her. Although there was work to be done outside, Meara stayed stubbornly in the hut. She cast smoldering glances in Rosamunde's direction and banged pots about to show her displeasure.

Finding the tiny hut uncomfortable with Meara in a rage, Rosamunde went out again and sat down upon a stone and studied the soft gray clouds that spun across the Irish sky. Rodrigue came back and gave her a frowning look. Rosamunde well knew what was bothering him, but forebore to talk about it. He spoke quietly to Meara, and the two strode off together. Soon Rosamunde, walking to the cliffs, saw the little fishing boat bobbing about in the sea below. Rodrigue and Meara were throwing out their nets, while she pondered.

How could you tell a man who was not your own that he stood a good chance of being killed by another man who was not your own either—and all for possession of
442

yourself, whom neither possessed or were likely to possess? She shook her head, trying to clear away the cobwebs, but as the days passed she was no nearer to a solution.

She had now begun to walk heavily as she prepared their meager meals, setting wooden bowls upon the rude table and beside it their wooden spoons. Rodrigue brought fresh grasses for their pallets and watched her anxiously as the stormy winter progressed. Sheets of rain fell, and when it was not raining—or sleeting—the sky was overcast and leaden. It was a cheerless winter, and Rosamunde, for all she looked forward to holding Harry's child in her arms, was borne down with depression.

O'Lear stayed away. For that Rosamunde was grateful, for his presence upset Rodrigue, and she had become more and more fond of her Spanish captain, thankful for his unfailing kindness—and grateful that he had made no more attempts to make love to her. She knew he watched her anxiously. Once he muttered that her time was coming and there was no midwife about. Rosamunde gave him a clear steady green-eyed look and told him she was not afraid—Meara had helped the sheep with difficult deliveries when she was but a young thing; she remembered birthing well. That was all very well, Rodrigue said, but that was sheep; she was a fragile woman and he was afraid for her. He cursed the gray weather and the cold and his own helplessness. Ever conscious of his concern for her, Rosamunde's demeanor toward him changed and grew noticeably gentle. He was a wordly man, she told herself, and she a wordly woman, and it was hard for them to be so cut off from civilization.

Indeed, they were completely cut off from news in Ireland, unaware that Europe was fast sinking into the Thirty Years War. In France the Huguenots had risen—and been crushed. In faraway America the Virginia Colonists struggled to tame a wilderness, while to the north of them a tiny town called Plymouth fought for existence. And in England King James was well embarked upon a course of corruption and tyranny which would eventually lead the British people to rise up in a bloody civil war.

443

But in Ireland Rosamunde and Rodrigue were concerned only with the miserable weather, the lack of food and comfort, the mending of fishing nets, the day-to-day problems of staying alive to meet each new dawn's challenge.

Once when the fishing was very bad and they had only crusts to eat, when Meara was out looking for roots or whatever was to be had, Rodrigue turned to Rosamunde as she sat despondently by the tiny peat fire and his face twisted.

"I am sorry," he whispered, "for all the evil that I have brought you."

Rosamunde looked up, startled by the raw anguish in his tone. "You have brought me no evil, Rodrigue. Indeed, you have always been kind to me. In Amsterdam," she added softly, "you gave me a lovely dress."

Rodrigue turned away as if he could not bear to look at her. "I am sorry for that too," he muttered.

"What?" She looked at him sharply. "You asked no price for it. 'Twas given out of kindness so that I might not appear in public looking like a domestic servant."

"No." His voice was ragged, ashamed. "It was a gown a man's mistress might wear—but not his wife. Not in Majorca. It showed I had no respect for you, no intention of making you my wife. All aboard the *Santa Cecilia* knew this. My claim of betrothal was only made so that I need not share you. They understood."

She was astonished. Such a gown would have been accounted sumptuous in England and worn by great ladies. Wistfully she looked down at the tattered green velvet gown, hardly recognizable now, at the torn and faded petticoat that had once been bravely shimmering red silk. She remembered with a pang the dainty green shoes with red heels that had been lost in the sea, the green leather gloves of which she had been so proud. "Great ladies in Spain wear black, don't they?" she asked slowly.

Rodrigue looked thoroughly miserable. " 'Tis the custom of the gentry. In Spain ladies wear black and very dark colors."

"So you were trying to degrade me in your own sight?" Her voice was sorrowful.

"I tried to—but it was useless." Inexorably his confessional went on. "From the first I fought my feelings for you. I told myself you were but another man's strumpet."

"And so I was, from the world's point of view."

"From *my* point of view. I wanted you—but on *my* terms."

Her expression was wry, remembering that whatever his feelings, he had abducted her, ravished her.

"So that was why you did not want your officers to know that I was a woman," she guessed shrewdly. "You had thought to take me even to Majorca posing as a man, even perhaps among your family . . . while at night . . . " Her voice reproached him. "Rodrigue, how could you?"

"Yes." He quivered as if she had struck him, but when he lifted his bowed head his face was set and haggard. "You have every right to despise me," he said intensely.

Rosamunde sighed. "I do not despise you, Rodrigue. I pity you."

He flinched.

"But all those aboard the *Santa Cecilia* are dead," she pointed out reasonably. "Whatever you have done, there are none to remember."

"*I* remember!"

"When I have borne my child and the ship comes and we can leave this place, you will soon forget me. I will be gone and you can go back to your usual way of life, whatever that is."

"But I do not want to go back to it!" he cried despairingly. "I want—"

Rosamunde regarded him steadily. The set of her jaw was such as to keep him at a distance. "I will not be your mistress, Rodrigue. I have told you that before."

Rodrigue rose and walked restlessly to the door. He opened it and peered down the path up which Meara would come. There was no one in sight.

Abruptly he closed the door and stood with his back

to her, hands clasped behind him. It was an irresolute pose, and the tension in his posture told her of the turmoil raging within him. When he spoke he did not turn to look at her.

"You are a heretic," he said quietly.

"I am no heretic. I am Church of England!" Rosamunde was indignant.

Rodrigue shrugged. "In my country it is accounted the same thing. There the Inquisition still prevails. We burn heretics."

Rosamunde felt a chill go through her. She remembered stories of the burning of Protestants in England during Bloody Mary's reign.

"If I am to give you my name," he said, "I do not ask that you accept my faith. But I do ask that you give lip service to it, else there will be reprisals—against you, against me, against my family. The Inquisition has a long reach."

If I am to give you my name! This proud Spaniard was proposing marriage! Rosamunde was stunned.

Rodrigue turned to her. "Your child will need a name, Rosamunde. I propose to give it mine."

"Rodrigue . . . " She did not know what to say to him. Her green eyes filled with tears. "You know that I am—that I have been—"

"Hush, do not say it," he said, coming over to her and touching his fingers to her lips. "I care nothing for what you have been. And as for the child you will bear, knowing you, I am sure its father was a good man."

"He was," she said wistfully. "A very good man."

"Then it is settled. The priest will marry us! When spring comes, I will find a ship to carry us away from this place. I will take you with me to Majorca—as my wife, Rosamunde. None need know the child is not mine. Indeed, I will claim it as my own."

Through wet lashes she looked up at him, knowing what this proposal had cost this proud man. "Rodrigue," she said huskily. "I am honored that you would want me for your wife, but—O'Lear will be back, and if he learns that I have wed you, he will kill you."

"O'Lear is not coming back."

"I did not tell you, Rodrigue, but he said he would be back for me—after the baby is born."

"O'Lear is not coming back," he repeated. "Father Paul tells me he has been taken."

Taken? Rosamunde felt a pang for the wild O'Lear, cooped up in some filthy jail, or tortured and hanged. He had given her a woolen cloak and a kindly smile. She thought he might have given her a little piece of his heart as well, and was sad for him.

"You are not grieving for O'Lear?" Rodrigue asked sharply.

She looked up. "He was kind to us, Rodrigue," she reminded him. "He brought us food—and clothing. Does Meara know?"

"I do not know," he said irritably. "If she knows, she conceals it well."

"She would," said Rosamunde sadly. "No wonder she has been so withdrawn of late."

"I am telling you that _you_ at least need think no more of Brian O'Lear; he is finished, he will not cross our paths again. But you, Rosamunde, you are young. You have all your life before you. And think of your child. Would you have your child brought up without a father, adrift in the world? I have a house and lands in Majorca. It is a lovely place, all blue seawater and blue sky and white beaches and olive trees. Could you give your child that?"

Rosamunde studied her hands. She knew she could assure her child of nothing, for her own future was uncertain. "I will not deceive you, Rodrigue. I am very fond of you, but—I do not love you as a wife should."

Rodrigue knelt beside her. His voice was eager. "You could learn to love me. I am a patient man." She gave him a wry look. Many virtues Rodrigue might possess, but certainly patience was not one of them. "I will wait for your love," he insisted. "See, you have proof of my patience, for though I have yearned to hold you in my arms, I have not touched you, not since . . . "

Not since the night he had taken her with such furious abandon on board the doomed *Santa Cecilia*.

"It is true," she said, "that I cannot fault your behavior since we were flung upon this shore." Her mind was in turmoil. She was trying to imagine herself as a Spanish lady with a house in Majorca, a sea captain's wife. Rodrigue had saved her from the English law, he had plucked her drowning from the wild sea. She owed him much. Still, another face kept crowding into her memory, a dark sardonic face, strong, gray-eyed and smiling—Harry's face. She told herself she must be practical. Her child would need a name and a home and a father. She was trembling when Rodrigue swept her hand to his lips and kissed it.

"Rosamunde," he entreated. "Be sensible. You know as well as I that it is the only way."

"You are right," she agreed hoarsely, pushing away that dark smiling face that haunted her dreams. "I will do it. And I will be a good and true wife to you, Rodrigue— by all I hold dear, I swear it."

Rodrigue straightened and his brow lost its furrow. Instantly he was all energy. He looked very young and alive. "I will go for the priest tomorrow," he said.

And so Rosamunde and Rodrigue were married, not in a church nor even in a house, but atop a wild cliff in Ireland in a gray winter landscape with the waves booming on the rocks below, and their faces turned to the south where far away lay the sunny land of Majorca, waiting for their safe return.

Rosamunde was wearing her tattered velvet dress and the warm woolen cloak O'Lear had given her. Meara had given her a sprig of myrtle to carry, and Rodrigue slipped on her finger a ring that was old in his family and had been with him all through the shipwreck. It was a gold signet ring with a dull-red stone, and though Rodrigue's fingers were slender for a man, Rosamunde must needs wear it upon her middle finger, though he had worn it always on his little finger.

She looked down at that gold ring and unbidden thought of Harry . . . one day she had thought to wear his
448

betrothal ring upon her white hand, to claim his old and honored name. She pushed the thought away guiltily as Rodrigue clasped her in his arms, gently, but with the surging urgency of a drowning man. "You will not regret this day," he whispered triumphantly against her blowing hair.

She looked up, smiling into his eyes, and made her own silent promises, vows she would never break. Father Paul gazed on them kindly and pronounced them wed under the laws of God—if not of this country—and Meara, who had languished ever since the word came that O'Lear had been taken, roused herself and laughed and clapped her strong hands and seized brother Patrick and Father Paul by the arms and brought them back to the hut, where she served a fat fish for the bridal supper.

It seemed incredible to Rosamunde that she was married . . . and to a man whose native tongue she did not even know.

Rodrigue set about correcting that at once. Every day he tutored her in Catalan Spanish and in Majorcan. Languages, she found, came as easily to her as they did to him. And it gave her an interest now that she was heavy and lumbering about.

Basically their marriage changed nothing. She was far gone in her pregnancy; Meara slept where she always had in the one-room hut, Rosamunde across the room, Rodrigue at the door in case of trouble. But Rodrigue walked straighter, he took a proprietary interest in everything she did, he was quicker to give her orders than before. She told herself wryly that he was Spanish, and in Majorca women were chattels.

But—her unborn child would have a name now. And a father.

32   *Early spring brought a ship. The priest came*
panting up to the shepherd's hut and told them of it. It
was anchored in the bay at the fishing village that lay
down the coast; he had been surreptitiously performing
a christening in the village and had seen it cast anchor.

"What flag?" Rodrigue asked anxiously, and his eyes
lit up when Father Paul replied, "The flag of Spain."

Rosamunde was near her time now, and Rodrigue hated
to leave her. But he left Meara with dozens of peremptory instructions, which caused Meara's eyebrows to ele-
vate, and Rosamunde to smile to herself at his concern.
Then he left for the ruined abbey. In company of the
priest's brother, Patrick the thatcher—for Father Paul
was too tired to attempt that long walk again—he slipped
into the village that night. They managed to avoid the
English authorities, and Rodrigue sought out the Spanish
ship's captain. The ship was one he knew, the *Infanta* out
of Barcelona. She was a rough sailer, and he had instant
forebodings at the thought of Rosamunde, heavy with
child, being thrown about in a tiny cabin . . . and what
if there should be a storm? He shuddered.

The *Infanta's* captain he did not know, but he was
greeted warmly, for they had mutual friends and Captain
Navarro had heard of Captain Rodrigue Avilo. Rodrigue
explained that he did not wish passage on the *Infanta,*
because his wife was near her time and he did not trust
the child to be born on shipboard in this gusty weather.
But he did wish Captain Navarro to carry a message to
his father and his partners in Barcelona, advising them of
the *Santa Cecilia's* fate, and to beg of the captain's char-

ity some clothing and provisions, for they had lost everything when the *Santa Cecilia* went down.

Graciously Captain Navarro, who was Portuguese, agreed to Rodrigue's requests. He knew one of the Barcelona partners slightly and had often heard fine reports of Captain Rodrigue Avilo of the *Santa Cecilia*. He expressed regrets at the loss of Rodrigue's ship, but he seemed a little uneasy that Rodrigue should discover that he was trading with the English—as his arrival in this port plainly showed. Rodrigue promptly set that fear at rest, telling Captain Navarro that he would be forever in his debt if he but had a ship's doctor who would come to the shepherd's hut and advise him on the state of Rosamunde's health.

Captain Navarro explained that the ship's doctor had died of an unfortunate accident on the way here—out of deference to the doctor's memory he did not elaborate that the doctor had become so drunk he had fallen overboard and drowned before anyone could reach him. But at Rodrigue's disappointed look, he suggested that he could easily arrange better quarters in the village for him than a shepherd's hut.

Rodrigue didn't doubt they'd be better, but he could imagine what Rosamunde would say if they were to bring disaster upon the brothers and Meara, who had helped them so selflessly. Nor did he care to explain to the English authorities his swift departure from the Cornish coast, with the Wild Rose aboard. Questions could bring discovery, and Rosamunde was still wanted by the English law. His jaw clenched. In Majorca she would be beyond their reach!

"I would be quite content with clothing and provisions," he told the Portuguese captain. And Captain Navarro, curious to see this lady who could hold a man who could go to Majorca on the grim shores of Ireland, accompanied the two sailors who packed in provisions to the shepherd's hut—provisions that would be paid for by the Barcelonan partners and charged to Rodrigue's account.

Captain Navarro saw Rosamunde's beautiful face—by

451

candlelight, for he had brought a gift of candles to replace the weak rushlights they had been using—and understood at once Rodrigue's desire to take no chances with his lady. He was moved, in fact, to send the next day some good Canary from his private stock to Captain Avilo's lovely wife.

Meara could scarcely believe this bounty. Cheeses and *bacon?* Fresh-baked bread from the village, and salted fish and wine—all packed up to them by the sweating sailors. Her eyes gleamed when Rodrigue bestowed on her one of the handsome cloaks brought from the *Infanta* by Captain Navarro. It was a man's cloak, for there were no women's garments on board. Meara murmured a prayer of thanksgiving in Gaelic, folded the cloak carefully, and set about preparing what for her was a feast.

"You have no midwife?" asked the Portuguese captain of Rodrigue during his visit.

"No." Rodrigue sighed. "For we are reluctant to call attention to ourselves here—it might endanger our friends, who disagree with the English law."

The Portuguese captain had easy ways. He shrugged at the evil snarl of English laws—his shrug said Spain's might be no better. "You should now have plenty of provisions for a short stay," he decided. "My sister ship, the *Coronada,* will be along in a few weeks, and you can leave aboard her. Doubtless your sentry, the priest, will see her sail into the bay."

Rodrigue brightened. "That is good news. Once the child is born, I would leave speedily!"

Captain Navarro gave him a sympathetic look. Any man from the sunny land of Majorca would surely be overjoyed to be quit of Ireland with its gray dampness and gloomy weather!

One of the *Infanta*'s sailors, a Morisco who had made the trek to the shepherd's hut carrying provisions, heard Rodrigue say that. As Captain Navarro prepared to depart, the Morisco turned for a last look at the beautiful face of the pregnant woman. Ah, he too would have stayed in Ireland to keep this woman safe! He sighed. There was an almond-eyed beauty waiting for him in Bar-

452

celona—if he but had the money for her hand. Her father was greedy. He wondered for a moment what this fair-haired beauty had cost Captain Avilo. Ordinary women might have dowries, but beauties must often be bought.

Captain Navarro kissed Rosamunde's hand gallantly as he left. For all that Rodrigue had lost his ship, at that moment Navarro envied him.

Rodrigue himself carried a load of bacon and wine over to the brothers at the abbey. He distributed his new largess as if he were accustomed to giving gifts. Rosamunde was proud of him. And she shrewdly guessed what it must have cost him to see the *Infanta* sail away without him —and this he had done because of her. She must see that he never regretted his bargain.

Meara had been distant with Rosamunde since O'Lear's visit, unbending only for the wedding, but the gift of the cloak and Captain Navarro's arrival with provisions seemed to break the ice. Now as Rosamunde's time grew closer her Irish heart warmed to the pale English beauty about to bear a child on foreign shores. She talked to Rosamunde and encouraged her, insisting that "birthing" was no great thing—look, all the animals bore their young alone!

Rosamunde smiled at Meara, big and determined and almost a savage herself. She guessed Meara could bear a child alone—if only she'd a father for it!

"Have you heard from O'Lear?" she asked, knowing that was the subject nearest to Meara's heart.

"I have heard Brian is imprisoned in a castle far to the south and may be brought north," said Meara, who often slipped down to the abbey to ask Father Paul for news.

The next day a former parishioner who came to the abbey to discuss a wedding next week brought word that O'Lear was indeed being moved, and Father Paul hastened over to tell Meara. Meara straightened up at the news and her eyes flashed. After Father Paul left, she went and got the stout staff which stood in the corner by her sleeping pallet and which she had always guarded so jealously. As Rosamunde watched, she gave the wood a twist, and Rosamunde saw that although it looked to be an innocent staff, in reality it was a scabbard and within reposed a keen-edged sword.

"I stole it," said Meara calmly, in answer to Rosamunde's curious glance. "While I worked for the English. And when I fled I took it with me."

"And what will you do with it, Meara?"

Meara had finished inspecting the blade. Now she tested it for sharpness against her finger, drew blood and sucked her finger before she turned to answer Rosamunde.

"I go to break Brian out of prison," she said in as calm a voice as if she was remarking on the weather. "Or if I should find him upon the road, to fall upon his jailers and set him free."

Rosamunde, heavy with child, felt a tingle of admiration for Meara, going out alone through wild country to face the English guns. There was a kind of glory about Meara this morning that made one forget her scars.

"You will die of your love for him, Meara," Rosamunde warned huskily—but she knew she would have done the same, for she had felt the same way about Harry.

"That well may be," said Meara in a grim voice. "But someday I will die anyway—all of us do. Rather would I die fighting to free Brian than of cold and starvation some winter when the fishing is bad—or locked in an English jail." Her bitter tone took no account of the fact that Rosamunde was English. This was Meara's wild heart that was speaking—and she spoke for Ireland as it had been before the invaders came.

Rosamunde, who was all English and would cheerfully have given ten years of her life to bring a certain English highwayman back to her, was silent in the presence of such great love—and such great hatred. Rather sadly she watched Meara pack a bit of food and start out. "You aren't taking enough," she told her, and pressed on her a bottle of wine.

"You'll need the rest here," said Meara bluntly. "For who knows when the ship will come? Anyway"—her blue eyes hardened—"I'll steal what I need from the lords of the land." She gave Rosamunde a sudden hard look that
454

said those lords of the land were Rosamunde's people—invaders, all of them!

"Aren't you going to tell Rodrigue goodbye?" wondered Rosamunde. "He'll be back from the abbey soon." For Rodrigue had walked back to the abbey with Father Paul, who had brought the news about O'Lear to the shepherd's hut.

"Nay, he'll try to dissuade me," said Meara carelessly. "You tell him goodbye for me." A sudden frown went over her face, a look of indecision. " 'Tis near your time," she muttered. "I promised I'd help ye, but I doubt I will be back in time to help you with your birthing." She ignored the fact that she might never be coming back, that she might die out there.

Rosamunde swallowed. That Meara should think of her at a time like this! "I can do it alone," she insisted sturdily. She had no idea whether she could do it alone or not, but she knew how she would have felt if it was Harry out there being moved from one castle keep to another.

Meara's brow cleared at so much fortitude.

"Aye, ye're a brave lass. Ye'll do fine," she agreed. She gave Rosamunde's shoulder a swift awkward hug, grasped her staff and provisions and swung through the door of the hut. Rosamunde stepped outside to watch her go, a tall gaunt woman moving with great determination. Her long stride carried her rapidly over the brow of a low hill and out of sight—hurrying away to save a man who did not love her. For a long time Rosamunde stood and studied the place where that strong yet tragic figure had disappeared across the horizon. Then she sighed and went back into the hut. Though she had given her friendship to Meara without reservation, she knew that Meara—who regarded her sometimes as a lost waif to be pitied and sometimes as a member of a conquering race to be scorned—would always have mixed feelings where she was concerned.

Rodrigue was enraged when he returned to find Meara gone.

"What?" he stormed. "When your time is so near? I
455

was counting on her to deliver the baby—she has told me she is proficient in such things."

"Proficient she may be, but present—not likely," said Rosamunde dryly. "She loves O'Lear, Rodrigue, and must find a way to help him if she can."

"I will go after her," he cried. "She cannot leave you like this—she promised to help with the birth!"

"No, you must not do that." Rosamunde laid a restraining hand on his arm. "She feels she can rescue O'Lear if she can but catch up with him as they are moving him."

Rodrigue gave her an amazed look. "But there will be a strong guard!"

"Even so, she must try it."

"But they will kill her!"

"She could not live with herself if she did not try," said Rosamunde simply.

"I cannot believe what I am hearing! A woman—to go up against a strong armed guard?"

"Yes."

Rodrigue shook his head. Then he shot her a keen look. "Are you saying that if I were taken, you—alone—would rush out to rescue me?" he challenged.

"I would try to get help," said Rosamunde reasonably. "Failing that, I would come for you alone. But please do not endanger yourself at the moment—pray wait until I am lighter!" she added with an attempt at humor.

A mixture of emotions played across Rodrigue's dark narrow face, and as if overcome by them, he strode toward her, enfolded her in his arms. "Nothing must happen to you. *Nothing*," he muttered.

"Nothing will happen to me. Come, let us walk about outside. The air will do me good."

He kept a sharp watch on her as they walked, would not let her go so far as the cliffs.

"This is far enough," he said. "Now you will rest for a while. Sit down on this smooth rock here." He brushed it off with his hand.

Rosamunde sank down; the short walk had tired her.

"We cannot do it alone," he said, running a distracted hand through his dark hair.

"Why not? Other women have."

"There are times when bravery is not enough. I will try to get a midwife from the village. Father Paul could bring her."

Rosamunde gave him a hopeless look. She knew the priest would advise against that, for the village had but one midwife and her doings were closely watched by the authorities. They had turned up more than one rebel that way—by following the midwife to some old ruin or distant campfire where some stout young outlaw awaited the birth of his first child. "Perhaps Meara will come back in time," she said, to comfort him. " 'Tis said they're bringing O'Lear north."

Rodrigue sighed and gazed at her tenderly, seated there on a big stone beneath the scudding gray sky with the wind blowing back her hair and her face looking almost ethereal. He had come to love this woman so much. If she should die in giving birth—! He turned away, unable to bear the thought.

"Rodrigue." Rosamunde had guessed what he was thinking, and her voice was tender. "I promise not to die. The baby will be here soon and we will all be going to Majorca."

"We will walk back," he said gruffly. "And tonight *I* will prepare dinner—you will sit and watch."

Rodrigue took tender care of her, but the baby was tardy in coming. Days passed. Each day Rosamunde grew larger, each day it was harder for her to get about, and her back ached. Spring had brightened the Irish landscape with a rich green, and the grass had sprung up everywhere like velvet. Rodrigue was never gone from the hut for long now, and his dark eyes had a watchful look. He still meant to get a midwife for Rosamunde—if there was time.

He was carrying a wooden bucket to the well for water when he heard Rosamunde scream. A tremor went through him as if he had been shot. He flung away the bucket and raced back to the hut. As he burst through the door he saw that Rosamunde was bent double, clinging to the wooden

457

table. She swayed and he leaped across the room and caught her.

"My God, is it your time?" he cried hoarsely.

Scarce able to speak, she nodded and gasped. "Yes. The baby is coming. Oh, Rodrigue—help me."

"I will go for the midwife!" he cried.

"No, that would take hours—oh, don't leave me here alone."

He watched her wildly from a white face. Gradually the pain subsided and she was able to collect her wits. "I feel better now," she said.

"I will take you to the midwife. I will carry you there."

Rosamunde shook her head. "We would never make it. Do you want me to have the baby on some cold damp hillside? Even if we reached the village, we might well be arrested! 'Tis best we stay here." She pushed him away, stood more firmly on her feet. "We can do it—together."

Rodrigue gave her a tormented look. His sole knowledge of giving birth came from helping his mare to foal, and from some questions he had sent by way of the priest, who had carried the answers from the village midwife. But he reacted promptly and with decision.

With a long arm he swept the table clear of wooden bowls and picked her up in his arms, laid her gently upon it. He folded his cloak and put it under her head for a pillow. She watched in wonder as he hurried about, heating water, gathering up the strips of clean linen Meara had hoarded for this occasion.

"Gather up the bowls," she said. "You may trip over them." And then another great pain struck her and rendered her breathless. Rodrigue sprang forward and loosened her clothing, lifted her skirts, and sponged her face with a wet cloth as she lay writhing.

The pains were spaced far apart at first, and Rosamunde had time between to consider her life. How fortunate she had been! she thought. To have known two such men—Rodrigue and Harry. Rodrigue, all kindliness and worried attention, was at her side, and when the pains came Harry's face seemed to hover near her, encouraging her.

458

"Rodrigue," she said in gratitude. "I—" And her voice ended in a smothered shriek as another great pain rent her body.

"It will be all right, Rosamunde. It will pass," Rodrigue promised in a tense voice. Beads of sweat gleamed on his own forehead as he watched her anxiously.

As the hours went by Rodrigue cursed himself for not going for the midwife at once. He knew a deadly fear as Rosamunde's pains grew worse. Afternoon deepened into dusk and dusk into darkness, and still she strained and cried out. A weak moon rose. The candles were nearly gone, for Rodrigue had been prodigal of them in this emergency. As they guttered, he lit rushlights. They flickered like fireflies in the darkness of the stone hut where the young woman in tattered green velvet lay in labor on a wooden table.

The pains were savage now, deep twisting pains that seemed to tear through Rosamunde's very flesh. They washed over her in waves of bright agony. Her nails bit into Rodrigue's hard comforting palms, and she could see by the flickering rushlight the gleam of sweat on his dark face as she drifted up out of wrenching blackness, as the time between pains grew shorter.

So fierce was the tearing within her that she had begun to think on death. Death was a river, men said. A dark boatman rowed you to the other side, and that farther shore was peopled with all those you had loved and lost. Harry was there. . . . Perhaps she would not wait for the boatman, perhaps she would just plunge into that river and let the current sweep her across. . .

Her fantasies grew wilder. She was walking down the wide stairway of Kenwarren House once again—and miraculously Harry was there. As she cried out to him in joy, a pain knifed through her stomach and she saw that it was Louisa, laughing and holding a bloody sword. Then someone swept Louisa back and she was looking into the face of Lord Matthew Waverclay. He was laughing and mocking her—now he was holding her baby high above his head beyond her reach. She screamed hysterically as he dashed it down the stairs.

"It is all right," Rodrigue cried distractedly. "Rosamunde, it is all right—I am here!"

But she did not hear him. The pain, the pressure had driven her half out of her head.

She did not hear the hut door burst open, did not notice Rodrigue's start as he turned to see who it was.

In the gray dawn Meara stood there. Gaunt and purposeful and travel-stained. She flung aside her heavy staff and moved to the table where Rosamunde lay straining.

"I heard her scream from yonder hill," she said tersely. "Stand aside, Rodrigue. Let me see how things are progressing."

Rodrigue moved aside a step to let Meara take over, but he kept Rosamunde's white fingers locked in his own. He could only hope he was giving her strength, for a terrible fear that she would die clutched at him.

"How long since the pains started?" asked Meara sharply.

"This afternoon."

Meara muttered something. She wiped off Rosamunde's brow with a damp cloth and murmured soothingly.

Rosamunde, swimming up from that dark sea of pain, recognized her. "Meara," she said wearily, then remembered Meara's mission to free O'Lear. "How did you find Brian?" she asked weakly.

"Already escaped and running before the hounds," reported Meara proudly. "They'll not catch him."

"No," agreed Rosamunde more strongly. "They'll not." And clenched her teeth as the agony seized her again. She heard herself screaming and could not stop. The pain seemed to surround her in bright waves. This time it did not go away. It stayed and stayed and lifted her up on a terrible wild sea of agony. She forgot where she was—she was being torn apart. "Harry!" she screamed. "Harry!"

White to the lips, Rodrigue gripped her hands and listened. His Rosamunde, in labor, was crying out for another man. His Rosamunde was giving birth to another man's child. *She loved another, she would always love another.* This was borne in on him in a terrible
460

loneliness as with all his strength he prayed that she would live.

"Can't you help her?" he demanded hoarsely of Meara

Meara's jaw was clenched; she shook her head. "I'm doing all I can." And then, with a cry of joy, "See—the baby's coming!"

In a last great burst of agony, the child slipped into Meara's competent waiting hands. Rosamunde sagged, sinking down and down into a spent, merciful oblivion. But Rodrigue's knees went weak. He disengaged those white fingers and staggered out into the open air and threw himself down upon the ground, for his legs would suddenly not hold him. Then he scrambled up in terror—would she live? The baby was born, but would she live?

He ran back into the hut, almost colliding with Meara, who was cradling a small bundle in her arms. From the bundle came a thin protesting wail.

"Ye've a daughter," Meara told him. Her eyes were shining.

"But Rosamunde," cried Rodrigue hoarsely. "What of her?"

"She is resting," said Meara, facing him down with her stern manner. "Do not disturb her."

"But is she all right?"

"She has had a hard time—but she will live."

Silently Rodrigue moved to the table and stood looking down at Rosamunde. The rushlights were flickering out in the murky dawn. A pinkish-gray light came through the hut's single window and bathed the woman lying exhausted on the table with a ghostly light. Though his ears still rang with her cry of "Harry! Harry!" his gaze was very tender—and very thankful. She looked so fragile and delicate as she lay crumpled there with her fair hair streaming back, wet from perspiration. He was reminded of the day he had wrested her from the sea's savage grip. She had seemed to him a mermaid then—a magical creature. Strangely, she still seemed so. Without a word he leaned over and pressed a kiss onto that wet pale cheek, felt her dark lashes brush his lips like angel wings.

She would live. Meara had promised it.

Tiredly, Rosamunde fought her way up out of the abyss, with memories of the pain-that-was flickering in and out of her consciousness like a shutter swinging idly in the wind. She seemed to remember strange dreams, terrible ones. She seemed to remember wading in the river of death, and feeling herself nearly swept away by the current. And Harry had been there, she had sensed his presence—no, that was Rodrigue.

She opened her eyes and let them drift shut again. Dawn was breaking and she could hear a child's thin cry. *Her* child. She tried to lift her hand to reach out for the child, to comfort it, but she had not the strength. But now the sea of anguish was washing away. And out of that terrible sea—wilder and darker than the great storm that had brought them to this coast—had been born her child.

"Rosamunde, you have a daughter," she heard Meara say.

A daughter! Smiling, exhausted, Rosamunde closed her eyes again. And drifted on a sea of remembered pain.

But when the sun rose, cutting through the murk, the small lovely child that lay in her sweat-soaked arms and suckled at her full breasts was worth all the pain, worth all the effort.

Rosamunde gazed upon her daughter with loving eyes.

"I will call her Elaine," she said softly, "for that was my mother's name."

"Rodrigue." Meara turned to him. "Now that a name has been chosen, would you not like to hold your daughter?"

Rodrigue drew a deep breath. Harry was dead, he reminded himself. And Rosamunde was his. "Yes," he said strongly, reaching out his arms to take the baby. "I would like to hold my daughter—my small Elena."

Rosamunde heard him say "my daughter" and her heart was full.

Rodrigue cradled the child in his arms, then carefully returned her to Rosamunde. She smiled up at him. "I promised you I would not die," she said.

Rodrigue bent and kissed her, and Meara watched with brooding eyes. The small baby had awakened an old

462

ache in her heart. O'Lear's baby should be in *her* arms now, just as O'Lear should all these months have been in her bed—and was not. No, all his thoughts, all his desires, were centered on this moon-fair Englishwoman. Meara liked Rosamunde. She was steady, proud, and openhearted. Nor could she fault Rosamunde's behavior when O'Lear was about, making a great oaf of himself over her. But before such dawning happiness, she flinched —as if she had been hurt.

As the days passed, Meara licked in silence the wounds life had given her, and at night dreamed of the wild O'Lear.

Rosamunde, now that her child was safely born, had discovered life again. She mended readily—she bloomed. On light feet she ran to the cliffs to watch the fishing boat carrying Rodrigue and Meara. She did not mourn for Harry now—she had a daughter to fill her empty life. All Ireland seemed to be celebrating Elaine's birth. The skies were bluer, the grass was greener—even Meara, now that the fishing was good, was filling out again. The gaunt angles of her body were becoming less sharp, more womanly.

Rosamunde would see Meara striding up the hill from the bay beside Rodrigue, carrying the catch as he carried the nets that would need to be mended, and always she was struck by the Irish woman's lithe distinctive walk, the proud way she held her head.

And always the regretful thought occurred to her: *Meara would be a beauty, were it not for her scars.* Sometimes she wondered if O'Lear had ever really looked at Meara. For when Meara turned her head so that only the left side of her face showed and the scarred right side was hidden, there was a clean beauty of line there that matched her flashing sapphire eyes. Her hair was long and thick and coarse and shining, with blue gleams on its black surface in the sunshine. How could O'Lear have missed it? A warrior's woman was Meara, though her chosen warrior seemed unaware of it.

It was a great day for Rosamunde and Rodrigue when Father Paul came puffing up to the shepherd's hut to

463

tell them importantly that the *Coronada*, sister ship to Captain Navarro's *Infanta*, had cast anchor in the bay and was trading goods with the English. There had been a man dying of dysentery aboard her when she had sailed in, and Father Paul, surreptitiously solemnizing a marriage, had been spirited aboard the *Coronada* under the very noses of the English, to give the man last rites. He had taken that opportunity to speak to the *Coronada*'s captain about their sailing with him.

Rodrigue would have departed for the village instantly, but Father Paul suggested it might be better to wait until tomorrow, when a cabin would have been prepared for them. Rosamunde guessed shrewdly that the ship might be overrun with Englishmen today, and that it might be better for Meara and Father Paul if she and Rodrigue slipped aboard after the first crush of interest subsided.

Meara was glum about their going. She had become very fond of Rosamunde, and she adored the baby. She kept finding reasons to delay them as they made ready to leave next day, and Rosamunde tried ineffectually to cheer her.

"Come, Rosamunde," called Rodrigue impatiently from outside the hut. "We have dallied long enough. We must reach the village before dusk."

"I am coming," Rosamunde called back. She turned to say goodbye to Meara before she picked up the baby and left, but Meara had disappeared.

Rosamunde stepped to the door. "Did you see where Meara went?"

"No, I was looking over these nets. We are leaving them in good shape for Meara. Are you ready?"

"As soon as I get the baby. But Rodrigue, we cannot leave without telling Meara goodbye."

"Perhaps she has gone down to the fishing boat," said Rodrigue. "I will go and find her." He hurried down the path that led to the bay.

Rosamunde went in and looked at the baby. Sleeping soundly. Meara was passionately fond of the child. Rosamunde guessed that Meara could not bear to part with little Elaine and had gone down to the boat to brood.

Ah, well, Rodrigue would find her and bring her back. She went back outside, stood in the sunlight, and studied the gentle gray clouds that promised rain. There seemed always to be rain in Ireland.

She was arrested by a deep voice and whirled.

"O'Lear!" she gasped.

Out of nowhere he seemed to have sprung. He looked very fit—they must have fed him well in jail. Or perhaps he had roasted an English sheep or two since his escape.

"I have come back," he said, lounging toward her, a red-bearded giant who seemed to fill the sky with his bulk. His bold gaze was admiring her new slenderness. "And now I will keep my promise and show you Ireland."

Show her Ireland! She must keep him talking while she thought.

"They told us you were taken, but Meara went to find you and came back saying you had escaped. She went looking for you, to break you out of jail."

"To break me out? Meara?" O'Lear looked amused. "No woman need break *me* out of jail. Sure, there's no jail can hold the O'Lear for long!"

Rosamunde didn't doubt it, but she wished he would stop walking toward her with that look in his blue eyes. "We all thought you would be far away by now."

"I was. But I came back for you." He was reaching for her arm.

Rosamunde drew back. "I—I cannot go with you, Brian," she said desperately.

O'Lear's brow was clouding up. "What's this?" he scowled.

"I am married. Rodrigue is now my husband."

" 'Tis a lie!" shouted O'Lear.

Suddenly Meara appeared, coming around the corner of the hut, carrying her fishing spear. She must have been listening. Rosamunde guessed she had been crouching there all along, watching O'Lear's approach. " 'Tis the truth, Brian," she said. "Father Paul married them before the babe was born."

O'Lear advanced threateningly on Rosamunde. "Then I will make you a widow!" he roared.

Out of the corner of her eye Rosamunde could see Rodrigue running up the hill path. He was pulling out his sword as he ran, and the blade flashed silver in the sun.

O'Lear saw him too and headed in that direction with long strides.

Before he had gone three steps, an iron cooking pot glanced off his shoulder. O'Lear turned with teeth bared, looking for a new antagonist.

Meara stood calmly watching him.

"*I* threw the pot, Brian," she announced in a fierce voice.

"And lucky 'twas you," growled O'Lear menacingly. "For I'd have skewered anyone else!"

Meara strode toward him. "I threw the pot to stop you, for I've something to say to you, Brian."

"It can wait until after I've killed the Spaniard."

"No, it cannot! It cannot wait another minute!"

The violence of her tone gave O'Lear pause, and he stood frowning and considering her, for Rodrigue was still some distance away. Rosamunde was wondering if there was some way she could fell O'Lear with a rock and give them time to make their escape when Meara suddenly hurled herself against O'Lear. His legs went out from under him and he went down like a felled ox with Meara on top of him. As they landed, Meara rolled nimbly off and scrambled to her feet. Stunned, Rosamunde realized that Meara had driven her fishing spear into his thigh—that was what had felled him. She must have driven it in with all her strength, for O'Lear was pinned to the ground by it.

"You will not do murder here, Brian O'Lear!" Meara cried ringingly. She glared down at him. "These two are married in the sight of God, and ye'll respect that! Ye'll let them go their way."

The huge red-bearded man lay on the ground staring up at her in slack-jawed astonishment. Rosamunde doubted that O'Lear had ever been attacked by a woman, and certainly never been felled by one. "Ye've taken leave of your senses!" he gasped.

"No, I have not!" Meara was more animated than Rosamunde had ever seen her; her sapphire eyes flashed. "I have had my say. But *that*"—she indicated the spear that pinned him down with a regal gesture—"is for refusing to see what's right before your eyes—that I'm the better woman and the only one for you!"

O'Lear's jaw dropped a shade further. He looked in amazement from his thigh, pierced by the fish spear, to the resolute Amazon before him. "It cannot be you, Meara," he muttered. "*You* would not have done this."

"Aye, 'tis myself, Brian," declared Meara. " 'Tis bringing you to your senses I am, you great hulk! 'Tis a crying shame I have to use force, but since that's the way of it, that's the way it will be!"

"Am I to understand," roared O'Lear, "that ye've pinned me to the ground with this bodkin for love of me?"

"Indeed." Meara gave an energetic nod. "Now do not be squirming about," she added sternly. "For 'twill aggravate the wound and cause me more trouble when I dress it."

Suddenly O'Lear began to laugh. His shoulders and his great red beard shook, and his loud booming laughter echoed along the cliffs.

Meara stiffened. She looked offended.

"Meara." O'Lear wiped his eyes. "Sure and ye'll be the death of me!"

"Not if you hold still and let me"—Meara was tugging on the spear as she spoke—"get this spear out!"

Rosamunde marveled that O'Lear did not even wince as the spear left the ground. "I'd be grateful to ye if ye'd take it out from the front," he told Meara politely. "That way 'twill not dirty the wound."

Meara nodded, preoccupied with her work. The left side of her face was turned to O'Lear, and her thick black hair spread like a heavy black satin shawl about her newly rounded shoulders, for she had gained some weight since coming back. Her brown homespun dress had fallen off one shoulder, and that bare white shoulder was presented to him temptingly.

But it was at her face that O'Lear looked. A beautiful face, unscarred on this side. And as he stared, Meara's

467

thick dark lashes lifted and she flashed him a smile that made her sapphire eyes sparkle teasingly.

"I'm thinking ye've not been won this way before, Brian O'Lear," she declared modestly.

O'Lear's big bearlike hand clamped over her wrist like a strong enveloping paw. "I think I should have noticed you before and this would ne'er have happened."

"That's true, Brian. I could not get your attention."

She had his attention now. O'Lear lay on the ground and gave this woman who would go to such lengths to gain his attention a steamy look. Forgotten for the moment were the Spanish captain and his blond English lady. Here before him was a woman as fierce as the storms that battered these coasts, as wild as himself and—strange he had not noticed it before—beautiful to boot!

The O'Lear had found his mate.

"Ye've never found a woman strong enough to march beside you and match ye stride for stride," declared Meara. "I am that woman!" She kept her good side turned toward him tantalizingly. "Nor am I afraid to wield a weapon—as ye may have noticed. Turn over."

"Faith, I could not help but notice it!" He gasped, doing her bidding. His tone, so fierce a moment ago, was surprisingly mild. "I do not see how it was I overlooked you," he marveled. "Ye're as fair as a rose, and I like a woman with spirit!"

"Yet it took a spear to call me to your attention!" Meara sounded indignant.

"Even so, be good enough to draw the spear out," said O'Lear. He was turned on his side, leaning on one huge arm. "Before all the good blood drains out of me and leaves me too weak to properly reward ye!"

With dignity, Meara drew out the spear—slowly and with care. "I am sorry," she cried in real distress as she saw the hole it left, and hurried to stanch the wound. O'Lear—for she had his attention at last—threw a careless arm about her as she worked on it, and her face flushed with pleasure.

"I've had worse scratches," he said, and rose to his feet to prove it. Meara promptly put his arm around her

468

shoulders and insisted he lean on her as he limped toward the hut.

Rodrigue had come up. He had sheathed his sword and was staring stupefied at this tableau. Even Rosamunde, who had known all along how much Meara cared for O'Lear, was dumbfounded by this turn of events.

"Away with you," called Meara over her shoulder, with a half-contemptuous wave of her hand. "I've enough to do to attend to my man without the likes of you staring at me!"

Rosamunde guessed that Meara wanted her quickly gone before O'Lear recovered his equilibrium enough to perhaps regret his sudden shift of affections.

"Goodbye, Meara!" she called. "Thank you for everything!" She ran past them to the hut, hurried inside and brought out her baby, and with a smile and a wave at them both, she hurried away beside Rodrigue.

"*Madre de Dios,* she drove that fish spear into his leg —and he did nothing!" marveled Rodrigue.

Rosamunde looked back. "He is kissing her," she reported, smiling. "I think perhaps he always cared for her—it just took an earthquake for him to realize it!"

Rodrigue laughed. "A fortunate earthquake!" he said.

They were halfway to the village when Meara caught up with them. She called to them and they stopped and waited for her. Meara was beaming. She held out her hand to Rosamunde.

" 'Tis for you. To remember me by," she said shyly, thrusting into Rosamunde's hand the silver-and-amber rosary Rosamunde had seen her use so often. It was Meara's dearest possession.

"But I can't accept this," protested Rosamunde. "It means too much to you, Meara."

" 'Tis the O'Lear that means the most to me." Meara laughed. "And thanks to you and my fish spear, I have him now!"

Sudden tears sprang to Rosamunde's eyes. This tall Irishwoman was giving her the most precious of her possessions. "I promise to treasure it, Meara," she said huskily.

"God go with you, Rosamunde," said Meara, suddenly hugging her with such force that Rosamunde was hard put to keep the baby from being crushed. Baby Elaine gave a spirited wail, and Meara laughed and brushed a kiss over that small cheek. "Should the English law come looking for you, I'll lead them astray," she promised Rosamunde cheerfully.

Rosamunde was too choked up to protest that the English law would hardly come looking for *her;* more likely they'd come looking for O'Lear! But Meara was already moving away from them, making her way back to the shepherd's hut and the only man she had ever loved.

Walking along beside Rodrigue, with tiny Elaine clutched in her arms, Rosamunde made her way to the little fishing village they had been afraid to take refuge in. They were met by a waiting ship's officer and hurried aboard. Rosamunde hardly saw the cluster of huts that made up the village. All her attention was riveted on the tall-masted ship anchored in the bay, to which they were rowed in a waiting longboat. She could read the painted name, *Coronada.* Sister ship to Captain Navarro's *Infanta.*

The *Coronada*'s rotund captain, Juan de Gaspar, was a voluble Portuguese. He made a handsome leg to Rosamunde and greeted Rodrigue with an outpouring of Spanish. Rosamunde had by now learned considerable Spanish and understood most of what he was saying: They would have a good cabin, large and pleasant. Rodrigue and his lady would have free run of the ship. They had taken on much fresh food, and the ship's cook was excellent.

But other matters preoccupied Rosamunde. As the anchor was hauled up and the great white sails caught the wind and billowed overhead, she stood by the ship's rail and studied the misty outlines of the Irish shoreline, slipping fast away. Then she turned to study the empty ocean that lay ahead. Somewhere far beyond her vision over brilliant sunlit seas lay the island of Majorca, and this tall white ship was taking her there.

"Rodrigue," she said suddenly to the tall Spaniard at her side, "what is Margarita like?"

He was startled. "She is tall and slender," he said finally. "Her hair is thick and dark, and her eyes—burn."

Rosamunde studied him. "And will she welcome me?" she asked dryly.

"I do not know," he muttered. "Margarita is very proud."

And considers you hers, Rosamunde finished for him silently. "Does she live near your house?" she asked.

Rodrigue started. "I do not live in my own house. It is old and in bad repair and situated across the island. I live in my father's house in San Telmo."

"But I thought you said—"

"I said only that I *owned* the house across the island and that you would like it. We will visit it from time to time, but we will live in my father's villa near the sea at San Telmo on Majorca's western tip. From there you can see the isle of Dragonera. It is beautiful. I promise, you will like it."

"Where do Margarita and your brother Ignacio live?"

"They also live with my father. The villa is very spacious. Ignacio and Margarita and their daughter Maria occupy one wing of the house; I occupy the other. My father enjoys the central portion."

So they were all to live in one house in Majorca. . . . Her brow furrowed.

"I see you do not like the arrangement." Rodrigue's voice was rather sharp. "But I beg you not to pass judgment until you have seen it. In my father's house I am treated as a prince."

Rosamunde was silent. The favorable winds that billowed the shrouds were not only speeding this tall white ship toward Majorca—they were speeding its passengers toward a handsome villa in San Telmo where a tall proud Spanish woman waited, a woman who up to now had counted Rodrigue her slave. . . .

they could have the broken-down stone wall that

3

Hot Winds
of Passion

Majorca 1622—1628

33   *Panting, Rosamunde pursued the nanny goat.*
The ever-blowing winds, which stunted the trees and made
the vegetation grow permanently aslant, had knocked
down part of the rude enclosure where the milch goats were
kept. Neither fat Pablo nor his spindly wife Juana were
able to catch the animal. It was July, and Majorca was
still in the grip of its annual drought—it had not rained in
months. Under the blistering sun, eastern Majorca burned.
Hot sand blew over Rosamunde's leather peasant sandals
and tingled against her bare legs as she ran. The goat's
path led upward over the rocks. Holding up the coarse
unbleached linen skirts of her loose peasant dress, Rosamunde pursued the fleet little animal over the stony path
that led up the cliffs.

Below her as she raced upward she could see the
parched cracked fields in which the peasants toiled ceaselessly to eke out a bare living, and before her rose the
barren rounded peaks of the mountains, reflecting the
burning heat of the sun like mirrors. Off to her right she
could see the cliffs falling sharply away into the sea. And
to her left was a sun-baked world, for in that direction
lay the arid steppelike *garriga*. Although the interior of
Majorca contained rich farmland laced by lemon and olive
trees, and figs and pomegranates and almonds, and when
there was enough rain produced four crops a year, the
barren *garriga* was a land of stunted pines and mastic
trees and dwarf palms.

The sun was in her eyes now, and she blinked and put
a hand over her face to shade it. Where had the goat gone?

Ah, there she glimpsed it! The little creature had headed for a favorite pasture—a ruined bronze-age village made of great rough-hewn stones, long deserted, mortarless and awesome. *Talayoti,* the people of Majorca called these towers, and there were both square towers and round. Among their tumbled stones, shaded from the sun's bright glare, grew succulent verdure beloved by goats. And true to her kind, this wandering nanny goat was contentedly grazing on a small bush that looked to be thorn.

Panting, Rosamunde sank down on a convenient stone and leaned her back against a broken wall. She was lucky to have found the goat so soon. She might have had to seek for an hour through this great jumble of overgrown hewn boulders. She would wait while the animal grazed, for the goat had run all the way here through this terrible heat—it would be cruel not to let her browse for a while on the green stuff she loved. And Rosamunde was fond of these gentle affectionate creatures that provided the milk and cheese for their table.

She loosened her bodice against the heat and tossed back her damp fair hair. The wind that blew endlessly across Majorca cooled her, and she leaned back against the rough-hewn stones and gazed about her. In the distance she could see another tower—this one built as a watchtower against the piratical Moors. It perched like a sentinel on a cliff that fell sharply away into the sea.

Pirates never came here now—nor any ships at all, for that matter. This was a quiet coast, and on a clear day one could see the island of Minorca in the distance across the brilliant blue sea.

Rosamunde curled her legs up under her and leaned back, enjoying the wind with exotic Majorca all around her. She thought wryly how very different was the entire island from anything she had imagined—and how different their reception from what Rodrigue had led her to expect.

It had been six years since they had sailed into the port of Palma. It had been July then too, and after Ireland's cool dampness, Rosamunde had found the heat suffocating. It shimmered from the streets, it seared the air, it beat at you like a living thing, scorching the lungs with every breath. Even the air in Palma, that town by the sea, burned, she thought, like a thousand deserts. She had looked about her uneasily. Majorca was beautiful—but to her English eyes it was alien.

They had arrived like beggars, Rodrigue and she, clad only in the clothes that had become rags during their stay in Ireland, for it was far too hot for cloaks, and the captain of the *Coronada* was anxious to get on and had stopped on the way only briefly to pick up water and more fresh fruit and vegetables, of which he was very fond.

In Majorca nothing had been as they had expected it to be.

As they neared the shore, Rodrigue had turned to her. "Are you wearing your rosary?"

"Yes." Rosamunde pulled aside her tattered collar, and he nodded in satisfaction.

"You must forget nothing that I have taught you," he warned in a stern undertone. "Since you are a foreigner, it is best to appear devout. For the Inquisition reaches even into Majorca."

Nervously Rosamunde fingered the beads that Meara had touched so reverently. The amber was warm to her touch but the silver was cold, and she repressed a shiver. The Inquisition . . . dread hooded questioners, torturers, chains, the rack, the fire. No, she promised herself, she would forget nothing that Rodrigue had taught her!

"And remember," he added, "that I have told the captain of this ship that you are Irish—not English."

"But you told Captain Navarro, when he touched port in Ireland, that I was English."

" 'Tis an oversight I will correct," said Rodrigue soberly. "Captain Navarro is broad-minded, a worldly man —he will understand. But I am not so sure about Captain de Gaspar."

Another chill came over her. She, who had ridden the highways of England as a counterfeit man, was now another kind of counterfeit. She must pretend to be Irish —for to be English was dangerous and might lead the Inquisition to question her; she must pretend to be Catholic, for to be Church of England on Spanish soil was to be a heretic and would lead promptly to torture and death.

For Rosamunde, Meara's rosary was like a talisman, a charm to ward off evil, and now as she watched the shore approach she fingered it with increasing anxiety.

She shifted baby Elaine in her arms, for her right arm was growing numb with the child's weight, and now she looked down at her daughter with a small tense smile. On this island Rodrigue's family awaited them; she hoped they would like her, for it was important to Rodrigue, but she was desperately anxious that they would like her daughter, for the child's whole future might depend on their approval. Then her gaze softened. Who could help but love the child, even if they cared nothing for the mother? she thought, gazing down into that sweet pure face.

Her hair, which she had bound up, was coming down again. It blew over her eyes. She turned to Rodrigue. "It is very windy here."

"Yes," he said absently. "In Majorca the winds always blow. We have named them all, as I have told you. You and I have arrived on the wings of the *mitjorn*—the sultry wind that blows to us out of Africa." He interrupted himself. "My father's house lies northwest of us at San Telmo. I could not persuade Captain de Gaspar to stop there, for the waters around the isle of Dragonera are dangerous and he would have needed to skirt Dragonera to reach San Telmo on Majorca. His excuse was that he had urgent business in Palma. But San Telmo is less than ten leagues away. We will arrive there tomorrow."

Rosamunde turned to peer into the dazzling sun to follow Rodrigue's gaze. Then she turned to consider Palma, coming up fast on the port bow. Her head was aching from the glare by the time they disembarked. Rodrigue held her arm with a fierce protectiveness that did nothing to allay her fears as they climbed into the longboat and were rowed ashore. There before them Palma slumbered in the sun.

No one met them, for they were not expected. As Rodrigue bargained with a cart driver near Cathedral Square,

Captain de Gaspar came hurrying up—he had remembered that they had no money for transportation. Graciously he advanced them the money for their journey; he would be in Palma a week and during that time Rodrigue could send money from San Telmo to repay him. They bade the captain a second warm goodbye and they were off, riding down the stately Paeso Maritimo and into open country. Rosamunde cushioned Elaine against the jolting as they passed white beaches marked by bizarre rock formations and sparse woods, bouncing along through alien country toward—what?

Fear of their arrival nagged at Rosamunde.

It was worse even than she had expected.

At dark they stopped and camped by the roadside. Rosamunde and small Elaine occupied the cart, while Rodrigue and the cart driver slept on either side of the road to be on the alert for robbers.

None had appeared. For Rosamunde it had been a sleepless night gilded by a white moon, and the sun had risen from the sea in a hot golden ball as they made their way over an already steaming roadway into the town of Andraitx. There the countryside had seemed to Rosamunde one vast perfumed garden looking down upon a white beach and a sapphire sea. Her spirits had lifted a little.

But they left Andraitx and wound through a wild and magnificent countryside. There were frequent majestic views, but the road was little more than an undiscernible track. It was the sort of road over which she and Harry and Will had so frequently lost their pursuers, she thought ironically. At last in the distance they could see San Telmo, and past it a strip of blue sea where rose the weird rocky cliffs of the islet of Dragonera.

Now they were jolting along through glaring light past walls that reflected the sun's rays punishingly. The sea below was a glassy blue mirror, and the sky was a hard pitiless blue. Rosamunde wondered if it was always like this. In the remnants of her green velvet gown—for Rodrigue had been unwilling to borrow more money from

478

Captain de Gaspar to outfit her—she felt as if she might faint.

"These walls—these surround my father's lands," Rodrigue told her, and she straightened, staring about her curiously.

"Remember," he muttered as they rode through a wide gateway into a sun-baked courtyard, "*I* will answer all questions. Your Spanish is poor and but recently learned —and no one in San Telmo speaks the Irish tongue."

"That is fortunate," said Rosamunde, speaking in English as he had (for the cart driver spoke only Majorcan), "for I speak Irish even less well than I speak Spanish. Yet you say I must claim to be Irish."

"For your life's sake," said Rodrigue sternly.

"Even with your family?" She gave him a wistful look.

Rodrigue hesitated, and she thought with a thrill of alarm, *He is not sure of his family; perhaps it is Margarita he does not trust.* "There are servants," he said vaguely, and let it go at that.

As he reached up to help her down from the cart there was a cry from the doorway, and one of the servants ran forward across the empty courtyard and greeted Rodrigue joyfully.

"This is Pablo," Rodrigue told her, and she smiled at the fat mustached fellow who bowed almost reverently. Rodrigue and Pablo conversed rapidly in Majorcan, which Rosamunde did not yet speak. She turned to study the iron grillwork and thick arching pillars of the great house before her. It was a strange exotic architecture to her English eyes, this architecture of colonial Spain, and after the burning heat of the cart the dimness within looked inviting.

At a sharp exclamation from Rodrigue, she turned in alarm. All the happiness had drained from his face. "My father is dead," he said in a flat voice. "Pablo tells me that he died last week and has already been buried."

Rosamunde did not know what to say to comfort him, but he seemed not to want comfort. With a face of stone he strode into the house, and Rosamunde followed.

The entire house seemed draped in mourning. But at

least it was cool inside, and the coolness of the thick walls struck her damp skin like balm. About her through the thick black hangings she could catch glimpses of the walls, which were painted white. All the furniture was rich and dark and heavy, of mahogany and olive wood, with tall-backed Spanish chairs and huge carved cupboards. The rooms were large and high-ceilinged, and their heels rang on the tile floors.

Before them a wide stairway with an iron railing led up to the second floor. Outside through a wooden grillwork door could be glimpsed a second courtyard. In this one a fountain tinkled, and there were flowers and waving palms. Exhausted from the heat, surrounded by funereal hangings, and with small Elaine asleep and weighing heavily in her tired arms, Rosamunde yearned for that courtyard.

A man came running down the stairs and clasped Rodrigue about the shoulders. He was about Rodrigue's height, but older and dressed in somber black. Even before Rodrigue presented her, Rosamunde was sure that this was his brother Ignacio—Margarita's husband.

Don Ignacio gave his brother's new wife a startled look, but he recovered quickly, made her an elegant leg and spoke to her in musical flowing Catalan. Rosamunde answered haltingly, trying to judge this man who, now that Rodrigue's father was dead, might well exert a strong influence upon their lives. He was a man of graceful expansive gestures, and under closer inspection she saw that he was a dandy, for all his garments were of the richest materials. She could not decide whether she liked him or not, for beneath his easy pleasant manner she thought she sensed insincerity—perhaps even dislike.

Ignacio took them into the palm-shaded courtyard, and there among the blooming roses she met Margarita.

Margarita was tall and thin as a whip. She had magnificent expressive dark eyes and thick, shining dark hair which was swept up and in which she wore a tall ornate tortoiseshell comb, which in turn supported a sweeping black lace mantilla. Mourning became her, setting off the pale-olive pallor of her cream-smooth skin. She was as richly garbed as her husband, and she had apparently
480

started up at the sound of Rodrigue's voice, but now she stiffened and fixed those large expressive dark eyes on Rosamunde in a kind of dawning horror. She flashed a startled glance at Rodrigue and at his wooden look, clasped her hands together, twisting her fingers so that her jet rings glittered. Rosamunde could see that her knuckles were white.

"Margarita has been much affected by my father's death," explained Ignacio in his musical Catalan. "She was very fond of him."

As if his voice had broken the spell that held his wife rigid, she now cast her eyes down at the stone paving of the courtyard and sank listlessly back into the carved stone bench on which she had been seated—dramatically, against a backdrop of blood-red roses. When she looked up again, all expression had been erased from her face. She greeted Rosamunde indifferently with a languorous outstretched hand. Rodrigue she favored with a brief but charming smile. Then she leaned back and gently wafted her black lace fan and studied Rosamunde with the concentrated interest with which a successful duelist might regard a new opponent.

Rosamunde sank down on a stone bench facing Margarita. Looking into those large glittering dark eyes she was inescapably reminded of a dangerous snake coiled to strike. Wearily she shifted the child to her other arm, and Margarita clapped her hands and when a servant appeared indicated she was to take the child. Rosamunde was nervous about surrendering Elaine to anyone, but this spindly woman—whose name was Juana and who was wife to fat Pablo, who had greeted Rodrigue in the courtyard—seemed so overjoyed to hold the child in her arms that she relented, smiling. As Juana rocked small Elaine, Rosamunde caught what bits of conversation she could, for it was all very fast and in Catalan. She knew Rodrigue was telling of their shipwreck, their eventual rescue. Even though she listened intently, she found Don Ignacio's rapid Catalan hard to follow. Margarita, with her staccato diction—even though her Spanish was more Castilian than Catalan—was easier to understand.

"Are we to understand that you met this lady in Ireland and that you were married and she bore you a child all in the short time after your shipwreck, Rodrigue?" Margarita inquired in a tone of lazy insult.

Rodrigue's dark face flushed and he looked at his sister-in-law sharply. She continued to wave her fan.

"I met this lady in England," he said harshly. "She is Irish but had been betrothed to an English lord and taken to England. 'Twas she who warned me that my ship was about to be attacked, and we escaped together. It was not until we reached Ireland that we could find a priest to marry us—and it was in Ireland that our child was born."

"And who was this English lord she chose not to marry?" wondered Margarita.

Apparently Rodrigue had not given thought to this question. For a moment his face went blank.

"Lord Matthew Waverclay," supplied Rosamunde, and her voice was bitter with remembrance.

Rodrigue looked relieved.

"And why did you not wish to marry the man to whom you had already been betrothed?" Margarita was fascinated.

"Because my guardian's wife was his mistress," said Rosamunde bluntly. "Among other reasons."

Margarita frowned and turned to Rodrigue. "But I thought you said—"

"When Rosamunde's father died, her mother went to live in England with kinsmen and died there. Her guardian was English," explained Rodrigue.

"But she grew up in Ireland?"

"Yes—her early days," Rodrigue answered for her.

Margarita turned her insolent gaze on Rosamunde. "It must have been terrible for you, living in that heretic country," she sympathized. "A terrible place, England— or so I have often heard. Did you not find it so?" There was an edge of mockery in her voice, and Rosamunde thought, *She does not believe us.*

"I—managed," said Rosamunde wearily. She shifted her weight on the stone bench and wished that Rodrigue had not invented for her an Irish background. Margarita
482

was sure to question her about Ireland, and she might stumble in her answers. And that would be dangerous. For she had no doubt that this handsome Castilian woman with her fierce dark eyes and pale-olive skin would be her bitter adversary. It was in the very way she looked at the newcomers, in the anger that underlay her quick light voice.

The fountain tinkled, a light breeze stirred the silvery branches of the fig tree beneath which Rodrigue sat, mopping his brow with his kerchief. Presently a servant girl—scarcely more than a child—came out and shyly offered them deep silver goblets of an iced fruit drink with which Rosamunde was unfamiliar—except that it was flavored with lime. When Rosamunde expressed surprise, Rodrigue told her moodily that it had been made with cistern water. She would learn that in Majorca good water was a rarity.

"No, I did not mean that," she exclaimed. "I meant the ice. In this heat!"

"The ice? Ah, for that we are indebted to the snow stampers."

When she turned to him a puzzled look, Ignacio explained courteously that in winter the "snow stampers" would climb the steep sides of the high peaks of the Sierra de Tramontana range and gather up the snow, packing it tightly into deep pits which he called the *casetas de sa neu.* They would stamp up and down on the snow in these pits with their feet until it had formed a hard icy mass in the biting winter air. They would sing as they worked, songs of festival, of revelry. And then they would bring the ice down into the valleys below, where it would be stored to cool the tall fruit drinks and furnish cool iced melons far into the blazing heat of summer.

"I am parched." Rodrigue drained his goblet, and the servant girl hurried forward to refill it with the clinking liquid.

"Enjoy it, Rodrigue." Ignacio laughed ruefully. "For it is the last of the ice. This heat would melt a mountain of snow."

"After the cool damp of Ireland, it would melt a man's brains," muttered Rodrigue, again mopping his brow.

Rodrigue and Ignacio fell to speaking of their father. They spoke with sadness, and Rosamunde, who had never known him, reached down and picked up a green fig that had fallen from the tree and fingered it as she sipped her cool drink. She was wondering if, in spite of everything, it would be possible to make a friend of Margarita. Her feminine intuition told her it would not be.

Margarita has always considered Rodrigue her property, Rosamunde thought soberly. *Even though she chose to marry his brother, she never meant to lose him—and never thought she would. And now I have come between them. Margarita will not easily forgive that.*

Now Margarita, a dramatic figure against the backdrop of red roses, was giving precise instructions to another servant as to how their rooms were to be prepared. Some of the words Rosamunde did not understand.

Not till Rodrigue had led her to the wing of the house he had always claimed as his own did she realize just what those instructions entailed—for she found their bedroom heavily draped in black.

"Margarita has sent you the black hangings from her own room," Rodrigue told her. "You must be sure to thank her."

"Yes, how—kind of her," murmured Rosamunde, giving a hopeless look at the funereal hangings. Doubtless Margarita was glad of an excuse to be rid of the depressing things!

Juana had brought little Elaine to her and left quietly. Now, restless and unnerved at the strangeness of this place and the uncertain warmth of their reception, Rosamunde did not fall into bed for a brief siesta as Rodrigue did, but walked about the room with the child in her arms.

"Come to bed," said Rodrigue abruptly, reaching out to offer her some pomegranates in an earthenware bowl.

Rosamunde continued to walk.

"One must rest in this heat."

He meant, *Let us make love, let our bodies join together in healing comfort and peace.*

But Rosamunde was too uneasy to feel like making

love in this gloomy room hung with heavy black. She gave him an impatient look.

"Women are like the winds," Rodrigue muttered moodily. "We name our winds in Majorca." He was fond of speaking of the winds; she had often heard him recount their various merits.

"And which wind am I like?" she asked lazily, humoring him.

He turned to regard her. "When you are angry you are like the *tramontana*, the wind from the north—and you chill me with your cold English ways and your cold English heart."

Obviously he was irritated that she had not come to bed when he called her. She lifted her finely arched brows. "And when I am not angry, Rodrigue?"

"Ah, then you are like the *mitjorn*—the sultry south wind that blows to us from the shores of Africa."

She gave him a mocking smile. But she laid the sleeping Elaine carefully down on a pile of black-draped cushions. The sight chilled her a little, for it looked to her like a funeral bier.

She straightened and shrugged out of her dress, letting it fall in tattered green velvet remnants onto the floor.

"Margarita has sent you a garment for siesta, Rosamunde."

Rosamunde looked at the pile of heavy black taffeta he indicated and repressed a shudder. Margarita would not get her to wear that! Without a word she let her chemise fall to the floor and stood naked in the heat, her pale body gleaming with perspiration.

Rodrigue sat up; his voice was irritable. "Close the shutters onto the gallery, Rosamunde. One of the servants might walk by and see you."

Rosamunde sighed. So they must shut off what little air there was in this stuffy room! She restrained an urge to march out and set up a barricade so that the servants might not walk by. Ah, well, Rodrigue had enough to plague him without her upsetting the household! Lazily she bent over and took a pomegranate from the earthenware bowl. She bit into it and went to the window, holding

485

it up to the brilliant light, looking at the glistening pink seeds. Past the gallery railing across the courtyard she could see Margarita, sweeping along with her light sure step, her back very stiff, her arrogant head held high. Margarita turned for a moment, and her gaze swept the gallery of that wing where Rodrigue lounged with Rosamunde. Rosamunde stepped quickly back so that Margarita might not see her naked form at the window and be shocked. But she had seen the fierce hot anger in that gaze that blazed up for a moment and then smoldered.

If I am like the moist seductive mitjorn, thought Rosamunde wryly, *then surely Margarita is like the* xalox—*that hot dry wind off the Sahara that stings the skin with sand lashed all the way from Africa.*

She closed the shutters and turned to Rodrigue with sudden sympathy, sensing that in his reckless life there had been much lust—but very little love.

She must make up to him for that lack and be all those things that the rapacious Margarita was not!

On the wings of that thought, she crossed the room, sank to the bed and twined her slim naked arms about him. She closed her eyes against the sight of the gloomy room and listened to Rodrigue's deep sigh of contentment as her soft breasts moved silkily against his lean chest.

"Rosamunde," he murmured. "This homecoming is not as I had thought it would be."

He did not have to tell her that; she knew it already. She silenced him with a kiss and felt her soft lips urgently pressed open by his probing tongue, felt her blood race fierily through her veins, and gave herself up to throbbing passion.

She told herself she loved Rodrigue. She would make him forget Margarita!

And as always, she found herself responding to his restless, moody, almost hurtful lovemaking, to the wild desperate passion that was unleashed in him and could find expression only in this way. Fiercer than the hot winds that blew from Africa across Majorca, his arms enveloped her on that sultry afternoon. Deeply he thrust, almost punishingly in his intensity. Wildly he roved within her.
486

He was like a man driven before a hurricane. In the white heat of that passion she could feel herself blown away, extinguished—like the Phoenix to rise again from the white-hot ashes refreshed and renewed.

It was not the way she had loved Harry, of course. Her memories of him, still too fresh to parade before her conscious mind, were relegated to a distant sacred place in her heart, covered over by countless curtains of gauze. And she had commanded the winds of memory not to blow, lest those curtains be swept aside and the truth gnash at her hurtfully.

For all her protestations to herself, she loved Harry still.

And on those nights when unbidden she had dreamed of him and waked to storms of tears, she had clenched her pillow and told herself fiercely that she loved Rodrigue, of course she did—she just loved him in an entirely different way.

It was a savage bond that held them together—and was it not as strong as any other?

In the courtyard below, Margarita—who could guess how Rodrigue and Rosamunde were spending their siesta—clenched her slender hands until the nails bit into the palms. Her proud spirit writhed. How dared Rodrigue bring another woman here? He must have known how it would hurt her!

She did not ask herself what that made her, she who had led Rodrigue to believe she loved him, then married his brother as the "better catch" and alternately teased and enraged Rodrigue ever since for her own entertainment. Margarita was not given to self-evaluation. Instead she contemplated with grim amusement the shock that would greet Rodrigue when he learned the terms of his father's will.

Rosamunde rose from her siesta languorously. She wished they could stay and have supper in their room, but she supposed it would offend Rodrigue to suggest it. Juana appeared and took charge of baby Elaine, and Rosamunde drifted down to supper on Rodrigue's arm, wondering what this great house looked like when it was not draped in mourning.

She had little chance to find out, for the cavernous dining room too was draped in black, and the candles in their heavy branched silver candlesticks made their faces seem to rise pale out of an enveloping night.

Margarita and Ignacio were both elegantly dressed in stiff rich brocades that must be suffocating, Rosamunde thought. Could Margarita actually be wearing beneath her gown one of those metal stomachers that were so popular in Spain? They flattened the breasts in the slim boyish Spanish style, but to Rosamunde, who had bound down her young breasts that she might ride the highroads of England disguised as a man, the thought of binding them down for *fashion* was as depressing as were the mournful hangings of the dining room.

For herself she would have left off her chemise in this heat, had Rodrigue not protested. As it was, she had chosen the lightest, though least fashionable, of the two dresses Margarita had sent to her—a dull-black silk of a heavy weave. Rodrigue was looking at her. Hastily she remembered to thank her hostess for her thoughtfulness in furnishing the clothes and the funereal hangings of their quarters. She was rewarded by a brief insincere smile on Margarita's pale-olive face.

"It is little enough to do for Rodrigue, who has had so much trouble these past months," declared Margarita sweetly, and Rodrigue gave her an approving smile.

Somewhat nettled, Rosamunde settled down to eat the tasty Majorcan food, which they washed down with ale and capped with chilled melon slices—apparently it was not quite "the last of the ice."

Across from her Rodrigue, freshly garbed in his own handsome clothes which he had left here at San Telmo, looked every inch the autocratic Spanish gentleman. He said little to her or Margarita—Rosamunde gathered that in Spain women were considered of little importance—but spoke mainly to his brother. Their conversation was subdued. Most of it concerned their father's last illness, for the old man had sickened and died very suddenly. Both Ignacio and Margarita emphasized that they had all believed Rodrigue dead when nothing was heard from him for so long.

But surely, Rodrigue protested, Captain Navarro had sent word of his shipwreck? He had sent word by Captain Navarro to the partners in Barcelona.

"No, no," said Ignacio quickly. "We heard nothing here—nothing."

Margarita's gaze was on Rosamunde as Ignacio spoke, and Rosamunde thought they held a mocking glitter.

The reason for her mockery was apparent when they learned the terms of the will. Rodrigue—always his father's favorite—had expected to inherit the great house at San Telmo. Now they were told that Rodrigue's father, as he lay dying, had changed his will. Whereas before he had left the house to Rodrigue and the remainder of his property to be divided equally between his two sons, now he had left the great house at San Telmo and all its lands and all his gold to Ignacio. To Rodrigue he had left the *Santa Cecilia*—Rodrigue had whitened to hear it, for the ship's bones lay bleaching beneath the sea off the Irish coast—and his share of her valuable cargo. The cargo was gone too.

So Rodrigue's inheritance was already at the bottom of the sea when it was willed to him. Rosamunde felt a burst of pity for Rodrigue as this was told to him.

"But my father would not change his will!" he blurted.

"Ah, but he did." Ignacio sighed, looking down at his enameled snuffbox as if he had never seen it before. He turned it nervously about in his hand. "You see, like us, Father believed you dead. But if you were to return he felt that the great ship *Santa Cecilia* would be more than sufficient for a seafaring man and a bachelor. And remember, he had already given you a house and land."

Rodrigue gave a short barking laugh. "A small strip of barren land and a house on the wild eastern coast at Cala Mesquida? He had promised me *this* house, Ignacio—as well you knew."

Ignacio shrugged, and shutters came down over his dark eyes. "Strange are the ways of fate," he murmured. "But it is done."

Rodrigue expelled a deep breath, and Rosamunde saw the bitterness in his eyes as he turned away from this pronouncement. He had been legally robbed of his inheritance.

But while Ignacio, with brotherly generosity, offered to let them stay at San Telmo as long as they liked, it was Rosamunde herself who insisted they go and occupy Rodrigue's own house across the island at Cala Mesquida.

Her decision came about very suddenly in a moment of terror.

Rodrigue, crushed at being dispossessed, had settled into a deep gloom. He drank deeply of strong wine, but he ate little and stalked restlessly about their funereally draped rooms. He stood for hours at the windows looking out to sea at the dark shape of the dragon island across from San Telmo. Rosamunde was deeply sorry for him, realizing that he was bearing a double loss—the loss of his beloved father and the loss of his inheritance.

And she had decided unhappily that he might not have lost either had it not been for her. Rodrigue had not hurried away from Amsterdam—because of her. Had he left sooner, he might have missed the terrible storms that had driven the *Santa Cecilia* at last to wreck on the rocky coast of Ireland. And if he had speeded safely home, he would have seen his father before the end, and Ignacio could not have pressured him to change his will. She knew the servants muttered that Rodrigue's father had died of a broken heart, believing his favorite son dead.

It was a bitter thought that she must live with.

In the meantime she was very tender with Rodrigue.

Out of his deep despondency he rose occasionally to take her in fierce wild bouts behind drawn shutters in the lazing heat of the afternoon . . . but the hot scented nights found him awake and walking like a caged panther in the moonlit gardens. Rosamunde watched him at night from her windows and sighed to see him like this.

She felt too that except in her bed, she had become a figure of gloom, for Margarita had been swift to provide her not only with a black-draped room but with the deep-black garments of mourning. Rosamunde had revolted at wearing the black night garment Margarita had provided.

"Who will know I am not wearing it?" she had demanded of Rodrigue. "No one save you—and surely you will not consider it disrespect of your father if I do not wear black both day and night!"

"I would prefer you to sleep naked," he said moodily. "Certainly the weather is hot enough."

And so she did.

Naked she lay in the darkened room at siesta time as well, fanning herself with a palm-leaf fan. Siesta was a difficult custom for her, but it was the way of the household. Rodrigue had urged her to let Luz, the nurse who took care of Margarita's frail toddler, Maria, take care of baby Elaine during siesta. Rosamunde did not like entrusting Elaine to anyone, but the child *did* have a way of crying at the wrong moments, and Luz did seem fond of her—though not so fond as Juana, who was kept occupied with other duties.

It happened one day at siesta time. Rosamunde had left Elaine—whom everyone, including Rodrigue, called Elena in the Spanish fashion—with big Luz on the shaded upper gallery. Maria, a dark thin child, was toddling about, getting under Luz's feet and being scolded by big Luz, who feared she would step on the child. Rosamunde sometimes felt sorry for little Maria, for Margarita was a stern taskmaster who did not lavish her love on children.

With a sigh, Rosamunde had left them and gone back to their bedroom, where Rodrigue waited. There she threw off her stiff black clothes and abandoned herself to love on the great square bed while bees buzzed outside the slatted shutters and glimmers of sun broke like fountains of light through the slats. Rodrigue's taking of her these days was wild, passionate, as if some great fire burned within him and only she could quench it. Rosamunde knew her body was a balm to his spirit. She felt a deep compassion for him—like her, he had been dispossessed. And that had waked in her a deep tenderness, almost akin to what she had felt for Harry. Now as he stroked her naked

491

body and murmured love words in Majorcan, she felt her own flaring passions ignite at the torch of his touch.

Together they shared and soared, together they found peace and contentment—even if it lasted only for an afternoon.

Rodrigue always slept afterward, but sometimes Rosamunde was restless. On this particular afternoon she rose, threw a black dressing gown about her naked body and slipped out to find Elaine. She walked down a long dim corridor and finally emerged through a shuttered door onto the empty second-floor gallery. The heat struck her like a clenched fist, and she stood by the railing, shading her eyes against the blinding light.

What she saw froze her blood.

34   *Directly across from her—across the courtyard* with its waving palms and tinkling fountain—on the other side of the gallery that ran in a U-shape around this side of the house, baby Elaine lay on the stone railing. Luz had disappeared. Only the toddler Maria was in sight, and she had climbed up on a bench beside the railing. As Rosamunde's shocked gaze took in the scene, Maria reached over to the baby, who laughed happily. If Maria tugged at the baby's long dress, the baby might fall to the hard stone floor of the gallery—or worse, a little push might knock her over the railing to the hard stone courtyard a full story below!

"Maria!" Rosamunde shouted. She had not known she could run so fast. On bare feet she flew around the gallery, the soles of her feet slapping against the hot tiles. She dashed past the surprised little Maria, swept up Elaine in her trembling arms—the child, not knowing her danger, was cooing—and shouted for Luz.

There was a clatter of feet up a stairway, a pounding of sandals on the corridor floor, and fat Luz came waddling up to her.

"What is wrong?" she panted.

"You left my child alone!" cried Rosamunde. "You left her lying on the railing! She could have fallen off and been killed!"

"But I did not leave her on the railing—nor was she alone!" protested Luz, babbling in her dismay. "Doña Margarita was holding the baby on her lap. She sent me for some lemonade. She—"

Her voice died away as another voice cut in coldly, "What are you saying to Doña Rosamunde, Luz? I was here earlier, but of course I did not leave the baby lying alone on the ledge! How dare you say it?"

Luz paled at the venomous gaze that met her muttered protests and fell silent.

Rosamunde had whirled as Margarita spoke. Now she watched that sinuous, almost languorous approach and was shocked at the light amusement in the tall Spanish lady's eyes at the sight of her trembling there with her baby in her arms.

There was no question in Rosamunde's mind who was telling the truth. Nor would it do any good to confront her with it. Margarita hated her—and hated Elaine as well, believing her to be Rodrigue's child. But Margarita was a clever adversary. She had not dashed the child to her death, she had merely abandoned her to let her fall off—and she would be in some other part of the house at the time, and would blame it all on poor Luz.

"Surely you believe me?" Margarita's face was insolent, her tone almost a taunt.

"I believe that my child is not safe in this house!" Holding Elaine cradled protectively in her arms, Rosamunde swept away from them, not caring that Margarita's gaze focused on the length of bare white leg that showed as she took a long step in the dressing gown, heedless of the Spanish lady's raised eyebrows.

493

What did she care what Margarita thought of her? That woman had tried to kill Elaine!

When she got back to her bedroom, she woke Rodrigue and told him what had happened.

He sat up and ran a distracted hand through his dark hair. He refused to believe it. She must have been mistaken, he insisted. The nurse, Luz, was having an affair with Alfredo, who was in charge of the stables; she must have set the child down for a moment to go to speak with him; had she not been within easy call, really but a few steps away?

Rosamunde wrenched open the shutters. The brilliant light knifed in and poured over her, haloing her fair hair. Her black silk dressing gown had fallen open, revealing a long streak of nude body to his gaze. She was a study in black and white and infinitely desirable.

Rodrigue, before this pulsating vision, caught his breath.

But Rosamunde was in no mood for love. She advanced on her husband like an avenging angel.

"I do not care what you say!" she raged, thrusting her face almost into his own. "I will not stay in this house with Margarita! She hates me, and she hates Elaine because she believes her to be our child, and—yes, I think she hates you too, Rodrigue, and wants to punish you. Because you dared to marry!"

Rodrigue's dark face whitened. "What are you saying?" he demanded hoarsely. "I have never laid so much as a finger on my brother's wife!"

"I believe you! But you could have—any day at all! She was waiting for you, expecting you!"

His palm lashed suddenly across her face, snapping her head back. "You will not speak so of Margarita!" he cried through clenched teeth.

So the Spanish woman still occupied a sacred place in his heart! A place she must not enter!

Rosamunde took a step backward and considered Rodrigue dispassionately. "Your Margarita may be as pure as you choose to believe," she said in a cold deliberate voice. "Nor do I care whether you have slept with her. But you have a house, Rodrigue, across the island from here—a
494

place where Elaine will be safe. And if you will not take me to your own house, I promise you that I will find a ship to carry me away from Majorca, for I will not live in your brother's house here in San Telmo another day!"

So desperate and so beautiful did she look standing there, with her blond hair streaming and her black silk dressing gown flowing away from her white body, that Rodrigue cast a wild look about him and his hands clenched. "I am sorry, Rosamunde," he said hoarsely. "I should not have struck you."

"I would take more than a blow for my daughter!" Rosamunde declared in a fierce voice. "What is your decision, Rodrigue? I would know it now, for I must pack."

Rodrigue heaved a deep sigh. "Very well, I will take you to my house at Cala Mesquida. But I warn you—you will not like it there."

"I will like it far better than here, anyway!" flashed Rosamunde and fell to packing.

As it turned out, they could not leave until the morrow. During that time Elaine never left Rosamunde's side—not even at supper, when Luz held out her arms for the baby and looked hurt that Rosamunde did not surrender her. It was at supper that Rodrigue announced his decision to leave for Cala Mesquida the next morning. He fended off the objections put forward by his brother Ignacio and Margarita, but Rosamunde thought he looked miserable. She did not care—they were going where Elaine would be safe!

She would never forget Margarita's last words to her. The tall Spanish woman had lain in wait for her in the dark corridor. When Rosamunde went by, carrying Elaine wrapped in a shawl, and a basket of bedclothing for the child over her other arm, Margarita had stepped out with an angry swish of black brocade skirts and confronted her.

Silently Rosamunde had waited for the words she knew would come.

Margarita's voice was low and full of venom. "Rodrigue is leaving San Telmo because you have told him lies about me," she accused. "You have told him I tried to kill your child!"

"You did," said Rosamunde flatly. "And had you suc-

495

ceeded"—her green eyes glinted—"I would have hunted you down and destroyed you—no matter where you hid."

"Liar!" Margarita drew herself up. "Do you think I would hide from you?"

Rosamunde saw that this conversation was pointless. "You will have no need to, Margarita," she said crisply. "For I do not expect to see you again."

"So! You will take Rodrigue away from his family!"

A shadow of a smile played around Rosamunde's mouth. "You mean I will take him away from you, don't you? And you wouldn't want that! After all, he's been your slave all these years!"

She ducked as Margarita's hand lashed out in fury. And her laughter floated back as she swept on down the hall, down the tile stairway and through the courtyard to the waiting cart that would take them to Cala Mesquida.

It was the last she had seen of Margarita. Rodrigue went to San Telmo from time to time, and he was always scrupulous in asking her to accompany him. But she thought he seemed relieved when she always made some excuse. She guessed it was because the Inquisition still reached into people's homes and he did not wish his heretic bride to attract attention in San Telmo—better to let it be known that Rodrigue's lady did not get along well with her in-laws.

Their journey across the island in the arid heat was uneventful. Their second night they spent in Palma, where Rodrigue had made a few purchases, things they would need to set up housekeeping at Cala Mesquida. The next morning as they were leaving Palma, Rodrigue reined in sharply to let a blue-and-yellow coach go by. There were several women and children running after it, shaking their fists and screaming something in Majorcan that Rosamunde could not understand.

"What are they saying?" she asked, turning to watch the coach's angry pursuers.

"They are crying out that the coach belongs to The Whip, and exhorting the driver to take it back to La Calobra—or to hell."

"La Calobra? The Whip?"

496

" 'The Whip' is the name the people call Don José Alvar. He was a favorite of the king of Spain who was sent away from the court for his misdeeds, and now he makes his home at La Calobra on the other side of the mountains." His face hardened. "I do not know if the stories they tell of him are true. . . . " His voice died away and he turned the wagon quickly into a side street.

Rosamunde turned her attention in the direction of his gaze. A procession of flagellants were trudging barefoot through the dust, their ankles hampered by chains. Each carried a little many-tailed whip. A collective moan rose up from them as they brought those whips up and then down again upon their own naked backs.

Rosamunde shuddered, the man at La Calobra forgotten. For she sensed that this bloody expression of public piety had made Rodrigue remember that the Inquisition would regard her as a heretic—and heretics were burned.

In silence they took the coast road out of Palma, then turned eastward across a flat and fertile plain. Past donkey carts and lumbering oxen, past *alquerias* or dairy farms, past almond groves and the ruined stone walls of ancient peoples who had been here before the Romans came, their cart jolted.

Pablo and his wife, Juana, accompanied them in their trek. They had been Rodrigue's personal servants and were loyal to him. Rosamunde was grateful for their company, even though she doubted their ability to pay them, for Juana was already very fond of baby Elaine and big Pablo seemed entirely trustworthy. Juana rode behind her in the first cart with little Elaine in her arms, while behind them Pablo drove another cart carrying a heavy bed and a carved cupboard. Rodrigue had traded the remainder of his furnishings at San Telmo to Ignacio for the carts and the donkeys that pulled them, and a little money. His own horse, an Arab stallion, trailed along on a lead, and Rosamunde yearned to leave the cart and leap astride him. But Rodrigue seemed to think it more suitable for her to jolt along demurely beside him, beneath a spreading sunshade made of woven straw.

497

Soon the land began to undulate and wind wheels appeared.

"Every house has its cistern," Rodrigue explained, "for in Majorca there is little water."

That fact was brought home to her when they passed primitive *norias,* old wells where horses or oxen walked around and around bringing up water on an endless chain of buckets.

That night they spent at Villafranca and at supper ate the melons for which the town was famous. Their road took them on to the large trading town of Manacor, whose church tower rose like a minaret from the plain, and thence through fields lined with fig trees to the town of San Lorenzo, where a green valley flowed down to the coast and occasional steep crags festooned with stunted trees rose like silent sentinels beside the roadway.

At San Servera they turned sharply north past fields cracked and parched by drought, past wilting corn and puny almond trees. The town of Arta seemed a green oasis in the midst of a line of round-topped heat-reflecting mountains. The glare hurt Rosamunde's eyes, and she was glad when Rodrigue announced they would stay the night in Arta so Rosamunde might see the wondrous cavern there. Rosamunde had never seen a truly great cave, and she was awed by the cathedral-like main chamber that reached upward to a height of almost eighty feet.

"And this is the Queen of the Columns." Rodrigue waved his torch proudly at the stalagmite that rose up and almost touched the cave's overarching roof. "You see, we do things well in Majorca!"

Rosamunde smiled and paced about the great chamber, which in the light of their torches seemed as long as the palace at Whitehall. It was cool here, a relief from the suffocating heat above. "I could stay here a week," she said ruefully.

"I think you would not like it so well after the torches went out," Rodrigue told her. "Then you would be groping around in the dark."

Rosamunde shivered. Lost . . . in a great cavern stretching endlessly away.

"But you would have no need to fear." Rodrigue's rich voice pulsated beside her. "For I would find you." His fingers ran intimately down her back so that she felt herself quiver. "There is no darkness through which I would not find you, Rosamunde."

She gave him a troubled look. Rodrigue loved her so intensely. Perhaps he even loved her too much. It might be difficult to prove worthy of that love. Silently she went out into the blazing sunshine and looked out at the hills which reflected that sun like mirrors.

"You are afraid to love me," he accused in a low voice, and kissed her ear.

"No, no, I am not afraid," she said guiltily. But she wondered in her heart if he was not right.

The next day they left Arta for the last lap of their journey. They had packed a lunch and ate it seated on a stone staircase amid the crumbling towers of the ancient *castillo* at Capdepera. Rosamunde shaded her eyes with her hand and looked past the worn stone steps and prickly pears at the brattices or covered wooden galleries, at the crenellated walls where windows peered out to sea with sightless eyes.

"On another day we will climb up to the little chapel at the top." Rodrigue gestured with a piece of dark bread to the top of this splendid ruin.

Rosamunde squinted up into the sun. "Who built this fortress, Rodrigue?"

He shrugged. "Some say the Romans, some say the Arabs. But the kings of Majorca enlarged it, and it was used as a place of refuge against attacks by pirates." She gave him a sharp look, and he smiled. "Pirates never come here anymore—nor, indeed, any shipping. This is a quiet coast." He sighed, and she knew he wished it were less quiet.

"You would have preferred your home to be at a busy port like Palma?"

"Yes," he said frankly. "I see from your face that you do not approve, but indeed I would. I do not care for all this desolation."

They finished their lunch and rode on through crystal-clear air that smelled of pines, and Rosamunde, surrounded by the beauty of sand-edged bays the blue of sapphires and picturesque cliffs, wondered why Rodrigue had lingered at San Telmo at all, why he had not come here at once. Certainly she would have!

Her first glimpse of the house at Cala Mesquida was a breathtaking one. It came into sight as they left a little stand of pine trees, a red-roofed white house situated on a low cliff overlooking the blue sea.

"My house," he said.

"But it's beautiful!" she burst out impulsively. "Oh, Rodrigue, you did not tell me it was so lovely."

Rodrigue gave her a worried look. "On a clear day you can see the island of Minorca from the windows. But," he added reluctantly, "the buildings are not in very good repair. It is a property my father took in payment of a debt and gave to me one day when I pleased him by swimming a great distance. I have not given it the attention that I should have."

As they came closer she saw that this was an understatement. There were huge cracks in one wall, a corner of the roof was gone, the wooden shutters hung disconsolately, and the nearby stable was entirely unroofed. In the barren courtyard several chickens scratched and a gnarled old olive tree fought for life. Juana looked daunted.

"It only needs a little effort," Rosamunde insisted cheerfully, jumping down from the cart before Rodrigue could assist her and holding out her arms for Juana to give her Elaine. "Soon it will be a wonderful place to live. We will all work at it."

"Yes. We will start tomorrow," agreed Rodrigue without enthusiasm.

Now from the ancient bronze-age village with its ruined *talayots*, where she had chased the little milch goat, Rosamunde looked down upon Rodrigue's house and smiled ruefully. From this distance it looked almost new with its red tile roof shining in the sun, but when one came closer one could see that it was still in bad repair. It had

500

been years now since they had come here, but the house was still not in shape. She supposed it never would be, for Rodrigue did not love it as she did.

But to his credit, on their arrival he had plunged at once with characteristic energy into a back-breaking effort to make the land produce. While Rosamunde and Juana had struggled to get the house, with its big echoing rooms, in order, Rodrigue and Pablo had worked with the two peasant families who tilled the fields. It was uphill work, for the land was arid and barren and the crops always seemed to wither and die in Majorca's annual six-month drought.

Nevertheless, Rodrigue persevered. When he came in from the fields, he worked on the house. In the evenings he and Pablo made the roof sound, cleaned out the big stone cistern, put back the fallen stones around the fireplaces and repaired the mortar around them. Though Pablo whistled, Rodrigue worked silently, as if punishing himself. It hurt Rosamunde to see how unhappy he was.

For she herself could have been very happy here at Cala Mesquida—but that Rodrigue was so miserable.

Now from the ruins she looked out at the land Rodrigue had tried so hard to make productive. As usual it was parched, the soil cracked from heat and dryness. Around the house she had carried buckets of water to the roses, to the vegetables, but out here that was not possible. The sun beamed down like a great lamp and the plants slowly dried up.

Rodrigue and she had had a thin time of it at first, for the harsh Majorcan seasons had all but destroyed their efforts. Only the goats seemed to flourish here, she thought ruefully.

She had not complained. It had been at her insistence that they had come here, and she had been stubbornly anxious to prove her decision right. It was right for baby Elaine, she thought, smiling as she pictured the dainty toddler building sand castles by the blue sea or playing with the gentle milk goats and their pretty silky-sided kids.

But . . . it had not been right for Rodrigue. It had never been right for Rodrigue. He had sat for long hours

501

staring out to sea, a sea empty of the ships he loved. And one day when the crop had failed again, he had shaken his fist at the diamond-blue sky from which no rain came. He had dashed the sweat from his sunburned brow and gone stamping back to the house. But he had not paused there. He had walked on to the stable, mounted up and ridden for Palma.

From the fields where she was laboring beside Pablo, Rosamunde had straightened up and watched him ride away—and guessed his mission. Rodrigue was going to try for a ship again. He was a seafaring man, but after he had lost his ship off Ireland, shipowners had turned a cold shoulder to him. Obviously he was going to try again.

This time he came back smiling, sitting proud and erect and graceful in the saddle. He had a ship. She was named *El Afortunado*. Her owners were Barcelonans. And he would have a one-fourth share in the cargo. *So he must have invested money of his own in the voyage,* she thought. She did not ask him how he had come by it. She guessed he had mortgaged his lands. But she was happy for him, for he walked with his old swagger and his dark eyes shone.

"Where will you take your ship?" she asked him.

"To Holland," he answered promptly.

Rosamunde frowned. "But the truce has long been over. Holland is again at war with Spain."

Rodrigue laughed and he lifted her up, set her in a wide windowsill with a vista of the sea behind her. "True. So there is much profit to be made in trading with her. I will paint a new name on the hull when we reach Dutch waters. The merchants of Amsterdam are a broad-minded lot—they will look the other way."

"But the guns of Spanish warships," said Rosamunde dryly. "Will *they* look the other way?"

"Guns?" he scoffed. "I have told *El Afortunado*'s owners they need have no fear—I will bring her through!"

So strongly did he say that, that Rosamunde's green eyes misted. At that moment she was fiercely proud of him. "Yes," she said huskily. "You will bring her through,
502

Rodrigue." And threw her arms about him, pulled him close.

They had been through so much together . . . and at that moment, she knew she loved him.

"What would you like me to bring you from Holland?" he teased, pushing her away a little to smile down into her face. "A length of satin? A necklace?"

"Yourself," she whispered. "Safe. I ask for nothing else, Rodrigue."

And Rodrigue clasped her to him and asked himself in his turbulent Majorcan heart if there had ever before been such a woman as Rosamunde.

That had been a few months ago. Rodrigue had returned from that voyage whistling, with money in his pockets and gifts for everyone. For Rosamunde he brought a dancing Arab mare—black as Nightwind had been, she thought stabbingly. And a rustling black silk dress. For Elaine he brought a lovely dress of china blue. For Pablo a pipe that made the man's eyes sparkle, and for Juana a new petticoat.

Rosamunde, who had labored in the fields while he was gone trying to salvage their wrecked crop, greeted him with joy. Her blond hair was bleached almost white by the fierce Majorcan sun and her fair skin was now the color of toast.

"You should wear a hat!" he told her sharply.

Rosamunde laughed and hugged him. He looked dark and handsome and prosperous—and he was wearing a new suit of fine black damask. The seams of the doublet were covered with a double row of satin braid. It became him.

"You do me honor!" she teased. "But you look too fine for your house—it does not match you."

"I have other gifts for you," he said, giving her a hot look. "We will get you out of that peasant's garb." He looked with distaste upon her worn brown homespun.

Rosamunde accompanied him as he carried his small sea chest to their bedroom. She was glad that with his new prosperity the servants would enjoy better food and she could refurbish their barren quarters as well as her own. Pablo and Juana had worked so hard—they deserved it!

And they could have the broken-down stone wall that bounded the property repaired so that the goats could range without forever getting lost. They could plant fruit trees and buy another billy goat, for the last one had succumbed to old age. Rodrigue would have a new saddle and Pablo another donkey on which he could ride to fiestas with Juana behind him. She would take lovely rides on the black Arab mare, which was named Shiraz—to the lighthouse at Cala Ratjada and to the green hills and freshwater pools of Cala Canyamel. And perhaps soon they could afford a tutor for Elaine!

So many lovely plans she made for the life at Cala Mesquida as she walked along beside Rodrigue.

In the bedroom he opened his sea chest and pulled out other gifts. A black mantilla, fragile as a spider web. A pair of silk stockings as sheer, he said, as the silky-sheer skin of her white thighs. A fan as fine as any Doña Margarita owned, and a high-backed tortoiseshell comb.

"So you are determined to make me into a Spanish lady." She laughed. "Even in this deserted place where no one ever comes!"

"*I* come here," said Rodrigue with a sweeping gesture. "And you are *my* lady. I would I could have brought you pearls. Someday I *will* bring you pearls!"

"Ah, Rodrigue, I do not need pearls—better we buy a new billy goat and have the wall repaired."

"Always the house," he murmured, "always the land. My practical Rosamunde! Ah, but it is good to be home! Come, let me see you wear my gifts—try them on!"

Swiftly she took off her clothes, leaving them in a soft pile on the floor. And while Rodrigue's eyes glinted, she dressed herself in the black silk dress and the sheer black stockings. She piled up her hair and stuck the tortoiseshell comb into it and let the drifting folds of the black lace mantilla drape over it. She struck a tempting pose by the window and let the sea breeze waft the mantilla, and waved her fan languorously.

Rodrigue loved it. He strode over and seized her and carried her, laughing and protesting, over to the big bed they had brought by cart from San Telmo, and made love
504

to her on the spot—even though she warned him flirtatiously that he well might tear her dress.

"Then we must get it off at once!" he exclaimed energetically, and divested her of it so rapidly that she thought he must have been practicing with the hooks on the way home.

Almost before the dress had cleared her body he was kissing her throat, her breasts, the whole writhing length of her. He tickled her and laughed delightedly as she twisted and protested, trying vainly to escape him. And then as she lay panting and gasping in the big bed, he divested himself of his new black damask garments and seized her—a strong man in his prime—and made wild love to her. Tenderly, but with a kind of controlled frenzy that told her how very much he had missed her.

When at last he had finished and slid away to lie exhausted beside her with his eyes shut, Rosamunde lay back on the bed, naked in the heat save for her long black stockings, which she had not had time to remove, and studied him. His lean body was taut and trim. His dark narrow face had lost its look of discontent. He was his old debonair self again, tempestuous and merry—a charming mate.

So why could she not forget Harry?

It was a question that tore at her, for Harry was never far from her thoughts. It was as if he were not dead . . . certainly he lived on in her heart. And it worried her that this should be so when she was married to Rodrigue, when he so obviously loved her, when indeed she returned that love.

Yet only last night she had dreamed of Harry and had wakened in the moonlight with tears shining on her lashes . . .

She gave a guilty start. Rodrigue had opened his eyes and was looking at her.

"I have missed you, Rodrigue," she said truthfully, trying to brush away her unfaithful thoughts.

"You will see more of me this time," he promised, reaching over to play with a round breast that trembled at his touch. "For I have not brought you these clothes
505

only to wear to church here in Cala Mesquida! I am taking you with me on my next voyage, and you can wear them then."

"Oh, Rodrigue!" Rosamunde sat up excitedly and her face lit up. "Where will we go?"

"We will sail to Ostend in the Spanish Netherlands—but perhaps we will also see your favorite town, Amsterdam!"

"Rodrigue, how wonderful!" She threw herself upon him, and he moved lithely under her soft weight, wrapped his arms about her tempting nakedness and took her again —gently and with love.

Rosamunde strained against him, giving affection for affection. She was grateful to Rodrigue and—yes, she loved him!

And not until this moment had she realized how very tired she was of the monotonous vista of a sea that was endlessly blue, of a diamond-hard blue sky, of the dry *garriga* stretching forever away.

Amsterdam! she thought as her senses swirled beneath his soft assaults. She was going back to Amsterdam!

That had been three weeks ago. During that time Rodrigue had gone back to Palma, where *El Afortunado* had been careened and was having her hull scraped and tarred.

Around her now the shadows were lengthing about the ruined *talayoti*. Rosamunde stood up and stretched and went to where the little nanny goat was daintly chewing on thorn. She leaned down and patted that soft head. "Come along," she said gently, and the little animal trotted ahead of her down the path that led back to the house and the goat enclosure.

Rosamunde followed, with her head full of dreams of Amsterdam. For Rodrigue was due back tomorrow, and the next day they would journey on horseback across the island to Palma and there embark on his tall white ship for the trading hub of the western world—Amsterdam.

Two

The Wanderer

London and Amsterdam 1622—1628

35 *While Rosamunde was speeding aboard the Coronada* from the shores of Ireland to the great house of the Avilo family at San Telmo, Harry had word from Barcelona. So many months had passed that even his stout heart was beginning to despair of ever learning the fate of the *Santa Cecilia* when he rode in the heat of July into London. He could almost feel Nightwind's indignation at the noisy crowded streets, the cobbles slippery with filth, the rude bawling of the carters and draymen as they tried to inch their carts and heavy wagons between darting pedestrians and street hawkers loudly calling out the merits of fish and fowl and baked pies.

Here was a busy corner where two crooked alleys ran together. Nightwind snorted and reared back to avoid a huge dray piled high with household goods on its way to the docks for removal to the Colonies. Harry soothed the big black horse with a word and a comforting pat, and Nightwind moved forward warily, his big hooves ringing on the uneven cobbles. Nightwind was brave as a lion in the country and had been known to do snorting battle with wolves in his day, but he was appalled by the raucous stream of city traffic. Harry didn't blame him; he preferred the country too.

Harry put up at the Star, ordering the sharp-eyed groom who led his nervous mount away to curry him and give him a good rubdown. The groom's nod was too careless to please him, so once he had arranged for his night's lodging, Harry went out to the stable and made sure that Nightwind was properly cared for. The big horse gave him a grateful look, nibbled the sugarcake Harry brought him and nuzzled Harry's broad shoulders gently, and Harry for a moment buried his dark head in that thick mane. They had been together a long time, horse and man. Nightwind was even beginning to forget his dazzling experiences among the mares in the night pastures of Surrey. He and Harry had slipped easily into their old roving life once again.

That evening Harry went around to the Hart, where his acquaintance Mr. Desmond, who had surreptitious dealings in various parts of the world, was wont to take his evening glass of port. The Hart's common room was crowded with a bunch of young rakes come from Surrey to attend a bearbaiting; their plumed hats swayed and their spurs jingled as they argued about whether the nearby cockfights might not be a better amusement. Near Harry's table two old men in plain black broad-brimmed hats consumed huge amounts of pigeon pie and lamented the occupation of the Palatinate by Spain, for Europe was already locked in what would become known as the Thirty Years War. At another table nearby a flushed-faced young man, whose brown Venetian tabby clothing had a startling amount of yellow-starched lace and gold buttons, talked to his fashionable companions in a loud aggrieved voice about one of the king's favorites who had well-nigh booted him out of Whitehall.

Seated alone and silent, his plain russet garb and serviceable sword and baldric guaranteed to attract little notice in this motley crowd, the lean highwayman whose fame resounded throughout England drank his ale from a pewter tankard and waited impatiently for Mr. Desmond to arrive.

At last he came, a slender bony little man with a habit of compressing his thin lips and squinting his small brown eyes to slits. Now those narrow slits swept the room and settled on Harry. A faint smile of recognition passed his lips and he moved toward that corner of the room, his progress impeded by hurrying tavern maids carrying trays and chargers and clattering armloads of empty tankards, for the Hart did a good business.

"Ah, I see I find you in good health, sir." Mr. Desmond

flopped down in the empty seat across from Harry and pulled his plum-colored cloak around him with a little shiver—Mr. Desmond was always cold, even in London in July.

"If you see me at all, I am probably in good health," said Harry sardonically. He turned to call a tavern maid to bring Mr. Desmond a glass of port.

"Aye, that's true, that's undoubtedly true," agreed Mr. Desmond, rubbing his perpetually cold hands together and studying the face opposite him. A dangerous man, he thought dispassionately. Mr. Desmond made his living dealing with dangerous men. He could have told you a great deal about many of the patrons seated at that moment in the Hart's common room. He could have told you which were the wastrels, and which the court favorites, and which could be had for a price. He knew, for instance, that Harry was a highwayman with a price on his head. It had not occurred to Mr. Desmond to essay to collect that price, for he had always found it more profitable to deal with such men, who of necessity paid above market for whatever they bought, whether it was goods or information.

"Have ye news of the *Santa Cecilia?*" prodded Harry impatiently, when Mr. Desmond, shivering and sipping his port, showed no sign of imparting any information.

"Aye." Mr. Desmond nodded. "But learning it has cost me dear," he added plaintively.

Harry had been prepared for this. He pulled out a velvet purse with what he considered the proper amount for Mr. Desmond already inside. It was not his only purse, for the man across the table would have bled him dry had he known Harry carried a purse filled with gold rings and jeweled baubles as well as coins.

Mr. Desmond reached out tentatively. He lifted the purse, hefted it, and set it down with a sigh. " 'Tis lighter than last time. Things have not gone well with you lately, I take it?" he inquired in a querulous voice.

For this too, Harry was prepared—'twas the way one dealt with Mr. Desmond. He gave a snort and moved to push back his chair. "If 'tis not enough, I'll take it back and buy my information elsewhere!"

"No, no! No need for that!" said Mr. Desmond hastily. His cold fingers made a swift snatch for the purse, and it disappeared from view beneath the cloak in which he huddled. He leaned forward and Harry waited tensely—now it would come. "The *Santa Cecilia*," Mr. Desmond informed Harry importantly, "was sunk off the coast of Ireland late last fall, gutted on the rocks that line that treacherous coast." Mr. Desmond, who hated to travel, shuddered at the thought of that coast.

Sunk! Harry paled. He seized Mr. Desmond's thin lace-clad wrist in a grip that made that gentleman blanch. "And what of the woman?" His voice was hoarse. "What of Rosamunde?"

His face convulsed by pain, Mr. Desmond struggled to withdraw his wrist from Harry's grasp. "I have heard no word of the woman," he gasped, managing to wrest himself free as Harry's grip loosened.

Harry slumped back. He waited as Mr. Desmond huddled back into his cloak with a shudder and massaged his benumbed wrist. "Ye have the devil's own grip!" complained Mr. Desmond. "Ye were nigh to breaking my wrist!"

"What else do you know?" growled Harry, for it was Desmond's way to let out information craftily a little at a time.

" 'Tis worth a heavier purse," insisted his informant in an aggrieved voice.

"Desmond . . ." Harry threw away caution. He leaned forward thrusting his face almost into Mr. Desmond's. "I am hard put to keep my hands from your throat. Tell me instantly what you know or I will break both your wrists!"

He would do it, too! Mr. Desmond's eyes widened in fright. "I do know that at least the *Santa Cecilia*'s captain survived the disaster. Don Antonio Navarro saw him in Ireland only this spring and has reported him to be alive and well."

"Navarro?"

"Captain of a merchantman out of Barcelona. My information says that Captain Navarro touched port at Cádiz and mentioned seeing Don Rodrigue Avilo, captain of the *Santa Cecilia*, who had been shipwrecked in Ireland." In point of fact Mr. Desmond's information had come by way of a French prostitute in a waterfront brothel in Cádiz, brought to England by her sometime lover, a man who espoused many nationalities and was loyal to none, but Mr. Desmond saw no reason to elaborate.

"*Where* in Ireland?" demanded Harry impatiently. "Where did the ship go down? Ireland has a long coastline."

His informant shrugged; the French prostitute had not been a mapmaker. "That I do not know, sir. But Captain Navarro was planning to return to his home in Lisbon for a time and then to leave on another voyage which would take him"—here he winked and laughed as if at a good joke—"to Amsterdam."

"Holland is at war with Spain," objected Harry, eyeing Mr. Desmond narrowly, for this *could* be a fabrication to drain him of his gold. "All know that the twelve-year truce between them has ended."

"Aye, the truce is over." Mr. Desmond nodded pleasantly; the circulation in his wrist had been restored again. "But Captain Navarro is a Portuguese. He cares little for Spanish wars and even less for Dutch ones."

"But Captain Navarro sails out of Barcelona, you say. Are not his backers Spanish?"

Mr. Desmond shrugged. "I believe they are, but they look the other way when Captain Navarro sails. The captain's voyages are very profitable for them." He smiled broadly. "Of course, ye would not be wise to sail to Barcelona, for there ye'd be an Englishman and a heretic and the Inquisition would roast ye on a spit or chain ye to the oars of their galleys—but if ye took ship at once, ye might catch Captain Navarro in Amsterdam."

Harry frowned and drummed his knuckles on the table. His instinct was to go at once to Ireland and look for Rosamunde—if she still lived. But that would be foolish. Ireland's coastline was long and jagged; there were many places where a ship could wreck itself upon the rocks. No, he'd best do as this shivering well-dressed rogue across the table from him suggested—go to Amsterdam and seek out Captain Navarro and learn from him just where the *Santa Cecilia* had broken up. *Then* he would go to Ireland, when he could pinpoint his destination.

"There was no word of the woman at all?" he asked wistfully.

Mr. Desmond shook his head. "None at all," he said in a cheerful tone, and drained his glass of port.

Harry wanted to hit him for that cheery note. Instead he asked the name of Captain Navarro's ship. Mr. Desmond shrugged; he did not know. Harry then inquired as to what the fastest ship leaving London for Amsterdam might be—for Mr. Desmond was always good for such information. On hearing that it was the *Albatross* and would sail day after tomorrow, Harry took his leave of his shivering companion, paid for the ale and wine, and hurried away to seek out the captain of the *Albatross* and arrange for passage. Having done so, he addressed himself to Nightwind's situation. He disliked leaving the horse stabled in London, when he did not know how long he would be gone, nor did he wish to take him on a dangerous voyage across the seas. Suddenly he remembered Chatsbury, the estate of the famous horse breeder Sir Wilfred Keyes, where Nightwind had been so happy among the mares.

It seemed the best solution. Harry rode away to Chatsbury.

It was late when he got there, a warm moonlit night with only a little breeze stirring the big sycamores that dotted the pleasant pasture, giving shade by day beneath long leafy branches. The moon picked out a clear little brook that trickled through the pasture and turned it to silver. Somewhere a hunting owl called. In the distance the great stone barn was a black hulk.

For the last mile Harry had felt excitement mounting in the great stallion he bestrode. Indeed he had been hard put to hold Nightwind back from a gallop as they skirted the little sleeping hamlet of Wentworth-Hastings and

512

neared Sir Wilfred's estate of Chatsbury. He was thankful there were no lights in any of the crofts they had passed; crofters here went early to bed. Like shadows, he and Nightwind had followed the hedgerows until they came to Chatsbury and Harry found the gate in the pasture fence he had used once before when he had traded another horse for Nightwind.

"Easy, boy," he murmured. "We must make sure there's no one about."

The black horse seemed to understand. He and Harry were both very still, listening, as Harry's keen gaze swung around the moonlit pasture. At one end of the long field they could see the mares standing together in a companionable group, as if having a social get-together. Suddenly one of them, a white mare, lifted her head. She had scented Nightwind.

The big black horse called to her with a low whinny and she trotted swiftly over, reached over the fence to rub her dainty muzzle eagerly against his. Harry watched Nightwind affectionately as the mare stepped back, dancing on her slender legs, and tossed her head coquettishly, letting the moonlight silver her silky mane. Then she seemed to realize that Nightwind—whose bridle Harry had prudently held onto—was still on the other side of the fence. She gave a low indignant snort and ran lightly away from him, swishing her plumelike tail. After a few steps she peered back to see if he was following.

Nightwind was trembling; he turned and gave Harry an anguished look.

Harry took off Nightwind's saddle and bridle. "You have found your lady again, Nightwind," he said softly, patting the big stallion's neck. "Pray God I may find mine as speedily—and that she be not harmed. Now—go to her."

He gave Nightwind a swat on the rump and stepped back. The black stallion needed no further invitation. He cleared the fence at a bound and the white mare turned and reared up, almost twirling in joy. More dignified now, Nightwind strolled over to her. He moved with a masterful stride, and when he reached her, turned about indifferently and stood looking fixedly in the other direction. Harry grinned. *You don't want her to know what a hold she's got on you*, he thought. The mare reached up and gave Nightwind's ear a playful nip, and he turned as if in surprise to see her there. Harry was chuckling as Nightwind trotted off beside the white mare. He was swaggering a little, Harry thought.

Sniffing the newcomer on the soft summer air, several horses had come up curiously to the fence which separated the stallions from the brood mares. Among them Harry saw the roan he had left before as a trade for Nightwind. The roan was watching Nightwind's progress into the group of mares a little sadly, Harry thought. Well, he'd give the roan an outing to ease his anguish!

It was the big roan on which Harry rode away, having transferred Nightwind's saddle and bridle to the roan's back. The roan seemed to appreciate the chance of a gallop, and once they had quietly skirted the hamlet of Wentworth-Hastings and were out on the open road to London, Harry let him run.

They arrived in London without incident, and Harry made his last arrangements and took his saddlebags aboard the *Albatross*.

Corpulent Sir Wilfred Keyes could not believe his ears when he learned at breakfast that the big black stallion was back and now the roan was gone! A stableboy ran, panting, to the big house with the news.

"What!" cried Sir Wilfred, leaping up and knocking over his bowl of porridge—for he had of late been dieting on oatmeal and barley bread in an attempt once again to fit into his favorite purple waistcoat. He sprinted past the stableboy, collided with the serving girl who was carrying in the barley bread, and charged on to the stables.

There he found Nightwind, who had strolled in through an open stable door and was contentedly munching hay. He looked up indifferently as Sir Wilfred approached, then returned to his meal.

Sir Wilfred's eyes bulged. "And the roan is gone, you say?" he asked raggedly.

"Aye, Sir Wilfred. He was in the pasture with the other stallions, and now he do be gone."

All day Sir Wilfred spent in the saddle, combing every place on his estate where he thought a horse might hide. He rode back empty-handed and puzzled.

"Mark my words," he told his faded once-pretty wife, as he balefully attacked a pasty of venison garnished with larks' tongues at dinner. "This is no—"

"Your diet, my dear," she interrupted cautiously.

"Diet?" Sir Wilfred's voice crackled. "You prate to me of diets when I'm near famished from a hard day's riding? Mark my words, I say. This is no ordinary theft. Vanished into thin air, has my roan? Not likely! Ye'll remember they were both blooded stallions, good breeding stock? 'Tis some rival horse breeder who shrewdly guessed I would not sell the black stallion and stole him from me and impudently substituted his roan! And now he'll have bred all his mares with the brute and he feared I might one day recognize my property—on *his* holdings—so he's brought the black stallion back lest I discover his villainy! And taken away the roan!" He rolled his eyes at the ceiling.

His wife hoped Sir Wilfred would not attack the great tart with the same enthusiasm with which he was demolishing the venison pasty. He would soon be able to wear none of his clothes!

"At least," she said repressively, "you have the black stallion back and in good shape, you say."

"Aye, but I'd give a packet to know where he's been." Sir Wilfred sighed.

Harry's "arrangements"—for he was sentimental about horses—had included sending the big roan back to Sir Wilfred by a circuitous route that could never be traced back to him.

When two days later the roan appeared in the pasture at Chatsbury, apparently having been ridden hard, and delighted at his return, Sir Wilfred almost had a stroke.

"It seems to me," soothed his wife, sensibly offering him her smelling salts and having them waved away, "that
515

you are the gainer in all this. You have your black stallion back—and you also have the roan!"

" 'Tis a horse breeder's done this," reiterated Sir Wilfred darkly. "Why, 'tis as if I had rented out the black stallion and received the roan in payment!"

He staggered out to the pasture and stared at the two stallions, pointedly ignoring each other across the pasture fence. Nightwind was grazing contentedly beside the white mare. Both their heads went up suspiciously as Sir Wilfred approached.

"Lord," said Sir Wilfred, looking from Nightwind to the roan, "but I wish you two could speak and tell me all about it!"

The wind blew fair for Holland, but it could not blow fair enough for Harry. Every slackening of sail he eyed with impatience. When the *Albatross'* captain told him jovially that they were making good time, he was somewhat put out that Harry's response was a frown and a sharp question as to how soon they would reach Amsterdam.

A dour fellow, this Mr. Howard, thought the captain—for Harry had signed aboard as Harry Howard. Restless and worried about Rosamunde, he had little to do with the other passengers, save for an old man named Grimshaw with whom he played frequent games of chess. Ignoring the sly smiles he got from the ship's female passengers, Harry strode about the deck taking the air and ate heartily of the ship's indifferent food. He had not thought to bring on board a supply of fresh fruit, but Mr. Desmond had. Mr. Desmond had appeared on the dock, wrapped as usual in his cloak and shivering, just before the *Albatross* sailed. Beside him was a lackey who hoisted a huge basket of fruit aboard.

"I think ye'll find these useful on your sea voyage," said Mr. Desmond, adding in honeyed tones, "I hope ye will find further use for my services on your return."

"Aye, I've no doubt of it," said Harry grimly. He'd borrowed money from Mr. Desmond before—Mr. Desmond charged forty percent per month—and he'd prob-
516

ably have to borrow from him again, for he doubted he'd return fat of purse—though he *did* intend to return with Rose by his side, God willing!

He thanked Mr. Desmond, shook the man's cold lifeless hand, and watched the anchor hauled up. By the rail he stood and watched the English shore depart, not dreaming that he would never live there again. Indeed all his thoughts were on the future, on finding Rosamunde.

Days aboard the *Albatross* were bearable, Harry found, for he managed to get some exercise by pacing up and down the deck, drinking in the fresh salt air that beat against his hard frame. But the nights were bad. He tossed sleeplessly in his small bunk—too short for a man the length of him—and memories flooded back of a slip of a girl naked and enticing in the moonlight, who had held out her white arms to him. He saw her again standing cool and fair in the cold brook water, saw her in the pink light of early morning splashing the silvery water about her bare legs. She would look up and smile at him invitingly, she would toss back her long blond hair, her soft breasts would ripple—and Harry would groan on his bunk and clench the wooden sides with his hands.

Sleepless, he swore a great oath:

He would find Captain Navarro—and through him Captain Rodrigue Avilo, who had sailed away with Rosamunde. By God, he would wrench the truth from them both if necessary! He would find out what Captain Avilo had done with Rosamunde. Horrible pictures flitted through Harry's tortured mind. She had been drowned in the shipwreck—he could see her deep down, her face pale and drowned-looking, her lovely hair tangled in seaweed. Or she had been sold to some wild Irish chieftain who had taken her deep into the trackless interior of Ireland to live with him the life of the hunted. Or perhaps Captain Avilo, finding himself a Spaniard on English-governed soil, had given her up to the English authorities to gain favor for himself. Perhaps even now she was swinging from a tall gibbet or rotting in an Irish jail!

So by night with these fancies Harry tortured himself. It was small wonder that by day he was cold and taciturn.

The *Albatross'* captain gave him a stiff goodbye when the ship docked in Amsterdam harbor. A lofty fellow, this Mr. Howard, he thought to himself. Ignoring everyone all through the voyage! A wonder it was that all the ladies had fancied him so, and sighed when Mr. Howard did not deign to notice them!

Harry did not even notice the coldness of the captain's goodbye. He was first among the passengers to alight on Dutch soil, carrying his worldly goods with him in a pair of saddlebags slung over his arm. Between the price he had paid Mr. Desmond for supplying him information and the cost of ship's passage, he had arrived in Amsterdam short of cash, although he had with him a small velvet pouch containing gold rings and fobs and two gold chains which were valuable.

He swung ashore on a blustery day of alternating clouds and sunshine, and forbore the urge to search the docks at once for Captain Navarro's ship, for he could see for himself that there must be a thousand ships or more in the harbor. Instead he plunged through the waterfront crowds into the busy city of canals and commerce. He took no time to appreciate the intricate brickwork of the crowded houses standing shoulder to shoulder, or the ornate step gables or the tall clusters of brick chimneys, or the international crowds, babbling in many tongues. Harry was intent on but one thing: finding Captain Navarro.

To that end he put up at a waterfront inn with gaily painted blue shutters, and proceeded to comb the docks, asking for the Portuguese captain. Silently he cursed the fact that Mr. Desmond had not found out the name of Captain Navarro's ship, for there seemed to be innumerable ships in the harbor, and more came and went each day, he was told.

As the day wore on, his tall figure, asking always the same question, was becoming a familiar one about the docks. But by evening he was no closer to finding Captain Navarro than he had been in England.

36

Wilhelm Van Hoorn was having a bad year. Low in funds after he had spent the advance Rodrigue had given him to drug Rosamunde, he had first gone back to his family home in Haarlem and there courted a slim bright-eyed girl named Lotje, daughter of a prominent local bulb grower. The bulb grower, knowing Wilhelm for a wastrel and the black sheep of his family, had locked up his daughter and slammed his oaken door in Van Hoorn's handsome face. Disgruntled, Van Hoorn had taken his brown-gold beard and his optimistic nature to Rotterdam, where he had an uncle living in a pretty little step-gabled house in the suburb of Delfshaven. But the commerce, the tall white ships with fluttering sails that passed through that great port where the Rhine—now named the New Maas River—emptied its waters into the North Sea, had interested Van Hoorn no more than had the flower fields around Haarlem. His uncle thought he knew how to straighten his errant nephew out. Some two years before he had given shelter to certain members of a group of Pilgrims who had sailed from there in the month of July to America. Their talk of a new land had fired in the older man an interest in emigrating, and he urged his nephew to join him. But Wilhelm Van Hoorn had no more taste for pioneering than he had for the sea or bulb growing. He spent his time in grog shops and roistering about the town, and on the day he gambled away his uncle's favorite long clay pipe and four valuable Delft plates, his uncle took a whip to him and turned him out.

Van Hoorn hurried back to Haarlem and talked his

widowed mother out of her life savings. His scheme was ingenious. He told her he wanted to elope with Lotje, buy a riverboat and ply the Spaarne River transporting flower bulbs to market. His mother, cajoled by the prospect of seeing her favorite son every time his boat drifted through Haarlem, gave him the money and saw him married to Lotje before she died when she slipped on her icy stoop and was run over by a heavy wagon wheel in the street. But her son Wilhelm never bought the boat. Instead he took Lotje to Leyden, where he had idled some time away at the university, and spent the money on high living.

When the money ran out, he abandoned the now-pregnant and disillusioned Lotje in Leyden and drifted by stages back to Amsterdam. There he at last put his education to use, for he reluctantly hired out as a clerk to one of Amsterdam's more successful merchant traders—that same Joost Van den Vondel whom he had bragged to Rosamunde of knowing. With his smooth manner and bland smile, Van Hoorn managed to work his way into a position of trust—and at the first opportunity absconded with some of Van den Vondel's funds. Tracked down by his irate employer—he had promptly headed for his native Haarlem—he had been saved from jail only by the enthusiastic intervention of his sister Mathilde, the only member of his family with whom he was still on speaking terms. Mathilde wept buckets, she implored; she was a handsome woman, and she finally won the day by making up Van den Vondel's losses herself. Mathilde's husband, Hooft, away from home at the time, had taken a dim view of having his hard-earned money wasted on his scoundrel of a brother-in-law. Unmoved by Mathilde's flowing tears, he had shoved Wilhelm Van Hoorn bodily through his front door into the street—he could do that because he was a giant of a man and hard-muscled—and warned him in a thunderous voice that had caused nearby shutters to fly open and heads to stick out that it was the last time he could expect help from this quarter.

Now an outcast from his family, who had supported him for so long, Wilhelm Van Hoorn had drifted back to Amsterdam. But word of his embezzlement from Van den

Vondel had spread, and he was cold-shouldered when he tried to find a job.

Of late Van Hoorn had been gambling for a living—which worked out well enough as long as the dice were his own. He had paid a handsome price for these "loaded" dice. But one night he overstepped himself and cheated a cold-eyed, hard-fisted Danish trader who snatched up the dice and broke them. On finding weights inside, the Dane promptly pursued Wilhelm down a narrow alley, cornered him where an overturned cart had blocked the street, and dragged the protesting Dutchman from a doorway where he was pounding and howling for entrance. There beneath the overhang of the lopsided buildings, the Danish trader had administered such a sound beating that Van Hoorn ached for a month.

With the loss of his weighted dice, Van Hoorn had drifted into even worse company, and had fallen to working with two waterfront cutpurses who were wont to lie in wait outside taverns for their prey. Van Hoorn had convinced them that such haphazard targets often netted little while the risk was great; 'twas better that he spend the evening drinking inside the tavern, observing who had a heavy purse and was too far gone in his cups to put up much of a fight. Van Hoorn's associates were the sort of men Harry would have scorned, but the life suited Van Hoorn well enough. It kept him in drinking money, and his share of the purses taken by his evil associates kept a roof over his head.

It was unlikely that the money he earned in this desperate manner would ever be enough to let him return to Lotje, who pined away for him in Haarlem, for her father had come to Leyden and taken her back to the bulb farm to have her baby, but Van Hoorn was a dreamer. He missed Lotje's warm white arms and bright smile. Not a night went by but that he imagined he would chance on some fellow with his life savings in his purse (there were such in Amsterdam, for people came there to buy and sell all manner of things, whole shiploads full; it was a town of great trading ventures), and then he would return, snatch Lotje from the bulb farm and set her and the

521

baby up in a fine brick home along one of the great canals.

On Harry's first night ashore in Amsterdam, Van Hoorn was posted in his favorite tavern watching Cornelis Van der Leyden grow drunk. Van Hoorn recognized Van der Leyden by sight—indeed, most of Amsterdam recognized Van der Leyden by sight, for he was one of that new-formed aristocracy of great merchant traders with a fine tall-gabled brick house on Rapenburg near that of the naval hero Piet Heyn.

Cornelis Van der Leyden was sure to carry a purse heavy with gold, thought Van Hoorn, noisily banging his brass tankard on the wooden table for a refill. It was unusual for Mynheer Van der Leyden to drink so much, the tavern maid confided when she brought Van Hoorn his ale; could he still be mourning his wife, who had died when a hoist broke and dropped a heavy load of lumber on her head as she walked to market?

Van Hoorn snorted. That had happened at least a dozen years ago. Who would mourn a woman so long? He made a ribald remark to the tavern maid, who frowned and tried to avoid his pinching fingers, just then reaching out for her bottom beneath her homespun skirts. Men like Van Hoorn made her life a problem!

Once she was gone, Van Hoorn forgot her, concentrating on his quarry, the rich merchant, a big gray-haired man soberly dressed in gray tabby trimmed with black ribands and black braid. Momentarily he expected Van der Leyden to leave, and he hoped Van der Leyden would not leave in the company of his fellow merchants, for his two confederates outside were cowardly and would never attack a band. He smiled over his tankard's rim as he saw the group rise and say their goodnights, leaving Van der Leyden sitting morosely alone. Soon Van der Leyden would be leaving too. But morosely the gray-haired man continued to drink.

When at last he saw Van der Leyden rise and lurch to the tavern door, Van Hoorn hastily swallowed the last of his ale, wiped his brown-gold beard with a dirty lace cuff, tossed some coins upon the table and sauntered out—not too fast—behind him. As the door closed behind him he looked quickly around—nobody in sight except the elderly merchant, pursuing a wavering path toward his home on Rapenburg. It was dark in the street. Clumps of clouds had drifted past all day, and now one such clump obscured the moon. As the moon broke cover, Van Hoorn lifted his white linen kerchief and waved it once toward the seemingly empty street down which Van der Leyden was making his halting way. At the signal two dark shapes emerged from the shadows of doorways where they had been lurking and began stalking the unsuspecting merchant.

It was this scene Harry chanced upon as he made his way back to his inn from a last look at the myriad ships in the harbor. He saw the kerchief waved as a signal, he saw the two dark shapes converge on Van der Leyden's lurching figure. He had no doubt what was afoot.

Harry's reaction was automatic. He sprang forward and gave a shout of warning.

Van Hoorn got a good look at Harry as he charged down the street—it was a murderous look he flung the Englishman, for Van Hoorn was in sore need of his one-third share of the gray-haired merchant's purse; his landlady, a big fierce *vrouw* with yellow teeth, had been pressing for the rent. He might have dashed forward to help his fellows, just now converging on the merchant, but Harry's shout had been heard down the street, and now a couple of upstairs windows swung open and nightcapped heads stuck out.

Van Hoorn had no desire to be taken, whatever happened to the pair down the street. Quickly he fell back within the tavern he had just departed.

"There are cutthroats abroad!" he gasped, holding his chest as if he might be in danger of a heart attack. "I saw them pounce upon a man down the street—I do believe it was Mynheer Van der Leyden, who had just quitted this place. Had I left but a moment sooner, they would surely have attacked *me!*"

The tavernkeeper gave Van Hoorn a jaded look. He was not unaware of Van Hoorn's new profession, but he chose to ignore it. This was a rough district, and he must deal with all comers. But several half-drunk patrons ran to the door and leaned out, alert to the clash of steel down the street. Fights were always a popular diversion and well attended.

Van Hoorn, in their van, saw bitterly that Harry had felled one miscreant and was fighting the second with his sword while Van der Leyden, who had been knocked to the street, dizzily regained his feet. Terror seized Van Hoorn—suppose his friends were taken? They'd name him as their accomplice!

Spurred by that frightening thought, Van Hoorn now ran down the street, calling out sturdily, "Stop, thief!"

From the gutter the fallen one scrambled up, gave a wild look toward that well-known voice denouncing him and took to his heels. Van Hoorn, in an apparent attempt to catch him, pretended to stumble against Harry from the rear, causing Harry to lose his balance for a second. In that second, Harry's second foe spun away and was lost in the shadows of a nearby alley, his feet clop-clopping over the bricks and dying away rapidly in the distance.

Furious at this clumsy "aid," Harry whirled on Van Hoorn. "I'd have had him, had you not charged into me!"

"Oh, my dear fellow!" Van Hoorn was now all smiling apologies. "I *am* sorry I fell against you there—I missed my footing. Ah, but we nearly had them!" He sighed and turned his solicitude onto Van der Leyden. "Mynheer Van der Leyden, what lawless streets we have that you should be attacked thus! Can I be of assistance?"

Cornelis Van der Leyden, considerably sobered, reared himself up to his considerable height and frowned at Van Hoorn. He had seen him before hanging about the tavern—a disreputable fellow; it was said he had bilked Van den Vondel of a considerable sum but that his family in Haarlem had prevented his going to jail. He was aware of where his assistance had come from. "Thank you," he said brusquely, "but it was *this* gentleman who came to my aid. Would you share a glass of Malmsey with me, mynheer?" he asked in English, for that was the
524

language he had heard Harry use. "My home is but a short distance away—if we can but reach it through the footpads." He gave Van Hoorn a distasteful glance, and Van Hoorn flushed angrily.

Harry, after his fruitless search of the docks, had nothing to look forward to but a sleepless night at an indifferent inn. He sheathed his sword and nodded. "I would be delighted, sir." He remembered to give his new alias. "Howard is my name—Harry Howard."

Seething with rage behind his bright smile, Van Hoorn watched the tall Englishman walk away with the gray-haired merchant. He saw Harry reach out a strong arm to steady his newfound friend.

"I am a bit wobbly on my legs tonight," admitted Van der Leyden with a rueful laugh. "I stayed too long at the tavern. I should have sent for my manservant Joris to walk me home, but he is old and I hated to drag him out in the night."

"I have stayed too long at many taverns," said Harry genially. "And fought my way out of more than one. But I have had not so much as a glass of wine this night, so I should be able to bring you home as safe as Joris."

"Safer," said Van der Leyden. "Joris is willing but he's no fighter. Never was, not even as a young man."

They were now walking down a quiet street of handsome houses. They climbed half a flight of stone steps and knocked on the door of one. After a few moments a manservant, looking a bit sleepy and resentful, peered out and then admitted them. He muttered something in Dutch.

Van der Leyden laughed. "Joris says I am unable to walk, that I should have sent for him and he would have brought me home in a barrow. Joris has been long in my service, and takes liberties. Speak English, Joris, 'tis the tongue our guest speaks—and bring us some Malmsey, the best you can find. Mynheer Howard here saved my life tonight, for I've no doubt that pair would have slit my throat after they'd slit my purse!" He turned to Harry. "Or would you prefer something else? My wine cellar is varied."

"But the Malmsey is the best," interposed Joris, looking more kindly on Harry. "Ye were a powerful man in your prime," he told his master severely. "But now your gray hair does invite footpads. A man with your experience of Amsterdam should know better than to walk alone by night."

"Especially in my cups, eh, Joris?" Cornelis Van der Leyden gave his old retainer an affectionate look. "Shall it be Malmsey, then?"

"Malmsey will do nicely," said Harry, his gray eyes kindling as he sensed that behind this handsome brick facade lay not only wine and companionship but information as well.

Joris closed and latched the door behind them, and Van der Leyden ushered Harry into a large and rather cozy room to the left of the entrance hall. It was easy to tell that the owner of this room was in the East India trade, for not only did a pair of tall Chinese vases flank the long wooden settle opposite the fireplace while a large woolen Oriental rug in harsh reds and blues adorned the clean-scoured floor, but the heavy oaken table in the center of the room was spread with a thick Chinese rug in rich ruby tones. On that table reposed a pair of heavy branched silver candlesticks, some fine linen napkins and an array of small fruit knives surrounding a Delft-blue bowl of ripe fruit. From a heavy dark cupboard nearby the manservant, Joris, extracted two heavy glass goblets and a bottle of Malmsey. Van der Leyden urged Harry to sit and himself sank down upon a heavy carved chair of some dark wood.

Joris was watching him in puzzlement, for the master never drank so much that he reeled into the house. Van der Leyden moved his shoulders uneasily under that frank inspection and for a moment passed his hands over his eyes. He had seen death coming twice tonight—once when those two cutpurses had jumped him in the dark street, and once much earlier before he had begun to drink his way into oblivion—and *that* death would not be denied. The old pains were back. He had always known they would come back and that when they did he would go downhill fast and it would be the end of him. He had felt it first, that familiar sickening pain in his side, as he was strolling home from his big brick warehouse on the Voorburgwal—that warehouse he had built and of which he was so justly proud. The pains had gone by the time he had reached the tavern, but he had known they would come back and that next time they would be worse. The tavern had been convenient, he had found a group of his fellow merchants there, and, loath to go home, he had lingered there drinking more than a man should.

Cornelis Van der Leyden was sixty-seven years old; he had lived a full life and except for his gray locks he looked to be still in his prime. But he knew. A year, he gave himself, possibly two, and then it would be over and he would be but a memory, one of the legendary figures who had helped to create what men were already calling Holland's Golden Age. It seemed strange to think that he would be dead, no longer controlling his great trading empire. The house on Rapenburg, the big brick warehouse, his shares in the Dutch East India Company, the three tall ships that rode the harbor, all would go—to whom? If only his son had lived. . . . Cornelis had never had any brothers; his sisters were all dead, and he had not liked them anyway— except smiling Jannet, who had had twin sons and died of the event. One of her sons had gone to New Amsterdam in America and had not been heard from for years and was presumed dead. The other was a strutting nincompoop named Jan whom Cornelis disliked to the point of hatred —he would not turn his fortune over to *him!* And his wife's family had come from Brussels, and all had died when the Plague visited there—no aid from that direction.

Cornelis Van der Leyden sighed and roused himself to entertain his guest. "Some fruit?" He indicated the Delft bowl on the table. "You will find it good, I think. The grapes and apples are from France, the plums from Holland, and the oranges from Spain."

"From Spain? I congratulate you. One would not know there was a war on!"

Van der Leyden smiled and shrugged. "There are always reckless fellows to run any blockade, and what moves in the western world moves usually through Amsterdam.

But come, a bit of fruit, a glass of wine, a night's lodging is hardly repayment for saving my life tonight. Is there not some more substantial way that I can thank you, Mynheer Howard?"

"There is," said Harry, sipping his Malmsey, which was excellent. "I seek information in Amsterdam, and perhaps you will be able to help me, Mynheer Van der Leyden."

The Dutchman nodded his leonine head. "I am in touch with much that goes on here," he admitted.

Harry leaned forward, studying the big man in gray tabby. "Then perhaps you can tell me the name of the ship commanded by Captain Navarro out of Barcelona. I'm told Captain Navarro himself is Portuguese."

"I can," replied Van der Leyden promptly. "She is named the *Infanta* when she sails from Barcelona to Ostend. But she changes her name to *Maartje* and flies the Dutch flag when she sails into Amsterdam. And she will again fly Spanish colors and metamorphose once again into the *Infanta* before she casts anchor in her home port of Barcelona."

Harry gave him a quizzical look. "The oranges?"

Van der Leyden nodded. "Now that the twelve-year truce between Spain and Holland is over, certain ships keep the trade alive—clandestinely. The Portuguese Captain Navarro is one of them. Such captains paint new names on their ships and hoist new flags, depending upon the port they are making for. It is a well-known practice; the authorities in some ports may know about it, but as a rule they look the other way."

Harry congratulated himself on his luck. Of all the men in the world he might have helped this night, he had given aid to one who knew Captain Navarro! And now he knew the name of Captain's Navarro's ship—the *Maartje!* He racked his brain, wondering if he had seen the *Maartje* in the harbor, but in upward of a thousand ships he could not remember the name.

The man in gray tabby was watching his English guest curiously. Both sat at their ease, leaning back with their legs crossed, and Harry could not but think how warm and inviting this room would be in winter when snow frosted the small-paned windows and a fire burned on the hearth and cast its warm glow upon that jewel-toned rug.

"You seek Captain Navarro?" asked the Dutchman.

"Yes. I am told that he is soon to put in to Amsterdam."

"I will correct you there. Captain Navarro is about to leave. He sailed in on a fair wind and has today finished loading his cargo. I would expect him to sail on the morning tide."

An exclamation from Harry brought a look of surprise to the Dutchman's face. In one swift movement, Harry's legs had uncrossed, his boots were now solidly on the floor, he had risen and was setting his half-empty goblet onto the carpet-covered table. "Faith, I'll see him tonight then!" he cried.

"Not so fast, my friend." The Dutchman waved him back to his seat. "Captain Navarro is a devil with the ladies. He will spend his last night before sailing enjoying the brothels of Amsterdam—and if you would find him, you must look between all the sheets of the city!"

"If need be!" Chagrined that he had not known before that Captain Navarro was here, Harry had already turned to go, for the night was short for him to seek his quarry.

"But if you will stay the night with me," pursued the gray-haired Van der Leyden, "I will have Joris take you to where the *Maartje* lies at anchor in plenty of time. Captain Navarro is very punctual. He will tear himself away from his warm bed and the clinging arms that hold him and be back on his ship at least an hour before sailing." He looked at Harry quizzically. "You would sail with him?"

"I would speak with him. 'Tis an urgent matter I have come all the way from England to discuss."

Cornelis Van der Leyden was not a prying man. If his curiosity was piqued by what matter would hurry a man from England to catch a Portuguese captain at a port in Holland, he did not show it. Instead he made Harry welcome, discussing the city and its trade. When, a few minutes later, an elderly serving woman appeared with both her white Dutch cap and collar askew as testimony to the speed with which she had dressed, he said kindly,

"Gretha, Joris should not have waked you. I could light Mynheer Howard to his room well enough."

Old Gretha gave him a quelling look. "And who would be making the room ready?" she inquired with asperity. "As soon as Joris told me we had a guest, I got out fresh linens. If ye will follow me, mynheer?"

"First let Mynheer Howard finish his drink," suggested Van der Leyden mildly. Harry swallowed the last of his Malmsey and smilingly announced himself ready for bed. He liked this easygoing Dutchman whose old servants regarded him more as a son than an employer and scolded him for his own good.

Old Gretha picked up her neat gray homespun skirts and white Dutch apron and lit Harry's way up the handsome wooden stair to his sleeping chamber on the floor above. Shadows leaped against the white-painted walls as he followed her, making dark grotesque shapes. She led him into a squarish front room whose small-paned windows looked out over Rapenburg. He saw that Gretha had already turned down the big square bed, which was spread with an embroidered coverlet and to a tired man looked infinitely inviting. She set down the candle in its round brass holder on a little carved chest by the bed.

"I think you will be comfortable here, mynheer," she told him.

Harry smiled at her. "I am sure I will, but 'twas not my intention to get you up in the night. My host could have lighted me to my bedchamber."

Gretha drew herself up and gave Harry a disapproving look from a pair of faded blue eyes. At the door she paused and said softly, "Joris and myself are both beholden to you, mynheer, for what you did tonight. Mynheer Van der Leyden forgets that he is no longer a young man—we worry about him, Joris and I."

The door closed firmly, and Harry smiled to himself at such loyalty. Wistfully he thought of old John at Locke Hall . . . John would have felt the same.

He took off his sword and baldric and his boots and made ready for bed. It was a deep soft feather bed of
530

goosedown into which he sank and sank—a far cry from the bedbuggy mattress he might have found at the inn.

But Harry was in no mood to appreciate all this luxury. His mind seethed. Tomorrow he would learn Rosamunde's fate!

37

Dawn found Harry dressed and booted, impatient to be taken to Captain Navarro's ship. His grayhaired host, up at daybreak despite his evening at the tavern, smiled at this impatience. "There is plenty of time for breakfast, Mynheer Howard," he told Harry. "Captain Navarro sails with the tide—he will not yet be back aboard the *Maartje*."

Breakfast was a stout affair: thick clotted cream and plum preserves, fat sausages and curds and delicious pancakes. Harry, anxious and uncertain, could not do it justice.

"However you spend your day, I will expect you back here for supper," announced Van der Leyden as they rose from the table. "Since you have rescued me from the footpads of the street, I can only hope that you will consider my home your own while you are in Amsterdam. For my sake," he added wryly, "more than your own!"

Harry, who had no idea what his plans would be, murmured his thanks and set off with taciturn old Joris as his guide. They had been walking briskly along the waterfront for some time when old Joris came to a halt. "There lies the *Maartje* at anchor, Mynheer Howard, and I think ye had best go aboard at once, for I see they are making ready to cast off." He turned and left him.

From the poop the Portuguese captain, Don Antonio

531

Navarro, watched Harry come aboard. He was an imposing figure, tall and supple and clad in the rich dark garments of his kind—the "Spanish styles" which had swept Europe and were being copied by fashionable gentlemen throughout the western world. A heavy gold chain glinted on the dark brocade that covered his considerable chest, but there was no glint at all in his hard appraising eyes.

"I seek Captain Navarro," the Portuguese captain heard Harry say in a clear carrying voice, and his jutting jaw jutted a little further. He regarded this tall newcomer to his ship with some malevolence. Captain Navarro's dark head ached from too much wine and too much wenching. He hoped with fervent sincerity that this tall fellow was not one of that little group of gentlemen he had offended in a tavern last night with his bawdy song about the Dutch, and from whom he had made his escape a bit tardily, losing his plumed hat in the resultant scuffle. Ah, but if by bad luck it was, the battle would be one to one instead of one to four, and he would certainly give this gentleman satisfaction! He loosened his sword in his baldric and strode forward to meet this formidable newcomer with all the bravado a man with a hangover that made every step clang like a gong through his head could muster. He stopped suddenly as his queasy stomach seemed to turn over and he closed his eyes. *Santa Maria,* what a night it had been!

When he opened his eyes, Harry was still there, surrounded by a non-English-speaking group on the deck.

Captain Navarro fought back an anguished groan and promised himself he would sing no more songs—bawdy or otherwise.

"Yusef." He spoke sharply to a nearby sailor. "Bring the gentleman who has just boarded us to me at once."

The sailor he had addressed was thin and dark and sharp-eyed, with aquiline features. He was a Morisco—a Moor whose people had been forcibly converted to Catholicism in Spain. He had noted the tall gentleman who walked with such authority coming aboard—and had eased closer to his captain. He always tried to be close
532

at hand when anything unusual happened—not because he cared anything for the handsomely clad Portuguese captain, but there was oftentimes money to be gained by having information, and it was a novel thing for an Englishman to come aboard this ship. Swiftly he brought Harry to the captain, then found something to tinker with so that he might appear busy and remain nearby. Yusef understood English passably well. Now he strained his ears to listen.

Captain Navarro watched Harry approach. Lord, he thought, the fellow was long of arm and grim of countenance! But if it was satisfaction he was after, the duel must be fought—and anyway, Captain Navarro was still smarting from the humiliation of having prudently run away last night. He should not have let that red-haired wench pull him out the tavern's back door—he should have stayed and faced them!

Now he stood with his legs wide apart and squared his shoulders.

"Ye seek me, sir?" he demanded in a truculent voice.

Without thinking, he had spoken in Portuguese, and Harry gave him a puzzled look. "I seek Captain Navarro," he reiterated.

Slowly it penetrated Captain Navarro's aching head that he was being addressed in English, and the wrathful gentlemen in the tavern last night had been Dutch to a man. He shook his head to clear it, was rewarded by a knifing pain that turned his olive skin pale. He glowered at Harry and reverted to English, which he spoke fluently.

"I am Captain Navarro," he admitted.

"Good," said Harry. "My name is Howard."

The captain listened in silence to what Harry wanted to know.

Captain Navarro had no love for the English—he had in fact traded shots recently with a British sloop when he'd strayed too close to that accursed coast. No damage had been done except to his mizzenmast and his pride, and though both had been soon repaired, he still nurtured a burning desire to make the English pay for it.

Now before him foursquare stood an Englishman, looking as resolute as any he'd ever encountered, not asking but *demanding* information, demanding it impatiently as if pressed for time.

Thoughtfully, Captain Navarro turned and spat—and narrowly missed the Morisco, Yusef, who dodged nimbly. When he turned back to this "Mr. Howard," he had made up his mind. The Englishman wanted Captain Rodrigue Avilo, did he? Captain Avilo had told him how he'd barely managed to bring his wounded ship from the English coast! Perhaps this arrogant Englishman had had something to do with that. . . .

"Am I to understand that you seek Captain Rodrigue Avilo?" he inquired, almost affably.

Harry hesitated. Best to lay the cards on the table, he thought. "I seek the woman with Captain Avilo," he explained bluntly. "The fair-haired woman under his protection."

Ah, this was more humorous than Captain Navarro had thought! Undoubtedly Rodrigue Avilo had stolen this Englishman's woman and sailed away with her—perhaps there'd been some reason for the English to fire after the departing *Santa Cecilia* after all! He considered stating bluntly that the lady was Captain Avilo's wife, decided against it—it would be more fun to play with this Englishman.

"I met this lady," he admitted slowly, and saw the Englishman's gray eyes flare up like a banked fire blazing to sudden heat. "A blond beauty with emerald eyes."

"In what health did you find her?" asked Harry, controlling with an effort his mad desire to throttle this fellow and make him spill out all the gems of information for which he hungered.

Captain Navarro was feeling better now that he had decided on a course of action. He shrugged his black damask shoulders and fingered his dark mustache. "In indifferent health. She was large with child," he added blandly, "which was why Captain Avilo would not embark with me. He feared for her life if the child were to come on a tossing ship during a storm." He saw with grim delight that his words had staggered the Englishman.
534

Large with child! The words rocked Harry. Ah, he had not known Rosamunde was pregnant! For a moment he found it hard to speak as he struggled to put a cap on his emotions. At least the Spanish captain who had taken Rosamunde to Ireland cared about her safety! Relief and jealousy warred in Harry's breast.

"And where is this lady now?" Harry burst out. He stepped forward, and his dark countenance was thrust almost into Captain Navarro's mustached face.

A pleading note at that moment might have softened the Portuguese captain's tough heart. But this fierce mien —and the ringing voice with which Harry demanded to know, a voice which sent a peal of agony through Captain Navarro's still sodden head—had just the opposite effect. He stepped back and his faintly scornful expression betrayed nothing. He was remembering those English nine-pounders that had shattered his mizzenmast. It amused him to mislead this overbold Englishman.

"I left them where I found them." He shrugged. "In a hut belonging to an Irish woman near a small fishing village—'tis a difficult place to make safe harbor, señor. Few ships cast anchor there."

"Then they are still there?" asked Harry excitedly.

"I do not know. As I say, few ships cast anchor there."

So Rosamunde must still be in Ireland. He could find her! Harry expelled a long deep breath. "Can you show me on your charts the exact location of this place?"

"I can do better than that," said Captain Navarro graciously. "I can point out a ship in this harbor—the *Geertje*—which sails for Ireland within the week. Her captain can carry you there—if he will."

Harry disregarded that careless "if he will."

"I'd be in your debt, sir!" he cried sincerely.

Sardonically Captain Navarro leaned over the rail and pointed out the merchant ship *Geertje*, which, Harry saw, flew the Dutch flag. "Her captain is named Jan Pieterzoon. Soon he will have finished loading her and be ready to sail. Be assured that he will know the cove. But come, I will show you." With a fine show of helpfulness he took Harry into his great cabin and showed him accurate

535

charts, smiled as Harry committed the location to memory. It amused Captain Navarro to watch the tall Englishman earnestly poring over his charts, for although he had scrupulously told Harry the absolute truth—no man could accuse him of lying—he had carefully omitted one all-important detail: that Captain Avilo had turned down his kind offer when he learned that the *Infanta's* sister ship the *Coronada* would be along in a month or so and decided to sail on her. The Englishman was not to know that he would arrive in Ireland only to find the Majorcan captain and the woman gone. Captain Navarro was having his own private revenge on the English who had riddled his mizzenmast.

But on deck Yusef the Morisco, who had overheard everything, was thinking. He'd been on board—and listening—when they were anchored in Irish waters. He'd been on deck—and listening—when Captain Avilo had regretfully refused passage on board the *Infanta*. He'd heard Captain Navarro tell Captain Avilo that the *Infanta*'s sister ship, the *Coronada*, would be along in a month or so and carry him and his lady away. Nor had Captain Navarro mentioned the word "wife" to the Englishman. That Captain Navarro was playing some kind of malicious game with this Englishman was readily apparent to the quick-witted Morisco. And there might be money to be had in setting matters aright.

When Harry and the Portuguese captain came once again on deck and the Captain was momentarily distracted by one of his ship's officers hurrying up to ask him a question, the Morisco lost no time in sidling up to Harry. His English, though heavily accented, was readily understood.

"There is more truth *el capitán* does not tell you, Englishman," he muttered.

Harry turned sharply to survey this thin dark-skinned man who was watching him with cynical dark eyes and holding out his hand in the age-old gesture that asked for money.

But someone else had overheard the Morisco's muttered words as well. The flat of a sword suddenly struck the Morisco's throat, rendering him speechless, and the point of that blade was suddenly pressed against the Morisco's breastbone.

"Truth, Yusef?" snarled Captain Navarro. "Lying dog, I will teach ye to tell the truth! Put this man in irons below!" And Yusef, grown sickly pale, was whisked away.

"What truth is this of which he speaks?" Harry's dark frown was turned dauntingly on Captain Navarro. His voice was cold. "What is it you have not told me, Captain Navarro?"

"The man sought to hoodwink you for your coins," insisted Captain Navarro, sheathing his sword and thinking how pleasant it would have been to have pinked this arrogant Englishman with it. "I know how to deal with such cattle. Before God, I have told you the truth, señor. I found Captain Avilo and the woman in the place I showed you on the charts. And now, unless you wish to sail with me, you must leave my ship."

At this dismissal, Harry nodded curtly and took his leave, with Captain Navarro's hearty "Good voyage, señor" ringing insincerely in his ears. He regretted losing his chance to question the dark-skinned sailor, who, for all he knew, might by now be having his tongue burned out as Captain Navarro's justice. Yet as he pondered all that had been said, he was convinced there had been the ring of truth in the Portuguese captain's voice when he spoke of seeing Captain Rodrigue Avilo and Rosamunde. And yet something in those flat dark eyes had given it the lie. . . .

There was *something* Captain Navarro had not told him, and Harry had a cold feeling in the pit of his stomach as he returned to the quay.

God grant no harm had come to Rosamunde!

Harry hurried at once to the *Geertje*, only to be told that Captain Pieterzoon was staying at an inn in the city and would be found there. Chagrined, Harry turned back into the city. In the bright sunshine he hastened down a crowded brick-paved street and over a humpbacked bridge. On the bridge he brushed by fresh-faced country girls in white aprons whose long braids emerged from intricate flaring starched white caps and whose wooden shoes clonked past him cheerfully. Over their arms were slung huge baskets of eggs, and flowers to be sold at the flower markets along the banks of the Singel. Next he made his way through a swaggering group of freshly disembarked Scandinavian sailors, their bodies sinewy, their hair bleached almost white by the sun and their blue eyes, pale as winter skies, alert for the pretty flirtatious Dutch girls, who giggled and blushed at sight of them. Now he must stop for a man bent under great pigeon coops, and now for an elderly merchant in long velvet robes, being carried by in a litter, to pass. And here he was surrounded by a number of carelessly dressed students, who were blocking the street as they conversed excitedly in Latin.

The colorful crowd, the bright sunshine, the screaming sea birds that wheeled overhead, all went unnoticed by Harry. Every impediment in his way was silently cursed by him until at last he plunged across the street through a dangerous medley of careening carts and hawkers and burst through the door of the inn.

The captain, he was informed, was not there either.

The next two hours of waiting were two of the longest in Harry's life. After talking with Captain Navarro he felt —he felt he had almost touched Rosamunde. She was alive, and now he knew where to find her! Tapping his boot with impatience, he sat by a window of the public room, nursing a tall tankard of ale and completely ignoring the blandishments of the voluptuous barmaid as he watched for Captain Jan Pieterzoon—for he had had from the innkeeper a description of the captain.

Ah, there he was at last, that heavy fellow with the rolling gait clad in serviceable—though unfashionable— brown woolen, ornamented only by plain black braid and missing most of its bone buttons. The one with the frizzy beard—for the innkeeper had laughed and said that Captain Pieterzoon was a good man but cared nothing for his appearance. An older man with weather-roughened skin and hair that was gray yet still streaked with the burnished gold of earlier years. A rotund level-eyed man who, met at the door by the tall form of the impatient Englishman, considered Harry for a second or two shrewdly sizing him
538

up, and then invited him into one of the inn's private rooms for a quiet discussion.

They seated themselves at a wooden table, and Captain Pieterzoon filled his long round-bowled clay pipe and listened quietly as Harry explained his need of fast passage to Ireland.

It was a troubled world, this world of the seventeenth century. Men fled for political reasons and were sometimes pursued—often to the detriment of the ships and captains who transported them. Captain Pieterzoon studied the tall determined Englishman with shrewd eyes that had seen much and tried to guess his profession. Hard and lean, not a farmer or a merchant. A soldier most likely, possibly a courier for a king—or more likely for rebellion, since he traveled in such haste and sought out strangers to transport him.

"If I am to take you on my ship, I would know why you make this voyage, Mynheer Howard."

"I seek a woman," answered Harry frankly.

The captain lit his clay pipe. Not political then. . . . "Ah, a woman," he said reflectively. "She has fled from you, mynheer?"

"She has fled—but not from me. I am told she sailed on the *Santa Cecilia,* which had put into an English port for repairs and was shipwrecked on the Irish coast. I am told she is alive, and I go to seek her."

Captain Pieterzoon frowned. "The *Santa Cecilia* has gone down? I am sorry to hear it. Irish waters are treacherous. And her captain? What of him?"

"I am told he is alive and well."

"But desolate at the loss of his ship, I am sure, for she belonged to his father and he set great store by her. I have quaffed a glass of Malmsey more than once with Captain Avilo and listened to his tales of his native Majorca."

Harry's head lifted. "You know him, then?"

"Aye, I do. Not well, but we nod to one another when we are in port and may have a glass together."

"What is he like?" Harry asked in a voice of studied casualness.

The Dutchman shrugged. "Captain Avilo is not quite
539

so tall as yourself, thinner—a merry fellow who has a way with women."

A way with women . . . and Rosamunde, his Rose, was with him! Jealousy clawed at Harry.

Now the Dutchman was leaning back, puffing his long pipe, considering him. There was a kind of amusement on his weathered face. The Englishman had not liked to hear that Captain Rodrigue Avilo had a way with women! "This woman," he asked softly. "Why do you follow her?"

Cynical and worldly-wise, Captain Pieterzoon expected to be told insincerely that the woman was "a favorite sister" whereas in reality she was probably a married woman fleeing her husband's wrath. He was surprised by Harry's answer, for Harry leaned forward—and threw away all the lies he had planned to tell.

"She is mine," he said shortly. "I would follow her to hell."

At this blunt admission, the old Dutch captain's eyes widened. There had been real sincerity and a twang of torment in Harry's voice when he said that. And Captain Pieterzoon was not so old that he could not remember how it had been to feel that way about a woman. In point of fact he had felt that way about three women in his time— and two of them had not been worth it. The third, a flaxen-haired girl from Zeeland, he had married and cherished and left in a grave near a windmill, well watered with his tears. Harry's fierce "I would follow her to hell" had struck a chord with him. He could remember the feeling well.

"Ah, yes," he said. "A man must seek his woman. . . ." He nodded decisively. "I will take you to Ireland, mynheer. Although I had not planned to stop at the little cove you mention, I will do so on my way to Galway— that is, if you have passage money. I sail with the tide on the morrow, God willing."

Passage money . . . Harry frowned. He had run out of coin, but he was not without resources. After a moment's hesitation, he pulled out a leathern pouch containing the store of rings and gold chains he had lifted on the English highroads. If the *Geertje* sailed on the
540

morning tide there might be little time to convert these into currency. He handed the pouch to Captain Pieterzoon. "I have no money, but these should be sufficient to pay for passage."

The grizzled Dutchman studied the contents of the pouch. "Indeed, more than sufficient," he murmured. Idly he held up two rings to the light that filtered through the small-paned windows into the dusky recesses of the common room. "These are signet rings here, mynheer, and I note that the crests and arms are—different."

"All are stolen," said Harry instantly. "But none of them were stolen in Holland."

Captain Pieterzoon handed back the leathern pouch with its precious store to Harry. A highwayman, then . . . he was not too surprised. "I will take your word that they were not stolen in Holland," he said thoughtfully, remembering a day when, hungry and cold, he had himself pilfered two loaves and some cheeses, and later a golden candlestick from a church. He might burn in hell for the candlestick, though he had since paid for it in gifts to the church a hundred times over, but it had been the beginning of his fortune. Without that candlestick, he was convinced, he would never have had his ship. He looked with favor upon the reckless Englishman, bent on finding his lady, wherever she was. "I will take you with me, mynheer Howard," he said. "The *Geertje* belongs to me, so you need not pay me in advance. Should you be unable to strike a bargain for these baubles here in Amsterdam, you may try again for a better price at any port we stop at."

Harry drew a deep breath and spoke his hearty thanks.

"There is no need to thank me so warmly," observed his host with a wry smile. "For I think, since you do not seek an English ship—and Ireland is governed by the English—you must be at odds with the English law. One of those crests I recognized—a powerful family who might reach even into Dutch waters to seek you out. But on my ship *I* make the law, and you may sail with me to find your lady. Have your goods brought aboard tonight, for the tide runs early tomorrow and we run with it."

"And the price of the passage?" asked Harry, wondering if there would be anything left after he disposed of the rings and chains.

Captain Pieterzoon named his price, a small figure.

"I will pay you double that," said Harry instantly, for he was used to the gouging ways of the road and knew that this Dutch captain already half suspected that he was a highwayman with a price on his head in England.

"Nay." Captain Pieterzoon shook his grizzled head. "My price for passage is fair, and it is enough. Where you got the money to pay for it is not my affair. I know only what you have told me—that you seek a woman who, you say, belongs to you—and it is all I want to know."

He did not add, nor did Harry guess, that the reason he was so willing to transport a man at odds with English law into English-governed Ireland where such a man could prove to be a dangerous cargo was that he saw in Harry his own young self again, in the days when he had recklessly hauled illegal cargo—and was in mad pursuit of a girl with flaxen hair.

That afternoon Harry sold the rings to a keen-eyed Italian trader who pursed his red lips and refused to give him enough money for the gold chains. Harry shrugged and took the chains elsewhere. In a tiny shop off the Warmoesstraat, a German trader in a velvet cap studied the chains carefully and gave him his price. Content that he now had enough money for passage to Ireland, Harry returned to the house of Cornelis Van der Leyden to sup.

Van der Leyden was delighted to see him and asked interestedly how his day had gone. On learning that Harry would sail on the morrow, he insisted Harry stay the night. And tomorrow he would see Harry off aboard the *Geertje*. Meanwhile there was supper, a feast upon which his household had labored in Mynheer Howard's honor.

Harry blinked at the groaning board: pheasant garnished with larks' tongues and parsley, a suckling pig flavored with thyme and stuffed with currants, eels simmered in butter and sweet herbs, a flavorful lamb pie and all manner of handsome pasties and rich sauces, cheeses
542

and sweetmeats—the household must indeed have labored in his behalf!

Unable to do justice to all these good things now that the pains were back, Cornelis Van der Leyden nibbled at his food and studied his English guest rather wistfully. This cool fellow who had, undoubtedly, saved his life last night was such a man as he would have wished his son to be, as his son *would* have grown up to be—had he not died of the green sickness, even though amply dosed with horehound and tansy, in his seventh year. Van der Leyden sighed; it would not do to look back. Ah, well, he could at least give his welcome guest a memorable dinner to remember through weeks of drab shipboard food!

After dinner he urged on Harry some of the very good Malmsey Joris hastened to bring.

"So you go to Ireland, Mynheer Howard?" Thoughtfully Cornelis studied Harry over the rim of his goblet. "And whence from there?"

"I do not know," said Harry frankly. He leaned back in his olive-wood chair and stretched out his long legs, noting again the solid comfort of this room. "Perhaps to England. Or perhaps the *Geertje*'s captain will be persuaded to carry us back to Amsterdam."

"Us?"

"I seek a lady," explained Harry. "And I am told she has been shipwrecked in Ireland."

"Ah . . . a lady." Van der Leyden drank that in. "And is this lady your wife, mynheer?" he wondered delicately.

Harry thought tenderly of Rosamunde—Rosamunde pursued, Rosamunde shipwrecked, bearing his child. "Not yet," he said softly. "But she will be, God willing."

The look on his face made Cornelis swallow suddenly and set down his goblet. He was thinking of his wife, who had filled these empty rooms with laughter, and who had left a void in his life that had never been filled. He roused himself. "If ye return to Amsterdam, Mynheer Howard, ye must seek me out at once," he insisted warmly. "Your word on it, mynheer!"

Good-naturedly Harry promised that he would indeed

look up Cornelis Van der Leyden the moment he returned to Amsterdam, but he found it hard to follow the older man's conversation. At the moment his mind was not on the spice trade, the Indies, or the war waxing hot between Spain and Holland. His thoughts were all concentrated on Rosamunde, Rosamunde with her glowing beauty and her emerald eyes filled with love—*his* Rose, waiting for him in Ireland!

38   *The Geertje's voyage to Ireland was uneventful.* They were blown forward by lazy winds that sometimes stopped altogether. Harry chafed whenever he looked aloft and saw the sails flapping idly as the great ship rode the waves like a floating gull. Although Captain Pieterzoon assured him jovially that they were making excellent time, considering the wind's lack of interest in their journey, Harry was not to be beguiled. A restless fever to find Rosamunde possessed him—and a kind of terror lest he arrive only to find her gone.

That she might be dead he shut out from his mind altogether. After all, had not Captain Navarro seen her? He had described her as "a blond beauty with emerald eyes"—ah, that was Rosamunde! And "large with child." That Rosamunde's child would have been born by now alarmed Harry, but he refused to dwell on it; he told himself staunchly that other women bore children and lived to tell of it—so would his Rosamunde!

That the child might not be his, might be someone else's—possibly Captain Rodrigue Avilo's—he refused to contemplate. But his strong hands clenched numbingly as the thought wandered through his tortured brain.

544

Rosamunde, Rosamunde, he could not wait to find her.

He spent long evenings in conversation with Captain Pieterzoon and long days on deck picking up sea lore and a knowledge of ships, for Captain Pieterzoon had observed Harry's interest in the vessel and was delighted to show him every nook and cranny and explain all that the sailors were doing both below and aloft. The ports they stopped at were only obstacles in the way to Harry—he was anxious to get on.

He was on deck when the cove they sought was sighted, and he could scarce restrain himself from climbing the rigging to get a better look as the rugged cliffs of Ireland hove into view. His heart was thudding as Captain Pieterzoon smiled and said, "This is the place you seek."

Harry peered at the tiny fishing village, scarcely more than a rude collection of huts, coming near and nearer. He would have clambered over the side into the longboat had not the captain's hand fallen heavily on his shoulder.

"From what you have told me, Mynheer Howard," Captain Pieterzoon cautioned, "you had best let me go ahead and make the inquiries. I can readily ascertain if the woman you seek is still in the area. But you are English, and the Irish hate the English—they might not tell you what you want to know. Also, you are not on the best of terms with the English law, and it is possible that the English authorities do not know that either Captain Avilo or the English lady are here."

Harry would have protested but he saw sense in the Captain's suggestion—and he would not endanger Rosamunde! It was almost physical pain for him to step back and watch the longboat leave without him.

On board the *Geertje,* waiting, Harry felt he aged several years. Mercifully, Captain Pieterzoon was quick in coming up with the information. At sight of the captain coming back aboard, Harry was up like a steel spring uncoiling, seizing his sword and cloak, eager to be gone. "What have ye learned?" he cried eagerly.

"There has been a changing of the guard this past month," announced Captain Pieterzoon cheerfully. "The Englishman who is in charge here now is a jaunty fellow—

one Charles Kingsford—who cares but little for regulations. He says the Irish have little reason to fear him, but 'tis best they do, for otherwise an Irish outlaw named O'Lear would move into the town and make it his headquarters—and then Kingsford would be forced to drive him out!"

"But what of Rosamunde?" Harry was goaded to interrupt.

"I am getting to that. The official who preceded Charlie Kingsford here"—Harry noted that Captain Pieterzoon was already on a first-name basis with Kingsford—"was a dour sort, a stiffnecked fellow who kept the countryside in subjection. When he left, he took his men with him, and Charlie and his staff are all new. The town does not confide in him, he tells me. He says there was a rumor of a Spanish captain who left by ship before he came here, but he knows nothing of a woman." At Harry's look of alarm, Captain Pieterzoon smiled. "Ah, but that is good, my friend! Perhaps she did not leave with him, perhaps she is still here in the shepherd's hut where the Spanish captain lived."

"I will find it!" cried Harry, galvanized.

Captain Pieterzoon put his hand on Harry's arm. "I have arranged with Charles Kingsford to guide you there."

Surprise arrested Harry's surge toward the longboat. "And why would he do that?" he demanded.

Captain Pieterzoon grinned and winked. "We plan to do a bit of business, Charlie and I. He is interested in contraband, and I will stop at this place on my next voyage to Ireland."

Ah, a bit of skulduggery! Harry relaxed.

"You have nothing to fear," Pieterzoon assured him. "Charlie knows nothing of your background. Indeed, I have told him you are a gentleman trader of Amsterdam."

Harry snorted. "It will seem strange to him then that I speak no Dutch!"

"No, he is relieved that you speak English. I told him you had an English mother—which of course is the absolute truth. And that the lady you seek is a shipwrecked

546

English cousin." Captain Pieterzoon flashed him a winning smile. "Now, into the longboat with you—Charlie is waiting for you on shore."

To Harry, a wanted highwayman with a price on his head in England, it seemed strange that he should be greeted on this Irish shore by a pink-cheeked English official who stepped gracefully forward to shake his hand and welcome him to Ireland. Greeted he was indeed by Charles Kingsford's entire staff—two smiling companions who greeted Harry cordially—mounted and with an extra horse already saddled to take him to his destination!

"I cannot take you all the way," Charles Kingsford told Harry as they rode north toward the shepherd's hut.

Harry, mounted on the borrowed horse and riding beside Charlie Kingsford's biscuit-colored stallion at the head of the two rakish young Englishmen who constituted Charlie's staff, looked surprised.

" 'Tis not that I would not enjoy the ride," explained his host with a charming smile. "But the woman who occupies the shepherd's hut is O'Lear's woman, and odds are she would either run away or attack us—in either case you would get no word of your English cousin. There is a slight rise before we reach the hut—my men and I will wait for you behind that lest we alarm her. Though for the life of me," he added, puzzled, "I cannot see why a shipwrecked Englishwoman would not immediately seek the help of the local English authorities, who would have been glad to aid her."

Harry could think of a reason or two why the Wild Rose of the English highroads would not seek out her countrymen in a strange land, but he kept silent.

"I suppose it was because she was in the company of a Spanish sea captain," decided Kingsford comfortably. "Things being as they are between England and Spain, doubtless he prevailed upon her to remain in hiding with an outlaw's woman!"

"Doubtless," agreed Harry, hard put not to gallop off ahead, leaving his genial host behind.

"A pity her mother had betrothed her to a Spaniard

sight unseen," added Kingsford. "No wonder you are come to bring her back!"

Harry gave him a worried look. How much of a wild tale had Captain Pieterzoon spun? he asked himself. Quickly he changed the subject to the misty weather, the clouds that hung low over the gray cliffs, the rich emerald green of the uneven ground, its grass cropped close by a flock of grazing sheep.

" 'Tis always damp here," said his host frankly, looking about him with distaste. "Lord, but I miss England!"

"Perhaps you will be returning soon," Harry suggested courteously.

"Not soon. But perhaps one day." Charlie Kingsford gave Harry a gloomy look. Harry hardly noticed. His eyes were intent on the terrain ahead.

On that ride he learned that his talkative companion, Charles Kingsford—whose biscuit-colored doublet and cloak had undoubtedly been carefully chosen to match his horse's elegant hide—was a wastrel younger son of an impoverished baronet who, at his wits' end what to do with Charlie, had pulled strings and got him sent out to Ireland.

"Where there isn't a pretty wench within miles," Charlie Kingsford confided to Harry. "And I learn there's been an English beauty residing a short ride away ever since I've been here!" He rolled his eyes in mock despair, reined up. "Ah, here's the place where you leave us. Over that rise is the hut of O'Lear's woman. Take your time, our horses will be glad to graze awhile—if the sheep have left them anything to eat!"

The mists had cleared away a little as Harry topped the rise and saw before him against the lowering gray sky the little stone hut where Rosamunde had wintered and borne her child in the spring. Checking his impatience, he walked his horse toward it, lest he alarm whoever was within. As he approached, he saw that the door was open and the hut apparently empty.

He turned the corner of the hut and found Meara bent over a flat stone, cleaning fish by the side of the hut. At the sudden appearance of a stranger, she straightened up,

548

threw back her long black hair and seized a stout staff. She sized Harry up at a glance. Tall he was and hard, but at least there was only one of him. If he had come to find out where O'Lear was hiding after his latest raid on the English, he would get no answers from her! O'Lear had been in and out of trouble ever since Rosamunde had left, and Meara, who loved the giant Irishman dearly, had spent most of her time in an agony of worry. It had made her expression bleak, and the look she leveled on Harry was one of silent menace.

Harry looked into that beautiful scarred face atop that gaunt homespun-clad body and came directly to the point.

"I am told you are O'Lear's woman," he said, dismounting.

An English voice! The sapphire eyes gave off a hostile gleam, the stout staff was clutched a little tighter. "And who told you that?" Meara snapped.

"Faith, 'tis well known!"

At Harry's calm rejoinder, Meara relaxed a bit. She studied the tall Englishman. "And why do you seek O'Lear?" she asked warily.

"I do not seek O'Lear. But I am told you sheltered a Spanish captain and a woman in this hut."

"Lies!" flashed Meara. "You can see for yourself the hut is empty!" She stepped briskly up on a flat-topped stone beside the hut wall. The height would give her an advantage if she had to fight him.

Harry guessed her intention and stepped back a pace. "Before you bring that staff down on my head, let me tell you it is the woman I seek."

But the added height that came of standing on the stone had enabled Meara to see three horsemen just over the rise. This Englishman was lying to her—he was but the advance man of a search party! Looking for O'Lear, no doubt!

"Search for yourself," she declared grandly, waving at the doorway with her free arm. "But you will find no one here."

"Then I ask you where she has gone, the blond lady you sheltered here."

Meara's mind was working fast, but she needed time to think. "What do you want with her?" she parried.

Harry's temper was fast wearing thin. "She is mine," he growled. "I have come all the way from England searching for her."

Faith, he *did* have the manner of a lover balked in his desire, this tall dark Englishman, thought Meara in bewilderment. Then suddenly it all came clear to her. Of course! *This* was the English lord to whom Rosamunde's guardian had betrothed her and from whom she had fled! *This* was the man who had driven her from her native land!

Meara had been about to blurt out that Rosamunde had married the Spanish captain and gone with him to Majorca, but now her jaws closed with a snap. Rage rose in her as she stared at Harry. A dangerous man he looked indeed—and doubtless he would pursue the slender Majorcan captain who loved Rosamunde so, and kill him with that serviceable sword he carried! Ah, but he would not! Rosamunde had been a good friend to her; she could have taken O'Lear away from her, yet she had not. And Meara paid her debts! Ah, she would arrange matters so that Rosamunde and her Spanish captain were left forever alone in their Majorcan paradise!

"I did shelter them here," she told Harry with deceptive calm. "But the Spanish captain is long gone, I know not where."

"And Rosamunde?" demanded Harry, tensing as he leaned forward.

Meara was almost beguiled by the vibrant concern in that voice. For a wavering moment she wished that O'Lear were here to advise her. But that great oaf had gone down to Cork, where there were wild doings afoot, and had stoutly refused to take her along—and all because she'd missed her last period! Ridiculous! As though she could not still fight as well as a man in the first months of her pregnancy! She was still angry at O'Lear for that, and now she turned a smoldering gaze on Harry, seeing in his lean hard body and wolfish countenance only another Englishman—to be fought and vanquished.

She heaved a deep sigh. "Rosamunde had fled from England and did live here for a time," she declared casually. "I was the last to see the poor lady alive."

She was watching Harry narrowly as she said that and felt a grim satisfaction at the tremor that went through his tall frame. His face had gone gray.

"How did she die?" he asked hoarsely.

"In childbirth. She bore the child there—on that table." Meara turned to point at the interior of the hut. " 'Twas a daughter. It lived but an hour."

His child . . . Rosamunde had died here bearing his child. Harry's voice was husky. "Where are they buried?"

Had Meara been looking at him she would have seen the deep pain that seared his gray eyes, but she was not—she was looking with distaste at the rising ground over which the mounted men could no longer be seen, for their horses were grazing lower down the slope. She turned with a start, realizing the Englishman had asked her a question.

"Over here," she said crisply, and stalked around the corner of the hut, led Harry down to the cliff's edge. A tall wooden cross of gray driftwood stood there. It was crudely made, and there was a mound of earth at its foot where grass was just beginning to spring up. Harry stood by that gray wooden cross looking down at that mound of earth with deep pain etched in his hard face. It was indeed a grave, but Harry had no way of knowing that it was the grave of O'Lear's dog, a hunting hound he had—like the rest of his living—"lifted" from the English overlords. The dog had met his death when he was gored by a wild boar and had been carried back here tenderly for burial. O'Lear had loved the dog. But the cross had been erected by Meara as a way of signaling O'Lear. If the cross stood upright, it was safe for O'Lear to come in—the hut was occupied only by Meara. If the cross was down—and Meara could always tell the English, if they came asking questions, that it had been blown down in the stiff winds that blew from the sea across these cliffs—then O'Lear knew to keep well back, for the hut was being watched or occupied by the English law.

Harry's face was as gray as the driftwood cross. He asked but one more question, huskily: "When did it happen?"

Meara shrugged. She was looking out to sea and forcing herself not to be moved by the pain in his voice. " 'Twas in the spring. A month or two before the Spanish captain left. About then."

His child for certain! Harry could not speak.

"There is no stone," Meara muttered. "For I have not been able to afford one."

"Here." Harry rummaged for coins, glad to be able to look down at his hands so that Meara could not see the savage bereavement on his face. "She and the child should not be without a stone to mark their passing." He gave Meara a handful of coins—all he had—and turned and stalked away so abruptly that Meara stared after his tall form in surprise. A strange lot, these English! Hard and cruel they could be in life, but in death . . . generous.

She would have to ask the O'Lear his opinion when he returned from Cork.

Harry flung himself blindly upon his borrowed horse and dug in his heels. The horse snorted and reared up. Together they plunged over the rise and thundered past Charles Kingsford and his rakish companions. All three took one look at Harry's gray face and moved hastily aside to let him pass.

"Closer than a cousin, I'll wager," said Kingsford softly.

"D'ye think the lass has fled him?" wondered one of them.

Kingsford shrugged. " 'Tis at least apparent she was not waiting for him with open arms. Well, we'd best back to town, gentlemen. It would seem our friend has had bad news."

They cantered along behind, but Harry had already far outdistanced them. His horse was fit and glad of a run, and Harry thundered along as if trying to outdistance his sorrow. Indeed, his vision was so blurred he had hardly seen the three mounted men he had shot past. His throat had closed up and there was a terrible burning ache behind his eyes. Gritting his teeth, Harry set his reckless
552

face into the wind that blew hard from the Atlantic and let the salt air dry the tears that sparkled on his dark lashes. They were speeding along the cliffs now, his horse's hooves thudding soft on the green turf. To his right and below him the sea crashed in, booming upon the wet rocks—even as his own life crashed and tumbled in ruins about him. Ah, not till this moment had he realized how much he'd missed her. Not till this moment had he known how very much he'd loved her.

Dead . . . his Rosamunde. Somehow he had never thought of that. Always he'd believed he'd find his Rose alive. In another man's arms perhaps, for 'twas hard for a woman to survive alone. He'd have forgiven her that, and he'd have wrested her from those other arms with a sharp blade thrust or a ball from his pistol. But—*dead. Never to see her again*. It was too much to bear.

A part of him died that day, a young believing part of him that had dared to hope that someday fate would smile and life would open its arms to lovers and he and his beloved would bask in the sunshine. It was not to be, he told himself bleakly, it was never to be. . . .

The fishing village rose before him, and Harry flung through it like a madman, looking neither to right nor left. He left his winded horse on the shore and plunged into the waiting longboat. His great muscles strained as if to make the boat fly across the water as he rowed himself out to where the *Geertje* lay at anchor.

The Dutch captain saw that Harry was returning alone. He saw the anguish on Harry's dark face as Harry climbed aboard.

"She does not wait for you, your lady?" he murmured.

"She is dead," said Harry, and flung on past to seek his cabin and make himself drunk on Irish whiskey.

39   *Harry might have gone back to England then,*
had the ship been bound for an English port after they left
the fishing village, but the *Geertje* was bound for Galway
and Le Havre and thence to Amsterdam.

And so Harry, who had paid scant attention to the land
of windmills and wooden shoes or its great trading city of
Amsterdam, discovered the world of the Dutch.

Amsterdam was made for Harry. He was a man of
parts and it was a city of parts. Its warehouse floors were
bent with the weight of its trade goods—it was said
enough corn alone was stored in the warehouses of Amsterdam to feed all of Europe through a bad harvest. Did
you wish to buy a weapon or a warship? Come to Amsterdam, you could probably get it on credit! Even the attics of
the merchants' houses were stuffed with merchandise
hauled up there on the jaws of cleverly concealed hoisting
beams, and wood and spices and foodstuffs and grain
moved in and out of this busy port at a speed that kept
the ships jostling each other in the harbor.

Cornelis Van der Leyden had asked to be informed
when the *Geertje* entered the harbor. He met Harry at
dockside, and on learning that Rosamunde was dead,
insisted Harry accompany him home—and that he accept
employment in his big warehouse.

"I need an assistant," he told Harry. "Old Vierkirk
cannot carry the load; we may lose him any day." And he
beat down Harry's objections.

For a man without prospects, who cared not where he
went, it was easier to agree than to argue. Still numbed
by his recent loss, Harry accompanied the old Dutchman
554

back to the house on Rapenburg, and the next day marched with him past a group of pasty-faced clerks on high stools in Cornelis' big brick warehouse on the Voorburgwal. There Cornelis introduced Harry to old Vierkirk with the cryptic remark in Dutch, "Treat Mynheer Howard as my son."

Old Vierkirk raised his bushy white brows and regarded the Englishman curiously. Harry, who spoke no Dutch, was unaware of what had been said. Now he looked around him with quickening interest at this busy high-ceilinged place where the cargoes of ships that ranged the world were stored.

Cornelis took him everywhere in Amsterdam. With him Harry visited the great Exchange. Grain was sold in buildings, but the largest transactions were made here at the Exchange. He witnessed Cornelis making one.

And of evenings they would sit and smoke their long clay pipes and discuss the never-ending war with Spain and the spice trade. Harry, with Rosamunde lost to him, was attempting to submerge his sorrow in a sea of work. Cornelis understood and sympathized. He encouraged Harry to offer suggestions on the conduct of his business.

One day Harry volunteered one:

"Ye sail empty ships to the Caribbean for salt," he said, "now that Spain has cut off Holland's salt supply."

"Aye," agreed Van der Leyden, puffing on his pipe. "Without salt, Holland's fishing industry would fail. And it can be had in those islands easily from salt pans near the sea."

"Yes, but why go empty? Why not carry contraband to some Spanish town in the Caribbean and make a double profit?"

Through the smoke Cornelis regarded Harry narrowly. "Ye're an apt pupil," he approved with satisfaction. "I've been thinking the same thing myself, and now ye bring it up. But who would go ashore to make the arrangements? 'Tis a dangerous thing!"

"I'd do it myself," volunteered Harry impatiently. "For that, I'd learn the language of Spain!"

555

Cornelis laughed. "Your eagerness does you credit. But be not so hasty, Hendrik. Your time will come."

It was not the last suggestion Harry made—nor the last Cornelis acted upon. For ambition tugged at Harry now. Had he not known Rosamunde, he might have been content to live out his wild life on the highroads, taking his fun where he found it with women like Nell, and ending up swinging from a tall gibbet while the crowd roared below him. But he had known Rosamunde, and the sweetness she had brought into his life had fired his energies and waked his ambition, so long buried under a drift of bitterness for his lost heritage. Instinctively he knew that although he would never forget her, work would help to ease this aching pain in his heart. So he plunged into the work at Cornelis' great brick warehouse, with its huge oaken doors and arched shuttered windows. He learned the working of Cornelis' shipping empire from the ground up. He learned how to operate the gigantic hoisting beam, operated from inside the warehouse by a great creaking windlass, that lifted up rare woods and spices and rich rugs and all the other treasures of the mysterious East—for Cornelis Van der Leyden was a heavy stockholder in the Dutch East India Company, which was making vast fortunes for so many merchants. He spent long hours talking with the captains of Cornelis' three tall-masted ships. He labored long hours over the books and came up with a new system of bookkeeping that cut the labor of the busy clerks by one-third.

He was ready for Cornelis' offer when it came.

It happened one morning as Harry accompanied the old Dutchman on his walk to the warehouse. Cornelis sighed. "Those oaken doors"— he indicated the warehouse doors that lay just ahead—"will not open for me very long. Gretha rails at me for not eating, but the truth is I can no longer get much food down."

Harry gave his friend and mentor a sharp look. The old man had indeed been looking frailer lately.

" 'Tis an old wound." Cornelis sighed. "I always knew one day I would die of it, and now my time has come. I count my future now in months—in weeks perhaps."

"Surely not!" Harry was dumbfounded.

Cornelis came to a stop and faced him, studying him with those keen eyes that had been weighing men for so long. "It is *your* future I would discuss with you, Hendrik."

"Nay, 'tis yourself you should think of!" exclaimed Harry. "For with all that you have taught me, I could go anywhere and make my way in the world of trade."

"Aye, that you could, Hendrik." Cornelis studied him wistfully, again wishing that Harry were his son. "But you will not have to go anywhere. I propose to leave all that I have to you—on one condition. No, wait!" as Harry would have spoken. "I am the last of my line, and there is no one to carry on my name. I would ask only that you change your name to Hendrik Van der Leyden and become in law my son, if not in fact."

For a moment Harry was startled by this request. "Cornelis," he said slowly. "You do me honor, but there are things you do not know about me. My past will not bear looking into."

"What you have been in other lands does not interest me. I know what you have been in Holland—and I respect you for it. I would you *were* my son, Hendrik. For I would be mightily proud of you!"

Harry felt tears sting his eyes. "Then I accept your offer and will bear your name with pride."

"Good." Cornelis reached out to steady himself against the brick warehouse wall. "I think I will accompany you no farther today, Hendrik," he gasped. "The old pains are back in force this time. I would creep home before I must be carried there."

Harry leaped forward. "Lean upon me; I will get you home!"

"That is why I brought this up," Cornelis said in a faint voice. "Now the legal details must be attended to."

Harry almost carried Cornelis back to his house. Both Gretha and Joris sprang forward as he bore him through the front door and lowered his burden into the nearest chair.

The next day Cornelis was feeling better. He spoke in a stronger voice. "Now that you are become my son in name if not in fact, Hendrik," he said energetically, "you must familiarize yourself with my ships. You must make voyages. My flagship, the *Volendam,* sails tomorrow for London with a cargo of spices and fine woods from the Far East. You will be on board her."

Harry's gray eyes kindled. To sail with the great trading ships!

"But will you not need me here?" he demurred, seeing how transparent was Cornelis' skin, how clawlike his hands.

"I will not see the ice freeze over the canals again," predicted Cornelis dryly. "But I have lived through tulip time and now I think I will live to see the fall harvest. If you do not choose to sail on the *Volendam*, Hendrik, I have another ship that sails in a fortnight for the Indies."

"No," said Harry thoughtfully. "I think this time I will choose the shorter voyage—to England."

For Harry, who missed his great black stallion, had decided to repossess himself of Nightwind.

So with Cornelis' "Safe voyage!" sounding in his ears, Harry, the one-time highwayman and now cloaked by a Dutch name and a Dutch ship, boarded the big East Indiaman and watched the wind catch the sails and carry the *Volendam* impetuously out of the harbor and into the wild North Sea.

Not only was it a safe voyage, as Cornelis had wished, it was a fast one, for the winds favored them all the way. Arrived in London, Harry left the *Volendam*'s captain occupied with unloading the cargo and bought a big bay stallion. He hoped Sir Wilfred Keyes had not sold Nightwind, for he might have difficulty tracing him, but he need not have worried. Nightwind waited in the same field where Harry had left him. Harry drew a deep breath of relief, for he was not a man to leave anything behind— he always went back for those he loved. At Harry's low whistle, Nightwind whinnied, left his beloved mares and trotted over to nuzzle Harry's hand and playfully nip at his gauntlets. Harry could see he was happy and might have left him there, but suppose after a couple of years Sir Wilfred decided there was too much inbreeding and sold Nightwind? The powerful stallion could end up dragging some huge coach or dray! Harry did not like the thought of Nightwind, who had charged so gallantly out of so many ambushes, struggling uphill lugging heavy loads over mired roads for his living. It would be a sad end indeed for such a gallant comrade.

"Easy there, Nightwind," murmured Harry affectionately. "Tell the mares goodbye, for this time I'm taking you with me for good. We'll not be parted again, old friend!"

As if he understood, Nightwind promptly left Harry and trotted back to the mares, rubbed his head against his favorites and then pawed the ground lightly with his forefeet and rushed back to Harry. Harry took that as an indication that Nightwind was ready to leave. He exchanged the bay stallion for Nightwind as he had before, and was about to mount when Nightwind turned and whinnied. The white mare came running lightly over to him. Her foal, a checkered black-and-white with a fluffy white mane, came running along too. The mare gave him a beseeching look and rubbed up against Nightwind.

Harry swore softly. He hated to part this charming equine family.

And after all, why should he? Nightwind was his by right of prior ownership, and he'd leave the big bay horse as payment for the white mare and her checkered foal. Cornelis would be delighted to see such fine breeding stock on his newly purchased *bouwerie* outside Amsterdam! Harry searched for a likely place in the fence to let the foal through, found a section he could pry loose. He took the bay's saddle and bridle and put them on Nightwind's back, tied the mare and her colt with a length of rope to the saddle. He chuckled as the pretty colt bucked and snorted at this cavalier treatment and eyed him evilly; she'd grow up to be as fine a horse as her dainty mother! He gave the bay a sharp smack on the rump, and the bay trotted contentedly into the pasture, eyeing the mares. With a twinkle in his eye, Harry replaced the loose section of fence. Let Sir Wilfred puzzle how the colt could have cleared that fence! He grinned as he rode away, imagining the amazement on Sir Wilfred's face at this newest switch of livestock.

But to the stableboys next morning, who viewed the solid fence and undisturbed locked gates, the replacement of the three horses by the bay stallion was little short of miraculous. They rushed to the manor house to acquaint their master of the event.

Sir Wilfred almost throttled the stableboy who brought him the news. Seated in his big dining room, breakfasting on sausages and wheaten cakes and honey from one of the crofter's hives, he turned pale. He threw down his napkin and ran out to the stable, outdistancing the stableboys. His eyes bulged with disbelief when he viewed the bay stallion, contentedly munching grass among the mares. Sir Wilfred smote the stable door with his fist hard enough to bruise his knuckles and said a few unprintable things about "animals shuffling in and out of the pasture as if it were some cursed innyard!" Then with blood in his eye, he repaired him to the best locksmith in the county, and after that the locks on Sir Wilfred's gates became famous —as did his fences, which were built up higher than a tall man's hand could reach.

He came home to denounce his wife's housekeeping, his inedible food, his thieving neighbors, and the state of the world in general.

"You are only upset because you have lost the black stallion again," said his wife at this choleric outburst.

"Aye!" cried Sir Wilfred waspishly. "The horse comes and goes like a wraith!" He sat and stared broodingly at the cold food on his trencher. "I am bewitched," he announced in hollow tones. "Horses come and go from my pasture at will. Locked gates do not deter them, nor high fences, nor watchful servants. I believe the black horse and this new one are one and the same. The black stallion has not left—he has merely changed the color of his coat to defy me!"

Shocked at this gloomy pronouncement, his wife dropped her knife with a clatter. "Surely you cannot mean it!"

"I do mean it." Sir Wilfred sighed gustily. He threw

560

down his napkin and rose. "I will seek me out a priest this very day!"

A priest was duly brought. An exorcism of evil spirits was performed in the great stables at Chatsbury. Sir Wilfred glowered at the new stallion throughout, and the horse gazed back calmly at his disgusted owner. Later Sir Wilfred confided to his wife in childish rancor that he had expected the great beast to turn into the black stallion before his eyes, but the brute had not.

His wife mollified him by remarking that the new stallion was indeed handsome, and surely a new strain would not be amiss.

Sir Winfred in later years was to pronounce the exorcism a complete success. The new bay stallion never showed any disposition to wander or change the color of his coat, and he sired fine foals until his death from eating foul hay some ten years later.

Harry's voyage to Holland was saddened because he had meant to bring old John with him too. But he had made inquiries and had discovered that Locke Hall had burned to the ground two months before and old John had died fighting the fire. Remembering his boyhood there, and the summer he had spent in the old wing with Rosamunde, Harry turned his face from England forever, and his countenance on the return voyage was described by the *Volendam's* captain as "formidable."

Harry returned to Amsterdam to find the house on Rapenburg draped in mourning. Cornelis had been wrong —he had not lived to see the fall harvest. Harry hurried in to comfort Gretha and old Joris, and found himself shortly accepting condolences from half the notables of Amsterdam.

It brought home to him sharply the new respect with which he was regarded. For Harry Waring, the sometime highwayman, had now become Hendrik Van der Leyden, sole owner of a vast trading empire.

But Harry's ideas of running that empire differed somewhat from Cornelis', and now he was able to put them into execution. He invested all he could raise or borrow in the Dutch West India Company, for he felt it had a great future. But he still pursued the spice trade, voyaging to the Orient on one or other of the three great East Indiamen that had been Cornelis' pride. Between voyages he spent time on the *bouwerie* outside Amsterdam where he had brought Nightwind and the white mare and her checkered foal. Sometimes he visited his newly purchased flower farm, near Haarlem, which was very profitable. There bright-eyed maidens in traditional white caps and white aprons and wooden shoes smiled a challenge at him over drifts of scarlet tulips and yellow daffodils.

But Harry was too restless to stay long in one place. He negotiated deals in Delft and Leyden and Rotterdam. Hendrik Van der Leyden became the darling of the bankers, for his deals were shrewd and he was prompt in repaying his loans. Eventually, sniffing money, he became a banker himself.

His was a busy life when Rosamunde came to Holland.

40   *It was wonderful to be in Amsterdam again.* *El Afortunado*'s voyage had been uneventful save that Juana had been constantly seasick and Rosamunde, who was never seasick, had had to care for six-year-old Elaine and Juana too. But on arrival Juana took over and Rosamunde was free to enjoy the delights of this Venice of the North. Rodrigue was busy unloading the cargo, and Rosamunde hurried on shore alone. Her days passed pleasantly.

She found the streets just as crowded, the brickwork of the elaborate facades just as intricate, the hoisting beams just as varied as she remembered. And the skies were just as blue—as blue as the eyes of smiling blond Dutchmen and yellow-haired Dutch women in their white caps who thronged past her. She decided the city had actually *grown* in her absence!

The crowd on Amsterdam's streets was as colorful as a box of jewels. There was a richly dressed Italian in purple velvet with a heavy gold chain encrusted with rubies. And there an English couple in cream-and-orange satins. And there a French lady with a powdered wig and a black patch to emphasize her dimple, in rustling violet taffetas and magenta plumes. In her handsome black silk —so correct for a Spanish lady of quality—Rosamunde felt garbed in mourning. She remembered the lovely sky-blue linen dress she had made here, and the white cambric chemise over which she had worn it—that dress Rodrigue had not thought "good enough" for her. And the beautiful green velvet gown he had bought her . . . gift for a light woman!

She smiled wickedly. Black might be just the thing for colonial Spain, but brilliant colors suited Amsterdam. She had money in her purse and she would visit her favorite markets on the water side of the streets that lined the canals. She would buy lovely delicate things for Elaine and for herself, sky-blue linen and green watered silk and—yes, red velvet! How she yearned for a length of rippling rich red velvet after such a long time in black! And even though she might never dare to wear such things in Palma or on visits to San Telmo, she could grace her own table at Cala Mesquida dressed any way she chose! On light feet, she made her way about the town—a town where last she had swaggered as a booted young dandy with a sword dangling at her side, or in a dress she had made herself. It seemed a lifetime ago.

Ah, she thought, if only she could have stayed here. Perhaps she could have picked up the threads of her old life, some semblance of the life she had known in England, instead of embarking on totally new alien ways in the burning heat of Majorca. She had reached a street of giant warehouses as she walked, and she paused to stare up, awed, at one mammoth building, some six stories high with pleasant arched openings that looked like barn doors rising one above the other, made of stout wood with massive iron hardware.

Such an interesting city! How Harry would have liked it! She missed a step, and her smiling face sobered. She must stop thinking about Harry. He was gone, gone forever. She had accepted that, hadn't she? Whole weeks, months even, had gone by in Majorca without a thought of him. She had been fully occupied in caring for Elaine, milking the goats, trying to patch up a near-ruined house and keep a roof over their heads and food on the table in Rodrigue's absence. But as *El Afortunado* had neared Amsterdam, she had remembered—as if Harry were suddenly close to her—and suffered all over again. She had dreamed he was taken, she had seen him lie on the road in his blood—and waked up screaming to see Rodrigue's face bending over hers in the darkness.

She hoped desperately that she had not cried out Harry's name, for she knew how jealous Rodrigue was of her memories.

This was not her first excursion into the town, for *El Afortunado* had docked in Amsterdam a week ago. Rodrigue had been all for putting up at an inn, but she—realizing he needed to save money to buy his own ship—persuaded him that they could as well stay aboard, using the ship for their hostelry, and come ashore by day to enjoy the city.

Rodrigue had taken her to a play—all spoken in Dutch, of which she understood nothing, but she had enjoyed the singing, the merry stamping dances and the mock duel on stage. They had dined at various inns and strolled like burghers over humpbacked stone bridges that arched over the quiet reflective waters of the canals. Light had filtered down through tall trees that shaded the sparkling waters, and in some places the branches had met overhead in leafy corridors. They had strolled at dusk down streets like the fashionable Herengracht where Amsterdam's wealthiest merchants were building their mansions. One of those houses was so beautiful that she remarked on it, and Rodrigue asked a passerby whose home it was. He was told it was being built by Hendrik

Van der Leyden. Rosamunde would have been shocked to learn that that was Harry.

In all the inns and taverns; the name of Piet Heyn was on everyone's lips, for word had just reached Amsterdam of a great haul in the Indies. The Dutch admiral Piet Heyn had captured the Spanish treasure fleet in Matanzas Bay and was headed home with a treasure so vast it would more than equal all the pirate trove taken from the Spanish since the discovery of the Americas!

Rodrigue was excited about that—after all, the treasure had been looted from Spain! But Rosamunde was determined not to let that spoil their vacation. She helped him walk off his displeasure in the crowded streets. Rodrigue was used to seaport cities, but she found the international flavor of the crowd exhilarating: tall-hatted Puritans, drab but richly dressed Quakers, stylish fops from every country prancing along in rosettes and beribboned canes and huge periwigs, light women from everywhere swaggering along swinging their hips and gazing boldly at the passing gentlemen with hot inviting eyes, silken-clad ladies being carried about in litters and chairs, and everywhere golden hair and blue, blue eyes and handsome Flemish beards and spurs that rang on the bricks and cobbles.

Amsterdam had come like a breath of fresh wind into her monotonous island existence, and today, while Rodrigue was busy supervising the loading of the new cargo, now that he had profitably disposed of the old one, she had left Elaine with Juana and ventured out by herself to roam the city and shop the canalside markets. Juana was still recovering from her long bout of seasickness and was glad to droop in her cabin, praying hourly to the small statue of the Virgin affixed to the wall for their safe and speedy return to Majorca. And Rodrigue, usually so strict about accompanying her everywhere, had smiled indulgently at Rosamunde's happy face and let her go without comment.

So today she was on her own, walking the streets of Amsterdam as she had some seven years ago.

She wandered through the Kalvertstraat, crowded with butcher shops, where calves were brought to market, admired the graceful tower of the Zuiderkerk, which had been almost new when she had been here before. Its tall spire had a delightful wedding-cake quality that reminded her she was hungry. She bought some sweet cakes in a little yellow-brick bakery and munched them as she strolled through the Warmoesstraat, Amsterdam's busy main street. There she made her purchases. A length of brilliant green satin, enough to make a dress. Some white cambric for dainty chemises, and sky-blue linen, handkerchief-fine, for summer dresses for herself and Elaine. A stone's throw away was the Schreierstoren, the Weeping Tower. She told herself those fortunate enough to live in Amsterdam should not weep.

A laughing crowd of young people carrying a picnic basket brushed by her, and she turned to look after them wistfully. If only she knew people here! But Rodrigue kept aloof and—save for one grizzled old sea captain named Sondergaard whose ship left the harbor the day after they arrived—he had not introduced her around to the captains and other ships' officers she had no doubt he knew in plenty. She suspected he would not have introduced her to Sondergaard had he not come surging out of a tavern with his rolling gait and almost collided with Rosamunde on their first night ashore. Rodrigue's jealousy again, she thought ruefully. Surely he must soon outgrow that!

With her arms full of packages she circled around a street vendor's small cart, nearly colliding with two tall-hatted gentlemen who gave her an approving look as they swept by in their short cloaks. She came to a stop when she found her way blocked by two men in leather jerkins, both carrying enormous wicker pigeon cages—for pigeon keeping was popular in Amsterdam, and many rooftops boasted shelters for them. She edged up against a brick building to let them pass, and when she looked up she saw coming toward her through the crowd a face she knew: It was Wilhelm Van Hoorn, the Dutchman who had drugged her so that Rodrigue could abduct her aboard the ill-fated *Santa Cecilia*.

Van Hoorn was thinner and looked older. He was very

down at the heel. His russet velvet clothes were not just worn but shabby, his brown-gold hair was unkempt, and his beard, of which he had once been so proud, was trimmed crookedly. He walked with a slight limp, and some of the wicked light had gone out of his blue eyes. He looked defeated by life, and she felt a sudden rush of sympathy for him.

Van Hoorn brushed by a street vendor, selling roasted chestnuts, and saw her. At first he looked startled and then disturbed. He stopped abruptly, and a big woman carrying a market basket bumped into him, said something sharply in Dutch and then clomped on by in her wooden shoes. He would have turned away into the crowd, but Rosamunde called out to him.

"Mynheer Van Hoorn!"

Reluctantly Wilhelm Van Hoorn slouched toward her, his limp more pronounced. "Mistress Rosamunde." He made her a sweeping bow, almost brushing the cobbles with the tattered yellow plume of his hat. "I am surprised to see you in Amsterdam."

She burst out laughing. "Did you think Rodrigue had boxed me up in some harem in Tangier? We are married now and live in Majorca."

Married? His tan-gold eyebrows elevated. So Rodrigue had ordered the lady drugged that he might marry her! A strange courtship where such desperate measures were needed! "I have been to Majorca," he told her. "To Palma."

"Our home is across the island from Palma, but my husband's family lives at San Telmo. Perhaps you have been there? It is not far from Palma."

Van Hoorn shook his head regretfully. "I am afraid not." He did not think it necessary to explain that the only part of Palma he had seen was the jail, a veritable dungeon as he remembered it, a place from which he had fortunately been bought out by charitable relatives, now dead. "It was very hot when I was there," he remembered, suppressing a shudder.

"Yes, summers are terrible in Majorca," agreed Rosamunde, stepping back hastily to let a woman carrying four live ducks pass. "The whole island simmers. But of course there is snow in winter in the mountains, and sometimes the *tramontana* blows."

"The *tramontana?*"

"The cold north wind which brings our icy weather. In Majorca even the winds have musical names."

Van Hoorn was looking at this woman of sunshine with some regret. "So you married him," he murmured.

"In Ireland, where we were shipwrecked. And have you married, Mynheer Van Hoorn?"

"Yes." Van Hoorn thought of his Lotje. When last he had seen her she had been working hard at the washtubs, scrubbing the dirt from the university students' clothes. Poor Lotje, with her yellow hair tied back and her plump round face perspiring as she carried the wooden tubs. Ah, well, her father had saved her from all that and she was back home in Haarlem. "We have a child now—a son," he added expansively—neglecting to mention he had abandoned them both.

"I am glad for you." Rosamunde smiled. She really was glad for him. She was glad for everybody today, this wonderful sunny windswept day with jostling crowds and sea birds wheeling noisily overhead. It seemed to her this bustling trading city was the very hub of the universe— you could run across anyone here.

" 'Tis hard to talk in this hubbub." Van Hoorn dodged a street hawker laden with fish, shrank back from a leper tolling a little bell as he shuffled along calling out for alms. "Could I buy you a tankard of ale?" He felt in his threadbare pocket to see if there were any coins left. "Or perhaps some wine?"

"I will buy *you* a tankard," Rosamunde said promptly. "And you will tell me about your life since last we saw each other. It must be more exciting than mine, for I spend much of my time chasing milk goats!"

Her laughter was infectious, and Van Hoorn joined her in it. She turned and would have marched directly into the small brick tavern that was nearest, but Van Hoorn touched her arm.

"There is a better place a little farther on," he said. He

568

did not tell her that he owed so much money in that tavern that the tavernkeeper was apt to chase him out on sight.

Rosamunde shrugged and accompanied the big Dutchman through the crowded street and into another tavern.

It was unfortunate for her that she had not insisted on the first tavern—for Harry, just returned from Delft, was seated in a corner there playing at cards with two other merchant traders of Amsterdam.

But Rosamunde did not know that. She was lonesome for someone to talk to, someone in touch with the great outside world, for Rodrigue, ever the Spanish gentleman, did not deign to discuss business ventures with his wife—and so she welcomed even the company of this shady character. She toyed with her wine and whiled away the time enjoying Van Hoorn's outrageous lies.

Meanwhile, Harry and his friends, Isaak Schrick and Dekker Schoone, finished their game. The loser paid for their wine and they rose to go their separate ways.

"I'll walk a way with ye, Hendrik," said Schrick eagerly, for he wanted to discuss a spice voyage to the Orient.

Harry smothered a sigh. Schrick's ideas were often excellent, but he kept two demanding mistresses and was always short of money. That French wench was costing him a packet; if he'd get rid of her, he wouldn't be so desperate for new ventures. Still, Schrick was a fine fellow and Harry felt like a stroll.

They moved through the dockside crowd discussing the price of silk and rum and spices before Schrick found his objective. In the forest of tall masts—for the waterfront was a jumble of ships of many nations being loaded and unloaded—he had sighted the one he wanted: the *Wilhelmina,* riding at anchor.

"Is she not a fine ship, Hendrik? I say she should be in the spice trade—but she is not."

Harry eyed the big merchantman with approval. The craft had a rakish seaworthy look to her. "She looks able to make the voyage," he agreed.

"I've been talking to her captain," said Schrick excitedly. "Ah, I see he is on the deck now." He waved his kerchief, and his greeting was acknowledged by a graceful bow from the lean dark figure on deck. "He is a sensible man and not averse to turning a guilder as best he can. He is a Majorcan and paints the name *Wilhelmina* on his ship when he is in Dutch waters—the rest of the time she is called *El Afortunado!*" He chuckled.

"Ah," said Harry thoughtfully. "One of those." For he was familiar with the clandestine trade that went on between Spain and Holland in spite of the war.

"Yes. His backers are Barcelonans and agreeable to his flying the Dutch flag as needs be. I've a voyage in mind that will take several backers to finance, and it could be that he is just the man for us, Hendrik!"

Just the man for us. As if Harry had already consented to Schrick's scheme! But—Schrick was a good fellow. Good-naturedly Harry accompanied him onto the deck of the merchantman.

"Ah, Captain Avilo," cried Schrick heartily. "Allow me to present my friend Mynheer Hendrik Van der Leyden. Captain Rodrigue Avilo."

Rodrigue Avilo. At the sound of that name something within Harry stilled and a great bell tolled. *This was the man.* Those liquid brown eyes into which he now looked had been the last to gaze upon his Rosamunde.

Rodrigue had met Schrick on a previous voyage and drunk a few rounds with him. He liked the fellow. "What, you are Dutch and I am Majorcan and yet we speak English?" he demanded jovially. "Come, Señor Schrick, what is this jest?"

"I was speaking English because it is Mynheer Van der Leyden's mother tongue and he prefers it when discussing business," explained Schrick hastily. His Simone was demanding a pearl necklace and pouting that if she did not get it, she would go back to Marseilles. He needed this venture! "There is a small business venture I hoped we could discuss—the three of us."

"But surely a man with a name like Van der Leyden is Dutch?"

Harry forced his features into a smile. "I am a some-
570

time Englishman, Captain Avilo. I came to these shores by way of Ireland."

A terrible apprehension seized Rodrigue. His heart was racing. A sometime Englishman . . . named Hendrik. In English "Hendrik" was "Henry," and Henry the Eighth had been called—*Harry*. And this man, this Harry, had come to Amsterdam by way of *Ireland*. No, no, it could not be—Rosamunde's Harry was dead, she had told him so. "Allow me to offer you gentlemen a glass of our fine Majorcan wine," Rodrigue said hospitably, but there was a faint tremor in his voice. "We can discuss Señor Schrick's business venture in my cabin."

Not by the slightest quiver did Harry betray his inner turmoil to the tensely smiling Spaniard who led these guests from shore into his great cabin and beckoned an olive-skinned cabin boy to pour for them great goblets of pale-golden wine. His dark face was impassive as Schrick, unconscious of these undercurrents, launched into the glories of the spice trade, the enormous profits to be gained from voyages to the Orient. Such a ship as this one could turn a huge profit!

"And this gentleman?" Rodrigue nodded suavely toward Harry. "Is he a captain too?"

"No, no, he is a merchant trader. He owns several great warehouses and four East Indiamen—one of them, the *Volendam,* is in the harbor now."

"A fine ship. I have seen her."

Harry acknowledged this compliment with a deprecating nod. Although his sardonic expression had not changed, he could not take his eyes off Rodrigue. Narrow, decisive, handsome, dressed in the rich Spanish fashion. A tense, tempery fellow, judging by the look of him, but he had been kind to Rosamunde, he had not taken her onto rough seas to have her child. It had ended badly anyway. . . . Harry looked quickly down into his wine goblet lest the pain in his eyes show.

Puzzled at the charged atmosphere in the cabin, Schrick waxed voluble. Rodrigue hardly heard him. At any time Rosamunde might be expected to come home from her day's shopping and—an unreasoning fear, cold as the *tramontana,* rushed over him—he did not want her to confront this tall Englishman. His thoughts raced. The child was safe aboard, being watched over by Juana, and sleeping. Thank God for that, for even at six, Elaine was a smaller version of Rosamunde.

"More wine?" he asked hurriedly.

"Yes!" cried Schrick, desperate to get Simone her pearls. "Majorcan, you say? Faith, 'tis the best I've tasted anywhere!"

"We are justly proud of our vines in Majorca," agreed Rodrigue absently. He was wondering how he could get rid of his guests before Rosamunde arrived. Tensely he wished for some minor disaster that would bring this conference to an abrupt conclusion.

Harry had no interest in the business venture Schrick outlined. He was already in the spice trade—quite profitably. Also it was clear that he would have to finance Schrick's part of the venture. But even though it was seven years now and he could wake at night without reaching over to touch her, could spend whole days, weeks even, without a wrenching pain at the memory of his loss, Harry still could not bring himself to let go by this chance to ask about her.

He straightened, and his gray eyes bored into Rodrigue's. "I knew the lady Rosamunde Langley," he said. "You will perchance remember her?" A foolish question, he decided, the moment he had uttered it. What man, having known Rosamunde, would not be drenched in memories of her?

The Majorcan captain sat very still. His suspicions had been correct, then. He felt his throat constrict; he had to clear it before answering. "You will be Harry, then, of whom she told me?"

This time a very real quiver went through Harry's tense muscles—and Schrick, noting it, gave his friend a puzzled look. Harry controlled it with an effort. "She . . . spoke of me?" he asked hoarsely.

"Often." That at least was the truth, Rodrigue thought grimly. Rosamunde had spoken of little else in Ireland! And in Majorca there had been a long succession of
572

nightmares in which she called out for Harry and woke with tears glimmering on her long lashes. He knew Rosamunde still thought of Harry, longed for him—on this very ship here in Amsterdam he had heard her cry out in her sleep, wild desperate cries of "Harry! Harry, save yourself!" He had clenched his strong fingers in the bedclothes and never betrayed by so much as a quiver that he had heard her start awake, or that he heard her shudder as tears for her lost Harry drenched her pillow.

So this was his rival, here before him at last in the flesh! Rodrigue's smoldering gaze raked the transplanted Englishman—and could find nothing to fault. He saw a tall lean man in his prime with cold gray eyes and a thoughtful look about him. The dull-finished gray satins he wore were casual but rich—even a Spaniard would approve them! A man whose broad shoulders swung with strength, who walked with a light step, and whose sinewy body looked as finely tuned as a harp. A man with a bold gaze who looked at him steadily, and whose sword had a serviceable look—observably not a man to trifle with.

A wild jealous rage possessed Rodrigue suddenly. What right had this cursed Englishman to come back from the dead to destroy all that Rodrigue Avilo loved?

Schrick gave them both a wild look. There were undercurrents here he did not understand.

"I was told she died in Ireland," said Harry, steadying his voice with an effort. "Did she leave me any message . . . at the end?"

Died in Ireland? For a moment Rodrigue was confused, then abruptly his senses righted themselves. So someone had told Harry that Rosamunde was dead? His clever mind leaped on that, came abruptly to the right conclusion. It must have been Meara, thinking Harry was the English law sent to track Rosamunde down. He laughed inwardly. She had done him a good turn with that lie, had Meara.

"Yes," he echoed pensively, not quite meeting the Englishman's eyes. "She died in Ireland."

God struck down liars. Rodrigue put the thought aside.

Harry fetched a great sigh. It came from the depths of him.

Looking into that hard and suddenly haggard face, Rodrigue knew a moment of compassion. If *he* had lost Rosamunde, he knew how desolate *he* would feel. Almost he burst out, *She is not dead. I have the honor to be her husband.* But his hands grew clammy and he stilled that outburst before it came. It had come over Rodrigue in a cold sweat that this man alone in all the world could take his Rosamunde away from him! He, Rodrigue, might hold her sweet body in his arms, but it was this damned Englishman who held her heart in keeping!

Time would change that! he told himself wrathfully. He would have all his life to make her love him! Meanwhile—his thoughts grew crafty—far better that Harry not know his Rosamunde had survived. Better Rosamunde not know that Harry lived either.

Rodrigue drew a breath so deep his chest strained against the black brocade of his doublet. By God, he had plucked her from the English guns, he had snatched her away from the mighty O'Lear—he would keep her from this Englishman too, whether she loved him or no!

But compassion made him speak kindly to Harry. "Her last words were for you," he lied gently. "She died with your name on her lips, saying"—he must be generous—"saying she loved you."

Harry looked abruptly away. His firm jaw was clenched, his gray eyes suspiciously bright. Like a bright flame, his mind seemed to burst asunder before the assault of that bittersweet goodbye. Rose . . . his lovely, gone-forever Rosamunde. . . .

"She was very brave," volunteered Rodrigue, breaking with a sigh the almost unbearable silence. "She never lost heart, not even when the *Santa Cecilia* broke up upon the rocks—and afterward, through all the hardships, very gallant."

"Aye," murmured Harry. "She was always brave, my Rose."

His Rose. To hear him say it shook Rodrigue like a
574

screaming gale. He took a big swallow of wine, almost choked.

Dumbfounded by this disastrous turn of events, Schrick cleared his throat. Something must be done to drag this conversation back to business, or sultry Simone would never have her pearls and he would never see her wriggling out of that black chemise again! He cast desperately about and tried an oblique approach.

"I did not know you were married, Captain Avilo," he said brightly. "But I was speaking to Captain Sondergaard the day he sailed, and he told me your wife is with you and that she is a great beauty." There, perhaps he would produce the lady and they could abandon this talk of dead women and Ireland!

At Schrick's words, Rodrigue's shoulders jerked so spasmodically that he spilled his wine. Hastily he pulled out a white linen kerchief and dabbed at his knee. "*I* consider her beautiful," he said in a voice gone suddenly falsetto.

Harry frowned. Even in his suffering, there had been a false note there that had struck him. "I should like to meet your wife, Captain Avilo," he said suddenly, for he had been seized by a great suspicion.

"I regret she is not here," said Rodrigue in a suffocated voice.

"Too bad." Harry's gaze was steely. "Perhaps I will rename the *Volendam* the *Santa Rosario* and call at Majorca on my next voyage."

Rodrigue felt as if he would faint. The terrifying thought that this dark sardonic Englishman might descend on Majorca—perhaps when he was away at sea!—and take Rosamunde away from him made his senses wheel about dizzily. When a woman's laugh sounded on deck, his taut nerves almost caused him to spill the wine again. But as before, his clever mind, scurrying like some trapped animal, served him well. And his plan would get rid of them too!

"You need not wait until you come to Majorca for that pleasure, señor," he told Harry thickly. "For it

575

seems she has returned. If you will accompany me, gentlemen?"

He hurried them out to the deck, closing the door quickly behind him. Over by the rail stood Juana, a thin figure in her black dress, her inky hair tightly bound. She was laughing raucously at something one of the Majorcan sailors had said. Rodrigue guessed she must have left the child asleep and come up for some air. He left Harry and Schrick and went over and seized her arm. He spoke in Majorcan. "Where is Elena?"

"Sleeping."

"Pray God she does not awaken!" muttered Rodrigue. "Come with me—and say nothing."

Surprised, Juana let him drag her along to where the two men waited. His voice rang out loudly, carrying to the dock, where several heads turned.

"Gentlemen, I have the honor to present my wife, Juana. I am afraid she speaks only Majorcan. Señor Schrick and Señor Van der Leyden."

Both men bowed deeply, and Juana gave them a bewildered curtsy.

Schrick regarded Juana in astonishment. Sondergaard had called this spindly little woman beautiful? He tried to recall Sondergaard's wife. A homely little dark-haired *vrouw*, as he remembered. Well, there was no accounting for tastes!

But faced by this bewildered olive-skinned woman, Harry's heart sank. It had been too much to hope, of course, that there had been some mistake, that Rosamunde still lived, that thinking him dead in England she had become the wife of this nervous captain from Majorca. Disappointment bit into him with sharp teeth, and he wished himself anywhere but here. Hardly knowing what he was saying, he exchanged a few pleasantries with the lady—all translated in courtly fashion by Rodrigue with answers which he invented on the spot for the bewildered Juana. At last Harry announced that he must go; he was expected elsewhere at a friend's house to sup.

Rodrigue tried to keep his relief at Harry's imminent departure from seeming too evident.

576

Harry bowed again to Juana and led a disconsolate Schrick to the gangplank. Simone would not have her pearls after all.

About to leave the ship, Harry paused.

Rosamunde, his lost love, was gone. But . . . this Spanish captain had been kind to her, had helped her at the end. Perhaps Captain Avilo needed money; captains frequently did not own their vessels, but only commanded them for their owners.

Abruptly he turned about. His hard face had a grayish tinge, and his features might have been carved in stone, but his voice, albeit a bit husky, was perfectly controlled. "I am much in your debt that you cared for Rose in her last days, Captain Avilo," he said. "For she was very dear to me. I am a man of some means. Is there aught you need? Perhaps backing for your share of Schrick's venture here?"

Schrick, who had given up hope, brightened. Perhaps Hendrik would be willing to finance the venture for all three! Simone would have her pearls after all! But to his surprise, Captain Avilo recoiled as if he had been struck, his face flushed a dark-olive hue.

Rodrigue felt suffocated. This Englishman, of his generosity, was offering him gold! Gold for sheltering Rosamunde! Gold for his lies! He could hardly keep his voice steady or his lips from quivering. "She came to me dressed as a man, and saved my life," he said stiffly. "That in itself was recompense enough for anything I may have done for her. For myself," he added in an austere tone, "I need nothing. This spice venture does not interest me. Good day, gentlemen."

"Just so." Harry was still numbed by the pain of his memories, but he strode back toward Rodrigue, and his big hand clapped warmly down on the Spaniard's shrinking shoulder. "But should you ever want, seek me out and I will aid you." His voice rang with sincerity.

He quitted the ship and shouldered his way onto the dock with Schrick.

"I was sure he would do it." Schrick, who had gloomily given up on the venture and had been turning over in his mind the puzzling impression he had had from Sondergaard that Captain Avilo's wife was a beautiful blonde, saw that Harry was eager to go. "Well, I'll bid you good day, Harry."

Harry nodded curtly. He would listen to Schrick's schemes another day.

Schrick fretted as Harry's broad shoulders disappeared into the dockside crowd. Why, Hendrik was striding along as if devils were after him! And then his round Dutch face cleared—the answer to his problem had come to him. He would buy Simone a fake pearl necklace with a real gold-and-ruby clasp—no woman would suspect the pearls to be fake when the ruby was so patently real! He would use the ruby from his watch fob—she knew its price! He would give it to her tonight in her bedroom—after he took her to the play. And then he would unhook her scarlet satin dress and she would wriggle out of her black chemise and stand there laughing, clad only in her black silk stockings. She would clasp him like the little cat she was and rake her claws down his naked back and purr—she would not go to Marseilles after all! With a jaunty step, Schrick moved away into the crowd, seeking a jeweler he knew.

His haste kept him from seeing something he would have considered interesting—perhaps even interesting enough to report later to Harry: a beautiful blond woman, loaded with bundles, was threading her way through the crowd, and now she went aboard Captain Avilo's ship.

Feeling suffocated by guilt, Rodrigue had watched his guests depart, then waved Juana away and stumbled back to the great cabin, where he sank into a carved chair. The encounter had given him a headache, and he pressed his fingers to his aching temples.

Fiercely he began to find excuses for what he had done. It was best for Rosamunde, he told himself. She had a settled life now, the life of a Spanish lady—surely better than anything this transplanted Englishman could offer her. And the child—what matter that it was Harry's child? Elena should not be uprooted.

But overweening all was the strength of his desire for

Rosamunde, a desire that would drive him to any lengths. Past reason, past judgment, past hope of heaven, Rodrigue Avilo loved the blond English beauty—and no accursed Englishman, returned from the dead or no, was going to take her from him!

When she had quitted the tavern with Van Hoorn, he had said whimsically, " 'Tis the first time such a lovely lady has ever paid for my wine!"

Rosamunde laughed. "It may be that I owe you a debt, Mynheer Van Hoorn," she said lightly. "For without your intervention, I would surely have remained in Amsterdam—and would never have had Captain Avilo for a husband."

"He has made you a good husband then?"

"The best." Rosamunde was in an expansive mood; she loved being here in Amsterdam—all was right with her world.

"I will walk you to the ship."

She could not have Rodrigue see her approaching the ship with Van Hoorn! It would arouse his jealousy. "No, I had forgotten a purchase I must make—some yellow ribands for Elaine's new dress. I will run and buy them now."

She walked back to a stall that sold ribbons and bargained for them. Van Hoorn waved goodbye and limped away, feeling vastly better for having met her. His aimless footsteps took him to the dock where *El Afortunado*, now renamed the *Wilhelmina*, lay at anchor. The wind was blowing in Van Hoorn's direction. He looked up at Rodrigue's loud introduction of Juana as his "wife."

Since Rosamunde had claimed to be Rodrigue Avilo's wife only minutes before, Van Hoorn seated himself upon a piling and awaited developments.

They were not long in coming.

Juana disappeared below—and Rodrigue vanished into his great cabin. Walking fast, with haunted eyes, Harry strode off into the crowd—and then Schrick, who had paused to watch Harry depart and then run away as if some great light had struck him. And there came Rosamunde, carrying her packages—and one new one she had not had when she had met Van Hoorn. It contained a length of yellow ribbon to trim Elaine's new dress.

Such little things control the world . . . for a length of yellow ribbon, Rosamunde lost her chance to meet Harry again.

With perfect aplomb she went aboard, never noticing Van Hoorn in the dockside throng. As she disappeared from view, Van Hoorn rose and stretched.

He considered going after Harry and telling him that the dark woman to whom he had just been introduced was but one of *two* wives—just to see the look of astonishment on the Englishman's face, for he still smarted over the night that Harry had cheated him out of taking Cornelis Van der Leyden's purse. But he remembered suddenly how glowing Rosamunde had looked, how forgiving she had been to him, the envious looks the tavern patrons had cast at him as they sipped their wine.

He sighed. If Rodrigue Avilo had succeeded in hood-winking the English girl into believing she was his only wife, so be it. At least she was happy.

Wilhelm Van Hoorn, who could at that moment have changed the shape of destiny for Harry and his beloved, shrugged and limped away into the dockside crowd. He would see if he could find a game of dice.

For him it was a rare quixotic gesture, for usually he came out on the side of the devil.

41   *Slumped in exhaustion from the violent churning* of his emotions, Rodrigue looked up when the cabin door opened to admit Rosamunde, weighted down with parcels.

"Rodrigue," she cried, tossing her parcels upon a chair, "you'll never guess whom I saw today."

Rodrigue's shoulders gave an involuntary jerk, and the wine he had been gulping down threatened to come up. He could certainly guess who she *might* have seen, and the thought made him blanch.

"Mynheer Van Hoorn," she told him gaily. "He walks with a limp now—a wound, he told me. Got in some tavern brawl, I would gather. He's lost weight and looks years older. He said—Rodrigue, are you all right? You look so pale."

Rodrigue relaxed his grip on the wine bottle he had been clutching and set it down beside him with a clatter. "I am in excellent health," he said in a choked voice. "What did Van Hoorn say?"

"He said he has a wife now—and a son."

"The world will be no better for that," said Rodrigue morosely.

"Oh, come, Rodrigue! He is our Cupid! After all, we might never have wed had you not hired him to drug me so you could abduct me!"

"But not to have you for himself," muttered Rodrigue, passing his right hand over the knuckles of his left, in silent memory of the blow he had given Van Hoorn that night some seven years ago.

"You were both wrong." She laughed, trying to cajole him out of his dark mood. "See where it has led you? You are saddled now with a wife and daughter—a wife who has just bought several lengths of beautiful material in colors that will shock your dignified Spanish soul!"

"You may wear them at Cala Mesquida, but—"

"But not to church and not to San Telmo!" she finished for him, reaching over to ruffle his hair affectionately. He gave her a haggard smile, and she pulled out a long length of brilliant green watered silk, whirled it about her like a shawl in a stamping dance she had seen the peasants perform on Majorca. She came to a wild whirling halt before him, her breast heaving from the exertion and her green eyes sparkling wickedly. "Come, Rodrigue," she coaxed, "have you not a smile for me? You once bought me a dress of this color right here in Amsterdam—a gift

581

for a light woman! You told me it was the color of my eyes!"

Rodrigue gave her a tormented look and essayed a wan smile. She was so lovely, so infinitely desirable, this woman of light and laughter. The thought of losing her burned his stomach and gripped his heart with ice. No, by God, he swore to himself, he would *not* lose her!

"I am glad you are back, Rosamunde," he said, his clever mind working again. "And doubly glad you have made your purchases."

She dropped easily down on the bunk, fanning herself with one slim hand, and gave him an inquiring look.

"If I am disturbed, 'tis with reason. While you were out I learned that there are several cases of the Plague in Amsterdam. We cast off tomorrow—you must not leave the ship again."

Her face fell. "The Plague!" she protested. "But Van Hoorn said nothing of it, and he—"

" 'Tis not widely known as yet," Rodrigue lied smoothly. "In a city that depends upon the flow of commerce, such evil tidings are closely guarded—until it can no longer be hushed up. A captain of my acquaintance gave me warning. He himself has already upped anchor and sailed away."

So this was all she was to have of Amsterdam, the lovely busy city she so loved. . . . Rosamunde lay back upon the bunk and turned her head away, trying to hide her disappointment. "You are right, of course," she mumbled. "We must not endanger Elaine."

Rodrigue gave her a miserable look. He hated crushing her bright spirit, hated himself for lying to her. "If there is anything else you wish to buy," he said quickly, "I will go ashore and purchase it for you."

She sat up, flashing him a surprised look. "But you must not endanger yourself by going ashore! If there is Plague in the city, we should sail today."

"We have not yet finished loading the ship. I will remind you that I have no share in the vessel—only in the cargo."

He turned and went out, to escape further questions.
582

Rosamunde stared after him, puzzled. There had been something in his voice. . . . Could it be that there was no Plague in Amsterdam? She doubted they could finish loading the cargo by tomorrow. Could Rodrigue be fleeing Amsterdam to keep her from seeing Van Hoorn again? She was familiar with the facile workings of Rodrigue's mind—and with his terrible jealousy. What a fool she had been to mention meeting the scoundrelly Dutchman!

In anger she almost leaped up and followed Rodrigue to the deck to have it out with him. Then her shoulders sagged in dejection. Perhaps there *was* Plague in Amsterdam. In any case, to imply that Rodrigue had lied to her would be sure to bring on an outburst.

So she reasoned, and again a small decision changed the course of her life.

For had she gone on deck at that moment, she would have seen Harry striding by on the dock. Harry, resplendent in a new blue velvet coat and wide-topped boots, with his serviceable sword swinging at his side, out to find what solace he could from the light women of Amsterdam.

He paused, looking at the ship. From the poop deck Rodrigue watched him, feeling his very soul crawl with fear.

This man could take from him everything—his wife, the child he had come to regard as his own, his every reason for living.

Harry saw him and bowed. Rodrigue returned the bow coldly and turned away to inspect the shrouds.

The Englishman could not have Rosamunde! She belonged to *him!*

In a cold sweat, Rodrigue piled on all the canvas his ship would carry and sailed out of Amsterdam as if pursued by devils. And indeed he was—but they were devils of conscience, and he carried them with him wherever he went. For once he had cleared the harbor, he faced the truth: Harry was wealthy now, powerful . . . he could give Rosamunde and Elaine so much more than Rodrigue could give them. In panic he told himself that he had stolen Rosamunde and the child—stolen them from

583

the Englishman, to whom they both truly belonged. He could not eat for thinking about it.

Restive after his encounter with Rodrigue, Harry put to sea on the *Volendam*, that great East Indiaman, bound for Madagascar and the Spice Islands. A faster sailor, she overtook *El Afortunado* off La Coruna.

It was dusk. In the warm breeze, Rosamunde leaned on the taffrail and watched the tall ship coming up to starboard.

"What ship is that?" she asked, peering into the dusk. "I cannot make out her name."

"It is the *Volendam*," said a ship's officer near her. "Out of Amsterdam. One of Hendrik Van der Leyden's fleet."

Was he never to be free of that cursed name? Rodrigue stared fiercely at the big East Indiaman. Rosamunde was his, *his!* "Whom God hath joined together, let no man put asunder," he muttered.

"What did you say?" asked Rosamunde.

Rodrigue started. He had not been aware he had spoken aloud. "I said this wind had grown piercing." Ignoring her protests, he hurried her back to her cabin, then gave hoarse orders to change course, draw nearer to the Spanish shore—and away from that cursed ship of Van der Leyden's that seemed to be pursuing him like the voice of conscience.

Having done that, he gripped the rail and watched those tall masts and billowing sails disappear into the deepening dusk. From the heavens a single star gazed down as if to peer into his very soul. *God will punish me,* he thought bleakly. *That I do not let them meet, that I do not let her choose.*

The Rodrigue who brought Rosamunde back to Majorca was not the lighthearted lover who had taken her to Amsterdam. Rosamunde was troubled by his restless tossing in bed, by the dark circles under his eyes that proclaimed yet another sleepless night. Sometimes she thought she should give up trying to understand this strange complex man who claimed her in nights of wild passion—yet at other times flung away from her and slept alone
584

or, head bent, walked the night away, pacing the courtyard below her window

She thought he would get over whatever tormented him in the tranquil beauty of Cala Mesquida. He did not. He remained irascible. Yet . . . still he lingered at Cala Mesquida.

Summer—the long dry burning Majorcan summer—had waned. Now it was autumn and the *ponent* was blowing—that wet west wind that would bring rain and flowers to Majorca. The green shoots of corn would break through earth that a short time before had been cracked and parched, and the muddy roads would be edged with green.

"Tomorrow the roads will be flooded," said Rosamunde, for by now she was accustomed to the violence of Majorcan weather.

Rodrigue nodded. "There was another message from Ignacio today—while you were off chasing the milch goats. He asks why the ship rots in Palma while I loll at Cala Mesquida."

"And why do you?"

He gave her a tormented look, but he did not answer. *We are too much alone,* she thought. *Perhaps if we took a house in Palma for a season . . .*

She chose her moment to mention it. It had rained for three days—hard punishing rain that had torn the topsoil from the barren *garriga*. But today the sun shone upon the steaming earth, and by evening it was balmy, pleasant.

At dusk when a deep rose-red sunset still lingered in the western sky, tinting the white walls of their house a soft pink and turning Rodrigue's dark-olive skin a ruddy hue and Rosamunde's fair hair to flame, they sat on the rude stone benches of the courtyard taking their ease. The air was heavy with the scent of roses, and Rodrigue was watching Elaine as she played.

"She has English eyes," he said moodily.

Rosamunde looked at the laughing child, pushing an orange across the flagged courtyard with an orange branch. *She has Harry's eyes,* she thought with a pang. For whenever Rosamunde looked in her daughter's eyes she was

585

reminded of Harry . . . Harry whom she had loved and lost. Those steady gray eyes brought it all back to her.

"Mine are English eyes too, Rodrigue," she reminded him.

"I know," he said painfully. "But for me, they have become—Majorcan."

She was touched. It was his way of saying: *mine*. It was then she brought up the subject of a house in Palma.

"No!" Rodrigue leaped to his feet and strode about the courtyard.

Rosamunde was alarmed. "I only thought we would see people and be less alone—"

He stopped before her. "Is that what you want? To see people? Is my company no longer enough for you?" His tone was brutal, and she shrank back before it. He continued staring at her, and his voice dropped so low she could almost believe she imagined it. "You loved the highwayman. You love him still."

"Is that what is troubling you?" she cried in amazement. "Rodrigue, I have been your wife for more than six years now. I have been faithful to you. What more do you want?"

"I want your heart," he said bitterly. *"And I have not got it."*

She threw him a withering look. "I will put Elaine to bed."

"And put to bed your fancies as well!" Rodrigue shouted after her. "I will not have him occupying a place between us! I feel we sleep three in a bed—you, myself and that damned Englishman!"

"Will you tell me that you are jealous of a man dead these seven years?" she asked cuttingly.

"He is not—" Rodrigue choked back the words. He had almost blurted out, *He is not dead.*

"He is not *what*, Rodrigue?"

"He is not dead to *you*. He lives in your heart."

She turned away with a scornful glance, but his lashing voice pursued her. "Tell me that he does not, Rosamunde. Tell me that!"

She fled from that voice. But as she tucked the child

586

into her bed and opened the windows that the sea air might waft through, she answered his question honestly to herself. When she went downstairs she found him seated on a stone bench with his head in his arms in an attitude of despair. So lightly had she trod he had not heard her, and now she held her breath as she looked at him. He was suffering, she knew, and it was a suffering hard for her to ease. Life was unfair. . . .

She went over and put her arms around him. The look he gave her was anguished.

"Rodrigue," she said softly, "you are a fool. Do you not know that if *you* were to die, you too would live on in my heart?

"If I died—?" His hurt naked gaze was on her face. *Do not lie to me,* it pleaded.

Rosamunde took a deep breath. "I would always love you, Rodrigue." *What matter that I would love Harry more?*

He shivered and grasped her like a drowning man, clutched her so fiercely that she was sure there would be blue bruises on her arms tomorrow. The fountain splashed and the scent of the roses was almost overpowering. From the goat enclosure came a gentle tinkle, and somewhere a land bird called to its nesting mate. Even the roar of the sea seemed muted, enticing.

She had said she loved him, would *always* love him. He crushed her to him wordlessly, for his love for this woman was overwhelming. It frightened him. He loved her beyond reason, beyond sense. He loved her more than God or Spain or church—he could not bear to be second in her heart, he must be first.

He had been derelict, he had tormented her! By God, he would woo her again, win her again! Caught on the wings of his powerful emotions, Rosamunde soared and thrilled in his arms. Now he was easing her down onto the stone bench. His face was dark above her, against the moon. She did not even feel the hardness of the stone against her back, so beguiled was she by the ardor of his lovemaking. Pulsing together with each sweet assault upon their senses, their clinging bodies reached a crescendo of desire and seemed to burst into flame like some great explosion.

When at last he carried her to bed, a nightingale was singing.

Winter came to Majorca and the icy *tramontana* blew across the land, turning the high sierras to white. But their home was by the sea, and the climate was milder. There were damp cold nights when they shivered in their beds and the chill sea fog crept in around the shutters, for at Cala Mesquida the windows were unglazed. But in February the almond trees in the garden bloomed and across the *garriga* at the base of the hills could be seen great drifts of white flowers, pure and lovely.

With the coming of spring, Rodrigue gained confidence. Harry was not coming to take Rosamunde away from him after all. His spirits lifted, and before he rode away in April to Palma through fields of horse beans and pale-green corn, he had made his peace with Rosamunde and with God.

She loved him. He was once more sure of that.

So it was a happy man who rode his big Arabian horse down a roadside aflower with white and yellow asphodels and golden marigolds. Rosamunde rode part of the way with him on Shiraz. The lovely mare was glad of a run, and after she had waved goodbye to Rodrigue, she galloped back across a wasteland awash with drifts of scarlet poppies and marguerites.

The next few years were the happiest they spent together.

Rodrigue prospered. Returning from one of his voyages, he brought Elaine a dainty Arabian mare, a fit companion for Shiraz. Her name was Yasmin, and Elaine was in raptures over her. Together the three of them would ride to picnic at those other beautiful bays that lay to the south: Cala Ratjada with its stunted trees and limpid transparent water that smelled faintly of pinewood, and Cala Canyamel, set among pleasant green hills where lofty pine branches sighed overhead. Most often they took the path to the soft warm sands of nearby Cala Guya and bathed in the warm clear water.

Once as they lazed there on the beach watching Elaine

play in the surf, Rosamunde dragged her fingers through the hot sand and turned luxuriously to Rodrigue. "This should be a smuggler's cove," she said dreamily, "with white-sailed ships standing out to sea in the moonlight and men rowing ashore in longboats filled with contraband."

Rodrigue cocked his head at her. "I once thought of it. But 'tis too far over rough roads to Palma, where goods could be sold. And smuggling on the northern coast from Alcudia to Soller is controlled by the coast watchers of Don José Alvar."

The Whip again . . .

"How strong is his grip?"

Rodrigue shrugged. "Don José puts to the lash any man who tries to bring in smuggled goods without first giving half of them to him. *I* would never deal with him," he added contemptuously, "although he once sent me a tempting offer at San Telmo."

"He puts them to the lash?"

"Don José is a man of strange tastes," said Rodrigue bluntly. "It pleasures him to cut a living back to ribbons. To him it is a form of artistry. I am told the graves of the unwary lie thick around La Calobra."

Rosamunde shivered in the bright sunshine. She was glad indeed that Rodrigue had refused to deal with this monster. Quickly she changed the subject to the repainting of the dining room, for the house at Cala Mesquida had benefited from Rodrigue's voyages too. When she had first come there, most of their furniture was crude but carved from the hard, beautifully grained olive wood. Rodrigue had showed her the grove from whence it came, slumbering in its antiquity, with thick misshapen trunks and weirdly reaching branches. Although the day was still, the silvery olive leaves had trembled at the lightest breath of wind and shimmered in the sun, casting moving lacy shadows on the rocky soil beneath.

But now he packed in two wagonloads of furniture—tables and chairs and cabinets of teak, of mahogany, Oriental things for which, he told her, he had traded casks of the strong Majorcan wine in Amsterdam.

Amsterdam . . .

"Could we not go with you on your next voyage?" she asked wistfully, for it was lonely here. "Elaine has no governess, and although I have taught her English and she speaks both Spanish and Majorcan, she knows so little of the world. It would benefit her."

Rodrigue looked harassed and ran nervous fingers through his hair. "The war—it is not safe." And when her face fell, "Perhaps I will take you to Barcelona."

But as it turned out, he did not even do that. For there was always the risk that he would be blown off course and put into some port where they would run into Harry. Here high above this lonely Majorcan bay, Rosamunde was safe from the Englishman. But Rodrigue knew—for he kept track of Harry—that Hendrik Van der Leyden roamed the world on one or other of his great ships. There was always the off chance that Rosamunde and Harry might come face to face in some far-off port.

He loved her too much—he could not chance it.

So the lady of Cala Mesquida lived a lonely life.

But it had its compensations: the wild lonely beauty of this place of sea and sky and scented winds; long rides up and down the rugged coastline on Shiraz.

Best of all, there was Elaine. Dainty and lovely and growing taller and more like her beautiful mother every day. Elaine built sand castles on the white beach, she cut roses from the garden—vibrant splashes of color to bring into the cool high-ceilinged house. She sat with her bare white legs dangling over the rocks of the clifftop and sang siren songs to an empty sea, she rode Yasmin out among the asphodels. It was lovely to be young and growing up in Majorca.

Her mother watched her fondly. Denied the exciting world Rodrigue frequented, Rosamunde had made another world for herself at Cala Mesquida. A world of tinkling goat bells among the ancient stones and a land that burst forth into bloom when the rains came. A world in which —except when Rodrigue was home from the sea and passions flowed like strong wine—she was like a princess in a fairy tale, cast under some witch's spell, dreaming her life away in a perfumed garden and spending far too much of her time in dangerous rememberings—of wild nights on the English highroads, and the tall man who had thundered down those highroads beside her: Harry . . . *how she had loved him.*

Later Rosamunde tried to pinpoint the exact time the change had come over Rodrigue. He had come back from one of his voyages morose and thoughtful, had had less to say than usual, had moped about the courtyard and taken little interest in the new fields his money had paid to clear, or the new crops which, God willing, would not fail again this year.

It was strange. Perhaps he was lonely, she thought. But when she again brought up the subject of voyaging with him, his response was like a pitcher of cold water.

"You will not!" he burst out. His sudden violence surprised her. It always surprised her. She would never accustom herself to the volatile Latin temperament. Rodrigue was sweet, he was charming as a child—but he was a madman when he was angry.

Seeing the consternation on her lovely face, he was instantly contrite. He moved forward to take her in his arms —and groaned suddenly and turned away. She watched him, puzzled.

"Rosamunde, I cannot stay," he said abruptly. "I came only to tell you that I have taken on another cargo and sail at once for Amsterdam. I must leave for Palma tonight."

"But you have just arrived!" she cried, bewildered. "Will you not even stay a fortnight?"

He did not meet her eyes. "I should not have come at all. The weather is good. A ship can make profitable voyages in weather like this."

"You drive yourself too hard!"

But argument could not move him. That night he rode for Palma and *El Afortunado.* Rosamunde found it hard to forgive his curt goodbye that day. He did not even kiss her. He gave her a long unfathomable look, and as she moved toward him, he mounted, set spurs to his horse, and rode away.

She stood looking after him, hurt.

Nothing ever was right between them after that.

The wild savage love that had bound them together

with golden ties was gone . . . and in its place was only emptiness. Rodrigue was seldom home, and when he was, he treated her politely—but like a stranger.

When he insisted on changing their sleeping arrangements and moved into a room across the hall, she rebelled. There was a wild stormy scene, and it ended with Rodrigue flinging out and riding away.

Rosamunde never knew that he rode only out of sight of the house and flung himself down on the ground and wept, deep wrenching sobs that came from the depths of him. After a while he rose and with shoulders sagging in defeat, rode away to Palma—and another voyage.

For there was a terrible reason behind Rodrigue's strange behavior. He now lived in deadly fear. But not of a human enemy.

Now every time he heard a leper's lonely bell or saw those sad groups of starving creatures, eyes gleaming through the slits of their enveloping hoods, as they groveled for alms at the gateways of seaport towns he visited, he shuddered—and for a new reason.

He had found a mark on his arm, and it had frightened him. He could not bear to seek medical advice lest his fears be confirmed. Instead, like his old nurse—from whom he now firmly believed he had contracted the disease on his visits to Barcelona—he kept his terrible secret.

Rodrigue Avilo, so brave about everything else, could not face the fact that he might have become—a leper.

Some days he was certain of it. At those times he told himself bitterly that it was a punishment from God for his lies, for his deceit in keeping Harry and Rosamunde apart. But even if he were to be struck dead for it, he would not have done other than he had done. . . .

On his long voyages, at night he would lean upon the taffrail of his ship and listen to the melancholy sounds of a *viola da gamba* and the sailors singing one of their haunting Majorcan refrains. Lulled by the music, he would dream of Rosamunde riding across the *garriga* on Shiraz, or bathing in the sparkling blue waters off Cala Mesquida. With quickening heart he would imagine himself coming back to her at the end of his voyage, seizing her in his arms, holding her, loving her, seeing the tender look on her lovely face.

And then he would turn a haggard gaze up to the cold night stars and remember that he must not touch her, dared not touch her. For the mark on his arm had not gone away as he had hoped. It had been joined by another.

He would lurch down to his cabin and find his sleep torn by strange wild nightmares where he was shut away, hooded, in some terrible place among horrors—and wake up screaming. And sometimes he would dream that Rosamunde came to that place and embraced him and told him that she would dwell there with him, that she would never leave him.

He woke up sweating at that. Oh, God, he must never let that happen! Not to the gallant girl he had married!

And then he would wake, feeling better. And he would tell himself the marks were something else, that he had *not* become a leper, that he would *not* need to absent himself from humankind—or from the woman he loved. He would sail on, carrying through another successful voyage —and on his return again be afraid to touch her.

It was a hell of his own making, but he lived in it by choice, for he knew that once he sought medical advice, he might well face a terrible decision.

When the time came, he promised himself, he would face it bravely.

There was a mark on his neck now. He took to wearing a wide concealing ruff—even though ruffs had gone out of fashion.

On one of his brief unsatisfying visits home, Rosamunde determined to have it out with him. If she had erred in some way, let him tell her so!

"Rodrigue," she pleaded, as he bade her goodnight and carried his candle dejectedly up the stairs toward his room, "Rodrigue, come back. Tell me what is troubling you. Let me help you, Rodrigue."

His stiff ruff gleaming in the candlelight, he turned and looked down at her with such sadness, such bitterness, that she flinched. To her surprise he gave a sharp barking laugh. "No one can help me, Rosamunde. I am being punished."

So, whatever it was, he had no intention of sharing it.

Now she leaned upon the newel post in the dark lower hall and listened to his retreating footsteps, the sound of his door closing.

He had shut her out—again.

For the first time she wondered if Rodrigue might be unfaithful to her. Dispassionately she summed him up in her mind: whipcord-lean, a ready smile, richly dressed in the narrow Spanish style that so became him, a man with a ready wit . . . he would tempt a woman, must have tempted many in the ports he visited.

Obviously, this time he too had been tempted.

Unfaith . . . it was something she had not considered. Somehow she had never thought such a thing would ever touch her life. That came, she told herself ironically, of having always been deemed a beauty. It had made her overconfident. She was as other women. She could be deserted, forgotten. Indeed, she was all but deserted now.

She lit a candle and studied her reflection in the mirror. She could not fault it. In no way was she changed. If a man had thought her lovely once, he still must think so. Unless *he* had changed.

She swallowed. Rodrigue had changed. Toward her. And there had to be a reason, for she had done nothing, nothing.

The reason must be a woman.

She lifted her chin and carried the candle up the stairs with her back very straight. It was with cool detached courtesy that she bade Rodrigue goodbye next day and wished him good voyage.

Rodrigue had walked his horses only a few paces before he reined in and turned to look at her. His heart ached to see her standing there in her blue dress, so strong, so gallant. That he had hurt her, he knew—and he must hurt her still more.

For if he was right—and he feared to have it confirmed—the terrible secret he carried in his body would be known soon enough.

594

He loved Rosamunde. He must not infect her.

He should tell her, he thought dully. But he shrank from that. He could not bear to see the dawning horror that would come over her face. Thank God he had had the strength to sleep in a separate room—it had been hard, so hard to do. And it had wounded her.

Always he must pretend to be in some great rage lest those he loved touch him! He even worried lest Pablo become infected when he pulled off his boots. Or Juana when she washed his clothes.

Ah, the danger to them all was too great! He must make *sure*. . . . He would see a barber-surgeon.

In Amsterdam he crashed blindly out of the barber-surgeon's office. For the barber-surgeon had confirmed his worst fears. He had contracted leprosy.

To be a leper! On his return voyage Rodrigue shivered in his cabin, his face gone gray. Leprosy was the most dread of all diseases, and so widespread that in Europe almost every town had its leprosarium on the outskirts where those unfortunates lived together, shunned by all.

He saw his future, and it was black.

For a little while he could keep the world from knowing —and then it would be all over for him. He would be shut away with the rest of the living dead.

A vision of Rosamunde drifted through his tortured mind—bold, beautiful, reckless, a woman of sunshine, a woman of laughter and gold. This evil that had come upon him was surely a judgment for his sin of loving her too much and keeping her away from the man she truly loved! He knew he should give her up now, send her to Amsterdam—to Harry, who loved her. He groaned and put his head in his hands. Even now, he could not bear to lose her.

But on that, his last voyage, Rodrigue Avilo made a great decision.

He converted all that he had—save the property at Cala Mesquida—into gold. And gave up the sea he loved and the ship.

And rode across Majorca to see his lady—one more time before the dark.

42   *This new estrangement from Rodrigue had made*
Rosamunde restless. Now she took long rides in which
she explored the countryside until she knew even the barren *garriga* like the back of her hand. Especially in spring
she loved riding Shiraz out onto its windswept expanse.
Through rock rose and gorse and rosemary the mare
would pick her dainty way, and sometimes Rosamunde
would alight by a burst of fan palms and walk through
milk vetch and spurge to pick an armload of the blue-
and-white asphodels and bring them back to old Juana,
who valued them greatly as medicine.

Her rides had been longer lately; sometimes she was
gone overnight, sleeping out beneath the stars. Alone.
Pablo and Juana shook their heads, not understanding
what drove the foreign lady to such lengths.

Today she would ride farther. Up early, she guided
Shiraz through the stone-age village, and under an arch
of giant boulders—an ancient gateway that reminded her
of Stonehenge in England. Once on the flower-strewn
garriga, she let Shiraz run.

Westward she rode, drinking from the wooden water
buckets of ancient *norias,* avoiding towns, buying her food
at isolated farmsteads. Her Spanish was flawless now, her
Majorcan nearly so, and in her simple homespun dress
with her fair hair covered by a discreet shawl, she attracted
little attention. Past olive groves and papyrus plants she
rode. Once or twice, as Shiraz grazed by the roadside, she
reached over a stone wall and lazily picked a pomegranate
or a fig. Over arched bridges built by the Romans she
rode, and into the high mountains. Across the ridge, skirt-

ing the Monastery of Lluch with its leprosarium, then past the wild whirlpool of Gorch Blau. She must be nearing The Whip's domain. She knew she should have turned back then, but she did not. Instead she crossed the saddle of Sa Corbata and let Shiraz pick her way down toward the coast.

Off in the distance now she could see a massive cream-colored building with high-flung windows and multiple chimneys and terraces with handsome stone balustrades. *Almost a palace!* she thought, surprised. Her view of it was partially obscured by tall dark cypress trees, but she could glimpse an olive grove too, with gray gnarled tree-trunks crouched like monsters. The house seemed to rear up arrogantly as if it wished to look about. It was so forbidding that she decided not to approach it.

As she turned Shiraz, she heard a whimper in the bushes and stopped to listen. It sounded like a child crying.

Rosamunde dismounted and walked stealthily toward the sound, pulled aside a tree branch and saw lying below it a young girl's crumpled figure. She was crying, soft muffled sobs that had a lost childlike quality, and her back—her back, naked to the waist, was covered with huge bleeding weals. *A whip had done that!*

This then must be La Calobra!

But Rosamunde's foot had caught in a root and announced her presence. With a muffled scream the girl sprang up. For a moment her staring terrified gaze fixed on Rosamunde; then she ran into a tangle of bushes and thorn and disappeared.

"Wait!" called Rosamunde in Majorcan. "Wait, I will help you!"

But the girl was gone. Rosamunde's search revealed not even a footprint, only a few drops of blood staining the leaves of a nearby bush.

Rosamunde looked around her uneasily. It was growing dusk. She would not like night to find her in these hills. She headed Shiraz northeast and broke through a stand of tall pines onto a tiny sheltered bay, walled in by cliffs. Below was a sandy beach.

It was lovely here, peaceful, balmy. The Whip and La

Calobra seemed far away. Besides, Rodrigue had not said The Whip attacked women. The olive-skinned girl—cruelly punished by her father, no doubt, for some infraction, and run away to weep—drifted from her mind before the beauty of that scene. She left Shiraz contentedly grazing beneath the pines and made her way down to the beach, swam in the warm water and spent the night beneath the pines, smelling the pungent pine scent mixed with the brisk salt air from the sea.

The next morning she bathed again in that tiny sheltered bay, dived under in the clear transparent water and swam through a great hole in the stone cliffs. She came up into a sea grotto, where light struck down from above. It was beautiful, and the shafts of light were sapphire-blue and turquoise. Rosamunde swam about it, marveling, before she went back through that underwater opening, back into the warm blue waters of the bay.

As she came up she saw something not visible from the land side, a black opening above her in the rocks—it must be a cave! Why, it could be reached from the beach if one were careful how one clambered up that rocky face. She swam ashore, shook herself, dressed and made for the cave. It was easy to reach, a gaping hole midway up the cliff. She sat for a while lazing in the entrance and then roused herself. She must not loll here; already she had been gone too long from Cala Mesquida. They would worry. She climbed down and from the beach cast a last wistful look back up the cliffs. How Harry would have loved this place!

Harry . . . she smiled wistfully as she thought of him. Ah, she had not forgotten Harry, though he had lain dormant in her heart for a long time. Strange, he had seemed so near, so close in Amsterdam. Now, with Rodrigue so neglectful and so strange, she took out the old memories and dusted them off, and her reckless highwayman rode with her in spirit across the hills beneath the blazing Majorcan sun.

Something else rode with her across the hills—pacing her from a discreet distance. Her way led her back past that forbidding pile of a house, and a pair of sharp eyes looking from an upstairs window had seen her crest the rise, her fair hair blowing. Now a lone horseman followed her trail.

Through the mountains to the eastward Rosamunde rode, unaware that she was being followed. Once she looked back and saw something glinting in the sun, perhaps the silver trimming of a saddle. But the sun's glare in these mirrorlike mountains blinded her, and the silver glint seemed to disappear.

At midday she dismounted in the shade of a great upflung boulder and flung herself upon the hot ground, exhausted. Shiraz too sought the shade. They were both asleep when the horseman who had patiently followed dismounted and approached carefully on foot.

Rosamunde woke, stirred by the toe of a dusty boot. She opened her eyes into the sun's bright glare and saw beside her a man's wide-topped leather boot. As she rolled away from it, she collided with his other boot and cried out as his spur raked her arm.

Towering above her, dark against the brilliant sky, the owner of the boots laughed. She looked up into a cruel, self-indulgent face. A pair of calculating brown eyes stared down at her, and a pair of red lips curved into a mocking smile. "Mademoiselle," purred a lazy voice, "why is a blond beauty like yourself riding the Majorcan hills alone?"

Rosamunde flushed. "Allow me to rise," she cried. "Or you will regret it!"

"You will rise soon enough—beneath me." He laughed. And lifted his booted foot and dragged his spur lightly over her skirt, making a long rip in the fabric— and a long bloody scratch on the white hip beneath.

Rosamunde reacted with the speed of an angry cat. She seized that boot and with all her strength threw herself to the side. Thrown off balance, the Frenchman went down, cursing. He fell across her, and her right knee caught him in the groin. With a howl of anguish he rolled off of her, writhing.

White-faced, Rosamunde scrambled to her feet. She

threw a last grim look at the Frenchman, rolling on the ground in agony, and galloped away on Shiraz.

She lost no time—others might be lurking. Like an arrow loosed from a bow, she flashed down out of the hills, sped past the mastic trees and dwarf palms and flower-strewn drifts of the *garriga* and thundered into the courtyard at Cala Mesquida, where old Pablo straightened up and regarded her reproachfully.

"We were worried, Doña Rosamunde."

She tossed him the reins. "I became lost in the hills."

Pablo sighed gustily and shook his head. He would never understand this Englishwoman.

After a brief visit to San Telmo, Rodrigue rode home to Cala Mesquida for the last time. The April drifts of flowers that seemed to flow beneath waving palms and Aleppo pines did not lighten his heavy heart, nor did the more dramatic sight, on the last leg of his journey, of banks of poppies and a veritable sea of white-and-blue asphodels.

In his bookish days when his father had urged him to enter holy orders, he had learned of a Greek legend that described the entrance to Hades as a meadow strewn with asphodels. Doomed, it seemed to him he was reliving that legend.

As he neared Cala Mesquida, he left the road and approached through a light pine forest. Around him was the chirping of cicadas and the tangy scent of resin. Then the land opened up, and below him was his red-roofed white house, and beyond it the clear blue sparkling waters of the bay.

Hastily he reined in. He would wait for dusk.

Dusk found him slipping down on foot, startling Pablo as he fed the milk goats—and silencing him with a warning finger to his lips. They spoke in low tones, and Pablo cried out sharply as he listened. Then he nodded in dumb acceptance. Sworn to secrecy, with shoulders drooping, Pablo carried a wooden ladder and stood it against the wall at Rosamunde's bedroom window.

When the moon was out, Rodrigue climbed that ladder and drank deep of the sight of her, lying naked on her bed in the heat, with her white arms outflung in the moonlight, a sleeping beauty, forever young. He leaned his arms upon the sill, dizzy with the sight of her and dying inwardly because he feared his resolve would weaken, that he would vault over the sill and stride to that big square bed and seize his woman—that he would hold her locked in his arms, would take her naked pliant body and have his way with it—and seal her fate forever! God, he must guard against that! Beads of perspiration glittered on his forehead as his inner battle raged. At last, still trembling from his inner turmoil, he made his way softly back down the ladder and padded away in the night. The first pink light that broke over the darkly glittering sea saw him riding away to the west through drifts of asphodels.

Rodrigue Avilo had found his Hades.

Now he would sort out his life, he would end this misery. He would never see Rosamunde again except through the eye slits of a leper's hooded robes.

He had made all of his arrangements already with his horrified brother, Ignacio—and bought Ignacio's reluctant cooperation with a chest of gold coins, the fruits of his labors these last years. Now he rode straight for the leprosarium outside the Monastery of Lluch and the dark world he had decreed for himself. At the Monastery he would pray before the altar of the Black Madonna—perhaps *she* would have the Answer.

Five days later Ignacio brought the news to Cala Mesquida that Rodrigue was dead.

It was growing dark in the bronze-age village that looked down on the red-roofed house, and the ancient *talayoti* stood out as beacons. On a hot flat stone, sixteen-year-old Elaine lay stretched out and sobbing.

Earlier her mother had ridden away on Shiraz alongside her Uncle Ignacio. She had heard what they were saying —that her father was dead! She would have run after them, but old Juana had grasped her by the arm. "It is

601

some trick," she hissed. "Your Uncle Ignacio robbed your father of his inheritance by a trick—and this is another. Your mother does not believe it. See, she does not cry, she rides away straight in the saddle. She goes to learn the truth."

Elaine had stumbled up the cliff path to the *talyotic* village, the Place of Stones as Juana called it. There she had flung herself down in the shade of a stunted palm and cried her heart out. No wonder her father had been irascible these last visits—he had been dying!

Below the cliffs the sea roared. Around her insects hummed and buzzed and palm fronds scraped in the wind. But gradually the sounds of the day died away like her sobs, and a little coolness came into the air. Elaine moved restively and opened her eyes. Dusk had fallen. Soon the swift Majorcan night would close down and the cliff path would be dark and treacherous.

Still she lay there, unwilling to move.

Behind her a stone was dislodged, and she sat up sharply. Then a low laugh rang out in the dusk and she was suddenly seized from behind. Even as she screamed, an arm like a steel band closed around her waist and a man's hot breath assaulted her ear.

Elaine was as brave as her reckless mother—and as cool.

Almost without conscious thought her hand closed over one of the round smooth stones beside her. With all her strength she brought that stone up past her head and smashed it blindly in the direction of her unseen captor's face.

There was a hoarse strangled cry and she was abruptly released, tumbling to the ground as her attacker staggered backward. She landed lithe as a cat and whirled to see a tall man clutching his face. Between his fingers blood was spurting—she had broken his nose. She took one terrified look at him, hardly seeing him in the dusk, and ran and stumbled back down the cliff path, burst in on Juana and told her what had happened. Pablo picked up a large club and searched the area, but came back to report he had found no one.

There was no sleep at Cala Mesquida that night.

Back from San Telmo rode Rosamunde, refusing escort. She galloped along as if to outrun the fact of Rodrigue's death. But as she rode, the anguish of these last days washed over her. First Harry had been taken from her, and now Rodrigue. Must she always go on alone? She felt bereft.

To her left a low wall bounded an orange grove. In the shadow of that wall she dismounted and sank to the ground, letting grief pour over her like a river. Then she rode on, dashing the tears from her face. *If only they had let her see him!* But the coffin had been already nailed shut when she arrived. She would have torn it open had not Ignacio stopped her. "Rodrigue slipped and fell from the rocks," he told her gravely. "His face was—ruined. He would not wish you to remember him that way." Then he had muttered about the heat, the need for a speedy funeral. In the end she had consented—and known a terrible suspicion when the coffin was lowered into the ground and there was a kind of rumbling sound as if rocks or—or chains were inside it. Could Rodrigue have gone mad? He had seemed so strange these last visits home. . . . Could he had been chained for his own safety, as the mad often were, and torn free and dashed himself to pieces on the cruel rocks? Was that what Ignacio was hiding from her? The thought pricked at her as she rode.

Juana ran forward to meet her when she dismounted in the palm-shaded courtyard at Cala Mesquida.

"It is true," she told Juana wearily. "Rodrigue is dead."

Juana gave a cry and rocked with misery. Then she stopped. "What of us?" she wondered. "Where shall we go? To San Telmo?"

Rosamunde's face hardened. "We will stay here, Juana. This is our home, here at Cala Mesquida."

"But we cannot," wailed Juana.

Even through her grief, Rosamunde sensed there was something here besides hysteria. "What are you saying, Juana?" she asked slowly. "What has happened?"

603

"The night you left, a man—it was too dark for her to see him clearly—tried to rape Doña Elena," whimpered Juana. "She fought him off but—she is beautiful like yourself; he will be back. Doña Elena said he was a strong man—perhaps too strong for Pablo to fight." She wrung her hands. "Oh, we must depart for San Telmo at once!"

"Elaine! Is she all right?" cried Rosamunde.

"Yes, yes, he did not hurt her, but—"

But the point was, he had *found* her. He knew where she lived. And Elaine at sixteen had a breathtaking beauty. Old Juana was right—he would be back.

Rosamunde grew thoughtful. She still had her pistol. But Elaine was young, restless, she could not always be guarded. Not on every casual stroll along the cliffs, not every time she chased an errant milch goat gone to graze among the *talayoti*. And—she felt a sudden chill—suppose he did not come alone? Cala Mesquida was remote. Suppose they were cut off, surrounded by determined men? They could not withstand a siege. Pablo could be picked off by a pistol as he went to the well to draw water. And Juana, and herself . . . leaving Elaine as their prey.

She shivered.

Even San Telmo was better than that.

"You are right, Juana," she said tiredly. "Pablo and I will share the watch tonight. But tomorrow we will all leave for San Telmo."

In Amsterdam the summer dusk settled down and the last rosy light turned to pink the white shrouds that decorated the forest of tall masts in the busy harbor. Seated at his ease in the high-ceilinged drawing room of his home on the fashionable Herengracht, was that greatest of Amsterdam's merchant traders, Hendrik Van der Leyden. His wide-topped boots rested on a red Turkey carpet and he drew slowly on the long curved meerschaum pipe Cornelis had bequeathed to him. Old Gretha—mistress of a platoon of servants now—had just supervised the lighting of the candles in the great branched silver candlesticks, and their yellow glow softened the hard
604

lines of Harry's face and emphasized, beneath the rich silver brocade and dull-gray silk of his doublet and trousers, the fine physique that had always been his, would be his till death.

Outside his aristocratic address, this being a pleasant evening, some of Amsterdam's most successful merchants would be strolling along the waterside with their wives. They would pause to admire the tall brick house Harry had built, and the wives would murmur that it was too bad such a wealthy man remained a bachelor. They would exclaim over the handsome flight of stone steps that led up to the impressive double doorway of heavy carved oak. And their husbands' gaze would rise speculatively to the great gabled attics that towered above them. There the hoisting crane was concealed by a majestic lion's head (which had caused it to become known to some as "Lion House"). For those capacious attics were rumored to contain much of Hendrik Van der Leyden's treasure.

They did not. Harry's treasure was in Dutch banks or shrewdly invested in the cargoes of his ever-larger fleet of ships, and in both the Dutch East India and West India Companies. But that did not keep the eyes of mothers of marriageable daughters from glittering almost as brightly as the tall-paned windows, five abreast, as they gazed at that brick facade with its weighty stone cornices, reflected in the shimmering waters of the canal. Fit home, they murmured, for a merchant prince—for such Harry had indeed become.

He had built the house—meticulously plaguing the master builders to use the finest of materials, imported from everywhere—as a monument to Rosamunde. It was the house he would have wished to give her—had she lived. And he had furnished it with the gifts he would have brought her—the finest treasures of his voyages east and west.

To this magnificent house on the Herengracht came Amsterdam's great men—and their wives. And unavoidably their daughters, for Mynheer Hendrik Van der Leyden was the catch of Amsterdam.

But Harry had turned his face from marriage. He had
605

thought about it once or twice when the girl in his arms was tempting, but always a pair of too-well-remembered green eyes got in the way. Instead he had plunged into the world of trade.

Harry was rarely at home among his Gobelin tapestries, his Ming vases, his imposing plate and carved teak and mahogany furniture that were the envy of Amsterdam. The huge carved front doors, which weighed hundreds of pounds and opened onto a marble entrance hall of vast height, swung wide more often to a servant's hand than to his own. He was always away voyaging on his great ships, coming home from each venture the richer, his lean body harder, his dark face more sardonic than ever. When he was at home he spent his time at the great Exchange, making deals

He was the despair of every matchmaking mother in Amsterdam.

"You will surpass me," Cornelis had predicted. "In ten years you will have doubled my holdings."

In point of fact, it had taken less than five. But that was partly because Harry had chosen to invest so heavily in the new West India Company. That investment alone would have made Harry rich beyond his dreams, for when Cornelis' old friend and neighbor Piet Heyn—paying Spain back for the years he had pulled oars in its galleys —had captured the Spanish treasure fleet off Cuba and brought the loot home to Holland, the Dutch West India Company had paid a single dividend of six hundred percent!

Now Harry sat moodily in the candlelight. Old Vierkirk —who, though he had seemed on the brink of dying all these years, had somehow survived—had been at him again today. He and others were urging Harry to marry. Harry smiled grimly. Old Vierkirk's dissolute son had come down with the "gallant disease" as a result of one of his drunken visits to the "women's district," and old Vierkirk was complaining loudly that no man should consort with prostitutes—all should take wives. Certainly there were many arguments for marriage! Fresh from a bitter session with his now chastened son, Vierkirk had railed at Harry. Suppose Hendrik were to die on one of his voyages—and none could say they were not dangerous!—who would Vierkirk have to turn to? A man should leave an heir! Surely there must be *some* likely wench who enticed him enough to marry her—all Amsterdam had offered their daughters!

Harry drummed his fingers restively, and unbidden thought of Rosamunde.

For while others had bewitched him for a while, their charms were not lasting. But Rosamunde . . . ah, Rosamunde had been his life.

If only she had lived. . . .

His face grew haggard and he set down his suddenly tasteless pipe. For he had all the rest of his life to live—without her.

Restless, he rose and strode out of his house. Almost curtly he returned the eager bows of his neighbors and hurried past them. He sought out a waterfront tavern—for he had need of solace this night.

The tavern was crowded when Harry entered. Filled with smoke and laughter and tankards clashing as toasts were proposed and drunk. In one corner Harry saw Schrick and some friends and threaded his way through the noisy throng to join them.

"Hendrik!" Schrick raised his tankard jovially. Simone had long since discovered her pearls were fake and gone back to Marseilles in a huff, but the very next week he had met Astrid, a statuesque blonde of such stamina that Schrick almost feared to go home at night. "Ye remember Captain Sondergaard, Hendrik."

Harry nodded to the company and gripped the grizzled old captain's hand warmly. It had been years since he had seen Captain Sondergaard, but before he had bought his own ship Sondergaard had captained the *Volendam*.

"Before I forget," rumbled Captain Sondergaard, making a place beside him for Harry. "I met Captain Rodrigue Avilo at Le Havre on my homeward voyage. He asked about you."

Rodrigue Avilo . . . the name gave Harry a twinge.

He remembered suddenly his long-ago promise to help the Majorcan captain. "Did he say what he wanted?"

"No." Sondergaard drew on his clay pipe. "I asked if his wife had accompanied him on his voyage. He said she never does anymore. 'Tis a pity, for she is easily the most beautiful woman I have ever seen."

Harry remembered skinny olive-skinned Juana with her dowdy black dress and pulled-back coiffure. *"Beautiful?"* he echoed.

"Yes." Sondergaard sighed. "A blond lady with eyes of an unusual clear green color—I was reminded of emeralds."   ..

"Blond, you say?" Harry's voice was sharp. "And her name?"

Captain Sondergaard frowned. "A flower's name, I think. Something in Latin. Rosamunde—that was it."

Rosamunde! Harry's face went white. "You are certain?" he asked in a dangerously controlled voice—for there must be no mistake when you go to kill a man.

"Aye." Sondergaard nodded his big head. "An English lady whom he had married in Ireland, as I remember."

So violently did Harry gain his feet that he nearly overturned the bench upon which Sondergaard sat. His visage was frightening.

"Lord, Hendrik, what's the matter?" cried Schrick in alarm. "Where are you going?"

Harry jammed his hat on his head hard enough to smash the crown. "I go to Majorca," he said hoarsely. "To throttle a Spaniard and take back my woman!"

"Ye'll be killed!" Schrick called after him. "Majorca is Spanish territory!"

"Men like Hendrik can survive a deal!" rumbled Sondergaard, watching Harry storm out. "Ten guilders that we see him again!"

There were several takers, for Majorca was in the Balearics off the coast of Spain, and that part of the Mediterranean was a Spanish sea.

Already Harry was striding toward the dock. He would make haste for Majorca. The *Volendam* would take him there! No, no, not the *Volendam*—that great East
608

Indiaman would attract too much attention from the Spanish warships that plied the Mediterranean. Some smaller ship . . . the *Anjanette,* that was it. She had unloaded her London cargo and been careened; she was waiting now at the dock to load her new cargo. By God, he would sail her empty! She would make better time. That damned Spaniard who had tricked him and stolen Rosamunde had lived too long already!

The weather favored Harry. Strong winds billowed the *Anjanette*'s sails past Ostend, swept her sleek hull through the choppy waters of the English Channel, then south through the Bay of Biscay. Now they must be on the alert for Spanish men-of-war, for the coast of Spain lay off their port bow. They gave Spain and Portugal a wide berth, slipped through the Straits of Gibraltar by night. Now they were in the Mediterranean Sea, and a hot dry wind from the Sahara seared them as they ran the gauntlet between Spain and North Africa on a course that would take them to that pearl of the Balearic Islands—Majorca.

Harry had learned that the Avilo family seat was at San Telmo. He would have sailed boldly to the coast and set ashore at San Telmo, but just north of Dragonera two Spanish galleons, both of forty guns, hove in sight. Prudently he sailed away to the northwest, and a freshening wind blew their more seaworthy craft out of sight of the warships. But the *Anjanette*'s captain was loath to return within reach of those guns—after all, the *Anjanette* was a merchant ship, no match for men-of-war.

Restless, Harry made his first mistake. He ordered himself put ashore by night in the bay at La Calobra— rowed there by two sailors. He would make his way across the island on foot and return to the ship. He would flash a signal from the shore—a signal fire by night with a cloak passed across it twice, to make it blink.

But the moon was bright that night and they were seen.

Hardly was the longboat beached upon the sand before the coast watchers of the man they called The Whip— always on the lookout for booty—pounced upon them. It was a short bitter fight, watched in horror from the distant deck of the *Anjanette*. But Harry and the surprised Dutch sailors were outnumbered five to one, and before a long-boat could be dispatched from the ship, the battle was over, all the combatants had disappeared into the pines and the beach was clear.

The *Anjanette*'s captain pondered what to do. He did not relish an attack upon the forbidding Majorcan coast. He decided to wait.

That night Harry made the acquaintance of The Whip.

Offers to bribe his captors had failed—they were too afraid of their vicious master. Harry and the others were dragged to a handsome villa, across the courtyard to a long beautiful room on the villa's second floor. And there, lying bound on the polished floor, Harry was forced to watch as The Whip—a man of vast bulk with shrunken legs—made mincemeat of his men with the great bullwhip he used as skillfully as a barber-surgeon used his scalpel.

Neither Harry's appeals to reason nor promises of rich ransom moved The Whip—not even his hoarse threats of bloody revenge. Some inner fury drove The Whip. His dark eyes burned with a fanatical light and his breath came hard with excitement as he sent the lash crashing again and again onto his screaming victims. A satin-clad fiend, he had sat in a heavy chair throughout—indeed, he could not leave it, for his shriveled legs would not support him. Suddenly he realized that the bodies he still flogged were long since lifeless and turned a sweaty face and gleaming eyes toward the Englishman.

Harry's jaw hardened. It was his turn now. He was determined to die well.

"Ye have mighty sinews," observed The Whip in guttural Dutch.

"Loose me and I'll match them against ye—whip and all!" roared Harry from the floor.

The Whip laughed. It was not a pleasant sound. "I think not." He passed a hand across his sweaty countenance, tossed the whip away. "I will save ye for a better occasion—my wedding night. For I think ye can withstand a hundred lashes—more, before ye lose your senses."

A chill went through Harry's hard frame. It was one
610

thing to die bravely in battle, or to be dragged beneath the cruel sea. But quite another to be trussed up like a goose, trying not to scream as a bullwhip cut one's flesh from one's bones. So he was to be the wedding-night entertainment for this voracious monster with the dead legs —his body would be reduced to a bloody pulp to amuse the bride!

For his wedding night! Harry knew he was looking at a madman and sawed in vain at his bonds until his wrists were raw. The Whip bellowed something and servants rushed in. Harry was seized and dragged along the polished floor, down the stairs, and plunged deep into the dungeons of La Calobra.

There he lay on the hard stone floor and gave thanks to all the gods who would listen that Rosamunde was not with him this night.

43   *The great house at San Telmo was in an uproar.* An offer of marriage had been made to Elaine! And it came from a nobleman of Spain, Don José Alvar, who at one time had been a confidant of the king himself and whose influence at court was legendary! But among the servants there were rolling scandalized eyes and whispers, and many crossed themselves, for Don José Alvar was known as The Whip, and his very name struck terror.

Don José's emissary had ridden in jauntily through the burning summer heat, resplendent in magenta satin doublet and peach satin breeches. He was to be forgiven these gaudy colors, for he was a Frenchman—himself of noble lineage, to hear him tell it. His name was Pierre Dumont, and he mouthed it so loftily, waving his lacy kerchief, that he might well have been a marquis.

The tension at San Telmo was the greater because Rosamunde was not at home when the offer came. She had ridden across the island with two carts to supervise the moving of her furniture from Cala Mesquida to Rodrigue's former wing of the great house at San Telmo. Don José's emissary was waiting impatiently for her return.

Four months had passed since Rodrigue's funeral. Four months in which Margarita had been unfailingly pleasant, Ignacio unfailingly kind—although adamant about discussing Rodrigue's affairs. All had been left in his hands, he told Rosamunde smoothly. She had nothing to worry about; let a man see to these matters.

Baffled, Rosamunde saw no alternative but to stay at San Telmo for the present, although she had already announced her intention to Ignacio of taking whatever was left to her and going with Elaine to live in Amsterdam.

"Be not so hasty," urged Ignacio. "Elena is beautiful. Perhaps she will be offered a great marriage—and then you will want to go and live with her."

Rosamunde had considered him uncertainly. This was not the Ignacio she remembered, but perhaps he wished to make amends for his neglect of Rodrigue's family. At his insistence, she had agreed to bring the furniture from Cala Mesquida—although privately she meant to sell it later in Palma if Ignacio did not choose to buy it. The furniture alone should be enough to buy passage to Amsterdam for Elaine and herself.

Rosamunde arrived back at San Telmo, riding ahead of the jolting carts, in the hot dusk of a blistering August day. She had barely dismounted before old Juana dashed forward and seized her arm and told her the news.

An offer for Elaine! And she barely turned sixteen!

"But the offer comes from La Calobra," cried Juana in a tragic voice. " 'Tis from Don José Alvar—the man they call The Whip."

"*The Whip!*" Rosamunde came to a full stop.

Old Juana wrung her hands. "They have kept me from her, so poor Elena does not know what he is. *You* must tell her. Don José is a cripple, of vast bulk. A fiend. It is said he hates the world because disease has deformed

612

him, and he vents his anger on innocent young girls and children. He has them brought to him for his pleasure and turns them out with their bodies marked by the lash. He can slice a mango with it, I am told! The peasants who live nearby are afraid to complain lest he revenge himself upon them!"

"And he lives in a massive stone villa with many terraces and balustrades, set in an olive grove and surrounded by tall cypresses," murmured Rosamunde remembering the girl with the stripped back. "I have seen it."

"Oh, do not let this marriage take place," begged Juana.

"Have no fear," said Rosamunde crisply. "It will not."

"The Whip's emissary is a Frenchman with a broken nose," said Juana nervously. "I fear he will not take no for an answer!"

Rosamunde gave a short laugh. "He will take *my* no for an answer! Where is this emissary?"

"In the inner courtyard. Don Ignacio says when you have changed your clothes—"

"I will see this emissary now!" Still in her dusty riding clothes, Rosamunde swept through the cool lower hall into the inner courtyard, where the gaudily clad Frenchman was bending down, smelling one of the deep-red roses that rioted over the balustrade. At her impetuous arrival, he turned and bowed deeply from the waist. Dark eyes, a red mouth . . . Rosamunde came to a sudden violent halt.

"You!" she cried incredulously. "*You* are the man who attacked me in the hills! Only—your nose was not broken then."

"True, it was not." Pierre Dumont's smile was wolfish, his voice cheerful and urbane. "If you accuse me, I will deny it—and how will you explain that you were across the island from your home at Cala Mesquida in your husband's absence—alone, unchaperoned? All will believe you went to meet a lover!"

It was true. Rosamunde bit her lip. Her green eyes narrowed. "How did you know I lived at Cala Mesquida?"

Pierre Dumont laughed. "I have been there."

A broken nose . . . Elaine had broken her attacker's

nose. "*You* are the man who attacked my daughter!" she accused.

He made her a mocking bow. "Forgive me the error —I thought it was you."

She gasped at that. His cool effrontery staggered her.

"Of course, if you choose to make an issue of it," he added casually, deliberately taking a pinch of snuff, "I shall deny everything."

"*You* will deny?" Her breath came fast. "*You,* a man who works for a monster like The Whip?"

"I would not call Don José that, were I you." Dumont closed his snuffbox with a snap. "Don Ignacio will take offense. You see"—a sly smile played about his mouth— "it is all arranged. At La Calobra, Don José heard stories of Elena's beauty."

"From *you.*"

"From me, yes. And he is so intrigued by it that he will use his influence at court—ah, yes, he still has influence even though he was banished for the death of that unfortunate girl in Madrid—he was never charged with it, you understand; her parents, the complainants, fortuitously disappeared."

"I suppose that was your doing!"

His wolfish smile deepened. "And for delivering this blond pastry to Don José, Doña Margarita may well become a lady-in-waiting to the queen of Spain."

Ah, now she understood! This had all been planned, discussed, a long time ago—and kept from her. God, perhaps Ignacio had killed Rodrigue so that this terrible marriage might take place—for Rodrigue would never have given his consent. No wonder Margarita had been so pleasant—she could destroy Elaine and at the same time further her own ambitions!

Blood throbbed in Rosamunde's temples at so infamous a scheme. She leaned forward, her emerald eyes dangerous. "The Whip will never have my daughter! Never!"

She spun about and went back into the house, her boots ringing on the tiles. Dumont stood languorously watching her. The smile on his ruined face had widened subtly to an expression of consummate evil.

"Ignacio!" called Rosamunde loudly in the lower hall. "Ignacio, where are you?"

Don Ignacio must have been watching the scene from a window, for he came down the stairs quickly, richly clad in his usual funereal black with a heavy gold chain dangling from his neck.

"Ignacio, I will never consent to this marriage!" she burst out.

"Pray do not excite yourself," Ignacio said smoothly. "In this heat, you could become ill."

"If you were looking for a human sacrifice to further Margarita's social ambitions"—Rosamunde's voice had a cutting edge—"why did you not betroth *me* to this monster at La Calobra? Why an innocent child like Elaine?"

Ignacio swallowed. He could hardly tell Rosamunde that she still had a living husband!

"You excite yourself needlessly. You will soon see that Elena does not share your views. She is delighted at the prospect of this marriage. Indeed, at this moment she is being fitted for her wedding gown. Come—I will show you."

Frowning, Rosamunde followed Ignacio up the stairs to the rooms she and Elaine occupied. He knocked discreetly, was bade to enter, and flung open the door with some ceremony.

Rosamunde was stunned. There before her was a smiling Elaine, twirling about delightedly in a wedding gown of heavy white lace over stiff white taffeta. At her feet crouched a swarthy sewing woman with a mouthful of pins.

"It fits perfectly—doesn't it, Uncle Ignacio? Oh, Mother, isn't it wonderful? I have an offer of marriage from a Spanish nobleman. They say he is young, handsome—"

"They have lied to you," said Rosamunde bluntly. "He is a deformed monster known as The Whip. He claws to pieces the backs of young girls. I have seen his work!"

The color left Elaine's cheeks, and the sewing woman almost swallowed her pins. "Mother, it cannot be true!"

"Take my word, it is true," said Rosamunde grimly.

615

"You will pack at once. We are going to Amsterdam." She turned to face Ignacio, who signaled the sewing woman to go; the woman fled in fright. "This time you cannot stop me, Ignacio. If you will not give me my inheritance from Rodrigue, I will turn the carts around. I will sell the furniture in Palma. It will bring enough to take us there."

Ignacio gave her a thin smile. "I would advise you to think it over. You may feel differently in the morning."

"Elaine and I will be gone in the morning!"

He shrugged and with a slight bow left the room. To her astonishment, she heard a key grate in the lock. Ignacio had locked her in! She went over and beat upon the door with her fists. "Ignacio, come back! Unlock this door at once!"

"The wedding will take place tomorrow," said Ignacio's voice on the other side of the door.

"It cannot!" Rosamunde shouted. "There is no groom!"

"The groom is infirm and cannot leave La Calobra. But he has sent his sword by Señor Dumont. The marriage will take place by proxy on the morrow. Elena will wed the sword."

Rosamunde whirled and ran to the cabinet where she had left Rodrigue's pistol. The cabinet was empty.

"Your supper will be sent up to you." Ignacio's voice floated back to them.

Rosamunde's gaze flew to the windows and a cold chill washed over her. She was looking at iron bars. Ignacio had thought of everything—he had known she would oppose this marriage. Heavy iron grillwork had been put over the windows in her absence. This lovely room had become her prison!

"I will fight them," declared Elaine in a trembling voice behind her. "I will rend my wedding veil and smash the sword upon the altar!"

"That would do no good," said Rosamunde absently. "They would only sedate you so that you would not know what you were doing and the wedding would take place anyway—even if they had to hold you upright."

616

"Then I will run away to Cala Mesquida—I could hide forever on the *garriga,* in the hills."

"One cannot hide forever," said Rosamunde bitterly, remembering England.

"What then?" cried Elaine in a tragic voice. "I cannot marry a monster!"

"Be quiet. I am trying to think." Rosamunde walked to the grilled window that looked out upon the garden, tested the heavy bars with distaste. No hope there! Dusk fell as she meditated, scanning the familiar shrubs and trees.

It came to her suddenly that there was something missing. Usually at this time a dark figure stood in the shadow of that clump of palms, just beyond the pomegranate and the yellow roses. He was always hidden by the shrubbery, although sometimes in the moonlight she had seen the gleam of his eyes. Ordinarily she might have been frightened by the steady way he watched her, but somehow she never was. Seeing that watching figure always gave her a feeling of peace, a sense of benediction.

Tonight he was gone, and she felt an odd sense of loss. More than that—chagrin. For she might have signaled to him.

She could not know that the lurking figure was Rodrigue, who would steal away from the leprosarium at Lluch, and at dusk with Pablo's connivance would slip in through the garden gate and watch his beloved Rosamunde as she walked by the candlelit windows. The hood he always wore, but he did not need it—his dark narrow face was as handsome and unmarred as ever. But a time would come, he knew, when it would not be, and Rosamunde must believe him dead, for too well he knew her gallant spirit. She would fling away everything and pursue him to Lluch to share his misery—and herself become a leper. That, at all costs, he must avoid. He wore the concealing hood so that no one would recognize him —and carry word to her.

But he could not resist any chance to view his beloved.

And so he would slip away from the leprosarium, and Pablo would let him through the garden gate. Lately he

617

had been camping in a grove near the house, and when he saw her leave with the carts, he guessed she was going to Cala Mesquida and had followed. There, hidden behind some rocks, he had feasted on the sight of her. But when the wagons left Cala Mesquida, he had gone back, reluctantly, to the leprosarium at Lluch to keep a promise made to a dying leper.

So he knew no more of the marriage offer than Rosamunde had.

Juana brought their supper. Two burly servants stood stolidly behind her as she entered. Rosamunde, who had intended to rush out when the door was opened, again wished she had Rodrigue's pistol.

"I need this woman to help me get my daughter out of this bridal dress," Rosamunde told the two men peremptorily, and shut the door in their faces. "Juana," she asked in a low tense voice, "where is Pablo?"

"Elena's horse, Yasmin, wandered away. Pablo went to find her."

"Then we must do this alone." Rosamunde leaned over and whispered in Juana's ear.

The older woman started. "But what of you?" she blurted.

"I will be all right. Do exactly as I have told you."

"What are you saying?" demanded Elaine in a worried voice.

"That you should eat your supper, to give you strength for tomorrow," said Rosamunde loudly, giving a significant nod toward the door and the two guards, who could hear if not see. She opened the door for Juana. "Tell Ignacio I would speak with him privately. My mind is clearer now."

Elaine gave her a puzzled look as she turned around. "What—what are you about, Mother?"

"Wait till I have talked to Ignacio."

That talk was not long in coming. Rosamunde was promptly—and ungently—escorted to a small room off Ignacio's bedchamber. He had prepared for bed and was already wearing his nightcap.

"What do you wish to see me about?" he inquired

618

testily. And to the servant, "No, do not leave us. I do not trust this lady. She may try to break and run if you release her."

Rosamunde's color heightened. "I have come to strike a bargain with you, Ignacio."

Her brother-in-law looked at her curiously. "And when did you come to that decision?"

"When I saw the iron bars you had placed on my windows," said Rosamunde sardonically. "It came to me with force that regardless of what happens to my daughter, I wish to be free to return to Amsterdam."

"What bargain do you offer?" asked Ignacio cautiously.

"I will consent to this marriage—yes, I will even convince Elaine that I have lied, that Don José is not The Whip."

Ignacio brightened. He had been dreading tomorrow's ceremony—the priest might balk if the bride and her mother screamed and pleaded! The priest might refuse to perform a marriage service with a proxy groom and hysterical participants and insist that the groom appear in person! And on this marriage did Margarita's future depend—for the marriage contract was a binding one with forfeitures if Don José did not carry out the terms. And it *must* be a hasty wedding, for if Rodrigue were to hear of it . . . ! Ignacio wiped perspiration from his brow. Leper or no, Rodrigue would surely kill him. But—of course Rodrigue would hear nothing, for he was shut away in the leprosarium at Lluch.

"If you do that," Ignacio said slowly, "I will buy your passage on the first ship to Ostend—from there you may make your way to Amsterdam. And I will give you money as well—on the promise that you will not return."

"Once I leave this accursed island"—Rosamunde's voice rang with sincerity—"you may count upon it that I will never return."

"But until the ceremony you will be under guard," he said, eyes glinting.

Rosamunde nodded carelessly. "I expected as much." She hesitated, frowned. "I may—I may not attend the ceremony. It would not do for me to regret my bargain.

I will go back to Elaine now and tell her she has nothing to fear."

"Good." Ignacio did not believe her; it was obvious to him that Rosamunde expected to spirit Elaine away after the ceremony, believing they would relax their security then. Wrong! The marriage contract said specifically that the bride must be delivered to La Calobra by Dumont. But Rosamunde would unwittingly have lent her cooperation, and afterward it would be too late to snatch the bride away!

Back in her room, Elaine asked her tensely, "What do you intend?"

"You will go through with the ceremony as planned."

Elaine stared at her. Her gray eyes had gone dark, but her voice was very composed. "Mother, I do not know what you plan, but I am sure that it is very dangerous—for you. I will not have you leap up with a pistol and be shot down on my account."

Rosamunde looked at her daughter. That determined face before her was *her* face, those level eyes were Harry's eyes. Elaine would never agree to what she had in mind.

She must lie to her.

"Elaine," she said dreamily, "I have a story to tell you. It concerns myself. I was not born in Ireland as you believe, but in England. . . ." Swiftly she told Elaine the story of her early years. "So you see," she finished, "though Rodrigue could not have loved you more, you are Harry's daughter—English, like myself. Somehow Ignacio has found that out. If you do not wed The Whip on the morrow, Ignacio has promised me that he will bring us both before the Inquisition—we will both die."

Elaine's head lifted stubbornly. "I do not fear death!"

Rosamunde regarded her daughter tenderly—how like Harry she was at that moment! "We will both live," she promised. "For I have made a bargain with Ignacio. I have told him—ignobly—that I will agree to this marriage if he will give me gold for passage to Amsterdam. You must go through with the ceremony—no, wait, hear me out," as Elaine's face grew stormy. "We will have the marriage annulled later, for it will not be consummated.
620

You will start for La Calobra with Dumont, but on the journey you will find a way to escape and join me in Palma. In the cathedral. I will pray there three times a day. By then I will have our passage money and we will go to Amsterdam together. Is it agreed?"

"Oh, yes." Elaine had been dazed at all these revelations, but now her young face brightened. She liked this plan. It appealed to her spirit of adventure and put her mother in no danger.

"Good. Now take off your wedding dress and we will both get some sleep."

But while Elaine slept, soundly as a child in her light chemise, Rosamunde sat by the window and stared out at the empty garden. For the plan she envisioned to save Elaine was not the plan she had outlined to her daughter.

In the morning she sent word to Ignacio that she and Juana would make the bride ready without assistance—the other servants might say something to upset Elaine and spoil their plans. Ignacio shrugged. They were plotting, of course, but as long as they were locked in together and the bride came out to be wed, who cared?

Juana brought up with her a bottle of wine, as Rosamunde had requested the day before. She tottered in, looking very old. Her face, sallow yesterday, was almost gray today.

"Are you ill, Juana?" asked Rosamunde in alarm.

"No," muttered Juana with an effort. "Just—worried. Pablo went seeking Yasmin and he has not returned."

"She must have strayed very far this time. You must not worry about him; he will be back soon." She studied Juana. Her whole plan depended on Juana. "You must not fail me," she whispered.

"I will not," said Juana faintly. "Are you sure—"

"Let us drink to success," Rosamunde interrupted. "It will take courage, Elaine, to escape and ride back to Palma without being recaptured. You must be careful."

Elaine's eyes flashed, and she lifted her glass with all the bright buoyancy of youth. How Rosamunde yearned to take her into her confidence—but she must not. She

621

watched Elaine drain her glass, set her own down untouched.

"Aren't you drinking to our success, Mother?"

"I feel—a little ill," said Rosamunde. "It is the excitement, I suppose. I will drink mine in a moment." She turned to busy herself getting out the wedding gloves and slippers. As she spread out the delicate underwear, the white silk stockings, she and Juana exchanged glances.

And now the wedding veil. Rosamunde stared at it. That veil, everything depended on that veil. She had got the idea yesterday when she had warned Elaine they might sedate her. Now she watched grimly as the drug Juana had put in the wine at her instigation took effect.

"Mother." Elaine sank to the bed. "I feel so strange. "I—" Her gray eyes widened in horror. "Mother, *you have drugged me!*"

"Hush, hush," hissed Juana. "Someone will hear!"

But even as she spoke, Elaine's body sagged and her long lashes fluttered shut. Rosamunde caught her and dragged her to the bed.

"She will sleep for several hours," promised Juana, pulling back the coverlet. "It is the same drug they gave my brother-in-law when the bull gored him. My sister gave me what was left of it."

"You did not tell her why you wanted it?" Rosamunde was disrobing as she spoke.

"No, no." Juana proffered the delicate chemise. "Elena's bridal gown may be a little tight for you. Not in the waist—your waist is as small as Elaine's—but she is slighter than you. Here, I will bind down your breasts."

Rosamunde thought wryly that in half the crises of her life, she had bound down her breasts! "I can do it myself." She waved Juana away. "Dress Elaine in my clothes. Pull the bedclothes well up around her and tumble her hair as if she slept restlessly. Let her arm dangle over the bed and put the bottle on the floor beside her hand—so. They will think I have made myself drunk for grief!"

Juana hastened to do as she was bid, but her fingers fumbled. They seemed to be growing numb lately, and her heart thumped when she climbed stairs. This scheme of Doña Rosamunde's was madness—if only Pablo would return!

Swiftly Rosamunde donned Elaine's bridal gown. It fit her slender figure admirably. For the first time in her life she gave silent thanks that Spanish gowns were modest and concealing. The white taffeta skirt was heavy and full and garnished with heavy white lace. It drifted along the floor, even concealing her feet in their white satin slippers. And the matching bodice was long-sleeved with white lace cuffs that flowed across her hands, while the prim neckline came up in a little ruff under her chin. Swiftly she combed her hair and swept it up into the style Elaine had been wearing, donned her white wedding gloves of soft delicate leather trimmed in seed pearls, and bent to let old Juana drape the heavy white lace mantilla over the high-backed ivory comb at the back of her hair. It flowed concealingly down over her face and her bright hair, reaching to her gloved hands in the front and flowing down her back to the hem of her skirt—perfect! If Dumont had mistaken Elaine for her in a thin revealing dress in the spring dusk at Cala Mesquida, he would certainly believe her to be Elaine now! But she must remember to keep her eyes down, for their brilliant emerald color would give her away.

"I cannot believe it," whispered Juana in amazement. "*Anyone* would believe you to be your own daughter!"

Rosamunde accepted this honest compliment with a glinting smile. "Do not look so worried, Juana. The Whip will be disappointed of a bride, for I mean to rejoin you within two days. Take care of Elaine for me."

"Oh, I will—I will." Emotionally, Juana embraced her. "I will take her away to the empty fishing hut by the shore, just as you bade me, and keep her safe till you return for her."

"I know you will, Juana." Rosamunde gave her a hug. "And I will not forget all you have done—I will send for you and Pablo and you can join us in Amsterdam."

"No, no," murmured Juana, wiping her eyes. "Just so ye both be safe."

There was a sharp knock on the door. "Are you ready?" Ignacio's voice, sounding harsh.

Juana watched mistily as Rosamunde the bride swept through that open door. Her head was modestly inclined, in a gesture of submission. Ignacio's swift gaze took in the bed, the dangling arm, the bottle—he looked pleased and turned to his pliant "niece" with satisfaction. She kept her eyes downcast.

"You will not regret this day, Elena," he assured Rosamunde with insincere heartiness, and beside him she walked down to the chapel.

The marriage ceremony, performed in that echoing vaulted room, seemed strange and alien to Rosamunde. She stood before the altar with her hand on the hilt of Don José's jeweled sword and was united in holy wedlock to that sword, symbolically, in his absence. It was a tense rather than a joyous occasion, and afterward she waved the wedding wine away.

"I see that she is anxious to be on the road north!" said Dumont jovially. "Where her eager young groom awaits her!"

It was a jarring note. The bride's slender shoulders moved convulsively, and Ignacio, warmed with wedding wine, looked at her with a sudden pang. So lovely, half-seen beneath that obscuring veil, so young and—unlike her rebellious mother—so compliant. Made maudlin with wine, he was beginning to have second thoughts.

Margarita's fierce look steadied him. "You and Elena should leave immediately, Señor Dumont. It is a long way to La Calobra—and slow by coach."

The bride stiffened. A coach! She had not seen a coach when she rode in from Cala Mesquida with the carts of furniture. She had counted on riding horseback and breaking away! Her pulse was racing as she was summarily bundled into the coach with Dumont.

"You were wise to come peaceably," he told her as the coach lumbered out of the courtyard. "For you would have come anyway. Bound and gagged—who knows?"

Rosamunde kept her head down and her mouth shut. He must not guess that she was not Elaine.

624

Dumont was content to jolt along in silence through the magnificent countryside. In fact, he seemed very pleased with himself. They had been riding for about an hour when his silence was broken by a low laugh.

"Come," he said cajolingly, "is it not time we end this charade—*Rosamunde?*"

Across from him Rosamunde's body went rigid. *He knew!* She threw back her white lace wedding veil, and a pair of dangerous emerald eyes searched his face.

The Frenchman was laughing. "I guessed you would do it," he boasted. "I wagered with myself what the tigress would do to protect her wild kitten—and I have won my wager. You have changed places with your daughter!"

How Rosamunde yearned for her pistol! It was too soon to throw open the door of the carriage and leap out. Juana would not have had time to secure Elaine.

"I suppose your daughter has fled somewhere?"

Rosamunde caught her breath.

Dumont laughed. "Have no fear, I have told no one. All has gone *as I wished*. I guessed what both the cat and the kitten would do."

"Then I am surprised you are not more uneasy, Monsieur Dumont," said Rosamunde in a tart voice. "Since the cat nearly unmanned you and the kitten broke your nose!"

"But this time the cat will be on a leash!" He sprang forward and seized her in a paralyzing grip. "Pepito!" he roared.

As Rosamunde struggled with Dumont, the coach jolted to a halt and the bulky coachman climbed down and opened the door. It was very wild here, overgrown with vines hanging from the trees. She could glimpse the blue sea in the distance.

"Scream all you like," said Dumont pleasantly. "Pepito, the bride should have a collar, don't you think?" From a chest at his feet he brought out a chain and fastened it at one end to a hook that protruded from the door of the coach, passed the chain around Rosamunde's neck, gestured Pepito to leave and fastened the chain's other end to the opposite door. "If the door should be opened before this is removed, it would break your neck." He smiled. "Do not worry, my dear, I will steady you when we jolt over rough roads." He reached forward and seized her breast familiarly. Rosamunde kicked at him.

His hand lashed across her face and she winced with pain as her head snapped back and the chain bit into her neck. Involuntarily her hands flew to the chain to loosen it.

"You see? You will learn to sit very still and hold on tightly to the chain. It will be a tiring ride for you, I am afraid." To the coachman he called, "Drive on, Pepito!" And as the coach jolted forward, "Here," he mocked. "There is a bump—I will steady you." He grasped her breasts, and she tore a hand loose from the chain and struck at him, groaned and choked as the coach lurched sideways and the chain bit in. Dumont laughed nastily. "You see?" he mocked. "To disobey me brings pain. It is a thing I learned from The Whip."

"If my neck is bruised from this chain," warned Rosamunde, hanging on as best she could to keep from being throttled in the lurching coach, "The Whip will know you have attacked me!"

"On the contrary, he will understand that you were reluctant to join your groom at La Calobra. He himself had the chain installed as an inducement to you to complete your wedding journey when he heard you were a woman of such spirit!"

Wedding journey! Half-fainting in the suffocating heat, Rosamunde hung on. When they passed through farmsteads or towns, Dumont would leap forward and stuff his linen kerchief into her mouth and hold it there until they had passed. By the time they had reached open countryside and the curtains had been pulled back, she would be past screaming and gasping weakly for air.

When they stopped to rest the horses and Dumont consumed a bottle of wine, watching her speculatively, she revived a little. He reached over and suddenly ran his hand up her skirts, and she gave him such a sharp kick on the shin that her toes were numbed in their satin slippers. Dumont drew back his arm and for a moment she thought it was all over for her, but he let it drop to his side with a sigh.

"Time enough for that later," he muttered. "Drive on, Pepito!"

Rosamunde clung with both hands to the bruising chain. "If you make any attempt upon me," she told Dumont fiercely, "I will tell The Whip what you have done! He will punish you."

"You do not understand," Dumont said pleasantly. "It is not the delights of your body he seeks—he is beyond that. It is the flesh of your delicious back he would rip to ribbons—my master delights in screams."

"He will hear no screams from me!"

"Then he will kill you. He always continues until his ears are filled with enough cries of agony that he is sated. I always advise his victims to scream as loudly as they can—that way they may escape with their lives. His first wife was proud like you, I am told—she refused to scream. He cut her to ribbons, and she died. That was in Madrid."

Rosamunde shivered. *That* was why Don José had been banished from the Spanish court; he had killed his young wife!

"But he will not enjoy hearing from my lips how you have defiled me on my journey to his lash," Rosamunde told him defiantly. "He might kill you for that, Monsieur Dumont!"

Dumont drew back. "He would also kill you," he said thoughtfully.

"We will die together!" she flashed.

Dumont sat back, considering his captive in mingled amusement and anger. Then he shrugged. "You will beg me to save you soon enough," he said indifferently. "You will beg for release from the pain, you will beg for death. And perhaps—if your beauty is not too much marred—I will listen."

Rosamunde turned her face from him. She did not want him to read fear in her eyes.

Dumont did not stop at an inn. Night found Rosamunde sagging in her chains. He let her remain there. Too exhausted to move, she listened to the night sounds of the

627

cicadas, the hunting owls, the stealthy rustling of the palm fronds. Surely they would rest somewhere! But Dumont stopped only to change horses and plunged on toward La Calobra. Dazed, only semiconscious by now, nearly unable to speak from her torment, Rosamunde could not help wondering if he feared pursuit.

It gave her hope. At noon of the second day she roused herself. She . . . must . . . escape. . . .

But again no opportunity presented itself. Dumont was savagely enjoying her discomfiture. The terrible journey wore on and the dark bruises on her throat deepened in color. She was hard put not to scream when the coach lurched.

At last they thundered into the courtyard of the cream-colored villa she remembered with dread. The terraces, the balustrades, the olive trees, the cypresses.

"Welcome to La Calobra," said Dumont in a voice of flint.

A terrible feeling of helplessness came over Rosamunde. Her senses reeled. She fainted.

44   *Pablo's feet were bleeding by the time he reached* the Monastery of Lluch. Yasmin had gone lame a long way back, and he had left her at a farmstead, promising to fetch her later. He had started out the moment he had learned that Rosamunde and Elaine were being held prisoner in an upstairs room until the proxy marriage could be held. Now he trudged wearily to the leprosarium and called out in a loud voice at the grating for Rodrigue. There was a shuffling of feet inside, then the wooden door swung open to admit a dark hooded figure.
628

"Have I not told you not to use my name?" growled Rodrigue. "Here I am known only as The Lost One." And then at Pablo's woebegone expression, "What has happened?"

The blood beat in Rodrigue's temples as Pablo's words gushed out, telling of this hasty marriage, which by now had taken place. His brother Ignacio had cheated him! He had paid Ignacio in gold to shelter and be kind to Rosamunde and Elena—and now Ignacio had wed the girl to The Whip!

"I lost much time when Yasmin went lame," explained Pablo humbly. "But perhaps we can still catch Dumont's coach before it reaches La Calobra."

Rodrigue flashed a tormented look at him. Poor Pablo . . . on foot. It was doubtful they could catch the coach. Still, it was worth a try. He took a deep breath. At the monastery he had prayed before the altar of the Black Madonna for the Answer—and now that Answer had been given him. At last he could do something for Rosamunde. He could rescue her daughter—he could save Elena.

That it was not Elaine but his beloved Rosamunde who was at risk he had no way of knowing.

Now his ever-agile mind gnawed at the problem. La Calobra was a stronghold, but from one of the lepers who had once worked for The Whip he had learned a secret way into the dungeons. From there a man could work his way upstairs into the master's quarters. For the first time Rodrigue thanked God for the terrible punishing strength of his leper's hands. They would do their work well! Galvanized to action, he almost seized Pablo's arm, and Pablo fell back instinctively.

"You must go back to San Telmo, Pablo. Tell Rosamunde Elaine will soon be back by her side. Go to her, Pablo. She will be in need of comfort."

Pablo hesitated. "And you?"

"I go to La Calobra."

" 'Tis a long way over the mountains," objected Pablo.

"There is a shortcut here from the monastery. I will go down the Torrente de Pareis."

"The canyon?" gasped Pablo, his eyes almost starting from his head.

Rodrigue nodded vigorously. "In dry weather there is a path that leads down the canyon to a little creek and the sea. 'Tis from that creek Don José's estate gets its name."

"You may be too late," worried Pablo.

"I have thought of that. I will not go alone. A fortnight ago a dying girl cut half to ribbons by a whip crawled up the canyon and died at the monastery door gasping out the name 'La Calobra.' The monks mutter, but the lepers are furious. One of them once worked in the dungeons of La Calobra. As his disease became apparent, The Whip kept him there on bread and water. When finally he was turned out to beg or starve, he came here. *And brought with him the key to the dungeons.* He meant to go back and wreak vengeance once he had regained his strength, but he was weakened from starvation and soon died. As he was dying, he gave me the key. The lepers know this, and I have promised to lead them there."

"To lead—to lead the lepers to La Calobra?" faltered Pablo.

"Yes," declared Rodrigue ringingly. "To empty The Whip's dungeons of his victims! 'Tis the reason I returned to Lluch, for I had given my word. There are still those who waver, who cannot decide—but this will make up their minds for them, when they learn my own daughter has been carried there!"

"The Whip is said to have a strong force," Pablo reminded him.

"All fear leprosy," announced Rodrigue in a voice of menace. "Some of that strong force will fear infection—they will run away. And for the rest, our lepers' hands are strong—we can crush bones with them. Go back to San Telmo."

Pablo limped away, and Rodrigue assembled his sad army.

Some of them quailed when they looked down the famous canyon that slashed the mountain landscape for some three miles. In places it cut into the karstic range to a depth of over fifteen hundred feet, and often the way was terrifyingly narrow, but a few yards across, and dark by daylight—for the sun never reached its depths. Rodrigue led his silent band, stumbling over the rocks with their heavy wooden staffs, in all some twenty men. Their shabby hooded robes contrasted oddly with the magestic eroded limestone of the gorge.

Deep in the dungeons of La Calobra, Harry heard a soft rustle that could be cloth rasping along the rough stone walls outside his cell. Instantly alert, he struggled to his knees and gained his feet, cursing his bound wrists. He padded softly to the heavy door, beneath which a faint glimmer of light now showed, ready to fall upon whoever opened it, using his bound hands like a bludgeon, and seek his freedom that way.

The rustling went on by, the light dwindled. There was the sound of bone cracking, a grunt, a thudding as if a body had slumped to the stone floor.

"Who is it?" asked Harry, his interest in these unusual sounds causing him to forget he was in Majorca and speak in English.

Outside in the corridor, Rodrigue stiffened. An English voice!

"Quiet," he growled, "and we will set ye free."

Hope leaped up in Harry. The crack of light beneath the door widened, there was the rasp of metal as a heavy bolt slid back and the door creaked open. His eyes unaccustomed to the light, Harry blinked at the hooded figure holding a pungently smoking torch. He would have seized his rescuer's other hand and shaken it with his own bound ones, but a voice from behind the hood warned, "Do not touch me. I am a leper."

It cost Rodrigue a deal to say those words. *This was the Englishman!* Rosamunde's Harry, whom he had thwarted in Amsterdam. From that torchlit face, Rodrigue looked up at the blackened ceiling. *He* could no longer protect Rosamunde—but here providentially, was someone who could. There was a God after all.

Rosamunde's eyelids flickered open and she struggled to sit up. Exhaustion still tugged at her and her throat ached, but the chain was miraculously gone and a refreshing sea breeze gave her strength. Someone—Dumont—was forcing wine into her mouth. Now he stepped back and smiled at her.

"Ah, I see you are with us again," he said cheerfully.

She looked around her, saw that she was lying on a purple velvet couch in a large high-ceilinged room. The breeze came through open casements that opened upon a wide balcony. Above the white wainscoting were walls painted with naked ladies and running stags pursued by huntsmen with bows. It was dark outside, and a chandelier of many candles illuminated a frieze of cupids that scampered across the ceiling.

So this was La Calobra!

Now she saw that she was not alone with Dumont. Across the polished floor, seated in a heavy armchair, a satin-clad man with gigantic shoulders was flicking a long bullwhip at the walls. As she watched, that whip flicked the naked breast of one of the painted women and chipped off a bit of paint and plaster at the nipple. Rosamunde shuddered.

This was The Whip—her husband!

The huge man with the lifeless legs turned to regard her. "So she is awake, Dumont? Bring her to me. I would view my bride."

Dumont caught her arm in a cruel grip and lifted her to her feet. "Remember what I told you," he muttered. "Scream loudly—it may save your life."

She shook him off and advanced defiantly toward The Whip.

"Throw back your veil," he commanded.

She tossed it back, stood looking down scornfully into his face.

"She is all that you told me, Dumont—and more," he murmured, his eyes kindling. "But are you blind to color? Her eyes are not gray—they are green!"

Dumont leaned over and peered at Rosamunde. "So they are," he said in a tone of surprise.

632

Rosamunde shot him a look. So Dumont meant to keep her impersonation of Elaine a secret between them!

"I have planned an evening's entertainment for you," her new husband told her. "One of your countrymen is in my custody. I will show you how deftly I can cut a man to pieces—with this." He patted the bullwhip.

Rosamunde felt revulsion rise in her. "I would rather you showed me your generosity and set him free!" she snapped.

He laughed. "No, this entertainment has been planned for some time."

"I will not watch!"

The admiring eyes narrowed to slits, and Dumont shot her a look of warning. "Perhaps I will sport with you *first*," said that guttural voice. "You will then be better able to appreciate my talent." And as her gaze flew to the doors, "You will find them locked."

Rosamunde turned desperately to Dumont. "You want me!" she cried. "I know you do. You have a sword—why don't you use it?"

A sickly hue spread over the Frenchman's face.

"Dumont is a man I have bought with gold," interposed The Whip. He chuckled, an evil sound in that cavernous room. "He desires you—but he desires the life I can give him more." His tongue ran over his thick lips even as his eyes ran heatedly over her slender body in its white dress. Rosamunde looked into those mad bulging eyes, saw the gleam of perspiration appear on his upper lip as he caressed the bullwhip. Instinctively she knew that he was mentally stripping her, mentally watching her writhe in anguish beneath the lash.

She would rob him of that pleasure!

"You will have no sport with *me* this night!" She whirled and and ran down the room toward the balcony, intending to hurl herself over the railing. It was her last slender chance of escape—and if she died of the fall, it was no worse than to die writhing beneath the lash!

Behind her the whip sang out. It caught her around the ankles, wrapped about them like a belt and sent her crashing to the floor. A scream tore from her hurt throat as she felt herself sliding back toward him, being pulled there inexorably by that entwining bullwhip.

At that moment Harry and Rodrigue burst through the locked doors.

Harry saw Rosamunde, clinging with both hands to the whip as she was dragged gasping back to the gigantic figure seated in the gilded armchair.

Rose—*it was Rose*!

Harry launched himself forward, and Dumont sprang to meet him, dragging at his sword hilt. Harry's fist caught Dumont squarely in the midsection, sending him doubled up to the floor.

The Whip, startled by this headlong entry and bewildered by the bedlam below, the hoarse shouts and sounds of battle that now rose from the floor below, sat for a moment transfixed. And in that moment Rosamunde struggled free of the binding whip. But The Whip was stunned only for a moment. He saw Harry coming; he lifted that great bullwhip and caught Harry around the waist with a great body-bruising blow that knocked Harry off balance. As Harry staggered and grasped at the whip, Dumont regained his feet and lunged toward him with sword drawn.

Rosamunde scrambled up and threw her heavy lace wedding veil like an imprisoning net over that sword and brought her weight down upon it, grazing the blade with her sleeve. The blade missed Harry by a breath.

By now Rodrigue had reached The Whip, and he threw himself upon that vast figure with silent hatred. His powerful leper's hands closed around the bullwhip, and the breath of the two antagonists rasped raggedly as they fought for possession of that terrible weapon.

Harry did not even try to understand how Rosamunde had come to be here—and in a bridal gown! It was enough that she was here and she needed him. Dumont had never seen such a face of hell as Harry's large fist caught him a smashing blow in the face and sent him crashing over backward to the floor. Elaine had once broken his nose, and it had set sideways. Harry smashed it across his face onto the other side. Dumont left the battle to crawl blindly across the floor, moaning and clawing at his bloody, twice-ruined face.

The wedding veil, tangled over Dumont's sword, was torn from Rosamunde's hands as the weapon crashed to the floor. She did not notice it. She was staring at Harry in disbelief. Harry—*here!* She wavered on her feet from shock and fatigue.

In a swift cunning move The Whip released his hold on his weapon and clamped his strong fingers around Rodrigue's throat. Harry leaped forward and brought the heel of his hand in a chopping blow across the nape of The Whip's neck. Those hands fell away from Rodrigue's throat, but the whole huge bulk of the man now turned on Harry, who gave the chair in which he sat a swift terrible kick that sent it skimming down the polished floor to bump into the balcony railing.

Rodrigue pursued that flying chair, and Harry seized Rosamunde and dragged her after him. "The men below are outnumbered," he cried. "With me, Rose!" He nodded to the leper. "We can climb down from this balcony."

But Rodrigue had seen that whip curl around Rosamunde's sweet ankles, seen her dragged along the floor. He wanted revenge.

"Not yet!" he panted—and hurled himself again at The Whip. The force of his lunge took The Whip—who had reared up on one arm in a convulsive gesture—over the low balcony railing. Locked together, their bodies pitched over the railing. Feeling himself airborne, The Whip gave a hoarse guttural cry and let go of Rodrigue, who fell to the side, landing harmlessly in a fig tree which broke his fall.

But The Whip was not so lucky. His heavy body plummeted straight down—down upon the sharp daggerlike wooden points of the shattered trunk of the old olive tree that had been climbed by his second wife's lover to effect her escape. The Whip had watched that flight, tied up in a chair, and it had driven him deeper into madness. That olive tree he had ordered chopped down, its branches cut into faggots. He had caught the lovers and tied them both —his second wife was a simple village girl—to a sharpened stake in the ground and piled those faggots up about them and burned them there together in a fiery screaming funeral pyre. It was upon the upthrust wooden points of that old trunk that his heavy body was now impaled, and as the splintered wood ripped through his torso he began to scream. Impaled there, he would scream his life away —just as *she* had screamed when first the flames blazed up bright around her. And in his rage and horror he thought he heard her voice—and at the last, her scornful laughter.

Beside Harry, Rosamunde swayed with fatigue. "Wait," he said. " 'Tis not much of a drop from here." He vaulted down. "Jump," he commanded. "I will catch you."

Rosamunde threw a long white leg over the balcony, swung down as far as she could—and dropped into Harry's waiting arms. He caught her easily and would have held her there, for the very miracle that she was in his arms again—but he stiffened as he smelled smoke and heard shouts and the sound of running feet.

"The house is burning," he said sharply. "We must away."

"There is a sea cave," she told him. "I can guide you."

Harry turned to that hooded figure on whom the gates of life had clanged shut, whose future lay in darkness— and yet who had so inexplicably helped them. "Come!"

Rodrigue's eyes through their leper's slits fixed on Rosamunde—Rosamunde in her white dress, held close in the Englishman's arms. It took all the strength of his will to force his gaze away from her.

"Take your lady," he cried hoarsely, his voice muffled by the material that concealed his face. "She has been given back to you. Take her and go! I will lead the pursuit up the gorge to Lluch."

In any other circumstance Harry would have stood beside the leper and taken whatever came. But he had Rosamunde to consider. Rosamunde, precious and newly found, who must not be endangered. He gazed down tenderly at the woman in his arms, then looked up at the leper.

"If ye live," he said huskily, "ask of me anything!"

Memory stirred in Rosamunde. Some timbre in the leper's voice had hauntingly reminded her of something . . . someone. Could she have known him once?

"God go with you," she called after him.

The hooded figure—already headed determinedly away from them—turned. There was the glimmer of tears behind the eye slits. "God has given me *this*," he said softly.

And with those enigmatic words he was gone, vanished into the darkness from whence he had come, and Harry and Rosamunde melted into the trees in the other direction.

From the first floor of the burning villa, where the clash between the lepers and the coast watchers had been fiercest, the sounds of battle were diminishing. The lepers were dying. Now the coast watchers broke from the house, pursuing stragglers.

And saw silhouetted in the moonlight the hooded figure of Rodrigue Avilo, tall and erect, waiting for them at the entrance to the gorge.

A collective roar rose from their throats and the pack ran in that direction.

Rodrigue smiled grimly. Up the steep path that led deeper into that dark narrowing canyon he moved swiftly. Behind him cursing, panting men struggled after him over the rough stones.

Rodrigue could easily have outdistanced them, for he was familiar with the treacherous path through the precipitous walls of this massive limestone formation. He could have outdistanced them and reached Lluch and safety.

But he did not. He stopped to give battle. For he meant to give them every chance, the lovers.

Because he had loved Rosamunde and could not bear to let her go, he had tricked the Englishman and kept Rosamunde on Majorca, a prisoner of his lies. Now he had given their lives back to them—gift of Rodrigue Avilo, gentleman of Spain!

So with the dawn he stopped where the way was narrowest. Standing in a narrow shaft between the sheer rock walls, he turned and faced his pursuers. Let them believe the pair they sought had already reached the monastery and safety! Soon there would be fewer to hunt down Harry and Rosamunde—for *he* would reduce their numbers!

The first who came panting and perspiring, stumbling along that rocky path, he seized with those hands charged with near-superhuman strength, and before the man could recover his wits, Rodrigue had cracked his head like an eggshell against the rocky wall.

The next foe—warned by a strangled cry from his predecessor—was more cautious. He stopped abruptly, peering forward into the dark recesses of the canyon. For a moment he thought he saw the shine of eyes, and then Rodrigue was upon him, carrying him backward with the surge of his assault so that he stumbled back against those who were toiling up, and three of them tumbled down the steep incline, one screaming that he had broken his leg.

Rodrigue stepped back in triumph, and the sun rose over the canyon cleft like a bright golden ball—they could see him now. Suddenly a dagger was thrown—and seemed to disappear into those black robes.

The hooded figure staggered forward, clutching at the hilt, and sagged to his knees. A kind of moan went up from those crowding forward, and they stumbled over him, stepping over his lifeless body on their futile journey to Lluch.

In the canyon's dark cleft the hooded figure lay where they had left him. They had cut him down in the bright sunshine of a new day, but he had died exultant, with a smile on his lips and gratitude in his heart. He had wronged Rosamunde, but at the end he had been able to save her—more, he had returned her to the Englishman she had always loved.

He had greatly sinned but—*he had atoned!*

Bending low, Harry carried Rosamunde through the tangled grasses and plunged into the cypresses and pines, and down the path that she indicated to him onto the beach that the tide would soon cover with water.

"They will search the cave," she told him in her soft exhausted voice as they reached the shore. "But there is a sea grotto—they will not think of it."

Together they plunged beneath the silver sea and came up inside the grotto, where light filtered down from above. It was like being inside a jewel. The walls were full of moving turquoise and sapphire light.

Tomorrow they would climb to the sea cave, taking with them yellow bursts of the giant fennel that rose among the boulders—its pith would burst into flames like tinder, and with it they would signal the ship. The coast watchers of La Calobra would be too disorganized to fight—and most of them would still be at Lluch. With their leader dead, his fortress a smoking ruin, they would not notice the glow from the cliffs or mount a resistance to the two heavily gunned longboats that would sweep in to shore and pick up the lovers and carry them out to the waiting *Anjanette*. The ship would spread her canvas wings and sail around the island to pick up Elaine at San Telmo.

And then she would carry them away to Amsterdam!

Tomorrow Rosamunde would ask Harry all the questions, hear all the answers, tomorrow she would tell him that he had a daughter.

But for her the miracle was now.

Her dress—that hateful wedding dress—had been half torn off her at La Calobra. Now she shrugged out of it, out of her soaking chemise and stockings, and once more lay back exhausted, a delicious misty fatigue stealing over her.

Harry rose on one arm and stared down at her. He caught his breath at the sight. She was so lovely it hurt to look at her. The rosy-tipped mounds of her delicately molded breasts rose mother-of-pearl in the shimmering light, and her long fair hair streamed out wet around her like a mermaid's, picking up blue and turquoise lights reflected from the grotto walls. The long undulating line of her lovely body that pulled in at the waist and rose sweetly at the hip sang like a line of poetry through his mind, something beautiful and half-forgotten come back with blinding light to torment him. Her dainty clean-cut limbs, so closely made at the thighs that he thought not even a blade of Toledo steel could pass through without disturbing the sweet flesh, seemed to beckon him, and the pale silky triangle of her hair at the crest of those thighs made him remember, remember, what it had been like to hold her, to possess her.

It was too much for him. With a tenderness that went deeper than anything he had ever felt before, he caressed her silken flesh, turned to ivory in the dawn's pale light.

She stirred and her green eyes fluttered open, gazed at him with such mounting splendor that he was shaken.

"Harry," she murmured in a soft voice. "Is it really you? Or am I dead and gone to heaven?"

"Rose, Rose, we are neither of us dead. Our lives have been given back to us." There was a tremor in Harry's voice, and his arms held her in a web of steel. She flinched as his ardent lips caressed her bruised throat, moved down her white bosom to nuzzle the soft tingling mounds of her breasts.

This was passion, but it was more than passion. She had longed for him so long. . . . As he gripped her to him, masterful now in his taking of her, her heart marched to a triumphant beat and her whole being thrilled with an inexpressible joy.

Harry, Harry, her heart throbbed. *Mine again. Mine forever.* She was lost in the dizzy radiance of it.

And for Harry, this joining was just as wondrous. His heart was a pounding drum that beat out her name, and his very veins ran fire that he should hold her in his arms again. So long he had thought her lost, yet all along—ah, but she was here now, and her pliant body spoke to him as richly of love as did her soft voice, whispering broken endearments warm against his ear. *Returned to me at last,* he thought, and aloud he murmured, *"This* time ye'll not escape me!"

Naked, and thrilling in his arms, Rosamunde gave a sigh of deep content and nestled deeper against him. From these arms she had no need to escape—ever!